DARKR

Other books by Glen Cook

DARKWAR

GLEN COOK

c.1
NIGHT SHADE BOOKS
SAN FRANCISCO

First Edition

ISBN: 978-1-59780-201-7

Printed in Canada

Night Shade Books
Please visit us on the web at
http://www.nightshadebooks.com

CONTENTS

DOOMSTALKER

BOOK ONE: THE PACKSTEAD

CHAPTER ONE

I

It was the worst winter in memory. Even the Wise conceded that early on. The snows came out of the Zhotak early, and by Manestar Morning they stood several paws deep. They came on bitter winds that found every crack and chink in the Degnan loghouses till in frustration the older females ordered the males out to cover the curved roofs with blocks of sod. The males strove valiantly, but the ice-teethed wind had devoured the warmth of the ground. The earth would not yield to their tools. They tried packing the roofs with snow, but the ceaseless wind carried that away. The ranks of firewood dwindled at an alarming rate.

It was customary for the young of the pack to roam the nearby hills in search of deadwood when they had no other chores, but this bitter winter the Wise whispered into the ears of the huntresses, and the huntresses ordered the pups to remain within sight of the packstead palisade. The pups sensed the change and were uneasy.

Nobody said the word "grauken." The old, terrible stories were put aside. Nobody wanted to frighten the little ones. But the adults all knew weather like this conjured the beast lying so near the surface of the meth.

Game would be scarce on the Zhotak. The nomad packs of the northland would exhaust their stored food early. They would come south before long. Some did even during the milder winters, stealing where they could, fighting if they had to seize the fruits of the labors of their sedentary cousins.

And in the terrible winters—as this promised to become—they even carried off young pups. Among meth, in the heart of the great winter, hunger knew no restraint.

In the fireside tales the grauken was a slavering beast of shadowed forests and rocky hills that lay in wait for careless pups. In life, the grauken was the hunger that betrayed civilization and reason. The Degnan Wise whispered to the huntresses. They wanted the young to develop the habit of staying close and alert long before the grauken came snarling up from its dark place of hiding.

Thus, another burden fell upon the harried males. They ventured out in armed parties, seeking firewood and long, straight logs suitable for construction. To their customary exhausting duties were added the extension and strengthening of the spiral stockade of needle-pointed logs and the bringing of snow into the loghouses to melt. The water produced, they returned to the cold, where they poured it into forms and froze it into blocks. With these ice cakes they sheathed the exteriors of the loghouses, bit by bit.

This winter's wind was like none the pack had ever known. Even the Chronicle did not recall its like. Never did it cease its bicker and howl. It became so cold the snow no longer fell. Who dared take a metal tool into a bare paw risked losing skin. Incautious pups suffered frostbitten muzzles. Fear glimmered in the eyes of the Wise as they bent their toothless heads together by the fires and muttered of signs and evil portents. The sagan, the wisest of the Wise, burned incense and made sacrifice daily. All the time she was awake her shaky, pain-deformed old paws wove powerful fetishes and banes to mount over the entrances to the loghouses. She commanded ceremonies of propitiation.

And the wind continued to blow. And the winter grew more cold. And the shadow of fear trickled into the bravest of hearts.

Huntresses found unfamiliar meth tracks just a few hours away from the packstead, up near the boundary with the Laspe hunting grounds. They might have been made by Laspe huntresses ranging out of their territory, seeking what small game did not hibernate. But the snow held no scent. Fears of the worst became haunting. Could it be that savages from the north were scouting the upper Ponath already?

Remnants of an old fire were found at Machen Cave, not far north of the packstead. Even in winter only the brave, the desperate, or the foolish nighted over in Machen Cave. The Laspe, or any other of the neighbors, would have traveled on by night rather than have sheltered there. So the Wise whispered and the huntresses murmured to one another. Those who knew the upper Ponath knew that darkness dwelt within Machen Cave.

II

Marika, Skiljan's pup, reached her tenth birthday during the worst of winters, when the fear lurked in the corners of her dam's loghouse like shadows out of the old stories the old females no longer told. She and the surviving pups of her litter, Kublin and Zamberlin, tried to celebrate the event in traditional pup fashion, but there was no breaking the gloom of their elders.

Skits drawn from folklore were customary. But Marika and Kublin had created their own tale of adventure, and over the protests of conservative Zamberlin, had rehearsed it for weeks. Marika and Kublin believed they would astonish their elders, Zamberlin that they would offend the hidebound Wise. In the event, only their dam proved insufficiently distracted to follow their story. All their expectations were disappointed. They tried flute and drums. Marika had a talent for the flute, and Zamberlin enthusiasm on the skins.

Kublin tried to sing.

One of the old females snarled at the racket. They failed to stop sufficiently soon. Skiljan had to interpose herself between the old female and the pups.

The pups tried juggling, for which Marika had an exceptional talent. In summertime the old females always watched and cooed in amazement. She seemed able to command the balls in the air. But now even their dam showed no interest.

Desolate, the pups slinked into a corner and huddled for warmth. The chill was as much of the heart as of the flesh.

In any other season their elders would have snapped at them, telling them they were too old for such foolishness. In this dread season the old ignored the young, and the young stayed out of the path of the old, for tempers were short and civilization's edge lay very near the surface. A meth who slipped over could kill. They were a race with only the most tenuous grasp on civilized behavior.

Marika huddled with her littermates, feeling the rapid patter of their hearts. She stared through the smoky gloom at her elders. Kublin whimpered softly. He was very frightened. He was not strong. He was old enough to know that in the hard winters weakling males sometimes had to go.

In name the loghouse was Skiljan's Loghouse—for Marika's dam—though she shared it with a dozen sisters, their males, several older females, and all their pups. Skiljan commanded by right of skill and strength, as her dam had before her. She was the best huntress of the pack. She ranked second in physical endurance and strength, and first in will. She was among the smartest Degnan females. These being the qualities by which wilderness meth survived, she was honored by all who shared her loghouse. Even the old females deferred when she commanded, though it was seldom she ignored their advice. The Wise had more experience and could see behind veils youth drew across the eyes. In the councils of the packstead she spoke second only to Gerrien.

There were six similar loghouses in the Degnan packstead. None new had been erected within living memory. Each was a half cylinder lying on its side, ninety feet long and a dozen high, twenty-five wide. The south end, where the entrance was, was flat, facing away from winter's winds. The north end was a tapering cone covering a root cellar, providing storage, breaking the teeth of the wind. A loft hung six feet above the ground floor, half a foot above the average height of an adult meth female. The young slept up there in the warmth, and much that had to be stored was tucked away in the loft's dark crannies and recesses. The loft was a time vault, more interesting than the Chronicle in what it told of the Degnan past. Marika and Kublin passed many a loving hour probing the shadows, disturbing vermin, sometimes bringing to light treasures lost or forgotten for generations.

The loghouse floor was earth hammered hard by generations of feet. It was covered with skins where the adults slept in clumps, males to the north, old females between the two central firepits, females of breeding age to the south, nearest the door. The sides of the loghouse were piled with firewood and tools, weapons, possessions, and such food stores as were not kept in the unheated point of the structure. All this formed an additional barrier against the cold.

A jungle of foods, skins, whatnots hung from the joists supporting the loft, making any passage through the loghouse tortuous and interesting.

And the smells! Over all was the rich smell of smoke, for smoke found little escape in winter, when warmth was precious. Then there was the smell of unwashed bodies, and of the hanging sausages, fruits, vegetables. In summer the Degnan pack spent little time indoors, fleeing the thick, rank interior for sleep under the stars. In summer adult meth spoke longingly of the freedom enjoyed by the nomadic meth of the Zhotak, who were not tied to such pungent spirit traps. (The nomads believed built houses held one's spirit prisoner. They sheltered in caves or pitched temporary hide tents.) But when the ice wind began to moan out of the Zhotak, old folks lost that longing. Settled meth, who raised a few scrawny vegetables and grains and who gleaned the forests for game and fruits that could be dried and preserved, survived the winters far more handily than their footloose cousins.

"Marika!" old Zertan snapped. "Come here, pup."

Marika shivered as she disentangled herself from her littermates. Her dam's dam was called Carque by all the pups of the packstead—a carque being a rapacious flyer of exceedingly foul temper. Zertan had bad teeth. They pained her constantly, but she would not have them pulled and refused to drink goyin tea. She was a little senile and a lot crazy and was afraid that enemies long dead would steal up on her if she risked the drowsiness caused by the analgesic tea.

Her contemporaries called her Rhelat—behind her back. The rhelat was a carrion eater. It had been known to kill things and wait for them to ripen. Zertan's rotten teeth gave her particularly foul breath.

Marika presented herself, head lowered dutifully.

"Pup, run to Gerrien's loghouse. Fetch me those needles Borget promised me."

"Yes, Granddam." Marika turned, caught her dam's eye. What should she do? Borget was dead a month. Anyway, she had been too feeble to make needles for longer than Marika could remember.

Granddam was losing her grip on time again. Soon she would forget who everyone was and begin seeing and talking to meth dead for a generation.

Skiljan nodded toward the doorway. A pretense would be made. "I have something you can take to Gerrien, since you are going." So the trip would not be a waste.

Marika shrugged into her heavy skin coat and the boots with otec fur inside, waited near the doorway. Zertan watched as if some cunning part of her knew the quest was fabulous, but insisted Marika punish herself in the cold anyway. Because she was young? Or was Zertan grasping for a whiff of the power that had been hers when the loghouse had carried her name?

Skiljan brought a sack of stone arrowheads, the sort used for everyday hunting. The females of her loghouse were skilled flakers. In each loghouse, meth occupied themselves with crafts through the long winters. "Tell Gerrien we need these set to shafts."

"Yes, Dam." Marika slipped through heavy hangings that kept the cold from roaring in when the doorway was open. She stood for a moment with paw upon the latch before pushing into the cold. Zertan. Maybe they ought to rid themselves of crazy old females instead of pups, she thought. Kublin was far more useful than was Granddam. Granddam no longer contributed anything but complaint.

She drew a last deep, smoky breath, then stepped into the gale. Her eyes watered instantly. Head down, she trudged across the central square. If she hurried she could make it before she started shivering.

The Degnan loghouses stood in two ranks of three, one north, one south, with fifty feet of open space between ranks. Skiljan's loghouse was the middle one in the northern rank, flanked by those of Dorlaque and Logusz. Gerrien's was the end loghouse on Marika's left as she faced south. Meth named Foehse and Kuzmic ruled the center and right loghouses, respectively. Seldom did any but Gerrien have much impact on Marika's life. Gerrien and Skiljan had been both friends and competitors since they were pups.

The packstead stockade, and the lean-tos clutching its skirts, clung close to the outer loghouses and spiraled around the packstead twice. Any raider would have to come in through a yard-wide channel, all the way around, to reach her goal. Unlike some neighboring packs, the Degnan made no effort to enclose their gardens and fields. Threats came during winter anyway. Decision had been made in the days-of-building to trade the risk of siege in growing time for the advantage of having to defend a shorter palisade.

The square between loghouse ranks seemed so barren, so *naked* this time of year. In summer it was always loosely controlled chaos, with game being salted, hides being tanned, pups running wild.

Six loghouses. The Degnan packstead was the biggest in this part of the upper Ponath, and the richest. Their neighbors envied them. But Marika, whose head was filled with dreams, did not feel wealthy. She was miserable most of the time, feeling deprived by birth.

In the south there were places called cities, tradermales said. Places where they made the precious iron tools the Wise accepted in exchange for otec furs. Places where many packs lived together in houses built not of logs but of stone. Places where winter's breath was ever so much lighter, and the stone houses turned the cold with ease. Places that, just by being elsewhere, by definition would be better than here.

Many an hour had she and Kublin passed dreaming aloud of what it would be like to live *there*.

Tradermales also told of a stone place called a packfast, which stood just three days down the nearby river, where that joined another to become the Hainlin, a river celebrated in the Chronicle as the guide which the Degnan had followed into the upper Ponath in ancient times. Tradermales said a real road started below the packfast, and wound through mountains and plains southward to great cities whose names Marika could never recall.

Marika's dam had been to that stone packfast several times. Each year the great ones who dwelt there summoned the leading females of the upper Ponath. Skiljan would be gone for ten days. It was said there were ceremonies and payments of tribute, but about none of that would Skiljan speak, except to mutter under her breath, "Silth bitches," and say, "In time, Marika. In due time. It is not a thing to be rushed." Skiljan was not one to frighten, yet she seemed afraid to have her pups visit.

Other pups, younger than Marika, had gone last summer, returning with tales of wonder, thrilled to have something about which to brag. But Skiljan would not yield. Already she and Marika had clashed about the summer to come.

Marika realized she had stopped moving, was standing in the wind and shivering. Dreamer, the huntresses and Wise called her mockingly—and sometimes, when they thought she was not attentive, with little side glances larded with uncertainty or fright—and they were right. It was a good thing pups were not permitted into the forest now. Her dreaming had become uncontrolled. She would find some early frostflower or pretty creekside pebble and the grauken would get her while she contemplated its beauty.

She entered Gerrien's loghouse. Its interior was very like Skiljan's. The odors were a touch different. Gerrien housed more males, and the wintertime crafts of her loghouse all involved woodworking. Logusz's loghouse always smelled worst. Her meth were mainly tanners and leather workers.

Marika stood before the windskins, waiting to be recognized. It was but a moment before Gerrien sent a pup to investigate. This was a loghouse more relaxed than that ruled by Skiljan. There was more merriment here, always, and more happiness. Gerrien was not intimidated by the hard life of the upper Ponath. She took what came and refused to battle the future before it arrived. Marika sometimes wished she had been whelped by cheerful Gerrien instead of brooding Skiljan.

"What?" demanded Solfrank, a male two years her elder, almost ready for the rites of adulthood, which would compel him to depart the packstead and wander the upper Ponath in search of a pack that would take him in. His chances were excellent. Degnan males took with them envied education and skills.

Marika did not like Solfrank. The dislike was mutual. It extended back years, to a time when the male had thought his age advantage more than overbalanced his sexual handicap. He had bullied; Marika had refused to yield; young teeth had been bared; the older pup had been forced to submit. Solfrank never would forgive her the humiliation. The grudge was well-known. It was a stain he would bear with him in his search for a new pack.

"Dam sends me with two score and ten arrowheads ready for the shaft." Marika bared teeth slightly. A hint of mockery, a hint of I-dare-you. "Granddam wants the needles Borget promised."

Marika reflected that Kublin *liked* Solfrank. When he was not tagging after her, he trotted around after Gerrien's whelp—and brought back all the corrupt ideas Solfrank whispered in his ear. At least Zamberlin knew him for what he was and viewed him with due contempt.

Solfrank bared his teeth, pleasured by further evidence that those who dwelt in Skiljan's loghouse were mad. "I'll tell Dam."

In minutes Marika clutched a bundle of ready arrows. Gerrien herself brought a small piece of fine skin in which she had wrapped several bone needles. "These were Borget's. Tell Skiljan we will want them back."

Not the iron needles. The iron were too precious. But… Marika did not understand till she was outside again.

Gerrien did not expect Zertan to live much longer. These few needles, which had belonged to her sometime friend—and as often in council, enemy—might pleasure her in her failing days. Though she did not like her granddam, a tear formed in the corner of Marika's eye. It froze quickly and stung, and she brushed at it irritably with a heavily gloved paw.

She was just three steps from home when she heard the cry on the wind, faint and far and almost indiscernible. She had not heard such a cry before, but she knew it instantly. That was the cry of a meth in sudden pain.

Degnan huntresses were out, as they were every day when times were hard. Males were out seeking deadwood. There might be trouble. She hurried inside and did not wait to be recognized before she started babbling. "It came from the direction of Machen Cave," she concluded, shuddering. She was afraid of Machen Cave.

Skiljan exchanged looks with her lieutenants. "Up the ladder now, pup," she said. "Up the ladder."

"But Dam…" Marika wilted before a fierce look. She scurried up the ladder. The other pups greeted her with questions. She ignored them, huddled with Kublin. "It came from the direction of Machen Cave."

"That's miles away," Kublin reminded.

"I know." Maybe she had imagined the cry. Dreamed it. "But it came from that direction. That's all I said. I didn't claim it came from the cave."

Kublin shivered. He said nothing more. Neither did Marika.

They were very afraid of Machen Cave, those pups. They believed they had been given reason.

III

It had been high summer, a time when danger was all of one's own making. Pups were allowed free run of forest and hill, that they might come to know their pack's territory. Their work and play were all shaped to teach skills adults would need to survive to raise their own pups.

Marika almost always ran with her littermates, especially Kublin. Zamberlin seldom did anything not required of him.

Kublin, though, hadn't Marika's stamina, strength, or nerve. She sometimes became impatient with him. In her crueler moments she would hide and force him to find his own way. He did so whining, complaining, sullenly, and slow, but he always managed. He was capable enough at his own pace.

North and east of the packstead stood Stapen Rock, a bizarre basalt upthrust the early Wise designated as spiritually and ritually significant. At Stapen Rock the Wise communed with the spirits of the forest and made offerings meant to assure good hunting, rich mast crops, fat and juicy berries, and a plentitude of chote. Chote being a knee-high plant edible in leaf, fruit, and fat, sweet, tuberous root. The root would store indefinitely in a dark, cool, dry place.

Stapen Rock was the chief of five such natural shrines recalling old Degnan animistic traditions. Others were dedicated to the spirits of air and water, fire and the underworld. The All itself, supercessor of the old way, was sanctified within the loghouses themselves.

Machen Cave, gateway to the world below, centered the shadowed side of life. Pohsit, sagan in Skiljan's loghouse, and her like visited Machen Cave regularly, propitiating shadows and the dead, refreshing spells which bound the gateway against those.

The Degnan were not superstitious by the standards of the Ponath, but in the case of shadows no offering was spared to avert baleful influences. The spells sealing the cave were always numerous and fresh.

Marika played a game with herself and Kublin, one that stretched their courage. It required them to approach the fane nearer than fear would permit. Timid, Kublin remained ever close to her when they ran the woods. If, perforce, he went with her.

Marika had been playing that game for three summers. In the summer before the great winter, though, it ceased being pup play.

As always, Kublin was reluctant. At a respectful distance he began, "Marika, I'm tired. Can we go home now?"

"It's just the middle of the afternoon, Kublin. Are you an infant that needs a nap?" Then distraction. "Oh. Look."

She had spotted a patch of chote, thick among old leaves on a ravine bank facing northward. Chote grew best where it received little direct sunlight. It was an ephemeral plant, springing up, flowering, fruiting, and wilting all within thirty days. A patch this lush could not have gone unnoticed. In fact, it would have been there for years. But she would report it. Pups were expected to report discoveries. If nothing else, such reports revealed how well they knew their territory.

She forgot the cave. She searched for those plants with two double-paw-sized leaves instead of one. The female chote fruited on a short stem growing from the crotch where the leaf stems joined. "Here's one. Not ripe. This one's not ripe either."

Kublin found the first ripe fruit, a one-by-one-and-a-half-inch ovoid a pale greenish yellow beginning to show spots of brown. "Here." He held it up.

Marika found another a moment later. She bit a hole, sucked tangy, acid juice, then split the shell of the fruit. She removed the seeds, which she buried immediately. There was little meat to chote fruit, and that with an unpalatable bitterness near the skin. She scraped the better part carefully with a small stone knife. The long meth jaw and carnivore teeth made getting the meat with the mouth impossible.

Kublin seemed determined to devour every fruit in the patch. Marika concluded he was stalling. "Come on."

She wished Zamberlin had come. Kublin was less balky then. But Zamberlin was running with friends this year, and those friends had no use for Kublin, who could not maintain their pace.

They were growing apart. Marika did not like that, though she knew there was no avoiding it. In a few years they would assume adult roles. Then Zambi and Kub would be gone entirely....

Poor Kublin. And a mind was of no value in a male.

Across a trickle of a creek, up a slope, across a small meadow, down the wooded slope bordering a larger creek, and downstream a third of a mile. There the creek skirted the hip of a substantial hill, the first of those that rose to become the Zhotak. Marika settled on her haunches a hundred feet from the stream and thirty above its level. She stared at the shadow among brush and rocks opposite that marked the mouth of the cave. Kublin settled beside her, breathing rapidly though she had not set a hard pace.

There were times when even she was impatient with his lack of stamina.

Sunlight slanted down through the leaves, illuminating blossoms of white, yellow, and pale red. Winged things flitted from branch to branch through the dapple of sunlight and shadow, seeming to flicker in and out of existence. Some light fell near the cave mouth, but did nothing to illuminate its interior. Marika never had approached closer than the near bank of the creek. From there, or where she squatted now, she could discern nothing but the glob of darkness. Even the propitiary altar was invisible.

It was said that meth of the south mocked their more primitive cousins for appeasing spirits that would ignore them in any case. Even among the Degnan there were those who took only the All seriously. But even they attended ceremonies. Just in case. Ponath meth seldom took chances.

Marika had heard that the nomad packs of the Zhotak practiced animistic rites which postulated dark and light spirits, gods and devils, in everything. Even rocks.

Kublin had his breath. Marika rose. Sliding, she descended to the creek. Kublin followed tautly. He was frightened, but he did not protest, not even when she leapt the stream. He followed. For once he seemed determined to outgut her.

Something stirred within Marika as she stared upslope. From where she stood the sole evidence of the cave's presence was a trickle of mossy water on slick stone, coming from above. In some seasons a stream poured out of the cave.

She searched within herself, trying to identify that feeling. She could not. It was almost as if she had eaten something that left her slightly irritable, as though there was a buzzing in her nerves. She did not connect it with the cavern. Never before had she felt anything but fear when nearby. She glanced at Kublin. He now seemed more restless than frightened. "Well?"

Kublin bared his teeth. The expression was meant to be challenging. "Want me to go first?"

Marika took a couple of steps, looked upslope again. Nothing to see. Brush still masked the cave.

Three more steps.

"Marika."

She glanced back. Kublin looked disturbed, but not in the usual way. "What?"

"There's something in there."

Marika waited for an explanation. She did not mock. Sometimes he could tell things that he could not see. As could she…. He quivered. She looked inside for what she felt. But she could not find it.

She did feel a presence. It had nothing to do with the cave. "Sit down," she said softly.

"Why?"

"Because I want to get lower, so I can look through the brush. Somebody is watching. I don't want them to know we know they're there."

He did as she asked. He trusted her. She watched over him.

"It's Pohsit," Marika said, now recalling a repeated unconscious sense of being observed. The feeling had left her more wary than she realized. "She's following us again."

Kublin's immediate response was that of any pup. "We can outrun her. She's so old."

"Then she'd know we'd seen her." Marika sat there awhile, trying to reason out why the sagan followed them. It had to be cruel work for one as old as she. Nothing rational came to mind. "Let's just pretend she isn't there. Come on."

They had taken four steps when Kublin snagged her paw. "There *is* something in there, Marika."

Again Marika tried to feel it. This sense she had, which had betrayed Pohsit to her, was not reliable. Or perhaps it depended too much upon expectation. She expected a large animal, a direct physical danger. She sensed nothing of the sort. "I don't feel anything."

Kublin made a soft sound of exasperation. Usually it was the other way around, Marika trying to explain something sensed while he remained blind to it.

Why did Pohsit follow them around? She did not even like them. She was always saying bad things to Dam. Once again Marika tried to see the old meth with that unreliable sense for which she had no name.

Alien thoughts flooded her mind. She gasped, reeled, closed them out. "Kublin!"

Her littermate was staring toward the mouth of the cave, jaw restless. "What?"

"I just..." She was not sure what she had done. She had no referents. Nothing like it had happened before. "I think I just heard Pohsit thinking."

"You what?"

"I heard what she was thinking. About us—about me. She's scared of me. She thinks I'm a witch of some kind."

"What are you talking about?"

"I was thinking about Pohsit. Wondering why she's always following us. I reached out like I can sometimes, and all of a sudden I heard her thinking. I was inside her head, Kublin. Or she was inside mine. I'm scared."

Kublin did not seem afraid, which amazed Marika. He asked, "What was she thinking?"

"I told you. She's sure I'm some kind of witch. A devil or something. She was thinking about having tried to get the Wise to... to..." That entered her conscious mind for the first time.

Pohsit was so frightened that she wanted Marika slain or expelled from the packstead. "Kublin, she wants to kill me. She's looking for evidence that will convince Dam and the Wise." Especially the Wise. They could overrule Skiljan if they were sufficiently determined.

Kublin was an odd one. Faced with a concrete problem, a solid danger, he could clear his mind of fright and turn his intellect upon the problem. Only when the peril was nebulous did he collapse. But Marika would not accept his solution to what already began to seem an unlikely peril.

Kublin said, "We'll get her up on Stapen Rock and push her off."

Just like that, he proposed murder. A serious proposal. Kublin did not joke.

Kublin—and Zamberlin—shared Marika's risk. And needed do nothing but be her littermates to be indicted with her if Pohsit found some fanciful charge she could peddle around the packstead. They shared the guilty blood. And they were male, of no especial value.

In his ultimate powerlessness, Kublin was ready to overreact to the danger.

For a moment Marika was just a little frightened of him. He meant it, and it meant no more to him than the squashing of an irritating insect, though Pohsit had been part of their lives all their lives. As sagan she had taught them their rituals. She was closer, in some ways, than their dam.

"Forget it," Marika said. By now she was almost convinced that she had imagined the contact. "We came to see the cave."

They were closer than ever they had dared, and for the first time Kublin had the lead. Marika pushed past him, asserting her primacy. She wondered what Pohsit thought now. Pups were warned repeatedly about Machen Cave. She moved a few more steps uphill.

Now she saw the cave mouth, black as the void between the stars when the moons were all down. Two steps more and she dropped to her haunches, sniffed the cold air that drifted out of the darkness. It had both an earthy and slightly carrion tang. Kublin squatted beside her. She said, "I don't see any altar. It just looks like a cave."

There was little evidence anyone ever came there.

Kublin mused, "There is something in there, Marika. Not like any animal." He closed his eyes and concentrated.

Marika closed hers, wondering about Pohsit.

Again that in-smash of anger, of near insane determination to see Marika punished for a crime the pup could not comprehend. Fear followed the thoughts, which were so repugnant Marika's stomach turned. She reeled away and her sensing consciousness whipped past her, into the shadows within Machen Cave.

She screamed.

Kublin clapped a paw over her mouth. "Marika! Stop! What's the matter, Marika?"

She could not get the words out. There *was* something there. Something big and dark and hungry in a way she could not comprehend at all. Something not of flesh. Something that could only be called spirit or ghost.

Kublin seemed comfortable with it. No. He was frightened, but not out of control.

She recalled Pohsit across the creek, nursing inexplicable hatreds and hopes. She controlled herself. "Kublin, we have to get away from here. Before *that* notices us."

But Kublin paid no attention. He moved forward, his step dreamlike.

Had Pohsit not been watching, and malevolent, Marika might have panicked. But the concrete danger on the far bank kept her in firm control. She seized Kublin's arm, turned him. He did not struggle. But neither did he cooperate. Not till she led him to the creekside, where the glaze left his eyes. For a moment he was baffled as to where he was and what he was doing there.

Marika explained. She concluded, "We have to go away as though nothing happened." That was critical. Pohsit was looking for something exactly like what had happened.

Once Kublin regained his bearings, he managed well enough. They behaved like daring pups loose in the woods the rest of the day. But Marika did not stop worrying the edges of the hundred questions Machen Cave had raised.

What was that thing in there? What had it done to Kublin?

He, too, was thoughtful.

That was the real beginning. But till much later Marika believed it started in the heart of that terrible winter, when she caught the scream of the meth on the breast of the cold north wind.

CHAPTER TWO

I

Having questioned Marika till she was sure her scream was not one of her daydreams, Skiljan circulated through the loghouses and organized a scouting party, two huntresses from each. After Marika again told what she had heard, they left the packstead. Marika climbed the watchtower and watched them pass through the narrows around the stockade, through the gate, then lope across the snowy fields, into the fangs of the wind.

She could not admit it, even to herself, but she was frightened. The day was failing. The sky had clouded up. More snow seemed in the offing. If the huntresses were gone long, they might get caught in the blizzard. After dark, in a snowfall, even the most skilled huntress could lose her way.

She did not stay in the tower long. A hint of what the weather held in store came as a few ice pellets smacked her face. She retreated to the loghouse.

She was frightened and worried. That scream preyed upon her.

Worry tainted the rank air inside, too. The males prowled nervously in their territory. The old females bent to their work with iron determination. Even Zertan got a grip on herself and tended to her sewing. The younger females paced, snarling when they got in one another's way. The pups retreated to the loft and the physical and emotional safety it represented.

Marika shed coat and boots, hung the coat carefully, placed her boots just the right distance from the fire, then scampered up the ladder. Kublin helped her over the edge. She did not see Zamberlin. He was huddled with his friends somewhere.

She and Kublin retreated to a shadow away from the other pups. "What did you see?" he whispered. She had asked him to scale the tower with her, but he had not had the nerve. For all his weakness, Marika liked Kublin best of all the young in the loghouse.

He was a dreamer, too. Though male, he wanted much what she did. Often they sat together filling one another's heads with imaginary details of the great southern cities they would visit one day. Kublin had great plans. This summer coming, or next at the latest, he would run away from the packstead when the tradermales came.

Marika did not believe that. He was too cautious, too frightened of change. He might become tradermale someday, but only after he had been put out of the packstead.

"What did you see?" he asked again.

"Nothing. It's clouded up. Looks like there's an ice storm coming."

A whimper formed in Kublin's throat. Weather was one of countless terrors plaguing him for which there was neither rhyme nor reason. "The All must be mad to permit such chaos." He did not understand weather. It was not orderly, mechanical. He hated disorder.

Marika was quite content with disorder. In the controlled chaos of a loghouse, disorder was the standard.

"Remember the storm last winter? I thought it was pretty."

The packstead had been sheathed in ice. The trees had become coated. The entire world for a few hours had been encrusted in crystal and jewels. It was a magical time, like something out of an old story, till the sun appeared and melted the jewels away.

"It was cold and you couldn't walk anywhere without slipping. Remember how Mahr fell and broke her arm?"

That was Kublin. Always practical.

He asked, "Can you find them with your mind-touch?"

"Shh!" She poked her head out of their hiding place. No other pups within hearing. "Not inside, Kublin. Please be careful. Pohsit."

His sigh told her he was not going to listen to another of her admonitions.

"No. I can't. I just have the feeling that they're moving north. Toward Stapen Rock. We knew that already."

Only Kublin knew about her ability. Abilities, really. Each few major moons since last summer, it seemed she discovered more. Other than the fact that Pohsit was watching, and hating, she had no idea why she should keep her talents hidden. But she was convinced it would do her no good to announce them. Driven by Pohsit, the old females often muttered about magic and sorcery and shadows, and not in terms of approbation, though they had their secrets and magics and mysteries themselves—the sagan most of all.

Carefully worded questions, asked of all her fellow pups, had left Marika sure only she—and Kublin a little—had these talents. That baffled her. Though unreliable and mysterious, they seemed perfectly natural and a part of her.

Considering mysteries, considering dreams and stories shared, Marika realized she and Kublin would not be together much longer. Their tenth birthdays had passed. Come spring Kublin and Zamberlin would begin spending most of their time at the male end of the loghouse. And she would spend most of hers with the young females, tagging along on the hunt, learning those things she must know when she came of age and moved from the loft to the south end of the loghouse.

Too soon, she thought. Three more summers. Maybe four, if Dam kept forgetting their age. Then all her freedom would be gone. All the dreams would die.

There would be compensations. A wider field to range beyond the stockade. Chances to visit the stone packfast down the river. A slim maybe of a chance to go on down the road to one of the cities the tradermales told tales about.

Slim chance indeed. While she clung to them and made vows, in her most secret heart she knew her dreams were that only. Huntresses from the upper Ponath remained what they were born. It was sad.

There were times she actually wished she were male. Not often, for the lot of the male was hard and his life too often brief, if he survived infancy at all. But only males became traders, only males left their packsteads behind and wandered where they would, carrying news and wares, seeing the whole wide world.

It was said that the tradermales had their own packfasts where no females ever went, and their own special mysteries, and a language separate even from the different language used among themselves by the males she knew.

All very marvelous, and all beyond her reach. She would live and die in the Degnan packstead, like her dam, her granddam, and so many generations of Degnan females before them. If she remained quick and strong and smart, she might one day claim this loghouse for her own, and have her pick of males with whom to mate. But that was all.

She crouched in shadows with Kublin, fearing her deadly plain tomorrows, and both listened to inner voices, trying to track their dam's party. Marika sensed only that they were north and east of the packstead, moving slowly and cautiously.

Horvat, eldest of the loghouse males, called dinner time. The keeping of time was one of the mysteries reserved to his sex. Somewhere in a small, deep cellar beneath the north end of the house, reached by a ladder, was a device by which time was measured. So it was said. None but the males ever went down there, just as none but the huntresses descended into the cellar beneath the southern end of the loghouse. Marika never had been down, and would not be allowed till the older huntresses were confident she would reveal nothing of what she learned and saw. We are strange, secretive creatures, Marika reflected.

She peeped over the edge of the loft and saw that none of the adults were hastening to collect their meals. "Come on, Kublin. We can be first in line." They scrambled down, collected their utensils quickly.

Two score small bodies poured after them, having made the same discovery. The young seldom got to the cookpots early. Oftentimes they had to make do with leavings, squabbling among themselves, with the weakest getting nothing at all.

Marika filled her cup and bowl, ignoring the habitual disapproving scowls of the males serving. They had power over pups, and used it as much as they dared. She hurried to a shadow, gobbled as fast as she could. There were no meth manners. Meth gobbled fast, ate more if they could, because there was no guarantee there was going to be another meal anytime soon—even in the packsteads, where fate's fickleness had been brought somewhat under control.

Kublin joined Marika. He looked proud of himself. Clinging to her shadow, he had been fast enough to get in ahead of pups who usually shoved him aside. He had filled his cup and bowl near spilling deep. He gobbled like a starved animal. Which he often was, being too weak to seize the best.

"They're worried bad," Marika whispered, stating the obvious. Any meth who did not jump at a meal had a mind drifting a thousand miles away.

"Let's get some more before they wake up."

"All right."

Marika took a reasonable second portion. Kublin loaded up again. Horvat himself stepped over and chided them. Kublin just put his head down and doggedly went on with his plunder. They returned to the shadow. Marika ate more leisurely, but Kublin gobbled again, perhaps afraid Horvat or another pup would rob him.

Finished, Kublin groaned, rubbed his stomach, which actually protruded now. "That's better. I don't know if I can move. Do you feel anything yet?"

Marika shook her head. "Not now." She rose to take her utensils to the cleaning tub, where snow had been melted into wash water. The young cared for their own bowls and utensils, female or not. She took two steps. Maybe because Kublin had mentioned it and had opened her mind, she was in a sensitive state. Something hit her mind like a blow. She had felt nothing so terrible since that day she had read Pohsit. She ground her teeth, on a shriek, not wanting to attract attention. She fell to her knees.

"What's the matter, Marika?"

"Be quiet!" If the adults noticed… If Pohsit… "I—I felt something bad. A touch. One of them… one of our huntresses is hurt. Bad hurt." Pain continued pouring through the touch, reddening her vision. She could not shut it out. The loghouse seemed to twist somehow, to flow, to become something surreal. Its so-well-known shapes became less substantial. For an instant she saw what looked like ghosts, a pair of them, bright but almost shapeless, drifting through the west wall as though that did not exist. They bobbed about, and for a second Marika thought them like curious pups. One began to drift her way as though aware of her awareness. Then the terrible touch ended with the suddenness of a dry stick breaking. The skewed vision departed with it. She saw no ghosts anymore, though for an instant she thought she sensed a feathery caress. She was not sure if it was upon her fur or her mind.

"They're in trouble out there, Kublin. Bad trouble."

"We'd better tell Pobuda."

"No. We can't. She wouldn't believe me. Or she would want to know how I knew. And then Pohsit…" She could not explain the exact nature of her fear. She was certain it was valid, that her secret talents could cause her a great deal of grief.

But Kublin did not demand an explanation. He knew her talents, and he was intimate with fear. Its presence was explanation enough for him.

"I'm scared, Kublin. Scared for Dam."

II

The scouting party returned long after nightfall. Nine of them. Two of those were injured. With them came two injured strangers and a wild, bony skeleton of a male in tattered, grubby furs. The male stumbled and staggered, and was dragged partway by the huntresses. His paws were bound behind him, but he did not cringe like the cowardly males Marika knew.

Because Skiljan had led the party, the Wise and adult females of all the log-houses crowded into her loghouse. Skiljan's males cleared room and retreated to their chilly northern territory. The more timid withdrew to the storeroom or their cellar. But Horvat and the other old ones remained watching from behind the barricade of their firepit.

The pups fled to the loft, then fought for places where they could look down and eavesdrop. Marika was big enough, ill-tempered enough, and had reputation enough to carve out a choice spot for herself and Kublin. She could not draw her attention away from the male prisoner, who lay in the territory of the Wise, watched over by the sagan and the eldest.

Skiljan took her place near the huntress's fire. She scanned her audience while it settled down with far more than customary snarling and jostling. Marika supposed the adults knew everything already, the huntresses having scattered to their respective loghouses before coming to Skiljan's. She hoped for enlightenment anyway. Her dam was methodical about these things.

Skiljan waited patiently. Three Degnan huntresses had not returned. Tempers were rough. She allowed the jostling to settle of its own inertia. Then she said, "We found eight nomads denned in a lean-to set on the leeward side of Stapen Rock. On the way there we found tracks indicating that they have been watching the packstead. They have not been there long, though, or we would have noticed their tracks while hunting. The cry heard and reported by my pup Marika came when they ambushed four huntresses from the Greve packstead."

That caused a stir which was awhile settling out. Marika wondered what her dam would have to say about neighbors poaching, but Skiljan let it go by, satisfied that the fact had sunk in. She ignored a call from Dorlaque for a swift demonstration of protest. Such an action could cause more trouble than it was worth.

"Four Greve huntresses ambushed," Skiljan said. "They slew two. We rescued the other two." The Greve in question were trying to appear small. Dorlaque had not finished her say, though no one but they were listening. Skiljan continued,

"The nomads butchered one of the dead."

Growls and snarls. Ill-controlled anger. Disgust. A little self-loathing, for the grauken never lurked far beneath the surface of any meth. Someone threw something at the prisoner. He accepted the blow without flinching.

"Our sisters from Greve packstead overheard some of their talk while they were captives. The speech of the Zhotak savages is hard to follow, as we all know, but they believe the group at Stapen Rock was an advance party charged with finding our weaknesses. They belong to an alliance of nomad packs which has invaded the upper Ponath. They number several hundred huntresses and are arming their males." She indicated the prisoner. "This group was all male, and very well armed."

Again an angry stir, and much snarling about stupid savages fool enough to give males weapons. Marika sensed a strong current of fear. Several hundred huntresses? It was hard to imagine such numbers.

"What became of the other nomads?" she wanted to ask. But she knew, really. Her dam was a cautious huntress. She would have scouted Stapen Rock well before doing anything. She would have made no move till she knew exactly what the situation was. Then she would have had her companions fill the shelter with arrows and javelins. That three Degnan huntresses had not returned said the nomads, male or no, had been alert and ready for trouble.

"I wonder if any nomads got away," she whispered. Then, "No. Dam would still be tracking them."

Kublin shook beside her. She could have shaken herself. This was bad, bad news. Too much blood. The nomads might appease their consciences with claims of blood feud now, and never mind that they were guilty of a dozen savage crimes. Meth from the Zhotak did not think like normal meth.

Near chaos reigned below. Each of the heads of loghouse had her own notion of what should be done now. Hotheads wanted to go out in the morning, in force, and hunt nomads before nomads came to the packstead. More cautious heads argued for buttoning up the stockade now, and forget the customary search for deadwood and small game. Some vacillated, swinging back and forth between extremes. Because Gerrien took no firm position, but simply listened, there was no swift decision.

Dorlaque shouted a proposal for arming the males within the stockade, a course never before taken except in utmost extremity. Males could not be trusted with weapons. They were emotionally unstable and prone to cowardice. They might flee from their own shadows and cost the packstead precious iron tools. Or in their panic they might turn upon the huntresses. Dorlaque was shouted down.

It went on till Marika grew sleepy. Beside her, Kublin kept drifting off. Many of the younger pups had gone to their pallets. Skiljan entered nothing into the debate but an occasional point of order, refereeing.

After all the arguments had gone around repeatedly, unto exhaustion,

Gerrien looked up from her paws. She surveyed the gathering. Silence fell as she rose. "We will question the prisoner." But that went without saying. Why else would Skiljan have brought him in? "And we will send a messenger to the silth packfast."

Marika came alert immediately. A low growl circulated among the Wise. Pohsit tried to rise, but her infirmities betrayed her. Marika heard her snarl, "Damned silth witches." Several voices repeated the words. Huntresses protested.

Marika did not understand.

Gerrien persisted. "Each year they take tribute. Some years they take our young. In return they are pledged to protect us. We have paid for a long time. We will call in their side of the debt."

Some began to snarl now. Many snapped their jaws unconsciously. There was a lot of emotion loose down there, and Marika could not begin to fathom it. They must be treading the edge of an adult mystery.

Skiljan shouted for silence. Such was her presence at that moment that she won it. She said, "Though I am loath to admit it, Gerrien is right. Against several hundred huntresses, with their males armed, no packstead is secure. Our stockade will not shield us, even if we arm our own males and older pups. This is no vengeance raid, no counting of coup, not even blood feud between packs. Old ways of handling attackers will not suffice. We cannot just seal the gate and wait them out. Hundreds are too many."

"Question the male first," Dorlaque demanded. "Let us not be made fools. Perhaps what the Greve huntresses heard was a lie by rogue males."

Several others joined her in arguing for that much restraint. Skiljan and Gerrien exchanged glances, Gerrien nodding slightly. Skiljan gave Dorlaque what she wanted. "We will send no messenger until we have questioned the captive."

Dorlaque carried on like she had won a major battle. Marika, though, watched Pohsit, who was plotting with her cronies among the Wise.

Skiljan said, "Two courses could be followed. We could scatter messengers to all the packsteads of the upper Ponath and gather the packs in one holdfast, after the fashion of those days when our foredams were moving into the territory. Or we can bring in outside help to turn away outside danger. Any fool will realize we cannot gather the packs at this time of year. The Wise and the pups would perish during the journey. Whole packs might be lost if a blizzard came down during the time of travel. Not to mention that there is no place to rally. The old packfast at Morvain Rocks has been a ruin since my granddam's granddam's time. It would be impossible to rebuild it in this weather, with Zhotak huntresses nipping around our heels. The reconstruction is a task that would take years anyway, as it did in the long ago. So the only possible choice is to petition the silth."

Now Pohsit came forward, speaking for her faction among the Wise. She denounced the silth bitterly, and castigated Skiljan and Gerrien for even suggesting having unnecessary contact with them. Her opposition weakened Skiljan in the eyes of her neighbors.

But the sagan did not speak for a unanimous body of the Wise. Saettle, the teacher of Skiljan's loghouse, represented another faction arguing against Pohsit. She and the sagan squared off. They were no friends anyway. Marika was afraid fur would fly, and it might have had the prisoner not been there to remind everyone of a very real external threat. Fear of the nomads kept emotions from running wild.

Who were these silth creatures? The meth of the packfast down at the joining of rivers. But what was so terrible about them? Why did some of the Wise hate them so? Pohsit seemed as irrational about them as she was about Marika herself.

Was it because they feared the silth would displace them? There seemed an undercurrent of that.

Unexpectedly, old Zertan shrieked, "Trapped between grauken and the All! I warned you. I warned you all. Do not stint the rituals, I said. But you would not listen."

After the first instant of surprise, Granddam was talking to air. Even her contemporaries ignored her. For a moment Marika pitied her. To this end an entire life. To become old and ignored in the loghouse one once ruled.

Marika firmed her emotions. Zertan had had her day. Her mind and strength were gone. It was best she stepped aside. Only, among the meth, one never stepped. One was pushed. All life long, one pushed and was pushed, and the strong survived.

And where did that leave the Kublins, brilliant but physically weak? Kublin, Marika knew, would not be alive now had he not been blessed with a mind that overshadowed those of the other pups. He was able to think his way around many of his weaknesses and talk his way out of much of the trouble that found him.

Below, the policy discussion raged on, but the real decisions had been made. The prisoner would be questioned, then a runner would be sent to the packfast. Everyone would remain inside the stockade till she returned. Food and firewood rationing would begin immediately, though there was plenty of both in storage. The loghouses would bring out their hidden stores of iron weapons and prepare them. The pack would outwait the nomads if possible, hoping that either hunger would move them toward easier prey or the packfast would send help. Hard decisions would await developments.

Hard decisions. Like winnowing the pack by pushing the old and weak and youngest male pups outside the stockade. Marika shuddered.

And then she fell asleep, though she had been determined to stay awake till the last outsider left.

III

With their interest thoroughly piqued, Marika and Kublin visited Machen Cave often. Each time they took advantage of their youth to shake Pohsit, running long circles, often dashing all the way down to the bank of the Hainlin before turning back to cross the hills and woods to where the cavern lay. The sagan could have tracked them by scent, had she the will, but after five miles of ups and downs old muscles gave out. Pohsit would limp back to the packstead, jaw grimly set. There she would grumble and mutter to the Wise, but dared not indict the pups before their dam. Not just for running her to exhaustion. That would be viewed as common youthful insolence.

Pohsit knew they were running her. And they knew she knew. It was a cruel pup's game. And Kublin often repeated his suggestion of escalated cruelty. Marika refused to take him seriously.

Pohsit never discovered that they were running to Machen Cave. Else she would have gone there and waited, and been delighted by what she saw.

That thing that Kublin had sensed first remained in or around the cavern. The sinister air was there always, though the pups never discovered its cause.

Its very existence opened their minds. Marika found herself unearthing more and more inexplicable and unpredictable talents. She found that she could locate anyone she knew usually just by concentrating and reaching out. She found that she could, at times, catch a glimmer of thought when she concentrated on wanting to know what was in the mind of someone she could see.

Such abilities frightened her even though she began using them.

It must be something of the sort that upset Pohsit so, she thought. But why were Pohsit's intentions so deadly?

There was a nostalgic, sad tone to their prowlings that summer, for they knew it was the last when they could run completely free. Adulthood, with its responsibilities and taboos, was bearing down.

After the ground became sufficiently dry to permit tilling, the Degnan began spring planting around their stockade. Upper Ponath agriculture was crude. The meth raised one grain, which had come north with tradermales only a generation earlier, and a few scrawny, semidomesticated root vegetables. The meth diet was heavy on meats, for they were a species descended of carnivores and were just beginning a transition to the omnivorous state. Their grown things were but a supplement making surviving winter less difficult.

Males and pups did the ground breaking, two males pulling a forked branch plow, the blade of which had been hardened in fire. The earth was turned up only a few inches deep. During the growing season the pups spent much of their time weeding.

Summers were busy for the huntresses, for the upper Ponath meth kept no domesticated animals. All meat came of game.

Their cousins in the south did herd meat animals. Several packs had had tradermales bring breeding stock north, but the beasts were not hardy enough to survive the winters.

Tradermales had suggested keeping the animals in the loghouses during the bitter months. The huntresses sneered at such silliness. Share a loghouse with beasts! Tradermales had shown how to construct a multiple-level loghouse, leaving the lowest level for animals, whose body heat would help warm the upper levels. But that was a change in ways. The meth of the upper Ponath viewed change with deep suspicion.

They suspected the traders of everything, for those males did not conform even remotely to traditional male roles.

Yet one of the high anticipations of spring was the coming of tradermales, with their news of the world, their wild tales, their precious trade goods. Each year they came trekking up the Hainlin, sometimes only a handful carrying their wares in packs on their backs, sometimes a train with beasts of burden. The magnitude of their coming depended upon what the Wise of the packs had ordered the summer before.

The dreamers Marika and Kublin awaited their coming with an anticipation greater than that of their packmates. They plagued the outsiders with ten thousand questions, none of which they seemed to mind. They answered in amusement, spinning wondrous tales. Some were so tall Marika accused them of lying. That amused them even more.

In the year of Machen Cave the anticipation was especially high, for Saettle had ordered a new book brought to the packstead, and much of the winter before the huntresses of Skiljan's loghouse had trapped otec to acquire furs sufficient to pay for it. The snows were gone and the fields were plowed. The greater and lesser moons approached the proper conjunction. The excitement was barely restrained. It was near time for spring rites as well as for the advent of strangers.

But the tradermales did not come.

While they were days late, no one worried. When they were weeks behind, meth wondered, and messengers ran between packsteads asking if tradermales had been seen. There was grave concern among packs which had ordered goods the lack of which might make surviving winter difficult.

They were very late, but they did come at last, without an explanation of why. They were less friendly than in the past, more hurried and harried, lacking in patience. At most packsteads they remained only hours before moving along. There was little spreading of news or telling of tales.

At the Degnan packstead a group nighted over, for the Degnan packstead was known as one of the most comfortable and hospitable. The traders told a few tales by firelight in the square at the center of the packstead, as though in token for their keep. But everyone could tell their hearts were not in the storytelling.

Marika and Kublin cornered an old tradermale they had seen every year they could recall, one who had befriended them in the past and remembered their names from summer to summer. Never shy, Marika asked, "What is the matter this summer, Khronen? Why did you come so late? Why are you all so unhappy?"

This old male was not as grave as the others. One reason they liked him so was that he was a jolly sort, still possessing some of the mischief of a pup. A bit of that shone through now. "The greater world, pups. The greater world. Odd things are stirring. A taint of them has reached this far."

Marika did not understand. She said so.

"Well, little one, consider our brotherhood as a pack stretching across all the world. Now think about what happens when there is argument between loghouses in your packstead. The loghouses of the brotherhood are at odds. There has been heated division. Everyone is frightened of what it may mean. We are all anxious to finish the season and return, lest something be missed in our absence. Do you see that?"

Both pups understood well enough. Skiljan and Gerrien often allied against other heads of loghouse. Within Skiljan's loghouse itself there was factionalism, especially among the Wise. The old females plotted and skirmished and betrayed one another in small ways, constantly, for the amusement of it. They were too old to be entertained by anything else.

Skiljan joined Marika, Kublin, and the old tradermale. She called him by name and, when the pups were surprised, admitted, "I have known Khronen many years. Since he was only a year older that Kublin."

Khronen nodded. "Since before I joined the traders."

"You are Degnan?" Marika asked.

"No. I was Laspe. Your dam and I encountered one another down by the river when we were your age. She tried to poach some Laspe blackberries. I caught her. It was a grand row."

Marika looked from the male to Skiljan and back. Seldom did she think of her dam having been a pup.

Skiljan growled, "You persist in that lie. After all these years I would think you could admit that you were trespassing on Degnan ground."

"After all these years I could still find my way to that berry patch and show that it is on Laspe ground."

Marika saw her dam was growing angry. She tried to think of a way to calm her. But Khronen stepped in instead. "That is neither here nor there, now," he said. To Kublin, he added, "She will never grow comfortable with males who do not whimper and cringe when she bares her fangs." Back to Skiljan, "You have something on your mind, old opponent?"

"I overheard what you said to the pups. I suspect that something which so stresses the tradermale brethren might affect the fortunes of my pack. It occurred to me that you might advise us in ways we might serve ourselves as a result."

Khronen nodded. "Yes. There are things I cannot say, of course. But I can advise." He was thoughtful for a time. Then he said, "I suggest you look to your defenses. It may be a harsh winter. I would suggest you invest in the best iron arrowheads, knives, and axes."

"You sell them too dearly."

"I am selling nothing. I am telling you what I believe the wise huntress would do if she were privy to the knowledge I possess. You are free to ignore me, as you so often do. Equally, you are free to buy. Or to make your own arrowheads and whatnot of stone, faithful to the old ways."

"You were always sarcastic, were you not?"

"I have always been possessed of a certain intolerance toward attitudes and beliefs held by the huntresses and Wise of the upper Ponath. Clinging to ways and beliefs obviously false serves no one well."

Skiljan bared her teeth. But Khronen did not submit, as a male of the Degnan might.

The pack's attitudes toward tradermale tools and weapons certainly baffled Marika. They dwarfed the stone in quality, yet seldom were used. Each summer the Wise and huntresses bought axes, arrowheads, knives both long and short, and even the occasional iron plowshare. Whatever they could afford. And almost always those purchases went into hiding and were hoarded, never to be used, deemed too precious to be risked.

What was the point?

Skiljan and Gerrien traded all their otec furs for worked iron that summer. And so that summer laid another shadow of tomorrow upon Marika's path.

CHAPTER THREE

I

The first enraged tentacles of the blizzard were lashing around the loghouse. Down on the ground floor, the argument persisted still, though now most of the spirit was out of it, most of the outside huntresses had returned to their loghouses, and those who remained did so purely out of perverse stubbornness.

Marika was just wakening, right where she had fallen asleep, when old Saettle left the press and approached the foot of the ladder. She beckoned. "Pups down here. Time for lessons."

"Now?" Marika asked.

"Yes. Come down."

Shivering, those pups old enough for lessons slipped down and eased past the still snarling adults. Saettle settled them on the male side, according to age and learning development, and brought out the books.

There were six of those, and they were the most precious possessions of the loghouse. Some had been recopied many times, at great expense in otec furs. Some were newer.

The pack, and especially those who dwelt in Skiljan's loghouse, was proud of its literacy. Even most Degnan males learned to read, write, and cipher. Though not consciously done as a social investment, this literacy was very useful in helping Degnan males survive once they were sent forth from the packstead. Such skills made them welcome in the other packsteads of the upper Ponath.

Early on Marika had noticed the importance of motivation in learning. Males, when young, were as bored by the lessons as were most of the female pups. But as the males neared adulthood and the spring rites which would see them sent forth from the packstead to find a new pack or perish, their level of interest increased exponentially.

The central thread of pack education was the Chronicle, a record that traced pack history from its legendary founder, Bognan, a rogue male who carried off a female and started the line. That had happened many hundreds of years ago, far to the south, before the long migration into the upper Ponath.

The story, the Wise assured the young, was entirely mythical. A tale wilder than most, for no male would dare such a thing. Nor would any be capable, the sex being less smart, weaker, and emotionally more unstable than the female. But it was a tale fun to tell outsiders, whom it boggled. Every pack had its black forebears. Once they drifted into the mists of time, they became objects of pride.

Six books in Skiljan's loghouse. Almost as many in the rest of the packstead. And the Degnan packstead possessed more than all the other packs of the upper Ponath. Ragged as the packstead was, it was a center of culture and learning. Some summers other packs sent favored female pups to study with the Degnan. Friendships were made and alliances formed, and the Degnan strengthened their place as the region's leading pack.

Marika was proud to have been born into such an important pack.

The lessons were complete and the morning was well advanced. The angry excitement of the night before had degraded, but the diehards were at it still. Rested huntresses returned from other loghouses. Tempers were shorter than ever.

The prisoner, unable to sustain his terror forever and overcome by exhaustion, had fallen asleep. He lay there ignored, huntresses stepping over and around him almost indifferently. Marika wondered if he had been forgotten.

Some common ground did exist. A watch was established in the watchtower, a task which rotated among the older pups. Most of the less interested adults began preparing for possible siege.

All those precious iron-tool treasures, so long hoarded, came out of hiding. The edges of axes and knives received loving attention. Arrows were mated to iron heads fearsome with many barbs. Marika noted that the heads were affixed to strike horizontally instead of vertically, as hunting arrows were. Meth ribs ran parallel to the ground rather than perpendicular.

More arrows, cruder ones, were made quickly. More spears were fashioned. Scores of javelins were made of sticks with their points hardened in the firepits. The older pups were shown basic fighting techniques. Even the males trained with spears, javelins, tools, and knives—when they were not otherwise occupied.

Skiljan, exercising her prerogative as head of loghouse, supported by Gerrien and most of the Degnan Wise, ended the everlasting debate by evicting all outsiders from her loghouse.

The Wise of the pack were more in concert than the huntresses. They issued advices which, because of the near unanimity behind them, fell with the force of orders. What had been preparations made catch-as-catch-can became orderly and almost organized. As organized and cooperative as ever meth became.

They first ordered a short sleep for the cooling of emotions.

Marika wakened from hers uneasy. Kublin was snuggled against her, restless. What was wrong? The psychic atmosphere was electric. There was a stench in it…. Pain. And fear. Like that touch when the huntresses were out seeking the source of the scream she had heard.

A true scream ripped up from the ground level. She and Kublin scrambled to the ladder's head, making no friends among pups already crouched there.

They were questioning the prisoner. Pohsit was holding his paw in the huntress's firepit. Another of the Wise sat at his head, repeating a question over and over in a soft voice. He did not respond, except to howl when Pohsit thrust his paw into the coals again.

The pups were neither upset nor disgusted, only curious. They battled for the best spots around the ladderhead. Marika was sure one would get pushed through the hole.

The torment went on and on. Marika whispered, "They won't get him to tell them anything."

Kublin nodded. He sensed it too.

Marika examined him. His nerves seemed frayed. Hers surely were. While she did not feel the prisoner's pain, she did catch the psychic scent of his fear and distress, the leak-over from his scrambled mind. She did not know how to push it away.

Kublin seemed to be feeling all that, too.

Pohsit looked up at them. Her lips pulled back over her teeth in a silent, promising snarl. Kublin inched closer. Marika felt his frightened shiver.

She did not need to touch the sagan's mind to know what she was thinking.

Pobuda, Skiljan's second, beckoned. "Down, pups. There is work to do." A massive rock of a female, she stood unmoved as pups tumbled about her, eager to be entrusted with something important. For that was what her tone and phrasing had implied. She had spoken as huntress to huntress.

"Marika. Kublin. You go see Horvat."

"Horvat? But—"

Pobuda's paw bounced off Marika's ear. Marika scooted around the prisoner and his tormentors. He was unconscious. She and Kublin awaited recognition at the edge of Wise territory. Receiving a nod from Saettle, they crossed over to the males' firepit, where Horvat was supervising some sort of expansion project. He was snarling because the hide umbrella, which gathered smoke to send it up a thin pottery flue, was cooked and smoked hard and brittle, and wanted to break rather than bend.

Marika said, "Horvat, Pobuda told us—"

"See Bhlase."

They found the young male, who had come to the pack only two years earlier. "Ah. Good," he said. "Come." He led them to the storage room. "Too dark in there. Kublin. Get a lamp."

Marika waited nervously. She had not visited this end of the loghouse since she was too small to know better. All the usual rules were falling....

Kublin arrived with an oil lamp. Bhlase took it and pushed through the doorskins. It was cold and dark in the storage room. It was more crowded than the loft.

But it was neat—obsessively neat, reflecting Horvat's personality. Bhlase moved about, studying this and that. Marika gawked. The male handed the lamp back to Kublin. Then he started piling leather bags and sealed pottery jars into Marika's arms. "Those go to the firepit."

Though irked by his tone, Marika did as she was told. Bhlase followed with a load of his own. He ordered their plunder neatly, set the pups down, gave Kublin and Marika each a mortar and pestle. He settled between them with his legs surrounding a kettle. He drew a knife.

Marika was astonished. The kettle was copper, the knife iron.

Bhlase opened one leather bag and used a ceramic spoon to ladle dried, crushed leaves into Marika's mortar bowl. "Grind that into powder. I'll need ten more like that."

Marika began the dull task. Bhlase turned to Kublin. More, but different, dried, crushed leaves went into his mortar bowl. These gave off a pungent odor immediately. "Ten from you, too, Kublin."

Marika recalled that Bhlase had been accepted by Skiljan because of his knowledge of herbs and such, which exceeded that of Pohsit.

But what were they doing?

Bhlase had brought several items Marika connected only with cooking. A sieve. A cutting board. A grater. The grater he set into the kettle. He cut the wax seal off one of the jars and removed several wrinkled, almost meth-shaped roots. He grated them into the bowl. A bitter scent rose.

"That is good enough, Marika." He took her mortar bowl, dumped it into the sieve, flung the bigger remains into the firepit. They flashed and added a grassy aroma to the thousands of smells haunting the loghouse. "Nine more will do it. How is yours coming, Kublin? Yes. That is fine. Dump it here. Good. Nine more for you."

"Are you not scared, Bhlase?" Marika asked. He seemed unreasonably calm.

"I have been through this before. When I was a pup, nomads besieged our packstead. They are ferocious but not very smart. Kill a few and they will run away till they have eaten their dead."

"That is awful."

"*They* are awful." Bhlase finished grating roots. He put the grater aside, sieved again, then took up the cutting board. The jar he opened this time contained dead insects the size of the last joint on Marika's smallest finger. He halved each longwise, cut each half crosswise, scraped the results into the kettle. After finishing the insects he opened a jar which at first seemed to contain only a milky fluid. After he poured that into the pot, though, he dumped several dozen fat white grubs onto his cutting board.

"What are we making, Bhlase?" Kublin asked.

"Poison. For the arrowheads and spearheads and javelins."

"Oh!" Marika nearly dropped her pestle.

Bhlase was amused. "It is harmless now. Except for these." He indicated the grubs, which he was dicing with care. "All this will have to simmer together for a long time."

"We have never used poisons," Kublin said.

"I was not here last time nomads came to the Degnan packstead," Bhlase replied. Marika thought she detected a certain arrogance behind his words.

"None of us were," she countered. "That was so long ago Granddam was leader."

"That is true, too." Bhlase broached another jar of grubs. And another after that. Kublin and Marika finished their grinding. Bhlase continued doing grubs till the copper kettle was filled to within three inches of its rim. He took that to a tripod Horvat had prepared, hung it, adjusted it just so over the fire. He beckoned.

"I am going to build the fire just as it must be," he said. "You two keep it exactly the same." He thrust a long wooden spoon into the pot. "And stir it each few minutes. The insects tend to float. The grubs sink. Try not to breathe too much of the steam."

"For how long?" Kublin asked.

"Till it is ready."

Marika and Kublin exchanged pained glances. Pups always got stuck with the boring jobs.

Over by the other firepit, the huntresses and Wise were still trying to get the prisoner to say something useful. He still refused. The loghouse was growing chilly, what with the coming and going of meth from other loghouses.

"Pohsit is enjoying herself," Marika observed, stirring the poison. She kept rehearsing the formula in her mind. She had recognized all the ingredients. None were especially rare. It might become useful knowledge one day.

Kublin looked at Pohsit, gulped, and concentrated on the fire.

II

So time fled. Sharpening of tools into weapons. Making of crude javelins, spears, and arrows. Males and older pups drilling with the cruder weapons over and over. The initial frenzy of preparation faded as nothing immediate occurred. The lookouts saw no sign of imminent nomad attack. No sign of nomads at all.

Was the crisis over without actually beginning?

The captive died never having said anything of interest—as Marika had expected. The huntresses dragged him out and hurled him off the stockade to lie in the snow before the gate, mute and mutilated. A warning.

Marika wished she had had a chance to talk with the prisoner. She knew next to nothing about the lands beyond the Zhotak.

The huntresses chafed at their confinement, though their restlessness sprang entirely from their minds. In winter they often went longer without leaving the packstead. There were disputes about whether or not the gate should be opened. Bitter cold continued to devour wood stores.

Skiljan and Gerrien kept the gate sealed.

The weather conspired to support them.

Marika took her turn in the watchtower and saw the nothing she expected to see. Her watch was not long, but it was cold. An ice storm had coated everything with crystal. Footing was treacherous everywhere. Males not otherwise occupied cleared ice and snow and erected platforms behind the stockade so huntresses could hurl missiles from their vantage. A few tried to break stones loose from the pile kept for use in a possible raid, but they had trouble. The ice storm had frozen the pile into a single glob.

Kublin called the alarm during his afternoon watch. The huntresses immediately assumed his imagination had gotten the best of him, he being a flighty pup and male to boot. But a pair of huntresses clambered up the tower, their weight making it creak and sway, as had been done with several earlier false alarms.

Kublin was not a victim of his imagination, though at first he had trouble convincing the huntresses that he was indeed seeing what he saw. His eyes were very sharp. Once he did convince them, they dismissed him. He returned to the loghouse to bask in unaccustomed attention.

"I saw smoke," he announced proudly. "A lot of smoke, far away."

Skiljan questioned him vigorously—"What direction? How far? How high did it rise? What color was it?"—till he became confused and frustrated.

His answers caused a stir.

Marika had less experience of the far countryside than did her elders. It took her longer to understand.

Smoke in that direction, east, at that distance, in that color, could mean only one thing. The packstead of their nearest neighbors, the Laspe, was burning. And packsteads did not burn unless intentionally set ablaze.

The Degnan packstead frothed with argument again. The central question was: to send scouts or not. Skiljan and Gerrien wanted to know exactly what had happened. Many of those who only hours earlier had demanded the gate be opened now wanted it kept closed. Even a large portion of the Wise did not want to risk huntresses if the nomads were that close.

Skiljan settled the question by fiat. She gathered a dozen huntresses of like mind and marched out. She had her companions arm as huntresses seldom did, with an assortment of missile weapons, hatchets and axes, knives, and even a few shields. Shields normally were used only in mock combats fought during the celebrations held at the turning of each season.

Marika crowded into the watchtower with the sentry on duty. She watched her dam's party slip and slide across the ice-encrusted snowfields till they vanished into the woods east of the packstead.

When she returned to her loghouse, they gave her the iron axe her dam had been sharpening, and showed her what to do. Skiljan had taken it from the nomads she had slain. It had not been cared for properly. Many hours would be required to give it a proper edge.

Not far away, Pobuda and several others—Wise, males, and huntresses who pretended to some skill in metalworking—were etching the blades of arrowheads and spears. Bhlase sat in the center of their circle with his pot of poison, carefully painting a brown, gummy substance into the etchings with a tiny brush. Marika noted that he wore gloves. The young huntress who carried the finished weapons away also wore gloves, and racked them out of the reach of the younger pups.

Marika soon grew bored with grinding the axe's edge. She had too much energy to sit still all the time. Too many strange thoughts fled through her mind while she ran the whetstone over that knicked piece of iron. She tried to banish the thoughts, to touch her dam.

There were distractions. The touch came and went. She followed the scouting party peripatetically. Mostly, she tasted their fear. Kublin kept coming to her with questions in his eyes. She kept shaking her head till his curiosity frayed her temper. "Get away!" she snarled. "Leave me alone! I'll tell you when there's something to tell."

Sometimes she tried to touch Grauel, who carried the Degnan's message to the packfast. She could not find Grauel. But she did not worry. Grauel was the best of the pack in field and forest. If she did not get through, none could, and there was no hope from that direction.

The scouts returned at dusk, unharmed but grim. Again Skiljan's loghouse filled with the adult female population of the packstead. This evening they were more subdued, for they sensed that the news was bad. Skiljan's report was terse.

"Nomads attacked the Laspe packstead. They managed to breach the palisade. They took the stores and weapons and tools, fired the loghouses, and ran away. They did not kill everyone, nor did they take many of the pups. Survivors we talked to said the nomads have taken the Brust packstead and are using it as their base."

End of report. What was not said was as frightening as what was. The Laspe, without stores or tools or weapons, would not survive. The Brust, of course, would all be dead already.

Someone suggested the Laspe pack's huntresses be brought into the Degnan packstead. "Extra paws to bear arms when the nomads come here. And thus the pack name would not die. Come summer they could take new males and rebuild."

Skiljan shook her head. "The nomads are barbarians but not fools. They did slay every female of pupbearing age. The huntresses forced them." She looked at the huntress who had spoken as though *she* were a fool.

That was the meth way—savagery to the last in defense of the pack. Only those too young or too old to lift a weapon would have been spared. The Laspe could be stricken from the roll of upper Ponath packs.

Marika was amazed everyone took the news with such calm. Two packs known obliterated. It had been several generations since even one had been overrun completely. It was a huge disaster, and portended far worse to come.

"What about the nomads?" someone asked. Despite tension, the gathering continued subdued, without snarling or jostling. "How heavy a price did they pay?"

"Not a price dear enough. The Laspe survivors claimed there were ten tens of tens of attackers."

A disbelieving murmur ran through the gathering.

"It does sound impossible. But they left their dead behind. We examined dozens of bodies. Most were armed males." This assertion caused another stir, heavy with distress. "They wore fetishes identifiable as belonging to more than twenty different packs. We questioned a young male left for dead, that the Laspe had not yet tortured. His will was less strong than that of our recent guest. He had much to say before he died."

Another stir. Then everyone waited expectantly.

Skiljan said, "He claimed the spring saw the rise of a powerful wehrlen among the nomads. A rogue male of no apparent pack, who came out of nowhere and who made his presence felt throughout the north in a very short time."

A further and greater stir, and now some mutters of fear.

A wehrlen? Marika thought. What was that? It was a word she did not know. There was so much she did not know.

At the far end of the loghouse, the males had ceased working and were paying close attention. They were startled and frightened. Their fur bristled. They knew, whatever a wehrlen was.

Murmurs of "rogue" and "male silth" fluttered through the gathering. It seemed Marika was not alone in not recognizing the word.

"He began by overwhelming the females of an especially strong and famous pack. Instead of gathering supplies for the winter, he marched that pack into the territory of a neighbor. He used the awe of his fighters and his powers to overcome its huntresses. He added it to the force he had already, and so on, expanding till he controlled scores of packs. The prisoner said the news of him began to run before him. He fired the north with a vision of conquest.

He has entered the upper Ponath, not just because it is winter and the game has migrated out of the north, but to recapture the Ponath from us, whose foredams took the land from the ancestors of the nomads. The prisoner even suggested that the wehrlen one day wants to unite all the packs of the world. Under *his* paw."

The Wise muttered among themselves. Those who had opposed the sending of Grauel to the packfast put their heads together. After a time one rose to announce, "We withdraw our former objections to petitioning the silth. This is an abomination of the filthiest sort. There is no option but to respond with the power of the older abomination."

Only crazy old Zertan remained adamantly against having any intercourse with the packfast.

Skiljan said, "Gerrien and I talked while returning from the Laspe packstead. It is our feeling that another message must be sent. The silth must know what we have learned today. It might encourage them to send help. If not that, they must know for their own sakes."

The motion carried. One of Gerrien's huntresses, Barlog, was selected for the task and sent out immediately. Meth did not enjoy traveling by night, but that was the safer time. By dawn Barlog should be miles ahead of any nomad who might cross her trail.

What could be done had been done. There was nothing more to discuss. The outsiders went away.

Saettle called the pups to lessons.

Marika took the opportunity to ask about the wehrlen. Saettle would not answer in front of the younger pups. She seemed embarrassed. She said, "Such monsters, like grauken, are better not discussed while they are howling outside the stockade."

It was plain enough there were no circumstances under which Saettle would explain. Baffled, Marika retreated to her furs.

Kublin wanted to talk about it. "Zambi says—"

"Zambi is a fool," she snapped without hearing what her other littermate had to say. Then, aware that she was behaving foolishly herself, she called, "Zambi? Where are you? Come here."

Grumbling surlily, her other littermate came out of the far shadows, where he had been clustered with his cronies. He was big for his age. He looked old enough to leave the packstead already. He had gotten the size and strength and endurance that Kublin had been shorted. "What do you want?" he demanded.

"I want to know what you know about this wehrlen thing."

Zamberlin rolled his eyes. "The All forfend. You waste my time...." He stopped. Marika's lips were back, her eyes hot. "All right. All right. Don't get all bothered. All I know is Poogie said Wart said he heard Horvat say a wehrlen is like a Wise meth, only a lot more so. Like a male sagan, I guess, only he don't have to be old. Like a male silth, Horvat said. Only I don't know what that is."

"Thank you, Zambi."

"Don't call me that, Marika. My name is Zamberlin."

"Oh. Listen to the big guy. Go on back to your friends."

Kublin wanted to talk. Marika did not. She said, "Let me go to sleep, Kub." He let her be, but for a long time she lay curled in her furs thinking.

Someone wakened her in the night for a brief stint in the watchtower. She bundled herself and went, and spent her time studying the sky. The clouds had cleared away. The stars were bright, though few and though only the two biggest moons were up, Biter and Chaser playing their eternal game of tag. The light they shed was not enough to mask the fainter stars.

Still, only a few score were visible.

Something strange, that sea of darkness above. Stars were other suns, the books said. So far away that one could not reach them if one walked a thousand lifetimes—if there was a road. According to Saettle's new book, though, the meth of the south knew ways through the great dark. They wandered among the stars quite regularly....

Silth. That name occurred in the new book, though in no way that explained what silth were, or why the Wise should fear them so. It was silth sisters, the book said, who ventured across the ocean of night.

Nothing happened during Marika's watch, as she had expected. Meth did not move by night if they could avoid it. The dark was a time of fear....

How, then, did these silth creatures manage the gulf between the stars? How did they *breathe*? Saettle's book said there was no air out there.

Marika's relief startled her. She felt the tower creak and sway, came back to reality with a guilty start. The nomads could have slipped to and over the palisade without her noticing.

She returned to her furs and lay awake a long time, head aswirl with stars. She tried to follow the progress of the messengers and was startled at how clearly the touch came tonight. She could grasp wisps of their thoughts.

Grauel was far down the river now, traveling by moonlight, and only hours away from the packfast. She had expected to arrive sooner but had been delayed by deep drifts in places, and by having to avoid nomads a few times. Barlog was making better time, gaining on the other huntress. She was thinking of continuing after sunrise.

Emboldened by her success, Marika strayed farther afield, curious about the packfast itself. But she could not locate the place, and there was no one there she knew. There was no familiar resonance she could home in on.

Still curious, she roamed the nearby hills, searching for nomads. Several times she brushed what might have been minds, but without any face she could visualize she could not come close enough to capture thoughts. Once, eastward, she brushed something powerful and hurried away, frightened. It had a vaguely male flavor. This wehrlen creature the Wise were so fussed about?

Then she gave herself a real nightmare scare. She sent her thoughts drifting up around Machen Cave, and there she found that dread thing she had sensed last summer, only now it was awake and in a malevolent mood—and seemingly aware of her inspection. As she reeled away, ducked, and fled, she had a mental image of a huge, starving beast charging out of the cave at some small game unlucky enough to happen by.

Twice in the next few minutes she thought she felt it looking for her, blundering around like a great, angry, stupid, hungry beast. She huddled into her furs and shook.

She would have to warn Kublin.

Sleep finally came.

Nothing happened all next day. In tense quiet the pack simply continued to prepare for trouble, and the hours shuffled away. The huntresses spoke infrequently, and then only in low voices. The males spoke not at all. Horvat drove them mercilessly. The Wise sent up appeals to the All, helped a little, got in the way a lot.

Marika did another turn on watch, and sharpened the captured axe, which her dam deemed a task suitable for a pup her age.

III

Autumn had come. High spirits were less often seen. Huntresses ranged the deep woods, ambushing game already migrating southward. Males smoked and salted with a more grim determination. Pups haunted the woods, gleaning deadwood. The Wise read omens in the flights of flyers, the coloration of insects, how much mast small arboreals stowed away, how deep the gurnen burrowed his place of hibernation.

If the signs were unfavorable, the Wise would authorize the felling of living trees and a second or even third gathering of chote root. Huntresses would begin keeping a more than casual eye on the otec colonies and other bearers of fur, seeing what preparations they made for winter. It was in deep winter that those would be taken for their meat and hides.

As winter gathered its legions behind the Zhotak, and the meth of the upper Ponath became ever more mindful of the chance of sudden, deadly storms, time for play, for romping the woods on casual expeditions, became ever more scarce. There was always work for any pair of paws capable of contributing. Among the Degnan even the toddlers did their part.

As many as five days might pass without Marika's getting a chance to run free. Then, usually, she was on firewood detail. Pups tended to slip away from that. Their shirking was tolerated.

That autumn the Wise concluded that it would be a hard winter, but they did not guess half the truth. Even so, the Degnan always put away far more than they expected to need. A simple matter of sensible precaution.

Marika slipped off to Machen Cave for the last time on a day when the sky was gray and the wind was out of the north, damp and chill. The Wise were arguing about whether or not it bore the scent of snow, about who had the most reliable aches and pains in paws and joints. It was a day when Pohsit was lamenting her thousand infirmities, so it seemed she would not be able to rise, much less chase pups over hill and meadow.

Marika went alone. Horvat had Kublin scraping hides, a task he hated—which was why Horvat had him doing it. To teach him that one must do that which one hates as well as that which one enjoys.

It was a plain, simple run through the woods for Marika, a few hours on the slope opposite that where Machen Cave lay, stretching her new sensing in an effort to find the shadow hidden in the earth. Nothing came of it, and after a time she began wandering back toward the packstead, pausing occasionally to pick up a nut overlooked by the tree dwellers. She cracked those with her teeth, then extracted the sweet nutmeat. She noted the position of a rare, late-blooming medicinal plant, and collected a few fallen branches just so it would not seem she had wasted an entire afternoon. It was getting dusky when she reached the gate.

She found Zamberlin waiting there, almost hiding in a shadow. "Where have you been?" he demanded. He did not await an answer. "You better get straight to Dam before anyone sees you."

"What in the world?" She could see he was shaken, that he was frightened, but not for himself. "What's happened, Zambi?"

"Better see Dam. Pohsit claims you tried to murder her."

"What?" She was not afraid at first, just astonished.

"She says you pushed her off Stapen Rock."

Fear came. But it was not fear for herself. If someone had pushed Pohsit, it must have been…

"Where is Dam?"

"By the doorway of Gerrien's loghouse. I think she's waiting for you. Don't tell her I warned you."

"Don't worry." Marika marched into the packstead, disposed of her burden at the first woodpile, spied her dam, went straight over. She was frightened now, but still much more for Kublin than for herself. "Dam?"

"Where have you been, Marika?"

"In the woods."

"Where in the woods?"

"Out by Machen Cave."

That startled Skiljan. "What were you doing out there?"

"I go there sometimes. When I want to think. Nobody else ever goes. I found some hennal."

Skiljan squinted at her. "You did not pass near Stapen Rock?"

"No, Dam. I have heard what Pohsit claims. Pohsit is mad, you know. She has been trying—"

"I know what she has been trying, pup. Did you decide you were a huntress and would get her before she got you?"

"No, Dam."

Skiljan's eyes narrowed. Marika thought her dam believed her, but also suspected she might know something she would not admit.

"Dam?"

"Yes?"

"If I may speak? I would suggest a huntress of Grauel's skill backtrack my scent."

"That will not be necessary. I am confident that you had nothing to do with it."

"Was she really hurt, Dam? Or just pretending?"

"Half and half. There is no doubt she took a fall. But she was able to walk home and raise a stink. A very inept murder attempt if it was such. I am inclined to think she was clumsy. Though what a meth her age was doing trying to climb Stapen Rock is beyond me. Go now. Stay away from Pohsit for a few days."

"Yes, Dam."

Marika went looking for Kublin immediately. She found him where she had left him. She started to snarl, but before he even looked up he asked, in a voice no one else could hear, "How could you do such a bad job of it, Marika? Why didn't you mash her head with a boulder while she was down, or something?"

Marika gulped. Kublin thought she had done it? Confused, she mumbled something about having had nothing to do with Pohsit's fall. She withdrew.

Not till next day did she become suspicious. By then trails and evidences were impossible to find. And Kublin adamantly denied having had anything to do with it himself, though Marika *was* able to isolate a period when no one had seen him around the packstead. She could establish him no alibi. She did not press, though. For Kublin, a male, even circumstantial evidence would be enough to convict.

In time even Pohsit began to wonder if the whole incident were not a product of her imagination. Imaginary or not, though, she let it feed her hatred, her irrational fear, her determination. Marika began to fear something *would* have to be done about the sagan.

Luckily, more and more of the Degnan were sure Pohsit was slipping into her dotage. Persecution fears and crazy vendettas were common among the Wise.

Marika did her best to stay out of the sagan's way. And when winter brought worse than anyone expected, even Pohsit relented a little, in the spirit of the pack against the outside.

CHAPTER FOUR

I

Marika's next night watch was very late, or very early in the morning. The stars had begun to fade as the sun's first weak rays straggled around the curve of the world. She stared at the heavens and daydreamed again, wondering incessantly about things hinted in the new book. What were these silth sisters? What were they finding up there among those alien suns? It was a shame she had been born to a pack on the very edge of civilization instead of in some great city of the south, where she might have a chance to enjoy such adventures.

She probed for the messengers again, and again the touch was sharp. Both had reached the packfast. Both were sleeping restlessly in a cell of stone. Other minds moved around them. Not so densely as in a packstead, where there was a continuous clamor of thought, but many nevertheless. And all adult, all old, as if they were all the minds of the Wise. As if they were minds of sagans, for they had that flavor. One was near the messengers, as if watching over them. Marika tried to touch it more closely, to get the feel of these distant strangers who so frightened the Degnan.

Alarm!

That mind shied in sudden fear, sudden surprise, almost slipping away. Marika was startled herself, for no one ever noticed her.

A countertouch, light for an instant, then hard and sudden like a hammer's blow. Marika whimpered as fractured thought slammed into her mind.

Who are you? Where? What?

There was darkness around the edges of that, and hints of things of terror. Frightened, Marika fled into herself, blanking the world, pinching herself with claws. Pain forced her into her present moment atop the watchtower, alone and cold beneath mocking stars. She stared at Biter's pocked face, so like an old meth Wise female, considering her from the horizon.

What had she done? That old female had been aware of her. Marika's fear redoubled as she recalled all the hints and half-heard talk of her elders that had made her determine to keep her talents hidden. She was certain many of her packmates would be terribly upset if they learned what she could do. Pohsit only suspected, and she wanted to kill....

Had she gone too far, touching that distant female? Had she given herself away? Would there be repercussions?

She returned to her furs and lay a long time staring at the logs overhead, battling fear.

The nomads came next morning. Everyone rushed to the stockade. Even the toddlers, whimpering in their fright. Fear filled the packstead with a stench the north wind did not carry away.

There were about a hundred of the northerners, and they were as ragged as Marika had pictured them. They made no effort to surprise the packstead. That was impossible. They stood off and studied it.

The sky was overcast, but not so heavily that shafts of sunlight did not break through and sweep over the white earth. Each time a rushing finger of light passed over the nomads, it set the heads of spears and arrows aglitter. There was much iron among them, and not all were as careless of their weapons as had been the owner of the axe Marika had sharpened for so long.

Skiljan went around keeping heads down. She did not want the nomads to get a good estimate of numbers. The packstead looked small because its stockade had been built close to the loghouses. Let them think the packstead weaker than it was. They might do something foolhardy and find their backs broken before they learned the truth.

Marika did not find that reasonable thinking. The nomad leaders would have questioned meth from captured packsteads, wouldn't they? Surely they would have learned something about the Degnan packstead.

She gave them too much credit. They seemed wholly ignorant. After a few hours of watching, circling, little rushes toward the stockade by small groups trying to draw a response, a party of five approached the gate slowly, looking to parlay. An old male continued a few steps more after the other four halted. Speaking with an accent which made him almost incomprehensible, he called out, "Evacuate this packstead. Surrender your fortunes to the Shaw. Become one with the Shaw in body and wealth, and none of you will be harmed."

"What is he talking about?" huntresses asked one another. "What is this 'Shaw'?"

The old male stepped closer. More carefully, trying to approximate the upper Ponath dialect more closely, he repeated, "Evacuate the packstead and you will not be harmed."

Skiljan would not deign to speak with a rogue male. She exchanged a meaningful glance with Gerrien, who nodded. "Arrows," Skiljan ordered, and named the five best archers among the Degnan huntresses. "Loose!" An instant later the nomads were down. "That is five we do not have to fight," Skiljan said, as pragmatic as ever.

The crowd on the field sent up a terrible howl. They surged forward, their charge a disorganized, chaotic sweep. The Degnan sent arrows to meet them. A few went down.

"They have ladders," Marika said, peeping between the sharpened points of two stockade logs. "Some of them have ladders, Dam."

Skiljan boxed her ear, demanded, "What are you doing out here? Get inside. Wise! Get these pups cleared off the stockade. Marika. Tell Rechtern I want her."

Rechtern was the eldest of all the Degnan Wise, a resident of Foehse's loghouse. The All had been kind to her. Though she had several years on the next oldest of the Wise, her mind remained clear and her body spry.

Marika scrambled down and, rubbing her ear, went looking for the old female. She found her watching over the pups of Foehse's loghouse as they fled inside. She said, "Honored One, the huntress Skiljan requests you come speak with her." The forms required one to speak so to the Wise, but, in fact, Skiljan's "request" amounted to an order. The iron rule of meth society was stated bluntly in the maxim "As strength goes."

Marika shadowed Rechtern back to the stockade, heard her dam tell the old female, "Arm the males. We may not be able to hold them at the stockade." Only the Wise could authorize arming the males. But a huntress such as Skiljan or Gerrien could order the Wise. There were traditions, and rules, and realities. "As strength goes."

Marika waited in the shadows, listening, shaking, irked because she could not see what was happening. There were snarls and crashes above and outside. There were cries of pain and screams of rage and the clang of metal on metal. The nomads were trying to scale the stockade. The huntresses were pushing them back. On the platforms behind the inner circle of the palisade, old females still able to bend a bow or hurl a javelin sped missiles at any target they saw.

A female cried out overhead. A body thumped down beside Marika, a nomad female gravid but skeletally thin. A long, deep gash ran from her dugs to her belly. Her entrails leaked out, steaming in the cold. A metal knife slipped from her relaxing paw. Marika snatched it up.

Another body fell, barely missing her. This one was an old female of the Degnan. She grunted, tried to rise. A howl of triumph came from above. A huge, lank male leapt down, poised a stone-tipped spear for the kill.

Marika did not think. She hurtled forward, buried the knife in the nomad's back. He jerked away, heaved blood all over his dead packmate. He thrashed and made gurgling sounds for half a minute before finally lying still. Marika darted out and tried to recover the knife. It would not come free. It was lodged between ribs.

Another nomad dropped down, teeth bared in a killing snarl. Marika squeaked and started to back away, eyeing the spear her victim had dropped.

The third invader pitched forward. The old Degnan female who had fallen from the palisade had gotten her feet under her and leapt onto his back, sinking her teeth in his throat. The last weapon, meth called their teeth. Marika snatched up the spear and stabbed, stabbed, stabbed, before the nomad could shake the weak grasp of the old female. No one of her thrusts was a killer, but in sum they brought him down.

Yet another attacker came over the stockade. Marika ran for her loghouse, spear clutched in both paws. She heard Rechtern calling the males out.

More nomads were over the stockade in several other places. A dozen were looking for someone to kill or something to carry away.

The males and remaining old females rushed upon them with skinning knives, hatchets, hammers, hoes, and rakes. Marika stopped just outside the windskins of her loghouse, watched, ready to dart to safety.

More nomads managed to cross the stockade. She thought them fools. Badly mistaken fools. They should have cleared the defenders from the palisade before coming inside. When the huntresses there—few of them had been cut down—no longer faced a rush from outside, they turned and used their bows.

There was no mistaking a nomad struck by an arrow on which Bhlase's poison had been painted. The victim went into a thrashing, screaming, mouth-frothing fit, and for a few seconds lashed out at anyone nearby. Then muscles cramped, knotted, locked his body rigidly till death came. And even then there was no relaxation.

The males and old females fled into the loghouses and held the doorways while the huntresses sniped from the palisade.

The surviving invaders panicked. They had stormed into a death trap. Now they tried to get out again. Most were slain trying to get back over the stockade.

Marika wondered if her dam had planned it that way, or if it was a gift from the All. No matter. The attack was over. The packstead had survived it. The Degnan were safe.

Safe for the moment. There were more nomads. And they could be the sort who would deem defeat a cause for blood feud.

Seventy-six nomad corpses went into a heap outside the stockade. Seventy-six leering heads ended up on a rack as a warning to anyone else considering an attack upon the packstead. Only nineteen of the pack itself died or had to be slain because of wounds. Most of those were old females and males who had been too weak or too poorly armed. Many fine weapons were captured.

Skiljan took a party of huntresses in pursuit of those nomads who had escaped. Many of those were injured or had been too weak to scale the stockade in the first place. Skiljan believed most could be picked off without real risk to herself or those who hunted her.

The Wise ruled that the Mourning be severely truncated. There was no wood to spare for pyres and no time for the elaborate ritual customary when one of the Degnan rejoined the All. It would take a week to properly salute the departure of so many. And they in line behind the three who had fallen near Stapen Rock, as yet unMourned themselves.

The bodies could be stored in the lean-tos against the stockade till the Degnan felt comfortable investing time in the dead. They would not corrupt. Not in weather this cold.

It occurred to Marika that they might serve other purposes in the event of a long siege. That the heaping of dead foes outside was a gesture of defiance with levels of subtext she had not yet fully appreciated.

So bitterly was she schooled against the grauken within that her stomach turned at the very thought.

She volunteered to go up into the tower, to watch Skiljan off.

There was little to see once her dam crested the nearest hill, hot on the tracks of the nomads. Just the males cutting the heads off the enemy, building racks, and muttering among themselves. Just the older pups tormenting a few nomads too badly wounded to fly and poking bodies to see if any still needed the kiss of a knife. Marika felt no need to blood herself.

She had done that the hard way, hadn't she?

But for the bloody snow it could have been any other winter's day. The wind grumbled and moaned as always, sucking warmth with vampirous ferocity. The snow glared whitely where not trampled or blooded. The trees in the nearby forest snapped and crackled with the cold. Flyers squawked, and a few sent shadows racing over the snow as they wheeled above, eyeing a rich harvest of flesh.

Where there is no waste, there is no want. So the Wise told pups more times than any cared to hear or recall.

The old females ordered a blind set in the open field, placed two skilled archers inside, and had several corpses dragged out where the scavengers would think they were safe. When they descended to the feast, the archers picked them off. Pups scampered in with the carcasses. The males let them cool out, then butchered them and added them to the larder.

There was a labor to occupy, but not to preoccupy. One by one, some with an almost furtive step, the Degnan went to the top of the palisade to gaze eastward, worrying.

Skiljan returned long after dark, traveling by Biter light, burdened with trophies and captured weapons. "No more than five escaped," she announced with pride. "We chased them all the way to Toerne Creek, taking them one by one. We could have gotten them all, had we dared go farther. But the smoke of cookfires was heavy in the air."

Again there was an assembly in Skiljan's loghouse. Again the huntresses and old females, and now even a few males deemed sufficiently steady, debated what should be done. Marika was amazed to see Horvat speak before the assembly, though he said little but that the males of the loghouse were prepared to stand to arms with the rest of the pack. As though they had any choice.

Pobuda rose to observe, "There are weapons enough now with those that have been taken, so that even pups may be given a good knife. Let not what happened today occur again. Let none of the Degnan meet a spear with a hoe. Let this plunder be distributed, the best to those who will use it best, and be so held till this crisis has passed."

Pobuda was Skiljan's second. Marika knew she spoke words Skiljan had put into her mouth, for, though fierce, Pobuda never had a thought in her life. Skiljan was disarming a potential squabble over plunder before it began—or at least putting it off. Let the bickering and dickering be delayed till the nomad was safely gone from the upper Ponath.

None of the heads of loghouse demurred. Not even Logusz, who bore Skiljan no love at all, and crossed her often for the sheer pleasure of contrariness.

Skiljan said, "Pobuda speaks wisely. Let it be so. I saw that several shields were taken. And a dozen swords. Let those be given huntresses on the outer stockade." A snarl of amusement stretched her lips. "They will make life difficult and death easy for the climbers of ladders." She held up a sword, did a brief battle dance in which she pretended to strike down a nomad coming at her from below.

Marika stared at the sword and was amazed. She had not seen the long knife during the fighting. It flickered in the light from the firepit, scattering shards of red light. She shivered.

It was the first weapon she ever saw which had no purpose other than the killing of members of her own species. Every other had as its primary function use in the hunt.

"But these new weapons will not be enough," Skiljan said. "Not nearly enough. There is much blood in this thing now. We have dared destroy those sent to destroy us. This wehrlen of the nomads, this ruler over many packs, if he is as mad as they say, will not let this lie. He cannot, for even a small defeat must reflect upon his power. He cannot have that firm a grip upon the huntresses who follow him. He cannot fail and survive. So we will see nomads again, tomorrow or the day after. He will come himself. And he will come in great strength, perhaps with his whole horde."

A mutter of anger and of fear rippled through the assembly. Skiljan stood aside so the Wise might speak their minds.

"I wish we knew about this wehrlen," Kublin whispered to Marika. "I wish we did not have to be enemies. It would be interesting to discover who he is, what he is trying to do really, why he is not content, like huntresses, just to take what he needs and go."

Marika gave him a baffled look. What was this?

Rechtern was first of the Wise to speak. She said, "I have little to tell. But a question to ask. Where did Zhotak nomads acquire swords? Eh? Twelve swords were taken, all were borne by huntresses in their prime. They were swords of quality, too. Yet we here, between the north and the cities where such things are made, have never seen such blades. In fact, we know of swords only from hero stories told us by such as Saettle. The question again: Where did nomads acquire weapons of such quality, meant only for the slaying of meth?"

The entire performance was rhetorical, Marika realized. No one could answer knowledgeably, or even speculatively. The old female merely wished to raise an issue, to plant a seed against the return of summer.

There were no smiths among the meth of the upper Ponath. Nor were there any known to be among the nomads. All things of metal came from the cities of the south, and were sold by tradermales.

There would be hard questions asked when the tradermales appeared again.

After Rechtern, almost all the Wise rose to speak in turn, including many who had nothing to say. That was the way of the old females. They talked long and long, harkening to ancient times to find something to compare with what had happened that day. Looking to precedent for action and response was second nature to the Wise.

The normal raid went nothing like what had happened. Seldom was a packstead destroyed, and then only in blood-feud, after a surprise attack. The last such in the upper Ponath had occurred in Zertan's time. Meth just did not go in for wholesale slaughter.

The pack were awed by the scale of the killing, but not sickened. Death was. Killing was. Their confusion arose from enemy behavior, which was, it seemed, based on reasoning entirely outside their ken. Though hunger drove them, the nomads now lying dead outside the stockade had not come to the packstead simply to take food by force.

There were lessons. Saettle, even wounded, allowed no respite from the lessons. Marika asked for a reading about something similar to what had happened.

"Nothing resembles what happened here, pup. It is unprecedented in our books. Perhaps in the chronicles of the silth, who practice darkwar and whose written memories stretch back ten thousand years. But you are not here to talk over what has been talked over for so many hours. You are here to learn. Let us get on with our ciphers."

"What is darkwar? What are the silth?" Marika asked. But her questions fell on deaf ears. The Wise could not be moved once their minds were set. She would be neither seen nor heard while she persisted. She abandoned the effort quickly.

Behind the students, arguments over tactics continued. Before them, and on the male side, weapons passed from paw to paw, being sharpened, being painted with poison once more. Both activities went on till well after Marika went to her furs and fell asleep despite all her curiosities and fears.

Once she wakened to what she felt might be a touch, panicky. But it did not come again. Restless, she reached toward the packfast, searching for the Degnan messengers. They were not in the place of stone.

She found them on the path homeward, hurrying by moonlight. Hope surged, but soon fell into the grasp of despair. Drawing closer to Grauel's thoughts, she saw that only three from the packfast accompanied them. Aching, frightened, she reached for Kublin and snuggled. He murmured in his sleep, but did not waken.

II

The stir below caused a stir above. The gouge of elbows and toes and paws as pups clambered over her wakened Marika. Kublin was gone from her side.

It was the middle of the night still. Other slow pups were rubbing their eyes and asking what was happening. Marika crawled to the head of the ladder, where Kublin had gotten himself a good vantage point. Marika squeezed in beside him, oblivious to the growls of those she pushed aside. "What is it?" she asked.

"I don't know. Somebody from Gerrien's loghouse came. The huntresses are getting ready to go out."

He was right. The huntresses were donning their heaviest furs. As if they expected to be out a long time. The males watched quietly from their end. Likewise the Wise, though Marika's granddam was holding forth in a subdued voice, ignored by everyone. Pohsit, too, was speaking, but seemed to be sending prayers up to the All.

Pobuda began checking weapons.

Something stirred in shadows where nothing should be moving. Startled, Marika stared at the storage area along the west wall, right were male territory met Wise. She saw nothing.

But now she caught a similar hint of motion from shadows along the base of the east wall. And again when she looked there was nothing there.

There had to be, though. She sensed something on that same level where she sensed the distant messengers and the dread within Machen Cave. Yes. It was something like that. But not so big or terrible.

Now she could almost see it when she looked at it....

What was happening?

Frightened, Marika crawled back to her furs. She lay there thoughtfully for a while, recovering. Then she began considering how she might get out and follow the huntresses. But she abandoned that notion quickly. If they were leaving the packstead, as their dress and weaponry implied, it would be folly for a pup to tag along.

The grauken was out there.

Skiljan strode about impatiently, a captured sword in paw, a bow and quiver across her back.

Something had happened, and something more was about to happen.

Marika pulled her boots on.

Below, the huntresses began leaving the loghouse.

Marika pushed through the pups and descended the ladder. Kublin's whisper pursued her. "Where are you going?"

"Outside." She jumped as a paw clasped her shoulder. She whirled, found Pobuda's broad face just inches from her own.

"What are you doing, pup?"

"I was going outside. To the tower. To watch. What is going on?"

Perhaps if she were not Skiljan's pup, Pobuda would not have answered. But, after a moment's reflection, the loghouse's second huntress said, "A nomad encampment has been spotted in the woods. Near Machen Cave. They are going to raid it."

Marika gaped.

"The tower, then. No farther, or I will chew your ears off and feed you to Skiljan when she gets back."

Marika gulped, dispensed with the last thread of her notion about following the huntresses. Pobuda made no idle threats. She hadn't the imagination.

Marika donned her otec coat under Pobuda's baleful eye. Pobuda wanted to go hunting with the others. But if Skiljan went out, she had to remain. She was not pleased. Skiljan never delegated the active roles.

Marika pulled her hat down over her ears and ducked through the windskins before anyone could call her back.

Pohsit sped a look of hatred after her.

The packstead was cold and dark. Only a few of the lesser moons were up, shedding little light. The last of the expedition were slipping into the exit spiral. Other huntresses were on the stockade, shivering and bouncing to keep warm. Most of the huntresses were going out. It must be an important raid.

Marika started climbing the tower. A face loomed above, unrecognizable. She ignored it. Her thoughts turned to the sky. It was clear again tonight. Why had the weather been so good lately? One ice storm and a few flurries. That probably meant the next storm would be especially brutal, charged as it would be with all the energies pent during the good days.

The sentinel proved to be Solfrank. They eyed one another with teeth bared. Then Solfrank backed away from the head of the ladder, unable to face her down. She scrambled into the precarious wicker basket. Out on the snowfields, the huntresses were spreading out and moving northward, dark, silent blotches against trampled white.

"There," Solfrank said, pointing. There was pride in his voice. He must be the cause of all the activity.

There was a glow in the forest in the direction of Machen Cave. A huge glow, as of a fire of epic proportion. A gout of sparks shot skyward, drifted down. Marika was astonished.

It must be some nomad ceremony. One did not build fires that could be seen for miles, and by potential foes, just to keep warm.

"How long has that been going on?"

"Only a little while. I spotted it right after I came on watch. It was just a little glow then. They must be burning half the forest now."

Why, Marika wondered, was Skiljan risking exposing so many huntresses? Hundreds of nomads would be needed to build such a conflagration. Those wild meth could not be so foolish as to presume their fire would not be seen, could they?

She became very worried, certain her dam had made a tactical mistake. It must be a trap. A lure to draw the Degnan into an ambush. She wanted desperately to extend her touch. But she dared not while Solfrank was there to watch her. "How long do you have left?"

"Only a few minutes."

"Do you want me to take over?"

"All right." He went over the side of the basket before she could change her mind.

Solfrank, Marika reflected, was impressed by nothing but himself. That fire out there had no meaning except as a small personal triumph. It would get him some attention. He was possessed of no curiosity whatsoever.

Fine. Good.

The tower stopped shaking to his descent. She watched him scurry toward the warmth of Gerrien's loghouse. The moment he entered, Marika faced north again and tried sensing her dam.

The touch was the strongest ever it had been. It seemed she was riding behind Skiljan's eyes, seeing what she saw, though she could not capture her dam's thoughts. Yet those became apparent enough when she directed the huntresses who accompanied her, for Marika could then see what they did, and even heard what they and her dam said part of the time.

Almost immediately the huntresses scattered to search out any nomad scouts who might be watching the packstead. They found none. They then filtered through the woods toward Machen Cave. They moved with extreme care, lest they alert sentinels.

Those did not materialize either. Marika sensed in her dam a growing contempt for the intelligence of the northerners.

Skiljan did not permit contempt to lessen her guard. She probed ahead carefully, lest she stumble into some trap.

But it was no trap. The nomads simply had not considered the possibility their bonfire might be seen from the Degnan packstead.

The fire lay on the south bank of the creek. It was huge. Marika was awed. Skiljan and her companions crouched in brush and watched as nomads piled more wood upon the blaze. The thunk of axes came from the opposite slope.

They were clearing the hill around the cave.

Hundreds of nomads hugged the fire's warmth.

Skiljan and Gerrien whispered together. Marika eavesdropped.

"What *are* they doing?" Skiljan asked. Scores labored upon the slopes. One particular nomad moved among them, giving orders that could not be heard. Little could be told of that person at a distance, except that it was someone the nomads considered important.

There were shouts. Boulders rumbled downhill. Nomads scrambled out of their path.

"The cave," Gerrien replied. "They're clearing the mouth of the cave. But why baffles me."

Back of all the other racket were the sounds of log drum and tambor and chanting. The nomad Wise were involved in some sort of ceremony.

"They would not be trying to draw the ghost, would they?" Skiljan asked.

"They might be. A wehrlen... They just might be. We have to stop that."

"Too many of them."

"They do not know we are here. Maybe we can panic them.'"

"We will try." The two separated. During the next several minutes Skiljan whispered to each of the huntresses on her side of the hill. Then she returned to center. Gerrien arrived seconds later.

Skiljan and her companions readied their bows. Marika's dam said, "Shout when you are ready."

Gerrien closed her eyes for half a minute, breathed deeply. Then she opened them, nodded, laid an arrow across her bow, rose. Skiljan rose beside her.

An ululating howl ripped from Gerrien's throat. In an instant it was repeated all across the slope. Arrows stormed downhill. Nomads squealed, shrieked, shouted. Dozens went down.

Skiljan's shafts, Marika noted, all flew toward the nomad Wise. And many found their marks.

Gerrien arced her arrows toward the meth leader on the far slope. It was a long flight in tricky light, and meth with shields had materialized around that one. None of Gerrien's shafts reached their mark.

A wild-eyed meth in bizarre black clothing suddenly materialized a few paces from Skiljan. She pointed something like a short, blunt spear. Skiljan and Gerrien were astonished by the apparition's appearance.

The meth cursed in a strange dialect and glared at the thing in her paws. She hefted it as a club. A pair of poisoned arrows ripped into her chest.

Gerrien then charged downhill. All the huntresses joined her. Javelins arced ahead of them. Nomads ran in circles. Already some were scattering into the darkness up the opposite slope. Only a handful dared counterattack. Their charge was met by huntresses with captured swords, and hurled back.

The panic among the nomads heightened. On the slope opposite, the leader screamed in dialect, trying to stiffen resistance.

Gerrien carried the charge two thirds of the way to the creek, then halted. Sheer numbers of nomads promised to make further going too difficult. After some bloody swordplay, spearplay, and javelin throwing, she loosed another ululating howl and withdrew.

Confused, terrified, the nomads did not press.

The Degnan huntresses loosed their remaining arrows. Every shaft that touched a nomad killed, for each was poisoned.

Once their last arrows flew, the Degnan ran. They left more than a hundred nomads slaughtered. Awe at what they had done would not touch them for some time, for they were too involved with fighting and surviving. But battle and slaughter were not meth customs. There was no precedent for this in the upper Ponath. Fighting in the mass meant holding the stockade against northern raiders, not taking death to the nomads before they struck.

Marika sensed the elation of the huntresses. They had done the nomads great damage while suffering no harm themselves. Perhaps this would compel them to seek easier looting. Now the Degnan needed do nothing but outrun their enemies.

Marika scrambled down the tower, ran to the loghouse. "Pobuda," she gasped. "They are coming back. The nomads are chasing them."

Pobuda asked no questions. Not then. She alerted the rest of the packstead. Everyone capable, males included, hurried to reinforce the palisade.

And found there was nothing to see.

Marika got up the tower again and tried to remain invisible. When she did look down she spied Pobuda staring up, paws on hips, looking angry.

A shout rolled out of the distance. Gerrien and Skiljan. Marika could not tell which. As if to offset its earlier perfection, the touch would not open at all. Perhaps she was too excited.

Those on the stockade heard. Weapons came to the ready. Dark shapes appeared on the snowfields, running toward the gate. The Degnan huntresses came in a compact group, with the strongest to the rear, skirmishing with a scatter of nomads darting around their flanks. The nomads were having no luck. But scores more now were pouring from the woods. It looked as though Skiljan and Gerrien would be caught against their own stockade.

Arrows reached out. Nomads went down. Those most imperiled held up. Skiljan and Gerrien faced their huntresses around and retreated more slowly, backing into the now open gateway. Well-sped poisoned arrows kept the pursuit at bay. Marika saw that her dam carried the club that had been wielded by the strange meth in black.

Skiljan was last inside. She slammed the gate. Gerrien barred it. The home-come huntresses rushed around the spiral and took their places upon the stockade, hurling taunts at the nomads.

The enemy made one ragged rush. It fell apart before it reached the foot of the palisade. The survivors fled ignobly. From a safe distance nomads who had taken no part howled ferocious threats and promises.

Marika abandoned the watchtower while all attention was concentrated elsewhere. She hastened to her loghouse and to her sleeping furs, where she tried to make herself vanishingly small against Kublin.

III

It was late fall, but not as late as the incident of Pohsit and Stapen Rock. The skies were graying and lowering with the promise of what was to come. The creeks often ran raging with runoff from small but virulent storms. All the portents were evil.

But a spirit of excitement filled the Degnan packstead. Runners from other packs came and went hourly. Wide-ranging huntresses brought in reports which Degnan just out of puphood sped off to relay to neighboring packs.

No sighting, said the reports. No sighting. No sighting. But each negative message only heightened the anticipation.

Marika was more excited than any of her packmates. This was a landmark autumn. This would be the first of her apprentice runs with the hunting pack.

"Soon, now. Soon," the Wise promised, reading the portents of wind and sky. "The herds must be on the move by now. Another day. Another two days. The skies are right. The forerunners will appear."

Up in the Zhotak a month or more ago, the kropek would have begun to gather. The young would be adolescent now, able to keep up during the migration south. The nomads would be nipping the flanks of the herds, but they seldom cooperated enough to take sufficient game to see themselves through their protracted winter.

The autumn kropek hunt was the major unifying force of the settled upper Ponath culture. Some years there were fairs. Occasionally two, three, even four packs gathered to observe an important festival. But only during the kropek hunt did the Degnan, Greve, Laspe, and other packs operate in unison—though they might not see one another at all.

The herd had to be spotted first, for it never followed the same route southward. Then an effort had to be made to guide it, to force it into a course that would allow a maximal harvest beneficial to all the Ponath packs.

Ofttimes the post-hunt, when the packs skinned and butchered and salted and smoked, became a gigantic fair of sorts. Sometimes tradermales arrived to take advantage of the concentration of potential customers. Frequently, charitable dams made arrangements on behalf of favored male offspring, saving them the more dangerous search for a new pack.

The kropek was not a large beast, but it was stubborn and difficult prey. Its biggest specimens stood three feet high at the shoulder. The animal had stubby legs and a stiff gait, and was built very wide. It had a thick skin and a massive head. Its lower jaw was almost spadelike. The female developed fearsome upthrust tusks as she matured. Both sexes were fighters.

In summer the kropek ran in small, extended-family herds just below the tundra, subsisting on grubs and roots. But the kropek was a true omnivore, capable of eating anything that did not eat it first. They did not hunt, though, being lazy as a species. Vegetables neither ran nor fought back. The only adventure in a kropek's life was its long vernal and autumnal migrations.

The meth of the upper Ponath hunted kropek only in the fall. In the spring, for the months bracketing the mating season, kropek flesh was inedible. It caused vomiting and powerful stomach cramps.

A young huntress raced into the packstead. The forerunners of the migration had been spotted in the high Plenthzo Valley, following that tributary of the east fork of the Hainlin. The near part of that valley lay only twenty miles east of the Degnan packstead. Excitement reached new heights. The kropek had not passed down Plenthzo Valley in generations. The good broad bottomland there made travel easy but gave meth room to maneuver in the hunt. There were natural formations where the migration could be brought under massed missile fire, the hunters remaining safe from counterattack.

Kropek were feisty. They would charge anything that threatened them—meaning mainly meth, for the meth were their most dangerous natural enemy. A meth caught was a meth dead. But meth could outrun and outsmart kropek.

Most of the time.

Huntresses double-checked weapons held ready and checked a dozen times since the season began. Messengers went out to the neighbors, suggesting meeting places. Males shouldered packs and tools. Pups being taken out to watch and learn scooted around, chattering at one another, trying to stay out of sight of those who ordered chores.

Skiljan finally gave Marika the light bow she had been hoping was meant for her. "You stay close, pup. And pay attention. Daydream around the kropek and you will find yourself dreaming forever. In the embrace of the All."

"Yes, Dam."

Skiljan wheeled on Kublin. "You stay close to Bhlase. Hear me? Do not get in the huntresses' way."

"Yes, Dam."

Marika and Kublin exchanged glances behind Skiljan's back, meaning they would do what they wanted.

A paw slammed against Marika's ear. "You heard your dam," Pobuda said. Her teeth were bared in amusement. "Put those thoughts out of your mind. Both of you."

Damned old Pobuda, Marika thought. She might be wide and ugly, but she never forgot what it was like to be young. You could not get away with anything with her around. She always knew what you were thinking.

Skiljan, and Barlog from Gerrien's loghouse, led the way. They set a pace the pups soon found brutal. Marika was panting and stumbling when they reached the Laspe packstead, where the Laspe huntresses joined the column. Marika did not, as she usually did, study the odd structure of the Laspe stockade and wonder why those meth did things so differently. She hadn't the energy. She had begun to realize that carrying a pack and bow made all the difference in the world.

Pobuda trotted by, mocking her with an amused grunt. Though Pobuda's pack weighed thrice what Marika's did, the huntress was as frisky as a pup.

Marika glanced back at Kublin, among the males. Her littermate, to her surprise, was keeping pace with Zambi. His face, though, betrayed the cost. He was running on pure will.

The pace slackened as they went up into the hills beyond the Laspe packstead. The scouts raced ahead, carrying only their javelins. The huntresses moved in silence now, listening intently. Marika never heard anything.

An hour later the Degnan and Laspe joined three packs coming up from the south. The enlarged party continued eastward on a broad front, still listening.

Marika finally surrendered to curiosity and asked why.

Skiljan told her, "Because kropek were spotted in the Plenthzo Valley does not guarantee that that is the route to be followed by the main herd. It could come some other way. Even over these hills. We do not want to be caught off guard." After walking some dozens of yards, she added, "You always hear the herd before you see it. So you always listen."

The pace remained slow. Marika recovered from her earlier strain. She wanted to drop back and lend encouragement to Kublin, but dared not. Her place was with the huntresses now.

The day began to fail as the packs descended toward the floodplain of the Plenthzo. Scouts reported other packs were in the valley already. The main herd was still many miles north, but definitely in the valley. It would be nighting up soon. There would be no hunting before tomorrow.

They came to the edge of the floodplain in the last light of day. Marika was amazed to see so much flat and open land. She wondered why no packstead stood on such favorable ground.

Only Pobuda felt inclined to explain. "It looks good, yes. Like a well-laid trap. Three miles down, the river enters a narrows flanked by granite. When the snows melt and the water rushes down, carrying logs and whatnot, those narrows block. Then the water rises. This land becomes one great seething brown flood, raging at the knees of those hills down there. Any packstead built on the plain would be drowned the first spring after it was built."

Marika saw the water in her mind, and the image suddenly became one of angry kropek. She began to comprehend the nervousness shown by some of the huntresses.

She did not sleep well. Nor did many huntresses, including her dam. There was much coming and going between packs, plotting and planning and negotiating. Messengers crossed the river, though meth disliked swimming intensely. Packs were in place on the far bank, too, for it was not known which way the kropek would follow, and those beasts had no prejudices against water.

Dawn arrived with unexpected swiftness. Pursuant to Skiljan's instructions, Marika placed her bedroll in a tree and memorized its location. "We will be running the herd," her dam said.

Marika expressed her puzzlement.

"The herd leaders must be kept moving. If we let them stop, the herd stops. Then there is no cutting individuals out or getting to those we might drop with arrows. They would not let us near enough."

The packs with which they had traveled moved out. Since first light scores of huntresses and males had been at work some distance down the plain, erecting something built of driftwood, deadwood, and even cut logs. Marika asked her dam about that.

"It is to scatter the herd. Enough for huntresses to dart in and out of the fringes, planting javelins in the shoulders of the beasts, or hacking at hamstrings." Skiljan seemed impatient with explanations. She wanted to listen, like the others. But her duty as dam was to relay what she knew to her young.

"They are coming," Pobuda said.

And a moment later Marika heard them, too. More, she felt them. The ground had begun to tremble beneath her feet.

The noise swelled. The earth shuddered ever more. And Marika's excitement evaporated. Her eagerness went away, to be replaced by growing apprehension. That sound grew and grew like endless thunder....

Then she spied the herd, a stain of darkness that spanned most of the plain.

"Both sides of the river," Pobuda observed. "Not running yet."

"The wind is with us," Skiljan replied. "Thank the All."

Pobuda spied Marika's nervousness, despite her effort to conceal it. She mocked, "Nothing to it, pup. Just dash up beside a male, leap onto his shoulders, hold on with your legs while you lift his ear, and slide a knife in behind it. Push it all the way to the brain, though. Then jump clear before he goes down."

"Pobuda!" Skiljan snapped.

"Eh?"

"None of that. Not from anyone of my loghouse. We have nothing to prove. I want everyone able to carry meat home. Not one another."

Pobuda frowned, but did not argue.

"Do they do that?" Marika asked her dam.

"Sometimes," Skiljan admitted. "To show courage. Behind the ear *is* a good spot, though. For an arrow." Skiljan cocked her head, sniffed the breeze. A definite, strong smell preceded the kropek. "Only place an arrow will kill one of them. Not counting a low shaft upward into the eye."

"Why use bows, then?"

"Enough hits will slow them down. It will be stragglers mostly, that we get. The old, the lame, the stupid, the young that get confused or courageous or foolish." She looked at Marika with meaning. "You stay outside me. Understand? Away from the herd. Use your bow if you like. Though that will be difficult while running. Most important, make plenty of noise. Feint at them when I do. It is our task to keep them running." As an afterthought, "There are some advantages to hunting in the forests. The trees do keep them scattered."

Skiljan had to speak loudly to be heard over the kropek. Marika kept averting her gaze from the brown line. So many of them!

The tenor of the rumble changed. The herd began moving faster. Faintly, over the roar, Marika heard the ululation of meth hunting.

"Ready," Skiljan said. "Just after the leaders come abreast of us. And do what I told you. I will not carry you home."

"Yes, Dam." All those venturesome thoughts she had had back at the packstead had abandoned her. Right now she wanted nothing more than to slink off with Kublin, Zambi, and the males.

She was scared.

Pobuda gave her a knowing look.

The roar of hooves became deafening. The approaching herd looked like a surge in the surface of the earth, green becoming sudden brown. Lean, tall figures loped along the near flank, screaming, occasionally stabbing with javelins.

"Now," Skiljan said, and dashed toward the herd.

Marika followed, wondering why she was doing such a foolish thing.

The Degnan rushed from the woods shrieking. Arrows arced in among the herd leaders, who put on more speed. Skiljan darted in, jabbed a male with her javelin. Marika made no effort to follow. At twenty feet she was as close as ever she wanted to be. The eyes of the ugly beasts held no fear. They seemed possessed of an evil, mocking intelligence. For a moment Marika feared that the kropek had plans of their own for today.

Distance fled. With speed came quick weariness. The meth who had been running the herd fell away, their hunting speed temporarily spent. They trotted while they regained their breath. The kropek seemed incapable of tiring.

There was endurance and endurance, though. Meth could move at the quick trot indefinitely, though they were capable of only a mile at hunting speed.

A male feinted toward Skiljan. Pobuda and Gerrien were there instantly, ready to slip between it and the herd if it gave them room. It moved back, ran hip to shoulder with another evil-eyed brute. Marika shuddered, imagining what would become of someone unlucky enough to fall in their path.

Another male feinted. Again huntresses darted in. Again the beast faded back.

Marika tried launching an arrow. She narrowly missed one of the huntresses. Her shaft fell with no power behind it, vanished in the boil of kropek. She decided not to try again.

Her lungs began to burn, her calves to ache. And she was growing angry with these beasts who refused to line up and die.

A third male feinted. And she thought, *Come out of there, you! Come out here where I can—*

It wheeled and charged her, nearly falling making so sudden a turn.

She did not stop running, but neither did she try to evade its angry, angling charge. She froze mentally, unable to think what to do.

Pobuda flung past, leaping over the kropek. She planted her javelin in its shoulder as she leapt. A second later Gerrien was on the beast's opposite flank, planting her own javelin as the kropek staggered and tried to turn after Pobuda. It tried to turn on Gerrien, then. Barlog jabbed it in the rear. It sprang forward, ran farther from the herd.

Then it halted and swung around, right into Marika. She had no choice but to jump up, over, as a big, wide mouth filled with grinding teeth rose to greet her.

She leapt high enough. Just barely high enough. Her toes brushed its snout.

"Keep running!" Skiljan yelled.

Marika glanced back once. The kropek stood at bay, surrounded.

Did I do that? Did I bring it out? she wondered. *Or was it coincidence?*

So try it again. But there was no time. They were approaching the obstacles built that morning. Marika watched her dam closely.

Skiljan slowed and turned away from the herd, to give the flood room to break around the barriers.

But the herd did not swing. It drove straight ahead at full speed, into the obstacles.

How many tons of kropek flesh in that raging tide? More than could be calculated. The barriers collapsed. Kropek climbed over kropek. The air filled with squeals of anger and agony.

Beyond, scores of huntresses were in flight. They had expected the herd to break up and pass around them. Now they used their speed advantage to angle away from that unstoppable wave. Most of them made it.

Skiljan did not pick up the pace again. When the Degnan came even with the barricade, they stopped, well away from the flow. Skiljan said, "There will be many stragglers here once the main herd passes."

Marika thought about loosing an arrow. Pobuda read her mind. "You would be wasting your shafts, pup. Save them."

It seemed hours before the last of the herd passed.

Skiljan was right. There were many stragglers, though those kropek that had gone down early were now little more than bloody stains in the trampled earth. The pack moved in, began the slaughter.

The stragglers clumped up in a compact mass. The heavily tusked females faced outward, held the line while the quicker, more agile males awaited a chance to leap upon their tormentors.

Down the valley the herd became congested at the narrow place. It had to force its way through a storm of missiles hurled by scores of huntresses safely perched atop high rocks. Over the next few days most of the wounded kropek would be run down and finished.

Marika tried luring one forth from the group encircled at the broken barrier. She had no luck.

Her talent—if such it was, and not a curse—was terribly unreliable.

The huntresses began picking on the more volatile males among the stragglers, one at a time. Tormented sufficiently, the beast would launch a furious charge that would expose it to attack from all sides. That made for slow work, but the number of animals dragged away for cooling out and butchering increased steadily.

There was no mercy in the huntresses, and seemingly no end to the hunt. With nightfall the males built fires from the remains of the barricades. Their light reflected redly from the eyes of the kropek still besieged. None of those rushed forward now. Which made it a standoff for the time being, though missiles kept arcing in, doing some damage. Very limited damage. Striking from head on, most just bounced off.

Fires burned all along the valley. Everywhere, on both sides of the river, meth were butchering, and gorging on organ meats. Marika thought her stomach would burst.

From the end of the floodplain came the continued squeal and rumble of kropek trying to force the narrows.

Skiljan finally allowed Marika to retrieve her bedroll, then to go settle down with the other pups, where she found Kublin in a state of exhaustion so acute she was frightened. But he did not complain. In that he was becoming something more admirable than Zamberlin, who carped about everything, though nature had equipped him far better to take it.

Before Marika parted from her dam, though, Skiljan said, "Think on what you have seen today. Reflect carefully. For meth sometimes behave very much like kropek. They develop momentum in a certain direction and nothing will turn them."

Marika reflected, but she would not understand the whole lesson for a long time.

CHAPTER FIVE

I

Marika was in the watchtower when the nomads returned the morning after her dam's night raid. She got no chance to descend.

Perhaps two hundred advanced toward the packstead, coming from the direction of the Laspe packstead. They halted beyond the reach of bows, howled, brandished weapons and fetishes. Their Wise moved among them, blessing. The huntresses among them carried standards surmounted by the skulls of meth and arfts, and the tails of kirns. Kirns were huge omnivores of the Zhotak, supposed by the nomads to be holy. Their ferocity and cunning and perseverance were legend. Thus the significance of their tails.

A big young male came forward, teeth bared as he stepped over and around bodies left from the night before. He shouted, "Abandon the stead and you will be forgiven all. Resist and your pups will be eaten."

A bold one for a male, Marika thought. He must be the rogue the Wise called the wehrlen. What other male would be so daring?

Skiljan sped an arrow. She was good, and should not have missed, yet her shaft drifted aside. A breeze, Marika supposed.

But her dam missed twice more, a thing unprecedented. No adjustment brought her nearer her mark. The nomads cheered. The mad male howled mockingly and offered his back. He stalked away slowly.

He had his answer.

Skiljan shouted, "Rogue! You dare the wrath of the All, flouting the laws of our foredams. If you truly believe yourself chosen, meet me in bloodfight."

A murmur of horror ran around the stockade. Was Skiljan mad too? Meet a *male* in bloodfight? Unheard of. Unprecedented. Disgusting. The creatures were not to be taken seriously.

Marika understood instantly, though. It was a ploy to weaken the wehrlen in the sight of his followers. They would believe him a coward if he refused. His position had to be precarious, for males did not lead and packs did not unite. Marika recalled the kropek hunt. Was this something like that, the nomads joining in the face of extremity?

The threat the wehrlen posed could be disrupted with a few well-chosen words, or by the proposed duel, the outcome of which could not be in doubt. No male could stand against a huntress of Skiljan's speed, ferocity, and skill.

The wehrlen turned, bared his teeth in mockery, bowed slightly, then walked on.

The ploy had failed. The nomads could not hear Skiljan's challenge.

The wehrlen reached them, took a spear from one, leaned upon it. After a moment he waved a languorous paw in the direction of the packstead.

The two hundred howled and charged.

The Degnan were better prepared today. All the archers faced the rush. Poisoned shafts stormed into the horde. Scores fell before the charge reached the stockade. Skiljan had placed half the archers where the rush could not reach them till it had crossed the outer stockade. Those huntresses kept speeding arrows once close fighting had been joined.

Old females still capable of bending bows were perched atop the loghouses. The females on the stockade were disposed so that those nomads who got over would find some paths easier than others. These paths concentrated them for the older archers. Skiljan had all the captured swords up front, and those were put to deadly use.

Nomads seized places on the shelf behind the stockade. They used their ladders to span the gap to the inner stockade, scrambled across. Many were hit and fell into the gap between barriers.

The armed males and older pups crouched in shadow under the inner platform. When nomads jumped down they attacked the invaders from in back. A great many nomads died there, and those who survived that found the loghouses sealed against them. When they turned on the males and pups, the archers atop the loghouses shot them down.

It was a great slaughter. Marika's heart hammered as she saw hope rising. They could do it again! Already over half the attackers were down. The others would flee, probably, as soon as they realized they had been set up for killing.

Hope died.

A horde of nomads came howling out of the forest from the direction of Machen Cave. They numbered several times the party which had attacked already. They were coming against the north wall, and the Degnan had concentrated at the point of assault on the east.

Marika screamed at her dam and pointed. Skiljan looked. Her face went slack. A nomad nearly got her before she recovered her equilibrium.

These new attackers surged up to the stockade, scarcely touched by arrows. They boiled around its base like maggots in an old carcass. Their ladders rose. Up they came, seized a foothold. Parties advanced along the platforms to right and left. Some spanned ladders across to the second circle. Others began chopping through the gate, seeking to penetrate the packstead by the traditional route.

That scores of them were dying under the hail of poisoned arrows seemed not to bother them at all.

There were so many....

Scores reached the interior unscathed. They hurled themselves upon the pups and males. Scores more died. Every weapon, no matter how crude, had been treated with the poison.

The old females atop the loghouses sped arrows as fast as they could bend their bows—and could do nothing to stem the endless flood. For a moment Marika recalled the kropek sweeping over the barricades in Plenthzo Valley. This was the same thing. Madness unstoppable.

Here, there, nomads tried to claw their way up the slick ice on the loghouses, to get at the old archers. At first they had no luck.

Marika whimpered. The stockade was almost bare of defenders. It would be but a matter of minutes.... Terror filled her. The grauken. The cannibal. The wehrlen had promised to devour the pups. And she could do nothing from her vantage. Nothing but wait.

She saw Gerrien go down under a pile of savages, snarling till the last, her teeth sunk in an enemy throat. She watched her dam fall a moment later in identical fashion, and wailed in her grief. She wanted to jump down, to flee into the forest, but she could not. Nomads surrounded the base of the watchtower.

No one was going to escape.

She watched Zamberlin writhe out his life, screaming, on a nomad spear. She saw Solfrank die after wielding an axe as viciously as any huntress. Three nomads preceded him into the embrace of the All. She watched the old females atop the loghouses begin falling to thrown axes and spears. These nomads carried no bows, little difference though that made now.

She saw Kublin race out from under a platform, side open in a bloody wound. He was trying to reach his dam's loghouse. Two slavering nomads pursued him.

Black emotion boiled inside Marika, hot and furious. Something took control. She saw Kublin's pursuers through a dark fog, moving in slowed motion. For a time it was as though she could see through them, see them without their skins. And she could see drifting ghosts, like the ghosts of all her foredams, hovering over the action. She willed a lethal curse upon the hearts of Kublin's pursuers.

They pitched forward, shrieking, losing their weapons, clawing their breasts.

Marika gaped. What? Had she done that? Could she kill with the touch?

She tried again. Nothing happened this time. Nothing at all. Whimpering, she strained to bring up that hot blackness again, to save what remained of her pack. It would not come.

The nomads began assaulting the loghouse doors. They broke through Gerrien's. In moments the shrieks of the very old and very young filled the square. A nomad came out carrying a yearling pup, dashed its brains out against the doorpost. Others followed him, also carrying terrified pups. Broken little bodies went into a heap. More nomads poured inside. Some brought out loot. Some brought torches. They began trying to fire the other loghouses—not an easy task.

The fighting soon dwindled to a single knot of huntresses clumped near Skiljan's door. Only two old females remained atop the roofs, still valiantly sending arrows. Nomads began to lose interest in battle. Some bore plunder out of loghouses already breached, or began squabbling over food. Others started butchering the pups taken from Gerrien's loghouse. Some prepared a huge bonfire of captured firewood. The victory celebration began before the Degnan were all slain.

And Marika saw it all from her watchtower trap.

A nomad came up the ladder. She drove her knife into his eye. He stiffened as the poison surged through him, plunged back down. His fellows below cursed her, threw stones and spears, harmed her not at all. The wicker of the stand turned their missiles.

She looked at the wehrlen, standing alone, leaning upon his spear, smug in victory. And the blackness came up without her willing it. It came so fast she almost missed her chance to shape it. She saw him naked of flesh, saw ghosts, and, startled, willed his heart to burst. Through the darkness she saw him leap in agony—then her thrust recoiled. It turned and struck back. She tried to dodge physically, crouched, whimpered.

Whatever happened, it did her no harm. It only terrified her more. When she rose and peeped over the wicker, she saw the wehrlen still rooted, clinging to his spear for support. She had not destroyed him, but she had hurt him. Badly. Only a powerful will kept him erect.

Gamely, Marika began seeking that blackness again.

The last defenders of Skiljan's doorway went down. Someone seized Kublin and hurled him away to fall among the countless bodies bloodying the square. He moved a little, tried to drag himself away. Marika screamed silently, willing him to lie still, to pretend he was dead. Maybe the cannibals would overlook him. He stopped moving.

The nomads began using axes on doors that would not yield to brute force. The door to Skiljan's loghouse boomed like a great drum. As each stroke fell, Marika jumped. She wondered how soon some nomad would realize that an axe was the tool to bring her down.

The door to Skiljan's loghouse went. Marika heard both Pohsit and Zertan shriek powerful curses. Her granddam sprang out with vigor drawn from the All knew where, slashing with claws painted with poison. She killed three before she went down herself.

Marika did not see what became of Pohsit. The tower began to creak ominously.

She sent up a prayer to the All and clutched her bloody knife. One more to go with her into the dark. Just one more.

II

Marika surveyed her homeland. This was what she would leave behind. To the north, forests and hills which rose in time to become the low mountains of the Zhotak. Beyond, taiga, tundra, and permanent ice. That was the direction from which winter and the grauken came.

Below, they were roasting pups already. The smell of seared meth flesh made Marika lose her breakfast. The nomads circling her tower cursed her.

Eastward lay rolling hills white with snow, looking like the bare bones of the earth. Beyond the Plenthzo Valley the hills rose higher and formed the finest otec territory.

Southward, the land descended slowly to the east branch of the Hainlin, then in the extreme distance rose again to wooded hills almost invisible because the line between white earth and pale gray cloud could not be distinguished. Marika never had traveled beyond the river. She knew the south only through stories.

The west was very like the east, except the rolling hills were mostly bare of trees and there were no higher hills looming in the far distance. In fact, the hills descended. The land continued a slow drop all the way to the meeting of rivers where the stone packfast stood so many days away.

Thought of the packfast made her recall the messengers, Grauel and Barlog. The messengers bringing help that would arrive too late.

She felt a hint of a touch.

For a moment she thought it just the tower vibrating to the pounding blows of the axes below.

Another hint.

This was the thing itself.

She spun, looked at the wehrlen. He had recovered somewhat. Now he was moving toward the packstead, using his spear like a crutch. He seemed totally oblivious to all the bodies and the racks of heads which his followers had overturned. Four-fifths of this meth had been slaughtered. Did he not care?

She noted his enfeeblement and gloried in what she had done. In what the Degnan had accomplished. There would be no more nomad terror in the upper Ponath.

A touch, though. If not from him, then who?

She recalled the messengers once more, and the response she had elicited from the old meth in the packfast. How close were Grauel and Barlog and their paltry aid? Maybe she had enough of this bizarre talent to at least speed them warning about the nomad.

She opened out, and reached out, and was astonished.

They were close. Very close. That way... She looked more closely at the land. For a moment she saw only the scrubby conical trees which dotted the snowscape. Then she realized that a few of those trees were different. They stood where no trees had stood before. And they were moving toward the packstead in short bursts.

Not trees at all. Three meth in black. Meth very like the one dam had slain near Machen Cave. Their clothing was like hers, like nothing Marika had ever seen, loose, voluminous, whipping in the wind. They came toward the packstead like the advance of winter, inexorable, a tall one in the middle, one of normal height to either side.

Behind them hundreds of yards, Marika now distinguished Grauel and Barlog crouched near a true tree. The two huntresses from Gerrien's loghouse had realized the magnitude of the disaster before them. They were too shaken to come ahead.

The axe kept slamming against the leg of the tower. They were taking long enough, Marika thought. Were they intentionally trying to torment her? Or was it just that the axe was in abominable condition?

The three black figures were two hundred yards away now, no longer making any effort to conceal their approach. A nomad spotted them, shouted, and pointed. Dozens more nomads clambered onto the platforms behind the stockade. The male chopping at the watchtower stopped for a moment.

The three dark figures halted. The one in the middle raised both paws and pointed forefingers at the palisade.

Marika saw nothing. It was nothing physical. But her mind reeled away from an impact as strong as the wehrlen's counterattack. And nomads began screaming and falling off the stockade, clawing at their chests just the way Kublin's attackers had.

The screaming ended. A deep silence filled the packstead. Nomads looked at nomads suddenly dead. The male below the tower dropped his axe. Mouths opened but nothing came forth.

Then an excited babble did break out. More nomads mounted the stockade.

This time all three dark meth raised their arms, and every nomad on the palisade fell, shrieking and clawing their chests.

Nomads boiled through the spiral, clambered over the stockade, all rushing the three, murder in their hearts and eyes. A handful besieged the wehrlen, who seemed to have halted to regain his breath. Marika could not guess what confused tale he heard, but did see him shudder and, as if by pure will, pull himself together.

Those nomads who chose to attack the meth in black died by the score. Not one got closer than a dozen feet.

The meth in black began circling round the stockade, toward the mouth of the spiral.

The wehrlen watched them come into view. He did something. One of the three mouthed a faint cry and dropped. The others halted. The taller did something with her fingers. The wehrlen stiffened. Marika felt his surprise.

Rigid as old death, he fell slowly forward.

Nomad witnesses howled in despair. They ran. It did them no good. The fastest and last to fall covered no more than twenty yards.

The two in black knelt over the third. Marika saw the tall one's head shake. They rose and walked the spiral into the packfast. A few dozen nomads remained inside. They scaled the stockade, trying to flee.

It was all very baffling to Marika.

The two entered the packstead's interior. A last few nomads died before they could hurl spears. Of the scores and scores of fallen, not one showed any sort of wound.

The dark two strode to the heart of the square, stepping over but otherwise ignoring the dead. There they halted, turned slowly, surveyed the carnage. They seemed aware of Marika but indifferent to her presence in the tower. The taller said something. The shorter went to the door of Logusz's loghouse. A moment later, inside, nomads began screaming. She moved across to Foehse's loghouse. Screams again. She then seemed satisfied.

Marika finally shook her knotted muscles into motion. Terror had left her so shaky she nearly fell twice getting down. She grabbed the axe from the male who had been chopping the tower leg, rushed toward the place where she had seen Kublin last.

Kublin was the only one of her blood who might still be living.

She had to dig him out from under a heap of nomads. He was breathing still, and bleeding still. She held him close and wept, believing, though she had neither healer's knowledge nor skill, that nothing could be done.

Somehow it all became concentrated in Kublin. All the grief and loss. The blackness welled within her. She saw ghosts all around her thickly, as though the spirits of the dead were reluctant to leave the place of battle. She looked inside Kublin, through Kublin, as though he were transparent. She saw the depth of his bruises and wounds. Angrily, she willed him health instead of death.

Kublin's eyes opened momentarily. "Marika?"

"Yes, Kublin. I'm here, Kublin. Kublin, you were so brave today."

"You were in the tower, Marika. How did you get down?"

"Help came, Kub. We won. They're all dead. All the nomads. The messengers came back in time." A lie. In time for what? Of all the Degnan other than the messengers themselves, only she and Kublin remained alive. And he was about to die.

Well, at least he could go into the arms of the All thinking something had been accomplished.

"Brave," Kublin echoed. "When it was time. When it counted. It was easier than I thought, Marika. Because I didn't have to worry."

"Yes, Kublin. You were a hero. You were as great as any of the huntresses today."

He rewarded her with that big winning look he got that made her love him above all her other siblings, then he relaxed. When she finally decided that he had stopped living, she wept.

Seldom, seldom did a meth female shed tears, unless in ritual. The two who wore black turned to stare at her, but neither made any move to approach her. They exchanged the occasional word or two while they watched.

The messengers came into the packstead. At last. Numb from shock, they surveyed the carnage. Grauel let out one prolonged, pained howl of torment. Barlog came to Marika, gently scratched the top of her head, as one did with infants in pain or distress. Marika wondered what had become of her hat. Why hadn't she felt the cold nipping at her ears?

Having collected herself, Grauel joined the two meth who wore black.

III

They sheltered the night in Skiljan's loghouse, which, having held the longest, had been damaged least. Marika could not get the stench of roast pup out of her nostrils. She kept shaking and hugging herself and slinking into shadows, where she closed into herself and watched ghosts bob through the loghouse walls. For a long time she was not very sane. Sometimes she saw meth who were not there and spoke with them as though they were. And then she saw one meth who might have been there, and she did not believe what she saw.

The messengers forced her to drink an infusion of chaphe, which finally pushed her down into a deep, long, dreamless sleep.

Nevertheless, in the deep hours of the night, she either wakened partially or dreamed she overheard the two in black. Grauel and Barlog and a tumble of ragged skins that might have contained a third body were scattered around one firepit. The outsiders sat by the other.

The taller said, "She is the one who touched us at Akard. Also the one who struck twice during the fighting. A strong one, well-favored by the All."

The rag-skin pile stirred.

"But untrained," the second outsider countered. "These ones who find themselves on their own are difficult to discipline. They never really fit in."

This meth was very old, Marika realized. She had not noticed before. She had not looked at these intruders closely at all. This one had to be older than her granddam. Yet she remained spry enough to have made a long journey in a forced march, traveling without rest, and then had had energy left to help drive away or kill hundreds of nomads. What manner of meth was she? What sort of creatures were these meth of the packfast?

"Silth bitches," she heard her dam murmur, as though she were still alive and crouching before the firepit, muttering about all the things she hated in her world. But at least Marika did not *see* her crouching there. Her mind was beginning to recover.

"We must take her back. That was, after all, the purpose of the expedition. To find the source of that touch."

"Of course. Like it or not. Fear it or not. Khles, I have a foreboding about this one. A name comes to me again and again unbidden, and I cannot shake it. Jiana. Nothing good will come of her. She has that air of doom about her. Do you not sense it?"

The other shrugged. "Perhaps I am not sufficiently Wise. What of the others?"

"The old one is useless. And mad. But the huntresses we will take, too. While they remain in shock, unready yet to race into the wilds to avenge their pack and get themselves killed in the avenging. We never have enough help, and they have no other pack to turn to. Myself, I foresee them becoming far more useful than the pup."

"Perhaps. Perhaps. Labor does have its value. Ho! Look there. See the little eyes glow in the firelight. She is a strong one, pushing back the chaphe sleep. Sleep, little silth. Sleep."

Behind the two strange meth the pile of rag skins stirred once again. Almost seethed, Marika thought.

The taller outsider extended a paw toward Marika. Fingers danced. Moments later sleep came, though she fought it with all her will, terrified. And when she wakened she remembered, but could not decide if what she recalled had been dream or fact.

The Wise made little distinction anyway. So what did it matter? She would accept all that as fact, though what she had heard made no sense.

CHAPTER SIX

I

Morning came. Marika awakened disoriented. Where were the noises of a loghouse beginning its day? The clatter, the chatter, the bickering were absent. The place was as still as death. Marika remembered. Remembered and began to whine.

She heard footsteps. Someone stopped behind her. She remained facing the wall. What a time to spend her first night in huntress's territory!

A paw touched her. "Pup? Marika?"

She rolled, looked into Grauel's face. She did not like Grauel. The huntress from Gerrien's loghouse had no pups of her own. She was very short with others' young. There was something indefinably wrong about her.

But this was a different Grauel, a changed Grauel, a Grauel battered by events. A Grauel shocked into gentleness and concern. "Come, Marika. Get up. It is time to eat. Time to make decisions."

Barlog was doing the cooking. Marika was amazed.

She surveyed her home. It seemed barren without the jostle and snarl. All outsiders surrounding the firepit. How many outsiders had ever eaten here? Very few.

And a huntress cooking. Times were odd, indeed.

The food was what one might expect of a huntress who had cooked only a few times in her life, and then in the field. A simple stew. But Marika's mouth watered anyway. She had not eaten since dawn the day before. Yet she did not gobble what Barlog handed her. She ate slowly, reluctant to get to what must follow. Yet the meal did end. Marika clasped her hands across her full stomach as Grauel said, "We three must decide what we will do now."

Barlog nodded.

Last of the Degnan. Last of the richest pack of the upper Ponath. Some things did not have to be said. They could not wait for summer, then take new males and begin breeding back up. Especially as Grauel could not bear pups. There were no Wise to teach, no males to manage the packstead. Of food and firewood and such there was such a plentitude that that wealth was

71

a handicap in itself.

Times were hard. If the nomads themselves did not come first, some pack left in tight straits by them would discover the wealth here and decide to plunder. Or move in. Two huntresses and a pup could not hold the palisade. Not unless the silth from the packfast stayed. And did so for years.

Marika suspected even a few days were out of the question.

Silently, she cursed the All. She stared into the embers at the bottom of the firepit, thinking of the wealth in iron and stores and furs that would be lost simply because the Degnan could not defend them.

Neighbors or nomads. There were plenty of both who would commit murder gladly now. Winter was ahowl and the grauken was loose in the world.

A few nomads had escaped the massacre yesterday. Marika did not doubt that there were others scattered about the upper Ponath. Were they gathering? Might their scouts be at Stapen Rock, watching, knowing the packstead could be taken easily once the strangers departed?

That was the worst of it. Thinking the nomads might get everything after all.

Grauel was speaking to her. She pricked up her ears. "What? I was thinking."

"I said the sisters offered us a place in their packfast." Loathing under strict control tautened Grauel's voice. These meth were the silth whom Marika's dam and granddam and Pohsit had so hated.

But why?

Grauel continued, "We have no choice if we wish to survive. Barlog agrees. Perhaps we can take new males and begin the line afresh when you have reached mating age."

Marika shook her head slowly. "Let us not lie to ourselves, Grauel. The Degnan are dead. Never will we grow strong enough to recover this packstead from those who claim it."

She had wanted to see the stone packfast inhabited by these meth called silth. But not at this price. "Run to the Laspe, Grauel," she said. "Tell them. For a while, at least, let our wealth aid someone who shares our misery. They will have a better chance of holding it. And they will become indebted, so we would have a place to return one day."

The silth, seated a short distance away, were paying no attention. Indeed, they seemed preoccupied with the male end of the loghouse. They whispered to one another, then did pay attention, as if very much interested in the huntresses' response to Marika's suggestion.

Grauel and Barlog were startled by the notion. It had not occurred to them, and probably could not have. Two packs sharing a stead was not unheard of, but it was rare.

Grauel nodded reluctantly. Barlog said, "She is as smart as her dam was." She rose.

Grauel snapped at her. For a moment they argued over who would carry the message.

Marika realized that both wanted to get away from the packstead and its uncompromising reminders of disaster.

"Both of you go. That will be safer. There are nomads around still."

The huntresses exchanged looks, then donned their coats. They were gone in moments.

For a long time the silth did nothing but sit staring into the firepit, as though trying to read something in the coals. Marika collected the eating utensils. As she cleaned them and stowed them away, the silth kept glancing at her. Occasionally, one whispered to the other. Finally, the tall one said, "It is time. She has not sensed it." She came and got one of the bowls Marika had cleaned, filled it from the pot, carried it to the trap closing the cellar belonging to the loghouse males. She set the bowl down, opened the trap, blew aroma into the darkness below. Then she retreated, looking amused.

Marika stopped working, wondering what was happening.

A wrinkled, meatless, gray old paw appeared. Marika frowned. Not even Horvat...

A head followed the paw fearfully.

"Pohsit!" Marika said.

Pure venom smoldered in the sagan's eyes. She snatched the bowl and started to retreat into the cellar.

"Stop," the tall silth ordered. "Come out."

Pohsit froze. She retreated no farther, but neither did she do as directed.

"Who is this, pup?"

"Pohsit," Marika replied. "Sagan of this loghouse."

"I see." The silth's tone said more than her words. It said that the feeling the sagan had for those of the packfast was reciprocated. "Come out of there, old fraud. Now."

Shaking, Pohsit came up. But she stopped when her feet cleared the cellar stair. She stared at the silth in stark terror.

For an instant Marika was amused. For the first time in her young life, she saw the sagan at a genuine disadvantage. And yet, there Pohsit stood, even while shaking, with her paw making slow trips from bowl to mouth with spoonfuls of stew.

"That is the male end of the loghouse, is it not, pup?" the taller silth demanded.

"Yes," Marika replied in a small voice. Pohsit was looking at her still, still poisonous with promise.

The sagan staggered. Her bowl and spoon slipped from her paws. Those flew to her temples. She screamed, "No! Get out of my head! You filthy witches. Get out."

The screaming stopped. Pohsit descended like a dropped hide, folding in upon herself. And for a moment Marika gaped. That was the exact rag pile she had seen during the night when she was not sure whether or not she was dreaming.

Had Pohsit been up here then? But the silth seemed surprised by her presence. Seemed to have discovered her only recently.

No sense here....

But she had seen her dam, too, hadn't she? And Pobuda. And many others who could not have been there because they were all dead. Or was that a dream?

Marika began to shake, afraid that she had begun to lose her grip on reality.

The alternative, that at times she was not quite firmly anchored in the river of time, she pushed out of mind the instant it occurred. That was too frightening even to contemplate.

"Just as I thought," the taller silth said. "Terror. Pure cowardice. She hid down there thinking the savages would not look for her there."

Hatred smoldered in the eyes that peeped out of the skin pile.

Marika sensed an opportunity to repay all the evil Pohsit had tried to do her. She had only to appeal to these meth. But Pohsit was Degnan. Crazy, malicious, poisonous, hateful, but still closer than any outsiders.

Grauel and Barlog would be pleased to learn that one of the Wise, and a sagan at that, had survived.

As though touching her thoughts, the older silth asked, "What shall we do with her, pup?" Marika now knew them for the creatures her elders had muttered against, but still did not know what silth were.

"Do? What do you mean, do?" She wished they would give names, so she could fix them more certainly in mind. But when she asked, they just evaded, saying their names were of no consequence. She got the feeling they were not prepared to trust her with their names. Which made no sense at all. The only other outsiders she had met, the wandering tradermales, insisted on giving you their names the moment they met you.

"We have looked into this one's mind. We know it as we know our own now." A whine escaped Pohsit. "We know how she tormented you. We know she would have claimed your life had she the chance. How would you requite such malice?"

The question truly baffled Marika. She did not want to do anything, and they must understand that. One did not demand vengeance upon the Wise. They were soon enough in the embrace of the All.

The older silth whispered, "She is too set in savage ways." But Marika overheard.

The other shrugged. "Consider the circumstances. Might we not all forgive our enemies in a like situation?"

There was something going on that Marika could not grasp. She was not sure if that was because she was yet too young to understand, or because these silth were too alien to comprehend.

She had been convinced that Pohsit was mad for at least a year. Now the sagan delivered final proof.

Pohsit hurled herself out of the rag pile at Marika. An iron knife flashed, its brightness dulled by traceries of Bhlase's poison. Marika made a feeble squealing sound and tried to crawl out of the way. Her effort was ineffective.

But Pohsit did not strike. She continued forward, bent at the waist, upper body way ahead of her feet. Her legs did not work right. Marika was reminded of a marionette one of the tradermales used to demonstrate at the night fire after the day's business was complete. The sagan had that same goofy, flailing gait.

It carried her the length of the loghouse and into the wall a few feet to one side of the doorway.

Marika watched the old meth rise slowly, a whimper sliding between her teeth. She faced around and met the cold stares of the silth, thinking of trying again. In a moment she put the thought out of mind.

Pohsit's behavior made no more sense than ever.

"What shall we do with her, pup?"

Still Marika would offer the sagan no harm. She shook her head. "Nothing.... I do not understand her. I do not hate her. Yet she hates me."

"That is the way of the false when faced with the true. You know you will not be safe while she lives."

Fear animated Pohsit now, and Marika suddenly knew the silth were right: she had hidden in the male fane out of cowardice. "Pohsit. Pohsit. What do you fear? You are so old death must be a close friend."

A spark of hatred for a moment glimmered through Pohsit's terror. But she did and said nothing more. Marika turned her back. "Let her do what she will. It is all the same to me."

The silth began ignoring Pohsit as studiously as did Marika. After a time the sagan quietly donned a coat—someone else's, way too big for her—and slipped out of the loghouse. Marika saw the tall silth nod slightly to the older.

She did not understand that till much later.

II

The silth questioned Marika about her talent. How had she grown aware that she was unusual? How had her talent manifested itself? They seemed convinced it would have caused her grave troubles had she let it become known.

"Your dam should have brought you to the packfast years ago. You and your littermates. As all pups are to be brought. It is the law."

"I know little about the packfast and the law," Marika replied. "Except that not many meth pay attention to either here in the upper Ponath. I have heard many jests made at the expense of that law. And I have heard our teacher, Saettle, say we came into the Ponath to escape the law."

"No doubt." The taller silth was extremely interested in Machen Cave. She kept returning to that. She asked Marika to be more specific about her experiences. Marika related each in as much detail as she could recall.

"You seem a little uncertain about something. As though there is more that you are afraid to tell."

"There is more," Marika admitted. "I just do not know if you will believe me."

"You might be surprised, pup. We have seen things your packmates would deny can exist." This was the older silth. Marika was not entirely comfortable with that one. In her way, she had a feel very like Pohsit. And she evidently had the power to be as nasty as Pohsit wished she could be.

"The last time I was there I really was not there. If you see what I mean."

The tall silth said, "We do not see. Why do you not just tell it?"

"The other night. When Dam and the others went out to raid the nomads. They were up at Machen Cave with a big bonfire and all their Wise doing some kind of ceremony. Anyway, I followed Dam through the touch. It was stronger than ever. I could see and hear everything she saw and heard." She choked on her words, eyed the silth oddly.

"You have remembered something."

"Yes. There was one of your kind there. With the nomads...."

Both silth rose suddenly. The tall one began pacing. The other hovered over Marika, staring down intently.

"Did I say something wrong? Did I offend?"

"Not at all," the tall one said. "We were startled and distressed. A sister like ourselves, you say? Tell us more."

"There is little to tell. Dam and Gerrien attacked the nomads. Most of them panicked and fled. But suddenly this one meth, dressed like you almost, appeared out of nowhere, and—"

"Literally?"

"Excuse me?"

"She materialized? In fact? She did not just step from behind a tree or something?"

"No. I do not think so. She just appeared right in front of Dam and Gerrien. She pointed something at them, then cursed it. It seemed like it was supposed to do something and did not. Then she tried to club them with it. Dam and Gerrien killed her. It was a strange weapon. All of metal."

The silth exchanged glances. "All of metal, eh? Where is this Machen Cave? I think we would be very interested in this metal club."

"Machen Cave is north. Several hours. But you do not have to go there. Dam brought the club home."

Excitement sparked between the silth. "Indeed? Where is it now, then?"

"I will have to find it. Dam put it away somewhere. She said she would trade the metal to the tradermales. Or maybe we could fashion tools from it."

"Find it, please."

While she talked Marika had begun setting the inside of the loghouse in order. When she kept paws and mouth busy, she did not have to think about what lay outside the loghouse. She continued distracting herself by searching for Skiljan's trophy. "Here it is."

The tall meth took it. Both sat down, facing one another, the metal club between them. They passed it back and forth, examined it minutely, even argued over a few small writing characters stamped into one side. They did so, though, in a language Marika did not understand. By the cautious way they handled the thing, Marika decided it was a dangerous something they had seen but never before touched.

"It is very important that you recall every detail about this meth you saw. The one who carried this club. It is certain she was our enemy. If we can identify her pack, by her clothing, say, we will be better equipped to protect our own. There should be no silth with the nomads."

"There should be no wehrlen either," said the older silth. "A wehrlen come out of nowhere, with skills as advanced as our own, or nearly so. This is an impossibility."

The taller meth was thoughtful a moment. "That is true." She looked at Marika intently. "Where does this Machen Cave lie again?" And Marika felt something brush her mind, a touch far lighter than that she had experienced the night the far silth had responded to her probing of the packfast. "Ah. So. Yes. Sister, I am going to go there after all. To see if the bodies remain. You learn what you can from the wehrlen."

The older silth nodded. She went out of the loghouse immediately.

The other dallied a moment, looking at Marika, saying nothing. Finally, she too departed, scratching Marika behind the ear lightly as she went. "It will all work out, pup. It will all work out."

Marika did not respond. She sat down and stared into the coals in the firepit. But she found no clues there.

III

She straightened the inside of the loghouse a bit more, moving in a daze. When she could find nothing more to preoccupy her there, she donned her coat. She had to go outside sometime and face the truth. No sense putting it off any longer.

It was every bit as terrible as she remembered, and worse. The carrion eaters had gathered. It would be a fat winter for them.

Though it was pointless, she began the thankless task of cleaning the packstead. One by one, straining her small frame to its limits, she dragged the frozen corpses of her packmates into the lean-to sheds. They would be safe from the carrion eaters there. For a time.

Near the doorway to Gerrien's loghouse she came on something that made her stop, stand as still as death for a long time.

Pohsit. Dead. Sprawled, one arm outstretched as if beseeching the loghouse, the other at her heart, her paw a claw. When Marika finally tore her gaze away she saw the elder silth in the mouth of the stockade spiral, watching.

Neither said a word.

Marika bent and caught hold of Pohsit's arm and dragged her into a lean-to with the others. Maybe, just a little, she had begun to understand what "silth" meant, and why her elders cursed and feared them.

Sometimes she could not reach her packmates because they were buried beneath dead nomads. Those she dragged around the spiral to the field outside, where she left them to the mercy of the carrion eaters. The wehrlen, she noted, had been both moved and stripped. The elder silth had searched him thoroughly.

There was no end to the gruesome task. So many bodies.... When her muscles began to protest, she rested by gathering fallen weapons instead, moving them near the doorway of her dam's loghouse, laying them out neatly by type, as if for inventory. She had tried to strip the better furs from the dead, too, but that had proven too difficult. The bodies would have to be thawed first.

Always the carrion eaters surrounded her. They would not learn to remain outside the stockade. They flapped away, squawking, only when she came within kicking distance. She sealed her ears to their bickering over tidbits. Listening might have driven her mad.

She was more than a little mad anyway. She drove herself mercilessly, carrying out a task without point.

After a time the taller silth returned, loping gracefully and easily upon the dirtied snow. She carried a folded garment similar to her own. She joined the other silth, and the two watched Marika, neither speaking, interfering, nor offering to help. They seemed to understand that an exorcism was in progress. Marika ignored them and went on. And went on. And went on till her muscles cried out in torment, till fatigue threatened to overwhelm her. And still she went on.

She passed near the silth often, pretending they did not exist, yet sometimes she could not help overhearing the few words they did exchange. Mostly, they talked about her. The older was becoming concerned. She heard herself called smart, stubborn, and definitely a little insane.

She wondered what the tall silth had learned around Machen Cave. They did not discuss that. But she was not interested enough to ask.

The sun rode across the sky, pursued by the specks of several lesser moons. Marika grew concerned about Grauel and Barlog. They had been gone long enough to reach the Laspe packstead and return. Had they fallen foul of nomad survivors? Finally, she scaled the watchtower, which threatened to topple off its savaged legs. She barely had the energy to complete the climb. She saw nothing when she did and looked toward the neighboring packstead.

She dug around inside herself, seeking her ability to touch, with increasing desperation. It just was not there! She had to reach out and make sure Grauel and Barlog were all right! The All could not claim them too, leaving her alone with these weird silth! But it was hopeless. Either she had lost the ability or it had gone dormant on her in her shock and fatigue.

She told herself there was no point worrying. That worry would do no good, would change nothing. But she worried. She stood there studying the countryside, unconsciously resting, till the wind penetrated her furs and her muscles began to stiffen, then she climbed down and lost herself in labor again.

She did not know, consciously, what she was doing, but she was avoiding grief, because it was a grief too great to bear. Even toughened Grauel and Barlog had needed something to occupy them, to allow some of the pressure to leak off unnoted, to give some meaning to having survived. How much more difficult for a pup not yet taught to keep emotion under tight control.

The silth understood grief. They stayed out of her way, and did nothing to discourage her from working herself into an exhausted stupor.

The shadows were long and the carrion eaters almost too overfed to fly. Marika had dragged most all of her packmates into the lean-tos. Suddenly she realized that she had not found Kublin. Zambi had been there, right where she remembered him falling, but not Kub. Kub should have been one of the first she reached, because she had left him atop one of the heaps of dead. Hadn't she?

Had she dragged him away and not noticed? Or had she forgotten? The more she tried to remember, the more she became confused. She became locked into a lack of movement, in complete indecision, just standing in the square while a rising wind muttered and moaned about her.

The sky above threatened new snow. A few random flakes danced around, dashed in to melt upon her nose or to sting her eyeballs. The several days' break in winter's fury would end soon. The white would come and mask death till spring pulled the shroud aside.

One of the silth came and led her into Skiljan's loghouse, settled her near a freshened fire. The other was building up the fire at the male end of the loghouse and setting out pots and utensils in preparation for a meal far too large for three. Neither spoke.

Grauel and Barlog arrived with the darkness, leading the Laspe survivors. They numbered just a few over three score, and all fit comfortably into the one loghouse. The silth dished up stew silently, watched while the Laspe ate greedily. After a time they prepared an infusion of chaphe and insisted Marika drink it. As she faded away, barely aware of them wrapping her in furs, she murmured, "But I wanted to hear about what you found at Machen Cave."

"Later, little silth. Later. Rest your heart now. Rest your heart."

She wakened once in the deep hours. The fire crackled nearby, sending shadows dancing. The taller silth sat beside the firepit, motionless as stone except when dropping another piece of wood into the flames. Her eyes glowed in the firelight as she stared at Marika.

A touch, gentle as a caress. Startled, Marika recoiled.

Easy, little one. There is nothing to fear. Go back to sleep.

Something enwrapped her in warmth, comfort, reassurance. She fell asleep immediately.

Morning found the packstead blanketed with six inches of new snow. The remaining bodies in the square had become vague lumps seen through slowly falling snowflakes. The air was almost still, the new flakes large, and the morning deceptively warm. It seemed one could go out and run without a coat. Grauel and Barlog rose early and went out to take up where Marika had left off. A few of the Laspe survivors joined them. There was little talk. The snowfall continued, lazy but accumulating quickly. It was a very wet snow.

Noon came. The silth made everyone come inside and eat a huge meal. Marika watched the Laspe Wise cringe away from the two in black, and wondered why. But she did not ask. She did not care enough about anything to ask questions just then.

Marika and Grauel were first to go back outside. Almost the instant they stepped into the snowfall the huntress snapped Marika's collar and yanked her down, clapped a paw over her mouth before she could speak. Holding Marika, she pointed.

Vague figures moved through the snowfall around Gerrien's loghouse. Nomads! And they could not be ignorant of the fact that the packstead was inhabited still, for Skiljan's loghouse was putting out plenty of smoke.

Marika wriggled her way back through the doorway. Grauel slid inside behind her. Once she was certain she would not be heard outside, the huntress announced, "We have company outside. Nomads. I would guess only a few, trying to steal whatever they can under cover of the snow."

The silth laid down their ladles and bowls, closed their eyes. In a moment the taller nodded and said, "There are a dozen of them. Quietly taking food."

Marika listened no more. Barlog had snatched up a bow and was headed for the door, not bothering to don a coat. Marika scampered after her, tried to restrain her. She failed, and in an instant was out in the snow again, still trying to hold the huntress back.

Her judgment was better than Barlog's. As the huntress pushed outside, an arrow ripped past her ear and buried itself in the loghouse wall.

Barlog drew her own arrow to her ear, let fly at a shadow as another arrow streaked out of the falling snow. The latter missed. Barlog's brought a yip of pain.

The door shoved against Marika's back. Grauel pushed outside, cursing Barlog for her folly. She readied her own bow, crouched, sought a target.

Marika flopped onto her belly. Barlog, too, crouched. Arrows whipped overhead, stuck in or bounced off the loghouse. They heard confused shouting in dialect as the nomads debated the advisability of flight. A shaft from Grauel's bow found a shadow. That settled the matter for the nomads. They hefted their wounded and ran. They were not about to stay in a place so well known to death.

Where were the silth? Marika wondered. Why didn't *they* do something?

Grauel and Barlog made fierce noises and chased after the nomads—making sure they did not catch up. Marika followed, feeling foolish as she yipped around the spiral.

The nomads vanished in the snowfall. Grauel and Barlog showed no inclination to pursue them through that, where an ambush could so easily be laid. Grauel held Marika back. "Enough, pup. They are gone."

During all the excitement Marika never felt a hint of touch. The silth had done nothing.

She challenged them about it the moment she returned to the loghouse.

The taller seemed amused. "One must think beyond the moment if one is to be silth, little one. Go reflect on why it might be useful to allow some raiders to escape."

Marika did as she was told, sullenly. After her nerves settled, she began to see that it might indeed be beneficial if word spread that the Degnan packstead was defended still. Beneficial to the remaining Laspe anyway.

She began to entertain second thoughts about emigrating to the silth packfast.

That afternoon the silth gave her another infusion of chaphe to drink. They made Grauel and Barlog drink of it and rest, too. And when night fell and Biter rose to scatter the world with her silvery rays, the two females said, "It is time to leave."

Between them, Marika, Grauel, and Barlog found a hundred reasons for delaying. The two females in black might have been stone, for all they were moved. They brought forth travel packs which they had assembled while the three Degnan slept. "You will take these with you."

Marika, too stupefied to argue much, went through hers. It contained food, extra clothing, and a few items that might come in handy during the trek. She found a few personal possessions also, gifts from Kublin, Skiljan, and her granddam that had meant much to her once and might again after time banished the pain. She eyed the silth suspiciously. How had they known?

Resigned, Grauel and Barlog began shrugging into the coats. Marika pulled on her otec boots, the best she owned. No sense leaving them for Laspe scavengers.

A thought hit her. "Grauel. Our books. We cannot leave our books."

Grauel exchanged startled glances with Barlog. Barlog nodded. Both huntresses settled down with stubborn expressions upon their faces.

"Books are heavy, pup," the taller silth said. "You will tire of carrying them soon. Then what? Cast them into the river? Better they stay where they will be appreciated and used."

"They are the treasure of the Degnan," Marika insisted, answering the silth but speaking to the huntresses. "We have to take the Chronicle. If we lose the Chronicle, then we really are dead."

Grauel and Barlog agreed with a fervor that startled the silth.

Few wilderness packs had the sense of place in time and history that had marked the Degnan. Few had the Degnan respect for heritage. Many had no more notion of their past than the stories of their oldest Wise, who erroneously told revised versions of tales passed down by their own granddams.

Grauel and Barlog were embarrassed. It shamed them that they had not thought of the Chronicle themselves. So long as it existed and was kept, the Degnan would exist somewhere. They became immovably stubborn. The silth could not intimidate them into motion.

"Very well," the taller said, ignoring the angry mutter of her companion. "Gather your books. But hurry. We are wasting moonlight. The sky may not stay clear long. The north spawns storms in litters."

The two huntresses took torches and left Skiljan's loghouse, made rounds of all the other five. They collected every book of the pack that had not been destroyed. Marika brought out the six from the place where Saettle had kept those of Skiljan's loghouse. When all were gathered, there were ten.

"They are right," she admitted reluctantly. "They *are* heavy."

They were big, hand-inscribed tomes with massive wood and leather boards and bindings. Some weighed as much as fifteen pounds.

Marika set the three volumes of the Chronicle aside, looked to the huntresses for confirmation. Grauel said, "I could carry two."

Barlog nodded. "I will carry two also."

That made four. Marika said, "I think I could carry two, if they were light ones." She pushed the massive Chronicle volumes toward the huntresses. Grauel took two, Barlog the other. No more than two would be lost if one of them did not reach the packfast.

Three books had to be selected from the remaining seven. Marika asked the huntresses, "Which do you think will be the most useful?"

Grauel thought for a moment. "I do not know. I am not bookish."

"Nor am I," Barlog said. "I hunt. We will have little real use for them. We just want to save what we can."

Marika exposed her teeth in an expression of exasperation.

"You choose," Grauel said. "You are the studious one."

Marika's exasperation became more marked. A decision of her own, a major one, as though she were an adult already. She was not prepared mentally.

On first impulse she was tempted to select those that had belonged to her own loghouse. But Barlog reminded her that Gerrien's loghouse had possessed a book on agriculture that, once its precepts had been accepted, had improved the pack's yields, reducing the labor of survival.

One of the silth said, "You will have no need of a book about farming. You will not be working in the fields. Leave it for those who will have more need."

So. A choice made.

Marika dithered after rejecting only one more book, a collection of old stories read for the pleasure of small pups. There would be no need of that where they were going.

The older silth came around the fire, arrayed the books before Marika after the manner of terrac fortune plaques, which the sagans so often consulted. "Close your eyes, Marika. Empty your mind. Let the All come in and touch you. Then you reach out and touch books. Those shall be the ones you take."

Grauel grumbled, "That is sheer chance."

Barlog added, "Witch's ways," and looked very upset. Just the way the Wise did whenever talk turned to the silth.

They were afraid. Finally, Marika began to realize what lay at the root of all their attitudes toward the silth. Sheer terror.

She did exactly as she was told. Moments later her paw seemed to move of its own accord. She felt leather under her fingers, could not recall which book lay where.

"No," said the older silth. "Keep your eyes closed."

Grauel grumbled something to Barlog.

"You two," the old silth said. "Pack the books as she chooses them. Place the others in the place where books are stored."

Marika's paw jerked to another book. For a moment it seemed something had hold of her wrist. And on the level of the touch, she sensed something with that darkshadow presence she associated with the things she called ghosts.

Again, and done.

The old silth spoke. "Open your eyes, pup. Get your coat. It is time to travel."

Unquestioning, Marika did as she was told. Coat on, she raised her pack and snugged it upon her shoulders the way Pobuda had shown her, finally, coming back from the hunt in Plenthzo Valley. She felt uncomfortable under the unaccustomed weight. Recalling the march to and from the hunt, and the deep, wet snow, she knew she would become far more uncomfortable before she reached the silth packfast.

Maybe she *would* end up discarding the books.

Maybe the silth had been trying to do her a favor, trying to talk her out of taking the books.

There were no farewells from or for the Laspe, who watched preparations for departure with increasing relief. As they stepped to the windskins, though, Marika heard the Laspe Wise begin a prayer to the All. It wished them a safe journey.

It was something.

As she trudged around the spiral of the stockade, the new snow dragging at her boots, Marika asked the silth ahead, "Why are we leaving now? Could we not travel just as safely in the daytime?"

"We are silth, pup. We travel at night."

The other, from behind Marika, said, "The night is our own. We are the daughters of the night and come and go as we will."

Marika shivered in a cold that had nothing to do with the wind off the Zhotak.

And around her, in the light of many moons, all the world glimmered black and bone.

BOOK TWO: AKARD

BOOK TWO

AKKARD

CHAPTER SEVEN

I

There was nothing to compare with it in Marika's brief experience of life. Never had she been so totally, utterly miserable, so cold, so punished. And the first night of travel was only hours old.

She knew how Kublin must feel—must have felt, she reminded herself with a wince of emotion—when trying to keep up with Zambi and his friends.

The new, wet snow was a quicksand that dragged at her boots every step, though they had placed her next to last in the file, with only Barlog behind her to guard their backs. Her pack was an immense dead weight that, she was sure, would crush her right down into the earth's white shroud and leave her unable, ever, to rise to the surface again. The wind off the Zhotak had risen, flinging tatters of gray cloud across the faces of the moons, gnawing at her right cheek till she was sure she would lose half her face to frostbite. The temperature dropped steadily.

That was a positive sign only in that if it fell enough they could be reasonably sure they would not face another blizzard soon.

All that backbreaking labor, trying to clear the packstead of bodies, came back to haunt her. She ached everywhere. Her muscles never quite loosened up.

Grauel was breaking trail. She tried to keep the pace down. But the silth pressed, and it was hard for the huntress to slack off when the older of the two could keep a more rigorous pace.

Once, during the first brief rest halt, Grauel and the taller silth fell into whispered argument. Grauel wanted to go more slowly. She said, "We are in enemy territory, sister. It would be wiser to move cautiously, staying alert. We do not want to stumble into nomads in our haste."

"It is the night. The night is ours, huntress. And we can watch where you cannot."

Grauel admitted that possibility. But she said, "They have their witchcrafts, too. As they have demonstrated. It would not be smart to put all our trust into a single—"

"Enough. We will not argue. We are not accustomed to argument. That

87

is a lesson you will learn hard if you do not learn it in the course of this journey."

Marika stared at the snow between her feet and tried to imagine how far they had yet to travel. As she recalled her geography, the packfast lay sixty miles west of the packstead. They had come, at most, five miles so far. At this pace they would be three or four nights making the journey. In summer it could be done in two days.

Grauel did not argue further. Even so, her posture made it obvious she was in internal revolt, that she was awed by and frightened of the silth, yet held them in a certain contempt. Her body language was not overlooked by the silth either. Sometime after the journey resumed Marika caught snatches of an exchange between the two. They were not pleased with Grauel.

The elder said, "But what can you expect of a savage? She was not raised with a proper respect."

A hint of a snarl stretched Marika's lips. A proper respect? Where was the proper respect of the silth for a huntress of Grauel's ability? Where was a proper respect for Grauel's experience and knowledge? Grauel had not been arguing for the sake of argument, like some bored Wise meth with time to kill.

It did not look that promising a future, this going into exile at the packfast. No one would be pleased with anyone else's ways.

She was not some male to bend the neck, Marika thought. If the silth thought so, they would find they had more trouble than they bargained for.

But defiance was soon forgotten in the pain and weariness of the trek. One boot in front of the other and, worse, the mind always free to remember. Always open to invasion from the past.

The real pain, the heart pain, began then.

More than once Barlog nearly trampled her, coming forward in her own foggy plod to find Marika stopped, lost within herself.

The exasperation of the silth grew by the hour.

They were weary of the wilderness. They were anxious to return home. They had very little patience left for indulging Degnan survivors.

That being the case, Marika wondered why they did not just go on at their own pace. They had no obligation to the Degnan, it would seem, in their own minds from the way they talked. As though the infeudation to which Skiljan and Gerrien had appealed for protection was at best a story with which the silth of the packfast justified their robberies to packs supposedly beholden to them. As though the rights and obligations were all one-sided, no matter what was promised.

Marika began to develop her own keen contempt for the silth. In her agony and aching, it nurtured well. Before the silth ordered a day camp set in a windbreak in the lee of a monstrous fallen tree, Marika's feeling had grown so strong the silth could read it. And they were baffled, for they had found her more open and unprejudiced than the older Degnan. They squatted together and spoke about it while Grauel and Barlog dug a better shelter into the snow drifted beneath the tree.

The taller silth beckoned Marika. For all her exhaustion, the pup had been trying to help the huntresses, mainly by gathering firewood. They had reached a stretch where tall trees flanked the river, climbing the sides of steep hills. Oddly, the land became more rugged as the river ran west, though from the plateau where the Degnan packstead lay it did not seem so, for the general tendency of the land was slowly downward.

"Pup," the taller silth said, "there has been a change in you. We would try to understand why overnight you have come to dislike us so."

"This," Marika said curtly.

"This? What does 'this' mean?"

Marika was not possessed of a fear the way the huntresses were. She did not know silth, because no one had told her about them. She said, "You sit there and watch while Grauel and Barlog work not only for their own benefit but yours. At the packstead you contributed. Some. In things that were not entirely of the pack to do." Meaning remove bodies.

The elder silth did not understand. The younger did, but was irked. "We did when there was none else to do. We are silth. Silth do not work with their paws. That is the province of—"

"You have two feet and two paws and are in good health. Better health than we, for you walk us into the earth. You are capable. In our pack you would starve if you did not do your share."

Fire flashed in the older silth's eyes. The taller, after another moment of irritation, seemed amused. "You have much to learn, little one. If we did these things you speak of, we would not be seen as silth anymore."

"Is being silth, then, all arrogance? We had arrogant huntresses in our pack. But they worked like everyone else. Or they went hungry."

"We do our share in other ways, pup."

"Like by protecting the packs who pay tribute? That is the excuse I have always heard for the senior huntresses traveling to the packfast every spring. To pay the tribute which guarantees protection. This winter makes me suspect the protection bought may be from the packfast silth, not from killers from outside the upper Ponath. Your protection certainly has done the packs no good. You have saved three lives. Maybe. While packs all over the upper Ponath have been exterminated. So do not brag to me of the wonderful share you do unless you show me much more than you have."

"Feisty little bitch," the taller silth said, aside to the elder.

The older was at the brink of rage, an inch from explosion. But Marika had stoked her own anger to the point where she did not care, was not afraid. She noted that Grauel and Barlog had stopped pushing snow around and were watching, poised, uncertain, but with paws near weapons.

This was not good. She had best get her temper cooled or there would be difficulties none of them could handle.

Marika turned her back on the silth. She said, "As strength goes." Though this seemed a perversion of that old saw.

She won a point, though. The tall silth began pitching in after, just long enough to make it appear she was not yielding to a mere pup.

"Be careful, Marika," Grauel snapped when they were a distance away, collecting wood. "Silth are not known for patience or understanding."

"Well, they made me mad."

"They make everyone mad, pup. Because they can get away with doing any damned thing they want. They have the power."

"I will watch my tongue."

"I doubt that. You have grown overbold with no one to slap your ears. Come. This is enough wood."

Marika returned to their little encampment wondering at Grauel. And at Barlog. The agony of the Degnan did not, truly, seem to have touched them deeply.

II

Neither Grauel nor Barlog said a word, but the covert looks they cast at the fire made it clear they did not consider it a wise comfort. Smoke, even when not seen, could be smelled for miles.

The silth saw and understood their discomfort. The taller might have agreed with them, once the cooking was finished, but the elder was in a stubborn mood, not about to take advice from anyone.

The fire burned on.

The huntresses had dug a hollow beneath the fallen tree large enough for the five of them, and deep enough to shelter them from the wind entirely. As the sun rose, the silth crept into the shelter and bundled against one another for warmth. Marika was not far behind. Only in sleep would she find surcease from aches both physical and spiritual. Grauel followed her. But Barlog did not.

"Where is Barlog?" Marika asked, half asleep already. It was a morning in which the world was still. There was no sound except the whine of the wind and the crackle of frozen tree branches. When the wind died momentarily, there was, too, a distinct rushing sound, water surging through rapids in the river. Most places, as Marika had seen, the river was entirely frozen over and indistinguishable from the rest of the landscape.

"She will watch," Grauel replied.

The silth had said nothing about setting a watch. Had, in fact, implied that even asleep they could sense the approach of strangers long before the huntresses might.

Marika just nodded and let sleep take her.

She half wakened when Barlog came to trade places with Grauel, and again when Grauel changed with Barlog once more. But she remained completely unaware of anything the next time Barlog came inside. She did not waken because that was when she was ensnarled in the first of the dreams.

A dark place. Stuffy. Fear. Weakness and pain. Fever and thirst and hunger. A musty smell and cold dampness. But most of all pain and hunger and the terror of death.

It was like no dream Marika had ever had, and there was no escaping it.

It was a dream in which nothing ever happened. It was a static state of being, almost the worst she could imagine. Nightmares were supposed to revolve around flight, pursuit, the inexorable approach of something dread, tireless, and without mercy. But this was like being in the mind of someone dying slowly inside a cave. Inside the mind of someone insane, barely aware of continued life.

She wakened to smoke and smells and silence. The wind had ceased blowing. For a while she lay there shuddering, trying to make sense of the dream. The Wise insisted dreams were true, though seldom literal.

But it slipped away too quickly, too soon became nothing more than a state of malaise.

Grauel had a fresh fire blazing and food cooking when Marika finally crawled out of the shelter. The sun was well on its way down. Night would be along soon after they ate, packed, and took care of personal essentials. She settled beside Grauel, took over tending the fire. Barlog joined them a moment later, while the silth were still stretching and grumbling inside the shelter.

"They are out there," Barlog said. Grauel nodded. "Just watching right now. But we will hear from them before we reach the packfast."

Grauel nodded again. She said, "Do not bother our superior witches with it. They know most all there is to know. They must know this, too."

Barlog grunted. "Walk warily tonight. And stay close. Marika, stay alert. If something happens, just get down into the snow. Dive right in and let it bury you if you can."

Marika put another piece of wood onto the fire. She said nothing, and did nothing, till the taller silth came from the shelter, stretched, and surveyed the surrounding land. She came to the fire and checked the cook pot. Her nose wrinkled momentarily. Travel rations were not tasty, even to huntresses accustomed to eating them.

She said, "We will pass the rapids soon after nightfall. We will walk atop the river after that. The going will be easiest there."

Aside, Barlog told Marika, "So we traveled coming east. The river is much easier than the forest, where you never know what lies beneath the snow."

"Will the ice hold?"

"The ice is several feet thick. It will hold anything."

As though the silth were not there, Grauel said, "There are several wide places in the river where we will be very exposed visually. And several narrow places ideal for an ambush." She described what lay ahead in detail, for

Marika's benefit.

The silth was irked but said nothing. The older came out of the shelter and asked, "Is that pot ready?"

"Almost," Grauel replied.

Rested, even the older silth was more cooperative. She began moving snow about so that their pause here would be less noticeable after their departure.

Grauel and Barlog exchanged looks, but did not tell her she was wasting her time. "Let them believe what they want to believe," Barlog said.

The taller silth caught that and responded with a puzzled expression. None of the three Degnan told her they thought the effort pointless because the nomads knew where they were already.

Biter rose early that night, full and in headlong flight from Chaser, which was not far behind. The travelers reached the river as that second major moon rose, setting their shadows aspin. Once again the silth wanted to push hard. This time Grauel and Barlog refused to be pushed. They moved at their own pace, weapons in paw, seeming to study every step before they took it. Marika sensed that they were very tense.

The silth sensed it too, and for that reason, perhaps, they did not press, though clearly they thought all the caution wasted.

And wasted it seemed, for as the sun returned to the world it found them unscathed, having made no contact whatsoever with the enemies Grauel and Barlog believed were stalking them.

But the huntresses were not prepared to admit error. They trusted their instincts. Again they set a watch during the day.

Again nothing happened during the day. Except that Marika dreamed.

It was the same, and different. All the closeness, pain, terror, darkness, hunger were there. The smells and damp and cold were there. But this time she was a little more conscious and aware. She was trying to claw her way up something, climbing somewhere, and the mountain in the dark was the tallest mountain in the world. She kept passing out, and crying out, but no one answered, and she seemed to be making no real ground. She had a blazing fever that came and went, and when it was at its pitch she saw things that could not possibly be there. Things like glowing balls, like worms of light, like diaphanous moths the size of loghouses that flew through earth and air with equal ease.

Death's breath was winter on the back of her neck.

If she could just get to the top, to food, to water, to help.

One of her soft cries alerted Grauel, who wakened her gently and scratched her ears till shuddering and panting went away.

The temperature rose a little that day and stayed up during the following night. With the temperature rise came more snow and bitter winds that snarled along the valley of the east fork, flinging pellets of snow into faces. The travelers fashioned themselves masks. Grauel suggested they hole up till the worst was past. The silth refused. The only reason they would halt, storm or no, was to avoid getting lost: There was no chance of that here. If they strayed from the river they would begin climbing uphill. They would run into trees.

Marika wished she could come through by day instead of by night in snow. What little she could see suggested this was impressive country, far grander than any nearer home.

There was no trouble with nomads that night either, nor during the following day. Grauel and Barlog insisted the northerners were still out there, though, tracking the party.

Marika had no dreams. She hoped the horror was over.

The weather persisted foul. The taller silth said, as they huddled in a shelter where they had gone to ground early, "We will be in trouble if this persists. We have food for only one more day. We are yet two from Akard. If we are delayed much more we will get very hungry before we reach home." She glanced at the older silth. The old one had begun showing the strain of the journey.

Neither huntress said a word, though each had suggested pushing too hard meant wasting energy that might be needed later.

Marika asked, "Akard? What is that?"

"It is the name of what you call the packfast, pup."

She was puzzled. Was Akard the name of the silth pack there?

The storm slackened around noon. The travelers clung to their shelter only till shadows began gathering in the river canyon. The sun fell behind the high hills while there were yet hours of daylight left.

The silth wanted to make up lost time. "We go now," the taller said. And the older hoisted herself up, though it was obvious that standing was now an effort for her.

Marika and the huntresses were compelled to admire the old silth's spirit. She did not complain once, did not yield to the infirmity of her flesh.

Again Grauel and Barlog would not be rushed. Both went to the fore, and advanced with arrows across their bows, studying every shadow along the banks. Their noses wriggled as they sniffed the wind. The silth were amused. They said there were no nomads anywhere near. But they humored the huntresses. The old one could not move much faster anyway. The taller one covered the rear.

Marika carried her short steel knife bared. She was not that impressed with silth skills, for all she knew them more intimately than did Grauel or Barlog.

It happened at twilight.

The snow on one bank erupted. Four buried savages charged. The silth were so startled they just stood there.

Grauel and Barlog released their arrows. Two nomads staggered, began flopping as poison spread through their bodies. There was no time for second arrows. Barlog ducked under a javelin thrust and used her bow to tangle a nomad's legs. Grauel smacked another across the back of the neck with her bow.

Marika flung herself onto the back of the huntress Barlog tripped, driving her knife with all her weight. It was a good piece of iron taken from her dead dam's belt. It slid into flesh easily and true.

Barlog saw that nomad down, whirled to help Grauel, dropping her bow to draw her sword.

Javelins rained down. One struck the older silth but did not penetrate her heavy travel apparel. Another wobbled past Marika's nose and she remembered what she had been told to do if they were attacked. She threw herself into the snow and tried to burrow.

A half-dozen huntresses streaked toward the stunned silth. Grauel and Barlog floundered toward them. Grauel still held her bow. She managed to get off two killing shafts.

The other four piled onto the silth, not even trying to kill them, just trying to rip their packs off their backs, trying to wrest the iron club away from the taller. Barlog hacked at one with her sword. The blade would not slice through all the layers of clothing the nomad wore.

Marika got herself up again. She started toward the fray.

Javelins intercepted her, drove her back.

There were more nomads on the bank now. At least another half-dozen. The cast was long for them, so they seemed intent on keeping her from helping.

Then she heard sounds from the other bank. She looked, saw more nomads.

For the first time since the fighting started she was afraid.

One of the nomads got the iron club away from the tall silth and started toward the south bank, howling triumph.

Marika reeled. There was an instant of touch, wrenchingly violent. Screams echoed down the canyon, to be muted quickly by sound-absorbent snow. In moments the nomads were all down, clawing their chests. Marika's own heart fluttered painfully. She scrambled nearer Grauel and Barlog to see if the touch had affected them, too.

For all the violence, only the older silth was badly injured. She made no complaint, but her face was grim with pain.

Curses in dialect rolled off the slopes.

"There are more of them," Marika told the taller silth. "Do something."

"I have no strength left, pup. I cannot reach that far."

There was a rattling *pop-pop-pop* from way up on the southern side of the canyon. Some things like insects buzzed around them. Some things thumped into the snow. The taller silth cursed softly and dragged Marika down.

The older gritted out, "You had better find some strength, Khles."

The tall silth snarled at Grauel and Barlog, "Get the old one to the bank. Get her behind something. All of you, get behind something." She closed her eyes, concentrated intently.

The popping went on and on.

"What is that?" Marika asked as she and the huntresses neared the north bank with their burden.

A new sound had entered the twilight, a grumble that started softly and slowly and built with the seconds, till it overpowered the popping noise.

"Up there!" Grauel snarled, pointing to the steepest part of the southern slope.

That entire slope was in motion, trees, rocks, and snow.

"Move!" the tall silth snapped. "Get as far as you can. The edge of it may reach us."

Her tone did more to encourage obedience than did her words.

The popping stopped.

The snow rolled down. Its roar sounded like the end of the world to a pup who had never heard anything so loud. She crouched behind a boulder and shivered, awed by the majesty of nature's fury.

She looked at the silth. Both seemed to be in a state of shock. The old one, ignoring her injuries, kept looking at the nearest dead nomads in disbelief. Finally, she asked, "How did they do that, Khles? There was not a hint that they were there before they attacked."

Without looking her way, Grauel said, "They have been with us since the first night, haunting the ridges and trails, waiting for an opportunity. Waiting for us to get careless. We almost did." She poked a nearby corpse. "These are the best-fed nomads I ever saw. Best dressed, too. And most inept. They should have killed us all three times over." She eyed the silth.

They did not respond. The tall one continued to stare up the slope whence the avalanche had come. There were a few calls in dialect still, but from ever farther away.

Barlog was shaking still. She brushed snow off her coat. A dying finger of the avalanche had caught her and taken her down.

The tall silth asked Grauel, "Were any of you hurt?"

"Minor cuts and bruises," Grauel said. "Nothing important. Thank you."

That startled the tall one. She nodded. "We will have to carry the old one. I am no healer, but I believe she has broken ribs and a broken leg."

Barlog made her own examination. "She does."

She and Grauel used their swords to cut poles from which they made a travois. They placed the old silth and their packs upon it, then took turns pulling. The tall silth took her turn, too. It was no time for insisting upon prerogatives. Marika helped later, when the going became more difficult and the travois had to be carried around obstacles.

Grauel and Barlog believed there were no nomads watching anymore.

"How did they sneak up on you?" Marika asked, trudging in the tracks of the tall silth.

"I do not know, pup." She searched the darkness more diligently than ever the huntresses had. Marika realized suddenly that the silth was afraid.

III

Nomads were no further problem. Enemies were not needed. Weather, hunger, increasing weakness due to exposure and short rations, those were enough to make the trek a misery. Marika took the travel better than her companions. She was young and resilient and not spending much energy pulling the travois.

Thus, when it came time to take shelter, the duty fell upon her. Grauel and Barlog were so exhausted they could do little but tend the fire and stir the pot—the pot that had so little to fill it. They snarled at one another for not having had sense enough to loot the nomads. The tall silth's pointing out that the nomads had carried nothing but weapons did not soften the dispute.

Meth did not withstand hunger well. Already Marika felt the grauken stirring within her. She looked at the others. If it came to that desperate moment, upon whom would they turn? Her or the old silth?

They had been five days making a two-day journey. Marika asked the tall silth, "How far must we travel yet? Surely we must be very close."

"Fifteen miles more," the silth said. "A quarter of the way yet. The worst quarter. Five miles down we have to leave the river for the trails. There are many rapids where the river will not be frozen over."

Fifteen miles. At the rate they had been progressing since the old one got hurt, that might mean three more days.

"Do not despair, pup," the silth said. "I have put aside my pride and touched those who watch for us in Akard. They are coming to meet us."

"How soon?" Grauel asked, her only contribution to the conversation.

"They are young and healthy and well fed. Not long."

Not long proved to be a day and a half. Every possible thing that could go wrong did, including an avalanche which destroyed the trail and compelled a detour. The grauken looked out of every eye, needing only a nudge to tear free. But meet those other silth they did, eight miles from the packfast, and they celebrated with what for Marika was the feast of her young life.

After that the cold and snow should have been mere nuisances. A meth with a full belly was ready to challenge anything. But not so. They had been too long hungry and exposed. The slide toward extinction continued.

Marika did not see Akard from outside on arriving, for they approached the stone packfast under a heavily clouded sky at a time when no moons were up. The only hints of size and shape came from lights glimpsed only momentarily. But by then she was not interested in the place except as journey's end. She half believed she would never make it there.

The journey from the Degnan packstead took ten nights, most spent covering the last twenty miles. For all she had food in her belly, Marika was exhausted, being half carried by the silth who had come to the rescue. And she was in better shape than any of her companions. She hoped that never again would she have to travel in winter.

They carried her into a place of stone and she collapsed. She did not think how much more terrible it had become for her companions, all of them having been carried the past few days, lingering on the frontiers of death. She thought of nothing but the all-enveloping warmth of her cell, and of sleep.

Sleep was not without its unpleasantness, though. She dreamed of Kublin. Of Kublin alone and terrified and injured and abandoned, surrounded by strange and unfriendly faces. It was not a dream that made sense. She began to whimper in her sleep and did not rest at all well.

For days no one paid Marika any heed. She was a problem the silth preferred to ignore. She ate. She slept. When she recovered enough to feel curious, she began roaming the endless halls of stone, by turns amazed, baffled, awed, frightened, disgusted, lost. The place was a monster loghouse—of stone, of course—surrounded by a high palisade of stone. Its architecture was alien, and there was no one to tell her why things were the way they were. The few meth her own age she encountered all were hurrying somewhere, were busy, or were just plain contemptuous of the savage among them.

The packfast was a tall edifice built upon limestone headland overlooking the confluence of the forks of the Hainlin. The bluffs fell sixty feet from the packstead's base. Its walls rose sixty feet above their foundations. They were sheer and smooth and in perfect repair, but did have a look of extreme age. There was a wide walkway around their top, screened by a stone curtain which looked like a lower jaw with every other tooth missing. The whole packfast was shaped like a big square box with an arrowhead appended, pointing downriver. There were huntresses upon the walls always, though when Marika asked them why, they did admit that Akard had seen no trouble within living memory.

"Still," one with more patience than most said, "it has been a hard winter, and the northerners are not known for their brains. They may yet come here."

"They are not completely stupid," Marika said. "They may come, indeed. They will look, and then they will go away. Packsteads are easier prey."

"No doubt. There have been rumors that nomads have been seen in the upper Ponath already."

Marika took a step back. She cocked her head in incredulity. "Rumors? Rumors? Do you not know why the huntresses and I came here?"

"You were brought because you have the silth talent."

"I came because I had nowhere else to go. The nomads destroyed all my pack but the two huntresses who came with me. As they destroyed several other packs and packsteads before ours. Within walking distance of ours. There are tens of hundreds of them in the upper Ponath. Ten tens of tens died at our packstead."

The huntress's disbelief was plain. "The sisters would not permit that."

"No? They did not do anything positive that I saw. Oh, they did finish the wehrlen leading the nomads, and they killed those who were plundering our packstead when they got there, but they did not go on to free the rest of the upper Ponath of invaders."

"Wehrlen," the huntress murmured. "You said wehrlen?"

"Yes. A very strong one. The silth said he was as powerful and well-trained as they." Warmed to her story, Marika added, "And there were silth with the nomad horde. My dam slew one. The tall sister, that the other called Khles sometimes, brought back her robe and weapon."

Marika suddenly turned to stare up the valley of the east fork. She had been baffled as to why the nomads had pursued them toward the packfast when they carried so little that was worth taking. Unless... The tall silth had acted as though that club and robe were great treasures.

Perhaps they were. For reasons she did not understand. The nomads *had* directed their attention toward the club and the taller silth's pack.

Already she knew life among the silth would be more complicated than it had been at the packstead. Here *everyone* seemed to be moved by motives as shadowed as Pohsit's.

The huntresses who patrolled the walls and watched the snows called themselves sentries. It was a word new to Marika.

She learned many new words, hearing them almost too fast to assimilate them. "Fortress" was another. Akard was what its meth called a fortress, a bastion which maintained the claim of a silth order called the Reugge, which had its heart in a far southern city called Maksche.

Marika was inundated with more new words when she discovered the communications center.

At the downstream tip of the fortress, at the point of the arrowhead, there was a great tall tree of metal. Marika discovered that her second day of roving. It looked like something drawn by a disastrously twisted artist trying to represent a dead tree. It had a dozen major branches. Upon those sat wire dishes with bowls facing south, each backed by a larger dish of solid metal. There were many smaller branches, seedling size, growing straight up from the main branches. Every inch of metal gleamed in the sunshine. Snow did not stick on the metal branches the way it did on the trees of the forest.

Below and in front of that mad tree there was one huge dish which faced the heavens above the southern horizon. Sometimes that dish moved the way a head did when the eye was following fast game.

What in the world? Very baffling for a pup from the upper Ponath, who found so much metal put to such inexplicable use criminal at the least. She wondered if Grauel or Barlog knew what was going on here. They had been to the packfast before. Surely they had unraveled some of its mysteries. She would have to become more insistent about being shown where they were recuperating.

Grauel and Barlog were sequestered apparently. She had not seen them since entering the packfast. No one would tell her where they were being treated. When she tried to use her own remarkable senses to locate them, something blocked her.

She did not think she was going to like the packfast Akard.

She knew she did not like the way the fortress's huntresses cringed and cowered around the silth. She knew there would be a confrontation of epic proportion the day the silth demanded that of her.

She went down to where the metal tree was and roamed around. But she could find nothing that explained what she saw. Or what she felt. While she was there she became dizzy and disoriented. It took all her concentration to overcome the giddiness and confusion long enough to find her way to a distance sufficient to reduce both.

Her secret senses seemed all scrambled. What had happened? Had she stumbled into some of the great magic for which the silth were so feared?

CHAPTER EIGHT

I

Marika could not stay away from that strange part of the packfast where her brain and talent scrambled. Three times that day of discovery she returned. Three times she reeled away, the third time so distressed her stomach nearly betrayed her.

There had been a true qualitative difference that last time, the strangeness being more intense.

She leaned against a wall and tried to hold her dinner down, panting, letting the chill north wind suck the sudden fever from her face. Finally, she pulled herself together enough to move on.

She ducked into the first doorway she encountered. The vertigo was less intense inside.

She halted. She heard odd voices ahead. Strange lights flickered around her. Lights without flame or much heat when she passed a finger near them. Quiet lights, constant in their burning, hard to the touch when she did rest a finger upon them. What witchery was this?

She became very nervous. She had been told she could go wherever she wanted and see anything she wanted. Yet the silth must have their ritual places, like the males and huntresses of the packstead, and those certainly would be off limits. Was this such a place? She dreaded the chance she would interrupt the silth at their black rites. They had begun to seem as dark as her packmates had feared.

Curiosity overcame fear. She moved forward a few steps, looked around in awe. The room was like nothing she had ever imagined. Some yards away a female in a blue smock moved among devices whose purposes Marika could not pretend to fathom. Some had windows that flickered with a ghostly gray light. The voices came from them. The female in the blue smock did not respond.

Devils. The windows must open on the underworld, or the afterworld, or… She fought down the panic, moved forward a few more steps toward the nearest of those ghostly portals.

She frowned, more confused than ever. A voice came through the window, but there was no one on the other side. Instead, she saw squiggles arranged in neat columns, like a page from a book in reversed coloration.

Flicker. The page changed. A new set of squiggles appeared. Some of those altered while she watched. She gasped and stepped closer again, bent till her nose was almost against the window.

The meth finally noticed her presence. "Hello," she said. "You must be the new sister."

Marika wondered if she ought to flee. "I do not know," she replied, throat tight. She was confused about her status. Some of the meth of the packfast did call her sister. But she did not know why. No one had taken time to explain. She did know that the word "sister" did not mean what it might have at home: another pup born of the same dam. None of these meth seemed to be related by blood or pack.

The society was nothing like that of a pack. Hierarchies and relationships were confusing. So far she had figured out for sure only that those who wore black were in charge and everyone else deferred to them in a curious set of rituals which might never make sense.

"What is this place?" Marika asked. "Is it holy? Am I intruding?"

"This is the communications center," the female replied, amused. "It is holy only to those hungry for news from the south." It seemed she had made a great jest. And was sorry to have wasted it on a savage unable to appreciate it. "You are from the stead in the upper Ponath that the nomads destroyed, are you not?"

Marika nodded. That story had gotten around fast once she had told the sentry. Many of the meth who wore colors other than black wanted to know all about the siege of the Degnan packstead. But when Marika told them the story, it made them unhappy. For themselves, not for the meth of the upper Ponath.

"Nomads running together in thousands. Ruled by a wehrlen. Times are strange indeed. What next?"

Marika shrugged. Her imagination was inadequate to encompass how her life could turn worse than it had already.

"Well, you are from the outside, so all this will be new to you. The upper Ponath is as backward a region as can be found on this world, bar the Zhotak, and deliberately so. That is the way the sisterhood and the brethren want it kept. Come. There is nothing here to fear. I will show you. My name is Braydic, by the way. Senior Koenic is my truesister, though blood means nothing here."

"I am Marika." Marika moved to the female's side.

Braydic indicated the nearest gray window. "We call this a vision screen. A number of things can be done with it. At the moment this one is monitoring how much water we have stored behind each of the three dams on the Husgen. That is what you call the west fork of the Hainlin. For us the east fork continues to be the Hainlin and the west fork becomes the Husgen. If you have been up on the ramparts at all, you must have seen the lower dam and its powerhouse."

Marika feared she might have walked into a trap quite unlike the one she had suspected. Meth did not chatter. They became very uncomfortable with those who did. Talkers were suspected of being unbalanced. Generally, they were just lonely.

Braydic poked several black lozenges among the scores ranked before the vision screen. Each lozenge had a white character inscribed upon it. The squiggles left the screen. A picture replaced them. After a moment Marika realized it represented a view up the west fork of the Hainlin, the branch Braydic called the Husgen. It portrayed structures about which Marika had been curious but had felt too foolish to ask.

"This is the powerhouse. This is the dam. The dam spans the river, forming a wall that holds back the water. The water comes down to the powerhouse through huge earthenware pipes, where it turns a wheel." Braydic poked lozenges again. Now the screen portrayed a big wooden wheel turning slowly as water from a pipe poured down upon blades. "The wheel in turn turns a machine which generates the power we use."

Marika was baffled, of course. What power? Did the silth generate the touch artificially?

Braydic recognized her confusion. "Yes. You would not understand, would you?" She stepped to a wall, touched something there. All the lights, except those near the vision screens, went out. Then on again. "I meant the power that works the lights and vision screens and such. I am monitoring the water levels behind the dams because the spring thaw will begin before long. We have to estimate how much to let water levels drop so the three lakes will be able to absorb meltoff without risk of overflow."

Marika remained lost. But she nodded, pretending to understand. If she did that, maybe Braydic would keep talking instead of sending her away.

She was lonely, too.

At home adults got impatient when you did not understand. Except for the studies in books, which said nothing of things like this, you were expected to learn by watching.

"Do not be afraid to say you do not know," Braydic told her. "Nor ashamed. If you do not admit ignorance, how are you to learn? No one will bother teaching you what you pretend to know already."

Marika studied the black lozenges. They were marked with the characters and numbers of the common symbology, but there were a dozen characters she did not recognize, too. Braydic pressed a larger lozenge which lay to one side. The vision screen went blank.

"Do you read or write, little sister?"

She wanted to say she was Degnan. Degnan were educated. But that seemed a fool's arrogance here. "I read. I do not write very well, except for ciphers. We had very little chance to practice writing, except when we made clay tablets or bark scrolls and could use a stick stylus or piece of charcoal. Pens, inks, and papers are all tradermale goods. They are too dear for pup play."

Braydic nodded. "I see. Think of a written word, then. All right? You have one?"

"Yes."

"Pick out the characters on the keyboard. Press them in the order you would write them. Top to bottom, the way you would read them."

Tentatively, Marika touched a lozenge. The first character of her name appeared on the vision screen. She pressed another and another, delighted. Without awaiting permission she pecked out her dam's name, and Kublin's.

"You should place a blank space between words," Braydic said. "So the reader knows where one ends and the next begins. To do that you press this key." Swiftly, all her fingers tapping at once, she repeated what Marika had done. "You see?"

"Yes. May I?"

"Go ahead."

Marika tapped out more words. She would have tried every word she knew, but one of the silth interrupted.

Braydic changed. She became almost craven. "Yes, mistress? How may I please you?"

"Message for Dhatkur at the Maksche cloister. Most immediate. Prepare to send."

"Yes, mistress." Braydic tapped lozenges swiftly. The vision screen blanked. A single large symbol took the place of Marika's doodlings. It looked like two comets twining around one another, round and round, spiraling outward from the common center. "Clear, mistress."

"Continue."

Braydic tapped three more lozenges. The symbol vanished. A face replaced it. It said a few words that Marika did not understand.

She gasped, suddenly stricken by the realization that the vision screen was portraying the image of a meth far away. This was witchcraft, indeed!

The silth spoke with that far meth briefly. Marika could not follow the exchange, for it was in what must be a silth rite tongue. Still, it sounded trivial in tone. More important the wonders surrounding her. She gazed at Braydic in pure awe. This witch ruled all this and she wasn't even silth.

The silth sister finished her conversation. She laid a paw on Marika's shoulder. "Come, pup. At your stage you should not be exposed to too much electromagnetic radiation."

Baffled, Marika allowed herself to be led away. She glanced back once, surprised a look on Braydic's face which said she would be welcome any time she cared to return.

So maybe she had found one meth here who could become a friend.

The silth scooted Marika through the door, then turned back to Braydic. In an angry voice she demanded of the meth in blue, "What are you doing? That pup came out of a Tech Two Zone. You are giving her Tech Five knowledge. Gratuitously."

"She is to be educated silth, is she not?" Braydic countered, with some spirit.

"We do not yet know that." The silth shifted from accented common speech to that she had used while speaking through the vision screen. She became very loud. Her temper was up. Marika decided to get away from there before that wrath overtook her.

II

They took her before the taller silth who had brought her out of the upper Ponath. That one, whom they all called Khles here, was confined to bed yet. Her one leg, only lightly wounded in the nomad attack, had begun to mortify during the long struggle to reach the packfast. She had spoken neither of the wound nor infection during the journey.

The sisters who brought Marika chattered among themselves beforehand, gossiping about the possibility that Khles's leg would have to be amputated. The healer sisters were having trouble conquering the infection.

"So," the tall one said, "they all forgot or ignored you, yes?" She seemed grimly amused. "Well, nothing lasts forever. The easy days are over."

Marika said nothing. The days had not been easy at all. They had been lonely and filled with the self-torment brought by memories of the packstead. They had been filled with the deep malaise that came of knowing her entire pack was going into the embrace of the All without a Mourning. And there was nothing she, Grauel, or Barlog could do. None of them knew the rites. Ceremonies of Mourning were the province of the Wise. The last of the Degnan Wise had perished—Marika was morally certain—through the agency of the silth.

When she slept, there were dreams. Not as intense, not as long, not as often, but dreams still edged with madness, burning with fever.

"Pay attention, pup."

Marika snapped out of a reverie.

"Your education will begin tomorrow. The paths of learning for a silth sister are threefold. Each is a labor in itself. There will be no time for daydreaming."

"For a silth sister? I am a huntress."

"You belong to the Reugge sisterhood, pup. You are what the sisterhood tells you you are. I will warn you once now. For the first and last time. Rebellion, argument, backtalk are not tolerated in our young. Neither are savage habits and customs. You are silth. You will think and act as silth. You are Reugge silth. You will think and act as Reugge silth. You have no past. You were whelped the night they brought us through the gates of Akard."

Marika responded without thinking. "Kropek shit!" It was the strongest expletive she knew.

As strength goes.

The silth was on her own ground now and not inclined to be charitable, understanding, or forgiving. "You will change that attitude. Or you will find life here hard, and possibly short."

"I am not silth," Marika insisted. "I am a huntress to be. You have no other claim upon me. I am here by circumstance only, not by choice."

"Even among savages, I think, pups do not argue with their elders. Not with impunity."

That did reach Marika. She had to admit that her lack of respect left much to be desired. She stared at the stone floor a pace in front of her toes.

"Better. Much better. As I said, your education will follow a threefold path. You will have no time to waste. Each path is a labor in itself."

The first path of Marika's education was almost a continuation of the process she had known at the packstead. But it went on seven hours every day, and spanned fields broader than any she could have imagined before becoming a refugee.

There was ciphering. There was reading and writing, with ample materials to practice the latter. There was elementary science and technology, which expanded her amazed mind to horizons she could hardly believe, even while sensing that her instructors were leaving vast gaps. That such wonders existed, and she had never known…

There was geography, which astounded her by showing her the true extent of her world—and the very small place in it held by the upper Ponath. Her province was but a pinprick upon the most extreme frontier of civilization.

She learned, without being formally taught, that her world was one of extreme contrasts. Most meth lived in uttermost poverty and savagery, confined to closed or semi-closed Tech Zones. Some lived in cities more modern than anything she saw at the packfast, but the lot of the majority was little better than that of rural meth. A handful, belonging to or employed by the sisterhoods, lived in high luxury and were free to move about as they pleased.

And there were the rare few who lived the dream. They could leave the planet itself, to venture among the stars, to see strange worlds and stranger races. But there was little said of that in the early days. Just enough to whet her appetite for more.

The second pathway of learning resembled the first, and paralleled it, but dealt only with the Reugge sisterhood itself, teaching the sisterhood's history, its primary rituals, its elementary mysteries. And mercilessly pounded away at the notion that the Reugge sisterhood constituted the axis of the meth universe. Marika tired of that quickly. The message was too blatantly self-serving.

The third course…

In the third pathway Marika learned why her dam had feared and hated silth. She learned what it meant to be silth. She studied to become silth. And that was the most demanding, unrelenting study of all.

Her guide in study, her guardian within the packfast, was named Gorry.

Gorry was the elder of the females who had brought her from the packstead. She never quite recovered from that journey. She blamed her enfeebled health upon Marika. She was a hard, unforgiving, unpleasant, and jealous instructress.

Marika preferred her to the one called Khles, though. The healer sisters did have to take her leg. And after that loss she became embittered. Everyone avoided her as much as possible.

Still they would not allow Marika to see Grauel or Barlog. She began to understand that they were trying to isolate her from any reminder of her origins.

She would not permit that.

III

Marika stood at the center of a white stone floor in a vast hall in the heart of Akard fortress. The floor around her was inlaid with green, red, and black stone, formed into boundaries and symbols. High above, glass windows—one of the marvels of the packstead—admitted a thin gray light come through a frosting of snow. That light barely illuminated the pillars supporting an all-surrounding balustrade forty feet above. The pillars were green stone, inlaid with red, black, coral, and white. Shadows lurked behind them. The glory of that hall ended at the columns, though. The stone of the wall back behind them was weathered a dark brownish gray. In places lichens patched it.

The white floor was a square forty feet to a side. The symbol at its center was that of the entwined comets, in jet and scarlet, three feet across. Marika stood upon the focus of the mandala.

There were no furnishings and no lighting in that chamber. It stirred with echoes constantly.

Marika's eyes were sealed. She tried to control her breathing so no sound would echo anywhere. She strove under Gorry's merciless gaze. Her instructress leaned on the rail of the balustrade, motionless as stone, a dark silhouette hovering. All the light leaking through the windows seemed to concentrate on Marika.

Outside, winter flaunted its chill and howl, though the spring melt should have begun. It was time trees were budding. Snowflowers should have been opening around the last branch-shaded patches of white. But, instead, another blizzard raged into its third day and third foot of gritty powder snow.

Marika could not put that out of her mind. It meant continued hard times in the upper Ponath. It meant late plantings, poor hunting, and almost certain trouble with nomads again next winter, no matter how mild.

Very little news from the upper Ponath reached the packfast. What did come was grim. The nomads had decimated several more packsteads, even without their wehrlen to lead them. Other packsteads, unable to sustain a winter so long, had turned grauken.

Civilization had perished in the upper Ponath.

Summer would not be much of a respite, for there would be little game left after a winter so cruel.

There had been no word from the Degnan packstead. The fate of the Laspe remained a mystery.

There were silth out now, young ones, hunting nomads, trying to provide the protection Akard supposedly promised. But they were few, unenthusiastic, and not very effective.

Something whispered in the shadows under the balustrade. Something moved. Marika opened her eyes....

Pain!

Fire crackled along her nerves. A voice within her head said, calmly, *See with the inner eye.*

Marika sealed her eyes again. They leaked tears of frustration. They would not tell her what to do. All they did was order her to do it. How could she, if she did not know what they wanted?

The sound of movement again, as of something with claws moving toward her stealthily. Then in a sudden rush. She whirled to face the sound, her eyes opening.

A fantastic beast leapt toward her, its fang-filled jaws opened wide. She squealed and ducked, grabbing at a knife no longer at her waist. The beast passed over her. When she turned, she saw nothing. Not even a disturbance in the dust on the floor.

Pain!

Frustration welled into anger. Anger grew into seething blackness. Ignoring the throbbing agony, she stared up at old Gorry.

Then she saw ghosts drifting through the shadows.

The old silth wavered, became transparent. Marika snatched at the pulsing ruby of her heart.

Gorry cried out softly and fell away from the railing.

Marika's pain faded. The false sounds went with the pain. She breathed deeply, relaxing for the first time that day. For a moment she felt very smug. That would show them that they could not—

Something touched her for an instant, like the blow of a dark fist. There was no pain but plenty of impact. She staggered off the center of the mandala, fell to her knees, disoriented and terrified.

She did not seem to be in control of herself. She could not make her limbs respond. What were they doing to her? What were they going to do to her?

More sounds. These genuine. Hurried feet moved above.

The paralysis relaxed. She regained her feet. Excited whispers filled the chamber. She looked up. Several silth surrounded Gorry. One pounded the old silth's chest, then listened for a heartbeat. "In time. Got to her in time."

The tall one who had come to the packstead, who now had only one leg, leaned her crutches on the railing and glared down at Marika. She was very, very angry. "Come up here, pup!" she snapped.

"Yes, Mistress Gibany."

Much to her embarrassment, Marika had discovered that Khles was not a name but a title. It marked Gibany as having a major role in Akard silth ritual. What that role was Marika did not yet know. She had not yet been admitted to any but the most basic rites.

In her own loghouse neither defiance nor the inclination to debate would have occurred to Marika. But here in the packfast, despite repeated warnings, she felt little of her customary reserve. These silth had not yet earned her respect. Few she saw seemed deserving of respect. She met Senior Koenic's eye and snapped, "Because she hurt me."

"She was teaching you."

"She was not. She was torturing me. She ordered me to do something I do not know how to do. I do not yet know what it was. Then she tortured me for not doing it. She taught me nothing. She showed me nothing."

"She was teaching you by forcing you to find the way for yourself."

"That is stupid. Even beasts are shown what they must do before their trainer rewards or punishes them. This way is neither reasonable nor efficient." She had thought out this speech many times. It rolled out almost without thought, despite her fright.

She believed what she said. Her elders in the Degnan pack had been impatient enough with pups, but they had at least demonstrated a thing once before becoming irritable.

"That is Gorry's way."

"It being her way makes it no less stupid and inefficient."

The senior was in a surprisingly tolerant mood, Marika reflected, as the fear-driven engine of her rage began to falter. Few adult meth would so long endure so much backtalk.

"It separates the weak from the strong. When you came here you understood—"

One more spark of defiance. "When I came I understood nothing, Senior. I did not even ask to be brought. I was brought blind, thinking I would become a huntress for the packfast, willing to come only because of circumstance. I never heard of silth before my dam sent messengers to ask you for help. All I know about silth I have learned since I have been here. And I do not like what I have learned."

The senior's teeth gleamed angrily in the lamplight. Her patience was about exhausted. But Marika did not back down, though now her courage was entirely bravado.

What would she do if she made them angry enough to push her out the gate?

The senior controlled herself. She said, "I will grant you that Gorry is not the best of teachers. However, self-control must be the first lesson we learn as sisters. Without discipline we are nothing. Field-workers, technicians, and guardians behave as you have. Silth do not. I think you had better learn to control your temper. You are going to continue in Gorry's tutelage. With this between you."

"Is that all?"

"That is all."

Marika made parting obsequies, as taught. But as she reached the heavy wooden door to the senior's quarters, the silth called, "Wait."

Marika turned, suddenly terrified. She wanted to get away.

"You must appreciate your obligation to your sisterhood, Marika. Your sisterhood is all. Everything your pack was, and your reason for living, too."

"I cannot appreciate something I do not understand, Senior. Nothing I see here makes sense. Forgive a poor country pup her ignorance. Everything I see implies this sisterhood exists solely to exploit those who do not belong. That it takes and takes, but almost never gives."

She was thinking of the feeble effort to combat the invasion of the nomads.

"You see beyond the first veil. You are on the threshold of becoming silth, Marika. With all that that implies. It is a rare opportunity. Do not close the door on yourself by clinging stubbornly to the values of savages."

Marika responded with a raised lip, slipped out, dashed downstairs to her cell. She lighted a candle, thinking she would lose herself in one of the books they had given her to study. "What?"

The Degnan Chronicle was stacked upon her little writing desk.

The next miracle occurred not ten minutes later.

Marika responded to a tentative scratching at her door. "Grauel!" She stared at the huntress, whom she had not seen since the trek to Akard.

"Hello, pup. May I?"

"Of course." Marika made way for her to enter. There was not much room in her cell. She returned to the chair at her writing desk. Grauel looked around, finally settled on Marika's cot.

"I cannot become accustomed to furniture," Grauel said. "I always look for furs on the floor first."

"So do I." And Marika began to realize that, for all she had been desperate to see either Grauel or Barlog for weeks, she really did not have much to say. "Have they treated you well?"

Grauel shrugged. "No worse than I expected."

"And Barlog? She is well?"

"Yes. I see they brought you the Chronicle. You will keep it up?"

"Yes."

For half a minute there did not seem to be anything else to say. Then Grauel remarked, "I hear you are in trouble." And, "We try to keep track of you through rumor."

"Yes. I did a foolish thing. I could not even get them to tell me if you were alive."

"Alive and fit. And blessing the All for this wondrous gift of snow. You really tried to kill your instructress? With witchcraft?"

"If that is what you call it. Not kill, though. Just hurt back. She asked for it, Grauel." Then, suddenly she broke down and poured out all her feelings, though she suspected the senior had sent Grauel round to scold her. "I do not like it here, Grauel." For a moment she was so stressed she slipped into the informal, personal mode, which among the Degnan was rarely used except with littermates. "They aren't nice. Can't you make them stop?"

Then Grauel held her and comforted her clumsily, and she abandoned the false adulthood she had been wearing as a mask since her assault on Gorry. "I don't *understand*, Grauel."

In a voice unnaturally weak for a grown female, Grauel told her, "Try again, Marika. And be patient. You are the only reason *any* of the Degnan—if only we—survive."

Marika understood that well enough, though Grauel was indirect. Grauel and Barlog were in Akard on sufferance. For the present their welcome depended upon hers.

She was not old enough to have such responsibility thrust upon her.

She could not get out of the more intimate speech mode, though she knew it made Grauel uncomfortable. "What are the silth, Grauel? Tell me about them. Don't just make warding signs and duck the question the way everybody did at home. Tell me what you know. *I* have to know."

Grauel became more uncomfortable. She looked around as though expecting to find someone lurking in the little cell's shadows.

"Tell me, Grauel. Please? Why do they want me?"

Grauel found her courage. She was one of the bravest of the Degnan, a huntress Skiljan had wanted by her when hunting game like kagbeast. She so conquered herself she managed to slip into the informal mode, too.

"They're witches, Marika. Dark witches, like in the stories. They command the spirit world. They're strong, and they're more ruthless than the grauken. They're the mistresses of the world. We were lucky in the upper Ponath. We had almost no contact with them, except at the annual assizes. They say we're too backward for the usual close supervision up here. This is just a remote outpost maintained so the Reugge sisterhood can retain its fief right to the Ponath. Tales tradermales bring up the Hainlin say they are much stronger in the south, where they hold whole cities as possessions and rule them with the terror of their witchcraft, so that normal meth dare not speak of them even as we do now. Tradermales say that in some cities meth dare not admit they exist even though every move and decision must be made with an eye to propitiating them. As though they were the All in Render's avatar. Those who displease them die horribly, slain by spirits."

"What spirits?"

Grauel looked at her oddly. "Surely you know that much? Else how did you hurt your instructress?"

"I just got angry and wished her heart would stop," Marika said, editing the truth. Her voice trailed off toward the end. She realized what she was doing. She recalled all those instances when she thought she was seeing ghosts. Were those the spirits the silth commanded? "Why are they interested in me?"

"They say you have the silth's secret eye. They say you can reach into the spirit world and shape it."

"Why would they take me even if that were true?"

"Surely by now you know that sisterhoods are not packs, Marika. Have you seen any males in the packfast? No. They must find their young outside. In the Ponath the packsteads are supposed to bring their young of five or six to the assizes, where the silth examine them and claim any touched by the silth talent. The females are raised as silth. The males are destroyed. Males with the talent are much rarer than females. Though it is whispered that if such sports ever die out completely, then there will be no more females of talent born either." One frantic glance around, and in a barely audible, breathy whisper, "Come the day."

"The wehrlen."

"Yes. Exactly so. They turn up in the wilds. Few of the Ponath packs and none of the nomads go along with the system. Akard is not strong enough to enforce its will throughout the Ponath. There are no silth on the Zhotak. Though there have been few talents found in the Ponath anyway."

"Dam suspected," Marika mused. "That is why none of my litter ever went to the assizes."

"Perhaps. There have been other pups like you, capable of becoming silth, but who did not. It is said that if the talent is not harnessed early, and shaped, it soon fades. Had this winter not been what it was, and brought what it did, in a few years you would have seen whatever you have as a pup's imagination." There was a hint, almost, that Grauel spoke with sure knowledge.

"I'm not sure it *isn't* imagination," Marika said, more to herself than to Grauel.

"Just so. Now, in the cities, they say, they do it differently. Tradermales say the local cloisters screen every pup carefully and take those with the talent soon after birth. Most sisters, including those here, never know any life but that of silth. They question the ways of silth no more than you questioned the ways of the Degnan. But our ways were not graven by the All. Tradermales bring tales of others, some so alien as to be incomprehensible."

Marika reflected for half a minute. "I still don't understand, Grauel."

Grauel bared her teeth in an expression of strained amusement. "You were always one with more questions than there are answers, Marika. I have told you all I know. The rest you will have to learn. Remember always that they are very dangerous, these witches, and very unforgiving. And that these exiled to the borderlands are far less rigid than are their sisters in the great cities. Be very careful, and very patient."

In a small voice, Marika managed to say, "I will, Grauel. I will."

CHAPTER NINE

I

In unofficial confinement, Marika did not leave her cell for three days. Then one of Akard's few novice silth brought a summons from Gorry.

Marika put aside her flute, which she had been playing almost continuously, to the consternation of her neighbors, and closed the second volume of the Chronicle. Already that seemed removed from her, like a history of another pack.

The messenger, whose name Marika did not recall and did not care about, looked at the flute oddly. As if Marika might look at a poisonous grass lizard appearing unexpectedly while she was loafing on a hillside, painting portraits in the clouds. "You have a problem?" Marika asked.

As strength goes. The other youngsters were afraid of her even before the Gorry incident. She was a savage, and clearly a little mad. And tough, even if smaller and younger than most.

"No. I never saw a female play music before."

"There are more wonders in the world than we know." She quoted a natural science instructress who was more than a little dotty and the target of the malicious humor of half the younger silth. "How fierce is her mood?"

"I am not supposed to talk to you at all. None of us are till you develop proper attitudes."

"The All has heard my prayers after all." She looked up and sped a uniquely Degnan *Thanks be* heavenward. And inside wondered why she was so determined to irk everyone around her. She had always been a quiet pup, given to getting in trouble for daydreaming, not for her mouth.

"You will make no friends if you do not stop that kind of talk."

"My friends are all ghosts." She was proud of being able to put a double meaning into a sentence in the silth low speech, which she had been learning so short a time.

The novice did not speak again, in the common speech or either of the silth dialects. She led Marika to Gorry's door, then marched off to tell everyone about the savage's bad manners.

Marika knocked. A weak voice bid her enter. She did so, and found herself in a world she did not know existed.

The senior did not live so well.

There was more comfort, and more wealth, in that one chamber than Marika had seen in her entire life at the Degnan packstead.

Gorry was recuperating upon a bed of otec furs stuffed with rare pothast down. The extremities of the room boasted whole ranks of candles supplementing the light cast by the old silth's private fire. Fire and candles were tended by a nonsilth pup of Marika's own age.

Marika saw many things of rich cloth such as tradermales brought north in their wagons, to trade for furs and the green gemstones sometimes found in the beds of streams running out of the Zhotak. There were metals in dazzling abundance, most not in the form of tools or weapons at all. Marika's head spun. It was a sin, that power should be so abused and flaunted.

"Come here, pup." The candle tender helped prop Gorry up in her bed. The old silth indicated a wooden stool placed nearby. "Sit."

Marika went. She sat. She was as deferential as she knew how to be. When the rage began to bubble she reminded herself that Grauel and Barlog depended upon her remaining in good odor.

"Pup, I have been reviewing our attempts to provide you with an education. I believe we have approached it from the wrong direction. This is my fault principally. I have refused to acknowledge the fact that you have grown up outside the Community. I have not faced the fact that you have many habits of thought to unlearn. Until you have done that, and have acquired an appropriate way of thinking, we cannot reasonably expect you to respond as silth in an unfamiliar situation. Which, I now grant, all of this is. Therefore, we will set a different course. But be warned. You will be expected to adhere to sisterhood discipline once it has been made clear to you. I shall be totally unforgiving. Do you understand?"

Marika sensed the tightly controlled rage and hatred seething within the silth. The senior must have spoken to her. "No, Mistress Gorry."

The silth shuddered all over. The candle tender wrung her paws and looked at Marika in silent pleading. For a moment Marika was frightened for the old meth's health. But then Gorry asked, "What is it that you do not understand, pup? Begin with the simplest question."

"Why are you doing this to me? I did not ask—"

"Did your dam and the females of your pack ask if you wanted to become a huntress?"

"No, mistress," Marika admitted. "But—"

"But you are female and healthy. In the upper Ponath a healthy female becomes a huntress in the natural course. Now, however, it develops that you have the silth talent. So it is the natural course that you become silth."

Marika was unable to challenge that sort of reasoning. She did not agree with Gorry, but she did not possess the intellectual tools with which to refute her argument.

"There is no choice, pup. It is not the custom of the sisterhood to permit untrained talents liberty within the Community demesne."

Oblique as that was, Marika had no trouble understanding. She could become silth or die.

"You are what you are, Marika. You must be what you are. That is the law."

Marika controlled her temper. "I understand, Mistress Gorry."

"Good. And you will pursue your training with appropriate self-discipline?"

"Yes, Mistress Gorry." With all sorts of secret reservations.

"Good. You will resume your education tomorrow. I will inform your other instructresses. Henceforth you will spend extra time learning the ways of the Community, till you reach a level of knowledge of those ways appropriate to a candidate of your age."

"Yes, Mistress Gorry."

"You may go."

"Yes, Mistress Gorry." But before Marika departed she paused for a final look around. She was especially intrigued by the books shelved upon the one wall beside the fireplace. Of all the wealth in that place, they impressed her most.

Sleep became a stranger. But just as well. There was so much to do and learn. And that way there were fewer of the unhappy dreams.

She was sure her haunt was Kublin's ghost, punishing her for not having seen the Degnan Mourned. She wondered if she ought not to discuss her dreams with the silth. In the end, she did not. As always was, what was between her and Kublin—even Kublin passed—was between her and Kublin.

II

The dreams continued. Spotted, random dreams unrelated to any phenomenon or natural cycle that Braydic could identify. They occurred unpredictably, as though at the behest of another, which convinced Marika that she was the focus of the anger of her dead. Ever more of her nights were haunted—though she now spent less time than ever asleep. There was too much to learn, too much to do, for her to waste time sleeping.

Braydic told her, "I think your dreams have nothing to do with your dead. Except within your own mind. You are just rationalizing them to yourself. I believe they are your talent venting the pressure of growth. You were too long without guidance or training. Many strange things befall pups who reach your age without receiving guidance or instruction. And that among the normally talented."

"Normally talented?" Marika suspected Braydic was brushing the edge of the shadow that had pursued her since she had noticed that something had passed among Akard's meth. All treated her oddly. The pawful of pups inhabiting the fortress not only, as expected, disdained her for her rude origins; they were afraid of her. She saw fear blaze up behind evasive eyes whenever she cornered one long enough to make her talk.

Only Braydic seemed unafraid.

Marika spent a lot of time with the communicator now. Braydic helped her with her language lessons, and let her pretend that she was not alone in her exile. Seldom did she see Grauel or Barlog, and when she did it was by sneakery and there was no time to exchange more than a few hasty words.

"Gorry has much to say about you to my truesister, Marika. And little of it good. Some reaches my humble ears." Nervously, Braydic set fingers dancing upon a keyboard, calling up data she had scanned only minutes before. Her shoulders straightened. She turned. "You have a glorious future, pup. If you live to see it."

"What?"

"Gorry knows pups and talents. She was once important among those who teach at Maksche. She calls you the greatest talent-potential Akard has yet unearthed. Maybe as remarkable a talent as any discovered by the Reugge this generation."

Marika scoffed. "Why do you say that? I do not feel remarkable."

"How would you know? At your age you have only yourself as comparison. Whatever her faults, Gorry is not given to fanciful speaking. Were I in your boots I would guard my tail carefully. Figuratively and even literally. A talent like yours, so bright it shines in the eyes of the blind, can become more curse than gift of the All."

"Curse? Danger? What are you saying?"

"As strength goes, pup. I am warning you. Those threatened by a talent are not shy about squashing one—though they will act subtly."

Again Braydic tapped at a keyboard. Marika waited, and wondered what the communicator meant. And wondered that she no longer felt so uncomfortable around the communications center. Perhaps that was another manifestation of the talent that so impressed Braydic. The communicator did say she was dealing instinctively with the electromagnetic handicap that others never overcame.

Braydic yanked her attention back to what she was saying. "It is no accident that most of the more important posts in most of the sisterhoods are held by the very old. Those silth were only a little smarter and a little stronger when they were pups. They did not attract attention. As they aged and advanced, they looked back for those who might overtake them and began throwing snares into the paths of the swifter runners."

What Pohsit would have done had she had the chance.

"They did not press those older than they."

Marika responded with what she thought would be received as a fetchingly adult observation. She was a little calculator often. "That is no way to improve the breed."

"There is no breed to improve, pup. The continued existence of all silthdom relies entirely upon a rare but stubbornly persistent genetic recessive floating in the broader population."

Marika gaped, not understanding a word.

"When a silth is accepted as a full sister, her order passes her through a ritual in which she must surrender her ability to bear pups."

Marika was aghast. That went against all survival imperatives.

In the packs of the upper Ponath, reproductive rights were rigorously controlled by, and often limited to, the dominant females. Such as Skiljan. Mating freely, meth could swamp the local environment in a very few years.

The right to reproduce might be denied, but never the ability. The pack might need to produce pups quickly after a wild disaster.

"A true silth sister must not be distracted by the demands of her flesh, nor must she be possessed of any obligation beyond that to her order. A female in heat has no mind. A female with newly whelped pups is neither mobile nor capable of placing the Community before her offspring. Nature has programmed her."

Braydic shifted subject suddenly, obviously in discomfort. "You have one advantage, Marika. One major safety. You are here in Akard, which has been called The Stronghold of Ambition's Death. None here will cut you in fear for themselves. They are without hope, these Akard silth. They are those who were kicked off the ladder, yet were deemed dangerous enough to demand lifelong exile. The enemies you are making here hate you because they fear your strength, and for less selfish reasons. Gorry dreads what you may mean to the Community's future. Long has she claimed to snatch glimpses of far tomorrows. Since your coming her oracles have grown ever more hysterical and dark."

Marika had assumed a jaw-on-paw attitude of rapt attention guaranteed to keep Braydic chattering. She did not mind the communicator's ceaseless talk, for Braydic gladly swamped the willing ear with information the silth yielded only grudgingly, if at all.

"The worst danger will come when you capture their attention down south. And capture it you will, I fear. If you are half what Gorry believes. If you continue in the recalcitrant character you have shown. They will have to pay attention." Braydic toyed with the vision screen. She seemed uneasy. "Given six or seven years unhindered, learning as fast as you have, the censure of the entire Community will be insufficient to keep you contained here." The communicator turned away, muttering, "As strength goes."

Marika had become accustomed to such chatter. Braydic had hinted and implied similar ideas a dozen times in a dozen different ways during their stolen moments. This time the meth was more direct, but her remarks made no more sense now than when Marika had first slipped in to visit her.

Marika was devouring books and learning some about her talent, but discovering almost nothing of the real internal workings of the Reugge sisterhood. She could not refrain from interpreting what she heard and saw in Degnan pack terms. So she often interpreted wrong.

Silth spoke the word "Community" with a reverence the Degnan reserved for the All. Yet daily life appeared to be every sister for herself, as strength goes, in a scramble that beggared those among frontier "savages." Never did the meth of the upper Ponath imperil their packs with their struggles for dominance. But Marika suspected she was getting a shaded view. Braydic did seem to dwell morbidly upon that facet of silth life.

It did not then occur to Marika to wonder why.

She left her seat, began pottering around. Braydic's talk made her restless and uneasy. "Distract them with other matters," Braydic said. "You are, almost literally, fighting for your life. Guard yourself well." Then she shifted subject again. "Though you cannot tell by looking, the thaw has begun. As you can see on the flow monitors."

Marika joined Braydic before one of the vision screens. She was more comfortable with things than with meth. She had a flair for manipulating the keyboards, though she did not comprehend a third of what Braydic told her about how they worked. In her mind electronics was more witchcraft than was her talent. Her talent was native and accepted fact, like her vision. She did not question or examine her vision. But a machine that did the work of a brain… Pure magic.

Columns of numeral squiggles slithered up the screen. "Is it warmer in the north than it is here, Braydic?" She had sensed no weakening of winter's grasp.

"No. Just warmer everywhere." The communicator made a minor adjustment command to what she called an outflow valve. "I am worried. We had so much snow this winter. A sudden rise in temperature might cause a meltoff the system cannot handle."

"Open the valves all the way. Now."

"That would drain the reservoirs. I cannot do that. I need to maintain a certain level to have a flow sufficient to turn the generators. Else we are without power. I cannot do my work without power."

Marika started to ask a question. A tendril of something brushed her. She jumped in a pup's sudden startle reaction. Braydic responded with bared teeth and a snarl, an instinctual reaction when a pup was threatened. "What is it, Marika?" She seemed embarrassed by her response.

"Someone is coming. Someone silth. I have to leave." She was not supposed to be in the communications center, exposed to its aura.

There were many things she was not supposed to do. She did them anyway. Like make sneak visits to Grauel and Barlog. The silth could not keep watch all the time. She slept so little. And the fortress's huntresses seemed disinclined to watch her at all, or to report observed behavior that was not approved.

She suspected Grauel and Barlog were responsible, for all they admonished her incessantly in their brief meetings. She caught occasional hints that her packmates had developed fierce reputations among Akard's untalented population.

Marika slipped away through a passage which led to the roof and the metal tree. Up there the aura still disoriented her, though not so she was unable to slide away in the moonlight and take a place upon the northern wall, staring out at the bitter snowscape.

To her, winter did not appear to be loosening its grip.

From the edges of her eyes she seemed to see things moving. She did not turn, knowing they would not be there if she looked. Not unless she forced her talent with hammer-blow intensity.

She did not look up at the great cold sky either, though she felt it beating down upon her, calling.

Someday, she thought. Someday. If Braydic was right. Someday she would go.

III

The moons tagged across the night in a playful band, in a rare conjunction that seemed impossible in the two-dimensional view available from the ground. They should be ricocheting off one another.

Sometimes smaller ones did collide with Biter or Chaser, according to Marika's instructresses. But the last showy impact had come two centuries ago, and the last before that a thousand years earlier still. For all the matter skipping across the nighttime skies, collisions remained rare.

"You are daydreaming again, Marika," a gentle voice said into her ear. She started, realized she had stopped marching. Barlog had overtaken her. Barlog, who was with the rear guard several hundred yards behind. There was a gentle humor in the huntress's voice when she asked, "Will you make these packfast meth over in your own image, rather than they you in theirs?"

Marika did not reply. She yanked the butt of her javelin from the soggy earth and trotted forward, up the topless hill. She understood. Barlog had made another of her sly observations about the stubborn resistance of a certain pup to assimilation into silth life. A resistance that was quiet and passive and almost impossible to challenge, yet immutable. She studied and she learned with a ravenous appetite, but she remained a savage in outlook, the despair of most silth.

Unconsciously, or perhaps instinctively, she had done the right thing to avoid coming to the attention of more distant members of the sisterhood. Pride would not permit the Akard silth to report the unconquerable wild thing among them.

Marika took her place near the rear of the main body, falling into the rhythm of placing her feet into the tracks of the sister before her. There were twelve silth and twelve huntresses in the party. They were far north of Akard. The moons appeared unnaturally low behind them. A few huntresses carried trophy ears, but it had not been the good hunt expected. The nomads were avoiding contact expertly. Sisters capable of the far-touch said the other parties had had no better hunting. It was as if the nomads knew where their stalkers were all the time. The few taken had been stragglers too weak to stay up with their packs, and mostly males.

A very frightening thing had happened. The nomad horde had not broken into its bickering constituent packs with the death of the wehrlen. The older silth in Akard were very disturbed. But they were not explaining why. At least not to Marika.

She had taken no part in the hunt so far, except to trudge along with the pack and learn what was to be learned, to marvel at endless alien vistas, at mountains and canyons and waterfalls and trees like nothing she had imagined while sealed up in her native packstead. To marvel at the world of the night, with its strangely different creatures and perils and aromas.

The hunting parties had departed Akard soon after winter's final feeble storm, while snow still masked the north. They had been instructed to harry the retreating nomads mercilessly, to press them back into the Zhotak, and beyond. Marika did not understand what the senior was doing, but had had no trouble comprehending why she had been sent along.

She was a disturbing influence in Akard. The old could not deal with her. They wanted her out of the way for a while, so they could regain their balance. And maybe so they could decide what to do about her.

She did not allow herself to dwell upon that. The possibilities were too grim. She was not as confident of her safety as Braydic said she should be. The senior and Khles and Gorry all had made the point repeatedly that she was at their mercy. And she had her responsibility to Grauel and Barlog. Why could she not conform more, at least outwardly? She tried, but invariably they would touch some unyielding chord of rebellion.

The party stopped moving. A huntress returned from the point to report, "We are there. Just beyond that loom of rock." She indicated a star-obscuring line ahead. Marika leaned on her javelin and listened, grateful for a chance to catch her breath. They had been climbing since sundown, and for three nights before that. And now they were just yards from the planned limit of their journey. Now they would turn and begin the long downhill return to Akard.

"You can see their campfires from the rim," the scout said. Marika became alert. The nomads? They were that close? And confident enough to show lights at night?

The pack responded with angry murmurs. Soon Marika found herself poised at the brink of an immense drop-off, staring at the patch of winking campfires, like a cloud of stars, many miles away.

"They feel safe beyond the Rift," muttered Rhaisihn, the silth who commanded the party. "They think we will not come on. Curse them. Far-toucher. Where is a far-toucher? I need instructions from Akard. I need to touch the other parties, to let them know that we have found the savages."

Even in the darkness the view's immensity awed Marika. When the others withdrew to carry out orders or begin making camp, she remained, staring at moonlight glinting off mists, streams, lakes, patches of unmelted snow. And at that constellation of campfires.

Whenever her gaze crossed that far camp, she suffered a startling resurgence of emotion she had thought fully dulled. But the hatred and anger remained, buried. She wanted revenge for what had been done to the Degnan.

The first ghost light of approaching day obscured the feeble eastern stars. Marika went down to her own camp, where she found Rhaisihn with two far-touchers, muttering angrily. Her request for permission to carry the pursuit beyond the Rift had been denied.

There were ceremonies upcoming at Akard, and it would be hard enough now to get back in time to participate. If they pressed on north the ceremonies would have to be forgone.

Marika was indifferent to ritual obligations. She interrupted. "Mistress? May I have the watch on the nomad camp?"

The silth looked up, startled. "You? Volunteering? I am amazed. I wonder what ulterior motive you may have. But go ahead. You may as well be of *some* use."

Rhaisihn did not like Marika. Marika did her share and more, yet Rhaisihn persistently accused her of malingering, perhaps because she tended to daydream. Marika stilled her anger and returned to the rim of the Rift. She found a prominence and seated herself.

The light had grown strong enough to obscure all but the westernmost stars.

There were few stars in the skies of Marika's world. No more than a few hundred. Most were so feeble only the sharpest eye could discern them. The only truly bright heavenly bodies were the moons and nearest planets.

The light continued to grow, and Marika continued to sit, as fixed as part of the landscape, her awe unabated. The lighter the dawn, the more grand the view. The lighter the dawn, the more she was astounded by the spectacle before her.

The Rift was a break in the earth's crust tilted like a monster paving stone ripped up by an earth giant's pry bar. The fall before Marika was at least two thousand feet. The Rift extended to either paw as far as she could see. The north spread out like a map. A map now partly obscured by mists over lakes and rivers and their verges. Most of the ground seemed flat and meadowy, maybe even marshy, but in the far distance there were darker greens that could only be forests. Beyond those the tundra began.

She looked to the east for some sign of the Great Gap, a wide break in the Rift wall through which both nomads and kropek migrated, and through which the nomads would have withdrawn. Those who had gone, for it was rumored that many had decided to remain in the upper Ponath. Parties from Akard were hunting them, too.

There was no sign of the Gap.

That vast sprawl of northland was hypnotic. There was no way Marika could gaze upon it and not fall into a daydream.

A light, wandering something touched her mind as lightly as gossamer on the wind. Startled, she evaded automatically, then focused her attention... And became very frightened.

That silth was not one of her party. That silth was out *there*.

For all her determination to learn, she had as yet mastered only the rudiments of silth mind exercise and self-control. She applied what she did know, calmed herself, let go of emotion, then went down inside herself seeking the gateway Gorry had been teaching her to find.

This was one of those rare moments when the gateway opened easily and she slipped through into the realm of ghosts, where the workaday world became as unreal as a chaphe dream. She captured a little fluttering wisp of a ghost, commanded it to carry her toward the nomad camp. To her astonishment, it complied.

She had tried that often before, and had had success only on a few occasions when she had wanted to do harm, when she had commanded by instinct, her will an iron engine driven by black hatred.

Luck was not enough. She could not guide the ghost with precision. She caught only random glimpses of the camp.

But those were enough.

She was aghast.

There were thousands of the nomads. Most were but fur and bones, clad in tatters, a little better shape than the few Marika's party had taken on the hunt. For all they had plundered the upper Ponath, they had done themselves little good. The sight of starving pups caused her the most discomfort, for it was hard to hate, and easy to have compassion, for the very young.

The ghost passed something in black. Someone not ravaged by malnutrition. Someone arguing with several dominant nomad huntresses. Marika tried to turn back, to take another look, but her control was inadequate. She caught one more glimpse of someone in black from a distance. The costuming appeared to be silth, yet it was different, subtly, from that which she knew.

A dwindling shrieking sound hammered upon her, filtering in from that other world where her flesh waited, petrified, upon an outcrop overlooking the sprawl of the north. There were harmonics of terror, of death, in that cry. She fought to drive her ghost away from the nomad encampment, back to her body.

She had no skill. It was like trying to herd a butterfly. It fluttered this way and that, only tending in the proper direction.

Her flesh relayed hints of a disturbance back there. Of excitement. Of danger. She felt tendrils of panic touch the edge of her. Then came the light caress of an investigative silth touch. A touch that became more firm, an anchor. A lifeline along which she could pull herself back to her flesh.

She returned to a body gripped by an intense flight-fight reaction. There were meth all around her, all chattering but Rhaisihn, who was just coming back from helping Marika return. The commander stared at her when she opened her eyes, slightly puzzled, slightly angry, a whole lot disconcerted. The leader turned to her chief huntress. "Get these meth out of here."

The huntress tried to do as instructed. But one meth would not go. One who carried a heavy hunting spear and appeared willing to fight rather than be budged. Barlog.

"What happened?" Marika asked in a small voice, certain something dramatic had happened while she was away.

"That was a foolish thing to try at your level," Rhaisihn said, her concern surprising Marika. "You *must* learn with a guide."

"What happened?" Marika demanded. "I sensed something terrible."

"Obrhothkask fell off the ledge." Rhaisihn indicated a point just two feet from Marika. "The All only knows what she was doing." Rhaisihn glared at Barlog. The huntress had not yet set the butt of her spear to earth. Her teeth were bared in a snarl so fierce Marika knew she would take anything as a challenge, and would fight rather than be moved an inch.

"We will discuss this later," Rhaisihn said. "Under more favorable circumstances. Settle her down. Then rest. We start south tonight."

"There are silth in that camp," Marika told Rhaisihn's back.

"Yes. There would be." Rhaisihn skirted Barlog carefully. The huntress faced her as she passed, turning slowly, spear at the ready. Only after the commander disappeared among the rocks did she begin to relax.

Marika practiced her calming exercises. She waited on Barlog. Once the huntress was no longer in the grip of her fury, she asked, "What happened? How did Obrhothkask fall?"

Barlog's eyes were hard and narrow and calculating as she settled beside Marika, stared at the nomad encampment. No awe of nature in her. "The butt of a spear struck her in the small of the back. She lost her balance."

"Oh?"

"Rumor says you were warned to remain alert. Perhaps you did not take the warning seriously." Barlog reached inside her jacket, produced a steel knife. It was the sort for which the tradermales demanded a dozen otec furs. "Let this talisman be a reminder. Save for a timely spear butt, it would be through your heart now. And you would lie where the witch lies."

Marika accepted the shining blade, barely able to comprehend. Barlog rose and strode toward the camp, spear upon her shoulder.

Marika remained where she was, thinking for half an hour, staring at that knife. Obrhothkask's knife. But Obrhothkask was only a few years her senior, and they had hardly known one another. Obrhothkask had no reason to attack her. Surely she would not have done so on her own. She was the most dull and traditional of silth trainees.

"Guard your tail," Braydic had said so often. And she had not taken the warning with sufficient seriousness. So a meth had died.

She snapped upright and peered over the edge. There was no sign of the fallen silth. The body was too far below, and in shadow. After a glance toward camp, Marika tossed the knife after its owner.

Twelve otec furs just thrown away. Barlog would have been appalled. But it might have been construed as evidence of some sort.

The homeward journey was a quiet one. Obrhothkask's death hung over the party, never forgotten. Silth and huntress alike avoided Marika and Barlog. The Degnan huntress seldom allowed Marika out of her sight.

Marika concluded that everyone knew exactly what had happened, and everyone meant to pretend that it had not. For the sake of history Obrhothkask's passing would be recalled as accidental.

Marika wondered about the form and substance of a silth Mourning. Would she be allowed to witness it? Would it be a form she could memorize and secretly apply to the account of her unMourned packmates?

Thinking of old debts and a time of life that now seemed as remote as the tale of another meth's puphood, she realized that she had had no dreams since leaving Akard's environs. Would that haunt be waiting when she returned?

After that she was not incautious again, ever. And never again was there so crude and direct an attempt to displace her.

Marika got the sense of much hidden anger and activity generated by the attempt, the death, and perhaps even the attempt's failure. She suspected the meth responsible was never identified.

She did not get to witness a silth Mourning. There was no such rite, as she understood a Mourning.

Summer fled quickly and early, and winter stormed into the world again.

CHAPTER TEN

I

It was a winter like the one preceding, when the doom had come to the upper Ponath. Harsh. But it began with a lie, hinting that it would be milder. After it lulled everyone, it bared its claws and slashed at the upper Ponath with storm after storm, dumping snow till drifts threatened to overtop Akard's northern wall. Its chill breath howled without respite, and left everything encrusted with ice. For a time the Akard silth lost touch with their Reugge sisters in the south.

It was a winter like the one preceding. The nomads again came down out of the north in numbers greater than before. Many of the packs that survived the first invasion succumbed to this one—though much of the bad news did not reach Akard till after winter's departure. Still, scores of refugees appealed for protection, and the silth took them in, though grudgingly.

Twice small bands of nomads appeared on the snowfields beyond the north wall, fields where during summer meth raised the fortress's food crops. They examined the grim pile of stone, then moved on, not tempted. Marika chanced to be atop the wall, alone and contemplating, the second time a group appeared. She studied them as closely as she could from several hundred yards.

"They are not yet suicidal in their desperation," she told Braydic afterward.

"The key phrase is 'not yet,' " Braydic replied. "It will come." The communicator was a little distracted, less inclined to be entertaining and instructive than was her custom. The ice and cold kept her in a constant battle with her equipment, and in some cases she did not possess the expertise to make repairs. "This cannot go on. There is no reason to expect the winters to get better. They had best send me a technician. Of course, they do not care if they never hear from us. They would be pleased if the ice just swallowed us."

Marika did not believe that. Neither did Braydic, really. It was frustration talking.

"No. They will not try it yet, Marika. But they will one day. Perhaps next winter. The next at the latest. This summer will see a stronger effort to stay in the upper Ponath. We have given them little difficulty. They will be less inclined to run away. And they are becoming accustomed to being one gigantic pack. This battle for survival has eclipsed all their old bitternesses and feuds. Or so I hear when my truesister and the others gather to discuss the matter. They foresee no turns for the better. We will get no help from Maksche. And without help we will not stem the flood. There are too many tens of thousands of nomads. Even silth have limitations."

What little news filtered in with the fugitives was uniformly grim and invariably supported Braydic's pessimism. There was one report of nomads being spotted a hundred miles south of Akard, down the Hainlin. Braydic received some very bitter, accusing messages because of that. Akard was supposed to bestride and block the way to the south.

The communicator told Marika, "My truesister will not send anyone—not even you—hunting nomads in these storms. We are not strong. We do not have lives to waste. Come summer. Then. When there is only the enemy to beware."

Enemy. As a group. The concept had only the vaguest possibility of expression in the common speech of the upper Ponath. Marika had had to learn the silth tongue to find it. She was not pleased with it.

Indeed, the senior and silth of Akard did nothing whatsoever to arrest the predations of the nomads. Which left Marika with severely mixed feelings.

Packs were being exterminated. Her kind of meth were being murdered daily. And though she understood why, she was upset because their guardians were doing nothing to aid them. When some pawful of refugees came in, bleeding through the snow, frostbitten, having left their pups and Wise frozen in the icy forests, she wanted to go howling through the wilderness herself, riding the black, killing ghosts, cleansing the upper Ponath of this nomad scourge.

It was in such moods that she made her best progress toward mastery of the silth magic. She had a very strong dark side.

That winter was a lonely one for her, and a time of growing self-doubt. A time when she lost purpose. Her one dream involved the stars ever obscured by the clouded skies. It seemed ever more pointless and remote in that outland under siege. When she reflected upon it seriously, she had to admit she had no slightest idea what fulfilling that dream would cost or entail.

She did not see Grauel or Barlog for months, even on the sly—which was just as well, probably, for they would have recognized her dilemma and have taken the side which stood against dreams. They were not dreamers. For wilderness huntresses maturation meant the slaying of foolish dreams.

Braydic encouraged the dreamer side, for whatever reasons she might have, but the communicator's influence was less than she believed. Coming to terms with reality was something Marika had to accomplish almost entirely for herself.

The lessons went on. The teaching continued throughout long hours.

Marika continued to learn, though her all-devouring enthusiasm began to grow blunted.

There were times when she feared she was a little mad. Like when she wondered if the absence of her nightmares of the previous year might not be the cause of her present mental disaffection.

The Degnan remained unMourned. And there were times now when she felt guilty about no longer feeling guilty about not having seen the appropriate rites performed.

It was not a good year for the wild silth pup from the upper Ponath.

II

The kagbeast leapt for Marika's throat. She did not move. She reached inside herself, through the loophole in reality through which she saw ghosts, and saw the animal as a moving mass of muscle and pumping blood, of entrails and rude nervous system. It seemed to hang there, barely moving toward her, as she decided that it was real, not an illusion conjured by Gorry.

A month earlier she would have been so alarmed she would have frozen. And been ripped apart. Now her reaction was entirely cerebral.

She touched a spot near the kagbeast's liver, thought fire, and watched a spark glow for a fragment of a second. The kagbeast began turning slowly while still in the air, clawing at the sudden agony in its vitals.

Marika slipped back through her loophole into real time and the real world. She stood there unmoving while the carnivore flailed through the air, missing her by scant inches. She did not bother to turn as it hit the white floor behind her, claws clacking savagely at the stone. She did not allow elation to touch her for an instant.

With Gorry directing the test, there might be more.

She was not surprised that Gorry had slipped a genuine killer into the drill. Gorry hated her and would be pleased to be rid of her in a fashion that would raise few questions among her sisters.

The old silth had warned her often enough publicly that her education could be deadly. She had made it clear that the price of failure might have to be paid at any time.

Gorry had had to explain the price of failure only once.

Marika could not sneak into Gorry's mind the way she had Pohsit's. But she did not need to do so. It was perfectly evident that Gorry had inherited Pohsit's mantle of madness. Gorry scarcely bothered concealing it.

The kagbeast howled and hurled itself at Marika once more. Once again she reached through her loophole. This time she touched a point at the base of its brain. It lost its motor coordination. When it hit the floor it had no more control than a male who had stolen and drunk a gallon of ormon beer.

She considered guiding the beast to the stair leading up to the balustrade. But no. She pushed that thought aside. There would come a better time and place.

The kagbeast kept trying. Tauntingly, Marika reached through and tweaked nerve ends so that it felt it was being stung.

While she toyed with her adversary, Marika allowed a tendril of touch to drift upward to where Gorry leaned upon the balustrade. She looked at the old silth much as she had done with the kagbeast. She did not touch the silth's mind, though. Did not alert Gorry to the true extent of her ability. That would come some time when the old silth was not alert.

Marika had waited almost two years. She could wait awhile longer to requite her torment.

Gorry's heart was beating terribly fast. Her muscles were tense. There were other signs indicating extreme excitement and fear. Her lips were pulled back in an unconscious baring of teeth, threatening.

Marika allowed herself one brief taste of triumph.

The old one was afraid of her. She knew she had taught too well in her effort to make the teaching deadly. She knew her pupil. Knew a reckoning had to come. And feared she could not survive it even now.

The faintest quiver at the edge of Gorry's snarl betrayed her lack of confidence. Pushed, she might well respond with one of the several yielding reflexes genetically programmed into female meth. Triggering reflexive responses in Marika—and robbing her of the taste of blood she anticipated.

Marika withdrew carefully. She would avoid arousing old instincts.

She brought her attention back to the kagbeast and to the space around him. Another of Gorry's taunts, selecting a male. Another of the old fool's errors of pride. Another stitch in her shroud of doom, as far as Marika was concerned. Another petty insult.

Something small and shimmering and red drifted close by, drawn by the kagbeast's pain. Marika snapped a touch at it and caught it. It wriggled but could not escape. She impressed her will upon it.

The ghost drifted into the kagbeast's flesh, into its right hindquarter, into a hip joint. Marika compressed it to the size of a seed, them made it spin. At that concentration the ghost was dense enough to tear flesh and scar bone.

The kagbeast shrieked and dropped to its haunches. It tried to drag itself toward her, to the end single-minded in its purpose. When she searched for it, Marika could feel the thread of touch connecting the beast's mind with that of her instructress.

She would shatter Gorry's control.

Each time the kagbeast pulled itself forward, Marika made her compressed red ghost spin again. Each time the kagbeast howled. Driven or not, it learned quickly.

As Marika had learned quickly, under Gorry's torments.

The beast screamed and screamed again, the power in its mind trying to drive it forward while the pain in its flesh punished every attempt to obey that will.

Gorry did have one advantage. She knew less of mercy than did her pupil.

Marika was sure one reason Gorry had volunteered to become her instructress was that she had no champions. No ties. No backing. Certainly not because she had seen a chance to waken and ripen a new silth mind. No. She had seen Marika as a barbarian who would make a fine toy for her secret desire to do hurt. An object on which she could use her talent to hurt. With a slight twist of the mind she was able to justify it all by believing Marika was a terrible danger.

All the Reugge sisters at Akard seemed to have twists to their minds. Braydic was not telling the truth, or the whole truth, when she insisted that these silth were in exile because they had made enemies elsewhere in the sisterhood. They had been sent to the edge of beyond because their minds were not quite whole. And the lackings were dangerous.

That Marika had learned, too. Her education ran broader than she had expected, and deeper than her teachers suspected. She had a feeling that Braydic herself was not quite what she pretended, was not quite sane.

The communicator pretended she had accompanied her truesister into exile for fear of reprisals once her protection vanished elsewhere. About that Marika was certain Braydic was lying.

Caution was the strongest lesson Marika had learned. Absolute, total caution. Absolute, total distrust of all who pretended friendship. She was an island, alone, at war with the world because the world was at war with her. She barely trusted Barlog and Grauel, and doubted she might retain that trust much longer. For she had not seen either huntress in a long time, and they had been exposed to who knew what pressures.

She hated Akard, the Reugge, silthdom.

She hated well and deeply, but she waited for the time of balance to ripen.

The kagbeast moved closer. Marika pushed distractions out of mind. This was not the time to reflect. Gorry might have more deadly tests in reserve. Might think to overwhelm her. It was a time to be on guard continuously, for Gorry did suspect the truth: that she was stronger than she pretended. There would be no more attacks like that on the Rift, but there would be something beyond the customary limits.

If the kagbeast was not an indication that the limits had been exceeded already. Marika knew of no other silth trainee who had been tested this severely this early in her training.

Had Gorry hoped she would be taken unsuspecting, thinking the monster an illusion?

Of course.

Enough. Toying with the beast was overweening pride. She was betraying herself, revealing hidden strength. She was giving too much information to one who meant her harm.

She reached through her loophole and stilled the beast's heart. It expired, almost grateful for the inflow of darkness and peace.

Marika spent a minute relaxing, then looked upward, her face carefully composed in an expression of inquiry.

Gorry continued to stare vacantly for several seconds. Then she shuddered all over, like a wet meth getting the water out of her fur. She said, "You did very well, Marika. My confidence in you has been justified. That is enough for today. You are excused from all classes and chores. You need to rest." All spoken in a feeble voice quivering with uncertainty.

"Thank you, mistress." She was careful not to betray the fact that she felt no weariness as she departed, pushing past servants hurrying to remove the kagbeast to the kitchens. Several eyed her warily, which she noted without paying attention. There were servants everywhere these days, and one paid them no mind at all. The influx of refugees meant work had to be created.

She went directly to her cell, lay on her pallet contemplating the afternoon's events, unaware that she had adopted a silth mind-set. Every nuance of what had—and had not—transpired had to be examined for levels of meaning.

Somehow, she was sure, she had gone through a rite of passage. A rite not planned by Gorry. But she was not sure what it was.

She willed her body to relax, muscle by muscle, as she had been taught, and pushed herself into a light sleep. A wary sleep, like that of a huntress in the field, overnighting in the forest far from her home packstead.

A part of her remained huntress. That would never change.

Never would she relax her guard.

III

Another year of exile passed. It was no happier than its predecessor.

Marika went to that part of the wall which overlooked the dam and powerhouse. There was a place there that she thought of as her own. A place only the newest refugees failed to respect as private and hers alone. A place surrounded by an invisible barrier that not even Gorry or her cronies among the old silth would cross when Marika was present. Marika went there when she wanted to be entirely free of care.

Each silth had such a place. For most it was their quarters. But the identity of such places developed in a tacit, unconscious fashion, within the shared awareness of the silth community. The silth of Akard gradually became aware that this place on the wall was the one where the wild pup was sovereign.

She liked the wind and the cold and the view. More, she liked the fact that she could not be physically approached without time to arrange her thoughts. There were those few who would and did dare intrude—the senior and Khles Gibany, for example—though they would do so only with sound cause.

The Husgen was frozen. Again. The silth had scores of refugee workers out keeping the ice from choking the pipes to the powerhouse. It was a winter worse than the previous two, and each of those had set new records for inflicting misery. There were fewer storms this year, and less snow, but the wind was as fierce as ever, and its claws of cold were sharper than ever. The ice wind found its way even into the heart of the fortress, mocking the roaring fires burning in every fireplace. The edge of the forest, a third mile beyond the bounds of the tilled ground, had retreated two hundred yards last summer. Deadwood had been gathered from miles around. Firewood clogged every cranny of the fortress. And still Braydic shivered when she ran calculations of consumption against time left to withstand.

Foraging parties were not going out this winter. No one was allowed beyond reach of the massed power of the Akard silth. It was rumored that none of the Zhotak nomads had stayed behind this winter.

That first bleak winter only a relative few had come south. Though the Degnan had been consumed, most of the upper Ponath packs had survived. The few nomads who had not fled north had been destroyed by the silth. The second winter had seen fully half the upper Ponath packs destroyed, and the summer following had been a time of constant blood as the silth strove to overcome those masses of nomads trying to hang on in the captured packsteads. Many nomads had perished, but the silth had failed to force a complete withdrawal.

The nomads had no wehrlen to lead them now, but they no longer needed one. They had become melded into one vast superpack. This year the northern horde had come early, during the harvest season. The silth did all they could, but the savages were not intimidated by slaughter or silth witchcraft. Always there were more desperate packs to replace those consumed by the Reugge fury.

Most of the surviving packsteads had been destroyed or overcome and occupied. Braydic predicted that none of the nomads would retreat come spring.

Marika sensed that this third winter of her exile marked the end of the upper Ponath as the frontier of civilization. This year the more mobile of the forerunner nomads were ranging far south of Akard. They gave the fortress a wide berth, then followed the course of the Hainlin, which had become a twisting road of ice carrying their threat down to the lands of the south. Only one other fastness of civilization remained unscathed, the tradermale packfast downriver, Critza.

Marika had seen Critza but once, briefly, from afar, during the nomad hunts of the previous summer. It was a great stone pile as forbidding as Akard itself. A great many refugees had fled there, too. More than to Akard, for the tradermales were not feared the way silth were.

They were not feared by the nomads either. The savages had attacked Critza once the second winter and twice already this year—without success. The tradermales were said to possess many strange and terrible weapons. The nomads had left many hundreds of dead outside Critza's walls.

Marika had been only vaguely aware of Critza's existence till she had seen it.

Then she had been amazed that the silth would permit so much independent strength to exist within their demesne. Especially in the hands of males. For the silth had very strong convictions about males. Convictions which beggared the prejudices of the meth of the upper Ponath.

They would not permit an unneutered male inside Akard. That imposed a terrible burden upon those pawfuls of survivors who fled to the fortress, especially those packs with hopes of someday breeding back up.

There was a small village of unneutered males almost below the point where Marika stood, scratching for life in shelters pitched against the wall and appealing to the All for help that would not come from those who protected them. Even a few stiff-necked huntresses stayed out there rather than bow to silth demands.

Marika suspected most of those meth would move on to Critza when travel became less hazardous.

But Critza—why did such a place exist here? Not one of the old silth had a kind word for the tradermales, nor trusted them in the least. They were the next thing to rogue, a definite threat to their absolute power, if only because they carried news between the packsteads.

Braydic said tradermales were necessary to the balance. They had a recognized niche in the broader law of the south, which was accepted by all the sisterhoods. The silth did not like the tradermale brotherhood, but had to accept it—as long as the tradermales remained within certain carefully defined professional strictures.

Marika shuddered but ignored the savage wind as she surveyed the view commanded by the packfast. Never in the entire history of the packfast—which reached back centuries before the coming of the Degnan to the upper Ponath—had there been a winter so terrible, let alone three in a row, each worse than the last.

Marika tried to recall winters before the coming of the nomads, and what the Wise had said about them. But she had only vague recollections of complaints that winters were becoming worse than they had been when the complainers were younger. The huntresses had scoffed at that, saying it was just old age catching up.

But the Wise had been right. These past three winters were no fluke. The sisters said the winters were getting harsher, and had been worsening for more than a generation. Further, they said this was only the beginning, that the weather would worsen much more before it began getting better. But what matter? It was beyond her control. It was a cycle she would not see end. Braydic said it would be centuries before the cycle reversed itself, and centuries more before normalcy asserted itself again.

She spied a familiar figure climbing the treacherously icy steps leading to the ramparts. She ignored it, knowing it was Grauel. Grauel, whom she had not seen in weeks, and whom she missed, and yet...

Grauel leaned into the teeth of the wind as she approached, determined to invade Marika's private space. Her teeth were chattering when she reached Marika. "What're you doing up here in weather like this, pup? You'll catch your death."

"I like it here, Grauel. Especially at this time of year. I can come out here and think without being interrupted."

Grauel ignored the hint. "They're talking about you down there, pup." Marika noted the familiar form of speech—which even now Grauel turned to only when she was stressed—but maintained her aloofness. Grauel continued, "I just heard them. I had the duty. Gorry again. Talking to the senior. As viciously as ever, but this time I think she may have found a sympathetic ear. What have you done?"

"Nothing."

"Something, certainly. You've frightened Gorry so badly she is insisting you be sent to the Maksche cloister come spring."

That startled Marika. It was an about-face for Gorry, who till now had wanted her very existence concealed from the cloister at Maksche, of which Akard was a subservient satellite. Though she had done nothing specific to alarm Gorry, the old instructress had read her better than she had suspected. Yet another argument for exercising caution. The old silth counted experience and superior knowledge among her advantages in their subtle, bittersweet, unacknowledged duel.

"I still don't understand them, Grauel. Why are they afraid of me?" Gorry she understood on a personal level. Gorry feared because she had whelped a powerful hatred in her pupil. But Gorry's fear was far more than just a dread of Marika's vengeance. Without comprehending, Marika knew it was far more complex than that, and knew that part of Gorry's fear was, to some extent, shared by all the older silth of the packfast.

Grauel said what had been said before, by herself, Barlog, and especially by Braydic. But Marika did not relate to it any better now.

"It's not that they fear what you are now, Marika. They dread what you might become. Gorry insists you're the strongest pupil she's ever encountered, or even heard of. Including those with whom she trained, and she claims those were some of the strongest talents of the modern age. What truth there? Who knows? They're all self-serving liars. But one fact remains undeniable. You have an air of doom that makes them uneasy."

Marika almost turned. This was something a little different from what she usually heard. "An air of doom? What does that mean?"

"I don't know for sure. I'm just telling you what I've heard. And what I've heard is, Gorry believes you are something more than you. Something mythic. A fang in the jaws of fate, if you will. Gorry came up with the idea a long time ago. The others used to scoff. They don't anymore. Even those who try to find ways to thwart Gorry. You have done something that makes even your champions uneasy."

Marika reviewed the past few months. There had been nothing at all that was different from what had gone before. Except that she had reached the brink of physical maturation and been ordered to take a daily draft of a potion which would prevent the onset of her first estrus.

"I don't see it, Grauel. I don't feel like I'm carrying any doom around."

"Would you know if you did, pup? Did Jiana?"

Gorry's word. Jiana. In a moment of anger the old silth had called her Jiana one day recently. "That's a myth, Grauel. Anyway, Jiana wasn't even meth."

The demigoddess Jiana had been the offspring of a rheum-greater and the all-father avatar of the All, Gyerlin, who had descended from the great dark and had impregnated Jiana's dam in her sleep. It was not accepted doctrine. It was a story, like many other tales from the dawn of time. A prescientific attempt to explain away mysteries.

When Jiana had become an adult, she had carried curses around the world, and in her wake all the animals had lost their powers of speech and reason. All but the meth, who had been forewarned by Gyerlin and had hidden themselves away where Jiana could not find them.

It was an ancient tale, distorted by a thousand generations of retellings. Any truth it might have held once had to have been leached away by the efforts of storytellers to improve upon the original. Marika accepted it only as what it was upon its face, an explanation of why the meth were the only intelligent, talking animals. She did not see that the myth had any connection with her present situation.

She said as much to Grauel.

"Myth or not, Gorry is calling you her little Jiana. And some of the others are taking her seriously. They are certain you have been touched by the All." Which expression could have two meanings. In this case Marika knew she could interpret it as a polite way of saying she was insane.

"Someone has been touched by the All, Grauel. And I don't think it is me. These silth are not very down to earth when you look at them closely."

Marika had been very much surprised to discover that the silth, for all their education and knowledge resources, were far more mystically and ritualistically inclined than the most primitive of nomads. They honored a score of days of obligation of which she had never before heard. They offered daily propitiation to both the All and the lesser forces with which they dealt. They made sacrifices on a scale astonishing to one for whom sacrifice had meant a weekly bowl of gruel set outside the packstead gate, with a pot of ormon beer, and a small animal delivered to Machen Cave before the quarterly conjunction of the two biggest moons. The silth were devil-ridden. They still feared specters supposedly cast down when the All had supplanted earlier powers. They feared shadows that had come with the All but which were supposed to be enchained irrevocably in other worlds. They especially feared those—always wehrlen—who might be able to summon those shadows against them.

Marika had observed several of the higher ceremonies by sneaking through her loophole. Those rituals had almost no impact upon those-who-dwell, as the silth called the things Marika thought of as ghosts. And those things were the only supernatural forces Marika recognized. At the moment she seriously questioned the existence of the All itself, let alone those never-seen shadows that haunted her teachers.

The ghosts needed no propitiation that Marika could see. Insofar as she could tell, they remained indifferent to the mortal plane most all the time. They responded to it, apparently only in curiosity, at times of high stress. And acted upon it only when controlled by one with the talent.

Doomstalker. That was Jiana's mystic title. The huntress in search of something she could never find, something that was always behind her. Insofar as Marika could see, the doomstalker was little more than a metaphor for change.

The doomstalker was a powerful silth myth, though, and Marika suspected that Gorry, fearful of what her own future held, was playing upon it cynically in an effort to gain backing from the other older sisters. None of the Akard silth liked Gorry, but they grudgingly respected her for what she had been before being sent into exile.

Even so, she would have to do some tall convincing before being permitted more blatant excesses toward her pupil. Of that Marika was confident.

Caution. Caution. That was all it would take.

"I am no doomstalker, Grauel. And I have no ambitions. I'm just doing what I have to do so we can survive. They need not fear me."

She had slipped into a role she played for Grauel and Barlog both, in their rare meetings, for she feared that Grauel, at least, in her own effort to survive reported her every remark. "I sincerely believe that I will become the sort of sister who never leaves the cloister and seldom uses her talent for anything but teaching silth pups."

Were her suspicions insane? It seemed mad to suspect everyone of malice. One meth, certainly. In any packstead there were enmities as well as friendships. Every packstead had its old-against-young conflicts, its Gorry-against-Marika. Pohsit had been proof of that. But to suspect the entire packfast of being against her, subtly and increasingly—even though the suspicion was encouraged by Braydic, Grauel, and Barlog—particularly for reasons she herself found mystical and inaccessible, stank of the rankest madness.

So it might be mad. She was convinced, and being convinced she dared do nothing but act as if it were true. Any concession to reason would be folly.

Why did the silth play their games of sisterhood? Or did every silth sister come to stand to all others as Marika was coming to stand to hers? Was sisterhood just a mask shown the outside world? An image with which the rulers awed the ruled? Was the reality continual chaos within the cloister wall? The squabble of starving pups battling over scraps?

Grauel intruded upon her thoughts. "I can't make you believe me, Marika. But I am bound to warn you. We are still Degnan."

Marika had definite, powerful feelings about that, but she did not air them. Grauel and Barlog both became sullen and hurt if she even hinted that the Degnan pack was a thing of the past. They had taken the Chronicle from her when they had discovered she was no longer keeping it up. Barlog had gone so far as to learn a better style of calligraphy so she could keep the Chronicle.

They were good huntresses, those two. They had given the packfast no reason to regret taking them in. They served it well. But they were fools, racked by sentimentality. And they were traitors to their ideals. Were they not working against her, their own packmate?

"Thank you, Grauel. I appreciate your concern. Please excuse my manners. I had a difficult morning. One of Gorry's more difficult tests."

Grauel's lips pulled back in a fierce snarl. For a moment Marika was tempted to press, to test the genuineness of the show. To employ Grauel as a blade in her contest with Gorry. But no. That was what someone had tried against her on the Rift. And the effort had earned nothing but contempt for the unknown one who had manipulated another into acting in her stead. The reckoning with Gorry was something she would have to handle herself.

So, when Grauel showed no sign of departing, she continued, "Thank you, Grauel. Please let me be. I need the song of the wind."

"It is not a song, pup. It is a death wail. But as you will."

Give Grauel that much. She did not subscribe to the clutch of honorifics which Marika was due, even as a silth in training. Had there been witnesses… But she knew Marika abhorred the whole artificial structure of honor in which the silth wrapped themselves.

As Grauel stalked away, cradling her spear-cum-badge of office, Marika reflected that she was becoming known for communing with the wind. No doubt Gorry and her cronies listed that as another fragment of evidence against her. Jiana had spoken with the wind, and the north wind had been her closest ally, sometimes carrying her around the world. More than one sister had asked—teasingly so far—what news she heard from the north.

She never answered, for they would not understand what she would say. She would say that she heard cold, she heard ice, she heard the whisper of the great dark. She would say that she heard the whisper of tomorrow.

CHAPTER ELEVEN

I

Gorry failed in her effort to rid Akard of its most bizarre tenant. Marika did not go to the Maksche cloister with the coming of spring. The senior was not yet sufficiently exercised with her most intractable student silth to accept the loss of face passing the problem would bring.

Hopeless as their hopes were, the exiles of Akard tried making themselves look good in the eyes of their distant seniors. Sometimes the winds of silth politics shifted at the senior cloisters and old exiles were derusticated. Not often, but often enough to serve as an incentive. A whip, Marika thought. A fraud.

Whatever, the senior did not wish to lose face by passing along such a recalcitrant student.

She was not shy, though, about getting her least favorite pupil out of Akard for the summer.

The orders had come not from Maksche but from beyond, from the most senior cloister of the Reugge sisterhood. The nomads were to be cleared from the upper Ponath. No excuses would be accepted. Dread filled Akard. To Marika that dread seemed unfocused, as much caused by the sisterhood's far, mysterious rulers as by the more concrete threat of the hordes close by.

Marika went out with the first party to leave. It consisted of forty meth, only three of whom were silth. One young far-toucher. One older silth to command. Thirty-seven huntresses, all drawn from among the refugees. And one dark-sider. Marika.

Maybe they hoped she would be inadequate to the task. Maybe they hoped her will would fail when it came time to reach down and grasp the deadly ghosts and fling them against the killers of the upper Ponath. Or maybe they had not had the webs drawn over their eyes the way she thought. Maybe they knew her true strength.

She did not worry it long. The hunt demanded too much concentration.

They went out by day, in immediate pursuit of nomads seen watching the fortress. The nomads saw them coming and fled. The huntresses slogged across the newly thawed fields. Within minutes Marika's fine boots were caked with mud to her knees. She muttered curses and tried to keep track of the prey. The nomads could be caught up when night fell.

Barlog marched to her left. Grauel marched to her right. The two huntresses watched their own party more closely than they watched the inimical forest.

"You look smug," Marika told Grauel.

"We are." Both huntresses were in a high good humor Marika initially assessed as due to the fact that they were outside Akard for the first time in six months. "We tricked them. They thought they would be able to send you out without us along to look out for you."

Maybe that explained the scowls from Arhdwehr, the silth in charge. Marika peered at the older silth's back and expressed her own amusement.

The hunt was supposed to follow the north bank of the east fork of the Hainlin as far as the nether edge of country formerly occupied by settled meth. Then it was to swing through the hills to the south, loop again north almost to the Rift, drift down to the east fork again, then head home. That meant five hundred miles of travel minimum, in no real set pattern after leaving the Hainlin in the east. Basically, they were to wander the eastern half of the upper Ponath all summer, living off the land and slaughtering invaders. Marika's would be but one of a score of similar parties.

For a long time very little happened. Once again, as in the summer of the journey to the Rift, the nomads seemed capable of staying out of their path. When the hunt passed below the site of the Degnan packstead, Marika, Barlog, and Grauel gazed up at the decaying stockade and refused to take a closer look. The Laspe packstead they did visit, but nothing remained there save vaguely regular lines on the earth and cellar infalls where loghouses had stood.

Stirring a midden heap, Marika uncovered a scorched and broken chakota doll—and nearly lost her composure.

"What troubles you, pup?" Barlog asked.

Throat too tight for speech, she merely held out the broken doll. Barlog was puzzled.

Marika found her voice. "My earliest memory is of a squabble with Kublin. I broke his chakota. He got so mad he threw mine into the fire." She had not thought of, or dreamed of, her littermate for a long time. Recalling him now, with a chakota in her paw, brought back all the pain redoubled. "The Mourning. We still owe them their Mourning."

"Someday, pup. Someday. It will come." Barlog scratched her behind the ears, gently, and she did not shy away, though she was too old for that.

Approaching the Plenthzo Valley, they happened upon a packstead that had been occupied till only a few hours before. "Some of them have changed their ways," Grauel observed.

It was obvious the place had been abandoned hurriedly. "They *do* know where we are and what we are doing," Marika said. She frowned at the sky for no reason she understood. And without consulting Arhdwehr—who was plundering deserted food stores—she ordered a half-dozen huntresses into the surrounding woods to look for signs of watchers.

Arhdwehr was very angry when she learned what Marika had done. But she restrained her temper. Though just a week into the venture, she realized already that the savages with whom she traveled responded far better to the savage silth pup than they did to her. Too strong a confrontation might not be wise.

Marika had sent those huntresses that Grauel felt were the best. So she believed them when they returned and reported that the party was not being stalked by nomad scouts.

"They must have their own silth with them," she told Grauel and Barlog. "So they sense us coming in time to scatter."

"That many silth?" Barlog countered. "If there were that many, they would fight us. Anyway, sheer chance ought to put more of them into our path." The only encounters thus far had been two with lone huntresses out seeking game. Those the Akard huntresses had destroyed without difficulty or requiring help from the silth.

While searching for the best food stores, Arhdwehr made a discovery. She told the others, "I know how they are doing it. Staying out of our way." But she would not explain.

Marika poked around. She found nothing. But intuition and Arhdwehr's behavior made her suspect it came down to something like the devices Braydic used to communicate with Maksche.

Which might explain how the packstead had been warned. But how had the reporter known where the hunting party was?

Ever so gently, so it would seem to be Arhdwehr's idea, Marika suggested that the party might spend a day or two inside that packstead, resting. It had been a hard trail up from Akard. Arhdwehr adopted the idea. Her point won, Marika collected Grauel and Barlog. "Did you find any of the herbs and roots I told you to watch for?"

"Everything but the grubs," Grauel replied. She was baffled. Almost from her first contact with them after their arrival at Akard, Marika had had them gathering odds and ends from the woods whenever they left the fortress.

She replied, "I did not think we would find any of those. It is far too early yet. And too cold. Even the summers have become so cool that they have become rare. However..." With a gesture of triumph she produced a small sealed earthenware jar she had brought from the fortress. "I brought some along. I found them the summer we went to the Rift. Find me a pot. And something I can use as a cutting board."

They settled apart from the others—which drew no attention because it was their custom already—and Marika went to work. "I hope my memory is good. I only saw this done once, when Bhlase made the poison for our spears and arrows."

"Poison?" Barlog looked faintly distressed.

"I am not without a certain low, foul cunning," Marika said lightly. "I have been gathering the ingredients for years, waiting for this chance. Do you object?"

"Not with the thought," Grauel said. "They deserve no better. They are vermin. You exterminate vermin." Her hatred spoke strongly. "But poison? That is the recourse of a treacherous male."

Barlog objected, too. Eyes narrow, she said, "Why do I think you will make poison here where none will know what you do, and test it on those none will object to seeing perish, and someday I will find myself wondering at the unexplainable death of someone back at the packfast?"

Marika did not respond.

The huntresses exchanged looks. They understood, though they did not want to do so. Barlog could not conceal her disgust. Perhaps, Marika thought, she would now discover if they were the creatures of the senior.

They continued to object. Poison was not the way of a huntress. Nor even of the Wise. The way of a stinking silth, maybe. But only the worst of that witch breed....

They said nothing, though. And Marika ignored their silent censure.

She cooked the poison down with the utmost care. And just before the hunting party departed the packstead—where everything had been left much as found, at her insistence—she put three quarters of the poison into those nomad food stores she thought likely to see use soon.

The hunting party crossed the Plenthzo and continued on eastward for three nights. Then, after day's camp had been set, Marika told Grauel and Barlog, "It is time to return and examine our handiwork."

Grauel scowled. Barlog said, "Do not spread the blame upon us, pup. *You* played the male's poison game."

They were very irked, those two, but they did not refuse to accompany her.

They traveled more quickly as a threesome with a specific destination and no need to watch for prey. They returned to the packstead the second evening after leaving camp.

The nomads had not been forewarned of their approach. Marika filed that fact for future consideration. Then she crouched outside the stockade and ducked through her loophole, went inside the packstead.

As she had guessed from evidence seen on site, the packstead was home to a very large number of nomads. More than two hundred adults. But now half those were dead or in the throes of a terrible stomach disorder. And there were no silth there to contest with her.

She did what she believed had to be done, without remorse or second thoughts. But dealing with so many was more difficult than she had anticipated.

The invaders realized the nature of the attack within seconds and responded by counterattacking. They very nearly got to her before she succeeded in terrorizing them into scattering.

Then it was over. And she was chagrined. She had managed to destroy no more than fifteen.

Grauel and Barlog, ever taciturn, were quieter than usual on the return trail as they pursued the main party. Marika pretended to be unaware of their continued displeasure. She said, "We were able to get close without difficulty. I wonder why. Two possibilities suggest themselves. The fact that we were a small party and the fact that we came by day. Which do you suppose it might have been? Or might it have been a combination of the two?"

Neither Grauel nor Barlog cared to sustain her speculations. She let them drop. And once they reached the site of the camp they had deserted, she bothered them no more, for from then on they were too busy tracking.

II

Arhdwehr flew into a rage. "You will not do that again, ever, pup! Do you understand? You will not go off on your own. If you had found more trouble than you could handle, there would have been no hope for you. No help. I had no idea where to look for you."

"If I had gotten into more trouble than I could handle, all your problems would have been solved for you," Marika countered. Her tone was such that Arhdwehr understood immediately exactly what she was implying. For a moment the older silth looked abashed, which was a happening so rare Marika savored it and decided she would treasure it.

Arhdwehr controlled herself. After a time, in a reasonable tone, she asked, "Have you decided how it was that you were able to approach them undetected?"

Marika shared her speculations.

"We will experiment. There must be other such packsteads. We will seek them out. We will pass them by if they are abandoned, then we will turn back and strike swiftly a few days later. We will try it with small parties, approaching both by day and by night."

Arhdwehr assumed that a large circle around the hunting party was alert to the presence of the hunting party. Given the nomad propensity for evasion, she felt safe scattering scouts widely in search of packsteads occupied by nomads.

Marika was pleased. "She has a temper," she told Grauel. "But she is flexible."

Still sullen, the huntress replied, "I admit it is seldom one sees that in a silth sister."

Marika was irked at the way her two packmates had distanced themselves, but she said nothing. They would have to learn flexibility themselves. Without coaching, which they would resist, if only because they were older and believed that gave them certain rights.

The huntresses discovered that a packstead could not be approached in large numbers by day, or even in small numbers by night. But by day twos and threes could close in and remain undiscovered till it was too late for the nomads.

The far-toucher reported the news to Akard. The sisters at the fortress passed the word to the other parties in the field, none of which had had much luck.

"They have their means of communication," Marika mused one evening. "They will figure it out and respond. Probably by abandoning their packsteads altogether. Which means we must begin considering ways to hunt them down once they revert to old ways."

Arhdwehr said, "That will be easier, if more work. Being on the move will rob them of much of their communications capacity." She would not expand upon that when Marika asked questions.

"They are weird, that is why," Grauel said when Marika later wondered why most silth refused to discuss some subjects with her. "Everything is a secret with them. Ask them what color the sky is and they will not tell you."

The daytime sneaking worked well for several weeks. The hills south of the Hainlin were spotted heavily by packsteads taken over by the nomads. The party fell far behind its planned schedule. Then a turn back found a packstead still empty. And the next packstead located had been abandoned a week.

Arhdwehr tightened the party up, not wanting to be too scattered if hostiles appeared. She expected the nomads to become less passive. She, though, seemed to be increasingly disaffected, muttering imprecations upon the silth of Maksche. Marika did not understand. And, of course, Arhdwehr would not explain.

III

The hunting party had given up hope of catching any more nomads unaware. They were headed toward the Hainlin, hoping for better hunting on the northward leg. Arhdwehr was pleased with what had been accomplished, though she would have liked even longer strings of trophy ears. Marika had begun to believe the entire hunt was an exercise in futility. She suspected that a score of nomads were escaping for each one even located, let alone destroyed. And Akard's strength was being sapped.

Out west of the fortress the nomads were fighting back.

There had to be a better way.

The far-toucher wakened suddenly in the middle of the day, when the party was just a day's travel south of the east fork. She squeaked, "A touch! Pain. A sister... just west of us. They are being attacked. She is the only silth left alive."

Marika stared at the far-toucher, who seemed panicky and confused. Then she felt the touch, too. It was a strong one, driven by the agony of a wound.

She felt the direction. "Up!" she snarled. "Everybody up. Weapons only. Leave your packs." She snatched her bow and javelin. Grauel and Barlog did likewise, questioning nothing, though they had many questions. Marika trotted toward the source of pain.

Two-thirds of the huntresses did not so much as glance at Arhdwehr for approval. The others scarcely delayed long enough to see the older silth begin to fall into a rage.

It had been coming from the beginning. Marika had not seen it, but Grauel and Barlog had and had spoken with most of the huntresses. Marika realized there was, and would be, a problem only after she had done the thing.

Grauel admonished her softly as they ran through the forest. "You must learn to reflect on the consequences of your actions, pup," the huntress said. "You could have done that politely and let Arhdwehr claim it as her own idea."

Marika did not argue. Grauel was right. She had not thought. And because she had not taken a few seconds there might be trouble. Certainly, what sympathy she had won from Arhdwehr was now dead.

Silth were extremely jealous of their prerogatives.

The party under attack was just five miles away. An easy run for huntresses. Half an hour. But half an hour was too long.

Forty-seven mutilated bodies in Akard dress lay scattered through the woods. Twice that many nomads lay with them, many twisted in that way they did after silth magic touched their hearts. Marika stared at the massacred, filled with a hard anger.

"They know we are close," Grauel said. "They fled without their dead." She knelt. "Mercy-slew their most badly wounded."

"Which way did they go?"

Grauel pointed. Marika looked to Arhdwehr, deferring this time. The older silth's lips pulled back in a snarl of promise. "How long ago did they run?"

Grauel replied, "Ten minutes at most."

The far-toucher said, "We left our things. We could lose them."

Marika gave her a fierce look. And, to her surprise, Arhdwehr did the same. The older silth said, "Marika, you and your friends take the point." To Grauel, she added, "Point out individual trails if they start scattering."

Everyone fell silent, froze. A far *tak-tak-tak*king echoed up the valley along which the nomads had fled. Then came several sounds like far, muted thunder.

"What in the All?" Arhdwehr exploded angrily. "Go! But slow down after the first mile."

Marika leapt down the trail a step behind Grauel. Barlog panted at her heels. The others came behind, making no effort to keep quiet. The rustle of brush would be heard by no one above that ferocious uproar ahead.

The sound swelled quickly. After a mile Grauel slowed as instructed. Marika guessed the noise's source to be a half-mile farther along. Grauel trotted another five hundred yards, then suddenly stabbed sideways with her spear and cut into the brush, headed uphill. Marika followed. Three minutes later Grauel halted. The hunting party piled up behind Marika.

The hillside gave a good view of a fire burn where tree trunks lay strewn like a pup's pick-up sticks. It was an old burn, with most of the black weathered away. Several hundred nomads crouched or lay behind the fallen trees. The *tak-tak-tak*king noise came from a slope beyond the nomads.

Something went *whump!* over there. Moments later earth geysered near a clutch of nomads. Thunder echoed off the hills. Meth screamed. Several nomads tried to flee. The *tak-tak* redoubled. All who were erect jerked around and fell, lay still.

They were dead. Marika sensed that instantly. "What is going on over there?" she asked Arhdwehr.

It was something secret. The older silth ignored her question. "You stay put," Arhdwehr told her. "Use your talent. The rest of you follow me." She let out an ululation that would have done any huntress proud.

The huntresses hesitated only a moment, saw Marika do as she was told, followed. A howl of despair went up from the nomads.

The chatter from the far woods lasted only moments longer.

Marika wasted only a moment more speculating. The odds were heavy against her party. The nomads would obliterate them unless she did what she was supposed to do.

It was not a long fight, and scarcely a pawful of nomads escaped. When Marika walked through the burn afterward, she stepped over scores of bodies contorted but unmarked by wounds. A bloody Arhdwehr watched her with an odd look. "You did exceptionally well today, pup." A trace of fear edged her voice.

"The rage came," Marika said. She kicked a weapon away from fingers still twitching. "Would it not have been wiser to have stayed on the hillside and used our bows?"

"The rage came upon me also. I wanted to feel hot blood upon my paws."

Marika stared up that slope whence the strange sounds had come. "What was that, Arhdwehr?"

The elder silth shrugged.

"Males," Marika said. "I sensed that much. And you must know. Why is it hidden?"

Arhdwehr's gaze followed hers. "There are rules, pup. There are laws." To the huntresses, most of whom had survived, she said, "Forget the ears. This day's work is not done." She started toward the source of the mysterious sounds, traveling in a squat, darting from one log to another.

The huntresses all looked to Marika. Even the far-toucher hesitated. Marika could not help being both flattered and dismayed. She waved them forward.

"You made the move," Grauel whispered.

"What move?" Instead of hurrying after Arhdwehr, she took time to examine her surroundings.

"As strength goes."

Marika slipped a finger into a hole something had drilled through four inches of hard word. She stared at the torn bodies lying near the site of the explosion she had witnessed. "No, Grauel. It was not that. I just did what needed doing without thinking about the politics." That was a word that existed only in the silth secret languages. "What could have done this?"

"Maybe you will find out if you are there when she catches whoever it is she is chasing."

Marika scowled.

Grauel was amused, but only briefly. She surveyed the carnage. "Who would have thought this could occur in this world? And for what, Marika?"

Barlog was studying the corpses nearby, trying to read pack fetishes and having no luck. Few of the dead even wore them. She rolled a corpse, knelt, pulled something from its chest. She presented it to Marika a moment later.

It was a blood-encrusted, curved fragment of metal. Marika examined it briefly, tossed it aside. "I don't know. We'd better catch up."

The run was long and hard. Marika sensed the males in front in a tight group of twenty, loping along at a steady, ground-devouring pace. They seemed to know exactly where they were going and what they were doing. And that a band of huntresses was on their trail. They increased their pace whenever Arhdwehr increased hers.

"Who would have thought it?" Grauel gasped. "That males could run us into the ground."

"We ran six miles before they started," Barlog countered.

"Save your breath," Marika snapped.

They moved up through the party till Marika was running at Arhdwehr's heels. She was young and strong, but the pace told. Why were they doing this?

Someone farther back said, "We will catch them after dark."

Arhdwehr tossed back one black look and increased her pace. Marika had to admire the silth. She was showing exceptional endurance for one who led a sedentary life. Marika started a warning. "Mistress…."

Arhdwehr held up. "I sense it," she gasped.

They had crested a ridge. The valley beyond reeked of many meth. All male meth.

Silth senses were not needed to detect the presence of meth, though. Smoke tainted the air, a smoke filled with the aromas of cooking and trash burning. There was another smell, too, an unfamiliar, penetrating, acrid scent that brought water into Marika's nose.

A flurry of activity broke out below, out of sight. There was a series of soft, rising whines that, one after another, in less than a minute began fading into the distance.

Arhdwehr cursed and sprang downhill at a dead run. She trailed an anger as great as any Marika had managed to inspire.

More whines faded away.

Marika charged after the older silth. Moments later Arhdwehr broke into a clearing, a dozen steps ahead. With a howl she launched her javelin. Marika broke cover just as the missile flashed into the darkness between two trees a hundred feet away. The gray curve of something big disappeared in that same instant, behind a swirl of dust and flying needles. The javelin did it no harm.

Marika gagged and gasped. She needed air desperately. But that male camp was choked with the foul smell that had stung her nose on the ridge. She fought for breath while she surveyed the clearing.

"Khronen!"

At least twenty males—tradermales—sat around a camp-fire to one side, all gazing at the huntresses. They appeared to be cooking and pursuing other mundane chores. Among them was the tradermale Khronen.

Grauel and Barlog recognized him, too. They followed as Marika stalked toward the males—none of whom bothered to rise or even to cease performing whatever tasks they had at paw. Marika noted the presence of a lot of metal, all of it pointed or edged.

Khronen rose. His eyes narrowed. "Do I know you, young sister?"

Marika glanced at Arhdwehr, who had gone to reclaim her javelin. Marika sensed the swift movement of males pulling away far beyond the elder silth. "Yes," she replied. "Or, say, you knew me when I was something else. What is this? What are you doing here?"

"Preparing our evening meal. We would invite you to join us, but I do not think we have enough to guest so many."

"So? Grauel. How many tradermale-made weapons have you seen these past two months?"

"I have not kept count. Too many."

"Look around. Perhaps we have found the source."

Grauel's teeth appeared in a snarl of anger and surprise. The thought had not occurred to her.

Barlog said, "Let me, Marika." Her tone suggested a strong emotional need.

"All right. You stay, Grauel."

Something flashed across Khronen's features when Barlog spoke. He had recognized her voice, perhaps. He said, "You have not answered my question directly."

"I will ask, male. You will answer."

Twenty-some pairs of eyes turned toward Marika. And she very nearly backed away, startled by the smoldering emotion she saw there.

"You think, perhaps, that we are some of your tame packstead chattels?"

Khronen asked. "Ah. The costume distracted me. I know you now. Yes. Very much the image of your dam. Even in your arrogance." He looked over her shoulder. Marika sensed that Arhdwehr had come up behind her. But she did not look back.

A hard-eyed male near Khronen said, "And at such a young age, too. Pity." His gaze never left her face.

All those eyes continued to bore into her.

It was a moment of crisis, she knew. A moment when the wrong word could cause a lot of trouble. Khronen was right. These were not the sort of males to which she was accustomed. She sensed that they would as soon battle her as be polite. That there was no awe of her in them, either because she was female or because she was silth.

What sort of male did not fear silth?

Barlog returned. "This is the only blade I found." Other than those close to male paws, of course.

Marika took it. "Grauel, give me one of those we captured." One was in her paw in a moment. She examined both blades, shrugged, presented both to Arhdwehr. Arhdwehr scarcely glanced at them.

"Not the same maker. Pup, suppose you take this opportunity to restrain your natural exuberance and allow one with a more diplomatic nature to handle communication?" She stepped past Marika, passed both weapons to Khronen, who was the oldest of the males. Some were little older than Marika. In fact, many had the look of upper Ponath refugees.

Grauel whispered, "That was well-done."

"What?" Marika asked.

"She saved you from trouble, salvaged your pride, and put you in your place with a single sentence. Well-done, indeed."

Marika had not seen that in it. But when she glanced around she saw that the other huntresses had read it that way. Instead of being irked, though, she was relieved to be out of the confrontation with Khronen.

She stepped up behind Arhdwehr, who had settled to the earth facing Khronen. The tradermale had seated himself, too. He barely glanced at the blades before passing them to the tradermale on his right. That one had not shifted his eyes to Arhdwehr. His gaze, frankly curious, bored into Marika as though trying to unmask her secret heart. There was an air of strength about him that made Marika suspect he was as important here as was Khronen.

He passed the blades back to Arhdwehr.

Khronen continued, "I know, sister. That is why we are here. Seeking the source. And doing much what you are."

"Which is?"

"Exterminating vermin."

"The last I heard, the upper Ponath was classified a Tech Two Zone."

"Your communications are more reliable than mine, sister. I have no far-toucher. I presume it still is. Is the pup your commer? I would not have guessed it of one of the Degnan."

Marika's ears twitched. Something about the way he said that…. He was lying.

"Dark-walker," Arhdwehr replied. She slipped a paw into a belt pouch, removed something shiny, passed it over. "Those who shatter the law should take care to clean up their back trail."

Khronen fingered the object, grunted, passed it to his right. Both males stared at Marika. Khronen's face became blank. "Dark-sider, eh? So young, and with her dam's temperament. A dangerous combination."

"Impetuous and undisciplined, yes. But let us discuss matters more appropriate to the moment. You will be in communication with Critza after we depart. Remind your seniors that Critza's walls mark the limit of brethren extraterritoriality in the upper Ponath. Only within those limits is overteching permissible. Most Senior Gradwohl is immutably determined on such points."

"We will relay your admonition, if we should discover a male far-toucher hidden in the crowd here. Though I doubt anyone there needs the reminder. How was the hunting, sister?" He did not look at Arhdwehr at all, but continued to stare at Marika. So did the male on his right.

She wondered what was on their minds.

"You would know better than I, I suspect," Arhdwehr replied. "You have eyes that see even where silth cannot."

"Here? In a Tech Two Zone? I fear not, sister. We have had a bit of luck, I admit. We have helped a few hundred savages rejoin the All. But I fear it is like bailing a river with a leaky teacup. They will breed faster than we can manufacture javelins."

Marika had noticed few pups anywhere. The numbers of old and young both were disproportionately small among the nomads she had encountered.

Some sort of fencing was going on between Arhdwehr and the tradermale. But whatever it was about, it was not dangerous. The other males went back to what they had been doing, occasionally glancing her way as though she were some strange beast that talked and behaved with inexcusable manners. She began to feel very young and very ignorant and very self-conscious.

She backed several steps away. "Grauel, there is more going on in this world than we know."

"You are catching on only now?"

"I mean—"

"I know what you mean, pup. And I had thought your innocence was feigned. Perhaps you do not hear as much in silth quarters as we do in ours."

"Silth do not gossip, Grauel."

Barlog said, "Perhaps she does not hear because she does not listen. She sees no one but that communicator creature." Barlog continued to watch Khronen with as much intensity as he watched Marika. "They say you may be in line for a great future, pup. *I* say you will never see it until you begin to see. And to hear. To look and to listen. Each dust mote has a message and lesson, if you will but heed it."

"Indeed?" Barlog sounded like one of her teachers. "Perhaps you are right. Do you know Khronen, Barlog? Is there something between you two?"

"No."

"He was Laspe. Dam knew him when he was a pup."

Barlog had no comment.

Arhdwehr rose, walked back to where she had left her javelin stuck into the earth. She yanked it free, trotted up the trail along which the hunting party had approached the male camp. The others followed in a ragged file. Baffled, Marika joined them. Grauel trotted ahead of her, Barlog behind. She glanced back before she left the clearing. Khronen was watching her still. As was his companion. They were talking.

Marika wondered if the party ought not to double back after a while....

Arhdwehr kept a steady pace all the way to the place where they had left their packs. Marika fell into the rhythm of the run and spent the time trying to unravel the significance of what had happened during that long and bloody day.

Two nights later the hunting party crossed the east fork of the Hainlin, headed north. The remainder of the season was uneventful. Marika spent most of her time trying to learn the lesson Barlog claimed she needed to learn. And she practiced pretending to be what she was supposed to be. She succeeded well enough. She managed to get back on Arhdwehr's good side. As much as ever anyone could be.

Early snows chased them back to Akard ten days earlier than planned. Marika suspected the upper Ponath was in for a winter more fierce than the past three.

She also felt she had wasted a summer. All that blood and anger had done nothing to weaken the nomads. The great hunt had been but a gesture made to mollify those shrill and mysterious silth who ruled the Reugge from afar. Only one result was certain. Many familiar faces had vanished from among Akard's population.

Marika visited Braydic even before she made her initial courtesy call upon Gorry. She told Braydic all about her summer, hoping the communicator's reactions would illuminate some of what she had seen. But she learned very little.

Braydic understood what she was doing. She was amused. "In time, Marika. In time. When you go to Maksche."

"Maksche?"

"Next summer. A certainty, I think, from hints my truesister has dropped. If we get through this winter."

If.

CHAPTER TWELVE

I

Marika was four years too young to be considered a true silth sister, yet she had exhausted the knowledge of those who taught her. In less than four years she had devoured knowledge others sometimes did not master in a lifetime. The sisters were more frightened of her than ever. They very much wanted to pass her on to the Maksche cloister immediately, but they could not.

It was yet the heart of the fourth winter. Nothing would move for months. The snows lay fifteen to twenty feet deep. In the north, in places, the wind sweeping across the fields had drifted it to the top of the packfast wall. The workers had dug tunnels underneath in order to connect the fortress with the powerhouse. It was essential that the plume water be kept running. If the powerhouse froze up, there would be no communication with the rest of the Reugge sisterhood.

The times were strange in more than the personal way Marika knew. By staying near Braydic whenever she was free, she had begun to catch snatches of messages drifting in from Maksche. Messages that disturbed the older silth more then ever.

For a long time the Reugge Community had been involved in a sort of low-grade, ongoing conflict with the more powerful Serke sisterhood. Lately there had been some strong provocations from the stronger order. There were some who suspected a connection with strange events in the upper Ponath, though no hard accusations were made even in secret. The Akard sisters were afraid there was truth in that, and that the provocation here would escalate.

As near as Marika could tell, it seemed to be packwar on a grand scale. She had never seen packwar, but she had heard. In the upper Ponath that meant a few isolated skirmishes, harassment of another pack's huntresses, a rather quick peak into a confrontation which settled everything. Often the fighting was ritualized and consisted entirely of counting coup, with the big battle ending the moment of the first death.

Unless there was blood in it. Bloodfeud was different. Bloodfeud might be fought till one side fled or boasted no more survivors. But bloodfeud was exceedingly rare. Only a few of the Wise of the Degnan had been able to recall the last time bloodfeud plagued the upper Ponath.

The louder the north wind howled and the more bitter its bite, the more Marika met it in her place upon the wall, and whispered back of the coldness and darkness that had found their homes within her mind. There were moments when she suspected she was at least half what Gorry accused, so savage were some of her hatreds.

So it was that she was in her place when the messengers came from Critza, with nomad huntresses upon their tails. She saw the males floundering, recognized their outer wear, saw they were on the edge of collapse from exhaustion. She sensed the triumph in the savages closing in behind them, climbing the slope from the river. She went down inside herself, through her loophole, and reached out over a greater distance than ever before. She ripped the hearts out of the chests of the savages, setting the Hainlin canyons echoing with their screams. Then she touched the messengers and guided them to a point where they could clamber up the snowdrifts to the top of the wall.

She went to meet them, gliding along the icy rampart, not entirely certain how she knew what they were or why their visit would be important, but knowing it all the same. She would bring them inside.

Males inside the packfast proper was unprecedented. The older silth would be enraged by the desecration. Yet Marika was absolutely certain she would be doing right by bringing them across the wall.

Their breaths fogged about them and whipped away on the wind. They panted violently, lung-searingly. Marika sensed that they had been forced to travel long and hard, with death ever snapping at their tails. One collapsed into the powder snow before she reached them.

"Welcome to Akard, tradermales. I trust you bear a message of the utmost importance."

They looked at her with awe and fear, as most outsiders did, but the more so because she was young, and because she still radiated the darkness of death. "Yes," said the tallest of the three. "News from Critza.... It is you. The one called Marika...."

She recognized him then. The male who had sat beside Khronen during last summer's confrontation with males. That unshakable self-certainty and confidence were with him no more. That anger, that defiance, had fled him. He shivered not only from the wind.

"It is I," Marika replied, her voice as chill as the wind. "I hope I have not wasted myself guarding you from the savages."

"No. We believe the sisterhood will be very interested in the tidings we bring." He was resilient. Already he had begun to recover himself.

"Come with me. Stay close. Do not stray. You know that an exception is being made. I alone can shield you once we go inside." She led them down, inside, into the great chamber where so often she had faced Gorry's worst, and where all the convocations of the cloister took place. "You will wait here, within the confines of this symbol." She indicated the floor. "If you stray, you will die." She went in search of Gorry.

Logic told her Gorry was not the one to inform. Gorry ran a bit short on basic sense. But tradition and custom, with virtually the force of law, demanded that she deal with her instructress first. It was up to Gorry to decide whether or not the situation required the attention of Senior Koenic.

Perhaps fate took a hand. For Gorry was not alone when Marika found her. Three sisters were with her, including Khles Gibany, who was her superior. "Mistress," Marika said, after impatiently working her way through all the appropriate ceremonials, "I have just come from the wall, where I watched a band of savages pursue three tradermales across the river. Deeming it unlikely that tradermales would be abroad in this weather and near Akard unless they had some critical communication to impart, I helped them to escape their pursuers and allowed them to scale the snowdrifts to the top of the wall. Upon inquiry, I learned that they did indeed bear a message from their senior addressed to the Akard cloister."

"And what was this message, pup?" Gorry asked. Her tone was only as civil as she deemed needful before witnesses. These days Gorry was civil only when appearances required. The passing of time made her ever more like Pohsit.

"I did not enquire, mistress. The nature of the situation suggested that it was not for me to do so. It suggested that I should turn to sisters wiser than I. So I led them down to the main hall, where they might shed the chill in their bones. I told them to wait there. They did suggest that their senior wished them to relate their message before the assembled cloister. It would seem the news they bring is bad."

Gorry became righteous in the extreme. Outsiders allowed into the packfast! *Male* outsiders. Her sisters, following the lead of Khles Gibany, proved to be more flexible. They shushed Gorry and began questioning Marika closely.

"I can tell you no more, sisters," she said, "unless you wish to review my feelings while I stood upon the wall, and the consequent reasoning which lent credence to them."

Gibany rose and manipulated herself onto her crutches. "I will be back soon. I agree with your feelings, Marika. There is something afoot. I will speak with the senior." She departed.

While Gorry glared daggers at Marika for further unsettling her life, the other two silth continued questioning her. They were only killing time, though. Already it was in the paws of Senior Koenic.

They saw the implications Marika had seen. The implications Gorry wished to ignore.

Once upon a time, years earlier, Khles Gibany had told Marika, in response to a question about Gorry: "There are those among us, pup, who prefer to live in myth instead of fact." Marika saw that clearly now.

Tradermales liked silth even less than the run of meth. The silth stand on male role assumption was harder than any packstead female's. The message brought by these males would have to be earthshaking, else they would not have come. And these days earthshaking news meant news about the nomads.

The myth-liver was the first to articulate what everyone was thinking. "The damned Critza fester has been overrun. They are trying to get us to take them in. No, say I. No. No. No. Let them stay out there in the wilderness. Let them fill the cookpots of savages. It is their ilk who have armed the grauken."

Grauken. Marika was startled to hear the word roll off a silth tongue.

"I do not believe they bear tidings of the fall of Critza, mistress. They did not look dispossessed. They just look exhausted and distressed." She did not put much force into her statement. She was being extremely careful with Gorry these days. And striving to build goodwill among the other sisters.

Gibany returned. "We are to report to the hall. We will hear what the males have to say. Nothing will be decided till they have spoken."

II

The leader of the tradermales, who made Marika so uneasy, called himself Bagnel. He was known to some of the sisters. He had spoken for his packfast before, though Marika did not recall having ever seen him anywhere but in that far clearing.

Another lesson: pay attention to everything happening. There was no telling what might become important in later days.

Bagnel's history of dealing with silth had led to his selection as leader of his mission.

"There were seven of us who left Critza," he said, after explaining his circumstances. "Myself and our six strongest, best fighters. Nomads caught our wind immediately, though we followed your own example and traveled by night. Four of us fell along the way, exhausted, and were taken by savages. We could not stop to help."

Gorry made nasty remarks about males and was ignored by all but a small minority of the assembled sisters. Clever Bagnel had placed a debt upon Akard with his opening remarks. He implied that the news he carried was worth four of his brethren's lives.

"Go on," the senior told him. "Gorry. Restrain yourself."

Marika stood behind her instructress, as was proper, and was embarrassed for her when she heard someone remark, "Old Gorry is getting senile." It was an intimation that Gorry would not be taken seriously much longer. Though Marika nursed her own black hatred, she felt for the old female.

"The journey took two days—"

"This is not relevant," the senior said. "If the tidings you bear are worthy, we will be in your debt. We are not here to trade. Be direct."

"Very well. Four days ago the nomads attacked Critza again. We drove them off, as we have before, but this time it was a close thing. They have acquired a quantity of modern weapons. They caused us a number of casualties. Their tactics, too, were more refined. Had they been more numerous the fortress would have fallen."

The senior stirred impatiently, but allowed Bagnel to establish the background. Silth exchanged troubled glances and subdued whispers. Marika felt the fur on her spine stir, though she did not quite understand what was being said.

Bagnel's gaze strayed her way several times while he spoke. That did nothing to make her more comfortable.

"We took prisoners," Bagnel continued. "Among them were several huntresses of standing. Upon questioning them we made several interesting discoveries. The most important, from the viewpoint of the sisterhood here, was the unmasking of a plan for an attack upon Akard."

That caused a stir, and considerable amusement. Attack Akard? Savages? That was a joke. The nomads would be slaughtered in droves.

"One of those prisoners had been in on the planning. We obtained all the details she knew." Bagnel drew a fat roll of hide from within his coat. He stripped the skin away to reveal a sheaf of papers. "The master directed that a copy of her testimony be given you." He offered the papers to the senior.

"You appear to take this more seriously than seems warranted," Senior Koenic said. "Here we are in no danger from savages, come they singly or in all the hordes of the north."

"That is not true, Senior. And that is why we risked seven fighters sorely needed at Critza. Not only have the nomads acquired modern weapons; they are convinced that they can neutralize most of your power. They have both silth and wehrlen with them and those will participate in the attack. So our informant told us. And she was incapable of invention at the time."

Bagnel's gaze strayed to Marika. To her consternation, she found she was unable to meet his eye.

From the reaction of the silth around her, Marika judged that what Bagnel had described was possible. The sisters were very disturbed. She heard the name "Serke" whispered repeatedly, often with a pejorative attached.

Senior Koenic struck the floor three times with the butt of her staff of office. Absolute silence filled the hall. "I will have order here," the senior said. "Order. Are we rowdy packsteaders?" She began to read the papers the tradermales had given her. Her teeth showed ever more as she proceeded. Black anger smoldered behind her eyes.

She lifted her gaze. "You are correct, tradermale. The thing they propose is hideous, but it is possible—assuming they surprised us. You have blessed us. We owe you a great deal. And the Reugge do not forget their debts."

Bagnel made gestures of gratitude and obeisance Marika suspected to be more diplomatic than genuine. He said, "If this is the true feeling of the Akard senior, the Critza master would present a small request."

"Speak."

"There is equally a master plan for the capture of Critza. And it will work even though we know about it. Unless…"

"Ah. You did not bring us this dark news out of love." The senior's voice was edged with a brittle sarcasm.

It did not touch the messenger. "The master suggests that you might find it in the Reugge interest to help sustain at least one other civilized stronghold here in the Ponath."

"That may be true. It may not be. To the point, trader."

"As you will, Senior." Bagnel's gaze strayed to Marika once again. "The master has asked that two or three sisters, preferably dark-siders, be sent to help Critza repel the expected attack. They would not be at great risk, as the nomads would not expect their presence. The master feels that, should the nomads suffer massive defeats at both fortresses in rapid succession, they will harass us no further. At least for this winter. Their own dead will sustain them through the season."

Marika shuddered.

The evidence had been undeniable in the packsteads she had seen last summer. The nomads had let the grauken come in and become a working member of their society. Whatever had shattered the old pack structure and driven them into hording up had changed much more than that.

"Your master thinks well. For a male. He may be correct. Presuming these papers carry the whole story." A hint of a question lurked around the edges of the senior's remark.

"I participated in the questioning, Senior. I am willing to face a silth truthsaying to attest to their authenticity and completeness."

Marika was impressed. A truthsaying was a terrible thing to endure.

"Send Marika," Gorry blurted. "She is perfect for this. And no one will miss her if she were lost."

"Ought to send you," someone muttered. "No one would miss you."

Gorry heard. She scanned the assembly, her expression stricken.

The senior glared at Gorry, angered by the unsolicited suggestion. But then she turned thoughtful.

Marika's heart fell.

"There is truth in what you say, Gorry," Senior Koenic said. "Even though you say it from base motives. Thus does the All mock the littleness in our hearts, making us speak the truth in the guise of lies. Very well, tradermale. You shall have your sisters. We will send three of our youngest and strongest—though not necessarily our most skillful—for they face a journey that will be hard. You will not want to lose any along the way."

Bagnel's face remained stone.

"So? What say you?"

"Thank you, Senior."

Senior Koenic clapped paws. "Strohglay." A sister opened a door and beckoned. A pair of senior workers stepped inside. The senior told them, "Show these males to cells where they may spend the night. Give them of the best food we possess. Tradermale, you will not leave your quarters under any circumstances. Do you understand?"

"Yes, Senior."

Koenic gestured to the workers. They led the males away.

The senior asked, "Are there any volunteers? No? No one wants to see the inside of the mysterious Critza fortress? Marika? Not even you?"

No. Not Marika. She did not volunteer.

Neither did anyone else.

III

Marika did not volunteer. Nevertheless, she went. There was no arguing with Senior Koenic.

Much of the time they traveled in Biter's light, upon snow under which, yards below, the waters of the Hainlin ran colder than a wehrlen's heart. In places that snow was well packed, for the nomads used the rivercourse as their highway through the wilderness, though they traveled only by day.

Braydic said most of the nomads were south of Akard now, harrying the meth who lived down there. She said the stream of invective and impossible instructions from Maksche never ceased. And never did any good. The only way they could enforce their orders was to come north themselves. Which was what Senior Koenic wished to compel.

Marika was miserable and frightened. The stillness of the night was the stillness of death. Its chill was the cold of the grave. Though Biter lingered overhead, she felt the Hainlin canyon was a vast cave, and that cave called up all her old terrors of Machen Cave.

There was something wicked in the night.

"They only sent me because they hope to be rid of me," she told Grauel and Barlog. Both her packmates had volunteered to come when they heard the call for huntress volunteers and learned that Marika had been assigned to go. Marika wondered if the silth could have kept them back had they wanted.

"Perhaps," Barlog said. "And perhaps, if one might speak freely before a sister, you attribute the motives of the guilty few to the innocent many."

Grauel agreed. "You are the youngest, and one of the least popular silth. None can dispute that. But your unpopularity is of your own making, Marika. Though you have been trying. You have been trying. Ah. Wait! Listen and reflect. If you apply reason to your present circumstance, you will have to admit there is no one in Akard more suited to this, the rest of the situation aside. You have become skilled in the silth's darkest ways. The deadly ways. You are young and strong. And you endure the cold better than anyone else."

"If one might dare speak freely before a sister," Barlog said again, "you are whining like a disappointed pup. You are shifting blame to others and refusing responsibility yourself. I recall you in your dam's loghouse. You were not that way then. You were a quiet one, and a dreamer, and a pest to all, but mistress of your own actions. You have developed a regressive streak. And it is not at all attractive in one with so much promise."

Marika was so startled by such bold chiding that she held her tongue. And as she marched, pressed by the pace the tradermales set, she reflected upon what the huntresses had said. And in moments when she was honest with herself, she could not deny the truth underlying their accusations.

She had come to pity herself, in a silth sort of way. She had come to think certain things her due without her having to earn them, as the silth seemed to think the world owed them. She had fallen into one of Gorry's snares.

There had been a time when she had vowed that she would not slip into the set of mind she so despised in her instructress. A time when she had believed her packstead background would immunize her. Yet she was beginning to mirror Gorry.

Many miles later, after much introspection, she asked, "What did you mean when you said 'so much promise,' Barlog?"

Barlog gave her a look. "You never tire of being told that you are special, do you?"

When Marika threatened to explode, Grauel laid one hard paw upon her shoulder. Her grip tightened painfully. "Easy, pup."

Barlog said, "One hears things around the packfast, Marika. They often talk about you showing promise of rising high. As you have been told so many times. Now they are saying you may rise higher than anyone originally suspected, if they teach you well at Maksche cloister."

"If?"

"They're definitely going to send you come summer. This is fact. The senior has asked Grauel and I if we wish to accompany you when you go."

There was a chance that had not occurred to Marika. Always she had viewed Maksche with great dread, certain she would have to face a totally alien environment alone.

A hundred yards along, Grauel said, "She is not all ice water and stone heart, this Koenic. She knew we would follow, even if that meant walking all the miles down the Hainlin. Perhaps she recalls her own pack. They say she came as you did, half grown, from an upper Ponath pack, and Braydic with her as punishment for their dam having concealed them from the silth. Their packstead was one of those the nomads destroyed during the second winter. There was much talk of it at the time."

"Oh." Marika marched on, for a long time alone with her thoughts and the moonlight. Three moons were in the sky now. Every riverside tree wore a three-fingered paw of shadow.

She began to feel a subtle wrongness in the night. At first it was just something on the very edge of perception, like an irritating but distant sound mostly ignored. But it would not be ignored. It grew stronger as she trudged along. Finally, she said, "Grauel, go tell that Bagnel to stop. We are headed into something. I need time to look ahead without being distracted by having to watch my feet."

By the time Grauel returned with Bagnel, she knew what it was. The tradermale asked, "You sense trouble, sister?" In the field, working together, he seemed to have an easy way about him. Marika felt almost comfortable in his presence.

"There is a nomad watchpost ahead. Around that bend, up on the slope. I can feel the heat of them."

"You are certain?"

"I have not gone out for a direct look, if that is what you mean. But I am sure here." She smote her heart.

"That is good enough for me. Beckhette." He waved. The tradermale he called Beckhette was what he called his "tactician," a term apparently from the tradermale cult tongue. The male arrived. "Nomad sentries around the next bend. Take them out or sneak past?"

"Depends. They have any silth or wehrlen with them?" The question was addressed to Marika. "Our choice of tactics must hinge on which course allows us the maximum time undiscovered by the horde."

Marika shrugged. "To tell you that I will have to walk the dark."

Both Bagnel and Beckhette nodded as if to say, go ahead.

She slipped down through her loophole, found a ghost, rode it over the slopes, slipping up on the nomads from the far side. She was cautious. The possibility that she might face a wild silth or wehrlen disturbed her.

They were sleepy, those nomad watchers. But there were a dozen of them huddled in a snow shelter, and with them was a male who had the distinctive touch-scent of a wehrlen. And he was alert. Something in the night had wakened him to the possibility of danger.

Marika did not withdraw to confer. She struck, fearing the wehrlen might discover her party before she could go back, talk, and return.

He was strong, but not trained. The struggle lasted only seconds. Pulling away, craft touched her. She squeezed her ghost down to where it could affect the physical world, undermined the shelter, brought tons of snow down upon the nomads before they fully realized they were under attack.

She returned to flesh and reported what she had done.

"Good thinking," Bagnel said. "When they are found it will look like a regrettable accident."

From that point onward Marika did not daydream. She lent all her attention to helping her sisters locate nomad watchers.

The tradermales insisted on taking the last few miles over a mountain. They were convinced they would encounter a strong nomad force if they continued to follow the watercourse. They did not want to waste their silth surprise by springing it in a struggle for the survival of a pawful.

They made that last climb in sunlight, among giant, concealing trees far larger than any Marika had yet seen in any of her wanderings. She was amazed that life could take so many different forms so close to her ancestral home—though she did reflect that she and Grauel and Barlog had wandered more of the world than any of the Degnan since the pack had come north in times almost immemorial.

They smelled smoke before they reached the ridgeline. Some of the huntresses thought it from the hearth fires of Critza, but the tradermales showed a frightened excitement which had nothing to do with an anticipation of arriving home. They hurried as if to an appointment with terrible news.

Terrible news it was.

From the heights they looked down on the hold which had been the traders' headquarters. Somehow, one wall had been broken. Smoke still rose, though no fire could be seen. The snowfields surrounding the packfast were littered with bodies. Marika did not immediately recognize what they were, for they appeared small from her viewpoint.

Bagnel squatted on his hams and studied the disaster. For a long time he said nothing. When he did speak, it was in an emotionless monotone. "At least they did not take it cheaply. And some of ours escaped."

Not knowing why she did so exactly, Marika scratched his ears the way one did when comforting a pup. He had removed his hat to better listen for sounds from below.

He looked at her oddly, which caused her to feel a need to explain. "I saw all this happen at my packstead four years ago. Help came too late then, too."

"But it came."

"Yes. As it did here. Seen from an odd angle, you might think me repaying a debt."

"A small victory here, then. At horrible cost we have gotten the silth to be concerned." He donned his hat, stood. His iron gaze never left the smoking ruins. "You females stay here. My brothers and I will see what is to be seen." He and the other two started down the slope. Ten paces along, he stopped, turned to Marika. "If something happens to us, run for Akard. Do not waste a second on us. Save yourselves. It will be your turn soon enough."

Return to Akard? Marika thought. And how do that? They had come south carrying rations for three days, no one having given thought to the chance that they might find Critza destroyed. They had thought there would be food and shelter at the end of the trail, not the necessity to turn about and march right back to Akard.

No matter. She would survive. She had survived the trek to Akard when she was much younger. She would survive again.

She closed her eyes and went into that other place she had come to know so well, that place where she had begun to feel more at home than in the real world. She ducked through her loophole into a horde of ghosts in scarlet and indigo and aquamarine. The scene of the Critza massacre was a riot of color, like a mad drug dream. Why did they gather so? Were they in fact the souls of meth who had died here? She thought not. But she did not know what to think them otherwise.

It did not matter. Silth did not speculate much on the provenance of their power. They sensed ghosts and used them. Marika captured a strong one.

She rode the ghost downhill, floating a few yards behind Bagnel.

He did not much heed the fallen nomads. Marika ignored them, too, but could not help noticing many were ripped and torn like those she had seen at the site of the tradermale ambush last summer. Only a few—and all those inside the shattered wall—bore cut or stab wounds. And she never saw a one with an arrow in his or her corpse.

Odd.

Odder still the fortress, much of which recalled Braydic's communications center. Though Marika was sure much of what she saw had nothing to do with sending or receiving messages. Strange things. She would have liked to have gone down and laid on paws.

The agony of the tradermales was too painful to watch. Marika withdrew to her flesh. With the others she waited, crouched in the snow, leaning upon her javelin, so motionless winter's breath might have frozen her at last.

Bagnel spent hours prowling the ruins of Critza while the silth and huntresses shivered on the hillside. When he returned, he and his companions climbed slowly, bearing heavy burdens.

They arrived. Bagnel caught his breath, said, "There is nothing here for any of us now. Let us return and do what we may for Akard." His voice was as cold as the hillside, edged with hatred. "There is a small cave a few miles along the ridge. Assuming it is not occupied, we can rest there before we start back." He led off, and said nothing more till Marika asked what he had learned in the ruins.

"It was as bad as you can imagine. But a few did break out on the carriers. The pups, I suppose. Unless the nomads carried them off to their pots. There was very little left, though they did not manage to break the door to the armory. We recovered what weapons and ammunition we could carry. The rest... you will know soon enough."

Marika looked at him oddly. Distracted, he was using many words she did not know.

"They stripped the place like scavengers strip a corpse. To the bone. Stone still sits upon stone there, but Critza is dead. After these thousand years. It has become but a memory."

Marika festered with questions. She asked none of them. It was a time for the tradermales to be alone with their grief.

A mile along his trail Bagnel halted. He and his brethren faced the direction they had come. Marika watched them curiously. They seemed to be waiting for something....

A great gout of fire-stained smoke erupted over the ridge recently quit. It rolled high into the sky. A great rumbling thunder followed. Bagnel shuddered all over. His shoulders slumped. Without a word he turned and resumed the march.

CHAPTER THIRTEEN

I

"Thank the All," Grauel said with feeling as they rounded the last bend of the Hainlin and dimly saw Akard on its headland, brooding gray and silver a mile away. "Thank the All. They have not destroyed Akard."

There had been a growing, seldom-voiced fear that their trek north would be rewarded with the sight of another gutted packfast, that they would round that final bend and find themselves doomed to the mocking grasp of the hunger already gnawing their bellies. Even the silth had feared, though logically they knew they would have received some sort of touch had the fortress been attacked.

But there the fortress stood, inviolate. The chill of the north wind was no longer so bitter. Marika bared her teeth and dared that wind to do its damnedest.

"This is where they ambushed us," Bagnel said. "One group pushed us while the other waited in that stand of trees there."

"Not this time," Marika replied. She looked through the blue-gray haze of lightly falling snow, seeing evidence of a nomad presence. The other silth did the same. The huntresses stood motionless, teeth chattering, arms ready.

Marika sensed nothing untoward anywhere. The only meth life lay within the packfast, brooding there upon its bluff.

"Come." She resumed walking.

There was no trail. Enough snow had fallen, and had been blown, to bury their southbound trail.

When they were closer and the packfast was more distinct, Marika saw that there had been changes. A long feather of rumpled snow trailed down the face of the bluff below the fortress, like the aftermath of an avalanche. Even as she walked and watched, meth appeared above and dumped a wheelbarrow load of snow, which tumbled down the feather.

The workers had been doing that all winter, keeping the roofs and inner courts clear, but the mound had never been so prominent. It had grown dramatically in five days. Marika was curious.

The workers saw them, too. Moments later something touched Marika. The other silth received touches too. The sisters would be waiting when they arrived, anticipating bad news.

Why else would they have returned so soon?

Marika sensed a distant alien presence as they began the climb from the river. The other silth sensed it, too. "On our trail," one said.

"No worry," the other observed. "We are far ahead, and within the protection of our sisters."

Even so, Marika was nervous. She watched the rivercourse as she climbed, and before long spotted the nomads. There were a score of them. They were traveling fast. Trail had been broken for them. But they never presented any real threat. They turned back after reaching the point where the travelers had begun their climb to the packfast.

The sisters—and many of their dependents—were waiting in the main hall. Many were males. Marika was astonished. She asked Braydic, "What happened? What is this? Males inside the fortress."

"My truesister decided to bring everyone inside the wall. Nomads were prowling around out there every day while you were gone. In ever greater numbers. Only the workers have been going out. Armed."

Marika had noted the workers clearing the snow away from the north wall, hoisting it to the wall's top and barrowing it around to the spill visible from the river.

"They have gotten very bold," Braydic reported. "My truesister feared they might have good reason. We might even need the males."

Senior Koenic called for a report from Marika's party.

Bagnel did the talking. He kept it simple. "They were all slain," he said. "Everyone in Critza, both brethren and those we gave shelter. Except a pawful who got out on the carriers. The wall was breached with explosives. The nomads took some arms and everything else. They were unable to penetrate the armory. We blew that before we left the ruin. Though I am sufficiently realistic to know you would not, if you were to ask my advice, I would tell you you should ask your seniors to evacuate Akard. The stakes have been raised. The game has sharpened. This is the last stronghold. They will come soon and come strong, and they will make an end of you."

Marika was both mystified and startled. The former because she did not understand all Bagnel was saying, the latter because Senior Koenic was considering the advice seriously. After reflection, Senior Koenic replied, "All this will be reported. We are in continuous contact with Maksche. I have my hopes, but I do not believe they will take us out. It seems likely the Serke Community is helping the nomads in an effort to push the Reugge out of the Ponath. I expect policy will be to stand fast even in the face of assured disaster. To maintain the Reugge face and claim."

The tradermale shrugged. He seemed indifferent to the world now that his mission was complete. His home had been destroyed. His folk were all dead. For what did he have to live? Marika understood his feelings all too well.

She worried his remarks about the Serke and evacuation. That baffled her completely. It had something to do with those parts of her education that had been left vague deliberately. She did know that competition between sisterhoods could become quite vigorous, and that there were centuries of bad blood between the Serke and Reugge. But she never imagined that it could become so intense, so deadly, that, as the senior implied, one sisterhood would help creatures like the nomads to attack another.

That meeting did nothing but frighten everyone. Only a few of the older silth, like Gorry, refused to believe that the danger was real. Gorry remained convinced that any nomad assault would see the surrounding countryside littered with savage corpses while leaving Akard entirely unscathed.

Marika was convinced that Gorry was overconfident. But Gorry had not seen Critza....

Even that might not have convinced the old one. She had reached that stage of life where she would believe only what she wished to be true.

II

Marika visited Braydic in the communications center the morning after her return. Even now she became mildly disoriented if she passed too near the tree and dish on top, but her discomfiture was nothing like that experienced by most of the Akard silth. Braydic believed she would conquer it entirely, given time.

Braydic had several communications screens locked into continuous operation. Each showed different far meth at work in very similar chambers. "Is that Maksche we are seeing, Braydic?" Marika asked.

"That one and that one. They are not going to evacuate us. You know that? But they want to keep close watch on what happens here. I believe they hope the nomads do attack."

"Why would they want that?"

"Maybe so they can find out for sure if the Serke are behind everything. The nomads will not be able to break in against silth without silth help. Though that would not be proof enough in itself. If we take prisoners and questioning reveals a connection, then Reugge policies toward the Serke would harden. So far it has been one of those cases where you know what is happening and who is doing it, but there has been no court-sound proof. No absolute evidence of malice." Braydic shuddered.

"What?" Marika asked.

"I was thinking of Most Senior Gradwohl. She is a hard, bitter, tough old bitch. Cautious on the outside but secretly a gambler. As we all do, she knows the Reugge are weaker than the Serke. That we stand no chance in any direct confrontation. She might try something bold or bizarre."

Marika did not understand all this talk of the Serke and whatnot. She did know there was no friendship between the Reugge and Serke communities, and that there seemed to be blood in it. But the rest was out of that knowledge that had been concealed from her for so long. Now the meth spoke as if she were as informed as they.

She was not as naive as she pretended either.

"What might be an example?"

Braydic was more open than the silth, but there were things she never discussed either. Now, in her distraction, she might be vulnerable to the sly question.

Braydic had learned her trade at the cloister in TelleRai, which was one of the great southern cities. In her time she had encountered most of the most senior sisters of the Reugge and other orders. She had been a technician of very high station till her truesister's error had gotten the pair of them banished to the land of their birth. Marika often wondered what had caused their fall from grace, but never had asked. About that time and that event Braydic was very closed.

"A sudden direct attack upon the Ruhaack cloister springs to mind. An attempt to eliminate the seniors of the Serke Community. Or even something more dire. Darkwar, perhaps. Who knows? Bestrei cannot remain invincible forever."

"Bestrei? Who is Bestrei? Or what?"

"Who. Bestrei is a Mistress of the Ship. The best there is. And she is the Serke champion, thrice victorious in darkwar."

"And darkwar? What is that?"

"Nothing about which you need concern yourself, pup. Of faraway meth and faraway doings. We are here in Akard. We would do well to keep our minds upon our own situation." Braydic eyed a screen spattered with numbers. Marika could now read displays as well as her mentor. This was a reference to a problem with a generator in the powerhouse. "You will have to leave now, pup. I have work to do. We are getting some icing out there, despite the fires." Braydic called the powerhouse technicians. While she awaited their response she muttered something about the All-be-damned primitive equipment given frontier outposts.

Braydic was not in a communicative mood. Marika decided there was no need pressing for something she could not get. She abandoned the communications center for her place upon the wall.

The wind was in its usual bitter temper. A steady but light snow was falling, confining the world to a circle perhaps a mile across. It was a world without color. White. Gray shadows. The black of a few trees, most of which appeared only as blobbish shapes floating on white. Marika wished for a glimpse of the sun. The sun unseen for months. The peculiar sun that had changed color during the few years she had been in this world, fading slowly through deeper shades of orange.

At long last Braydic had let fall what the winters were about. She said the sun and its gaggle of planetary pups had entered a part of the night that was extremely thick with dust. This dust absorbed some of the sun's energy. It had hastened a planetary cooling cycle already centuries old. The system would be inside the dust cloud for a long time to come. The world would get very much colder before it passed out. That would not happen in Marika's time.

She shivered. Much worse before it got better.

Below, workers continued the endless task of carrying snow away from the wall. The restless north wind brought drifts down almost as fast as they could carry it away.

Farther up the headland, other workers were building a plow-shaped snowbreak intended to divert blowing, drifting snow into the valley of the eastern fork of the Hainlin, away from both the wall and the powerhouse on the Husgen side.

Marika spotted Grauel among the huntresses watching over the workers on that project. She raised a paw. Grauel did not see her. She was wasting no attention on the packfast.

Nomad parties had come within touch of the silth twice during the past night. One party had been large. Their movements suggested they were maneuvering according to the plan Bagnel had wrung from a prisoner down at Critza.

Several silth were out with the workers, adding their might to that of the guardian huntresses. Marika was surprised to see Khles Gibany among them. But Gibany never had permitted her handicap to control her life.

She looked very strange bobbing around on crutches specially fitted so she could travel on snow.

Marika went inside herself and found her loophole. She slipped through into the realm of specter. And was startled to find it almost untenanted.

Strange. Disturbingly strange.

There were moments when the population of ghosts numbered more or less than normal, times when finding one appropriate to one's purpose was difficult, but never had she seen the realm so sparsely occupied. Marika came back out and looked for a sister on watch.

The first she found answered her question without her having to ask. The truth was graven on the silth's face. She was frightened.

This, if ever there was one, was a time for a nomad attack. The power of the Akard silth would never be weaker.

Marika hurried back to her place, waved at the workers and Grauel.

The news had reached Senior Koenic, Marika saw. The silth of Akard had begun to come to the rampart. Outside, the working parties had begun gathering their tools. Everything seemed quite orderly, indicating preparation beforehand.

Indicating planning not communicated to Marika.

She was irked. They never bothered telling her anything, though *she* considered herself an important factor in Akard's life and defense. What was wrong with these silth? Would they never consider her as more than a troublesome pup? Did she not have a great deal to contribute?

Workers already within the walls were being armed. Another facet of planning of which she had been left ignorant. She was surprised to see males mount the walls bearing javelins.

Marika sensed the nomads approaching before the last workers started for the packfast gate. She did not bother reporting. She reached out and touched Khles Gibany. *They come. They are close. Hurry up.*

Hobbling about, Gibany hurried the workers and formed a screen of huntresses bearing spears and shields. But she allowed no one to become precipitate. Even for silth tools were too precious to abandon.

Marika sensed the enemy in the snow. They were approaching Akard all across the ridge. There were thousands of them. Even now, after so many years of it, Marika could not imagine what force could have drawn so many together, nor what power kept them together. The horde the wehrlen had brought south had been implausible. This was impossible.

The forerunners of the host appeared out of the snow only a few hundred yards beyond Khles Gibany and the workers. They halted awhile, waiting for those behind to come up. Gibany remained cool, releasing no one to return to the fortress unburdened with tools.

Perhaps she was unconcerned because she believed she was safely under the umbrella of protection extended by her silth sisters.

Marika sensed a far presence not unlike that of her sisters. She tried to go down through her loophole to take a look, but when she got down there she could not find a single usable ghost. Without ghosts she could but touch, and there was little chance of touching without her reaching for someone she knew. It was certain she could effect nothing.

She returned to the world to find the forerunner nomads howling toward Gibany's group. Fear seized her heart. Grauel was out there! Javelins arced through the air. A couple of nomads fell. Then the attackers smashed against huntress's shields. Spears and swords hacked and slashed. The nomads screeched war cries. The line of huntresses staggered backward under the impact of superior numbers. A few nomads slipped through.

Marika realized that these attackers were the best the nomads had. Their most skilled huntresses. They were trying to effect something sudden. One nomad suddenly shrieked and clasped her chest, fell thrashing in the snow. Then another and another followed. The silth had found something to use against them, though their range seemed limited and the killing was nothing so impressive as other slaughters Marika had witnessed.

The swirl of combat began to separate out. Still forms scattered the snowfield. Not a few were Akard huntresses, though most were nomads. The nomads retreated a hundred yards. The silth seemed unable to reach them there. Marika went down through her loophole and found that it was indeed difficult to reach that far. There were a few ghosts now, but so puny as to be jokes. She retired and watched the nomad huntresses stand watch while the Akard workers and huntresses continued their withdrawal.

Khles Gibany. Where was Gibany? The crippled silth was no longer there to direct the retreat. Marika ducked through her loophole again and went searching.

She could not find a body.... There. Somehow, the nomad huntresses had managed to take Gibany captive. What had they done? The Khles was unable to call upon her talent to help herself. And Marika, though she strained till it ached, could not apply enough force to set her free.

Nomad males with farming tools came forward. Two hundred yards from the snow break they began excavating trenches in the old hard-packed snow. They threw the dugout snow to the Akard side of the trench, used their shovel to beat it into a solid wall.

Marika became aware that someone had joined her. She glanced to her right, saw the tradermale Bagnel. "They learned at Critza," he said. "Curse them." He settled down on the icy stone and began assembling a metal contraption he had been carrying since his initial appearance at Akard. Marika saw his two brothers doing likewise elsewhere.

Out on the snow, beyond the trench, nomad workers had driven a tall post deep into the snow. Now they were laying a layer of rock and gravel around it. Others stood by with arms loaded with wood. Marika was puzzled till she saw several huntresses drag Gibany to the post.

They tied the one-legged silth so her foot dangled inches from the surface. They then piled wood around her. Even from where she watched, Marika could sense Gibany's fear and rage. Rage founded in the fact that she could do nothing to halt them, for all she was one of the most powerful silth of Akard.

"They are taunting us," Marika snarled. "Showing us we are powerless against them."

Bagnel grunted. He mounted his metal instrument upon a tripod, peered through a tube on top. He began twisting small knobs.

A runner carrying a torch came out of the snowfall, trotted up to where Gibany was bound. Marika slipped through her loophole once more, hearing Bagnel mutter "All right," as she went.

There was not a ghost to be found. Not a thing she could do for Gibany, unless—as several silth seemed to be doing already—she extended her touch and tried to take away some of the fear and agony soon to come.

Thunder cracked in her right ear.

Marika came back to flesh snarling, in the full grip of a fight-flight reflex. Bagnel looked at her with wide, startled eyes. "Sorry," he said. "I should have warned you."

She shook with reaction while watching him fiddle with his knobs. "Right," he said. And the end of his contraption spat fire and thunder. Far out on the snowscape, the nomad huntress bearing the torch leapt, spun, shrieked, collapsed, did not move again.

Marika gaped.

Facts began to add together. That time in the forest last summer, when she had heard those strange *tak-takk*ing noises. The time coming down the east fork with Khles Gibany and Gorry when the nomads attacked…

The instrument roared again. Another nomad flung away from Gibany.

Marika looked at the weapon in awe. "What is it?"

For a moment Bagnel looked at her oddly. Along the wall, his brethren were making similar instruments talk. "Oh," he murmured. "That is right. You are Tech Two pup." He swung the instrument slightly, seeking another target. "It is called a rifle. It spits a pellet of metal. The pellet is no bigger than the last joint of your littlest finger, but travels so fast it will punch right through a body." His weapon spat thunder. So did those of his brethren. "Not much point to this, except to harass them." *Bam!* "There are too many of them."

Below, the last of the workers and huntresses were coming in the gate. Only one of Akard's meth remained unsafe: Khles Gibany, tied to that post.

The nomad huntresses and workers had thrown themselves into the trench the workers had begun. Now Marika saw another wave hurrying forward from the forest beyond the fields. She could just make that out now. The snowfall was weakening.

Pinpoints of light flickered along the advancing nomad line, accompanied by a crackle like that of fat in a frying pan.

"Down, pup!" Bagnel snapped. "They are shooting back."

Something snarled past Marika. It took a bite out of the earflap on her hat. Another something smacked into the wall and whined away. She got down.

Bagnel said, "They have the weapons they captured at Critza, plus whatever else someone gave them." He sighted his weapon again, fired, looked at her with teeth exposed in a snarl of black humor. "Hang on. It is going to get exciting."

Marika rose, looked out. Someone had managed to get the torch into the wood piled round Gibany's foot. Gibany's fear had drawn her…. Once more through the loophole. Once more no ghosts of consequence. She reached with the touch to help Gibany endure. But half the silth on the wall were doing that, almost in a passive acceptance of fate. "No!" Marika said. "They will not do that. You. Bagnel. Show me how to use that thing." She indicated his weapon.

He eyed her a moment, shook his head. "I am not sure what you want to do, pup. But you will not do it with this." He patted the weapon. Snowflakes touching its tube were turning to steam. "It takes years to learn to use it properly."

"Then you will do it. Put one of your deadly pellets into Khles, to free her from agony. We cannot save her. The talent is denied us today. But we can rob the savages of their mockery by sending her to rejoin the All."

Bagnel gaped. "Mistress…."

Her expression was fierce, demanding.

"I could not, mistress. To raise paw against the silth. No matter the cause…."

Marika stared across the snow, ignoring the insect sounds swarming past her. Gibany had begun writhing in her bonds. The pain of the fire had torn all reason from her mind. She knew nothing but the agony now.

"Do it," Marika said in a low and intense voice so filled with power the tradermale began looking around as if seeking a place to run. "Do it now. Free her. I will take all responsibility. Do you understand?"

Teeth grinding, Bagnel nodded. Paws shaking, he adjusted knobs. He paused to get a grip on himself.

His weapon barked.

Marika stared at Gibany, defying the nomad snipers.

The Khles bucked against her bonds, sagged. Marika ducked through her loophole, grabbed the best ghost available, went looking.

Gibany was free. She would know no more pain.

Back. "It is done. I am in your debt, tradermale."

Bagnel showed her angry teeth. "You are a strange one, young mistress. And soon to be one joining your elder sister if you do not get yourself down." A steady rain of metal pounded against the wall. Swarms whined past. Marika realized most must be meant for her. She was the only target visible to the nomads.

She sped them a hand gesture of defiance, lowered herself behind a merlon.

One of Bagnel's brethren shouted at him, pointed. Out on the snowfield meth were running forward in tight bunches. Each bunch carried something. Bagnel and his comrades began shooting rapidly, concentrating on those groups. Some of the silth, too, managed to reach them. Marika saw nomads go down in the characteristic throes of silth death-sending. But three groups managed to carry their burdens into the snow trenches, where workers were still digging. Marika now understood why they were heaping the snow the way they were. It would block the paths of the pellets from the tradermales' weapons.

More nomads came from the woods. Some carried heavy packs, some nothing at all. The latter rushed to the burdens their predecessors had dropped, grabbed them up, hustled them forward.

The crackle of nomad rifles continued unabated. Twice Marika heard someone on the wall shriek.

"Get down as flat as you can," Bagnel told her. "And snuggle up tight against the merlon. They are going to start throwing the big stuff."

Puffs of smoke sprouted and blossomed above the nomad trenches, vanished on the wind. Muted crumpings came a moment later, a sort of soft threatening thumping. Where had she heard that before? That time when tradermales ambushed the nomads she and Arhdwehr were chasing...

"Down," Bagnel said, and yanked at her when she did not move fast enough to suit. He pressed her against the icy stone.

Something moaned softly in a rising pitch. There was a tremendous bang outside the wall, followed by a series of bangs, only one of which occurred behind the wall. That one precipitated a shriek which turned into the steady moan of a badly injured meth.

"They are getting the range," Bagnel explained. "Once they find it the bombs will come steady."

Where were the ghosts? How could silth battle this without their talents?

Why were the ghosts absent just when the savages elected to attack?

A second salvo came. Most fell short, though closer. Several did carry past the wall. They made a lot of noise but did little damage. The packfast was constructed of thick stone. Its builders had meant it to stand forever.

The entire third salvo fell inside the fortress. Marika sensed that that presaged a steady hammering.

A river of meth poured from the woods, burdened with ammunition for the engines throwing the bombs. Workers left their trenches and darted forward, hastily dug shallow holes in which to shelter. They worked their ways toward the snow break. Nomads carrying rifles followed them, only sporadically harassed by Bagnel and his brethren. The crackle of nomad rifle fire never slowed.

Several more packfast meth were hit.

"This is hopeless," Marika whispered. "We cannot fight back." She went down through her loophole again, and again found the ghost world all but barren. But this time she stayed, hoping for the stray chance to strike back. She sensed that many sisters were doing the same, with occasional success. Those who did find a tool spent their fury upon the crews of the bomb-throwing instruments.

Why was the ghost world so naked?

Marika waited with the patience of a hunting herdek, till the ghost she needed happened by. She pounced, seized it, commanded it, rode it out over the snowfields, past the nomads and their strange engines, through woods where thousands more nomads waited to move forward, and on to the very limit of her ability to control that feeble a ghost. And there she found the thing that she had sensed must exist, if only on the dimmest level.

A whole company of silth and wehrlen, gathered in one place, were pulling to them all the strong ghosts of the region. The air surrounding them boiled with color, denser than ever Marika had imagined. She thought the ghosts must be so numerous they would be visible to the eyes of untalented meth.

They were weak, these wild silth and wehrlen. Poorly trained. But in the aggregate they were able to summon the ghosts to them and so deny the Akard sisters access to their most potent defense.

Marika sought a focus, one strong silth controlling the group. Sometimes her Akard sisters linked under the control of the senior to meld into a more powerful whole.

A greater whole there was here, but not under any immediately evident central direction.

Straining her ghost, Marika picked a female and plucked at her heart.

The distance was too extreme. She was able to injure the wild silth but not to kill her.

Might that not be enough?

She moved among the nomads rapidly, stinging, and for a moment they lost control. A moment was enough. The ghosts scattered, driven by some mad pressure.

Marika felt her hold on her self growing tenuous. She had strained it too much. She hurried back to Akard. She was a moment slow getting through her loophole, and nearly panicked. There were stories about silth who did not get back. Terrible stories. Some might be true.

It took a moment to get oriented in her flesh.

She opened her eyes to discover the nomad rifle fire grown ragged, to the sight of nomads fleeing toward the woods, and many not making it.

This was the slaughter Gorry had prophesied and insisted would be visited upon the savage.

Feebly, Marika attained her feet and made her way toward Senior Koenic. The senior was out of body when she arrived. She waited till her elder came back from the place of ghosts. When the senior's eyes focused Marika reported all that she had seen and done.

"You are a strong one, pup," Koenic said while a nearby Gorry scowled at such praise. "I sensed them out there myself, but I did not have the strength to reach them. Will you be able to do it again?"

"I am not certain, mistress. Not right away. It is an exhausting thing to do." She was shaking with fatigue.

Senior Koenic stared out across the snowfields. "Already they begin to gather those-who-dwell to them again. Soon they will resume their attack. In an hour, perhaps. Marika, go down into the deepest cells, where their weapons cannot reach you. Rest. Do not come back up, for you are our final weapon and you must not be risked. When you are ready, scourge them again."

"Yes, mistress."

Gorry glowered, angered because her pupil should receive so much direct and positive attention. A glance told Marika that her instructress was scheming to take advantage of the day. She would have to watch her back. The moment the danger receded....

Senior Koenic mused, "Those of us who can will seize what you give us and punish the savages. They may take Akard from the Reugge, but they will pay dearly for the theft."

Marika was surprised at such negativity in the senior. It frightened her.

Grauel appeared from somewhere unseen. Marika felt pleased, restored, knowing her packmate was watching over her. The huntress followed her down into the courtyard, where bombs had destroyed everything not constructed of the most massive stone. In a strained, flat tone, Grauel said, "We had four years, Marika. Four more than seemed likely when last the nomad threatened us."

"Yes? You, too? Even you have surrendered to despair?" She could think of nothing else to say. "Express my regards to Barlog."

"I will. She will not be far away."

Marika passed through the great hall. It was a shambles. The overhead windows had been shattered by bombs. Its interior had been damaged badly. Though there had never been much in that chamber not made of stone, a few small fires burned there, being fought by worker pups too young to make a stand upon the wall. Marika paused to watch.

The word seemed to have run ahead. The pups looked at her in awe and fear and hope. She shook her head, afraid that too many meth, for whatever reason, had suddenly invested all their hopes in her.

It did not follow logically in her mind that because she had aborted the savage strategy once she should become the heartpiece of the packfast's defense.

While she stood there she thought of going to the communications center to see what news Braydic had, in hopes there would be a hope from Maksche, but she decided she would be drained too much by the electromagnetic fog. If she was to be the great champion of Akard—foolish as that seemed to her—then she must conserve herself.

She went down to her own cell, not as deep inside the fortress as Senior Koenic might have liked, but deep enough to be safe from bombs, and psychologically more comfortable than anyplace but her retreat upon the wall.

CHAPTER FOURTEEN

I

Jiana! You have brought this upon Akard and the Reugge.

Marika started out of her resting trance, shaken by the touch. What?...

Someone scratched at her cell door. She sat up. "Enter."

Barlog came in. She carried a tray laden with hot, high-energy food. "You'd better eat, Marika. I hear the silth need much energy to work their witchery."

The smell of food made Marika realize how hungry she was, how depleted her energies were. "Yes. You are wise, Barlog. I had not thought of it."

"What is the trouble, pup? You seem distracted."

She was. It was that touch. She took the tray without answering, dug in. Barlog stationed herself beside the door, beaming approval like a fussy old male.

Another scratch. Barlog met Marika's eye. Marika nodded. Barlog opened the door.

Grauel stepped inside, apparently relieved to see Barlog there. She carried a whole arsenal of weapons: shield, sword, knives, heavy spear, javelins, even a bow and arrows, which would be useless inside the fortress's tight corridors. Amused, Marika asked, "What are you supposed to be?"

"Your guardian."

"Yes?"

Grauel understood. "The old one. Gorry. She is saying wicked things about you."

"Such as?"

"She is walking the walls calling you doomstalker. She is telling everyone that the nomads have come down upon Akard because of you. She is telling everyone that you are accursed. She is saying that to end the threat the packfast must rid itself of the Jiana."

"Indeed?" That was a change from moments ago. "I thought that the senior had designated me Akard's great hope."

"There is that school of thought, too. Among the younger silth and hunt-resses. Especially those who have shared the hunt with you. Arhdwehr follows her around, giving the lie to all she says. But there are those among the oldest

174

silth who live in myth and mystery and hear only the magic in Gorry's claims. One savage packstead pup is a cheap price to pay for salvation."

"It is sad," Marika said. "We have ten thousand enemies howling outside the walls, so we divide against ourselves."

Grauel said, "I know huntresses who have served the Reugge elsewhere. They say it is ever thus among silth. Always at one another's throats—from safely behind the back. This time could be dangerous. There is much anxiety and much fear and a great desire for a cheap, magical solution. I will stand guard."

"I, too," Barlog said.

"As you will. Though I think you two would be of more value upon the wall."

Neither huntress said a word. Each had a stubborn look that said no command would return them to the wall while they fancied Marika threatened. Barlog took weapons from Grauel. After a last look at their charge, the two stepped outside.

Marika wondered if a bomb would blast them away from her door.

She did feel more secure, knowing they were there.

She ate, and returned to her resting trance.

Jiana. Your time is coming.

Angrily, Marika flung back, *Someone's time is near. The grauken is about to snap at someone's tail.* She felt Gorry reel under the impact of the unexpected response. She felt Gorry's terror.

She was pleased.

Yes. Someone's time was near, be it hers or that of the mad old instructress.

For a time Marika had difficulty resting. Memories of kagbeasts and other surprise horrors kept creeping into her mind.

II

She felt the bombs falling in the far distance, sending muted vibrations running through Akard's roots. The nomads were back. Their silth had recovered control of the ghost realm. She ignored the sounds, remained calm, waited till she had regained her full strength. Then she probed out through the cold stone, searching for a suitable ghost.

The hunt took much longer this time. In time she captured a weaker one and rode it farther afield in her search. And it was while she hunted that she witnessed the disaster on the Husgen.

The third dam, the far dam, up the Husgen several miles, erupted suddenly. A wild volcano of ice and snow went charging down the river, driven by the reservoir water. So mighty was its charge that it smashed through the ice upon the middle lake, poured over the face of the middle dam, gnawed at its foundations where it abutted the canyon walls, and broke it, too. The combined volume of two lakes rushed toward the final dam.

The disaster seemed to occur in slow motion because of its scale. Marika had ample time to grow angry.

Her anger, perhaps, allowed her to scale another barrier, as she had done during the attack upon the Degnan packstead. She found she was able to detect the presence of a far, strong ghost. She called it to her, mounted it, took it under control as the fury in the canyon reached the third dam, broke it, swamped the powerhouse, and bit deep into the face of the bluff on which Akard stood, so that great pillars of stone collapsed into the flood, taking a section of fortress wall with them. Several score huntresses, silth, and dependents tumbled down with the wall.

Whipped by rage, Marika drove her ghost steed out to the gathering of nomad silth. She hit them the way a kagbeast hit a herd of banger, slaughtering everything in reach. There would be time to savor and linger over the kill later.

Once again the nomad silth lost their concentration. And once again Marika's strength expired and she had to race back to her self, past the second rout of the besiegers, who were scourged much more terribly this time.

This time, as she parted from the wild silth gathering, Marika did sense the presence of a central control, a trained silth. But this control was stationed far from the main gathering, directing them from both safety and anonymity in the eyes of the sisters of Akard.

A trained silth, yes, certainly. And a powerful one. Perhaps the Serke guiding influence the senior suspected, and so wanted to capture.

Perhaps she was the key, Marika thought.

Marika slipped into her own flesh and lay there gasping.

"Are you ill, pup?"

Grauel was bending over her, face taut with concern.

"No. It is hard work, making the silth magic. Bring me some sweetened tea. A lot of sweetened tea." Her head was pounding. "Make it one cup of goyin to begin." She tried to sit up. Grauel had to help her. "I stopped them, Grauel. For a while. But they destroyed the dams."

She wondered what Braydic was doing now she could get no more power from the powerhouse. What would they be thinking down in Maksche? Would loss of contact force them to move finally? When it was too late?

Grauel went for the teas while Barlog stood in the doorway, heavy spear in one paw, sword in the other. When Marika gave her a querying look, she said only, "Gorry has found a new slander to spread. She is accusing you of murdering Khles Gibany, and of trafficking with males."

An accusation that would be hard to deny, Marika realized. Anyone who had been trying to help Gibany weather the agony of burning would have realized a tradermale projectile had ended her trial.

Senior Koenic came down soon after Grauel returned with the teas. It seemed an age since she had come back to flesh, but it could not have been more than fifteen minutes. "You did very well this time, pup." There was a light in the senior's eyes that baffled Marika. Mixed fear and respect, she supposed.

"Senior... Senior, I think I touched a true silth that time. She was beyond the nomads, hiding, but I am sure she was fully trained and exceptionally strong. And there was an alien flavor about her."

"Ah! Good news and dark. We may not die in vain. I must relay this to Maksche immediately, before Braydic's reserve power fails. It is not proof, but it is one more hint that the Serke are moving against us." She vanished in a swish of dark clothing.

Marika allowed the goyin free run and lay back to sleep. Many hours passed while her body recovered from the drain she had placed upon it. When she finally awakened, she was instantly aware that there was fighting inside the packfast proper. Panicky, she dove through her loophole and explored.

Nomad huntresses had gotten inside, coming around the end of the wall where it had collapsed. More were coming all the time, despite the arrows of Akard's huntresses and the rifles of the tradermales. Two thousand nomads lay dead upon the snowfields, but still they came, and still they died. They were a force as unstoppable as winter itself.

It was insanity. It was nothing any meth of the upper Ponath could have imagined in her worst nightmare. It was blood-soaked reality.

Most of the day had passed. It was late. If she could turn the attack once more, Akard would have the night to recuperate, to counterattack, to something. Night was the world of the silth....

Grauel and Barlog heard her stirring. They looked in. "Finally coming around?" Barlog asked.

"Yes. You look awful. You need some rest."

"No. We have to guard this door." And there was that in Barlog's stance which said that the guardianship had been tested, though the huntress appeared unwilling to say how.

Grauel said, "There are those now willing to appease the All with the sacrifice of a doomstalker."

"Oh."

Just the slightest hint of fear edged Barlog's voice as she asked, "Is there anything you can do to stop the nomads, Marika? They are inside the packfast now."

"I was about to do what I can. Try to have me some tea and food here when I come back."

"It will be here," Grauel promised.

Marika slipped through her loophole. Desperately, she hunted for an appropriate ghost. And the thing she finally found was a monster, discovered hovering high above the packfast. It never had occurred to her to seek upward before. A set of mind she realized was shared by all the silth she knew. All were surface oriented.

Once she bestrode the monster, she immediately became aware of others, higher still, even more monstrous, but the sensing of them was dim, and they were too strong to control. She stayed with the ghost she had, and rushed it toward the nomad silth.

This time she sensed the control of the silth clearly as she approached. Marika was stronger than she had ever been. She located the strange sister and stole toward her, and took her entirely by surprise.

She pounced. There was an instant of startled "Who are you?" before she ripped the female's flesh, scattering her heart and blood across an acre of snow.

Marika was appalled. The silth had, almost literally, exploded.

It was a strong ghost.

She savaged the nomad silth as well, slaying several score before she became so body-loose she had to withdraw. She fled to Akard, where her sisters were again slaughtering nomads by the hundreds.

But there were hundreds inside the fortress, unable to flee, and they continued fighting, as cornered huntresses would.

Too many silth sisters had been slain during the attack. Those who survived were hard pressed, even with their powers restored. And, one by one, they were succumbing to exhaustion.

Marika grabbed her flesh before she lost her grip entirely.

Grauel recognized her arrival in flesh, had her sitting up with a cup of sweet tea to her muzzle almost before she recognized her surroundings. "Drink. Did you do well? Is there hope?"

Marika drank. Almost immediately she felt the sugar spreading through her body, giving her a near high. "I did very well. But maybe not enough. Maybe too late. More of that. And chaphe. I will have to go back right away. The others haven't the strength to hold."

"Marika...."

"You want a hope? The only hope I saw was for me to strike again. Soon. Closer to the fortress. The way it stands now, silth or no silth, we are destroyed."

Grauel nodded reluctantly.

"What of Gorry?"

"As vicious as ever. But lately she has been too busy to stir trouble. I think most of those who supported her have been killed in the fighting. So she may be no problem after all."

Marika downed another long draft. Her limbs were trembling. She knew risking the ghost realm in her state was not wise. But it was necessary. It seemed to be the choice between grave risk and certain death. Also, there was something she had to do....

"Stay with me this time, Grauel. I don't know you could, but if something seems bad wrong, try to bring me back."

"All right."

Marika lay back and closed her eyes. She slipped through her loophole. A glance upward showed her the giant ghost she had used before still hovering over the packfast. She snatched at it, seized it, brought it down amid the ruins of the broken wall.

She spied Gorry almost immediately, surrounded by scores of nomad bodies, exulting in her killing. Gorry, whom she hated above all else in her world. Gorry, who was totally engrossed in her work. Gorry, who was wounded and likely to be struck down by some nomad missile at any moment.

That could not be. No nomad would steal the pleasure of that death.

It was time.

Marika reached, found the point at the base of Gorry's brain, struck quickly but lightly, paralyzing not only the old silth's body but her talent. She held Gorry there for a long moment, letting the terror build.

It is time, Gorry. And, *Good-bye, Gorry.*

She left the paralyzed silth for the nomads. Their imaginations were far more gruesome than hers. She hoped Gorry suffered a long wait in impotent terror.

She hacked, slashed, battered, left a hundred nomads twisted and torn. Then she could stay out no longer. Blackness hovered at the edges of her perception. If she did not get out of the ghost realm soon, she never would.

She slipped into her own present and fell into a sleep of total exhaustion. Her final thought was that she needed food if she were to recover. She had pressed too hard, taken herself too far.

Self-mockery echoed through her fading consciousness. This was the last sleep from which she would never return.

She tried to beg the All to spare her awhile longer. She had one mission yet to perform before she departed the world. The Degnan dead remained unMourned.

III

To Marika's amazement, she wakened. The hammer of tradermale weapons wakened her. She opened her eyes. She was lying on a pallet in Braydic's comm room. Grauel sat beside her, a bowl of soup in her paw. Relief flooded her features.

Marika turned her head slowly. It ached terribly. She needed more goyin tea. She saw Bagnel and one of his comrades firing through narrow windows. Huntresses with bows waited behind them, occasionally stepped forward to loose an arrow while the males reloaded. Bombs were falling outside. They did little damage. Occasionally a metal pellet whined through one of the windows. Most of Braydic's beautiful equipment had been wrecked. All of it was dead. Marika could not feel a specter of the electromagnetic fog.

Barlog knelt beside Grauel. "Are you all right, Marika?"

"My head aches. I need a double draft of goyin tea." She then realized it was daylight out. She had slept a long time. "How bad is it? How did I get here?"

"It is very bad, pup." She presented the tea, which had been prepared. "We are the last." She gestured. The two tradermales. A dozen huntresses, counting herself and Grauel. Braydic. A dozen worker pups cowering in the nether reaches of the room. "We carried you up when it became clear the nomads would take the underparts of the packstead. Take as little of that tea as you can. You have been drinking too much."

"The sisters. Where are the sisters?"

"All fallen. All but you. A valiant struggle, I am sure. One the savages will recall for a thousand generations. We will be sung into their legends."

Grauel exchanged glances with Barlog. "Are you too weak, Marika? You are the last silth. And we need to hold them off awhile longer. Just awhile."

"Why? What is the point? Akard is fallen."

Braydic replied, "Because help is coming, pup. From the Maksche cloister. Because of what you discovered about the Serke sister. They want to see the body for themselves. You see? Never abandon hope. You may then be too late to profit from what the All has in store."

"I killed her," Marika said. "Gruesomely. They will not find enough left of her to identify."

"They did not need to know that down there," Braydic countered. "Shall we turn them away?"

A burst of explosions sounded outside. Marika turned to Grauel and Barlog. "Help is too late once again, eh?"

Barlog looked at her oddly, with a hint of awe. "Perhaps. And perhaps the All is moving through the world."

Puzzled, Marika glanced at Grauel and surprised the same look there. What were they thinking?

She said, "More food. I am starving. Famished." When no one moved, she pouted. "Find me something to eat. I can do nothing till I have eaten." Her body did feel as though she had fasted for days. "Those pups are beginning to look tasty."

They brought her food. It was dried trail rations of the sort prepared for the summer nomad hunts. Tough as hide. And right then very tasty.

Outside, the racket of the siege continued to rise. Bagnel and his comrade looked ready to collapse. But those two were, for the moment, the only line of defense.

Marika went among the ghosts again, for the last time at Akard. They were few, but not so few as when the nomad silth had been more numerous. And the big dark killer still hovered on high, as though waiting to be used and fed. She called it down.

She ravened among the besiegers, fueling herself with fear and anger and an unquenchable lust for requiting what had been done to the Degnan. She allowed all the hidden shadows, so long repressed, to the fore, and gave them free rein. But she was one silth alone, and the nomads were growing skilled at evading silth attack, at hiding under a mantle of protection extended by their own wild silth, who were in the packfast themselves. Blood ran deep, but Marika feared not deep enough. The savages continued to hammer at the last bastion.

The day proceeded, and despite Marika's efforts the siege turned worse. One after another, her companions were hit by fire coming through the two windows. There was no place to hide from ricochets. The nomads tried to throw explosives inside, and that she forestalled each time, but each time it distracted her from her effort to destroy the wild silth.

Collapse was moments away. She knew she could hold no longer, that her will *did* have its limits. And as she faced the absolute, resolute, and unyielding herself, she found that she had only the old regret. There would be no Mourning for the Degnan. And a new. There would be no journey to Maksche, which might have been the next step on her road leading toward the stars.

The hammer of weaponry rose toward the insane. Bagnel dared not return fire, for a swarming buzz of metal now came through the windows. The pellets were chewing Braydic's machines into chopped metal and glass.

The firing ceased. Bagnel bounced up for a look. Braydic whimpered. "Now they will come."

Marika nodded. And did something she never did before. She hugged Grauel and Barlog in turn.

Pups of the upper Ponath packs hugged no one but their dams, and that seldom after their first few years.

The two huntresses were touched.

Stray nomad weapons resumed a sporadic fire apparently meant to keep Bagnel away from his window.

Grauel rejoined the tradermale. She was trying to learn to use a rifle. Bagnel's companion could no longer lift his.

A slumping Marika suddenly went rigid. Her jaw dropped. "Wait! Something…."

Something mighty, something terrible in its power, was roaring toward her up the valley of the Hainlin. For a moment she was paralyzed by her terror of that raging shadow. Then she hurled herself to the one window facing down the river.

She saw three great daggerlike crosses hurtling up the river's course, above the devastation left by the flood released with the collapse of the dams. They charged into the teeth of the wind, flying like great raptors fifty feet above the surface in an absolutely rigid V formation.

"What are they?" Grauel whispered from Marika's side.

"I do not know."

"Looks like meth on them," Barlog murmured from Marika's other side.

"I do not know," Marika said again. She had begun shaking all over. A fierce and dreadful shadow-of-touch rolled ahead of the crosses, boiling with a mindless terror.

A tremendous explosion thundered out behind them. Its force threw the three of them together, against the stone of the wall. Marika gasped for breath. Grauel turned, pointed her rifle. It began to bark counterpoint to Bagnel's, which was speaking already.

Nomad shapes appeared in the dust boiling around the gap in the wall blown by the charge.

Marika clung to the window and stared out.

The three rushing crosses rose, screaming into the sky, parting.

WARLOCK

BOOK THREE: MAKSCHE

CHAPTER FIFTEEN

I

The universe of the touch, the ghost plane into which silth like Marika ducked to work their witchery, had gone mad. Some mighty shadow, terrible in its power, was raging up the valley of the Hainlin River, which this last bastion of the fortress Akard overlooked. For a moment Marika was paralyzed by the power of that shadow. Then she flung herself to a south-facing window.

Three great daggerlike crosses stormed up the frozen river. They drove into the fangs of the wind in a rigid V. That fierce and dreadful shadow-of-touch preceded them, flaying the mind with terror. Upon each cross stood five black-clad silth, one at each tip of each arm, the fifth at the axis. The incessant north wind howled around them and tore at their dark robes. They seemed to notice it not at all.

"They are coming," Marika shouted to Grauel and Barlog, who crowded her against the windowsill.

An explosion thundered out behind them. It threw them together. Marika gasped for breath. Grauel turned, pointed her rifle. It barked in unison with that of the tradermale Bagnel as savages appeared in the dust swirling in the gap created by the explosion.

Marika clung to the windowsill, looking out, waiting for death.

The rushing crosses rose as they neared Akard, screaming into lightly falling snow, parting. Marika slipped through her loophole into the realm of ghosts and followed them as they plunged toward the attacking nomads, spreading death and terror.

Grauel and Bagnel stopped firing. The nomads had fled the breach. In minutes the entire besieging horde was in full flight. Two of the flying crosses harried the savages northward. The third returned and hovered over the confluence of the forks of the Hainlin, above which Akard brooded on a high headland.

Akard's pawful of survivors crowded the window, staring in disbelief. Help had come. After so long a wait. In the penultimate moment, help had come.

The cross drifted closer till the tip of its longest arm touched the fortress on the level above the communications center. Marika pushed weariness aside and went to meet her rescuers. She was only fourteen, as yet far from being a full silth sister, but was the senior silth surviving. The *only* silth surviving. Through eyes hazed with fatigue and reaction, she vaguely recognized the dark figure which came to meet her. It was Zertan, senior of the Reugge Community's cloister at Maksche.

It looked like she would get to see the great city in the south after all.

A moment after she had fulfilled the necessary ceremonial obsequiences, exhaustion overtook her. She collapsed into the arms of Grauel and Barlog.

Marika wakened after the fading of the light. She found herself perched precariously upon the flying cross. In one hasty glance she saw that she shared the strange craft with the other survivors of Akard. Grauel and Barlog were as near her as they could get—as they always were. Bagnel was next nearest. He rewarded her with a cheerful snarl as her gaze passed over him. Communicator Braydic seemed to be in shock.

The wind seemed almost still as the cross ran with it. To the left and below, the ruins of Bagnel's home, Critza, appeared. "No bodies anymore," Marika observed.

In a hard, low voice, Bagnel said, "The nomads feed upon their dead. The grauken rules the Ponath." The grauken, the monster lying so close beneath the surface of every meth. The archetypal terror of self with which every meth was intimately familiar.

The Maksche senior eyed Bagnel, then Marika from her standing place upon the axis of the cross. She pointed skyward. "It will get worse before it gets better. The grauken may rule the entire world. It comes on us with the age of ice."

Marika looked skyward, trying to forget the dust cloud that was absorbing her sun's power and cooling her world. She tried to concentrate on the wonder of the moment, to take joy in being alive, to forget the horror of the past, of losing first the pack with which she had lived her first ten years, then the silth packfast where she had lived and trained the past four. She tried to banish the terror lurking in her future.

Jiana! Doomstalker! Twice!

The voice in her mind was the voice of a ghost. She could not make it go away.

The hills of the Ponath gave way to plains. The snowfall faded. And the flying cross fled with the breath of the north wind licking behind.

II

For months Marika had seen nothing but overcast skies. Always the bitter north wind had been present, muttering of even colder times to come. But now the gale could not catch her. She mocked it quietly.

Cracks began to show in the cloud cover. One moon, then another, peeped through, scattering the white earth with silver.

"Hello, strangers," Marika said.

"What?"

The response startled Marika, for she had been enclosed entirely within herself, unmindful of her bizarre situation. "I was greeting the moons, Grauel. Look. There is Biter. One of the small moons is running behind her. I cannot tell which. I do not care. I am just glad to see them. How long has it been?"

The huntress shifted her weapon and position gingerly. It was a long fall to the frozen river. "Too long. Too many months." Sorrow edged Grauel's voice. "Hello, moons."

Soon Chaser, the second large moon, showed its face too, so that shadows below looked like many-fingered paws.

"Look there!" Marika said. "A lake. Open water." She too had not seen unfrozen water in months.

Grauel would not look down. She clung to their transport with a death grip. Marika glanced around.

Five strangers, five friends. All astride a metal cross the shape of a dagger, running with the wind a thousand feet above the earth and snow. Grauel and Barlog, known since birth. Bagnel, known only months, strange, withdrawn, yet with the aroma of someone who could become very close. At that moment she decided he would become an integral part of her destiny.

Marika was silth. The Akard sisters had called her the most powerful talent ever to be unearthed in the upper Ponath. Sometimes the strongest silth caught flashes intimating tomorrow.

Braydic. The only friend the exile pup had made in her four years at Akard. Marika was glad that Braydic had survived.

Finally, two pups of meth who had served the silth, holding one another, terrified still, not yet knowing their fates. She realized that she did not know their names. She had saved them, as she had saved herself, for redoubled exile. Shared terror and last-second salvation ought to account for more intimacy.

"So," she said to Grauel and Barlog. "Here we go again. Into exile once more."

Barlog nodded. Grauel merely stared straight ahead, trying to keep her gaze from taking in the long fall to the silvered snows.

The Hainlin twisted away to the west and out of sight for a time, then swept back in beneath. It widened into a vast, slow stream, though mostly it remained concealed behind a mask of white. Time passed. Marika shook off repeated fits of bleak memory. She suspected her companions were doing the same.

Meth were not reflective by nature. They tended to live in the present, letting the past lie and allowing the future to care for itself. But the pasts of these meth were not the settled, bucolic pasts of their foredams. Their pasts reechoed with bloody hammer strokes. Their futures threatened more of the same.

"Lights," Grauel croaked. And in a moment, "By the All! Look at the lights!"

Ten thousand pinpricks in the night, like a nighttime sky descended to earth. Except that the sky of Marika's world held few stars, filled as it was with a dense, vast cloud of interstellar dust.

"Maksche," Senior Zertan said. "Home. We will reach the cloister in a few minutes."

The flying crosses pacing them suddenly swept ahead, vanished into the darkness. The lights ahead bobbed and rocked and swelled, and then the first passed below, maybe five hundred feet down. Marika felt no awe of the altitude. She exulted in the flying.

Soon the cross settled into a lighted courtyard, to a point between crosses already arrived. Scores of silth in Reugge black waited silently. The cross touched down. Zertan stepped off. Several silth approached her. She said something Marika did not catch, gestured, and stalked away. The other silth left their places at the tips of the cross.

A meth female in worker apparel approached Marika and the others. "Come with me. I have been instructed to show you quarters." She assessed them cautiously. "Not you," she told Bagnel, diffidently. "Someone from your Bond is coming for you."

Marika was amused, for she knew this meth saw only savages out of the Ponath. Even her, for all she was silth. And she knew this city meth was frightened, for savages from the Ponath had reputations for being unpredictable, irrational, and fierce.

Marika gestured. "We go. You, lead the way."

Bagnel stood aside, looking forlorn, one paw raised in a gesture of farewell.

Grauel followed the worker. Marika followed her. Barlog stayed close behind, weapon at port. Braydic and the pups tagged along at the end.

The Degnan refugees searched every shadow they passed. Marika listened with that talented silth ear that was inside her mind. She felt silth working their witcheries all around her. But the shadows were haunted by nothing more dangerous than projected fears of the unknown.

The servant led them through seemingly endless hallways, dropping first the pups, then Braydic. Marika sensed Grauel and Barlog becoming edgy. Their sense of location was confused. She grew uncomfortable herself. This place seemed too large to encompass. Akard was never so vast or tortuous that she had feared for her ability to get out.

Get out. Get out. That built within her, a smoldering panic, a dread of being unable to escape. She was of the upper Ponath, where pack meth ran free, at will.

The worker detected their mounting tension. She led them up stairs and outside, to the top of a wall at least vaguely reminiscent of the north wall at Akard, where Marika had made her away place, the place she went to be alone and think.

Each silth found such a place wherever she might be.

"It is huge," Barlog breathed from behind Marika. Marika agreed, though she knew not whether Barlog meant the cloister or city.

The Maksche cloister was a square compound a quarter-mile to a side. Its outer wall stood thirty feet high. It was constructed of a buttery brown stone. The structures it enclosed were built of the same stone, all topped with steep roofs of red tile. The buildings were all very old, very weathered, and all very rectilinear. Some had corner towers rising like obelisks peaked by triangles of red.

The worker said, "A thousand meth live in the cloister, separate from the city. The wall is the edge of our world, a boundary that is not to be passed."

She meant what she said, no doubt, but the fierceness that rose in her charges made her drop the subject. Marika growled, "Take us where we are supposed to go. Now. I will hear rules from those who make them, and will decide if they are reasonable then."

Their guide looked stricken.

Grauel said, "Marika, I suggest you recall all that has been said about this place."

Marika stared at the huntress, but soon her gaze wandered. Grauel was right. At the beginning she had best submit to the local style.

"Stop," she said. "I want to look." She did not await approval.

The cloister stood at Maksche's heart, upon a contrived elevation. The surrounding land was flat all the way to the horizons. The Hainlin, three hundred yards wide, looped past the city in a broad brown band two miles west of Marika's vantage. Neat squares of cropland, bounded by hedgerows or lines of trees, showed through the snow covering the plain.

"Not a single hill. I think it will not be long before I become homesick for hills." Marika used the simple dialect of her puphood, and was surprised when the worker frowned puzzledly. Could the common speech be so different here?

"I think so. Yes," Grauel replied. "Even Akard was less foreign than this. It is like ten thousand little fortresses, this thing called a city."

The buildings were very strange. But for Akard and Critza, every meth-made structure Marika had ever seen had been built of logs and stood under twenty-five feet high.

"I am not allowed much time away from my regular duties here," the worker said, her tone whining. "Please come, young mistress."

Marika scowled. "All right. Lead on."

The quarters assigned had been untenanted for a long time. Dust lay thick upon what tattered furniture there was. Marika coughed, said, "We are being isolated in some remote corner."

Grauel nodded. "Only to be expected."

Barlog observed, "We can have this livable in a few hours. It is not as bad as it looks."

Feebly, the worker said, "I must take you two to… to…" She fumbled for a word. "I guess you would say, huntress's quarters."

"No," Marika told her. "We stay together."

Grauel and Barlog snarled and gestured toward the door with their weapons.

"Go," Marika snapped. "Or I will tie a savage's curse to your tail."

The female fled in terror. Grauel said, "Probably whelped and raised here. Scared of her own shadow."

"This is a place where shadows are terrors," Barlog countered. "We will hear from the shadow mistresses now."

But Barlog was wrong. A week passed without event. It was a week in which Marika seldom left her quarters and had no intercourse at all with the Reugge of Maksche. She let Grauel and Barlog do the physical exploration. No one came to her.

She began to wonder why she was being ignored.

The time free began as a boon. In her years at Akard she had spent most of every waking hour in study, learning to become silth. The only respite had come during summers when she had joined hunting parties stalking the nomadic invaders who brought Akard and the Ponath to ruin.

Once her quarters were clean and she had sneaked a few exploratory forays into nearby parts of the cloister, and had penetrated the rest of it riding ghosts, and had found herself an away place in a high tower overlooking the square where she had arrived, she grew bored. Even study became appealing.

She snarled her dissatisfaction at the worker who brought their meals. That was on her tenth day in Maksche.

Things seemed to move slowly in Maksche. Marika's complaints continued for a week, growing virulent. Yet nothing happened.

"Do not cause trouble," Grauel cautioned. "They are studying our conduct. It is all some sort of test."

"Pardon me if I am skeptical," Marika said. "I have walked the dark side a hundred times since we have been here. I have seen no indication that they even know we are here, let alone are watching. We have been put out of sight, out of mind, and are imprisoned in a dungeon of the soul."

Grauel exchanged glances with Barlog. Barlog observed, "All things are not seen by the witch's inner eye, Marika. You are not omnipotent."

"What is that supposed to mean?"

"It means that one young silth, no matter how strong, is not going to use her talent to see what a cloister full of more practiced silth are doing if they do not want her to see."

Marika was about to admit that that might be possible when someone scratched at the door. She gestured. "It is not time to eat. The drought must be over."

Barlog opened the door.

There stood a silth older than any Marika had encountered before. She hobbled in, leaning on a cane of some gnarled dark wood. She halted in the center of the room, surveyed the three of them with rheumy cataracted eyes. Her half-blind gaze came to rest upon Marika. "I am Moragan. I have been assigned as your teacher and as your guide upon the Reugge Path." She spoke the Reugge low speech with an intriguing, elusive accent. Or was it a natural lisp? "You are the Marika who stirred so much controversy and chaos at our northern fastness." Not a question. A statement.

"Yes." Marika had a feeling this was no time to quibble about her role at Akard.

"You may go," Moragan told Grauel and Barlog.

The huntresses did not move. They did not look to Marika for her opinion. Already they had positioned themselves so that Moragan stood at the heart of a perilous triangle.

"You are safe here," Moragan told Marika when no one moved.

"Indeed? I have your sworn word?"

"You do."

"And the word of a silth sister is worth the metal on which it is graven." She had been studying the apparel of the old sister and could not make out the significance of its decorations. "As we who were under the sworn guardianship of the Reugge discovered. Our packsteads were overrun without aid coming. And when we fled to the Akard packfast for safety, that too was allowed to be destroyed."

"You question decisions of policy about which you know nothing, pup."

"Not at all, mistress. I simply refuse to allow policy to snare and crush me in coils of deceit and broken oaths."

"They said you were a bold one. I see they spoke the truth. Very well. We will do it your way. For now." Moragan hobbled to a wooden chair, settled slowly, slapped her cane down atop a table nearby. She seemed to go to sleep.

"Who are you besides Moragan?" Marika asked. "I cannot read your decorations."

"Just a worn-out old silth so far gone she is past being what you would call Wise. We are not here to discuss me, though. Tell me your story. I have heard and read a few things. Now I will assess your version of events."

Marika talked, but to no point. A few minutes later Moragan's head dropped to her chest and she began to snore.

And so it went, day after day, with Moragan doing more asking and snoring than teaching. That day of her first appearance, she had been in one of her more lucid periods. Sometimes she could not recall the date or even Marika's name. Most of the time she was of little value except as a reference guide to the cloister's more arcane customs. Always she asked more questions than she answered, many of them irritatingly personal.

Her role, though, provided Marika with a role of her own. As a student she occupied a recognized place in cloister society and was answerable principally to Moragan for her conduct. Safely knit into the cultural fabric, Marika felt more comfortable teaching herself by exploring and observing.

Marika liked little of what she did learn.

Within the cloister the least of workers lived well. Outside, in the city, meth lived in abject want, suffering through brief lives of hunger, disease, and back-breaking labor. Everyone and everything in Maksche belonged to the Reugge silth Community, to the trademale brotherhood calling itself the Brown Paw Bond, or to the two in concert. The Brown Paw Bond maintained its holdings by Reugge license, under complicated and extended lease arrangements. Residents of Maksche who were neither trademale nor silth were bound to their professions or land for life.

Marika was bewildered. The Reugge possessed meth as though they were domestic animals? She interrogated Moragan. The teacher just looked at her strangely, evidently unable to comprehend the point of her questions.

"Grauel," Marika said one evening, "have you figured this place out? Do you understand it at all? That old carque Moragan cannot or will not explain anything so it makes any sense."

"Take care with her, Marika. She is more than she seems."

"She is as All-touched as my granddam was."

"She may be senile and mad, but she is not harmless. Perhaps the more dangerous for it. It is whispered that she was not set to teach you but to study you. It is also whispered that she was once very important in the order, and that she still has the favor of some who are very high up. Fear her, Marika."

"I should fear someone I could break?"

"As strength goes? This is not the upper Ponath, Marika. It is not the strength of the arm that counts. It is the strength of the alliances one forms."

Marika made a sound of derision. Grauel ignored her.

"Marika, suppose that some of them hope you try your strength. Suppose some of them want to prove something to themselves."

"What?"

"Our ears are sharp from many years of hunting the forests of the upper Ponath. When we go among the huntresses of this place—and sorrier huntresses you will never see—we sometimes overhear whispers never meant for our ears. They talk about us and they talk about you and they talk about the thinking of those around Senior Zertan. In a way, you are on trial. They suspect—maybe even know—about Gorry."

"Gorry? What about Gorry?"

"Something happened to Gorry in the final hours of the siege. There was much speculation, overheard by everyone. We said nothing to anyone about that, but we are not the only survivors brought out of the ruins of Akard."

Marika's heart fluttered as she thought of her one-time instructress. But she felt no remorse. Gorry had deserved the torment she had suffered, and more. All Marika felt was a heightened apprehension about being ignored. It had not occurred to her that it was that sort of deliberateness. She would have to be careful. She was in no position of strength.

Grauel watched expectantly while Marika wrapped her mind around the implications.

"Why are you looking at me that way?"

"I thought you might have some regrets."

"Why?"

"She was—"

"She was a carque of an old nuisance, Grauel. She would have done it to me if she could have. She tried often enough. She got what she asked for. I do not want to hear her mentioned again."

"As you wish, mistress."

"Have you found Braydic yet?"

"She was assigned to the communications center here, as you might expect. Students are not permitted entry there. And technicians are not allowed out."

"Why not?"

"I do not know. This is a different world. We are still feeling our way. They never tell you what is permitted, only what is not."

Marika realized that Grauel was upset with her. When Grauel was distressed, she insisted on using the formal mode of speech. But Marika had given up trying to interpret the huntress's moods. She was exercised about something most of the time.

"I want to go out into the city, Grauel."

"Why?"

"To explore."

"That is not permitted."

"Why not?"

"I do not know. Rules are not explained here. They are enforced. Ignorance is no excuse."

What was the penalty for disobedience?

Marika banished the thought. It was too early to challenge constraints. Still, she felt compelled to say, "If this is life in the fabulous Maksche cloister, Grauel, I may go over the wall."

"Barlog and I have very little to do either, Marika. They think we are too backward."

III

The absolute, enduring stone of the cloister became a hated enemy. It crushed in upon Marika with the weight of massively accumulated time and alien tradition. Enforced inactivity made it almost intolerable. Each day she spent more time in her towertop away place. Each day meditation did less to ease her spiritual malaise.

Her place overlooked nothing but the courtyard, the city, and the works of meth. There was a constant wind, a north wind, but it did not speak to her as had the winds at Akard. It carried the wrong smells, the wrong tastes. It was heavy with the sweat of industry. It was a foreign, indifferent wind. That wind of the north had been her friend and ally.

Often she did not leave her cell at all, but lay on her pallet and used a finger to draw stick figures in the sweat on the cold wall.

Sometimes she went down through her loophole into the realm of ghosts, but she found little comfort there. Ghosts were scarce where so many silth were gathered. She sensed a few great monsters way high above, especially in the night, but she could not touch them. She might as well reach for Biter.

There was a change in atmosphere in the cloister around the end of Marika's sixth week there. It puzzled her till Barlog showed up to announce, "Most Senior Gradwohl is coming here." Most Senior Gradwohl ruled the entire Reugge Community, which spanned the continent. "They are frantic trying to get ready."

"Why is she coming?" Marika asked.

"To take personal charge of the effort to control the nomads. Two days ago nomads were seen from the wall of the packfast at Motchen. That is only a hundred miles north of Maksche, Marika. They are catching up with us already." In a lower voice Barlog confided, "These Maksche silth are frightened. They have a contract with the tradermales that obligates them to protect traders anytime they are in Reugge territory. They have been unable to do that. Critza is just one of three tradermale packfasts that were overrun. There is a rumor that some tradermales want to register an open petition for the Serke sisterhood to intercede in Reugge territories because the Reugge can no longer maintain order."

"So?" Marika asked indifferently.

"That would affect us, Marika."

"How? We have no part in anything. We are tolerated for some reason. Barely. We are fed. And otherwise we are ignored. What do we have to fear? If no one sees us, who can harm us?"

"Do not talk that way, Marika."

"Why not?"

"These sisters can go around unseen. One of them might hear you."

"Don't be silly. That's nonsense."

"I heard it from..." Barlog did not finish for fear of compromising her source.

"How much longer can you tolerate this imprisonment, Barlog? What does Grauel think? I won't endure it much longer, I promise you that."

"We can't leave."

"Says who?"

"It's not permitted."

"By whom? Why not?"

"That's just the way it is."

"For those who accept it."

"Marika, please…."

"Go away, Barlog. I don't want to hear you whine." As Barlog was about to leave, she added, "They've tamed you, Barlog. Made a two-legged rheum-greater out of a once fine huntress." Use of the familiar mode made Marika's words all the more cutting.

Barlog's lips parted in a snarl of fury. But she restrained herself and even closed the door gently.

Marika went to her tower to observe the most senior's arrival. Gradwohl came in on one of the flying crosses, standing at its axis. Marika watched it drop past the tower, the silth at the tips of its arms standing rigidly with their eyes closed. There was a thrumming rhythm between them that Marika had missed during her flight south. But then she had been exhausted physically, drained mentally and emotionally, and had been interested in little but leaving a shattered fortress and life behind.

She went down inside herself and through her loophole and was astonished to find the cross surrounded by a roiling fog of ghosts, great ghosts similar to the dark killing ghosts she had ridden in the north. The sister at the tip of the longer arm controlled them. They moved the ship. The other sisters provided reservoirs of talent from which the senior sister drew. The most senior did nothing. She was but a passenger.

This, finally, was something about which Marika could get excited. How did they manage it? Was it something she could learn to do? It would be fantastic to ride above the world by night upon one of those great daggers. She studied the silth. What they were doing was different from killing, but it did not appear difficult. She touched the senior sister, trying to read what was happening, as the cross neared the ground.

Her touch distracted the silth. The cross dropped the last foot. Marika recoiled quickly. A countertouch brushed her, but was not specific. It did not return.

A great deal of pomp and ceremony followed the most senior's landing. Marika remained where she was. The most senior, her party, and those who welcomed her, vanished into the labyrinthine cloister. Marika gazed over the red rooftops at the horizon. For once the wind carried a hint of the north. That chill breath of home worsened her feeling of alienation.

Grauel found her still there near midnight, chin on arms on stone, eyes vacant, staring at the far fields of moon-frosted snow as if awaiting a message. "Marika. They sent me to bring you."

Grauel seemed badly shaken. There was something in her voice that stirred the dangerous flight-fight response within her. "Who sent you?"

"Senior Zertan. On behalf of the most senior. Gradwohl herself wants to talk to you. That Moragan was with them. I warned you to watch yourself with her."

Marika bared her teeth. Grauel was terrified. Probably of the possibility that they would get thrown out of the cloister. "Why does she want me?"

"I don't know. Probably about what happened at Akard."

"Now? They're interested now? After almost two months?"

"Marika. Restrain yourself."

"Am I not perfectly behaved before our hosts?"

Grauel did not deny that. Marika even treated Moragan with absolute respect. She made a point of giving no one cause to take offense—most of the time.

Nevertheless, she was not liked by the few sisters who crossed her path. Grauel and Barlog claimed the Maksche sisters feared her. Just as had the sisters at Akard.

"All right. Show me the way. I'll try to mind my manners."

They made Grauel stop at the door to the inner cloister, the big central structure opened only for high ceremonies and days of obligation. Marika touched Grauel's elbow lightly, restraining her. Grauel responded with a massive shrug of resignation—and, Marika thought, just the faintest hint of amusement in the tilt of her ears. It was a hint only one who knew Grauel well would have caught.

What was she up to? And where was Grauel's rifle? She had not been parted from the weapon since she had received it from Bagnel. She *slept* with it, it was so precious. Her carrying it all the time had to be cause for consternation and comment.

Almost, Marika looked back. Almost. Native guile stopped her.

Two silth led her to a vast, ill-lighted chamber. No electricity there, just tapers shuddering in chilly drafts. As must be in a place where silth worked their magics. Electromagnetic energies interfered with their talents.

This was the chamber where the most important Reugge rites were observed. Marika had been there before only as a dark-walker. Other than in its symbolic value, the place was nothing special.

Two dozen ranking silth waited, perched silently upon tall stools. Only the occasional flick of an inadvertently exposed tail betrayed the fact that anything was happening behind their cold obsidian-flake eyes. Every one of those eyes was fixed upon Marika.

She was less intimidated than she expected.

Several worker-servants moved among the silth, managing wants and refreshments. One with a tray approached Marika. She was an ancient whose fur had fallen in patches, leaving only ugly bare spots. She dragged her right leg in a stiff limp. As Marika waved her away, she was startled by the meth's scent. Something familiar....

In a low voice the servant said, "Mind your manners, pup." She hitch-stepped off to the sideboard that seemed to be her station.

Barlog!

Barlog. With a limp. And Grauel's treasure was missing.

With that rifle Barlog could cut down half the silth in the room before any even thought of employing their witchery.

Marika was pleased by the resourcefulness of Grauel and Barlog. But she felt no more confident of her ability to handle the subtleties of the coming interview.

Of the silth in that room, Marika recognized only two. Zertan and Moragan. Marika faced the senior and performed the appropriate ceremonial greeting to perfection. She would show Barlog who could mind her manners.

"This is the one from Akard?" a gravelly voice asked.

"Yes, mistress."

The most senior, Marika assumed. Younger than she had expected. She was a hard, chunky, grizzled female with slightly wild eyes. Like a Gorry still sane. A sister who was as much huntress as silth, and a hungry huntress at that.

"I thought she would be older. And bigger," the most senior said, echoing Marika's own thoughts.

"She *is* young," Moragan said, and Marika noted that she was completely awake and vibrant and alive. Moragan's stool stood between those of Zertan and the most senior, an inch nearer that of the latter, subtly proclaiming her most important tie.

Senior Zertan said, "We do not know what to do with her. Her history is repellent at best. She is an astoundingly strong feral detected accidentally four years ago. Akard took her in. That was soon after the first nomadic incursions into the upper Ponath. Her hamlet was one of the first overrun. It seems that, with no training whatsoever, purely instinctively she drew to the dark and slew several savages. Her latent ability in that respect so disturbed some of our sisters that they labeled her Jiana, after the mythological and archetypal doomstalker Jiana. A sister, Gorry, who had a Community-wide reputation before the necessity for her rustification arose—"

A revenant shrieked in Marika's mind. *Jiana! Doomstalker!*

"Zertan." Most Senior Gradwohl's voice was coldly cautionary.

Zertan shifted her emphasis slightly. "Gorry had very strong, very negative feelings about the pup. In one way of seeing, Gorry was correct. She has twice been almost the only survivor of monstrous disasters that befell those who nurtured her. Gorry was very much afraid of her, but was her teacher. Thus her training there was haphazard at best. Reliable reports do indicate that she achieved a commanding ability to reach and command the darkest of those-who-dwell."

The object of discussion was growing more irate by the moment. Barlog's cold stare helped her control her tongue.

"Zertan," Gradwohl said again. "Enough. I have seen all the reports you have, and more." For a moment the Maksche senior seemed startled. "Can you tell me anything new? Anything I do not know? How does she feel about the sisterhood?"

After a silence that began to stretch painfully, Zertan admitted, "I have no idea how she feels. But it does not matter. A pup's attitudes are the clay that the teacher—"

Gradwohl did not seize upon Zertan's clumsiness. Instead, she shifted approach. "Senior Koenic reported to me shortly before Akard fell. Among other things, we discussed a feral silth pup named Marika. This Marika, though only fourteen years old, was directly responsible for the deaths of several hundred meth. Senior Koenic was as scared of her as Gorry was. Because, as she put it, this Marika was an embryonic Bestrei or Zhorek—without the intellectual handicaps of those two dark-walkers. Senior Koenic knew Bestrei and Zhorek before *her* rustification. She watched Marika for four years. She was in a position to form an intelligent estimate of the pup."

Gradwohl eased down off her stool, surveyed the assembly. "What does it matter what a pup thinks of the Community? Consider two ideas. Trust, and personal loyalty.

"For all the backbiting that goes on, trust cements the Reugge Community. We *know* we are in no physical danger from one another. We *know* none of our sisters will *willfully* work to the detriment of the order. Our subordinates *know* we will protect and nurture them. But Marika believes none of that.

"Why? Because her hamlet and hundreds of others were overrun by savages the Reugge were pledged to repel. Because genuine attempts have been made upon her life. Because she has not been educated to see the good of the Community as paramount."

Gradwohl sounded like some windy Wise meth giving the convocation on a day of high obligation. The longer Gradwohl talked, the less closely Marika listened and the more she became wary. There was some silth game running and she was just a counter.

"About personal loyalty, few of you know a thing," the most senior continued in a hard voice. "Let us experiment. Moragan. Proceed."

Moragan got off her stool. She drew a long, wicked knife from inside her robe, presented it to Senior Zertan.

Gradwohl said, "Carry out your instructions, Zertan."

Zertan left her stool with obvious reluctance. She looked at Marika for a moment.

She flung herself forward.

Marika's response was instantaneous and instinctive. She ducked through her loophole into the ghost realm. A thought captured a ghost. A mental shout scattered the few others before any other silth could come through and seize them. She hurled her ghost at the vaguely perceived form plunging toward her.

She returned to reality while the bark of a rifle still reverberated through the chamber. Zertan was pitching forward, dropped knife not yet to the floor. Gradwohl was turning, spun by Barlog's bullet. Marika flung up a paw, restraining Barlog before she commenced a massacre.

The chamber door exploded inward. The guards posted outside tumbled through. Grauel leaped through with a Degnan ululation, shield on one arm, javelin poised for the cast. Behind her, a quivering Braydic menaced the guards with a sword she had no idea how to use.

Not one of the silth on the stools moved more than the tip of a tail.

Some silth game.

Most Senior Gradwohl recovered. The bullet had but clipped her shoulder. She met Marika's cold stare. "I seldom miscalculate. But when I do, I do it big." Her paw went to her shoulder, where moisture seeped into the fabric of her robe. "I did not anticipate firearms. Halechk! See to Zertan before she dies on us."

A silth with healer's decorations left her stool and hastened to Zertan.

Gradwohl said, "Personal loyalty. Even in the face of certain disaster." Her teeth ground together. Her wound had begun to hurt.

Zertan's knife had come to rest only inches from the tip of Marika's right boot. She kicked it across the floor to the most senior's feet.

Gradwohl's cheek began to twitch. She whispered, "Have a care, pup. Had it been real, you *might* have gotten through it by having surprise on your right paw."

"Had it been real, there would be only three meth alive in this room right now." Marika spoke with conviction. She broke eye contact long enough to glance at the knife. "We had a saying in the Ponath. 'As strength goes.'" She had to say it in dialect. Gradwohl did not react. Perhaps it went past her.

"When I am manipulated or pushed, mistress, I must push back."

Gradwohl ignored her. She surveyed the silth, still perched upon their stools. "This assembly has served its purpose. It is as I suspected. Someone has been remiss. Someone allowed prejudice to overwhelm reason. Listen! This pup ambushed and destroyed a *ranking* sister of the Serke Community. And I promise you, that House is giving that fact a lot more attention than this one has."

Gradwohl stared at Marika hard. Marika continued to meet her gaze, refusing to be intimidated. Beneath, beyond the test of wills, she sensed a kindred soul.

"This assembly is at an end," Gradwohl said, still holding Marika's gaze. "Go. All but you, pup."

Silently, silth began filing out. Two helped carry Senior Zertan.

Barlog and Grauel did not move.

Braydic, though, Marika noted, had disappeared. Ever-cautious and timid Braydic.

Just as well, perhaps. Just as well.

Marika focused upon this meth strong enough to rule the fractious Reugge Community.

CHAPTER SIXTEEN

I

Gradwohl climbed onto a stool. "Sit if you like," she told Marika.

Marika settled crosslegged upon the floor, as had been the custom among the packs of the upper Ponath. Furniture had been unknown in her dam's loghouse.

"Tell me about yourself, pup."

"Mistress?"

"Tell me your story. I want to know everything there is to know about you."

"You know, mistress. Through your agent Moragan."

Gradwohl seemed amused. "She was that transparent?"

"Only looking back."

"Nothing substitutes for direct examination. Begin simply. Tell me your story. What is your name?"

"Marika, mistress."

"Tell me about Marika. From her birth to this moment."

Marika sketched an autobiography which included her first awarenesses of her talent, her unusually close relationship with her male littermate Kublin, her troubles with one of the Wise of her dam's loghouse, and all her troubles during her stay at the fortress Akard.

Gradwohl nodded. "Interesting. But possibly even more interesting in complete privacy."

"Mistress?"

"You have told me very little about Marika inside."

Marika grew uneasy.

"Do not be frightened, pup."

"I am not, mistress."

"Liar. I met a most senior when I was your age. I was petrified. There is no need. I am here to help. You are not happy, are you? Honestly, now."

"No, mistress."

"Why not?"

She thought she had made that clear. Perhaps their backgrounds were too alien. She rambled till Gradwohl lost patience. "Get to the point, pup. There are no ears here but mine. Even were there, your sisters would make no reprisals for what you say. I will not permit that. And do not lie. I want to know what the real Marika thinks and feels."

Irked, Marika tested the water with a few mild remarks. When Gradwohl did not explode, she continued till she had revealed most of her dissatisfactions.

"Exactly what I suspected. An absolute lack of vision from the very beginning. I was not a feral myself, but I endured similar troubles. They sense strength and power, and it frightens them. In their way, silth have minds as small as any common meth. Those who might be surpassed want to stifle you before you develop the skills to command them. It is a severe shortcoming of the society silth have developed. Now. Tell me more about Akard."

Gradwohl spoke no more of Marika's place in things, nor of her feelings. Instead, she concentrated upon a minute examination of events during Akard's final days. "What has become of the other survivors? Especially the commtech and the tradermale?" She used the Ponath dialect word tradermale as though it was unfamiliar.

Marika reflected carefully before saying, "Braydic was assigned work in the communications center here." Had the most senior noted the sword-carrying meth who had threatened the guards behind Grauel, keeping them from interfering? "They will not let me see her. Bagnel vanished. I assume he rejoined his brotherhood. They say there is a tradermale place here in Maksche."

"Presumably I could reach him through his factors."

"Darkship, mistress?"

"The flying cross. That was you in the tower, was it not? You touched Norgis just before we set down."

"Yes, mistress."

"What did you think?"

"I was awed, mistress. The idea of riding such a thing.... I rode one coming down from Akard, but most of that escapes me."

"You are not frightened by it?"

"No, mistress."

"You do not find those-who-dwell frightening?"

"No, mistress."

"Good. That will be all, pup. Return to your quarters."

"Yes, mistress."

"There will be changes in your life, pup."

"Yes, mistress," Marika said as she walked toward the doorway.

Grauel went through first, surveyed the hallway, nodded. Barlog backed out behind Marika, rifle still trained on the most senior.

Not one word about the confrontation passed between the three of them.

The changes began immediately. The morning following the interview, a silth the age of Marika's dam came to her cell. She introduced herself as Dorteka. "I am your instructress, detached from the most senior's staff for that purpose. The most senior has ordered an individualized program for you. We will get started now." Plainly, Dorteka did not like her assignment, but she was careful to avoid saying so.

Marika would soon note a cloisterwide shift of attitude toward one who had caught the most senior's interest.

That first morning Dorteka took her to a meditation chamber. They sat upon the floor, across a table of the same stone as the cloister, in the eerie light of a single oil lamp. On Dorteka's side lay a clipboard and papers. Dorteka said, "Your education has been erratic. The most senior wants you to go back and begin at the beginning."

"I would be with pups…."

"You will proceed at your own pace, independent of everyone else at every level. Where your training has been adequate, you will advance rapidly, to your limits." Dorteka straightened a paper. "What would you like to do for the sisterhood?"

Marika did not hesitate. "Fly the darkships. To the starworlds."

A trace of amusement showed in the tilt of Dorteka's ears. "So the most senior suggested. The darkship is possible. The starworlds are not."

"Why?"

"We were too late going out. We looked in the wrong places. The starworlds are all enfiefed, and they are guarded jealously by the sisterhoods who own them. Even to leave the planet now would mean an immediate challenge to darkwar. So darkwar can be our only reason for entering the dark. We will not. We have no one capable of challenging."

Puzzled, Marika asked, "What is darkwar? No one will explain."

"At your level it will be difficult to comprehend. In essence, darkwar is a bloodduel between the leading Mistresses of the Ships of Communities in conflict. The survivor wins the right of the dispute. Darkwar is rare because it usually seals the fate of an entire Community."

Bloodduel Marika understood. She nodded.

"Time enough for such things after you gain a solid foundation. You wish to become involved with the ships. Then you shall become involved, if you remain interested once you become qualified. There are never enough sisters willing to work them. You do read and write?"

"Yes, mistress."

Dorteka handed her a sheet of paper. "This is our schedule. We will adjust it as needed."

Marika looked it over. "Not much time left for sleep."

"You wish to fly darkships, you must learn to endure sleeplessness. You wish to see your friend Braydic, you will remain stubbornly devoted to your studies." Dorteka pushed a scrap of paper across the table. The notes on it were in a paw almost mechanically perfect. *"Suggested motivators for the feral subject Marika."*

"The most senior?"

"Yes."

The interest shown by the most senior was a bit intimidating.

The sheet was filled with a complicated diagram for earning the right to visit Braydic or the city.

"As you see, a visit to your friend requires you to accumulate one hundred performance points. Those are mapped out for you there. Leave to go outside the cloister will be more difficult to obtain. It is subject to my being satisfied with your progress. You will never get out if I feel you are giving less than one hundred percent."

Crafty old Gradwohl. She had speared to the heart of her and tapped forces which could *make* her learn. The thought of seeing Braydic sparked an immediate urge to begin. The opportunity to get into the city, too, stirred her, but less concretely.

"I doubt that I will permit a city visit anytime soon. Perhaps we will accumulate several opportunities for later."

"Why, mistress?"

"The streets could be dangerous for an untrained silth. We have been having a problem with rogue males. I expect the Serke are behind that, too. Whatever, silth have been assaulted. Last summer ringleaders were rounded up and sentenced to the mines, but that did little good. The brethren—those you call tradermales—may have a paw in the movement."

"The world is not so complicated on an upper Ponath packstead," Marika observed.

"No. You see the schedule and rewards. Are they acceptable?"

"Yes, mistress."

"You will become a full-time student, with no other duties. You will accept the discipline of the Community?"

"Yes, mistress." Marika was surprised to find herself so eager. Till this morning she had cared about nothing. "I am ready to begin."

"Then begin we shall."

II

Marika's education commenced before the next dawn. Dorteka wakened her and took her to a gymnasium for an hour's workout. A bath followed.

Marika's determination almost broke. She nearly broke her vow to obey and conform.

A bath! Meth—of the upper Ponath, at least—*hated* water. They never entered it voluntarily. Only when the populations of insects in one's fur became too great to stand....

The bath was followed by a hurried meal prior to the first class of the day, which was an introduction to being silth. Rites and ceremonies, dogma and duties, and instruction in the secret languages of the sisterhood, which she hardly needed. She discovered that there were circles of sisterhood mysteries silth were supposed to penetrate as they became older and more skilled. Till Dorteka, she had no idea how much she had been shut out.

She ripped through those studies swiftly. They required rote learning. Her memory was excellent. Seldom did she need to be shown anything more than once.

She excelled in the gymnasium. She was her dam's pup. Skiljan had been fast, strong, hard, and tough.

The second class lay across the cloister from the first. Dorteka made her run all the way. Dorteka made her run everywhere, and ran with her. The second class was not as susceptible to rote learning, for it was mathematics. It required the use of reason. Silth naturally tended to favor intuition.

After mathematics came the history of the sisterhood, a class which Marika devoured in days. The Reugge were a minor Community with a short, uneventful past, an offshoot of the Serke that had established independence only seven centuries earlier. Sustenance of that independence was the outstanding Reugge achievement.

Silth had a history that stretched into prehistory, countless millennia back, when all meth lived in nomadic packs. The earliest sisterhoods existed long before the keeping of records began. Most silth had little interest in those days. They lived in an eternal now.

Marika's pack had maintained a record of its achievements called the Degnan Chronicle. That it had been kept in her dam's loghouse had been a source of pride to the pup. Barlog still kept it up, for she and Grauel believed that as long as it survived and remained current, the Degnan pack survived. As a historical instrument, the Degnan Chronicle was superior to any kept by the Reugge even now. For the Reugge Community, history was an oral tradition mainly of self-justification.

Broader historical studies proved no more informative. They raised more questions than they answered, as far as Marika could see. What were the origins of the meth? In olden times—as now among the nomads of the north—they were pack hunters. Physically, they resembled a carnivore called a kagbeast. But kagbeasts were not intelligent, nor did their females rule their packs. In fact, female meth did not rule the primitive packs of the southern hemisphere, where silth births were rare. There the males hunted on equal footing.

When Marika asked, Dorteka theorized, "Female rule developed because of the high incidence of silth births in northern litters. So I have heard.

"Primitive packs such as your own are structured around the strong. When the strong become weakened by time or disease, they are pushed aside. But a silth could stave off challengers even though she was weak physically, and once in command would tend to be partial to those who shared her talent. In primitive packs where breeding rights are reserved for the dominant females, silth dominance would mean especial favor to the spread of the silth strain."

Marika observed, "Then an old female like my instructress Gorry, at Akard, could stay in control till she died, yet could not lead or make rational decisions, really."

Dorteka snorted. "Which indicts the silth structure, yes. For all the most senior said about trust and whatnot in your interview—yes, I have heard all about that—we live under rule by terror, pup. The most capable do not run the Communities. The most terrible do. Thus you have a Bestrei among the Serke without a brain at all but in high station because she is invincible in darkwar. She is one of many who would not survive long if stripped of her talent."

After general history came another meal, followed by a long afternoon spent trying to harness and expand Marika's talents.

Dorteka went through everything with her, side by side. She graded herself, making herself the standard against which Marika should perform.

Marika almost enjoyed herself. For the first time since the fall of the Degnan packstead, she felt like her life was going somewhere.

The exercises, the entire program, were nothing like what she had had to suffer through with Gorry. There were no monsters, no terrors, no threats, no abuses. For silth class Marika seated herself upon a mat, closed her eyes, led herself into a trance where her mind floated free, unsupported by ghosts. Dorteka adamantly insisted she shun those-who-dwell.

"They are treacherous, Marika. Like chaphe is treacherous. You can turn to them too often, till you become dependent upon them and turn to them every time you are under pressure. They become an escape. Go inside and see how many other paths lie open."

Marika was amazed to discover that most silth could not reach or manipulate the deadly ghosts. That was a rare talent, dark-walking. The rarest and most dread talent of them all was being able to control the giants that moved the darkships—the very giants she had summoned at Akard for more lethal employment against nomads.

Her heart leapt when she learned that. She would fly!

Flight had become a goal bordering upon obsession.

"When can I begin learning the darkships, mistress?" she asked. "That is what interests me."

"Not soon. Only after you have a sound grounding in everything it takes to become true silth. The most senior would like you to become a flying sister, yes, but I feel she wants you to be much more. I suspect she plans a great future for you."

"Mistress?" At Akard there had been much talk of a great future, little of which anyone had been willing to explain.

"Never mind. Go through and see how far you can extend your touch."

"To whom, mistress?"

"No one. Just reach out. Do you need a target?"

"I always have."

"To be expected of the self-taught, I suppose." Dorteka never became exasperated, even when she had cause. "It is not necessary. Try it without."

Despite the grind, which left little time for sleep, Marika often visited her tower, sat staring at the stars, mourning the fate that had enlisted her in a sisterhood incapable of reaching them.

Dorteka's sessions could be as intense as Gorry's, if not as dangerous. Marika found herself grasping skills instinctively, progressing so rapidly she unsettled her instructress. Dorteka began to see what the most senior had intuited. That much talent in the paws of one raised to the primitive huntress world view, with its harsh and uncompromising values.... The possibilities were frightening.

Evenings after supper, Marika's education turned to the mundane, to the sciences as the Reugge knew them. Though they were laden with a mysticism that left Marika impatient, her progress was swift, and limited only by her ability to grasp and internalize the principles of ever more complex mathematics.

Word came down from the most senior: expand the time given math. Let the sisterhood trivia slide.

Dorteka was offended. The forms of silthdom were important to her. "We are our traditions," she was fond of saying.

"Why is the most senior doing this?" Marika asked. "I do not mind. I want to learn. But what is *her* hurry?"

"I am not sure. I am certain she would disapprove of my guessing. But I believe she may be thinking in terms of sculpting some sort of liberator for the Reugge. If the Serke keep pressing us and the winter keeps pushing south, we could be devoured within ten years. She does not want to be remembered as the last most senior of the Reugge Community. And she has begun to feel her mortality."

"She is not that old. I was surprised when first I saw her. I thought she would be ancient."

"No, she is not old. But always she hears the Serke baying behind her. However, that is not our worry. Mine is to teach. Yours is to learn. The whys are not relevant now. Time will unfold its leaves."

Marika continued to advance at a rate that shocked Dorteka. The teacher observed, "I begin to suspect that, despite themselves, our sisters at Akard taught you a great deal. At this rate you will, in every way, surpass your own age group before summer. In some ways you already exceed many sisters accounted full silth."

Much of what Marika encountered was new. She did not tell Dorteka that, afraid of frightening her teacher with the ease with which she learned.

After evening classes there was an events-of-the-day seminar conducted by the Maksche senior's second, a silth named Paustch. This took place in the hall where Marika had confronted Gradwohl, and Marika was required to attend. She kept the lowest profile possible. Her presence was tolerated only because Gradwohl insisted. No one asked her opinion. She offered none. She had no illusions about her presence there. She was the senior's marker, but she did not know in what game. She ducked out first when the seminar ended.

Thus she stayed close to the warming feud with the Serke, with the latest on nomad predations, gained an idea of the shape of politics between sisterhoods, heard of all their squabbles, caught rumors about the explorations of distant starworlds. But mostly the Maksche leadership discussed the nomads and the ever-more-common problem of male sedition.

"I came into this in the middle," Marika told Dorteka. "I am not certain I understand why the problem is such a problem."

"These males are few and really only a minor irritant," Dorteka said. "Taken worldwide their efforts would not be noticeable. But they have concentrated their terrorism in Reugge territories, especially around Maksche. And a large portion of their attacks have been directed against guests of the Reugge—clearly an effort to make us appear weak and incapable of policing our fiefs. And the Serke, as you might expect, have been making the most of the situation. We have been subjected to a great deal of outside pressure. All part of the Serke maneuver against us, of course. But we cannot prove they are behind it."

"If the behavior of males here is unusual.... Are these rogues homegrown?" As an afterthought, she added the appropriate, "Mistress?"

Dorteka's ears tilted in mild amusement. "You strike to the heart of the matter. In fact, they are not. Our native males are perfectly behaved, though they often lend passive support by not reporting things they should. Sometimes they even grow so bold as to provide places of hiding. Certainly they sympathize with the rogues' stated goals."

Those goals were nothing less than the overthrow and destruction of all silthdom. A grand vision indeed, considering the iron grip the Communities had upon the world.

III

Marika's first attempt to visit Braydic did not go well at all. Called out of the communications center, the technician met her with evasive eyes and an obvious eagerness to be away. Marika was both amused and pained, for she recalled who it was who had held the door guards at bay in the heat of crisis.

"No one saw you, Braydic," she said. "You are safe. I doubt the guards themselves could identify you. They were on the edge of hysteria and probably recall you as being a demon nine feet tall and six wide."

Braydic shuddered and stared at the floor. Marika was disappointed, but knew what that momentary commitment had cost Braydic. She had risked everything.

"I owe you, Braydic. And I will not forget. Go, then, if you fear having me for a friend. But I promise my friendship will not falter for it."

Marika returned two weeks later. Braydic was no more sure of herself. Pained, Marika determined that she would not return again till she had attained some position of power, the shadow of which could fall upon Braydic.

She had begun to grow aware of the value and uses of power, and to think of it. Often.

That second visit, cut short, left her an hour free. She went to her away place in the tower.

Spring now threatened Maksche. The city lay under a haze from factories working overtime to fulfill production quotas before their workers had to report to the fields. Because of the shortening growing seasons, every worker now had to labor in the fields to get sufficient crops planted, tended, and harvested. Else the city would not make it through the winter.

This failing winter had been the worst in Maksche's history, though it was mild compared to those Marika had seen in the upper Ponath. But succeeding winters would be worse. The Maksche silth were now driving their tenants, their dependents, their meth property, so Maksche would be prepared for the worst when it came.

A darkship rose from the square below. The blade of the dagger turned till it pointed northward. Once it was above Maksche's highest structures, it fled into the distance.

From the date of the most senior's arrival, darkships had been airborne every day the weather permitted, hunting nomads, tracking nomads, scouting out their strong points and places of meeting, gathering information for a summer campaign. The Reugge could not challenge the Serke directly. They had neither the strength nor proof other Communities would consider adequate. So the most senior meant to defeat their efforts by obliterating their minions.

She was tough and bloodyminded, this Gradwohl. She meant to fertilize the entire northern half of the Reugge province with nomad corpses. And if she could manage it, she would add several hundred troublesome rogue males to the slaughter.

The cloister was ahum with an anticipation Marika hardly noticed. She did not expect to become involved in Gradwohl's campaign.

How long before Dorteka allowed her to explore Maksche? She was eager to be away from the cloister, to break for a few hours from this relentless business of becoming silth.

Maksche was odd, a city of marked contrasts. Here sat the cloister, all but its ceremonial heart electrically lighted and heated. One could get water simply by lifting a lever. Wastes were carried away in a system of sewage pipes. But outside the cloister's walls few lights existed, and those only candles or tallow lamps. Meth out there drew their water from wells or the river. Their sewers consisted of channels in the alleyways, washed clean when it rained.

It had not rained all winter.

Meth out there walked, unless they were the rare, rich, favored few who could rent dray beasts, a driver, and a carriage from the tradermales of the Brown Paw Bond. Silth sisters going abroad in the town usually rode in elegant steam coaches faster than any carriage. If Dorteka allowed her out, would she be permitted the use of such a vehicle? Not likely. They were guarded jealously, for they were very expensive. They were handcrafted by one of the tradermale underbrotherhoods not part of the local Brown Paw Bond, and imported. They were not silth property.

The traders sold no vehicle outright, but leased them instead. Lease contracts demanded huge penalty payments for damages done. Marika suspected that was motivated by a desire to keep lessees from dismantling the machines to see how they worked.

A tradermale operator came with every vehicle. Outsiders were not allowed to learn how to drive. Those males obligated to the vehicles of the cloister lived in a small barracks across the street from the cloister's main gate, whence they could be summoned on a moment's notice.

When her hour was up, Marika went to Dorteka and asked, "How many more points do I have to accumulate before I can go into the city?"

"It is not a point system, Marika. You can go whenever I decide you deserve the reward."

"Well? Do I?" She had held back nothing. Having been used as a counter in a contest she did not understand, for reasons she could not comprehend, she had gone all out to arm herself for her own survival. Dorteka could not have demanded more. There was no more she could give.

"Perhaps. Perhaps. But why go out into that fester at all?"

"To explore it. To see what is out there. To get out of this oppressive prison for a while."

"Oppressive? Prison? The cloister?"

"It is unbearable. But you grew up here. Maybe you cannot imagine freedom of movement."

"No. I cannot. At least not out there. My duties have taken me into the city, Marika. It is disgusting. I would rather not traipse around after you while you crawl through the muck."

"Why should you, mistress?"

"What?"

"There is no reason for you to go."

"If you go, I have to go."

"Why, mistress?"

"To keep you out of trouble."

"I can take care of myself, mistress."

"Maksche is not the Ponath, pup."

"I doubt that the city has dangers to compare with the nomad."

"It is not danger to your flesh I fear, Marika. It is your mind that concerns me."

"Mistress?"

"You do not fool me. You are not yet silth. And you are no harmless, eager student. A shadow lives behind your eyes."

Marika did not respond till she carefully stifled her anger. "I do not understand you, mistress. Others have said the same of me. Some have called me doomstalker. Yet I do not feel unusual. How could the city harm my mind? By exposing me to dangerous ideas? I have enough of those myself. I will create my own beliefs here or there, regardless of what you would have me believe. Or could it harm me by showing me how cruelly Reugge bonds live so we silth can be comfortable here? That much I have seen from the wall."

Dorteka did not reply. She, too, was fighting anger.

"If I must have company and protection, send my packmates, Grauel and Barlog. I am certain they would be happy to accept your instructions." Her sarcasm was lost on Dorteka.

She and Grauel and Barlog had been at odds almost since the confrontation with the most senior. The two huntresses had been making every effort to appear to be perfect subjects of the Community. Marika did not want them to surrender quite so fast.

"I will consider that. If you insist on going out there."

"I want to, mistress."

The great ground-level gate rolled back. Grauel and Barlog stepped out warily. Marika followed, surprised at their reluctance. Behind her, Dorteka said, "Be back before dark, Marika. Or no more passes."

"Yes, mistress. Come on!" She ran, exulting in her freedom. Grauel and Barlog struggled to keep pace. "Isn't it wonderful?"

"It stinks," Grauel said. "They live in their own ordure, Marika."

And Barlog: "Where are you going?" Already it was evident that Marika had a definite destination in mind.

"To the tradermale enclosure. To see their flying machines."

"I might have guessed," Barlog grumbled. "Slow down. We're not as young as you are. Marika, all this obsession with flying is not healthy. Meth were not meant for it. Marika! Will you slow down?"

Marika glanced back. The two huntresses were struggling with the cumbersome long rifles they carried. "Why did you bring those?" She knew Grauel preferred the weapon she had gotten from Bagnel.

"Orders, Marika. Pure and simple and malicious orders. There are some silth who hope you'll get killed out here. The only reason you get a pretense of a bodyguard is because you have the most senior's favor."

"Pretense?"

"Any other silth would have at least six guards. If she was insane enough to come out on foot. And they would not be so shoddily armed. They would not have let *us* come except that we are two they won't miss if something happens."

"That's silly. Nobody has been attacked since we've been here. I think all that is just scare talk. Good old grauken in the bushes."

"No one has been foolish enough to walk these streets either, Marika."

Marika did not want to argue. She wanted to see airships. She pressed ahead. The tradermales built machines that flew. She had seen them in her education tapes and from her tower in the nether distance, but it was hard to connect vision screen images and remote specks with anything real. The airfield lay too far from the cloister for examination from her tower.

An aircraft was circling as Marika approached the fence surrounding the tradermale enclave. It swooped, touched down, rolled along a long concrete strip, and came to a halt with one final metallic belch. Marika checked Grauel and Barlog for their reactions. They had seen nothing like it before. Servants of the silth saw very little of the world, and tradermale aircraft were not permitted to fly near the cloister.

They might have been watching carrion birds land upon a corpse.

"Let's get closer," Marika said. She trotted along the fence, toward a group of buildings. Grauel and Barlog hurried after her, glancing over their shoulders at the aircraft and at two big transport dirigibles resting in cradles on the far side of the concrete strip.

The advantage of being silth, Marika believed, was that you could do any All-bedamned thing you wanted. Ordinary meth would grind their teeth and endure. She breezed into an open doorway, past a desk where a sleepy tradermale watched a vision screen, dashed down a long hallway and out onto the field proper, ignoring the startled shout that pursued her. She headed for the freighters.

The nearest was a monster. The closer she ran, the more she was awed.

"Oh," Grauel said at last, and slowed. Marika stopped to wait. Grauel breathed, "All bless us. It is as big as a mountain."

"Yes." Marika started to explain how an airship worked, saw that she had lost both huntresses, said instead, "It could haul the whole Degnan pack. Packstead and all. And have room left over."

Tradermale technicians were at work around the airship's gondola. One spotted them. He yelled at the others. A few just stared. Most scattered. Marika thought that was amusing.

The fat flank of the ship loomed higher and higher. She leaned back, now as awed as Grauel and Barlog. She beckoned a male either too brave or too petrified to have fled. He approached tentatively. "What ship is this, tradermale?"

He seemed puzzled by that latter, dialect word, but got the sense of the question. *"Dawnstrider."*

"Oh. I do not know that one. It is so big, I thought it must be *Starpetal.*"

"No. *Starpetal* is much larger. Way too big for our cradles here. Usually only the smaller ships come up to the borderlands."

"Borderlands?" Marika asked, bemused by the size of the ship.

"Well, Maksche is practically the end of the world. Last outpost of civilization. Ten miles out there it turns into Tech Three Zone and just gets worse the farther you go." He tilted his ears and exposed his teeth in a way that said he was making a joke.

"I thought I hailed from the last outpost," Marika countered in a bantering tone. "North edge of the Tech Two." If she could overcome his awe, he might have something interesting to say. She did realize that most meth considered Maksche the end of the world. It was the northernmost city of consequence in the Hainlin basin, the limit of barge traffic and very border of Tech Four-permitted machine technology. It had grown up principally to service and support trade up the Hainlin, into the primitive interior of the vast and remote northern Reugge provinces. "Well, savagery is relative. Right? *We* are civilized. *They* are savages. Come, Barlog. Grauel."

"Where are you going?" the tradermale squeaked. "Hey! You cannot go in there."

"I just want to look at the control cabin," Marika said. "I will not touch anything. I promise."

"But... wait..."

Marika climbed the ladder leading to the airship's gondola. After a moment of silent debate, Grauel and Barlog followed, shaking visibly, driven onward only by their pride. A Degnan huntress knew no fear.

Dawnstrider was a freighter. Its appointments were minimal, designed to keep down mass so payload could be maximized. Even so, the control cabin was bewildering with its array of meters and dials, levers, valves, switches, and push-buttons. "Do not touch anything," Marika warned Grauel and Barlog for the benefit of the technician, who refused to leave them unsupervised. "We do not want this beast to carry us away."

The huntresses clutched their weapons and stared around. Marika was puzzled. They were not ignorant Ponath dwellers anymore. They had been exposed to the greater meth universe. They should have developed some flexibility.

She did not remain impressed long. *Dawnstrider* was a disappointment, though she could not pin down why. "I have seen enough. Let us go look at the little ships."

She went down the ladder behind the technician, amused by the emotion betrayed in his every movement. She was getting good at reading body language.

She did not sense the wrongness till she had moved several steps from the base of the ladder. Then it was too late.

Tradermales rushed from beneath the airship, all of them armed. Grauel and Barlog snapped their weapons to the ready, shielded Marika with their bodies.

"What is this?" Marika snapped.

"You do not belong here, silth," a male said. "You are trespassing on brethren land."

Marika's nerve wavered. Yet she stared the male in the eye with the arrogance of a senior and said, "I go where I please, male. And you mind your manners when you speak—"

"You are out of line, pup. No one comes into a brethren enclave without permission of the factors."

He had the right of it. She had not thought. There were compacts between the Reugge and the tradermales. She had overlooked them in her enthusiasm.

A stubborn something within her refused to back down, insisted that she up the risk. "You better have these males put their weapons aside. I do not wish to harm anyone."

"I have twenty rifles, pup. I count two on your side."

"You are speaking to a darkwalker. I can destroy the lot of you before one trigger can be pulled. You think about dying with your heart ripped out, male."

His lips peeled back in a snarl. He was ready to call her bluff. The set of Grauel's shoulders said that the huntress thought her mad to provoke the male so, that she would get them all killed for nothing.

Fleetingly, Marika wondered why she did provoke almost everyone who ever challenged her.

"We shall see." The tradermale gestured.

Marika felt an odd tingling, like that she experienced around high-energy communications gear. Something electromagnetic was being directed at her. She spotted a tradermale in the background aiming a boxlike device her way.

She dived down inside herself, through her loophole, snagged a ghost, and slammed it into the guts of the box. She twisted that ghost and compressed it into an ever more rapidly spinning ball, all within an instant. She watched it shred wires and glass.

She came back in time to watch the box fly apart, to hear the technician's startled yelp. He raised a bleeding paw to his mouth.

Fingers strained at triggers. The leading tradermale betrayed extreme distress. "You see?" Marika demanded.

"Hold it! Hold it there!" someone shouted from the distance. Everyone turned.

More males were running along the airstrip. In a moment Marika realized why one seemed familiar. "Bagnel," she said softly. Her spirits rose. Maybe she would escape the consequences of her own stupidity after all.

The instant she began to see hope, she started worrying about the consequences that would follow the report that would reach the cloister. There would be a complaint, surely. Tradermales were said to be militant about their rights. They had struggled for ages to obtain them. Their organization was by-the-rules where those were concerned.

Marika was mildly amazed to discover she was more afraid of Dorteka than she was of this potentially lethal confrontation.

A few tradermale weapons sagged as they awaited those approaching. Tension drooped with them. Grauel and Barlog relaxed, though they did not lower their weapons.

Bagnel rushed up, puffing. "Timbruk, what have you got here?" He peered at Marika. "Ha! Well! And I actually thought of you when they told me. Marika. Hello." He interposed himself between Marika and the male he had called Timbruk. "Can we have a little relaxation here, meth? Everybody. Put the weapons down. There is no call to get anyone hurt."

Timbruk protested, "Bagnel, they have trespassed…"

"Obviously. But no harm done, was there?"

"Harm is not the point."

"Yes. Yes. Well, Timbruk, if they need shooting we can do that later. Put the weapons down. Let me talk. I know this sister. She saved my life in the Ponath."

"Saved your life? Come on. She is just a pup. She is the one who…?"

"Yes. She is that one."

Timbruk swallowed. His eyes widened. He looked spooked. He stared at Marika till she became uncomfortable. Twice his gaze seemed pulled toward a group of buildings at the north end of the field. Each time he jerked it back to her with sudden ferocity. Then he said, "Relax, brothers. Relax. Weapons on safety."

Marika said, "Grauel, Barlog, stand easy. Put your weapons on safe."

Grauel did not want to do it. Her every muscle was tense with a rigidly controlled fight-flight response. But she did as she was told, though her eyes continued to smolder.

Barlog merely heaved a sigh of relief.

Bagnel did likewise. "Good. Now, shall we talk? Marika, what in the name of the All did you think you were doing, coming in here like that? You cannot just walk in like you own the place. This is convention ground. Have they not taught you anything over there?

"I know. It was stupid." She stepped closer, spoke more softly. "I was just wandering around, exploring. When I saw the airships I got so excited I lost my head. I forgot everything else. I just had to look. Then these males…" She broke off, realizing she was about to make accusations that would be unreasonable and provocative.

Bagnel was amused. But he said, "Did you have to be so… I see. They have taught you—taught you to be silth. I mean, the way silth here understand being silth. Cold. Arrogant. Insensitive. Never mind. As they say, silth will be silth.

Timbruk. It is over. There is no need for you here now. This is to be forgotten. No record. No formal protest. Understand?"

"Bagnel…"

Bagnel ignored him. "I owe you a life, Marika. But for you I would have become meat in a nomad's belly more than once. I repay a fraction of the debt here. I forgive the trespass." In soft humor, he added, "I am sure your seniors would have a good deal to say to you if they heard about this."

"I am sure they would. Thank you."

Timbruk and his males were stalking away, some occasionally glancing back. Except for the male who had tried to use the box. Despite his wound, he was crouched over the remains, prodding them with a finger, shaking his head. He seemed both baffled and disturbed.

"Come," Bagnel said. He started toward the buildings through which Marika had made her dash.

She asked, "What are you doing here?"

"I am assigned here now. As assistant security chief for the enclave. Since I did such a wonderful job as security officer at Critza, they awarded me a much more important post." His sarcasm was thick enough to cut. Marika could not determine its thrust, though. Was he his own target? Or were the seniors who had given him the job?

"That was what you were doing up there? I always had a feeling you were not a regular wander-the-forests-with-a-pack-on-your-back kind of tradermale."

"My job was to protect the fortress and manage any armed operations undertaken in the region of its license."

"Then you were in charge of that hunting party you were with the first time we met."

"I was."

"I thought old Khronen was in charge."

"I know. We allowed you think so. He was just our guide, though. He had been in the upper Ponath all his life. I think he knew every rock and bush by name."

"He was a friend of my dam. At least as near a friend as she ever had among males."

Bagnel, daring beyond belief, reached out and touched her lightly. "The memories do haunt, do they not? We all lost so much. And those who were never there just shrug it off."

Marika stiffened her back. "Can we look at the small aircraft on the way to the gate?"

Bagnel rewarded her with a questioning look.

"The crime is committed," she replied. "Can I compound it?"

"Of course." He altered course toward a rank of five propeller-driven aircraft.

"Stings," Marika said as they approached. "Driven by a single bank nine-cylinder air-cooled radial engine that develops eighteen hundred meth power. Top speed two hundred ten. Normal cruising speed one sixty. Not fast, but capable of carrying a very large payload. A fighting aircraft. Who do tradermales fight, Bagnel?"

"You amaze me. How did you find out? We fight anyone who attacks us. There are a lot of wild places left in the world. Even here in the higher Tech Zones. There is always a demand for the application of force."

"Are these ones here for the push against the nomads?"

"No. We may reoccupy our outposts if the Reugge manage to push the nomads out, but we will not help push."

"Why not? The Brown Paw Bond suffered more than we did, if you do not count the packs. Posts all along the Hainlin…"

"Orders, Marika. I do not pretend to understand. Politics, I guess. Little one, you picked the wrong sisterhood at the wrong time. Strong forces are ranged against the Reugge."

"The Serke?"

"Among others. They are the most obvious, but they do not stand alone. That is off the record, though. You did not hear it from me."

"You did not tell me anything I did not know. I do wonder why, though. No one has bothered the Reugge since they split from the Serke. Why start now?"

"The Reugge are not strong, Marika, but they are rich. The Hainlin basin produces a disproportionate amount of wealth. Emeralds out of the Zhotak—those alone might be reason enough. We Brown Paw Bond traders have done very well trading junk for emeralds."

Marika harkened to younger days, when tradermales had come into the upper Ponath afoot or leading a single rheum-greater, exchanging a few iron tools, books, beads, flashy pieces of cloth, and such, for the clear green stones or otec furs. Every year Dam's friend Khronen had come to the Degnan packstead, bringing precious tools and his easy manner with pups, and had walked away with a fortune.

The Degnan had been satisfied with the trades. Emeralds were of little value on a frontier. Otec fur was of more use, being the best there was, but what it would bring in trade outweighed its margin of value over lesser furs.

Junk, Bagnel called the trade goods. And he was right from his perspective. Arrowheads, axe heads, hoes, hammers, rakes, all could be manufactured in bulk at little cost in Maksche's factories. One emerald would purchase several wagonloads here. And books, for which a pack might save for seasons, were produced in mass in the city's printshops.

"Is that why the Ponath is kept savage?"

Meth, with the exceptions of tradermales and silth, seldom moved far from their places of birth. Information did not travel well in the mouths of those with an interest in keeping it close. How angry Skiljan would have been had she known the treasures she acquired for the pack cost the traders next to nothing. She would have believed it robbery. Just another example of innate male perfidy.

"Partly. Partly because the silth are afraid of an informed populace, of free movement of technology. Your Communities could not survive in a world where wealth, information, and technology traveled freely. We brethren would have our troubles. We are few and the silth are fewer still. Between us we run everything because for ages we have shaped the law and tradition to that end."

They walked around the fighting aircraft. Marika found its presence disturbing. For that matter, the presence of *Dawnstrider* was unsettling. Trade in and out of Maksche did not require a vessel so huge. There was more here than met the eye. Maybe that explained Timbruk's hostility.

"The Sting's main disadvantage is its limited range when fully fight-loaded," Marika said, continuing with the data she had given earlier.

"You are right. But where did you learn all that, Marika? I would bet only those of us who actually fly the beasts know all you have told me."

"I learned in tapestudy. I am going to be a darkship flyer. So I have been learning everything about flying. I know everything about airships, too."

"I doubt that." Bagnel glanced back at *Dawnstrider*.

"But those craft..." Marika indicated several low, long, ovoid shapes in the shadow of a building on the side away from the city. "I do not recognize those."

"Ground-effect vehicles. Not strictly legal in a Tech Four Zone, but all right as long as we keep them inside convention ground. You came close to catching us using them that time you first met me."

"The noise and the smell. And Arhdwehr getting so angry. Engines and exhaust. Of course."

"Every brethren station has a few for emergency use. Mainly for hurried getaways. You remember the odd tracks going away from Critza? Where I said some of our brethren got out? Ground-effect vehicles made those. They leave a pretty obvious trail in the snow." He went on to explain how the machines worked. Marika had no trouble grasping the concept.

"There is much I do not yet know, then," she said.

"No doubt. There is much we all do not know. Let me give you some advice. Try to consider the broader picture before you let impulse carry you away again."

"What?"

"There is a great deal of tension between the Brown Paw Bond and the Reugge right now. Our factors not only refused to help reclaim the provinces overrun by the nomad, they would not lease the fighting aircraft the Reugge wanted. I do not pretend to understand why. It was a chance for us to sweep up a huge profit."

"I see." Marika considered the fighting aircraft once more. It was a two-seat, open-cockpit biplane with two guns that fired through the airscrew, four wing-mounted guns, and a single gimbal-mounted weapon which could be fired rearward by the occupant of the second seat. "I would love to fly one of those," she said. The tapes mentioned capabilities that could be matched by no darkship.

"It is an experience," Bagnel agreed.

"You fly?"

"Yes. If there was trouble and the aircraft had to be employed, I would be a backup flyer."

"Take me up."

"Marika!" Grauel snapped.

Bagnel was amused. "There is no limit to her audacity, is there?"

"Marika," Grauel repeated, "you exceed yourself. You may be silth, but even so we will drag you back to the cloister."

"Not today, Marika," Bagnel said. "I cannot. Maybe some other time. Come back later. Be polite at the gate, ask for me, and maybe you will be permitted entrance—without all this fuss. Right now I think you had better leave before Timbruk goes over my head and gets permission to shoot you anyhow." Bagnel strode toward the gateway buildings. Marika followed. She was nervous now. There would be trouble when she got home.

Bagnel said, "I do not think your sisters would be upset if Timbruk did you in either. You still have that smoky look. Of the fated outsider."

"I have problems with the silth," Marika admitted. "But the most senior has given me her protection."

"Oh? Lucky for you."

They parted at the gate, Bagnel with a well-wish and repeated invitation to return under more auspicious circumstances.

Outside, Marika paused to scan the field, watched Bagnel stride purposefully toward distant buildings. Her gaze drifted to those structures in the north. Cold crept down her spine. She shivered.

"Come. We are returning to the cloister right now," Grauel said. Her tone brooked no argument. Marika did not protest, though she did not want to go back. She did have to cling to the goodwill of Grauel and Barlog. They were her only trustworthy allies.

CHAPTER SEVENTEEN

I

Marika went from the gate to her tower, where she sat staring toward the tradermale compound. Several dots soared above the enclave, roaming the sky nearby.

Grauel came to her there. She looked grim. "Trouble," she said.

"They have registered their protest already? That was fast."

"Not that kind of trouble. Home trouble. Somebody got into our quarters."

"Oh?"

"After we turned in the weapons they gave us, we went up to clean up. My rifle was gone."

"Anything else?"

"No. The Degnan Chronicle had been opened and moved slightly. That is all."

"The most senior should spend more time here instead of talking about spending more time here."

Marika had noted that in Gradwohl's absence she was treated far more coolly. She wished that most senior would move into Maksche in fact as well as name. Despite declarations of intent, she just visited occasionally, usually without warning.

"I will not tolerate invasions of my private space, Grauel. No one else in the entire Community has to suffer such intrusions. Back off and give me a few minutes of quiet."

She slipped down through her loophole and cast about till she found a ghost she thought sufficiently strong. She took control and began roaming the cloister, beginning in places she thought were most likely to reveal the missing weapon.

Finding it took only minutes. It was in the cloister arsenal, where some sisters argued it belonged anyway. A pair of silth were dismantling it.

Marika returned to flesh. "Come."

"You found it? That quickly?"

"It is not hidden, actually. It is in the arsenal. We will take it back."

"And I was right there a few minutes ago."

The arsenal door was closed and locked now. Marika had no patience. Rather than scratch, wait, ask permission to enter, and argue, she recalled her ghost and squeezed it down as she had done when she had destroyed the electronic box belonging to the tradermale. She shoved the ghost into the lock and destroyed the metal there.

That made enough noise to alert the silth inside. They peered at her with fear and guilt when she stalked into the room where the parts of Grauel's weapon were scattered upon a table. One started to say something. Marika brushed her soul lightly with the ghost. "Grauel. Put it back together. You. Where is the ammunition? I want it here. Now."

The sister to whom she spoke thought of arguing, eyed Marika's bare teeth, thought better of it. She collected the ammunition from a storage box. After placing it upon the table, she retreated as far as the walls would allow. She choked out, "The orders came from Paustch. You will be in grave—"

"Ask me how much I care," Marika snapped. "This is for you to remember. And perhaps even share. The next meth who enters my quarters without my invitation will discover just how vicious a savage I really am. We invented some truly fascinating tortures to get nomads to tell us things we wanted to know."

Grauel cursed under her breath.

"Is it all there?"

"Yes. But they have mixed things up. It will take me a few minutes."

Marika used the time to glare at the two sisters till they cringed.

She heard Grauel slam the magazine home and feed a round to the chamber. "Ready?"

"Ready," Grauel said, sweeping the weapon's aim across the silth. Her lips pulled back in a snarl that set them on the edge of panic. "I do suppose I should thank them for cleaning it. They did that much good."

"Thank them, then. And let us be gone."

Gradwohl might not have been present in Maksche, but her paw was firmly felt. Darkships began arriving, bearing Reugge whose accents seemed exotic. They paused only to rest and eat and further burden their flying crosses. Some of the darkships lifted so burdened with meth and gear they looked like something from the worst quarters of the city.

"Everyone that can be spared," Barlog said as she and Marika and Grauel watched one darkship lift and another slide in under it. "That is the word now. The cloister is to be stripped. They have begun soliciting workers from the city, offering special pay. I would say the most senior is serious."

There had been some silth, at the evening meetings Marika attended, who had thought Gradwohl's plans just talk meant to form the basis for rumors that would reach the Serke. Rumors that would make that Community chary of too bold interference. But the lie had been given that view. The stream of darkships was never ending. The might of the Reugge was on the move, and impressive might it was.

Mistresses of the Ship could be seen in the meal halls almost all the time. Bath—the sisters who helped fly the darkships from their secondary positions at the tips of the shorter arms—sometimes crowded Maksche silth out of the meal lines. Scores seemed to be around all the time. Marika spent all her free time trying to get acquainted with those bath and Mistresses. But they would have little to do with her. They were an order within the order, silent, separate beings with little interest in socializing and none in illuminating a pup.

Three small dirigibles, contracted to the Reugge before the Brown Paw Bond elected not to support the offensive, appeared over the cloister and took aboard workers and silth and construction equipment. The cloister began to have a hollow feel, a deserted air. A shout would echo down long, empty halls. No one was there to answer.

The dirigibles would all make for Akard, which the most senior wanted rebuilt and reoccupied. It would become the focal point of a network of satellite fastnesses meant to interdict any nomad movements southward.

"I do not think she realizes how many nomads there are," Marika told Grauel. "Or really how vast her northern provinces are. All that might is not a tenth enough."

"She knows. I believe she is counting on the nomads having spent the best they had in the past few years. I think she expects it to be a job of tracking down remnants of the real fighting bands, then letting next winter finish the rest."

"I think she would be wrong if that is the basis of her strategy."

"So do I."

"We shall see, of course. Let us hope the answer is not savages in the cloister."

The early reports from the north told of a big harvest of nomads, of kills far more numerous than anyone expected. The numbers caused a good deal of uneasiness. They implied other numbers that might prove troublesome. For everyone agreed that there would be a dozen live and concealed nomads for every one dead.

II

The dream was a nightmare Marika had not known for several years, but it was old and familiar.

She was trapped in a cold, dark, damp place, badly hurt, unable to call for help, unable to climb out.

The dream had tormented her every night since her return from the tradermale enclave. She had told no one, but Grauel and Barlog sensed that something was torturing her.

Marika wished she could go visit Braydic. The last time the dreams had come, soon after her arrival at Akard, following the destruction of the Degnan packstead, she had shared her pain with the communications technician. Braydic had been unable to interpret the dream. Eventually, she had agreed it must be Marika's conscience nagging her because the dead of the Degnan pack had not gone into the embrace of the All with a proper Mourning.

After the return of the dreams, she had asked Grauel and Barlog where they stood in regard to that unsettled debt.

"We can do nothing now," Barlog told her. "Someday, though, we will take care of it. Perhaps when you are important and powerful. The score is not forgotten, nor considered settled."

That was good enough for Marika. But meantime she had to endure the horror of her nights.

Dorteka wakened her from this dream. She was early, but Marika was too fuddled to realize that till after they had been into their gymnasium routine for some time. "Why are we up so early?" she asked.

"We have new orders, you and I. We are headed north."

"Up the river? To chase nomads?" Marika was astonished. It was the last thing she expected.

"Yes. The great hunt is in full cry. The most senior is sending everyone who has no absolute need to remain. She sent a note saying that means us especially."

Just last evening word had come round that the most senior had ordered all patrolling darkships to destroy any meth they found upon the ground. They were to operate on the assumption that no locals had survived. No mercy was to be shown.

"What is it all about, mistress?" Marika asked. "Why is Gradwohl so determined? I have heard that winter may not break this year, at least in the upper Ponath. That the ground will remain frozen. No crops could be planted there. So why fight for useless territory?"

"Someone exaggerated, Marika. There will be a summer. Not that it matters. We are not going to send settlers into the Ponath. We are simply validating our claim to our provinces. In blood. Gradwohl is leading us in a fight against the Serke, and this is the only way we can battle them. Indirectly."

"Why are the Serke so determined, then? I am told wealth is the reason. I know about the emeralds, and there is gold and silver and copper and things, but nobody ever did any mining up there. It is a Tech Two Zone. There must be some other reason the Serke risk conflict."

"Probably. We do not know what it is, though. We just know we cannot allow them to steal the Ponath. Them or the brethren."

"You think the reason the tradermales will not help us is because they want to steal the Ponath, too?"

"I expect the Brown Paw Bond would stand with us if they could. We have been close associates for centuries. But higher authority may have been offered a better cut by the Serke."

"Could we not impose sanctions?"

Dorteka appeared amused by her naiveté. "Without proof? Wait. Yes. You know, and I know, and everyone else alive knows what is happening. Or we think we do. We *suspect* that the brethren and the Serke Community have entered into a conspiracy prohibited by the conventions. But no Community extant will act on suspicion. The Serke have Bestrei, and flaunt it. As long as the Reugge cannot present absolute and irrefutable proof of what is happening, no other Community faces the disagreeable business of having to take sides. They would rather sit back and be entertained by our travails."

"But if the Serke get away with this, they will be a threat to everyone else. Do the other orders not see that? Armed with all our wealth, and Bestrei besides…"

"Who knows what is really going on? Not you or I. The other sisterhoods may be in it with the Serke. There are ample precedents."

"It all seems silly to me," Marika said. "Will Grauel and Barlog be able to go with me?"

"I am sure they will. You are a single unit in most eyes."

Marika glanced at her instructress, not liking her tone. She and Dorteka tolerated one another because the most senior insisted, but there was no love between them.

Marika, Grauel, Barlog, and Dorteka, with their gear, boarded a northbound darkship about the time Marika should have begun her mathematics class. The bath, before going to their places at the tips of the short arms, made certain the passengers strapped themselves to the darkship's frame. All gear went into bins fixed around the cross's axis.

Marika paid much more attention to the darkship and its operators this trip. "Mistress Dorteka. What is this metal? I have seen nothing like it before." It seemed almost invisible when probed with the touch.

"Titanium. It is the lightest metal known, yet very strong. It is difficult to obtain. The brethren recover it in a process similar to that they use to obtain aluminum. They fairly rob us for these ships."

"They make them?"

"Yes."

"I would think it something we would do for ourselves. Why do we let them rob us?"

"I am not sure. Maybe because to argue is too much trouble. We do buy them, I think, because their ships are better. We have been buying them for only about sixty years, though. Before that most of the orders made their own. There was a lot of artistry involved. Most of those old darkships are still in service down south, too, around TelleRai and the other big cities."

"What were they like? How were they different? And what do you mean, buy? I thought the tradermales only leased."

"Questions, questions, questions. Pup…. They do not lease darkships. We would not let them get away with that. In some ways they have us too much in their power now.

"The old ships are not much different from those you have seen. Maybe smaller, generally. They were wooden, though. A few were pretty fanciful because they were seen as works of art. They were pawcrafted from golden fleet timber, a wood that is sensitive to the touch. The trees had to be at least five hundred years old before they could be cut. They were considered very precious. The groves are protected by a web of laws even now. So-called poachers can be slain for even touching a golden fleet tree.

"Every frame member and strut in the old ships was individually carved from a specially selected timber or billet. The way I hear, a shipbuilder sister might spend a year preparing one strut. It might take a building team twenty years to complete a ship. No two darkships were ever alike, unlike these brethren products. These things are plain and all business."

All business maybe, but hardly plain. This one was covered with seals and fanciful witch signs that, Marika suspected, had something to do with the Mistress and her bath.

"You say those old ones are still around?"

"Most of them. I have seen some in TelleRai that are said to be thousands of years old. Silth have been flying since the beginning of time. The Redoriad museum at TelleRai has several prehistoric saddleships that are still taken up once in a while."

"Saddleships?" Here was something she had missed in her search for information on flying.

"In olden times that sort of silth who today would become a Mistress of the Ship usually flew alone. Her ship was a pole of golden fleet wood about eighteen feet long with a saddle mounted two-thirds of the way back. You would find the Redoriad museum interesting, what with your interest in flight. They have something of everything there."

"I sure would. I will find out about it if I ever get to TelleRai."

"You will get there soon enough if Gradwohl has her way."

"Then I suppose the reason for buying metal ships is because that is easier than making them."

"No doubt."

"Are there any artisans left? Sisters who could build darkships if necessary?"

"I am sure there are. Silth are conservative. Old things take a thousand years to die. And about darkships there are many still devoted to the old. Many who prefer the wooden ships because the golden fleet wood is more responsive than cold metal. Also, many who feel we should not be dependent upon the brethren for our ships.

"The brethren keep taking over chunks of our lives. There was a time when touch-sisters did everything comm techs do now. Their greatest bragged that they could touch anyone anywhere in the world. That far reach is almost a lost art now."

"That is sad."

The darkship was fifty miles north of the city already. Ahead, Marika could just distinguish the fire-blackened remains of a tradermale outpost. Kharg Station. It marked the southernmost flow of nomad raiding for the winter. Its fall had been the final insult that had driven Gradwohl into the rage whence this campaign had sprung. Its fall had come close to costing Senior Zertan her position, for she had made no effort to relieve the besieged outpost.

"I think so, too. We live in the moment, we silth, but many long for the past. For quieter times when we were not so much dependent upon the brethren." Dorteka eyed the ruins. "Zertan is one of those. Paustch is another."

The darkship moved north at a moderate pace. After marveling at the view of the plain and the brown, meandering Hainlin, Marika slid down inside herself. For a time she studied the subtle interplay of talent between the bath and the Mistress of the Ship. These were veterans. They drew upon one another skillfully. Fatigue would be a long time coming.

Once she thought she understood what they were doing, Marika began cataloging all she knew about her own and others' talents. She found what she was seeking. She returned to the world.

"Dorteka, could we not make our own metal darkships? Assuming we want to produce the ships quickly? We have sisters who could extract the metal from ore with their talents. It could not be difficult to build a ship if the metal was available."

"Silth do not do that kind of work."

Marika ran that through her mind, looking at it from every angle but the logical. She already knew the argument made no logical sense. She must have missed something because she still did not understand after trying to see it as silth. "Mistress, I do not understand."

Dorteka had forgotten already. "What?"

"*Why* should we not build a metal darkship if it is within our capacity? When it is all right for us to build a wooden one? Especially if the tradermales are working against us." There was some circumstantial evidence that a tradermale faction was supporting the ever-more-organized efforts of the rogue males plaguing the Reugge.

Dorteka could not explain in any way that made sense to Marika. She became confused and frustrated by her effort. She finally snapped, "Because that is the way it is. Silth do not do physical labor. They rule. They are artists. The wooden darkships were works of art. Metal ships are machines, even if they perform the same tasks. Anyway, we have tacitly granted that they fall inside the prerogatives of the brethren."

"We could have our own factory inside the cloister...." Marika gave it up. Dorteka was not interested in a pup's foolish notions. Marika invested in a series of mental relaxation exercises so she could clear her thoughts to enjoy the flight.

The darkship did not pursue a direct course toward Akard. It roamed errati-cally, randomly, at times drifting far from the river, on the off chance contact would be made with nomads. The day was far advanced when Marika began to see landmarks she recognized. "There, Grauel. What is left of Critza."

"The tradermales will not be restoring that. That explosion certainly took it apart."

Bagnel had set off demolition charges in what the nomads had left of the packfast, to deny it value to any nomads who thought to use it later.

"Now. There it is. Straight ahead," Barlog said as the darkship slipped around a bend in the river canyon.

Akard. Where Marika had spent four miserable years, and had discovered that she was that most dreaded of silth, a strong darkwalker.

The remains of the fortress were perched on a headland where the Hainlin split into the Husgen and an eastern watercourse which retained the Hainlin name. It was webbed in by scaffolding. Workers swarmed over it like colony insects. The darkship settled toward the headland.

It was a scant hundred feet off the ground when Marika felt a sudden, strong touch.

Hang on. We have a call for help.

That was the Mistress of the Ship with a warning so powerful even Grauel and Barlog caught its edges.

Marika barely had time to warn them verbally. The darkship shot forward, rose, gained speed rapidly. The robes of the Mistress and bath crackled in the rushing wind. Marika ducked down through to examine the altered relation-ship between the Mistress and bath. The Mistress was drawing heavily on the bath now.

The darkship climbed to three hundred feet and arced to the east, into the upper Ponath. A few minutes later it passed over the site of the Degnan packstead, where Marika had lived her first ten years. Only a few regular lines in the earth remained upon that hilltop clearing.

Marika read grief in the set of Grauel's upper torso. Barlog refused to look and respond.

The darkship rushed on toward the oncoming night. Way, way to her left Marika spotted a dot coming down from the north, angling in, occasionally spilling a crimson flash as sunlight caught it. Another darkship. Then to the south, another still. All three rushed eastward on intersecting courses.

Marika's ship arrived first, streaking over a forest where rifles hammered and heavier weapons filled the woods with flashes. A clearing appeared ahead. At its center stood an incomplete fortress of logs. It was afire. Huntresses enveloped in smoke sniped at the surrounding forest.

Something black and wicked roiled around Marika. The darkship dropped away beneath her, plunging groundward. The darkness cleared. The Mistress of the Ship resumed control of her craft, took it up. Chill wind nibbled at Marika's face.

Screams came from the forest.

The second and third darkships made passes while Marika's turned. Marika went down through her loophole, located a ghost not bearing the ship, and went riding. She located a band of wild silth and wehrlen. They were feeble but able to neutralize the three silth who commanded the besieged workers and huntresses.

A hum past her ear pulled Marika back. The Mistress was into her second pass. Rifles flashed ahead. Bullets whined past the darkship. One spanged against metal and howled away.

Marika dived through her loophole, found a steed, lashed it toward the wild silth. She allowed her anger full reign when she reached them.

She was astonished by her own strength. It had grown vastly during her brief stay at Maksche. A dozen nomads died horribly. The others scattered. In moments the nomad fighters followed.

The darkships began flying fast, low-level circles, spiraling outward from the stronghold, exterminating fugitives. Marika's Mistress of the Ship did not break off till after three moons had risen.

III

Paustch was in charge of the reconstruction of Akard. She was no friend of that uppity pup Marika or her scandalously undisciplined savage cohorts, Grauel and Barlog. She tolerated their presence in her demesne only a few days.

During those days Marika wangled a couple of patrol flights with the Mistress on whose darkship she had come north. The Mistress was not being sociable or understanding of the whims of a pup. She respected Marika's darker abilities and hoped they would help her survive her patrols.

No contact came during either flight.

On her return from the second venture, Marika found Dorteka packing. "What is happening, mistress? Have you been recalled?"

"No. *We* have been assigned the honor of establishing a blockhouse directly astride the main route from the Zhotak south into the upper Ponath, some-where up near the Rift." The look she gave Marika said much more. It said this was an exile, and that it was all Marika's fault because she was who and what she was. It said that they were being sent out into the wilderness because Paustch wanted her both out of her fur and into a difficult position.

Marika shrugged. "I would rather be away from here anyway. Paustch and her cronies persist in aggravating me. I am long-suffering, but under the circumstances I might eventually lose my temper."

Dorteka first tilted her ears in amusement, then came near losing *her* temper. "This hole is primitive enough. Out there there will be nothing."

"The life is not as hard as you imagine, mistress. And you will have three experienced woodsmeth to show you how to cope."

"And how many nomads?"

Marika broke away as soon as she could. She did not want to argue with Dorteka. She had plenty of firm enemies already among those who had power over her. Dorteka would never be a friend, but at present she could be counted upon for support as an agent of the most senior.

She *was* pleased to be assigned to a blockhouse garrison. It meant a respite from the grinding silth life, with all its ceremony and all the animosity directed her way. She did not enjoy that, though perforce she must live with it.

Next morning a school of darkships lifted Marika, Grauel, Barlog, Dorteka, and another eight huntresses and ten workers across the upper Ponath. The assigned site overlooked the way that had been both the trade route with and invasion route for the nomads of the Zhotak. Marika did not anticipate any real danger from nomads. She believed the savages all to have left the Zhotak long since. The vast majority should be looking for easy hunting far to the south of the upper Ponath.

"Dorteka. The nomads have lived hard lives ever since I have been aware of their existence. The Zhotak was a harsh land even before the winters worsened. Before they became organized, the raids they made were all acts of desperation. Now that they are fighting everywhere, all the time, they do not seem so desperate."

"What are you driving at, pup?" They had just landed at the site, a clearing on a slope overlooking a broad, meadowed valley. There was a great deal of snow among the trees on the opposite slope yet.

"In the past they did not have time free from trying to get ready for the next winter to spend their summers attacking and plundering. Now they have that time. To me it would seem their problems getting food have lessened. But I do not see how that could be. They are hunters and gatherers, not farmers. The winters have wiped out most of the game animals. So where are they getting food? Besides from eating their dead?"

"From the Serke, I suppose. I do not know. And I do not care." Dorteka surveyed the valley, which Marika thought excitingly beautiful. "I do not see why we bother fighting them for this wasteland. If they want it so badly, let them have it."

She was in a mood. Marika moved away, joined Barlog and Grauel, who were helping the workers unload supplies and equipment.

"We will need some sort of barrier right away," Grauel said. "I hear there are still a few kagbeasts in these parts. If so, they would be hungry enough to attack meth."

"I saw some snarltooth vines just west of here as we were coming in," Marika said. "Drive stakes and string some of those with some briars from the riverbank down there. That will do till we get a real palisade up."

"Grauel and I will work out a watch rotation. We will need big fires at night. Do we have permission to harvest live wood if there is not enough dead?"

"If necessary. But I think you will find plenty of deadwood. The winters are killing some of the less hardy trees already."

The outpost had to be built from the ground up. The task took a month. That month passed without incident, though on a couple of occasions Marika sensed the presence of strange meth on the far side of the valley. When she grabbed a ghost and went to examine them, she found that they were nomad scouts. She did not bother them. Let them prime themselves for falling into a trap.

Marika was unconcerned for her own safety, so unconcerned she sometimes wandered off alone, to the distress of Grauel and Barlog, who tracked her down each time.

Marika often joined in the physical work, too. She found it a good way to work out the frustrations she had accumulated during her months in Maksche. And in labor she found temporary surcease from concerns of the past and future.

This close to the Degnan packstead she could not help thinking often of the Mourning she owed. But there were no nightmares. Could that be because of the work? That did not seem reasonable.

After a time most of the southern huntresses joined the work, too, for all of Dorteka's disapproving scowls. There was nothing else to do but be bored.

The workers appreciated the help, but did not know what to make of it. Especially of a silth who actually dirtied her paws. Marika suspected they began to think well of her despite all the rumors they had heard. By summer's end she had most of them talking to her. And by summer's end she had begun consciously trying to cultivate their affection.

Dorteka refused to do anything but tutor Marika. That assignment she pursued doggedly, as if motivated mainly by an increasing desire to get the job over with. Their relationship deteriorated as the summer progressed, and Marika steadfastly refused to be molded into traditional silth shape.

Though the summer gave Marika a respite from her concerns and fears, she did spend a lot of time thinking about the future. She approached it with a pragmatic attitude suitable for the most cynical silth.

The only attack came soon after the blockhouse was complete. It was not a strong one, though the savages thought it strong enough. They cut through the snarltooth vine fencing and evaded the pit traps and booby traps. They used explosives to breach the palisade. Distressed, Dorteka reached out to Akard with the touch and asked for darkship support.

Marika obliterated the attackers long before the one ship sent arrived.

She deflected and destroyed the attackers almost casually, using a ghost drawn from high in the atmosphere. She had learned that the higher one could reach, the more monstrous a ghost one could find.

Afterward, Dorteka shied away from her the way she might from a dangerous animal, and never did get over being nervous when Marika was close.

Marika did not understand. She was even pained. She did not need Dorteka's friendship, but she did not want her fear.

Was her talent for the dark side that terrible? Did she exceed the abilities of other silth by so much? She could not believe that.

Soon after the first snowflakes flew, a darkship arrived bearing winter stores and a replacement silth. Marika and Dorteka received orders to return to the Maksche cloister.

"I am not going," Marika told Dorteka.

"Pup! I have had about all of your insubordination that I am going to stand. Get your coat on and get aboard that ship." Dorteka was so angry she ignored Grauel and Barlog.

"This is the last darkship that will come here till spring, barring a need for major support if the blockhouse comes under attack. Not so?"

"Yes. So what? Do you love these All-forsaken woods so much that you want to stay here forever?"

"Not at all. I want to go home. And so do these workers."

That caught Dorteka from the blind side. She could do nothing but look at Marika askance. Finally, she croaked, "What are you talking about? So what?"

"These meth were hired for the season. They were promised they would return home in time for the Festival of Kifkha. The festival comes up in four days. And no transportation has been provided them yet. You go ahead. You go south. You report to the most senior. And when she asks why I did not come back with you, you tell her why. Because once again the Reugge Community is failing to live up to a pledge to its dependents."

Dorteka became so angry Marika feared she would have a stroke. But she stood there facing her teacher in a stance so adamant it was clear she would not be moved. Dorteka went inside herself and performed calming rituals till she was settled enough to touch someone at Akard.

The workers went out next morning. From all over the upper Ponath they went, with an alacrity that said that Gradwohl herself must have intervened. Before they left, two workers very quietly told Marika where they could be reached in Maksche if ever she needed them to repay the debt. Marika memorized that information carefully. She had Grauel and Barlog commit it to memory too, protecting it through redundancy.

She meant to use those workers someday.

She had plans. During that summer she had begun to look forward in more than a simpleminded, pup-obsessed-with-flying sort of way. But she was careful to mask that from everyone. Even Grauel and Barlog remained outside.

"Will your holiness board her darkship now?" Dorteka demanded. "Is the order of the world arranged to your satisfaction?"

"Indeed. Thank you, Dorteka. I wish you understood. Those meth may be of no consequence to you. Nor are they to me, really. But a Community can only be as good as its honor. If our own dependents cannot trust our word, who else will?"

"Thank the All," Dorteka muttered as Marika began strapping herself to the cold darkship frame.

"Such indifference may well be the reason the cloister is having so much trouble keeping order in Maksche. Paustch is determined not to do right and Zertan is too lazy or too timid."

"You will seal your mouth, pup. You will not speak ill of your seniors again. I still have a great deal of control over how happy or miserable your life can be. Do I make myself understood?"

"Perfectly, mistress. Though your attitude does not alter the truth a bit."

Dorteka was furious with her again.

CHAPTER EIGHTEEN

I

In most respects Marika had attained the knowledge levels expected of silth of her age. In many she had exceeded those. As she surpassed levels expected, she found herself with more and more free time. That she spent studying aircraft, aerodynamics, astronomy, and space, when she could obtain any information. The Reugge did not possess much. The brethren and dark-faring sisterhoods clung to their knowledge jealously.

Marika had a thousand questions, and suspected the only way to get the answers was to steal them.

How did the silth take their darkships across the void? The distances were incredible. And space was cold and airless. Yet darkships went out there and returned in a matter of weeks.

She ached because she would never know. Because she was stuck in a sisterhood unable to reach the stars, a sisterhood that might not survive much longer.

To dream dreams that could not be attained, that was a horror. Almost as bad as the dreams that came by night.

The nightmares resumed immediately upon her return to Maksche. They were more explicit now. Often her littermate Kublin appeared in them, reaching, face tormented, as if crying for help. She hurt. She and Kublin had been very close, for all he was male.

Most Senior Gradwohl had shifted from TelleRai to Maksche in fact as well as name while Marika was in the north. Four days after Marika's return, the wise ones of Maksche, and many others from farflung cloisters of the Community, gathered in the ritual hall. Marika was there at Gradwohl's command, though she had not as yet seen the most senior.

After a few rituals had been completed, Gradwohl herself took the floor. Meth who had accompanied her from TelleRai began setting up something electrical, much to the distress of Zertan. They tried to argue that such should not be permitted within the holy place of Maksche.

Gradwohl silenced them with a scowl. It was well-known that the most senior was not pleased with them. Though she remained outside the mainstream of cloister life, Marika had heard many rumors. Most made the futures of the Maksche senior and her second sound bleak.

The device set up projected a map upon a white screen. Gradwohl said, "This is what the north looked like at its low ebb, last winter. The darker areas are those that were completely overrun by savages.

"Our counterattack seems to have caught them unprepared. I would account the summer's efforts a complete success. We have placed a line of small but stout fortresses up the line of the Hainlin, running from here to Akard. A second line was gone in crosswise, here, roughly a hundred miles north of Maksche. It runs from our western boundary to the sea. Each fastness lies within easy touch of its neighbors. Any southward movement can be detected from these, and interdicted with support from here in Maksche.

"Akard is partially restored. It now forms the anchor for a network of fastnesses in the Ponath. They will allow us to maintain our claim there without dispute. A small fleet of darkships based there will thwart any effort to reduce the fastnesses. Work on Akard should be completed next summer.

"Next summer also, I hope to begin squeezing the savage packs from the north, south, and east, giving them no choice but to flee west into the territories of our beloved friends the Serke. Where they may do more evil than they have done. The Serke raised them up like demons. May they suffer as a witch whose demon breaks the ties that bind."

Gradwohl scanned the assembly. Nearly a hundred of the most important members of the Reugge Community were present. No one seemed inclined to comment, though Marika sensed that many disapproved of Gradwohl and her plans.

"As strength goes," Marika murmured. Gradwohl was getting her way only because she was the strongest of Reugge silth.

"Also next spring we will begin restoring several brethren strongholds that will be of use to us. Especially the fortress Mahede. From Mahede it will be possible to mount year-round darkship patrols and up the pressure on the savages even more."

Gradwohl tapped the screen with a finger. Mahede lay halfway between Maksche and Akard. She used a claw to draw a circle around Mahede. It was obvious that circles of the same size centered upon Akard and Maksche would overlap, covering the entire Hainlin rivercourse north of the city. The Hainlin was the main artery of the northern provinces.

"Meantime, this winter we will continue hunting the savages the best we can, with all the resources we can bring to bear. We must keep the pressure on. It is the only way to beat the Serke at their own game."

Several senior silth disagreed. A murmur of discontent ran through the audience. Marika scanned faces carefully, memorizing those of her mentor's opponents. They would be her enemies, too.

In the course of the discussion that followed, it began to appear that those who opposed Gradwohl's scheme did so principally because it interfered with their comfort and their abilities to exploit their own particular demesnes. Several seniors of cloisters complained because they had been stripped of their best silth and, as a result, were having trouble maintaining order among their workers. Especially among the males.

The pestilence of rebellion was spreading.

"I suspect our problems with workers are the shadows of the next Serke move against us," Gradwohl said. "It is unlikely that they expected me to collapse under pressure from the savages. The northern packs were expendable counters in their game. So will our workers be. But we will deal with that in its turn. The most critical task facing us is to make sure the northern provinces are secure no matter what troubles plague us elsewhere."

"Why?" someone demanded. The shout was anonymous, but Marika thought the voice sounded like that of Paustch.

"Because the Serke want them so desperately."

Once the grumbling faded, Gradwohl expanded somewhat. "I see it this way, sisters. The Serke appear willing to spend a great deal, and to risk even more, in order to wrest the north from our paws. They must have very powerful reasons for their behavior. If they have reasons, then we have reasons for taking every measure to retain our territories. Even though we do not know what they are.

"But I will find out what they are. And when I do, you will be informed immediately."

More grumbling.

"While I am most senior none of this is subject to debate. It will be done as I have decreed. In coming days I will speak to each of you individually and have more to say at that time. Meantime, this assembly is adjourned. Senior Zertan. Paustch. I wish to speak to you immediately. Marika. I want you to remain here. I will call upon the rest of you as I have the opportunity."

That was a dismissal. Silth rose from stools and began drifting out. Marika studied the groups they formed, identifying alliances of interest. She heard several seniors grumbling about being tied down at Maksche when they had problems at home demanding immediate attention.

Paustch and Zertan left their stools and moved forward to face Gradwohl. Marika remained upon her stool in the shadows, well away. The Maksche senior and her second did not need to be reminded of her presence.

Gradwohl said, "Mildly stated, I am not pleased with you two. Zertan. You are walking close to the line. Your problem is plain laziness compounded by indifference and maybe a dollop of malice. I will be here for some time now, watching over your shoulder. I trust my presence will lend you some incentive to become more ambitious.

"Paustch. For a number of years you have been the true moving spirit here in Maksche. You have been responsible for getting done most of what has gotten done. It is my sorrow that most of that has been negative. I have in mind several directives that you carried out to the letter but managed to sabotage in spirit. I cannot shake the feeling that I have clung too close to TelleRai since becoming most senior. My paw should have been more evident in the outlying cloisters.

"I will no longer tolerate undermining and backstabbing by subordinates. To that end, you will be transferred to TelleRai immediately. A courier darkship will be leaving at dawn. You will be aboard. When you reach TelleRai, you will report to Keraitis for assignment to duties there. Understood?"

Her entire frame shaking with rage, Paustch bowed her head. "Yes, mistress."

"You may leave us."

Paustch drew herself up, turned, marched out of the hall. Marika thought she might become trouble unless Gradwohl made further moves to neutralize her malice. Unless by its very nature her new assignment placed her where she could do no harm.

Gradwohl turned to Zertan once Paustch was outside. "Do you feel a spark or two of wakening ambition, Zertan? Do you feel you can become more productive?"

"I believe I do, mistress."

"I thought you might. You may go, too."

"Yes, mistress."

Only the sounds of Zertan's slippers disturbed the silence of the hall. Then she was gone, and Marika was alone with the most senior. Silence reigned. Lamplight set shadows dancing. Marika waited without fear, without movement.

Finally, Gradwohl said, "Come forward."

Marika left her stool and approached the most senior.

"Come. Come. Not to be frightened."

"Yes, mistress." Marika slipped into the role she assumed with every superior, that of simplicity.

"Marika, I know you, pup. Do not play that game with me. I am on your side."

"My side, mistress?"

"Yes. Very well. If you insist. How was your summer?"

"A pleasant break, mistress. Though the Ponath is colder now."

"And going to get a lot colder in years to come. Tell me about your day on the town."

"Mistress?" The debacle in the tradermale enclave had slipped her mind completely.

"You visited the brethren enclave, did you not?"

"Yes, mistress." Now she was disturbed.

Her reaction was not well concealed. Gradwohl was amused. "You had quite an adventure, I gather. No. No need to be concerned. The protest was an embarrassment, but a minor one, and a blessing as well. Am I right in assuming that the male Bagnel is the male we brought out of Akard?"

"Yes, mistress."

"And you are on friendly terms? He kept the fuss to a minimum."

"He thinks I saved his life, mistress. I did not. I was saving myself. That the others were saved was incidental."

"The fact is seldom as important as the perception, Marika. Illusion is the ruling form. Shadow signifies more than substance. Silth always have been more fancy than fact."

"Mistress?"

"It is not important whether or not you made an effort to save this male. What signifies is his belief that you saved him. Which in fact you did."

Marika was puzzled. Why the interest in Bagnel?

"You have been away for a while. Living in rather primitive, difficult circumstances. Would you like another day on the city?"

Yes, she thought excitedly. "I have studies, mistress."

"Yes. I hear you have added your own regimen to Dorteka's."

"Yes, mistress. I have been studying flying, space, and—"

"When do you sleep?"

"I do not need much sleep, mistress. I never have."

"I suppose not. I was young once, too. Are you learning anything?"

"There is not much information available, mistress. Most paths of inquiry lead to dead ends where tradermales or other Communities have invoked a privilege."

"We will find you fresh sources. About this Bagnel."

"Yes, mistress?"

"Will he accept a continued friendship?"

Warily, Marika replied, "He invited me to return, mistress. He told me I should ask for him, and he would see that there was no trouble."

"Excellent. Excellent. Then go see him again. By all means."

"Mistress? What do you want?"

"I want you to cultivate him. The brethren are supporting our enemies for reasons we do not understand. It is not like them to compromise their neutrality. You have a contact. See more of him. In time you might learn something to help us in our struggle with the Serke."

"I see."

"You do not approve?"

"It is not my place to approve or disapprove, mistress."

"You have reservations then?"

"Yes, mistress. But I cannot say what they are exactly. Except that the thought of using Bagnel makes me uncomfortable."

"It should. We should not use our friends. They are too precious."

Marika gave the most senior a calculating look. Had she meant more than she had said? Was that a warning?

"Yet at times greater issues intervene. I think Reugge survival warrants pursuit of any path to salvation."

"As you say, mistress."

"Will you pursue it? Will you cultivate this male?"

"Yes, mistress." She had decided instantly. She would, for her own purposes. For information *she* wanted. If some also fell the most senior's way, good. It would keep the cloister doors open.

"I thought you would." The most senior's tone said she knew Marika's mind. It said also that she was growing excited, though she concealed it well.

Perhaps she could read minds, Marika thought. Some silth could touch other minds and steal secrets. Was that not how a truthsaying worked? And would that not be a most useful talent for one who would command an entire unruly Community?

"I will tell Dorteka to let you out whenever you want. Do not overdo it. You will make the brethren suspicious."

"Yes, mistress."

"There is plenty of time, Marika. We will not reach the time of real crisis for many years yet."

"Yes, mistress."

Gradwohl again expressed restrained amusement. "You could become one of the great silth, Marika. You have the proper turn of mind."

"They whisper behind my back, mistress. They call me doomstalker and Jiana."

"Probably. Any of us who amount to anything endure a youth filled with distrust and fear. Our sisters sense the upward pressure. But no matter. That is all for today. Unless there is something you want to discuss."

"Why do we not make our own darkships, mistress? Why depend upon tradermales?"

"Two answers come to mind immediately. One is that most sisters prefer to believe that we should not sully our paws with physical labor. Another, and the one that is more close to the honest truth, is that we are dependent upon the brethren in too many other areas. They have insinuated tentacles into every aspect of life. If they came to suspect that we were trespassing on what they see as their proper rights, they might then cut us off from everything else they do for us.

"There is an ecological balance between male and female in our society, as expressed in silth and brethren. We are interdependent, and ever more so. In fact, I suspect an imbalance is in the offing. We have come to need them more than they need us. Nowadays we would be missed less than they."

Marika rose. "Maybe steps ought to be taken to change that instead of pursuing these squabbles between Communities."

"An idea that has been expressed often enough before. Without winning more than lip service support. The brethren have the advantage of us there, too. Though they have their various bonds and subbonds, they answer to a central authority. They have their internal feuds, but they are much more monolithic than we. They can play one sisterhood against another."

"*Find* ways to split them into factions," Marika said from the doorway. And, "We built our own ships for ages. Before the tradermales."

Gradwohl scowled.

"Thank you, mistress. I will visit Bagnel soon."

II

Grauel and Barlog were beside themselves when Marika announced another expedition to the tradermale enclave. They did everything possible to dissuade her. She did not tell them she had the most senior's blessing. They gossiped. She knew, because they brought her snippets about the Maksche sisters. She did not doubt but what they paid in kind.

The huntresses became suspicious soon after they left the cloister. "Marika," Grauel said after a whispered consultation with Barlog, "we are being followed. By huntresses from the cloister."

Marika was not pleased, but neither was she surprised. A silth had been set upon by rogue males not a week before her return from the upper Ponath. "It's all right," she said. "They're looking out for us."

Grauel nodded to herself. She told Barlog, "The most senior protecting her investment."

"We'll be watched wherever we go," Marika said. "We have a friend."

"One is more than we did have."

"Does that tell me something?"

"Did you know that we were not supposed to come back from the Ponath?"

"We weren't?" The notion startled Marika.

"The story was whispering around the barracks here. We were sent out to build that blockhouse behind the most senior's back. We were not supposed to get out of it alive. That is why Paustch was demoted. It was an attempt to kill us."

Barlog added, "The senior councillors here are afraid of you, Marika."

"We survived."

Grauel said, "It is also whispered that nomad prisoners confessed that our blockhouse wasn't attacked once they found out who the keeper was. You have gained a reputation among the savages."

"How? I don't know any of them. How could they know me?"

"You slew the Serke silth at Akard. That has been bruited about all the Communities, they say. The one who died had a great name in her order, though the Serke aren't naming it. That would mean admitting they were poaching on the Ponath."

"I love this hypocrisy," Marika said. "Everyone knows what the Serke are doing, and no one will admit it. We must learn the rules of this game. We might want to play it someday."

"Marika?"

Grauel's tone warned Marika that she had come too far out of her role. "We have to play the silth game the way it is played here if we are to survive here, Grauel. Not so?" She spoke in the formal mode.

"I suppose. Still…"

Barlog said, "We hear talk about the most senior sending you to TelleRai soon, Marika. Because that is where they teach those who are expected to rise high. Is this true? Will we be going?" Barlog, too, shifted to the formal mode.

Marika shifted back. "I don't know anything about it, Barlog. Nothing's been said to me. I don't think there's anything to it. But I will not be going anywhere without you two. Could I survive without touch with my pack?"

How could she survive without the only meth she had any reason to trust? Not that she trusted even them completely. She still suspected they reported on her to curry favor, but to do that they had to stay close and remain useful.

"Thank you, Marika," Barlog said.

"Here we are. Do not hesitate to admonish me if I fail to comport myself properly." Marika glanced back. "Any sign of our shadows?" She could have gone down through her loophole and looked, but did not care enough.

"None, Marika."

"Good." She touched the fence lightly, examined the aircraft upon the field. Today the airstrip was almost naked. One small freight dirigible lay in one of the cradles. Two Stings sat near the fence. There were a couple of light craft of a type with which she was unfamiliar. Their design implied them to be reconnaissance or courier ships.

She went to the desk in the gateway building. The same guard watched the same vision screen in the same state of sleepy indifference. He did not notice her. She wondered if his hearing and sense of smell were impaired, or if he just enjoyed being rude to meth from the street. She rapped on the desk.

He turned. He recognized her and his eyes widened. He sat up.

"I would like to speak to Assistant Security Chief Bagnel," Marika told him.

He gulped air, looked around as if seeking a place to hide, then gobbled, "Yes, mistress." He hurried around the end of his desk, down the hallway leading to the airfield. Halfway along he paused to say, "You stay here, mistress." He made a mollifying gesture. "Just wait. I will hurry him all I can."

Marika's ears tilted in amusement.

The guard turned again at the far door, called back, "Mistress, Bagnel is no longer assistant chief. He was made chief a few months ago. Just so you do not use the wrong mode of address."

"Thank you." Wrong mode of address? What difference? Unless it was something the nervous guard had let carry over from the mysteries of the tradermale brethren.

She supposed she ought to examine the relevant data—what was known—if she was going to be dealing with Bagnel regularly.

Time enough for that later. After today's encounter had shown its promise, or lack thereof. "Grauel, go down the hall and keep watch. Barlog, check the building here, then watch the street." She stepped around the desk and began leafing through the guard's papers. She found nothing interesting, if only because they were printed in what had to be a private male language. She opened the desk's several drawers. Again she found nothing of any interest.

Well, it had been worth a look. Just in case. She rounded the desk again, recalled Grauel and Barlog. To their inquisitive looks she replied, "I was just curious. There wasn't anything there."

The guard took another five minutes. He returned to find them just as he had left them. "Kentan Bagnel will be here shortly, mistress. Can I make your wait more comfortable somehow? Would you care for refreshments?"

"Not for myself, thank you. Barlog? Grauel?"

Each replied, "No, mistress," and Marika was pleased with their restraint. In years past they would have chastised any male this bold.

"You called Bagnel Kentan. Is that a title or name?"

The guard was fuddled for a moment. Then he brightened. "A title, mistress. It denotes his standing with the brethren."

"It has nothing to do with his job?"

"No, mistress. Not directly."

"I see. Where does a kentan stand with regard to others? How high?"

The guard looked unhappy. He did not want to answer, yet felt he had to conform to orders to deal with her hospitably.

"It must be fairly high. You are nervous about him. The year has treated Bagnel well, then."

"Yes, mistress. His rise has been…"

"Rapid?"

"Yes, mistress. We all thought your last visit would cause him grave embarrassment, but…"

Marika turned away to conceal her features. A photograph graced the wall opposite the desk. It had been enlarged till it was so grainy it was difficult to recognize. "What is this place?"

Relieved, the guard came around his desk and began explaining, "That is the brethren landhold at TelleRai, mistress."

"Yes. Of course. I have never seen it from this angle."

"Marika?"

She turned. Bagnel had arrived. He looked sleek and self-confident and just a bit excited. "Bagnel. As you see, I'm behaving myself this time." She used the informal mode without realizing it. Grauel and Barlog gave her looks she did not see.

"You've grown." Bagnel responded in the same mode. His usage was as unconscious as Marika's.

Grauel and Barlog bared teeth and exchanged glances.

"Yes. Also grown up. I spent the summer in the Ponath, battling the nomad. I believe it changed me."

Bagnel glanced at the guard. "You've been grilling Norgis. You've made him very uncomfortable."

"We were talking about the picture of the Tovand, kentan," the guard said.

Bagnel scowled. The guard retreated behind the barrier of his desk. He increased the volume of the sound accompanying the display on his screen. Marika was amused, but concealed it.

"Well," Bagnel said. "You're here again."

Grauel and Barlog frowned at his use of the familiar mode.

"I hoped I could look inside the aircraft this time. Under supervision, of course. Nothing secret seems to be going on now. The fighting ships and the big dirigibles are gone."

"You tease me. Yes, I suppose we could look at the light aircraft. Come."

As they stepped outside, Marika said, "I hear you've been promoted."

"Yes. Chief of security. Another reward for my failure at Critza."

"You have an unusual concept of reward, I'd say."

Grauel and Barlog were displeased with Marika's use of the familiar mode, too.

"I do?" Bagnel was amused. "My superiors do. I haven't done anything deserving." Softly, he asked, "Do you need those two arfts hanging over your shoulder all the time?"

"I don't go anywhere without Grauel and Barlog."

"They make me nervous. They always look like they're planning to rip my throat out."

Marika glanced at the huntresses. "They are. They don't like this. They don't like males who can or dare do more than cook or pull a plow."

He gave her a dark look. She decided she had pushed her luck. Time to become Marika the packless again. "Isn't this a Seifite trainer?" She indicated an aircraft standing straight ahead.

"Still studying, are you?"

"Always. When I can get anything to study. I told you I plan to fly. I have flown three times, on darkships. Each flight left me more convinced that flight is my tomorrow." She glanced at several males hurrying toward them. Grauel and Barlog interposed themselves quickly, though the males were not armed.

"Ground crew," Bagnel explained. "They see us coming out here, they expect us to take a ship up."

The males slowed when they discerned Marika's silth garb. "They're having second thoughts," she said.

"You can't blame them, can you? Silth are intimidating by nature."

"Are they? I've never seen them from the outside."

"But you grew up on a packstead. Not in a cloister."

"True. And my pack never mentioned them. I was silth before I knew what was happening." She made the remark sound like a jest. Bagnel tried to respond and failed.

"Well?" he asked. "Would you like to go up? As long as you're here?"

"Can you do that? Just take off whenever you want?"

"Yes."

"In cloister we would have to have permission all the way from the senior." She climbed a ladder to the lower wing of the aircraft. "Only two places. No room for Grauel and Barlog."

"Unfortunately." Bagnel did not sound distraught.

"I don't know if they'd let me."

"You're silth. They're just—"

"They're just charged on their necks with bringing me back alive. Even if that means keeping me from killing myself. They don't trust machines. It was a fight just getting to come here again. The idea wasn't popular at the cloister. Someone made a protest about last time."

"Maybe another time, then. When they understand that I don't plan to carry you off to our secret breeding farm."

"What? Is there such a place? Oh. You are teasing."

"Yes. We recruit ragtag. Especially where the traditional pack structures still predominate. A lot of the Brown Paw Bond youngsters came out of the Ponath."

"I see."

Each spring newly adult males had been turned out of the packsteads to wander the hills and valleys in search of another pack willing to take them in. They had had to sell themselves and their skills. Thus the blood was mixed.

Many, though, never found a place. A pack did not need nearly as many males as females. Marika had not wondered much about what had become of the unsuccessful. She had assumed that they died of exposure or their own incompetence. Their fates had not concerned her, except that of her littermate Kublin, the only male for whom she had ever held much regard.

"Well? Up? Or another time?"

Marika felt a longing so intense it frightened her. She was infatuated with flight. More than infatuated, she feared. She was obsessed. She did not like that. A weakness. Weaknesses were points where one could be touched, could be manipulated. "Next time," she grated. "Or the time after that. When my companions have learned to relax."

"As you wish. Want to sit in it? Just to get the feel?"

And so it went, with Marika getting a look at every ship on the field, including the Stings. "Nothing secret about them," Bagnel assured her. "Nothing you'd understand well enough to tell our enemies about."

"You have enemies?"

"A great many. Especially in the sisterhoods. Like that old silth—what was her name? Gorry. The one who wanted us thrown back to the nomads when we came to Akard asking help. Like all the other dark-faring silth have become since we joined the Serke and Redoriad in their interstellar ventures."

"What?" Why had that not been in the education tapes? "I was not aware of that. Brethren have visited the starworlds?"

"There are two ships. One is Serke, one is Redoriad. The silth move them across the void. The brethren deal on the other end."

"How is that possible? I thought only specially trained silth could stay the bite of the dark."

"Special ships. Darkships surrounded with a metal shell to keep the air in. Designed by brethren. They put in machines to keep the air fresh. Don't ask me questions because that's all I know. That is another bond entirely, and one we have no contact with."

"And the other sisterhoods are jealous?"

"So I gather. I don't know all that much. The Brown Paw Bond is an old-fashioned bond involved in trade and light manufacturing. Traditional pursuits. The only place you could get the kind of answers you want would be at the Tovand in TelleRai. I tell you, the one time I saw that place it seemed more alien than the Reugge cloister here. Those are strange males down there. Anyway, I was telling about the Serke and the Redoriad. Rumor says they asked the brethren to help them with their star ventures. That could be why the Reugge have become so disenchanted with the Serke."

"Don't fool yourself. The disenchantment did not begin with us. The Serke are solely responsible. There's something in the Ponath that they want." She studied Bagnel closely. He gave nothing away.

"The brethren won't go back to Critza, Bagnel. I thought you said trade was lucrative up there."

"When there was someone to trade with. There isn't anymore."

"Nomads?"

"What?"

"They're getting their weapons somewhere. They were better armed than ever this summer. They shot down two darkships. There is only one source for firearms."

"No. We haven't sold them weapons. Of that I'm certain. That would be a self-destructive act."

"Who did?"

"I don't know."

"They had to get them from you. No one else is allowed to manufacture such things."

"I thought you said the Serke were behind everything."

"Undoubtedly. But I wonder if someone isn't behind the Serke. No. Let's not argue anymore. It's getting late. I'd better get home or they won't let me come again."

"How soon can I expect you?"

"Next month maybe. I get a day a month off now. A reward for service in the Ponath. As long as I'm welcome, I'll keep coming here."

"You'll be welcome as long as I'm security chief."

"Yes. You owe me, don't you?"

Startled, Bagnel said, "That, too. But mostly because you break the tedium."

"You're not happy here?"

"I would have been happier had the weather never changed and the nomads never come out of the Zhotak. Life was simpler at Critza."

Marika agreed. "As it was at my packstead."

III

"Well?" the most senior demanded.

Marika was not sure what to say. Was it in her interest to admit that she suspected Bagnel had been given an assignment identical to her own?

She repeated only what she thought Barlog and Grauel might have overheard. "Mostly we just looked at aircraft and talked about how we would have been happier if we had not had to leave the Ponath. I tried to avoid pressing. Oh. He did tell me about some ships the dark-faring Serke and Redoriad had built special so the brethren could—"

"Yes. Well. Not much. But I did not expect much. It was a first time. A trial. You did not press? Good. You have a talent for the insidious. You will make a great leader someday. I am sure you will have him in your thrall before long."

"I will try, mistress."

"Please do, Marika. It may become critical down the path."

"May I ask what exactly we are doing, mistress? What plans you have for me? Dorteka keeps telling me—"

"You may not. Not at this point. What you do not know you cannot tell anyone else. When it becomes tighter tactically…. When you and I and the Reugge would all be better served by having you know the goal and able to act to achieve it, you will be told everything. For the present, have faith that your reward will be worth your trouble."

"As you wish, mistress."

CHAPTER NINETEEN

I

It was the quietest time of Marika's brief life, at least since the years before the nomads had come to the upper Ponath and destroyed everything. The struggle continued, and she participated, but life became so effortless and routine it fell into numbing cycles of repetition. There were few high points, few lows, and each of the latter she marked by the return of her nightmares about her littermate Kublin.

She could count on at least one bout with dark dreams each year, though never at any time predictable by season, weather, or her own mental state. They concerned her increasingly. The passing of time, and their never being weaker when they came, convinced her that they had little to do with the fact that the Degnan remained unMourned.

What else, then? That was what Grauel, Barlog, and even Braydic asked when she did at last break down and share her distress.

She did not know what else. Dreams and reason did not mix.

She did see Braydic occasionally now. The comm technician was less standoffish now it was certain Marika enjoyed the most senior's enduring favor.

Studies. Always there were studies. Always there were exercises to help her expand and increase her silth talents.

Always there were frightened silth distressed by her grasp of those talents.

Years came and went. The winters worsened appreciably each seasonal cycle. The summers grew shorter. Photographs taken from tradermale satellites showed a swift accumulation of ice in the far north. Glaciers were worming across the Zhotak already. For a time they would be blocked by the barrier of the Rift, but sisters who believed themselves experts said that, even so, it would be but a few years before that barrier was surmounted and the ice would slide on southward, grinding the land.

It never ceased to boggle Marika, the Serke being so desperate to possess a land soon to be lost to nature.

The predictions regarding the age of ice became ever more grim. There were times when Marika wished she were not in the know—as much as she was. The world faced truly terrible times, and those would come within her own life span. Assuming she lived as long as most silth.

Grauel and Barlog were inclined to suggest that she would not, for she never quite managed to control her fractious nature.

The predictions of social upheaval and displacement, most of which she reasoned out for herself, were quite terrifying.

Each summer Marika served her stint in the north, from the time of the last snowfall till the time of the first. Each summer she exercised her ability to walk the dark side, as much as the nomads would permit. Each summer poor Dorteka had to endure the rustification with her, complaining bitterly. Each summer Marika helped establish a new outpost somewhere, and each summer the nomads tried to avoid her outpost, though every summer saw its great centers of conflict. She sometimes managed to participate by smuggling herself into the strife aboard a darkship commanded by a pliable Mistress.

Gradwohl's strategy of driving the nomads west into Serke territories seemed slow in paying off. The savages clung to Reugge lands stubbornly, despite paying a terrible price.

The Reugge thus settled into a never-ending and costly bloodfeud with the savages. The horde, after continuous decimation through attack and starvation, no longer posed quite so serious a threat. But it remained troublesome because of the rise of a warrior caste. The crucible of struggle created grim fighters among the fastest, strongest, and smartest nomads. Composed of both male and female fighters, and supported by ever more skillful wild silth and wehrlen, it made up in ferocity and cunning what the horde had lost in numbers.

Gradwohl's line of blockhouses north of Maksche did succeed in their mission. The final southward flow crashed against that barrier line like the sea against an uncrackable breakwater. But the savages came again and again, till it seemed they would never withdraw, collapse, seek the easier hunting to the west.

As the nomad threat waned, though, pressure against the Reugge strengthened in other quarters. Hardly a month passed that there was not some incident in Maksche involving rogue males. And that disease began to show itself in other Reugge territories.

But none of that touched Marika. For all she was in the middle of it, she seemed to be outside and immune to all that happened. None of it affected her life or training.

She spent the long winters studying, practicing, honing her talents, making monthly visits to Bagnel, and devouring every morsel of flight- or space-oriented information Gradwohl could buy or steal. She wheedled more out of Bagnel, who was pleased to help fill such an excited, eager mind.

He was learning himself, turning his interests from those that had occupied him in the Ponath to those of the future. His special interest was the web of communications and weather satellites the brethren maintained with the aid of the dark-faring silth. The brethren created the technology, and the silth lifted the satellites aboard their voidfaring darkships.

Marika became intrigued with the cycle and system. She told Bagnel, "There are possibilities that seem to have escaped everyone."

"For example?" His tone was indulgent, like that of an instructress watching a pup reinvent the wheel.

"Possibilities. Unless someone has thought of them already and these ridiculous barriers against the flow of information have masked the fact."

"Give me an example. Maybe I can find out for you."

It was Marika's turn to look indulgent. "Suppose I do have an original thought? I know you tradermales think it unlikely of silth, but that possibility does exist. Granted? Should I give something away for nothing?"

Bagnel was amused. "They make you more a silth every time I see you. You're going to be a nasty old bitch by the time you reach Gradwohl's age, Marika."

"Could be. Could be. And if I am, it'll be the fault of meth like you."

"I'd almost agree with you," Bagnel said, his eyes glazing over for a moment.

Those quiet years were heavily flavored with the most senior's favor. With little fanfare, initially, Marika rose in stature within the cloister. In swift succession she became a celebrant-novice, a celebrant-second, then a full celebrant, meaning she passed through the stages of assistanceship in conducting the daily Reugge rituals, assistanceship during the more important rites on days of obligation, then began directing rites herself. She had no trouble with the actual rituals.

There were those who resented her elevation. Of course. Traditionally, she should not have become a full celebrant till she was much older.

Each swift advancement meant someone else having to wait so much longer. And older silth did not like being left behind one who was, as yet, still a pup.

There was far more resentment when Gradwohl appointed Marika junior censor when one of the old silth died and her place among the cloister's seven councillors was taken by the senior censor. Zertan was extremely distressed. It was a cloister senior's right to make such appointments, without interference even from superiors. But Zertan had to put up with Gradwohl's interference or follow Paustch into exile.

Marika questioned her good fortune less than did Grauel or Barlog, who looked forward to a dizzying fall. Those two could see no bright side in anything.

The spring before Marika's fourth Maksche summer, shortly before she set out for her fourth season of counterattack, death rested its paw heavily upon the cloister leadership. Two judges fell in as many days. Before Marika finished being invested as senior censor, Gradwohl ordered her elevated to the seventh seat on the council.

Tempers flared. Rebellion burned throughout the halls of the ancient cloister. Marika herself tried to refuse the promotion. She had much more confidence in herself than did any of the Maksche sisters, but did not think she was ready for the duties of a councillor—even though seventh chair was mainly understudy for the other six.

Gradwohl remained adamant in the face of unanimous opposition. "What will be is what I will," she declared. "And time only will declare me right or wrong. I have decreed it. Marika will become one of the seven judges of this house."

As strength goes. There was no denying the strong, for they had the power to enforce their will.

But Gradwohl's will put Marika into an unpleasant position.

The sisters of Maksche had not loved her before. Now they hated her.

All this before she was old enough to complete her silth novitiate. Officially. But age was not everything. She had pursued her studies so obsessively that she was the equal or superior of most of the sisters who resented her unnaturally fast advancement. And that was half their reason for hating her. They feared that which possessed inexplicable strength and power.

The strengthened resentment caused her to turn more inward, to concentrate even more upon studies which were her only escape from the misery of daily cloister life. Once a month, there was Bagnel.

And always there was a touch of dread. She suspected doom lurking in the shadows always, at bay only because Gradwohl was omnipresent, guarding her while she directed the northern conflict. While she let the sisterhood beyond Maksche run itself.

Marika was sure there would be a price for continued favor of such magnitude. She believed she was prepared to pay it.

Gradwohl had plans for her, shrouded though they were. But Marika had plans of her own.

II

The summer of Marika's fourth return to the Ponath marked a watershed.

It was her last summer as a novice. On her return to Maksche she was to be inducted full silth, with all the privileges that implied. So she began the summer looking beyond it, trying to justify the ceremonies in her own mind, never seeing the summer as more than a bridge of time. The months in the north would be a slow vacation. The nomads were weak and almost never seen in the Ponath anymore. The snows up there were not expected to melt. There was no reason to anticipate anything but several months of boredom and Dorteka's complaints.

Gradwohl assigned her the entire upper Ponath. She would be answerable only to Senior Educan at Akard. She made her headquarters in a log fortress just miles from the site of the Degnan packstead. In the boring times she would walk down to the site and remember, or venture over hill and valley, through dead forest, to Machen Cave, where first she became aware that she had talents different from those of ordinary packmates.

A great shadow still lurked in that cave. She did not probe it. Because it had wakened her, she invested it with almost holy significance and would not desecrate the memory by bringing it out into the light for a look.

She was responsible for a network of watchtowers and blockhouses shielding the Ponath from the Zhotak. It seemed a pointless shield. The Zhotak was devoid of meth life. Only a few far arctic beasts lingered there. They were no threat to the Reugge.

That Gradwohl considered the northernmost marches safe was indicated by Marika's command. She had twenty-three novices to perform the duties of silth, and Dorteka to advise her. Her huntresses and workers—commanded by Grauel and Barlog, who had risen by being pulled along in the wake of her own rise—were ragtag, of little use in areas more active. Except inasmuch as the command gave her some experience directing others, Marika thought the whole show a farce.

The summer began with a month of nonevents in noncountry. The Ponath was naked of meth except for its Reugge garrisons. There was nothing to do. Even those forests that were not dead were dying. The few animals seen were arctic creatures migrating south. Summer was a joke name, really. Despite the season, it snowed almost every day.

There was a momentary break in the boredom during the third week. One of the watchtowers reported sighting an unfamiliar darkship sliding down the valley of the east fork of the Hainlin, traveling so low its undercarriage almost dragged the snow. Marika dived through her loophole, caught a strong ghost, and went questing.

"Well?" Dorteka demanded when she returned.

"There may have been something. I could not make contact, but I felt something. It was moving downstream."

"Shall I inform Akard?"

"I do not think it is necessary. If it is an alien darkship, and is following the east fork down, they will spot it soon enough."

"It could have been an unscheduled patrol."

"Probably was."

A darkship out of Akard patrolled Marika's province each third day. Invariably, it reported a complete absence of nomad activity. What skirmishing there was was taking place far to the south. And the few nomads seen down there were now doing as Gradwohl wished. They were migrating westward, toward Serke country.

There were rumors that Serke installations had been attacked.

"Looks like the Serke have lost their loyalty," Marika told Dorteka after having examined several such reports.

"They have used them up. They will be little more than a nuisance to our cousins."

"I wonder what the Serke bought them with. To have held them so long on the bounds of death and starvation."

Dorteka said, "I think they expected to roll over us the year they took Akard. The intelligence says they expected to take Akard cheaply and follow that victory with a run that would take them all the way to Maksche. Maksche certainly could not have repelled them at the time. The glitch in their strategy was you. You slew their leading silth and decimated their best huntresses. They had nothing left with which to complete the sweep."

"But why did they keep on after they had failed?"

"Psychological momentum. Whoever was pulling the strings on the thing would have been high in the Serke council. Someone very old. Old silth do not admit defeat or failure. To me the evidence suggests that there is a good chance the same old silth is still in charge over there."

"By now she must realize she has to try something else. Or must give up."

"She cannot give up. She can only get more desperate as the most senior thwarts her every stratagem."

"Why?"

"The whole world knows what is happening, Marika. Even if no one admits seeing it. Our hypothetical Serke councillor cannot risk losing face by conceding defeat. We are a much weaker Community. Theoretically, it is impossible for us to best the Serke."

"What do you feel about that?"

"I feel scared, Marika." It was a rare moment of honesty on Dorteka's part. "This has been going on for eight years. The Serke councillors were all old when it started. They must be senile now. Senile meth do things without regard for consequences because they will not have to live with them. I am frightened by Gradwohl, too. She has a disregard for form and consequence herself, without the excuse of being senile. The way she has forced you onto the Community...."

"Have I failed her expectations, Dorteka?"

"That is not the point."

"It is the only point. Gradwohl is not concerned about egos. The Reugge face the greatest challenge of their history. Survival itself may be the stake. Gradwohl believes I can play a critical role if she can delay the final crisis till I am ready."

"There are those who are convinced that your critical role will be to preside over the sisterhood's destruction."

"That doomstalker superstition haunts my backtrail still?"

"Forget legend and superstition—though they are valid as ways of interpreting that which we know but do not understand. Consider personality. You are the least selfless silth I have ever encountered. I have yet to discern a genuine shred of devotion in you, to the Community or to the silth ideal. You fake. You pretend. You put on masks. But you walk among those who see through shadows and mists, Marika. You cannot convince anyone that you are some sweet lost pup from the Ponath."

Marika began to pace. She wanted to issue some argument to refute Dorteka and could not think of a one she could wield with conviction.

"You are using the Reugge, Marika."

"The Reugge are using me."

"That is the way of—"

"I do not accept that, Dorteka. Take that back to Gradwohl if you want. Though I am sure she knows."

Grauel witnessed this argument. She grew very tense as it proceeded, fearing it would pass beyond the verbal. Dorteka had been having increasing difficulty maintaining her self-restraint.

Marika had worked hard to bind Grauel and Barlog more closely to her. Again and again she tested them in pinches between loyalties to herself and loyalties to the greater community. They had stuck with her every time. She hoped she was laying the foundations of unshakable habit. A day might come when she would want them to stick with her through extreme circumstances.

For all she had known these two huntresses her entire life, Marika did not know them very well. Had she known them well, she would have realized no doubt of their loyalties ever existed.

Barlog entered the room. "A new report from Akard, Marika."

"It's early, isn't it?"

"Yes."

"What is it?"

"Another sighting."

"Another ghost darkship?"

"No. This time it's a possible nomad force coming east on the Morthra Trail. Based on two unconfirmed sightings."

"Well, that is no problem for us."

The Morthra Trail was little more than a game track these days, lost beneath ten feet of snow. At one time it had connected Critza with a tradermale outpost on the Neybhor River, seventy miles to the west. The Neybhor marked the western frontier of Reugge claims in that part of the Ponath.

"Sounds like wishful thinking," Marika said. "Or a drill being sprung on us by the most senior. But I suppose we do have to pass the word. Dorteka, you take the eastern arc. I will take the western." Marika sealed her eyes, went inside, extended a thread of touch till she reached an underling in an outlying blockhouse. She relayed the information.

Two days later touch-word brought the news that Akard had lost contact with several western outposts. Darkships sent to investigate had found the garrisons dead. An aerial search for the culprits had begun.

One of the darkships fell out of touch.

Senior Educan sent out everything she had.

When found, the missing darkship was a tangle of titanium ruin. It had buried itself in the face of a mountain, evidently at high speed. The Mistress of the Ship and her bath appeared to have suffered no wounds before the crash.

"That is silth work," Marika said. "Not nomads at all, but Serke." She shivered. For an instant a premonition gripped her. Grim times were in the offing. Perhaps times that would shift the course of her life. "This must be the desperate move you predicted, Dorteka."

The instructress was frightened. She seemed to have suffered a premonition of her own. "We have to get out of here, Marika."

"Why?"

"They would send their very best. If they would go that far. We cannot withstand that. They will exterminate us, then ambush any help sent from Maksche."

"Panic is not becoming in a silth," Marika said, parroting a maxim learned at Akard. "You are better at the long touch than I am. Get Akard to send me a darkship."

"Why?"

"Do it."

"They will want to know why. If they have lost one already, they will want to hoard the ones that are left."

"Invoke the most senior if you have to."

Sighing, Dorteka started to go into touch.

"Dorteka. Wait. Find out which outposts were silenced. And where that darkship went down."

"Yes, mistress," Dorteka replied.

"Sarcasm does not become you. Hurry. Before those fools panic and run away."

Dorteka went into touch. Her strained, twisting face betrayed her difficulty getting through, then an argument ensuing. Marika told Grauel, "If those fools don't come across, I'll hike down there and take a darkship myself. Why did they put Educan in charge? She is worse than Paustch ever was. She couldn't..." Dorteka had come out of touch. "What did they say?"

"The darkship is coming. I had to lie, Marika. And I had to invoke Gradwohl. I hope you know what you are doing."

"What state were they in?"

"You can guess."

"Yes. Educan was packing. Grauel. Get my coats, boots, and weapons." On the frontier Marika dressed as one of the huntresses, not as silth.

Dorteka studied a map while Marika dressed. Marika glanced over her shoulder. "A definite progression, yes?"

"It does look like a developing pattern."

"Looks like? They will hit here next, then here, here, and then try Akard. No wonder Educan is in a dither. They will reach the Hainlin before dawn tomorrow."

"You have that look in your eye, Marika. What are you going to do?"

No particular thought went into Marika's answer. "Ambush them at Critza." It was the thing that had to be done.

"They would sense our presence."

"Not if we use our novices to keep our body heat concealed."

"Marika...."

"We will hit them on huntress's terms initially. Not as silth. They will not be looking for that. We will chew them up before they know what is happening."

"Critza is not inside your proper territory."

"If we do not do something, Educan will run off and leave us here. The Serke will not have to come after us. They can leave us to the grauken if they take Akard."

"True. But—"

"Perhaps one of the reasons Gradwohl favors me is that I am not bound by tradition. Not if form's sake means sticking my head into a kirn's den."

"Perhaps."

"Contact the outposts. We will gather everyone. Grauel. Prepare for two days of patrol for the whole force."

III

Marika kept the darkship aloft continuously, bringing huntresses to Critza, till she felt the Serke party could be within an hour of her ambush. The western outposts had fallen as she had predicted. Akard was in a panic. The leadership there had so wilted, Marika no longer bothered trying to stay in touch.

A pair of darkships raced over, fleeing south, practically dripping meth and possessions. "That," Marika observed, "is why we silth are so beloved, Dorteka. Educan has saved everything she owns. But how many huntresses and laborers were aboard?"

Dorteka did not try to defend Educan. She was as outraged as Marika was, if not quite for the same reasons. The Akard senior's flight was indefensible on any grounds.

"Everyone in place?" Marika asked. There were no tracks in the snow, nothing to betray the ambush physically. The huntresses had dropped into their positions from the darkship. "See if you can detect anybody, Dorteka. If you do, get on the novice covering." She could detect nothing with her own less skillful touch.

Fear proved to be a superb motivator. The novices hid everyone well.

"That is it for Chaser," Marika said as the last of the major moons settled behind the opposite ridge. But there was light still. Dawn had begun to break under a rare clear sky. Long shadows of skeletal trees reached across the Hainlin. The endless cold had killed all the less hardy. They were naked of needles. Occasionally the stillness filled with the crash following some elder giant's defeat in its battle with gravity. Farther north, where the winds kept the slopes scoured of snow, whole mountains were scattered with fallen trees, like straw in a grain field after harvest.

A far hum began to build in the hills opposite Critza. "Utter silence now," Marika cautioned. "Total alertness. Nobody move for any reason. And hold your fire till I give the word. Hold your fire." She hoped it would not be much longer. The cold gnawed her bones. They had dared light no fires. The smell of smoke would have betrayed them.

A machine thirty feet long and ten wide eased down the far slope, sliding between trees. It slipped out onto the clear highway of the rivercourse, surrounded by flying snow. For a moment Marika was puzzled. It seemed like a small darkship of odd shape, floating above the surface. It made a great deal of noise.

Then she recalled where she had seen such a vehicle. At the tradermale station at Maksche.

Ground-effect vehicle. Of course.

A second slithered through the trees, engine whining as it fought to keep from charging down the slope. Marika silently praised Grauel and Barlog for having established superb discipline among the huntresses. They were waiting as instructed.

They dared not open fire till all the craft were in the open.

She could see meth inside them, ten and an operator for each of those first two. At a guess she decided two silth and eight fighters aboard each. And definitely not nomads.

What had Bagnel told her about ground-effect vehicles? Yes. They were not sold or leased outside the brethren. Ever.

This ambush would stir one hell of a stink if she pulled it off.

A third and fourth vehicle left the forest. These two appeared to be supply carriers. No heads were visible through their domes, only unidentifiable heaps.

A fifth vehicle descended the slope, and a sixth. And still those already on the river hovered, waiting.

Marika ground her teeth. How much longer could fire discipline hold among huntresses already badly shaken by what faced them?

Not long. As the eighth vehicle appeared, making four carrying meth and four carrying supplies, a rifle cracked.

The huntress responsible was a competent sniper. Her bullet stabbed through a dome and killed an operator. The vehicle surged forward, gained speed rapidly, rose, and smashed into a bluff a third of a mile upriver. Its fuel exploded.

Long before that happened Marika's every weapon had begun thundering at the Serke. For a while the vehicles were hidden by smoke and flying snow.

Two more vehicles came down into the storm of death.

"Get that darkship up over the trail," Marika snapped at the Mistress of the Ship. "Wait. I am going with you. I do not want you following Educan. Dorteka. Keep hitting them. Get the personnel carriers first."

A vehicle broke out of the fury and scooted away north, sideslipping around the burning vehicle upstream. "That was a transport. We will catch it later. Take it up."

The darkship rose. At a hundred feet Marika could see that the remaining craft had been disabled. Huntresses had come out of some and were returning fire.

A fuel tank blew, spread fire to other crippled vehicles. The conflagration generated a battle between volatile fuel and melting snow. Burning fuel spread atop the running melt.

Marika reached with her touch and found several silth minds among the survivors, all bewildered, shocked, unready to respond. She jerked back, ducked through her loophole, grabbed the first suitable ghost she found, and hurtled down there. Slap. Slap. Slap. She dispatched three silth.

There were at least four more vehicles in the forest, all carrying silth and huntresses. They had halted. Marika flung herself that way, hammered at silth hearts and minds till she encountered one that hurled her back and nearly broke through her defenses.

She ducked back into the world long enough to order the darkship forward. The bath carried automatic weapons and grenades. She would wrestle the Serke sisters while the darkship crew demolished them with mundane weapons.

And so it went for a few minutes, the bath crippling two of the vehicles. Marika fenced with the strong Serke sister, and ducked around her occasionally, discovered that hers was the only Serke silth mind still conscious.

On the river the survivors of the ambush were getting organized. The Serke silth ducked away from Marika and went to prevent Dorteka and the novices from overwhelming her fighters.

The huntresses on the mountainside headed down to help their sisters. They fired on the darkship as they went.

You are a strong one, the Serke silth sent. *But you will not survive this.*

I have survived the Serke before, Marika retorted. *This is the end of the Serke game. Here, today, you will all die. And you will leave the Reugge the proof needed to call the wrath of all the Communities down upon the Serke. You have fallen into the trap.*

You are the one called Marika?

Yes. Which great Serke am I about to destroy?

None.

The silth slammed at her. Marika barely turned the blow, interposing her ghost between herself and that ruled by the Serke. She had made a tactical error. She had issued too strong a challenge before fully assessing the strength of the other's ghost. It was more powerful than hers.

Bullets hummed around the darkship. One spanged off the metal framework. Marika wondered why the ship was not moving, making itself a more difficult target. She ducked into reality for a second, saw that one bath had been wounded and another had been knocked entirely off the darkship. The Mistress had only one bath to draw upon. She could do little but remain aloft, a target for rifle fire.

Marika flung a hasty touch Dorteka's way. *Dorteka. Get some mortar fire into the woods up here. Under the darkship. Before they bring us down and we are all lost.*

The Serke attacked again. She wobbled under the blow, fought its effects, tried to locate a more powerful ghost. There was none to be reached quickly enough. There were some great ones high above that might have been drawn in had she had time, but the Serke would give her no time.

She dodged another stroke, slipped back into reality. Bombs had begun to fall on the slope below. Had she had the moment, Marika would have been amused. Those mortars were all captured weapons, taken from slain nomads. The brethren were adamant in their refusal to sell such weapons to the Reugge.

She located the Serke silth visually. The female stood beside her disabled vehicle. Marika tried a new tack, hammering at the snow in the trees above the meth.

A shower fell, distracting the silth. Marika used the moment won to stab at the huntresses firing on the darkship. She slew several. The others broke and ran.

The silth regained her composure, punched back, adding, *You do not play the game by the rules, pup.*

Marika dodged, sent, *I play to win. I own no rules.* She struck at a tree instead of the silth. The brittle trunk cracked. The giant toppled—in the wrong direction. She cracked another, then fended off the silth again.

This was not going well. The Serke was wearing her down. And the darkship had begun to settle toward the surface. For the first time she felt uncertainty. The Serke sensed it, hurled mockeries her way.

Angered, she cracked several more trees. This time the Serke was forced to spend time dodging the physical threat.

Marika used the time to unsling her rifle and begin firing. Her bullets did not touch the silth, but they forced her to keep moving, ducking, too busy evading metal death to employ her talent.

Marika hurled a pair of grenades. One fell close. Its blast threw the silth ten feet and left her stunned.

Marika took careful aim, pumped three bullets into the sprawled form, the last through the brain.

"That should do—"

The darkship began to wobble, to slide sideways, to tilt.

The Mistress of the Ship had been hit by a stray bullet.

She had wanted to fly for so long. Marika's thoughts were almost hysterical. She hadn't wanted her first opportunity at flight to come at a time like this! She grabbed at the ship with her mind, trying to put into practice what she knew only as theory, while she edged out the long arm toward the wounded Mistress.

Tree branches crackled as the darkship settled. Marika was afraid a giant would snap and in its fall sweep her and the darkship to the surface.

Without her and the darkship, the Serke would win still.

The darkship was low. She'd probably survive the fall. Still, she had to do more than survive. She had to save the darkship. She had to be available to support her huntresses, who were in a furious firefight with the Serke huntresses. She had to…

She reached the Mistress of the Ship. Despite the meth's salvageable condition, Marika pitched her off the position of power, ignored her cry of outrage as she fell. There was no time for niceties.

Marika closed into herself, felt for those-who-dwell, who had begun scattering, summoned them, made them stabilize the craft before it fell any farther. She drew upon the bath and willed the ship to rise.

It rose. Smoothly and easily, it rose, amazing her. This was easy! She turned it, drove it toward Critza, brought it down a little roughly just a few feet from its original hiding place.

The wounded bath died moments later, drained of all her strength. The other passed out. Marika had drawn upon them too heavily.

Marika had nothing left herself. Darkness swam before her eyes as she croaked, "Dorteka! What is the situation?"

"They have gotten dug in. There are too many of them, and they still have a few silth left. Enough to block our dark-side attacks. We dare not assault them. They would cut us apart. I am hoping the mortars will give us the needed edge. You killed the leader?"

"Yes. It was a close thing, too. I had to trick her, then shoot her. Keep using the mortars to pin them down till I recover. No heroics. Hear?"

Dorteka gave her a look that said she was a fool if she expected heroics from her teacher.

Marika drained her canteen, ate ravenously, rested. Weapons continued to crackle and boom, but she noticed them not at all.

The Serke huntresses had gotten out of their transport with nothing but small arms. Thank the All for that. Thank the All that she had been able to think quickly aboard the darkship. Else she would be dead now and the Serke would soon be victorious.

The moment she felt sufficiently strong, she ducked through her loophole, found a monster of a ghost, flung it toward where the surviving Serke silth cowered, arguing about whether or not they should try to retreat to the two unharmed vehicles and flee.

They were terrified. They were ready to abandon their followers to their fates. The one thing that held them in place was their certain knowledge of what defeat would mean to their Community.

Marika sent, *Surrender and you shall live.*

One of them tried to strike at her. She brushed the thrust aside.

She killed them. She touched their huntresses and told them to surrender, too, then slaughtered those who persevered till she had no more strength. She returned to flesh. "The day is yours, Dorteka. Finish it. Round up the survivors."

When it was all done neither Marika nor Dorteka had strength enough to touch Akard and let the garrison there know that the threat had been averted.

Grauel started fires and began gathering the dead, injured, and prisoners inside the ruins of Critza. She came to Marika. "All rounded up now."

"Many surrender?"

"Only a few huntresses." Her expression was one of contempt for those. "And five males. Tradermales. They were operating those vehicles."

"Guard them well. They mean the end of the threat against the Reugge. I will examine them after I have rested."

CHAPTER TWENTY

I

The moons were up, sprawling skeletal shadows upon the mountainsides. As Marika wakened, it seemed she could still hear the echoes of shots murmuring off the river valley walls. "What is it?" Barlog had shaken her gently. The huntress wore a grim expression.

"Come. You will have to see. No explanation will do." She offered a helping paw.

Marika looked at Grauel, who shrugged. "I've been here watching over you."

Barlog said, "I moved the prisoners over here, where I thought we could control them better. I did not notice, though, till one of the males asked if they could have their own fire. I spotted him when the flames came up. Before that it was like he was somebody else."

"What are you talking about?" Marika demanded.

"I want you to see. I want to know if I am wrong."

Marika eased between fallen building stones, paused. "Well?"

Barlog pointed. "There. Look closely."

Marika looked.

The astonishment was more punishing than a physical blow. "Kublin!" she gasped.

The tradermale jerked around, eyes widening for a moment.

Kublin. But that was impossible. Her littermate had died eight years ago, during the nomad raid that destroyed the Degnan packstead.

Grauel rested a paw upon Marika's shoulder, squeezed till it hurt. "It is. Marika, it is. How could that be? Why did I not recognize him earlier?"

"We do not look for ghosts among the living," Marika murmured. She moved a couple steps closer. All the prisoners watched, their sullenness and despair for a moment forgotten.

The tradermale began shaking, terrified.

"Kublin," Marika murmured. "How?… Grauel. Barlog. Keep everybody away. Don't say a word to anyone. On your lives." Her tone brooked no argument.

261

The huntresses moved.

Marika stood there staring, remembering, for a long time. Then she moved nearer the fire. The prisoners crept back, away. They knew it was she who had brought them to this despair.

She settled onto a stone vacated by a Serke huntress. "Kublin. Come here. Sit with me."

He came, sat on cold stone, facing away from the other prisoners, who pretended not to watch. Witnesses. Something would have to be done....

Was she mad?

She studied her littermate. He was small still, and appeared no stronger than he had been, physically or in his will. He would not meet her eye.

Yet there was an odor here. A mystery more than that surrounding his survival. Something odd about him. Perhaps it was something in the way the other males eyed him beneath their lowered brows. Was he in command? That seemed so unlikely she discarded the notion immediately.

"Tell me, Kublin. Why are you alive? I saw you cut down by the nomads. I killed them..." But when the fighting ended, she recalled, she had been unable to find his body. "Tell me what happened."

He said nothing. He turned slightly, stared into the fire. The other males came somewhat more alert.

"You'd better talk to me, Kublin. I'm the only hope you have here."

He spat something derogatory about silth, using the dialect they had spoken in their packstead. He mumbled, and Marika no longer used the dialect even with Grauel and Barlog. She did not catch it all. But it was not flattering.

She patted his arm. "Very brave, Kublin. But think. Many of my huntresses died here today. Those who survived are not in a good temper. They have designs on you prisoners. Especially you males. You have broken all the codes and covenants. So tell me."

He shrugged. "All right."

He was never strong with her, Marika reflected. Only that time he tried to murder Pohsit.

"I crawled into Gerrien's loghouse after dark. There was still a fire going in the male end. I tried to get to it, but I fell into the cellar. I passed out. I do not remember very much after that. I kept trying to get out again, I think. I hurt a lot. There was a fever. The Laspe found me several days later. I was out of my mind, they said. Fever and hunger."

Marika drew one long, slow, deep breath, exhaled as slowly. Behind closed eyes she slowly played back the nightmare that had haunted her for so long. Being trapped in a dank, dark place, badly hurt, trying to climb a stair that would not permit climbing....

"The Laspe nursed me back to health, out of obligation. I must have been out of my head a long time. My first clear memories are of the Laspe three or four weeks after the nomads came. They were not pleased to have me around.

Next summer, when tradermales came through, I went away with Khronen. He took me to Critza. I lived there till the nomads came and breached the walls. When it became obvious help from Akard would not arrive in time, the master put all the pups aboard the escape vehicles and helped us shoot our way out. We were sent someplace in the south. When I became old enough, I was given a job as a driver. My orders eventually brought me here."

A true story, Marika thought. With all the flesh left off the bones. "That's it? That's all you can tell me about eight years of your life?"

"Can you say much more about yours?"

"What were you doing here, Kublin?"

"Driving. That is my job."

A truth that was at least partly a lie, Marika suspected. He was hiding something. And he persisted in using the formal mode with her. Her. When they had been pups, they had used only the informal mode with one another.

"Driving. But driving Serke making an illegal incursion into Reugge territory, Kublin. You and your brethren knowingly violated age-old conventions by becoming directly involved in a silth dispute. Why did you do that?"

"I was told to drive. Those were my orders."

"They were very stupid orders. Weren't they?"

He would not answer.

"This mess could destroy the brethren, Kublin."

He showed a little spirit in answering, "I doubt that. I doubt it very seriously."

"How do you expect the Communities to respond when they hear what brethren have done?"

Kublin shrugged.

"What's so important about the Ponath, that so many must die and so much be risked, Kublin?"

He shrugged again. "I don't know."

That had the ring of truth. And he had given in just enough to have lapsed into the informal mode momentarily.

"Maybe you don't." She was growing a little angry. "I'll tell you this. I'm going to find out."

He shrugged a third time, as though he did not care.

"You put me in a quandary, Kublin. I'm going to go away for a little while. I have to think. Will you be a witness for me? Before the Reugge council?"

"No. I will do nothing for you, silth. Nothing but die."

Marika went away, amazed to find that much spirit in him. And that much hatred of silth. So much that he would not accept her as the littermate he had shared so much with.

Marika squatted beside Grauel. She nodded toward the prisoners. "I don't want anyone else getting near them," she whispered. "Understand?"

"Yes."

Marika found herself a place beside the main fire, crowding in among her surviving novices. She did not pay them any heed.

Kublin! What was she to do? All they had shared as pups....

She fell asleep squatting there. Despite the emotional storm, she was too exhausted to remain awake.

Marika wakened to the sting of cold-blown snow upon her muzzle and the crackle of small-arms fire. She staggered up, her whole body aching. "What now?"

Snow was falling, a powder driven by the wind. A vague bit of light said it was near sunrise. She could see just well and far enough to discover that yesterday's bodies and wreckage already wore a coat of white. "Dorteka! What is happening?"

"Nomads. There was a band following the Serke force. They stumbled onto the voctors I had going through the vehicles on the far slope."

"How many are there?"

"I do not yet know. Quite a few from the sound of it."

Marika moved out into the open to look across the valley. She was surprised at the effort it took to make her muscles carry out her will. She could see nothing through the falling snow. "I am still worn out. I used up far more of me than I thought yesterday."

"I can handle this, Marika. I have been unable to detect any silth accompanying them."

Marika's head had begun to throb. "Go ahead. I must eat something. I will be with you when I can."

The firing was moving closer. Dorteka hurried off into the falling snow. Marika turned, stiffly returned to the fire where she had slept, snatched at scraps of food. She found a half-finished cup of soup that had gone cold, downed it. That helped some almost immediately.

Stiffly then, she moved on to the prisoners.

Grauel sat watching them, her eyes red with weariness. "What is all the racket, Marika?"

Marika glared at the prisoners. "Nomads. Our friends here had a band trailing them, probably to take the blame." They must have known. "I wondered why the reports mentioned sighting nomads but not vehicles." She paused for half a minute. "What do you think, Grauel? What should I do?"

"I can't make a decision for you, Marika. I recall that you and Kublin were close. Closer than was healthy, some thought. But that was eight years ago. Nearly half your life. You've gone different paths. You're strangers now."

"Yes. There is no precedent. Whatever I do will be wrong, by Degnan law or by Reugge. Get some rest, Grauel. I'll watch them while I'm thinking."

"Rest? While there is fighting going on?"

"Yes. Dorteka says she can handle it."

"If you say so."

"Give me your weapons. In case they get ideas. I don't know if my talents would respond right now."

"Where are your weapons?"

"I left them where I fell asleep last night. Beside the big fire. Go on now."

Grauel surrendered rifle and revolver, tottered away.

Marika stared at the prisoners for a few minutes. They were all alert now, listening to the firing as it moved closer. Marika suspected they would be very careful to give no provocation. They nurtured hopes of rescue, feeble as those hopes might be.

"Kublin. Come here."

He came. There seemed to be no defiance left in him. But that could be for show. He was always a crafty pup.

"What do you have to say this morning?" she asked.

"Get me out of this, Marika. I don't want to die."

So. He knew how much real hope there was for a rescue by the nomads. "Will you stand witness for me?"

"No."

That was an absolute, Marika understood. The brethren had won Kublin's soul.

"I don't want you to die, Kublin. But I don't know how to save you." She wanted to say a lot more, to lecture him about having asked for it, but she refrained. She recalled how well he had listened to lectures as a pup.

He shrugged. "That's easy. Let me run. I overheard your huntresses saying there were two vehicles that weren't damaged. If I could get to one...."

"That's fine for you. But where would it leave me? How could I explain it?"

"Why would you have to explain anything?"

Marika indicated the other prisoners. "They would know. They would tell when they are interrogated. You see? You put me into a terrible position, Kublin. You face me with a choice I do not want to have to make."

The firing beyond the river rose in pitch. The nomad band seemed to be very large. Dorteka might be having more trouble than she had expected.

"In the confusion that is causing, who is going to miss one prisoner? You could manipulate it, Marika."

She did not like the tone of low cunning that had come into his voice. And she could not shake the feeling that he was not entirely what he seemed.

"My meth aren't stupid, Kublin. You would be missed. And my novices would detect you sneaking toward those vehicles. They would kill you without a thought. They are hungry for blood. Especially for male blood, after what they have learned here."

"Marika, this is Critza. Critza was my home for almost four years. I know this land...."

"Be quiet." Marika folded in upon herself, going away, opening to the All. It was one of the early silth lessons. Open to intuition when you do not know what to do. Let the All speak to your soul.

The dream returned. The terrible dream with the pain and the fever and the fear and the helplessness. That had been Kublin. Her mind had been in touch with his while he was in his torment. And she had not known and had not been able to help.

Grauel was right. Though he appealed to the memory, this Kublin was not the Kublin with whom she had shared the loft in their dam's loghouse. This was a Kublin who had gone his own way, who had become something.... What *had* he become?

That horrible dream would not stay away.

Perhaps her mind was not running in appropriate channels. Perhaps her sanity had surrendered briefly to the insanity of the past several dozen hours, to the unending strain. Without conscious decision she captured a ghost, went hunting her novices, touched each of them lightly, striking them unconscious.

Dorteka, though, resisted for a moment before going under.

She returned to flesh. "All right, Kublin. Now. Start running. Go. Take one of your vehicles and get out of here. This may cost me. Don't slow down for anything. Get away. I can't cover you for long."

"Marika...."

"Go. And you'd better never cross my path again, in any circumstances. I'm risking everything I've become for your sake."

"Marika...."

"You damned fool, shut up and get out of here!" She almost shrieked it. The pain of it had begun gnawing at her already.

Kublin ran.

The other prisoners watched him go, a few of the males rising, taking a pace or two as if to follow, then freezing when they saw the look in Marika's eye. Their mouths opened to protest as, slowly, as if of its own volition, Grauel's rifle turned in her paws and began to bark.

They tried to scatter. She emptied the rifle. Then she drew the pistol and finished it.

Grauel and the surviving bath sister rushed out of the snowfall. "What happened?" Grauel demanded.

"They tried to run away. I started to nod off and they tried to run away."

Grauel did not believe her. Already she had counted bodies. But she did not say anything. The bath looked studiedly blank. Marika asked her, "How do you feel this morning? Able to help me move ship?"

"Yes, mistress."

"Good. We'll start toward Akard as soon as Dorteka finishes with the nomads."

The firing was rolling toward the river quickly, Marika realized.

Then she gasped, suddenly aware of what she had done. By knocking out the novices so Kublin could slip away, she had robbed her huntresses of their major advantage in the fight. They had no silth to support them. She plunged into the hollowness inside herself, reached out, found a ghost, flogged it across the river.

She had done it for sure. The huntresses were in retreat from a nomad party that had to number more than two hundred. Most of the novices had been found and slain where she had left them unconscious.

Stupid. Stupid. Stupid.

She captured a stronger ghost. With it she hit the nomads hard, decimating them. They remained unaware of what was happening because so few could see one another through the snowfall. They came on, and they kept overtaking Marika's huntresses.

She extricated Barlog from a difficult situation, scanned the slopes, killing here and there, and by the time she returned to Barlog found the huntress trapped again.

Only a dozen of her meth made it to the river.

Only when they assembled before taking up the pursuit in the open did the nomads discover how terribly they had been hurt.

Marika ravened among them then, and they panicked, scattered.

She searched for Kublin. She found him starting up the far slope safely downstream from the action. She stayed with him till he reached an operable vehicle, silencing any nomad who came too near. Though he seemed aware of their presence almost as soon as she, and shied away. And as he had said, he knew the land and made use of its masking features.

Even so, she hovered over him while he transferred fuel to fill one vehicle's tanks, then got it going. As it began climbing the trail over which the attack had come, Marika hurried back to her proper form.

When she came out she was more exhausted than she had been the evening before.

"Marika?" Grauel asked. "Are you all right?"

"I will be. I need food and rest. Get me something to eat." The firing had stopped entirely. "Any word from over there?"

"Not yet. You went?"

"Yes. It looked awful. There were hundreds of savages. And Dorteka guessed wrong. There were silth with them. Wild silth. Most of our meth are dead, I think. Certainly most of the novices are. I could find no sign of them."

Grauel's lips twitched, but she said nothing. Marika wondered what thoughts lay behind her expressionless eyes.

Huntresses began to straggle in almost as soon as Grauel had gotten a cookfire going. Only seven showed. Marika turned inward and remained that way, loathing herself. She had fouled up about as bad as it was possible to do.

That All-be-damned Kublin. Why did he have to turn up? Why couldn't he have stayed dead? Why had fate dragged him across her trail just now?

"Marika? Food." Grauel gave her of the first to come from the fire. She ate mechanically.

Dorteka staggered out of the snowfall fifteen minutes after Marika began eating. She settled beside the fire. Grauel gave her food and drink. Like all the rest of them, she ate and stared into the flames. Marika did not wonder what she saw there.

After a while Dorteka rose and trudged toward where the prisoners had been held. She was gone fifteen minutes. Marika was only marginally aware that she had gone.

Dorteka returned. She settled beyond the fire, opposite Marika. "The prisoners tried to get away during the fighting?"

"Yes," Marika said, without looking up. She accepted another cup of broth from Grauel. The broth was the best thing for a silth who reached this exhausted state.

"One got away. A trail runs down the slope. I heard an engine over there while I was coming back. Must have been one of the males."

"I do not know. I thought I got them all." She shrugged. "If one got away he will take warning to the rest."

"Who was he, Marika?"

"I do not know."

"You helped him. Your touch cannot be disguised. You were directly responsible for the deaths of all of our novices and most of the huntresses. Who was he, Marika? What is this thing you have with males of the brotherhood? Why was the escape of this one so important you destroyed yourself?"

Was there no end to it?

Marika clutched Grauel's revolver beneath her coat. "You believe what you have said. Yes. I see that. What are you going to do about it, Dorteka?"

"You have left me no choice, Marika."

Powder burned Marika's paw. The bullet struck Dorteka in the forehead, threw her backward. She lay spasming in the snow, her surprise lingering in the air of touch.

The huntresses yelped and began to rise, to grab for weapons. Grauel and Barlog did the same, but slowed by tangled loyalties.

This would be the ultimate test of their faith, Marika thought as she slipped through her loophole, grabbed a ghost, and struck at the seven.

The last fell. Marika waited for the bullet that would tell her Grauel or Barlog had turned against her. It did not come. She returned to flesh, found both huntresses staring at her in horror. As was the bath from the darkship, who had been sleeping for so long Marika had forgotten her.

She summoned what remained of her strength and energy and rose, collected a rifle, put several bullets into each of the downed huntresses so it would look like nomads had slain them.

"Marika!" Barlog snarled.

Grauel laid warning fingers upon her wrist.

Marika said, "The snow will cover everything. We will report a huge battle with savages. We will be the only survivors. We will be stricken with sorrow. The Reugge do not Mourn their dead. There is no reason anyone should investigate. Now we rest."

Her companions radiated the sort of fear huntresses betrayed only in the presence of the mad. Marika ignored them.

She would pull it off. She was sure she would. Grauel and Barlog would say nothing. Their loyalties had passed the ultimate test. And now their fates were inextricably entwined with hers.

II

Just a few minutes more, Marika thought at the All. Just a few more miles. They had to be close.

The limping darkship was just a hundred feet up, and settling lower all the time. And making but slight headway. Snowflakes swirled around Marika. The north wind pushed at her almost as hard as she was able to push against it. When she risked opening her eyes to glance back, she could barely distinguish the bath at the girder's far end. Grauel and Barlog, riding the tips of the crossarm, were scarcely more visible.

The huntresses had little strength she could draw, but she took of them as well as of the bath. She also dredged deep into her own reserves. She knew she was not doing this right, that she was devouring far more energies than needful in her crude effort, but survival was the prize.

Only savage will kept the darkship aloft and moving.

Will was not enough. Cold gnawed without mercy. Weariness ravened as Marika rounded the last bend of the Hainlin before it forked around Akard, the ship's rear grounding strut began to drag in the loose snow concealing the river's face. Marika sucked one final dollop of strength from the bath and herself, raised the darkship a few yards, and threw it forward.

The draw was too much for the bath. Her heart exploded.

The rear of the darkship dropped into the snow. The ship began tilting left. The left arm caught. Grauel and Barlog tumbled off. The flying dagger tried to stand on its point. Marika arced through bitter air and, as snow met her, flung one desperate touch at the shadowy fortress looming above her.

III

Marika opened her eyes. She was in a cell walled with damp stone. A single candle provided weak light. She could not distinguish the features of the face above her. Her eyes refused to focus.

Had she damaged them? A moment of panic. Nothing was so helpless as a blind meth.

"Marika?"

"Is that you, Grauel?"

"Yes."

"Where are we? Did we make it to Akard?"

"Yes. Most Senior Gradwohl is on comm from Maksche. She wants to talk to you."

Marika tried to rise. Her limbs were quicksilver. "I can't...."

"I'll have you carried there."

The face disappeared. Darkness and dreams returned. The dreams were grim. Ghosts wandered through them, taunting her. The most prominent was her littermate, Kublin.

She was lying in a litter when she revived. The smell of soup tempted her. She opened her eyes. Her vision was better this time. Barlog walked beside her, her gait the strained labor of a tired old Wise meth. She carried a steaming stoneware pot. Her face was as empty as that of death. The bitter chill behind her eyes when she met Marika's gaze had nothing to do with weariness.

"How did we get here?" Marika croaked.

"You touched someone. They sent huntresses out after us."

"How long ago?"

"Three days."

"That long?"

"You went too far into yourself, they say. They say they had trouble keeping you anchored in this world." Did she sound the slightest disappointed?

So many times Dorteka had warned her against putting all her trust in those-who-dwell. There were ways less perilous than walking the dark.... So close.

Barlog said, "They sent huntresses to Critza to find out what happened there. In case you did not make it. Their far-toucher reported by touch this morning. The most senior wanted to know when she did. She wanted you wakened when that happened. Even she was not certain you could be drawn back."

Gradwohl had taken a direct interest? Mild trepidation fluttered through Marika. But she hadn't the energy for real fear. "Give me a cup of that soup."

Barlog stopped the stretcher-bearers long enough to dole out a mug of broth. Marika gulped it down. In moments she felt a surge of well-being.

The soup was drugged. But not with chaphe. That would have propelled her back into the realm of nightmare.

Barlog said, "The most senior did not think to question simple huntresses such as Grauel and I."

Marika understood the unstated message.

Grauel met them at the comm room door. "I have placed a chair facing the screen, Marika. I will be over here, out of hearing, but watching. If you have trouble, signal me and we will develop technical difficulties." The huntress chased the technicians out. There would be no outside witnesses.

"I can handle it," Marika said, wondering if in fact she *could* match her show of confidence with actions. The most senior was difficult enough to fool even when Marika had full control of her faculties.

She kept her eyelids cracked as Grauel and Barlog levered her into the chair.

The face on the screen was not that of the most senior at all, but of Braydic. Braydic looked as if she had put in some hard hours of worry. Good Braydic. She would have to be remembered in times to come.

The distant communications technician said something to someone at her end, moved out of view of the pickup.

Gradwohl replaced her. The most senior appeared concerned but neither suspicious nor angry. Maybe the effort to make it look like the nomads had wiped out the ambush had been successful.

Marika opened her eyes. "Most senior. I am here."

"I see. You look terrible."

"They tell me I did stupid things, mistress. I may have. It was a desperate and narrow thing. But I think I will recover."

"Tell me about it."

Marika told the story exactly as it had happened till the moment she had discovered Kublin. She left her littermate out of it. She left her treachery out of it. Of course. "I am not sure why the nomads were following so far behind. Maybe the Serke outdistanced them in their eagerness to reach and silence Akard before help was summoned. Whatever, I was unprepared for the advent of nomads. They surprised us while I was unconscious and my huntresses were scattered, going through the damaged vehicles. They overran everyone and crossed the river before anyone wakened me. Then the prisoners broke away and added to the confusion.

"Had the snowfall not been so heavy the savages might have been intimidated by their losses. But they could not see those. It came to hand-to-hand fighting in our camp before I managed to slay the last silth protecting them. And then I did not have the strength to finish them. All I could do was lie there while my huntresses died around me.

"Mistress, I must take responsibility for this disaster. I have betrayed you. Through my inattention I turned victory into defeat."

"What defeat, Marika? It was costly, yes. I will miss Dorteka. But you broke the Serke back. You saved the Ponath. They will not try anything like this again."

"Mistress, I…"

"Yes?"

"I lost my command. I lost Dorteka. I lost many valuable novices. I lost everything. This is not a thing to celebrate."

"You won a triumph, pup. You were the only one to stand her ground. Your seniors lost heart and fled before the battle was joined. And I am certain the Serke did not make it easy for you. Or you would not be in the state you are now."

"There was one of their great ones with them," Marika reiterated. "I bested her only through trickery."

Gradwohl ignored her remarks. Her voice took on a flint-knife hardness. "Educan is going to rue her male cowardice. The tall tales she told when she reached Maksche will cost her every privilege she has." A glint of humor appeared in the most senior's eye. "You would have appreciated her expression when the news came that you had saved Akard. That the garrison she abandoned there never saw hair of the invaders."

"Mistress, I fear what might happen if news of this gets out to other Communities."

"I am two steps ahead, pup. Let the villains quake and quiver. Let them wonder. What happened is not going to leave the circle of those who know now. We will let the snows devour the evidence."

Marika sighed.

"We are not ready for the upheaval going public would cause. We have years yet to go."

Marika was puzzled by what Gradwohl said. She told herself not to underestimate the most senior. That female had a labyrinthine mind. She was but a little animal being run through its maze, hoping she could keep her head well enough to use as much as she was used. "Yes, mistress. I was about to suggest that." *Let* the snows devour the evidence.

"I think we will have less trouble with the Serke now. Do you agree? Yes. They will walk carefully for a while, now. Come back to Maksche, Marika. I need you here."

Marika could think of nothing to say. Her mind refused to function efficiently.

"You flew the darkship blind, untrained, with but one bath to support you. I am impressed and pleased. You give me hope."

"Mistress?"

"It is time your education moved into new, more practical areas."

"Yes, mistress."

"That is all for the moment, Marika. We will examine this more closely after you return. When you are more fully recovered. A darkship will come for you soon."

"Thank you, mistress."

The most senior stepped off pickup. Braydic reappeared for a moment, made an encouraging gesture. Then the screen blanked.

"You ducked that one, didn't you?" Grauel asked. When Marika glanced her way, she found the huntress's back turned.

The most senior turned out the cloister in Marika's honor. Because only a very few knew the whole story, the older sisters acclaimed her only grudgingly.

"What do they want of me?" Marika asked Grauel. "No matter what I accomplish, they resent it." She was surprised that, after all these years facing the disdain of the Reugge Wise, she could still be hurt by their attitudes.

"I do not know, Marika." Grauel's voice was tired, cold, remote. "You are a heroine now. Your future is assured. Is that not enough?" She would not criticize, but censure choked her body language.

For a very long time she and Barlog would speak to Marika only when the course of everyday business required it.

CHAPTER TWENTY-ONE

I

For a year the Reugge were free from outside pressures. The Serke Community assumed a posture of retrenchment that baffled the silth world. They seemed to be digging in quietly in anticipation of some great fury while overtly shifting more of their energies into offworld ventures. But nothing happened.

Some who watched the brethren closely noted that they, too, sought a lower profile. Some of the constituent bonds, especially those strongest politically within the brotherhood, also seemed to anticipate some great terror. But nothing happened.

Except that Most Senior Gradwohl of the Reugge gathered legates of the Communities at the Reugge complex in TelleRai to formally announce a major victory over the savages plaguing the Reugge northern provinces. She declared those territories officially pacified.

The savages had come to concern several other Communities whose lands bounded the Reugge and would have been threatened had the Reugge campaign been unsuccessful. Those Communities were pleased by Gradwohl's declaration.

Gradwohl publicly announced that a young Reugge sister named Marika had engineered the end of the savages' tale.

Privately, Marika did not believe the threat to be extinct. She thought it only dormant, a weapon the Serke would unsheathe again if that seemed profitable.

TelleRai, where many silth Communities maintained their senior cloisters, simmered with speculations. What was the truth behind this bland bit of Reugge folkloring? Who was this deadly Marika, of whom there had been rumors before? Why was Gradwohl taking so little genuine note of what in fact amounted to a withering defeat for Serke intrigues? What was the Reugge game?

Already Gradwohl was a shadowy, almost sinister figure to the silth of TelleRai, known by reputation rather than by person. Her intensity and determination on behalf of a relatively minor, splinter Community, while she

274

herself remained an enigma, were making of her an intimidating legend, large beyond her actual strength. Her spending most of her time away from TelleRai only strengthened the aura of mystery surrounding her.

Was the legend striving toward some goal greater than plain Reugge survival? Her plots were intricate, complex, though always woven within the law.... She made more than the Serke ruling council uncomfortable.

Once a month, on no set day, Marika left the Maksche cloister and walked to the brethren enclave. The only escort she accepted consisted of Grauel and Barlog.

"I will not be loaded down with a mob of useless meth," she insisted the first time after her return from the north. "The more I drag along, the more I have to worry about protecting."

It had become customary for a silth sister daring the streets to surround herself with a score of armed guards. Invariably there would be at least one sniping incident.

Marika wanted to get the measure of the rogue infestation. In the back of her mind something had begun to see them as potentially useful, though she had as yet formulated nothing consciously.

Silth learned to listen to their subconscious even when not hearing it clearly.

The rogues did not bother her once, though she presented an inviting target.

Grauel and Barlog invariably chided her. "Why are you doing this? It's foolish." They said it a dozen ways, one or the other, every time.

"I'm proving something."

"Such as?"

"That there is a connection between the rogue problem and the nomad problem."

"That has been the suspicion for years."

"Yes. But the Serke always get blamed for all our troubles. This is more in the nature of a practical experiment. If they feel I really burned their paws in the Ponath, maybe they'll be afraid to risk troubling me here. I want to be satisfied that the same strategists are behind both troubles."

She had other suspicions that she did not voice.

More than once Barlog admonished, "Do not become too self-important, Marika. The fact that we do not draw fire in the street may have nothing to do with it being you that is out there."

"I know. But I think if we are ignored often enough, it would be safe to say it's purposeful. Especially if everybody else still gets shot at. Right?"

Reluctantly, both huntresses admitted that that might be true. But Grauel added, "The Serke will now think that they have a blood debt to balance. They will want your life."

"*I* might stoop to murder to achieve my ends," Marika admitted. "But the Serke will not. That's more a male way of doing things, don't you think?"

Grauel and Barlog looked thoughtful.

Marika continued, "The Serke are too tradition-bound to eliminate an important enemy that way." She did not add that others with, perhaps, an equal interest in her death would not be bound by silth customs. Let the huntresses figure that out for themselves.

Those untraditional meth might be the ones who controlled the rogues tactically.

"You're in charge, Marika," Grauel said. "You know what you are doing, and you know the ways of those witches. But that city out there is wild country, for all its pretense to civilization. The wise huntress remains always alert when she is on the stalk."

"I will keep that in mind."

She did not need the admonition. She made each trip by a different route, carefully keeping near cover, with more wariness than even Grauel demanded. She probed every foot of the way with ghosts before she traversed it.

Not once did she divine the presence of would-be assassins.

Did that mean the Serke in fact controlled their unholy alliance with the brethren—or only that all her enemies were equally intimidated?

During that, the year of silence, Marika and Bagnel sparred carefully and subtly, each gently mining the other for flecks of information. Marika often wondered if he was as conscious of her probable mission as she was of his. She suspected he was. He was quite intelligent and perceptive. For a male.

Halfway through the year Bagnel began teaching her to fly one of the brethren's simplest trainers. His associates and hers alike were scandalized.

The visits to Bagnel relieved a growing but as yet unspoken pressure upon Marika. On returning from the Ponath she had been eligible for the final rites of silth adulthood, the passage that would admit her into full sisterhood among the Reugge. But she had not asked to be passed through the ritual. She evaded the subject however obliquely it arose, hinting that she was too busy with her duties, too involved with learning the darkship, to take out the months needed for preparation.

She did spend most of her waking time studying and practicing the methods of the silth Mistresses of the Ship, driving herself to exhaustion, trying to become in months what others achieved only after years.

II

It was not her darkship, of course, but she fell into the habit of thinking of it that way. It was the cloister's oldest and smallest, its courier and trainer. There were no other trainees and few messages to be flown. Its bath were old and drained, no longer fit for prolonged flights. They were survivors of other crews broken up by time or misfortune during the struggle with the savages. They did not mesh perfectly, the way bath did after they had been together a long time, but they did so well enough to give a young Mistress-trainee a feel for what she had to learn.

Marika had the most senior's permission to avail herself of the darkship anytime it was not employed upon cloister business. It almost never was. She had it to herself most of the time. So much so that when an occasion for a courier flight did arise, she resented having it taken from her.

She spent as much time aloft as the bath would tolerate.

They did have the right to refuse her if they felt she was using them or herself too hard. But they never did. They understood.

One day, drifting on chill winds a thousand feet above Maksche, Marika noticed a dirigible approaching. She streaked toward it, to the dismay of Grauel and Barlog, and drifted alongside, waving at the freighter's master. He kept swinging away, disturbed by silth attention.

She thought of Bagnel, realized she had not seen him in nearly two months. She had been too engrossed in the darkship.

She followed the freighter in to the enclave.

She dropped the darkship onto the concrete just yards from Bagnel's office building. Tradermales surrounded her immediately, most of them astonished, many of them armed, but all of them recognizing her as their security chief's strange silth friend.

Bagnel appeared momentarily. "Marika, I swear you'll get yourself shot yet." He ignored the scowls his familiarity won from Grauel and Barlog.

"What's the matter, Bagnel? Another big secret brethren scheme afoot out here?" She taunted him so because she was convinced such schemes did exist. She hoped to garner something from his reactions.

"Marika, what am I going to do with you?"

"Take me up in a Sting. You've been promising for months. Do you have time? Are you too busy?"

"I'm always busy." He scratched his head, eyed her and her huntresses and bath, all hung about with an outrageous assortment of weapons. Marika refused to leave the cloister unarmed, and even there usually carried her rifle. It was her trademark. "But, then, I've always got time for you. Gives me an excuse to get away from my work."

Right, Marika thought. She grew ever more certain that *she* was his primary occupation. "I've got a better idea than the Sting. You're always taking me up in your ships. Let me take you up on mine."

Grauel and Barlog snapped, "Marika!"

The eldest of the bath protested, "Mistress, you forget yourself. You are speaking to a male." She was scandalized by Marika's use of the familiar even more than by her invitation.

"This male is my friend. This male has ridden a darkship before. He did not defile it then. He will not now. Come on, Bagnel. Do you have the courage?"

Bagnel eyed the darkship. He examined the small platform at the axis, usually shared by Grauel and Barlog. He licked his lips, frightened.

Marika said, "Grauel, Barlog, you stay here. That will give him more room."

The huntresses surveyed the unfriendly male crowd with narrowed eyes. Unconsciously, Barlog unslung her rifle. Grauel asked, "Is that wise, Marika?"

"You'll be all right. Bagnel will be my hostage for your safety. Come on, tradermale. You claim to be the equal of any female. Can you fly with no cushion under your tail and no canopy to keep the wind out of your whiskers?"

Bagnel licked his lips and approached the darkship.

Grauel and Barlog stepped down. Marika suggested, "Use the harness, Bagnel. Don't try to show off the first time. First-timers have been known to get dizzy and fall if they aren't harnessed."

Bagnel was not too proud to harness himself. He did so carefully, under the grim gaze of the leading bath.

They were angry, those old silth. Marika expected them to resist when she tried to take the darkship up, so she lifted off before they were ready, violently, shocking them into assuming their roles for their own safety's sake.

She made a brief flight of it, stretching her capabilities, then brought the darkship down within inches of where it had settled before.

Bagnel unfastened his harness with trembling fingers. He expelled a great breath as he stepped down to the concrete.

"You look a little frayed," Marika teased.

"Do I, now? Ground crew! Prepare the number-two Sting. Come with me, Marika. It's my turn."

Grauel, Barlog, and the bath watched, perplexed, as Bagnel seated Marika in the Sting's rear seat and strapped her in.

"What's this?" Marika asked. She had worn no harness when they had flown in trainers.

"Parachute. In case we have to jump."

Bagnel wriggled into the forward seat, strapped himself in. One of the ground crew spun the ship's airscrew. The engine coughed, caught, belched smoke that stung Marika's eyes and watered her nose. The ground crew jerked the blocks away from the ship's wheels.

The aircraft bucked and roared with a power unlike any Marika had seen in the trainers. Its deep-throated growl swelled, swelled. When Bagnel let off the brakes, the ship raced down the airstrip, jumped into the air, climbed faster than was possible for any darkship.

Bagnel leveled off at one thousand feet. "All right, smart pup. Let's see about *your* courage."

The Sting tilted, dove. The airstrip swelled, spun. Buildings whirled dizzyingly. "You're getting too close," Marika said.

The ground kept coming up. *Slam!* It stopped spinning. *Slam!* Marika's seat pressed into her back hard. Her guts sagged inside her. The ground slid away ahead. The horizon appeared momentarily, then whipped upward as Bagnel dumped another fifty feet of altitude. It reappeared and rotated as Bagnel rolled the aircraft. It seemed she could pluck the frightened growls from the lips of Grauel and Barlog as the ship roared past them.

The great engine grumbled more deeply as Bagnel demanded more of it. Clouds appeared ahead—and slid away as Bagnel took the ship over onto its back. He completed the loop, resumed the climb, reached five thousand feet, and went into a stall. The ship spun and fluttered.

Bagnel turned, said, "I've been meaning to ask you about that business in the Ponath last summer. What happened anyway? I've heard so many different stories…."

Marika could make no sense of what was happening outside. She clung to her courage by a thread. "Shouldn't you be paying attention to what you're doing?"

"No problem. I thought this would be a chance to talk without those two arfts hanging over your shoulder."

"I ambushed a mob of nomads. It was a tough fight. Hardly anybody got out on either side. That's all there was to it." Her eyes grew wider as the surface drew closer.

"Really? There are so many rumors. I suppose they're exaggerated."

"No doubt." He was digging. Carrying out an inquiry on instructions from his masters, she supposed. The brethren seniors would be getting nervous. They would want to know the Reugge game. That amused her mildly. She did not know the game herself. The most senior kept its strings held close to her heart.

"Looks like time to do something here," Bagnel said. "Unless you'd like to land the hard way?"

"I'd rather not."

"You're a cool one, Marika."

"I'm scared silly. But silth aren't allowed to show fear."

He glanced back, amused, then faced forward intently. He took control. The world stopped rocking and spinning. Then Bagnel went into a hard roll.

Something popped in the right wing. Marika watched a strut tear away, dragging fabric and wire. The ship staggered. The fragment spun behind, whipping at the end of a wire, threatening to pull more wing with it. "I think we might have trouble, Bagnel."

"I think you might be right. Hang on. I'll take us down."

His landing was as stately and smooth as any he had made in a trainer. He brought the wounded ship to a halt just yards from his ground crew, killed the engine. "What did you think, Marika?"

The roar in her ears began to fade. "I think you got even. Let's don't do that to each other anymore."

"Right." He unbuckled, climbed out, and dropped from the lower wing to the concrete. Marika followed. When he finished briefing the ground crew about the strut, he told Marika, "You'd better leave now. My masters won't be happy as it is."

"Why not?"

"You dropped in unannounced. Better give warning from now on. Every time."

Marika glanced at the freighter. She wondered if it really had brought in something the tradermales did not want seen by silth eyes. "All right. Whatever you say. Oh. I wanted to tell you. The most senior says it's all right if you want to visit me at the cloister. If you have time off and have nothing better to do. My time isn't as tight as it once was. I spend most of it learning the darkship. Maybe we could try another flight on one."

News of that permission had scandalized the older sisters. Already they considered her friendship with Bagnel a filthy reflection upon the cloister, a degradation, though there was nothing even a little scandalous in the relationship. When her periodic estrus threatened, Marika was scrupulous about sinter, the self-isolation of silth who had not yet completed the Toghar ceremonies leading to full sisterhood.

The pressure remained silent, but it was mounting. Her resistance was becoming more conscious.

III

Marika learned to manipulate a darkship as well as any Mistress of the Ship assigned to the Maksche cloister. And she did so in months instead of years.

She was not accepted within the select group of Mistresses, in their separate and sumptuous cloister within a cloister, though they did condescend to speak with her and give her advice when she asked it. No more was she accepted by the bath, who, in their way, formed a subCommunity even more exclusive than that of the Mistresses. They, like everyone else, had become frightened of the talent she showed.

There was nothing more she could learn from them anyway. She told herself she did not hurt for lack of their society. She had become the best again.

She received a summons to Gradwohl's presence. She believed her accomplishments were the reason for it, and felt vindicated in her belief when, after the amenities and obeisances, Gradwohl said, "If you belonged to a major Community, Marika, you would be destined for the big darkships. For the stars. There are moments when I hurt because the Reugge are too small for you. Yet, there *is* tomorrow."

In private Gradwohl seemed partial to such cryptic remarks. "Tomorrow, mistress?"

"You once asked why we do not build our own darkships anymore. When the brethren announced that they would no longer replace darkships lost by the Reugge, I started looking into that. I located sisters willing to soil their paws on the Community's behalf. I found more of them than I expected. We are not as far gone in sloth and self-importance as one like yourself might think. I have them hidden away now, with a good crew of workers to help them. They have begun to report modest successes. Extracting the titanium is more difficult than we expected.

"But there are several golden fleet groves within the Reugge territories. Those most immediately threatened by the advancing ice I have ordered harvested. Old shipwrights with the ancient skills promise me that we do not need to be fancy, and that wood can be substituted many places even in the brethren designs.

"So we will no longer be dependent. May a curse fall upon all male houses. If this works out the way I expect, we may even be able to build our own void darkships."

Marika arrayed her face in a carefully neutral expression. Now she understood the additional, intensified silth exercises she had been assigned on her return from the Ponath.

There was little more she could learn from teachers available at Maksche. Indeed, she seemed to have exhausted the Reugge educational resources. Her responsibilities as a councillor took up very little time. She was free to pursue private studies and to expand her silth capacities. Gradwohl insisted she do the latter, feeling she was especially weak in her grasp of the far-touch.

The far-touch was a talent increasingly rare because the use of telecommunications was so much easier. One side of Marika was lazy enough to want to ignore the talent—just as that lazy side throughout the Reugge Community was responsible for the talent's diminution. She rebelled against that laziness, hammered away at learning. And at times was very amused at herself. She, the outsider, the cynic about silthdom's traditional values, seemed to be the Community's most determined conservator of old ways and skills.

Often she wrestled the question of why Gradwohl wanted her to become the complete silth when what she really wanted was to create a Mistress of the Ship able to darkwar for the Reugge.

In one of her more daring moods, Marika asked the most senior, "Is Bestrei getting old, mistress?"

"You cannot be fooled, can you? Yes. But we all age. And the Serke, knowing how much their power depends upon their capacity for darkwar, have other strong darksiders coming up behind Bestrei."

"Yet you believe I will be able to conquer them."

"In time, pup. In time. Not now. I have never encountered anyone with your ability to walk the dark side. Not even Bestrei herself. And I have met her. But you are far from ready for such a confrontation. The Reugge must survive till you have been tempered, and hardened in your heart, and till we have built ourselves a true voidfaring darkship, and assembled bath who can fare the dark with you."

"So that is why you have been avoiding confrontation when you knew you could force it and probably win the backing of the other Communities."

"Yes. I am playing this game for the biggest stakes imaginable."

Marika put that aside. She said, "I have had an idea for a device I think would be useful. To test it I would need someone from communications to modify one of the receivers for taking signals off the satellite network."

"You are zigging when I am zagging, Marika." Gradwohl appeared mildly baffled.

"I want to try to steal the signals of other sisterhoods, mistress. From what Bagnel has said, doing so should not be difficult. Just a matter of altering one of the receivers so it will accept signals other than our own."

Gradwohl reflected for a moment. "Perhaps. The males would be most incensed if ever they discovered the fact." Like mechanized transport, communications equipment came from the brethren on lease. Only minor repairs were permitted the lessees.

"They will not find out. I will use receivers we took away from the nomads."

"All right. You have my permission. But I suspect you will find it more trouble than it is worth. Any messages of importance will be couched in the secret languages of the Communities sending them. And in code besides, if they are critical. Still, much could be learned from the daily chatter between Serke cloisters."

Marika was more interested in intercepting data returned from tradermale research satellites, but she could not have interested the most senior in that. Gradwohl was an obsessive, interested only in defeating the Serke and augmenting Reugge power. "We might even find out what is so important about the Ponath," Marika said. "If we knew that we might become a more powerful Community simply by possessing the knowledge."

"That is true." Gradwohl did not seem much interested in pursuing the thought, though. Something else was on her mind. Marika had a glum suspicion. Gradwohl said, "Let us get to the point, Marika. To the reason I called you here."

"Yes, mistress?"

"Utiel is about to retire."

"Mistress?" Marika knew what was coming. Utiel was fourth on the Maksche council. Only first chair, or senior, held more real power.

"I want to move you to fourth chair, Marika."

"Thank you, mistress. Though there will be protests from—"

"I can quiet the egos of those passed over, Marika. Or I could if I did in fact move you up. I said I want to move you. I cannot. Not the way things stand."

Marika slipped into her cautious role. "Mistress?" She controlled her emotions rigidly. Fourth chair she wanted badly. It could become her springboard into the future.

"Fourth chair is understudy for third as well as being responsible for cloister security, Marika."

She knew that well. In the security responsibility she saw opportunities that seemed to have evaded those who had held the chair before.

Gradwohl continued, "Third chair is liaison with other cloisters, Marika. A coordinating position. A visible, public position. As fourth, understudying, you would be expected to begin making contacts outside the Maksche cloister. As fourth you would become known to the entire sisterhood as my favorite. As fourth you would be seen to have ambitions beyond Maksche.

"For all those reasons your behavior and record would be subjected to the closest scrutiny by those who hope to place obstacles in your path.

"From fourth chair, Marika, it is only a step to an auditor's seat at conventions of the Reugge seven at TelleRai."

"I understand, mistress."

"I do not think so, Marika."

"Mistress?"

"Never has one so young sat upon the Maksche council. Or any other cloister council, except in legend. But the sisters here accept your age, if grudgingly, because of your demonstrated talent, because of all you have done for the Community, and especially because you have my favor. They can brag about you before sisters from other cloisters. You have helped put a remote cloister upon the map, so to speak. But there are limits to what their pride and my power can force them to swallow."

"Mistress?"

"They would revolt before they permitted you to assume a position in which you would represent this cloister elsewhere, pup."

"You have lost me, mistress."

"I doubt that. I doubt that very much. You know exactly what I am talking about. Don't you? I am talking about Toghar, Marika. You have been eligible for the ceremony since you returned from the Ponath. You have put it off repeatedly, calling upon every excuse you can muster."

"Mistress…."

"Listen, Marika. I am speaking of roads to the future opened and closed. If you continue to evade the ceremony you will not only not rise any higher than you are now, you will begin to slide. And there will be nothing I can do. Tradition must be observed."

"Mistress, I—"

"Marika, you have many dreams. Some I know, some I infer, and some must be entirely hidden. You are one moved by dreams." The most senior stared at her intently. "Listen, pup. Marika. Your dreams all live or die with that ceremony. No Toghar, no stars. And the darkship will go. We cannot invest so much of the Reugge in one who will not invest of herself in the Community."

She awaited an answer. None came.

"Pay the price, Marika. Demonstrate your dedication. So many smaller, weaker, less-dedicated silth have done so before you."

Still Marika did not respond.

She had witnessed the Toghar ceremonies. They were not terrible, just long. But the cost…. The price of acceptance as an adult silth, with full privileges….

She had no plans to birth pups, ever. She did not wish to be burdened with trivial, homey responsibilities. Yet to surrender the ability to dam them…it seemed too great a price.

She shook her head. "Mistress, do you have any idea what Grauel would give to possess the ability you are asking me to surrender? What she would *do?* We came out of the Ponath, mistress. I carry the burden of ten years of living with and accepting those frontier values that—"

"I know that, pup. The entire cloister knows. That is why I am being pressed to push your ceremonies. There are those who hope you will stumble upon that early training."

She had already. When she had released her littermate Kublin. Where was he now? There had been none of the terrible nightmares since that day on the Hainlin. Had she laid some ghosts?

"Make up your mind, Marika. Will you be silth? Or will you be a Ponath huntress?"

"How long do I have, mistress?"

"Not long. There are pressures I cannot resist forever. So make it soon. Very soon."

Smug bitch, Marika thought. Gradwohl was sure what the decision would be. She thought she had Marika's every emotional end tied to a puppet string.

"But enough of that now, Marika. I also want your thoughts on the rogue situation. Did you hear that there was another factory explosion last night?"

"At another place belonging to someone friendly to us?"

"It was at the tool plant. That pushes the brethren down the list of suspects, does it not?" When she spoke in council, Marika always insisted the brethren were connected with the rogues.

"No."

There had been a series of explosions lately, all of which had damaged meth bonded to the Maksche cloister. One bomb had gone off in a farm barracks during sleeping hours, killing twenty-three male field workers. Rumor blamed disaffected males. As yet there had been no captures of those responsible.

Marika, like everyone else in the cloister, believed the Serke were responsible. But unlike everyone else, she believed the rogues were drawing support from within the tradermale enclave. Were, perhaps, striking from there, and thus remaining unseen.

"There is no such evidence, Marika," the most senior argued. "Males are naturally foolish, I admit, but there are few fools among the Brown Paw Bond—with whom we have had an understanding for centuries."

"There is no evidence because no one is trying to collect it, mistress. Why is it that Utiel cannot catch the males responsible for these explosions? Is she not trying? Or is she just inept? Or could it be that she still does not believe the rogues to present a threat worth taking seriously? Do they have to start throwing bombs over the cloister wall before we take direct action? I have heard that several of the Communities have begun watching us here."

"Do not lecture me, pup. Utiel has tried. She is old and has her faults, I admit, but she has tried. She has been unable to detect them. It is almost as if the rogues have found a way to hide from the touch."

"So must we be so dependent upon our talents? Must we be wholly committed to one method of looking? We cannot assume a reactionary stance and expect to handle this sort of threat."

"You have a better idea?"

"Several. Again, does Utiel take all this seriously enough? I do not believe she does. Old silth grumble about rogues but just go on about their business. They say there are always a few rogues. It is a pestilence that will not quite go away. But this is a disaffection that has been growing for years. As you know. And it is clear that there is organization behind it. Organization and widespread communication. It is worst here in Maksche, but the same shadow falls upon a dozen other Reugge cloisters. I think we would be fools to just try waiting it out. Before long we would be watching the Educans run away when reality closes in."

"You will not forgive her, will you?"

"I lost a lot of meth because of her. If she had not lost her nerve, we could have devoured the nomads and Serke before they knew what hit them."

The most senior looked at her hard. Marika was sure Gradwohl had not swallowed her whole story about what had happened at Critza. But she was equally certain that the most senior did not suspect the truth.

She hoped Kublin had had sense enough to keep his mouth shut.

"I would have had her shot, mistress. Before the assembled cloister."

"Perhaps. You think you can do better with the rogues? You think you can handle the security function of fourth chair? Then take charge."

"Mistress?"

"It is fourth chair's responsibility."

"Will you assign me the powers I will need to get the job done?"

"Will you take the Toghar rites?"

"Afterward."

Gradwohl eyed her coldly. "This is your watershed, pup. You had better. There will be no more bargaining. Be silth, or be gone. You can have whatever you need. Try not to walk on too many toes."

CHAPTER TWENTY-TWO

I

Marika moved quickly, drafting every silth and huntress she respected. Two nights after receiving the most senior's blessing, she began moving small teams into every site she believed to be a potential rogue target. She followed the dictum of the ancient saw, "The night belongs to the silth." She moved in the dark of the moons, by low-flying darkship, unseen even by those who managed the places she chose to protect.

She was certain there would be an attack soon. Some show of strength. She had written Bagnel bragging about her appointment, transparently implying that she suspected his bond of being behind the rogues.

If he was what she believed, and reported the contents of her letter to his factors, there should be a move made in an effort to show nothing so simple would frighten them off. Or to make it appear the Brown Paw Bond really had no control over the rogue group.

She hoped.

Her planted teams kept themselves concealed from those who worked and dwelt in and around the potential targets. Marika herself shifted to a nighttime schedule, remaining aloft on the trainer darkship she had made her own.

The rogues waited four days. Then they walked into it. It could not have gone better for Marika had she been giving the villains their orders.

Three were slain and two captured in an action so swift no shots were fired. Marika lifted the captives out quietly and carried them to the cloister aboard her darkship.

One of those two managed to poison himself. The other faced a truthsaying.

He yielded names and addresses.

Marika threw teams out aboard every darkship the cloister possessed, ignoring all protests, invoking the most senior where she had to. By dawn seven more prisoners had been brought into the cloister. Five lived long enough to be questioned.

A second wave of raids found several rogues forewarned or vanished completely. This time there was some fighting. Few rogues were taken alive.

Even Marika was surprised at how many rogues Maksche boasted.

The third wave of raids took no prisoners at all. Few rogues were found. But weapons and explosives enough for an arsenal were captured, along with documentary evidence of rogue connections in TelleRai and most cities where the Reugge maintained cloisters.

Marika had the captured arms laid out upon the cloister square. The dead rogues joined them.

"Very good, Marika," Gradwohl said as she and the Maksche councillors inspected the take. "Very impressive. You were right. We were too passive, and even I underestimated the scale and scope of what was happening. No one could see this and remain convinced that we are dealing with the usual scatter of malcontents. I will order all the Reugge cloisters to—"

"Excuse me for interrupting, mistress. It would be too late for that. The rogues will have vanished everywhere. Posting rewards might help a few places, if they are large enough. A point that I have to make, over and over till everyone understands, is that for all their broad antisilth sentiments, and all that the evidence shows them established almost everywhere, these rogues are attacking nobody but the Reugge."

"Noted," Gradwohl replied. "And right again. Yes, Marika. The Serke are behind them somewhere, though the rogues themselves would not know that."

"They did not when we questioned them."

"Where did they go? Those who disappeared?"

Marika felt certain the most senior knew the answer she was about to give—and did not want to hear it. "Mistress?"

"You did not collect two-thirds of those you identified. I know this. So where did they go?" Gradwohl seemed resigned to a great unpleasantness.

"Into the tradermale enclave, mistress. I had the gate watched. As a sort of experiment. Inbound traffic grew rapidly after we began raiding. It peaked before our third round. Almost no one came out."

"So they are safe from retribution. Accursed—"

"Safe? Mistress? Are you certain? What are the legalities? Is there no mechanism for extracting fugitives from convention territories?"

"We shall see." Gradwohl flung a curt gesture at the rest of the council. "Come."

"If there is no mechanism, I will make one," Marika said softly.

The most senior gave her a narrow look. "I believe you would, pup." A few paces later, "Take care, Marika. Take care. Sometimes this world will show a toughness that is different from that of the Ponath. Sometimes losing can be the better path to winning."

"You didn't let me know you were coming," Bagnel complained. "How come you're back already? You usually stall around." He looked abashed. He also looked as if he was under a strain.

"Official business this time." Marika glanced at the clipboard she carried, though she knew the names and numbers by heart. She turned it so he could see the list. "These meth, all fugitives from the law, were seen entering this gate yesterday."

His lips peeled back in an unconscious snarl, and she knew the cause of the strain that had him so edgy.

"I have brought the orders necessary for their removal from the enclave. They have a future in the mines."

"There must be some mistake."

"None whatsoever, Bagnel. Each of these meth has been convicted in court, on evidence presented by confederates. Sentence has been passed. Each was seen entering here. Would you like photographs of them doing so? I will have to send to the cloister for them." She ran a spur-of-the-moment, inspired bluff with that remark. Photo surveillance had occurred to her only in retrospect.

"Holding the job you do, by now you have heard about the ruckus in town. I presume your staff were involved in this behind your back." Give him a ready-made excuse. "The males on this list fled here. They are here still. No airships have left the enclave. You have two hours to deliver them to Grauel and Barlog. If you do not, you will be considered in violation of the conventions and your charter."

Bagnel looked aghast.

Grauel and Barlog waited outside with a dozen armed huntresses.

"Marika…" Bagnel's tone was plaintive. "Marika, that sounds like a threat."

"No. Here I have a copy of the charter negotiated before your brethren assumed control of this enclave. I have added a map for your personal information."

Bagnel examined the map first. "I do not understand." He couched his speech in the formal mode.

"You will note that it shows your enclave surrounded entirely by land belonging directly to the Reugge Community. At the time they assumed control, the Brown Paw Bond had no aircraft. Now they do. You must know that the conventions say that no aircraft of any sort may be flown over silth lands without direct permission of the sisterhood involved."

"Yes, but—"

"The Brown Paw Bond have never obtained that permission for the Maksche enclave, Bagnel. They have never applied. The enclave is in violation of the conventions. Overflights will cease immediately. Otherwise sanctions will be applied."

"Sanctions? Marika, what in the world is going on here?"

"Any aircraft or airship attempting to leave this enclave will be destroyed. Come." She led him to the doorway, showed him three darkships slowly circling the enclave.

Bagnel opened and closed his mouth several times, said nothing.

Marika presented a fat envelope. "This contains a formal notice of the Reugge Community's intent to cancel all Brown Paw Bond charters that now exist within Reugge territories."

"Marika…." Bagnel began to get hold of himself. "These fugitives. You really want them that badly?"

"Not really. Not personally. It would not matter now if you did sneak them out. They are dead. Bounties have been posted on them—very large bounties. As you once noted, the Reugge are a very wealthy Community. No. What is at stake is a principle. And, of course, my future."

Bagnel looked puzzled. She had come at him hard, from unexpected directions, and had managed to keep him off balance.

"I have reached a position of substance within my sisterhood, Bagnel. I am very young for it. My age alone has made me many foes. Therefore I have to consolidate my position and fashion a springboard to a greater future. I have chosen to do that in my usual way, by taking the offensive against enemies of the Community. My opponents inside the sisterhood are unable to fault that." A pause for effect. "Those who get in my way can expect the worst."

"You intend to climb over *me?*"

"If you get in my way."

"Marika, I am your friend."

"Bagnel, I value you as a friend. I have treasured your friendship. Often you were the only one I could turn to."

"And now you are so strong you do not need me anymore?"

"Now I am so strong I do not need to blind myself to what you are doing. Nor was I ever so weak as to allow crimes to be committed simply because a friend was involved."

"Involved?"

"Drop the act, Bagnel. You know the brethren are backing the Serke effort to steal the Ponath from us. You know the brethren have been sponsoring the terrorism practiced by disaffected males. It is another ploy against us. You use criminals now that there are no more nomads to be your proxies. You even flew in males from outside because Maksche did not produce enough villains of its own. Now, is that something I should ignore simply because one of the behind-scenes movers is a friend?"

"You are mad, Marika."

"You will stop. Cease. Give me my prisoners and do nothing more. Or I will see the Brown Paw Bond torn apart like an otec rent by kagbeasts."

"You are totally insane. They have given you a taste of power and it has gone to your head. You begin imagining nonexistent plots."

"Phoo! Think, Bagnel. I struck near the mark, yes? Insofar as you know? Naturally, you have not been trusted with full knowledge. You deal with me. You traffic with silth. Can they trust you? When they hoard knowledge the way old Wise females hoard metal in the Ponath? You recall my great triumph up there, so called? Did you know that nomads had very little to do with it? Did you know that what I defeated was actually an invasion carried out by Serke and armed brethren, with a few hundred nomads along for show? If you do not know these things, then you have been used worse than I suspect."

Almost out of pity she stopped hitting him. She could see that he was hearing much of this for the first time. That, indeed, he had been used. That he did not want to believe, yet his faith was being terribly tested.

"Enough of that. Friend. When you report to your factors, as inevitably you must before you dare yield the criminals I want, tell them for me that I can produce thirteen burned-out ground-effect vehicles, with their cargoes and the corpses of their drivers and passengers, anytime I feel inclined to assemble delegates from the various Communities."

Bagnel composed his features, but could not help staring.

"You do not have to believe me, Bagnel. Just tell them what I said. Nice word, 'driver.' It is from the brethren secret speech, is it not? Not everyone aboard those vehicles died in the ambush."

"What is this madness you're yammering?"

He was innocent of guilty knowledge, she was now sure. A tool of his factors. But he had heard so many wild rumors that she now had him on the edge of typical male panic. Composed as he kept his face, his eyes glittered with fear. His hackles had risen and his head had dropped against his shoulders. She wanted to reach out to him, to touch him, to reassure him. To tell him she did not hold him personally responsible. She could not. There were witnesses. Any softening would be perceived as weakness by those who were not here and did not know them.

"The message will register once you pass it along, Bagnel. Tell them the price of silence is their desertion of the Serke. Tell them they can tell the Serke that if they want to do us in, henceforth they must come at us directly, without help."

He began to understand. At least, to understand what she wanted him to understand. He whispered, "Marika. As a friend. Not as Bagnel the tradermale or Bagnel the security chief of this enclave. Don't push this. You'll get rolled under. I know nothing of the things you have talked about. I do know that you cannot withstand the forces that are ranged against the Reugge. If you really have the sort of evidence you claim, and I report it, they will kill you."

"I suspect they'll be reluctant to try, Bagnel." She spoke in a whisper herself, and pointed to one of the circling darkships, to make those watching think she was talking about her threats. "Their force commander in the Ponath was the Serke number four. Stronger than anyone but Bestrei herself. She's dead.

And I'm here."

"There are other ways to kill."

Marika rested a paw upon the butt of her rifle. "And I know them. They may have their way with the Reugge. But they will pay in blood. And pay and pay and pay. We have just started fighting, Gradwohl and I."

"Marika, please. You're too young to be so ruled by ambition."

"There are things I want to do with my life, Bagnel. This struggle with the Serke is a distraction. This scramble is something I want to get over early. If I sound confident of the Reugge, that's because I am. In the parlance of your brethren, I believe the hammer is in my paw. I'd rather you and your silth allies just went away and left us alone. I'd rather not fight. But I am ready to bring on the fire if that is the way they want it. You may tell them that we Reugge believe we have very little to lose. And more to gain than they can imagine."

Bagnel sighed. "You always were headstrong and deaf to advice. I will tell my factors what you've said. I'll be very much interested in their response myself."

"I'm sure you will. As you walk over there, keep one eye on the darkships up top. Keep in mind that they have orders to kill anyone who tries to leave the enclave. You can shoot them down if you like. But I don't think even the Serke will tolerate that."

"I hope you know what you're doing, Marika. I really do. I think, though, that you don't. I think you have made some grave and erroneous accusations, and based serious miscalculations upon them. I fear for you."

She *was* making a long bet, setting the price of protecting the rogues so high the brethren factors would have no choice but to surrender them. A success would cement her standing within the Community.

She did not care if the silth liked her, so long as they respected and feared her.

"I intend to be very careful, Bagnel. I give these things more thought than you credit me for. Go. Grauel and Barlog will be waiting here at the gate." She walked through the building beside him, halted at the door to the airstrip, counted silently while he walked fifteen steps. "Bagnel!"

"What?" he squeaked as he whirled.

"Why is the Ponath worth risking the very existence of the brethren?"

An instant of panic betrayed him. If he did not know, he had firmly founded suspicions. Perhaps because the tradermales of Critza had been involved from the beginning?

"The plan is for the brethren to betray the Serke after they take over, isn't it? The brethren think they have some way to force the Serke out without a struggle."

"Marika...."

"I questioned some of the drivers who were with the Serke invaders, Bagnel. What they didn't know was as interesting as what they did."

"Marika, you know very well I do not know what you are howling about. Tell me. Does Most Senior Gradwohl know what you are doing here?"

"The most senior has ambitions greater than mine."

That was not a direct answer, but Bagnel nodded and resumed walking, his step tentative. He glanced at the circling darkships only once. His head lowered against his shoulders again.

She had rattled him badly, Marika knew. Right now he was questioning everything he knew and believed about his bond. She regretted having had to use him so harshly. He *was* a friend.

Given her victory, the day would come when things would balance.

When she returned to the street outside the enclave, Grauel asked, "Are they going to cooperate?"

"I think they will. You can put anything over on anybody if you sound tough enough and confident enough."

"And if they are guilty as charged?"

"That will help a lot."

Barlog looked at one of the darkships. "Did you really order…?"

"Yes. I could not run the bluff without being willing to play part of it out. They might test me."

Barlog winced, but said nothing.

II

Grauel received the rogue prisoners within the deadline. "But nine of them were given over dead, Marika," she reported.

"I expected that. They resisted being turned over, did they?"

"That is what Bagnel told me."

"Want to bet the dead ones could have connected the brethren of the enclave with their movement?"

"No bet. They had to get their weapons and explosives somewhere. Bagnel slipped me a letter, Marika. A personal communication, he said."

"He did?" She was surprised. After what she had put him through? "Let's see what he has to say."

Bagnel said much in few words. He apologized for his brethren having betrayed the conventions. He had not believed her at the gate, but now he had no choice. He was ashamed. As his personal act of contrition, he appended two remarks. *"Petroleum in the Zhotak. Pitchblende in the western Ponath."*

Petroleum she understood instantly. She had to go to references to make sense of the other.

She hurried to Gradwohl's quarters. "My cultivating the male Bagnel has finally paid a dividend, mistress," she reported. She did not mention the brethren yielding the criminals. Gradwohl's meth would have reported all that already. "He has told me what is so important about our northern provinces."

"You broke him down? How? I had begun to think him as stubborn as you."

"I shamed him. I showed him how his factors had been making a fool of him, using him in schemes he would not have touched had they asked him directly. But no matter. He has turned over the rogues, and he has given me the reason behind all the years of terror.

"Petroleum and pitchblende. Our natural resources. Considering what they were willing to risk, the deposits must be huge."

"Petroleum I understand." It was a scarce commodity, very much in demand in the more advanced technological zones farther south. "But what is pitchblende? I have never heard of it."

"I had to look it up myself," Marika admitted. "It is a radioactive ore. A source of the rare heavy elements radium and uranium. There is very little data available in our resources, but there is at least the implication that the heavy elements could become an energy source far more potent than petroleum or other fossil fuels. The brethren already use radioactives as power sources in some of their satellites."

"Space. I wonder.... Now I wonder why the Serke would....?"

"Yes. Suddenly, it looks like we have seen everything backward, does it not? For a long time I thought the Serke were using the brethren. Now I think the brethren have been using the Serke the way the Serke used the nomads. The Serke promised a great prize and secret support. The savages had little real choice, pressed as they were by the onset of the ice age. The brethren in turn baited their snare with the petroleum of the Zhotak. And the Serke leapt on it like an otec onto the scraps of greasy bread huntresses use in their traps along the side creeks. I am sorry. The brethren. I believe they are interested in the pitchblende."

"You have evidence?"

"Only intuition at this point."

Silth accepted intuition as a reliable data base. Gradwohl nodded. "Can you guess what their motives might be?"

"I think that brings us full circle, back to the problem that put me in a position to learn what I have. I think their ultimate goal is the destruction of the silth. Not just the Reugge, a minor Community, but all silth everywhere."

"That is stretching intuition into the wildest conjecture, Marika. Into implausible conjecture."

"Perhaps. Yet there were those who said that about the connection between the rogues and the enclave brethren. And there is no evidence to the contrary. Nothing to show any great tradermale love for silth. Not so? Who does love us? We even hate ourselves."

"I will not permit that kind of talk, Marika."

"I am sorry, mistress. Sometimes I grow bitter and am unable to contain myself. May I proceed upon my assumptions?"

"Proceed? It seems to me that you have handled the situation." Gradwohl glared suspiciously, sensing that Marika wanted to cling to power momentarily gained. "Now it is time we started planning your Toghar ceremonies."

"There will be more incidents, mistress. The brethren have been allowed to create an alternative society. One with far greater appeal to the mass of meth. One in which silth are anachronistic and unnecessary. In nature, the species that is unnecessary soon vanishes."

"I am becoming fearful for your sanity, Marika. Intuition is a fine thing, but you persist in going far beyond intuition, into the far realms of speculation, then treating your fantasies as though they are fact. That is a dangerous habit."

"Mistress, the brethren have created a viable social alternative. Please think about that. Honestly. You will see what I mean. Their technology is like a demon that has been released from a bottle. We have let it run free for too long, and now there is no getting it back inside. We have let it run free so long that now it nearly possesses the power to destroy us. And we have no control over it. They have cunningly held that in their own paws so long that tradition now has the virtual force of law. Our own traditions of not working with our paws cripple us."

"My head understands your arguments. My heart insists you are wrong. But we cannot listen to our hearts always. I will reflect."

"We cannot confine ourselves to reacting to threats only, mistress. As in the old folklore, devils spawn devils faster than they can be banished. They will keep on gnawing off little chunks of us unless we go straight after the demons who raise the demons."

Gradwohl set aside a traditionalist silth's exasperation with ideas almost heretical. That, more than her grasp of silth talents, was the ability that had fueled her rise to the first position among the Reugge. "All right, Marika. I will accept your arguments as a form of working hypothesis. You will be replacing Utiel soon. By stretching the imagination, the problems you conjure will fall within the purview of fourth chair. You may pursue solutions. But be careful who you challenge. It will be years yet before the Reugge are in any position to assert independence from the brethren."

Marika controlled her features carefully. She exulted inside. Saying that, Gradwohl revealed far more than she knew. She did believe! And somehow, though she did not want it known, she was moving to loosen the chains of tradermale technology.

"As you wish, mistress. But let us not remain so enamored of our comforts that we allow ourselves to be destroyed for fear of losing them."

"The ceremonies, Marika. All your arguments, all your desires, all your ambitions are moot without Toghar. Will you stop ducking and changing the subject? Are we going to secure your future? Or deliver it into the paws of those who would see you fail?"

Marika sighed. "Yes, mistress."

"Can we set a date, Marika? Sometime soon?"

Fear twisted Marika's guts. What was the matter with her? Toghar was simple.

Countless silth had survived it. None that she had heard of had not. It was less to be feared than facing down the brethren over a few dozen criminals. Why could she not overcome her resistance? "Yes, mistress. I will begin my preparations immediately."

Maybe something would come up to delay it.

III

"Grauel…. I'm terrified."

"Thousands have been through it, Marika."

"Millions have been through birthing."

"No one has ever died." Hard edge to Grauel's words.

The birthing remark was the wrong thing to say before her two packmates. "It's not that. I don't know how to explain. I'm just scared. Worse than when the nomads came to the packstead. Worse than when they attacked Akard and we all *knew* we were not going to get out alive. Worse than when I was bluffing Bagnel about attacking brethren aircraft if they tried to leave the enclave."

"You were not bluffing."

"I guess not. I would have done it if he had forced me. But I didn't want to. And I don't want to do this."

"I know. I know you're scared. When you're genuinely terrified, you can't shut up."

Startled, Marika asked, "Really? Do I give myself away so easily?"

"Sometimes."

"You will have to educate me. I can no longer allow myself to be easily read."

Barlog stepped around Grauel, held out the white under-shift that was the first of the garments Marika would don. She appeared less empathetic than did Grauel. But when Marika leaned forward to allow her to slide the shift over her head, Barlog hugged her.

Each huntress, in her own way, understood well the price of becoming silth. Grauel, who never could bear pups, and Barlog, who had not been allowed since accepting the Reugge bond. Barlog said, "It isn't too late to leave, Marika."

"It's too late, Barlog. Far too late. There's nowhere we could go. Nor would they tolerate us trying. I know too much. And I have too many enemies, both within and outside the Community. The only way out is death."

"She's right," Grauel said. "I've heard the sisters talking. Many hope she won't go through with it. There is a powerful faction ready to take all our heads."

Marika walked to a window, looked out on the cloister. "Remember when we rated nothing better than a cell under Akard?"

"You've come a long way," Grauel admitted. "You've done many things of which we couldn't approve. Things I doubt we can forgive, even knowing what moved you. There are moments when I can't help but believe what some say, that you're a Jiana. But I guess you've only done what the All demands, and that you've had no more choice than we do."

"There's always a choice, Grauel. But the second option is usually the darker. Today the choice is Toghar or die."

"That's why I say there really isn't any choice."

"I'm glad you understand." She turned, let Barlog pull the next layer of white over her head. There would be another half-dozen layers before the elaborate outer vestments went into place. "I hope you'll understand in future. There will be more evil choices. Once I fulfill Toghar, my feet will settle onto a path from which there will be no turning aside. It is a path into darkness, belike. A headlong rush, and the Reugge dragged right along with us, into a future not even the most senior foresees."

Grauel asked, "Do you really believe the tradermales want to destroy the silth? Or is that just an argument you're using to accumulate extraordinary powers?"

"It's an argument, Grauel, and I'm using it that way. But it also happens to be true. An obvious truth to which the sisters have blinded themselves. They refuse to believe that their grasp is slipping. But that's of no moment now. Let's move faster. Before they come to find out why I'm taking so long."

"We're right on time," Barlog said, arranging the outer vestments.

Grauel slipped the belt of arft skulls around her waist. Barlog placed the red candidate's cap upon her head. Grauel passed her the gold-inlaid staff surmounted by a shrunken kagbeast head indistinguishable from a meth head in that state. In the old days it would have been the head of a meth she had killed.

Grauel brought the dye pots. Marika began staining her exposed fur in the patterns she had chosen. They were not traditional silth or Reugge. They were Degnan patterns meant for a huntress about to go into single, deadly combat. She had learned them as a pup, but never had seen them worn. Neither had Grauel or Barlog, nor anyone or the pack that they could recall. Marika was confident none of today's witnesses would understand her statement.

She stared at herself in a mirror. "We are the silth. The pinnacle of meth civilization."

"Marika?"

"I feel as barbaric as any nomad huntress. Look at me. Skulls. Shrunken head. Bloodfeud dyes." For weeks she had done nothing but prepare for the ceremonies. She had gone into the wild to hunt arfts and kagbeasts, wondering how other candidates managed because the hunting skills were no longer taught young silth.

The hunt had not been easy. Both arfts and kagbeasts were rare in this winter of the world. She had had to slay them, to bring the heads in, and to boil the flesh off the arft skulls and to shrink the head of the kagbeast. Grauel and Barlog had assisted only to the limits allowed by custom. Which was very little.

They had helped more preparing the dyes and sewing the raiments. They were better seamstresses than she, and the sewing had been done in private.

"Do you want to go over your responses again?" Grauel asked. Barlog dug the papers out of the mess on Marika's desk.

"No. Any more and it'll be too much. I'll just turn off my mind and let it happen."

"You won't have any problems," Barlog prophesied.

"Yes," said Grauel. "Overstudy.... I studied too hard when they made me take the voctor exams." "Voctor" was the silth word that approximated the Degnan "huntress," though it also meant "guard" and "one who is trusted in the silth presence bearing weapons." "There were questions where I just went blank."

Barlog said, "At least you got a second chance at the ones you missed. Marika won't."

It did not matter terribly, insofar as the outcome of the ceremonies proper, if Marika stumbled occasionally. But to be less than perfect today would lend her enemies ammunition. They would use any faltering as a sign that she was less than wholly committed to the silth ideal.

Appearances, as always, were more important than substance.

"Barlog. Are you still keeping the Chronicle?"

"Yes."

"Someday when I have the free time I'd like to see what you have said about what has happened to us. What would Skiljan and the others have thought if they could read what you've written, only fifteen years ago? If they'd had that window into the future."

"They would have stoned me."

Marika applied the last daub of vegetable dye. Gathering the dyes had been as difficult as collecting the animal heads. There had been no choice but to purchase some, for the appropriate plants were extinct around Maksche, destroyed by the ongoing cold.

Marika went to the window again, stared north, toward her roots. The sky was clear, which was increasingly rare. The horizon glimmered with the intensity of sunlight reflected off far snowfields. The permanent frostline lay only seventy miles from Maksche now. It was expected to reach the city within the year. She glanced at the heavens. The answer lay up there, she believed. An answer being withheld by enemies of the silth. But there would be nothing she could do for years. There would be nothing she could do, ever, unless she completed today's rites.

"Am I ready?"

"On the outside," Grauel said.

"We haven't forgotten a thing," Barlog said, referring to a checklist Marika had prepared.

"Let's go."

Turmoil twisted into hurricane ferocity inside her.

The huntresses accompanied Marika only as far as the doorway to the building where the ceremonies would be held. The interest was such that Gradwohl had set the thing for the great meeting chamber. Novices turned the huntresses back. Ordinarily the Toghar rites were open to everyone in the cloister. Only those involved and their friends turned out. But Marika's ceremonies had drawn the entire silth body. She was no ordinary novice.

Her enemies were there in hopes she would fail, though novices almost never did so. They were there in hopes their presence would intimidate her into botching her responses, her proper obeisances. They were there in hopes of witnessing a stumble so huge that it could not be forgiven, ever.

Those who were close to Gradwohl, and thus to the most senior's favorite, were there to balance the grim aura of Marika's enemies.

The enemies made sure no nonsilth were present. Marika was more popular among the voctors, whom she had given victories, whom she treated as equals, and who liked the promise of activity she presented.

Marika stepped through the doorway and felt a hundred eyes turn upon her, felt the disappointment in enemies who had hoped she would not show. She took two steps forward and froze, waiting for the sisters not yet seated to enter the hall and take their places.

Fear closed in.

It was not a proper time. Gradwohl and Dorteka both repeatedly had tried to tell her not to place all her trust in those-who-dwell. Even knowing she should not, she slipped down through her loophole, into that otherworld that overlapped her own, and sought the solace of a strong dark ghost.

She found one, brought it in, and used it to ride through the chamber ahead, reassuring herself that the ceremonies would proceed in the usual way. It was a cold world out there, with the ghosts. Emotion drained away. Fear dribbled into the ether, or whatever it was through which the ghosts swam. The coldness of that plane drained into her.

She was ready. She had control. She could do it now. She could forget what it would cost her, could forget all her nurture as a huntress-to-be, dam-to-be, of the Degnan pack. She released the ghost with a stroke of gratitude, pulled back to the world of everyday, of continuous struggle and fear. She scanned the hall ahead with cold eyes. All the sisters had taken their places.

Coolly, she stepped forward, standing straight, elegant in her finery. She paused while two novices closed the door behind her. She faced right and bent to kiss the rim of an ancient pot that looked like a crucible used till it had had to be discarded. She dipped a finger in, brought thick, sweet daram to her lips and tongue.

That pot was older than the Reugge. Older, even, than the dam Community, the Serke. Its origins had been lost in the shadows of time. Its rim had been worn by the touch of countless lips, its interior crusted by residue from the tons of daram that had filled it over the ages. It was the oldest thing in the Reugge world, an icon-link that connected the Community with the protosilth of prehistory, the symbolic vessel of the All from which silth were granted a taste of infinity, a taste of greater power. It had been the kissing bowl of seven gods and goddesses before the self-creation of the All.

The glow of the daram spread through Marika, numbing her as chaphe would, yet expanding her till she seemed to envelope everyone else in the hall. They, too, had tasted daram. Their mind guards were down a fraction. Touch leaked from everyone, pulling her into a pool of greater consciousness. Her will and personality became less sharply defined and singular. It was said that in the ancient lodges, before civilization, silth had melded into a single powerful mind by taking massive doses of daram.

That part of her, the majority, which remained wholly Marika, marveled that hidden beyond this welcoming glow there could be so much fear, spite, enmity, and outright irrational hatred.

Her sponsor Gradwohl and the chief celebrants waited at the far end of the hall. She spoke her first canticle, the novice requesting permission to approach and present her petition for recognition. A silth somewhere to her right asked a question. She replied automatically, with the proper response, noting in passing that her primary interrogator would be Utiel, the old female she would replace in fourth chair. All the Maksche councillors seemed to have assumed roles in the ceremonies, even the senior, who had been all but invisible since falling out of favor with Gradwohl.

Before she realized what was happening, the initial interrogatory ended. She approached the celebrants. Again there were questions. She did not become involved on a conscious level. She responded crisply, automatically, made her gestures at the exact appropriate instant. She felt like a dancer perfectly inserted into her dance, one with the music, leaping, twisting, turning with absolute grace, the thing itself instead of an actor, the ultimate and ideal product of a perfect sorcery. Her precision, her *artistry,* fed back to the celebrants so that they, too, fell into her matchless rhythm.

The slight tension brought on by the presence of enemies faded from the shared touch of the daram, expunged by the experience of which she was heart. That experience began to swell, to grow, to drown everything.

And yet, deep within her, Marika never wholly surrendered to the commitment the rite was supposed to represent.

The celebrants completed the final interrogatory. One by one, Marika surrendered her staff, her belt of skulls, her cap, her ceremonial raiments to the kettle of fire around which the celebrants stood. Noisome smoke rose, filled the hall. In moments she stood before the assembly wearing nothing but her dyes.

Now the crux. The stumbling stone. The last hope of those who wished her ill. The truly physical part, when they would stretch her on the altar and a healer sister would reach into the ghost realm and summon those-who-dwell, lead a ghost into her recumbent form, and destroy forever her ability to bear young.

Marika met Gradwohl's eye and nodded. The most senior stepped around the smoking kettle, presented the wafer. Marika took it between her teeth.

And added her bit of style, her own fillip to the ceremony. She faced the assembly before biting down, chewing, swallowing. She felt the stir in the entwined touch, the slight, unwilling swell of admiration.

The wave of well-being came over her as concentrated chaphe spread through her flesh. The celebrants stepped around the kettle and allowed her to settle into their arms. They lifted her to the altar. The healer sister loomed over her.

That reluctant something tried to wriggle forth, tried to scream, tried to will her to move, break away, flee. She stifled it.

She felt the ghost move inside her. Felt her ovaries and tubes being destroyed. There was no pain, except of the heart. There would be little discomfort later, she had been promised.

She turned inward, felt for the ghost world, fled there for several moments.

It was all over when she returned. The observers were filing out. The celebrants and their assistants were cleaning up. Gradwohl stood over her, looking down. She seemed pleased. "That was not so bad, was it, Marika?"

Marika wanted to say the hurt was all in her mind, but she could not. The daram and chaphe held her. She reflected momentarily upon a pack still unMourned and wondered if their spirits would forgive her. Wondered if she could ever forgive Gradwohl for forcing her into this crime against herself.

It would fade. The heart's pains all faded.

"You did very well, Marika. It was a most impressive Toghar. Even those who dislike you had to admit that you are extraordinary."

She wanted to protest that they never had denied that, that that was the reason they feared her, but she could not.

Gradwohl patted her shoulder. "You are fourth chair now. Utiel officially announced her retirement the moment the ceremony was complete. Please use your power wisely. Your two voctors will be in to help you shortly. I will tell them to remind you that I want to see you after you have recovered." Gradwohl touched her gently, almost lovingly, in a fashion her own dam never had managed. For a moment Marika suspected there might be more to her patronage than simple interest in the fate of the Reugge.

She forced that out of mind. It was not difficult with the chaphe in her blood.

"Be well," Gradwohl murmured, and departed.

Grauel and Barlog appeared only several minutes after the last of the silth departed. Marika was vaguely amused as she watched them prowl the chamber, peering into every shadow. They, who believed silth could render themselves invisible with their witchcraft. Finally, they came to her, helped her down off the altar.

"How did it go?" Barlog asked. She seemed under a strain.

"Perfectly," Marika croaked through a throat parched by drugs.

"Are you all right?"

"Physically, I'm fine. But in my soul I feel filthy."

Again both huntresses scanned the shadows. "Can you speak business? Are you too disoriented?" Grauel asked.

"I can. Yes. But take me away from here first."

"Storeth found those workers," Grauel told Marika, after they had taken her to her quarters. "She reported while you were in that place. They were reluctant to talk, but she convinced them she came from you. They acknowledged their debt. They knew very little, but they did say there is a persistent rumor that the rogues have found themselves a powerful wehrlen. One who will be able to defeat silth at their witchcraft when he is ready. So the thing is not done. As you thought."

In the questioning of all the rogues taken, there had been that thread of belief in something great about to befall the criminal movement. Marika had not been able to identify it clearly. In the end she had decided to seek out two Maksche workers who had served her in the Ponath years ago, workers who had vowed they would repay an imagined debt.

"Warlock," she murmured. "And a great one, of course. Or he would not be able to inspire this mad hope."

She had not mentioned anything of this to the most senior. Intuition told her this was a thing best kept to herself. For the present, at least.

"We must find him. And kill him, if he cannot be used."

For once Grauel and Barlog concurred in a prospective savagery.

They remembered the wehrlen who first brought the nomads out of the Zhotak.

BOOK FOUR:
TELLERAI

CHAPTER TWENTY-THREE

I

Barlog relayed the message that had been left at the cloister gate. "A communication from Bagnel, Marika. And I wish you would do as the most senior suggests and move to quarters more suitable to one of your status. I am growing too old to be scampering up and down stairs like this."

"Poo. You're only as old as you think, Barlog. You're still in your prime. You have a good many years ahead of you. What is it?"

"But are they all years of up stairs? I don't know what it is. It's sealed."

"So it is." Marika opened the envelope. It was a large one, but contained only a brief note.

"Well?"

"He wants a meeting. Not a visit. A meeting." She pondered that. It implied something official. Which further implied that the tradermales were aware of her official elevation to fourth chair and her brief for dealing with rogue males. She had not wanted the news to get out of the cloister so quickly. But outside laborers would talk. "I guess a month of secrecy is enough to ask. Barlog. I want to talk to Braydic. In person. Here. Don't let her give you any of the usual excuses."

Ever since the confrontation in the main ceremonial hall, Braydic had bent every effort to avoid compromising herself further by avoiding Marika.

"Yes, mistress."

Braydic's evasions had done her no good. Marika had made her head of a communications-intercept team. Like it or not. And Braydic did not.

Marika did not quite understand the communications technician. From the first a large part of her friendship for the refugee pup had been based upon her belief that Marika would one day become powerful and then be in a position to do her return favors. But now she was afraid to harvest what she had sown.

Braydic was too conservative. She was not excited by new opportunities and new ideas. But she carried out her orders and did so well. In the nine days since she had gotten the intercept system working, she had stolen several interesting signals.

Marika paced while waiting. She was not sure where she was going now. There had been a time when she thought to displace Gradwohl and head the Reugge Community in her own direction. But Gradwohl seemed to be steering a course close to her own ideal, if sometimes a little cautiously and convolutedly, and not seizing control of the sisterhood meant not having to deal with the flood of minutiae which swamped the most senior.

She lamented having so few trustworthy allies. She could not do everything she wanted herself, yet there was no one she could count on to help move the sisterhood in directions she preferred.

Was she getting beyond herself? Looking too far down the path?

She went to a window, stared at the stars. "Soon," she promised them. "Soon Marika will walk among you."

She returned to her desk and dug out the file containing outlines of Braydic's reports.

The critical notation to date was that Braydic had identified signals from more than one hundred orbital satellites. Though the spacefaring sisterhoods did not announce an orbiting, the available data suggested that they had helped boost no more than half that number into orbit. Which meant that the brethren had somehow put the rest up on their own, trespassing upon silth privilege by doing so. The space codicils to the conventions specifically excluded the brethren from the dark, except as contract employees of the sisterhoods.

Intriguing possibilities there.

Braydic entered tentatively. "You sent for me, mistress?"

"Yes. I want to know what you have intercepted recently. Especially today."

"I sent a report not two hours ago, mistress."

"I know, Braydic. A very long, thick, dull report that would take forever to get through. It will take less time if you just tell me if there was anything worth overhearing. Especially from our male friends at the enclave."

"There has been heavy traffic all day, mistress. Much has been in cant or in the brethren cult language. We have not been able to decipher much of it, but we think they are expecting an important visitor."

"That would make sense," Marika murmured to herself. "That is all?"

"All we could determine without an interpreter. If you expect me to unravel the content of these messages, you are going to have to give me interpreters or scholars capable of discovering the meaning of the secret languages. Neither I nor any of my team are capable."

"I will see what I can do about that, Braydic. It would please me, too, if we could understand everything being said. Thank you for taking time to come up here. And I want you to know I appreciate your efforts."

"You are welcome, mistress. Oh. Mistress. The Serke network has also been carrying a heavy traffic load today."

"There might be a chance of a connection? Yes? Good. Thank you again. This calls for reflection." Marika seated herself, closed her eyes, allowed herself to sink into the All. She waited for intuition to fuel her thoughts.

She came out to find Barlog poised near the doorway, waiting, doing nothing to disturb her. "Barlog?"

"Is there to be an answer to the message, Marika? The messenger is waiting."

"Indeed? Then tell him to tell Bagnel that I will be there an hour after midnight." She consulted her calendar. "An hour and thirteen minutes after, to be precise."

The major moons would attain their closest conjunction of the month at that time. The tides would rise high enough to halt the flow of the Hainlin. The hour would be one considered especially propitious to the silth. Bagnel would understand. She was sure he had been studying everything known about the silth with as much devotion as she studied everything known about flying and space. He might not be wholly aware of the part he was playing in this game, but he was as dedicated as she. A pity he could not become her prime opponent. He would make a good one. The tension of their friendship would add spice.

From Bagnel she shifted thought to the rumored wehrlen. Was that anything but wishful thinking by rogues? She could catch the odor of nothing even remotely concrete. Her resources were inadequate.

Ten minutes before she was due at the enclave, Marika assumed her position at the tip of the dagger of her darkship. She had elected to fly to avoid the chance of rogue ambush. She did not fear ambush, but it would be too much of a distraction.

Grauel and Barlog accompanied her, standing at the axis of the cross. Marika and they carried their weapons. She made the bath go armed. The moment they were airborne Grauel used a portable transceiver to contact the tradermale controller. She followed procedures identical to those Bagnel used on landing approaches.

Marika thought that amusing. Especially if the brethren were up to some wickedness.

She brought the darkship down near Bagnel's headquarters. Barlog and Grauel dismounted quickly and took their places to either paw. One bath went ahead of Marika, two followed. The party bristled with weapons. Marika herself carried a revolver and automatic rifle taken from enemies in the Ponath. She hoped the tradermales would see the symbolism.

Bagnel handled her irregular arrival well. She wondered if she could surprise him anymore. He greeted her pleasantly. "Right on time. Come into the back."

Marika was startled. Never before had he offered her entrance to his private quarters.

"Is all the hardware necessary?" Bagnel asked.

"That remains to be seen. We live in strange times. I don't believe in taking needless chances."

"I suppose." He sounded as though he thought his honesty had been questioned.

"It's not personal, Bagnel. I trust you. But not those who use you. I want to be able to shoot back if somebody shoots at me. More sporting than obliterating them with a blow from the touch. Don't you think?"

"You've developed a bloodthirsty turn, Marika."

She wanted to tell him it was calculated. But even with him there were truths best kept close to the heart. So she told him an incomplete truth. "It's my upbringing. I spent so much time getting away from meth who wanted to eat me. What did you expect anyway? This can't be social. You've never invited me over in the middle of the night. That would be an impropriety."

Marika gestured. Grauel, who retained the sensitive nose of a Ponath huntress, stepped up and sniffed the fruit punch Bagnel had begun preparing. The tradermale eyed her with a look of consternation.

"I didn't think you'd be fooled," he said. "Knowing you, you have it half figured out."

"You want me to meet someone who is going to try to bribe me or twist my arm. I trust that you were a good enough friend to warn them that their chances of success are slight."

"Them?"

"I expect there will be more than one, and at least one will be female, of exalted rank, representing the Serke."

A door opened. Marika glimpsed a sleeping room. Bagnel had spartan tastes in private as well as public. She credited him with a point to his account of positives. He worked to fulfill his tasks, not to acquire a more luxurious life.

Several meth came out of the sleeping room. None were armed and none were of low status. Their trappings reeked of power and wealth. Marika's party seemed incongruous in their presence, all of them clad for the field, all armed, the bath and Grauel and Barlog nearly fight-alert against the walls.

Marika had hit near the mark. There were two silth and two males. The males were so old their fur had a ratty, patchy look. Both exuded a strong presence seldom seen even in females. She recognized neither, but there were few photographic records of those who were masters among the brethren.

One of the males stared at her in a fashion she found too bold. Too much like a butcher sizing up livestock.

"Marika," Bagnel said, stirring the punch, "I want to be on record as having arranged this meeting under orders. I don't know what it's about, so don't blame me personally if you don't like the way it goes."

"I know that, Bagnel. It would be unreasonable to expect thieves to give any consideration to friendship. Few of them are aware that it exists. I'll bet the word does not occur in the Serke secret tongue, or even in your tradermale cant." She turned. "Greynes. Natik. Korth. Guard the outside. One of you take the hall doorway. The other two patrol around outside. I doubt you will see anyone, as these bandits will not want it known what they are doing and orders will have been given keeping everyone away from here. But, just in case, shoot first and ask questions later."

The moment the door closed behind the bath, she asked, "What are you going to offer?" She brought her gaze ripping across four sets of hard but mildly unsettled eyes.

The silth looked back blankly, careful students of their art. Marika judged them to be high in their order. Almost certainly from the Serke controlling council itself. They would want a close look at the Reugge youngster who had slain two of their number.

The tradermales remained blank, too.

None of the four spoke.

"But surely you have something to offer. Some way of getting me to betray my Community so you can work your wicked wills. Think of the prizes at stake. Our Reugge provinces are floating on oil. Those parts that are not sinking beneath the weight of rare heavy elements." She revealed her teeth as she tilted her ears in a contrived expression of amusement. "But look at you, crinkling around the corners of your eyes and wondering what is this creature? It is just me. The troublesome savage Marika. The shin-kicker who forestalls the conspiracies of thieves. Trying to drive a wedge between you."

Teeth began to show. But for some reason they had made it up to allow her all the initial talking. Perhaps a test?

"Yes. I am forthright. I tell you right out front that I am going to put you at one another's throats. No proxies and no lies. Sisters, did your friends here ever tell you about the pitchblende in the western Ponath?"

One of the tradermales jerked upright, lip peeling back in an unconscious snarl. The silth did not miss that. Grauel and Barlog snapped their rifles down, aimed at his chest.

"Pitchblende is a source of radioactives, rare and dangerous heavy metals. They have very limited technological applications at the moment—primarily as power sources in satellites. But it takes no imagination to see that major surface installations could be built by an advanced technology. I suspect the brethren could have something operating within ten years. Sisters, do look up radium and uranium when you get back to Ruhaack, or wherever. While you are checking things, see if you can get an accurate count on the number of satellites orbiting our world. Compare that number with the number that the dark-faring Communities have lifted."

Marika faced the tradermales. "I am perfectly transparent, am I not? It is your turn. You, of course, have been anticipating Serke treachery from the beginning. That is the way those witches are. You have been preparing for the scramble for the spoils. But suppose we could short-circuit the process? Lovely technical term, short-circuit. Suppose you did not have to deal with the Serke at all? Suppose I offered you a Reugge license allowing you access to all the pitchblende you want? Without your having to sneak through the wilds outside the law, hoping you can survive the malice of your accomplices."

The males exchanged looks.

"There? You see? I have been perfectly obvious, and yet I have given you much on which to think. Why not get what you want the cheaper and safer way? I understand you better than you think. I know what moves you." She shifted her gaze to the silth. "You, though, remain enigmas. I do not know if I will ever fathom your motives for committing such hideous crimes."

She settled into the one chair standing on her side of the room, waiting. A shaken Bagnel hovered in no-meth's land. He sped Marika a look of appeal.

"I am waiting," she said after half a minute of silence.

They had found their strategy wanting, though they took its failure well. One of the males finally said, "Not long ago you placed the brethren in a tight position. You tied us up so we had no choice but to do something we considered despicable."

"That is just beginning, old-timer. If you persist in arming, training, sending out criminals to attack silth, you are going to find yourselves in even tighter places. You will find the Reugge have so many criminals under sentence we will be selling their sentences to Communities that have a shortage of condemned laborers."

Her confidence rattled the male for a moment. But he recovered, held unswervingly to what had to be a prepared line of argument. "We have decided to do unto you as you did unto us."

"Really? Why do I get the feeling I am about to witness the unfolding of a grand delusion?"

"We do not delude ourselves!" he snapped. She could almost hear him thinking, *You silth bitch.*

"*Arrogant* silth bitch," she corrected aloud. "Come ahead, then. Try me."

For the first time the Serke looked genuinely uncertain. The appearance of confidence becomes confidence, Marika reminded herself.

The male who had not yet spoken did so now. From several glances he had thrown Bagnel's way, Marika inferred that he must somehow be her friend's superior. He said, "Some time ago you ambushed a joint force in the Ponath. You once threatened to make the circumstances public. We would like it noted that the same event can be used to *your* detriment. If you refuse to cooperate with us."

Marika was not surprised. She had expected that Kublin would come back to haunt her eventually. But she had let the matter float, hoping she could do the right thing intuitively when he did.

The male suggested, "You might want to send your guards outside."

"I might not. There are two Serke of exalted status here. I might not be able to kill both of them quickly enough to keep you from sticking a knife into me. Go ahead with your threats."

"As you wish. You allowed a littermate to escape that ambush. Surrounding circumstances suggest that you did more than that to assure his safety. Suppose that were made known?"

The one thing Marika *had* done about the matter was to send a group of huntresses, picked by Grauel, to Critza. They were under instructions to lie low and capture any snoopers. So she controlled the physical proofs. "Go ahead. If that is your best."

"What we have in mind is presenting the evidence to your most senior. She, I believe, is your principal anchor within the Reugge Community."

Marika shook her head, honestly less worried by the moment. "Go with it. See what it gets you. While you are at it, though, why not up the stakes? Why not try to buy me somehow?"

That caused more consternation.

"We *will* present Most Senior Gradwohl with the evidence."

"I said go ahead. You will have assembled a fair file on me by now. You know I do not bluff."

"We know your bluff has not been called. We know you are young. A characteristic of youth is that it takes long risks, betting that older, more cautious heads will not hazard stakes as dangerous."

"Play your stakes," Marika said. "Grauel, our presence here seems pointless. Tell the bath to ready the darkship."

"Wait," one of the silth said. "You have not heard what we want."

"To tell the truth, I do not care what you want. It would not be anything in my interest, or in the interest of the Reugge Community."

"You could become most senior of the Reugge if you cooperated."

"I have no wish to become most senior. That is a job that would distract me too much from those things that do interest me."

"Is there any way to reach you?"

"Almost certainly. We all want some things so badly we will befoul ourselves to get them. Witness yourselves. But I cannot think of anything that is within your power to offer. At least nothing I cannot take for myself. I suggest you stop trying to steal the Ponath. Accept the fact that the Reugge control it. Deal for the petroleum and pitchblende. Frankly, I find it impossible to comprehend your frenzy for outright control."

Marika looked at the tradermales, hoping they would understand that she actually had no trouble at all understanding. "I will go now. You four squabble over the ways you may have planned to stab one another in the back."

With Grauel and Barlog covering her, she backed to the doorway. She paused there, added, "The most senior is away this month, as she often is. You will not be able to contact her for some time. However, she will return to Maksche for a two-week period beginning the fifth day of Biter—if you feel compelled to present *your* evidence. My own proofs are held by a trusted sister at TelleRai, under seal. She is under bond to break the seal in the event of my death or prolonged disappearance." She left. But after she had taken a few steps, she turned back to add, "After me, my fine thieves, the end of the world. At least for you and yours."

Her feet flew as she dashed to the darkship. She had gotten away with yanking their whiskers. Very nearly with yanking them out by the roots. She had left them completely at a loss.

It was wonderful.

It was the sort of thing she had wanted to do to some of her elders almost from the time she had grown old enough to reason.

She took the darkship up, on a long flight, pursuing the rogue orbit of a small retrograde moon. She pushed hard, glorying in the cold air's rush through her fur.

After the crude joy began to fade, she halted, floated high, where the air was thin but cut like knives of ice. She looked southward. Far, far down there were the great cities of the world. Cities like TelleRai, which spawned the Gradwohls and silth like the Serke she had faced tonight. And thousands of miles farther still lay the equator, over which orbited many of the tradermale satellites.

The ice was advancing because the world had cooled. The world had cooled because not enough solar radiation impinged upon it now that it had entered the interstellar cloud. To halt the ice required only an increase in the amount of solar energy reaching the surface of the planet.

Someday, and perhaps not that long now, she would begin throwing more coals on the fires of the sun—as it almost had to be said in the dialect of her puphood, naked as it was of technical and scientific terms.

II

Marika had won again, apparently. Neither the Serke nor brethren appeared inclined to test her.

A quiet but busy year passed.

Three months after the confrontation in Bagnel's quarters, third chair came open. Gradwohl moved her up. Marika clung to those security functions pertaining to the rogue male problem. She continued to expand them as much and as often as she dared, though she operated with a more delicate paw than had been her custom. With more to lose and more to gain, she invested much thought before making more enemies.

Third chair meant having to monitor meetings of the Reugge council at TelleRai. Tradition insisted third chair accompany first chair, or senior, at each such gathering. Marika refused to attend in person, though Gradwohl herself often urged her to make herself known to the sisters of the ruling cloister.

She audited the meeting electronically. She did not feel comfortable leaving the heart of the network she had begun building.

She spent seven months in third chair, then second came open. The All was a persistent taker during those years at Maksche, an ally almost as valuable as Gradwohl herself, hastening her rise till it rattled her almost as much as it did her detractors.

At every step of her elevation she was the youngest ever to hold her position.

Gradwohl moved her into second chair. And within the month her ally the All passed its shade across the order's ruling council itself. Gradwohl appointed her seventh chair, a step which shook the entire Community. Never before had an order-wide chair been held by one less than a cloister senior. Never before had two chairs been held by sisters from the same cloister.

Marika ignored the grumbles and uproar. Let the most senior deal with it if she insisted on elevating her favorite over others who felt themselves more deserving.

Again the most senior urged her to make herself known at TelleRai. Her arguments were basic and irrefutable. One day she would have to deal with those meth regularly. She should get to know them now, while they could yet become comfortable with her.

Again she demurred, wishing to remain near the root of a growing political power.

She did not have to be in TelleRai to know what they were saying down there. It was the same old thing, on the larger scale of the sisterhood. They did not like one so young, from the wilds, acquiring so much power within the Community. They were afraid, just at the sisters of Maksche and Akard had been afraid. But the resistance down in TelleRai was even more resistance of the heart than of the mind. They did not know her at all. Only a few had encountered her during the campaigns in the Ponath. The silth there recognized her accomplishments. They were not as bitter as the silth at Maksche. Even those silth gave her very little real trouble, preferring to hate her in their hearts and minds while hoping she set herself up for a fall.

Marika slept very little that year. She pushed herself hard, developing her antirogue force, making of it a personal power base she insinuated into every Reugge cloister. Cynically, she made strong use of the rumors about a great wehrlen lurking among the rogues. If Gradwohl understood what she was doing, she said nothing.

With Braydic's reluctant help Marika developed stolen technology into tools suited to her tasks. Her finest became a listening device she planted in the quarters of those she suspected of trying to thwart her. Toward the end of the year she began having such devices installed in the quarters of anyone she thought might someday get in her way.

The listening devices, unknown outside her circle, gave her a psychological edge on her enemies. Some of her more superstitious sisters came to believe that she could indeed become invisible as in old silth myth. Her revenges were subtle but emotionally painful. Before long all Maksche lived in fear of offending her. The terror of her sisters remained mainly a terror of what she might become, not a fear of what she was.

Each such tiny triumph of intimidation strengthened her. In building her power base she switched back upon her past, in other cloisters, and tried to recruit the most reactionary silth to manage the rogue program.

Her efforts in that direction yielded results sufficient to convince the most doubting silth that there was a grand conspiracy against the sisterhoods, with the Reugge the chosen first victim. Every criminal male taken and questioned seemed to provide one more fragment fitting into a grand mosaic of revolution.

The warlock began to take substance, if only as a dreadful shadow.

Marika's first contacts outside her own Community came not as a result of her place on the council at TelleRai but because several of the more friendly sisterhoods became interested in creating their own rogue-hunting apparatus before the problem in their territories swelled to the magnitude of that in the Reugge. They came to Marika for advice.

The parade of outsiders impressed the Maksche sisters. Marika made of that what she could, gradually silencing more of her strongest critics.

Yet silence bought nothing. The more widely known she became, the more hated she became by those who had chosen to stand against her in their hearts.

There was no conquering irrationality. Especially not among silth.

There were nights when she lay awake with the pain of unwarranted hatred, vainly consoling herself with the knowledge that all silth who attained any stature did so at the cost of hatred. Few of the Maksche council were well liked. No one liked Gradwohl. Were the most senior there more often, instead of away doing what no one knew what, she might have absorbed some of the hatred directed her favorite's way.

Often when Marika did sleep she fell into a strange dream wherein she rode a surrealistic, shifting beast across a night infested with stars, without a wind stirring her robes and fur, without a planet below. There was peace in that great star-flecked void.

Mornings afterward she would waken with her determination refreshed, no longer caring if anyone loved her.

She was alive for the sake of a creature called Marika, not for anyone else. She would salvage the freedom of the Reugge if she could. She owed the Community something. If she succeeded, so much the better. If she did not, she would not much care.

She would help the Serke if there were no other way of opening her pathway into the great dark.

She was second chair, yet Gradwohl tinkered with it in a manner that there were no duties for her at Maksche. In time her campaign against the rogues was so successful she had little to do but monitor reports of ever-dwindling criminal activity. She began to find herself with time on her paws. That left her time to brood. She began to feel hemmed in, pressured, restless.

III

It was the anniversary of Marika's confrontation in Bagnel's quarters. She had extended her morning exercises by an hour, but they had done nothing to stay her restlessness. A call to Bagnel had proven fruitless. He was tied up, unable to entertain her. She faced a long and tiresome day of poring over stolen texts, searching for something she did not already know; of skimming reports from Braydic's intercept teams and plant listeners, finding the same old things; of scanning statements from informants seeking rewards for helping capture members of the rogue movement.

She had had all she could stand of that. She wanted to be free. She wanted to fly.

"This is not what I want to do with my life. How do they get anyone to take first chairs? Barlog! Tell the bath to prepare my darkship."

"Marika?"

"You heard me. I am sick of all this. We're taking the darkship up."

"All right." Barlog disapproved. She had found herself a niche, helping direct the movement of information, which suited her perfectly. And she did not like Marika's laying claim to the ship. It was not yet assigned her formally. It still belonged to the cloister generally, though no one else had used it all year. Barlog was becoming very conscious of place and prerogative. "Where will you be going?"

"I don't know. I'll just be going. Anywhere away from all this. I need to feel the wind in my fur."

"I see. Marika, we have come no nearer finding the warlock."

Marika stifled a sharp reply. She was tempted to believe the warlock a product of rogue wishful thinking. "Inform Grauel. She'll need to find a sub if she has cloister duty today."

"Do you expect to be up long?" Barlog looked pointedly at a heap of reports Marika had yet to consider.

"I think so. I need it this time." She had done this before, but only for brief periods. Today, though, demanded an extended flight. The buildup of restlessness and frustration would need a while to work off.

"As you command." Barlog departed.

Marika scowled at her back. For one who had come to set so much stock in place, Barlog was getting above herself. She shuffled papers, looking for something that might need immediate attention.

For no obvious reason she recalled something Dorteka had said. About a museum in TelleRai. The Redoriad museum? Yes.

TelleRai. Why not? She was secure enough now. Both in her power and within herself.

She summoned one of the novices assigned to run and fetch for her. "Ortaga, get me some medium-scale maps of the country south of here. The Hainlin to the sea, the coast, and everything west to and including the air corridor to TelleRai. As far south as TelleRai."

"Yes, mistress."

The maps arrived before Barlog returned. Marika laid out a flight path that would pass over outstanding landmarks she had heard mentioned by bath and Mistresses of the Ship with whom she had spoken. She told the novice, "I will be gone all day. I expect to return tonight. Have the other novices sort the papers the usual way. Tag any that look important."

"Yes, mistress."

"Barlog. At last. Is the darkship ready?"

"It will be a short time yet, mistress. The bath told me that they will want to fulfill the longer set of rites if you intend an extended flight."

"I see." Marika did not understand the bath. They had their own community within the greater Community, with private rites they practiced before every flight. The rites apparently amounted to an appeal to the All to see them through unscathed.

There were Mistresses, like Bestrei of the Serke, who considered their bath in the same class as firewood. They cared not at all for them as meth. They drew upon them so terribly they burned them out.

Even lesser and more thoughtful Mistresses had been known to miscalculate and destroy their helpers.

Marika took some coin from her working fund, then donned an otec coat. Otec fur was rare now. The coat was her primary concession to the silth custom of exploiting one's status. Otherwise she lived frugally, dressed simply, used her position only to obtain information. Any sort of information, not just news about rogue males or about the space adventures of the dark-faring Communities. She had accumulated so much data she could not keep track of it all, could not keep it correlated.

Grauel joined her as she and Barlog reached the grand court where the dark-ships came and went. Workers were removing hers from its rack. It was so light only a half dozen were needed to lift it down and carry it to the center of the square. They unfolded the short arms and locked them into place. Marika eyed the line of witch syrinxes painted on shields hung along the main beam.

"Someday I will have a darkship all my own. I will have it painted all in black," she said to no one in particular. "So it can't be seen at night. And we will add Degnan symbols to those of the Reugge."

"The tradermales could still follow you with their radar," Grauel said. "And silth could still find you with the touch."

"Even so. Where are they? Do their rituals take so long? Barlog, where are your weapons? We don't go anywhere without our weapons." She herself carried the automatic rifle and revolver captured in the Ponath. She carried a hunting knife that had belonged to her dam, a fine piece of tradermale steel. She never left her quarters unarmed.

Grauel still carried the weapon Bagnel had given her during the siege of Akard. It remained her most precious treasure. She could have replaced it with something newer and more powerful, but she clung to it superstitiously. It had served her well from the moment it had come into her paws. She did not wish to tempt her fates.

Barlog was less dramatically inclined. Marika often had to remind her that they were supposed to be living savage roles. Marika *wanted* other silth to perceive them as terribly barbaric. It amused her that those with the nerve sometimes asked why she did not wear ceremonial dyes as well as always going armed.

She never bothered telling them that the daily dyeing of fur was a nomad custom, not one indigenous to the Ponath. For all there had been a deadly struggle of years, most of the Reugge could not understand the difference between Ponath and Zhotak meth.

There was a chill bite to the morning wind. It made her eager to be up and away, running free, riding the gale. Someday she wanted to take the darkship up during a storm, to race among growling clouds and strokes of lightning. Other Mistresses thought her mad. And she would never be able to try it. The bath would refuse to participate. And they had that right if they believed a flight would become too dangerous.

Marika had worked long and hard to develop and strengthen her natural resistance to electromagnetic interference with her silth talents. But in her more realistic moments she admitted that even she would be overwhelmed by the violent bursts of energy present in a thunderstorm. Flight among lightnings would never be more than a fantasy.

Barlog came hustling back armed as though for a foot patrol against the nomad. She even carried a pod of grenades. Marika ignored the silent sarcasm, for the bath appeared at the same time, each with her formal greeting for the Mistress of the Ship. All bath seemed to be very much creatures of ceremony.

Each of the bath was armed as a huntress. They knew Marika's ways.

They did not like serving with her, Marika knew. But she knew it was nothing personal. The Reugge bath did not like any of the Reugge Mistresses of the Ship. It was part of their tradition not to like anyone who held so much power over their destinies.

"Positions," Marika said.

"Food?" Grauel asked. "Or have I guessed wrong? Will it be a brief flight?"

"I brought money if we need it. Board and strap, please."

The bath counted off the ready. "Stand by," Marika called, and stepped onto her station. Unlike the bath, she often disdained safety restraints. This was one of those times when she wanted to ride the darkship free, in the old way, as silth had done in the days of slower, heavier wooden ships.

"Be prepared!"

Marika went down inside herself, through her loophole, and sent a touch questing. Ghosts were scarce around the cloister. They did not like being grabbed by silth.

She knew the cure for that. A whiff of the touch, like the sense of one of their own calling. A lure laid before them and drawn slowly closer. They were not smart. She could draw in a score at a time and bind them, and reach for another score.

The grand court was aboil within a minute with more ghosts than any other Mistress could have summoned. There were far more than Marika really needed to lift and move the darkship. But the more there were, the safer she would be. The more there were, the farther she could sense and see through that other level of reality. And the higher and faster she could fly—though speed was determined mainly by her ability to remain aboard the darkship in the face of the head wind of her passage.

She squeezed the ghosts, pressed them upward. The darkship rose swiftly. Grauel and Barlog gasped, protested, concerned for her safety. But Marika always went up fast.

She squeezed in the direction she wished to travel. The titanium cross rushed forward.

She rose as high as she dared, up where the air was cold and rare and biting, like the air of a Ponath winter, and maintained control of the ghosts with a small part of her mind while she gazed down on the world. The Hainlin was a wide brown band floating between mottled puzzle pieces of green. From that height she could not make out the flotsam and ice which made river travel hazardous. The dead forests of the north were coming down, seeking the sea. She glanced at the sky overhead, where several of the smaller moons danced their ways through the sun's enfeebled light. She again wondered why the tradermales did nothing to stay the winter of the world.

She would, one day. She had mapped out a plan. As soon as she had garnered sufficient power.... She mocked herself. She? A benefactor? Grauel and Barlog would be astonished if they knew what she had in mind.

Well, yes. She could be. Would be. After she had clambered over scores of bodies, of sisters, of whoever stood in her path. But that was far away yet. She had to concentrate upon the present. Upon the possibilities the Serke-brethren conspiracy presented. She had to get back to them, to sound them out. There might be more there than she had thought.

IV

Marika followed the Hainlin for a hundred miles, watching it broaden as two mighty tributaries joined it. She was tempted to follow the river all the way to the sea, just to see what the ocean looked like. But she turned southward toward the Topol Cordillera, not wishing to anger anyone by trespassing upon their airspace. She was not yet in the position of a Bestrei, who could fly wherever and whenever she wished. That lay years in the future.

Quietly, she admonished herself against impatience. It all seemed slow, yes, but she was decades ahead of the pace most silth managed.

The Topol Cordillera was a low range of old hills which ran toward TelleRai from the continent's heart. The airspace above constituted an open, convention corridor for flights by both the sisterhoods and the brethren. The hills were very green, green as Marika recalled from the hills of her puphood. But even here the higher peaks were crowned by patches of white.

The world was much cooler. The waters of the seas were being deposited as snow at an incredible rate. "And it need not be," she murmured. She wondered that meth could be so blind as to miss seeing how the ice could be stopped. Never did she stop persisting in wondering if they did see, know, and do nothing because that was to their advantage. Whose?

The tradermales', of course. They were the technicians, the scientific sort. How could they help but see?

Who would hurt most? The nomads of the polar regions first. Then the pack-living meth of remote low-technology areas. Then the smaller cities of the far north and south, in the extremes of the technologized regions. The great cities of the temperate zones were only now beginning to catch the ripple effect. They would not be threatened directly for years.

But the silth who owned them and ruled from them drew their wealth and strength from all the world. They should *try* to do something, whether or not anything could be done.

Ordinary meth would direct their anxieties and resentments toward the sisterhoods, not toward the brethren, who were careful to maintain an image as a world-spanning brotherhood of tinkerers.

The real enemy. Of course. Always it added up when you thought in large enough terms. The brethren pursued the same aim as the rogues. Secretly, they supported and directed the rogues.

Then they had to be broken. Before this great wehrlen came out of the shadows.

Her ears tilted in amusement. Great wehrlen? What great wehrlen? Shadow was all he was. And break the brethren? How?

That was a task that could not be accomplished in a lifetime. It had taken them generations to acquire the position they held. To pry them loose would require as long. Unless the Communities were willing to endure another long rise from savagery.

The mistake had been made when the brotherhood had been allowed to become a force independent of the Communities. The attitude that made it unacceptable for a sister to work with her paws had become too generalized. The brethren's secrets had to be cracked open and spread around, so silth-bonded workers could assume those tasks critical to the survival of civilization.

Her mind flew along random paths, erratically, swiftly curing the world's ills. And all the while the darkship was driving into the wind. The world rolled below, growing greener and warmer. Ghosts slipped away from the pack bearing the darkship. Others accumulated. Marika touched her bath lightly, drawing upon them, and pushed the darkship higher.

The Cordillera faded away. A forested land rolled out of the haze upon the horizon, a land mostly island and lake and very sparsely inhabited. The lakes all drained into one fast watercourse which plunged over a rift in a fall a mile wide, sprinkled with rainbows. The fall's roar could be heard even from that altitude. The river swung away to Marika's left, then curved back beneath her in a slower, wider stripe that, after another hundred miles, left the wilderness for densely settled country surrounding TelleRai. TelleRai was the most important city on the continent, if not on the meth homeworld.

The silth called this continent the New Continent. No one knew why. Perhaps it had been settled after the others. None of the written histories went back far enough to recall. Generally, though, the cities on other continents were accepted as older and more storied and decadent. Several were far larger than TelleRai.

The outskirts of the city came drifting out of the haze, dozens of satellite communities that anchored vast corporate farms or sustained industrial enclaves. Then came TelleRai itself, sometimes called the city of hundreds because its fief bonds were spread among all the sisterhoods and all the brethren bonds as well. It was a great surrealistic game board of cities within the city, looking like randomly dropped pieces of a jigsaw puzzle, with watercourses, parks, and forests lying between the cloisters.

Marika slowed the darkship and came to rest above the heart of the city, a mile-wide circle of convention ground enfiefed to no Community, open to everyone. She harkened to the map in her mind, trying to locate the skewed arrowhead shape of the Reugge cloister.

She could not find it.

She touched her senior bath. *Greynes. You have been here before. Where is our cloister?*

Southwest four miles, mistress.

Marika urged the darkship southwestward at a leisurely pace. She studied the city. It seemed still and lifeless from so high above. Till she spied a dirigible ascending. That must be one of the tradermale fastnesses there.

Now she saw the Reugge cloister. Even from close up it did not resemble the picture she had had in mind. She took the darkship down.

From a lower altitude the cloister began to look more as it should. It had tall, lean spires tapering toward the sky. Almost all its structures were built of a white limestone. It was at least three times the size of the Maksche cloister and much more inviting in appearance.

The city itself looked more pleasant than Maksche. It lacked the northern city's grim, grimy appearance. It did not suffer from the excessive, planned regularity of Maksche. And the poverty, if it was there, was out of sight. This heart of the city was more beautiful than Marika had imagined could be possible.

Meth scurried through the visible cloister as the darkship descended. Several startled touches brushed Marika soon after it became obvious her darkship would land. She pushed them aside. They would not panic. They could see the Reugge insignia upon the underframe of the darkship.

She drew on Greynes for word of the proper landing court, drifted forward a quarter mile, completed her descent as silth and workers rushed into the courtyard.

The landing braces touched stone. Marika relaxed, released the ghosts with a touch of gratitude. They scattered instantly.

Grauel and Barlog were there when she was ready to step down. The three bath positioned themselves a step behind. "A beautiful flight, sisters," she told the bath. They seemed fresher than she was.

The eldest bowed slightly. "You hardly drew upon us, Mistress. It was a pleasure. It is seldom we get a chance to see much of the country over which we travel. If from ever so high." She removed her gloves and rubbed her paws together in a manner meant to suggest that Marika might refrain from going up into such chill air.

Several silth rushed to Marika, bowed according to their apparent status. One said, "Mistress, we were not informed of your coming. Nothing is prepared."

"Nothing needs to be prepared," Marika replied. "It was an impulse. I came to visit the Redoriad museum. You may arrange that."

"Mistress, I am not sure—"

"Arrange it."

"As you command, mistress."

They knew who she was. She smelled the fear in the courtyard. She sensed a subtle flavor of distaste. She could read their thoughts. Look at the savage. Coming into the mother cloister under arms. With even her bath carrying weapons. Carrying mundane arms herself. What else could be expected of a feral silth come from the northern wilderness?

"I will view the highlights of the cloister while arrangements are being made."

The level of panic did not subside. More silth arrived, including several of the local council. They appeared as distressed as their lesser sisters. One asked, "Is this a surprise inspection, Marika?" The name stuck in the silth's throat. "If so, you certainly have taken us off our guard. I hope you will forgive us our lack of ceremony."

"I am not interested in ceremony. Ceremony is a waste of valuable time. Send these meth back to work. No. This is not an inspection. I came to TelleRai to visit the Redoriad museum."

Her insistence on that point baffled everyone. Marika enjoyed their confusion. Even the senior silth did not know what to make of her unannounced arrival. They went out of their way to be polite.

They knew she had the favor of the most senior, though. And the most senior's motives were deeply shadowed. They refused to believe this a holiday excursion.

Let them think what they would. The most senior was not around to set them straight. In fact, she was not around much at all anymore. Marika often wondered if that did not bear closer examination.

"How *is* the most senior?" one of the older silth asked. "We have had no contact with her for quite a long time."

"Well enough," Marika replied. "She says she will be ready to begin what she calls the new phase soon." Marika hoped that sounded sufficiently portentous. "How soon will a vehicle be ready?"

"The moment we obtain leave from the Redoriad. Come this way, mistress. You should see the pride of the cloister."

Marika spent the next hour tagging after various old silth, leaving a wake of staring meth. Her reputation had preceded her. Even the lowliest of workers wanted to see the dangerous youngster from the north.

A novice came running while Marika's party was moving through the most senior's private garden, where fountains chuckled, statues stood frozen in the midst of athletic pursuits, and flowers of the season brightened the soft, dark soil beneath exotic trees.

Marika said, "I cannot see Gradwohl having much taste for this, sisters."

The eldest replied, "She does not. But many of her predecessors liked to relax here. Yes, pup?" she snapped at the panting novice.

"The Redoriad have given permission, mistress. Their gate has been informed. Someone will be waiting."

Marika's companions seemed surprised. She asked, "You did not expect them to allow me to see their museum?"

"Actually, no," one of the old silth said. "The museum has been closed to outsiders for the last ten years."

"Dorteka did not mention that."

"Dorteka?"

"My instructress when I first came to Maksche. She reminisced fondly of a visit to the Redoriad museum when she was a novice herself."

"There was a time, before the troubles began, when the Redoriad opened their doors to everyone. Even bond meth and brethren. But that has not been true since rogue males tried to smuggle a bomb inside. The Redoriad have no wish to risk their treasures, some of which date back six and seven thousand years. After the incident they closed their gates to outsiders."

Another silth explained, "The Redoriad take an inordinate interest in the past. They believe they are the oldest Community on the New Continent."

"May we go, then?" Marika asked. "Is a car ready?"

"Yes." The old silth seemed displeased.

In a merry tone, Marika said, "If you really want to be inspected, I can come back later. I must become acquainted with this cloister, as I no doubt will be moving here soon."

Deep silence answered that remark. The older silth started walking.

"Why are they this way?" Grauel asked. "Feeling hateful, but being so polite?"

"They fear that I'm Gradwohl's chosen heir," Marika replied. "They don't like that. I am a savage and just about everything else they don't like. Also, my being heir apparent would mean that they would have no chance of becoming most senior themselves. Assuming I live a normal life span, I will outlast them all."

"Maybe it's a good thing we arrived unannounced, then."

"Possibly. But I doubt they would go to violent extremes. Still, be alert when we get into the streets. There has been time for news of our arrival to have gotten out of the cloister."

"Rogues?"

"And the Serke. They aren't pleased with me either."

"What about these Redoriad? They are the other major dark-faring Community. Might not their interests parallel those of the Serke? Getting into their museum so easily…."

"We'll find out. Just don't let them move me out of your sight."

"That has not needed saying for years, Marika." Grauel seemed almost hurt by the reminder.

Marika reached out and touched her arm lightly.

CHAPTER TWENTY-FOUR

I

The vehicle selected for Marika's use proved to be a huge steam-powered carriage capable of carrying twelve meth in extraordinary comfort. Silth began climbing aboard. Marika snapped, "Leave room for my companions. Barlog, you sit with the driver."

She hustled the bath and Grauel inside, climbed aboard herself. The coach's appointments were the richest she had ever seen. She waited indifferently while the silth jockeyed for seats. She intervened only to make certain her TelleRai deputy in the antirogue program found a place. She confined her conversation to business while the coach huffed along TelleRai's granite-cobbled streets at a pace no faster than a brisk walk. Grauel watched the world outside for signs of any special interest in the coach. Marika occasionally did the same, ducking through her loophole to capture a ghost. She would flutter with it briefly, trying to catch the emotional auras of passersby.

She detected nothing that warranted excessive caution.

The Redoriad were the largest of all sisterhoods as well as the oldest upon the New Continent. Their cloister showed it. It was a city in itself in an ornate, tall architectural style similar to that of the Reugge cloister.

The steam vehicle chugged to a gate thirty feet high and nearly as wide. The gate opened immediately. The vehicle pulled through, halted. Silth in dress slightly different from the Reugge formed an honor guard. An old female with the hard, tough look of the wild greeted Marika as she descended from the coach.

"They told me you were young. I did not expect you to be this young."

"You have a beautiful cloister. Mistress...?"

"Kiljar."

Marika's local companions made small sounds of surprise.

"You honor me, mistress." She was surprised herself. The Kiljar whose name she knew would be second or third of the Redoriad, depending upon one's information source.

"You know me, then?"

"I am familiar with the name, mistress. I did not expect to be snowed under with notables on a simple visit to a museum."

"Simple visit?" The Redoriad silth began walking. Marika followed, staying just far enough away to allow Grauel and Barlog room. Kiljar was not pleased but pretended not to notice. "Do you really expect anyone to believe that?"

"Why not? It is true. I wakened this morning feeling restless, recalled an old instructress's wonder at the Redoriad museum, decided to come see it for myself. It was sheer impulse. Yet everyone is behaving as though my visit has some sort of apocalyptic portent."

"Perhaps it does not, after all. Nevertheless, the name can be the thing. What is expected is what is believed. Recent times have made it seem that the fate of the Reugge Community may revolve around you. Your name has become known and discussed. Always twinned with that of Most Senior Gradwohl, as strange and unorthodox a silth as ever became a most senior."

"I will agree with that. A most unusual female."

Kiljar ignored that remark. "Young, ambitious silth everywhere are militating for agencies similar to that you created within the Reugge. Old silth who have had brushes with you or yours follow your every move and wonder what each means. Brethren beg the All to render you less a threat than you appear."

Marika stopped walking. The column of Reugge and Redoriad halted. She faced Kiljar. "Are you serious?"

"Extremely. There has not been a day in months when I have not heard your name mentioned in connection with some speculation. Usually it is on the order of, 'Is Marika the Reugge behind this?' Or, 'What is Marika the Reugge's next move?' Or, 'How does Marika the Reugge know things as though she were in the room when they were discussed?'"

Marika had had some success with her signal intercepts, but not that much. Or so she had thought. Penetrating the various secret languages was very difficult, with the results often unreliable. "I am just one young silth trying to help her Community survive in the face of the most foul conspiracy of the century," she replied. She awaited a response with both normal and silth senses alert.

"Yes. To have a future you must have a Community in which to enjoy it. But I have heard whispers that say the Serke made a proposal in that regard."

Marika did not miss a step or feel a flicker of off-beat heart, but she was startled. Word of her encounter with the Serke and brethren had gotten out? "That is not quite true. The Serke approached me once, in their usual hammer-fisted way. They tried to compel me to turn upon my sisters. Nevertheless, the Reugge are stronger today, and the Serke are more frightened."

"Do they have cause?"

"Of course. A thief must be ready to pay the price of getting caught."

"Yes. So. But these are thieves with considerable resources, not all of which have entered the game yet."

"Bestrei?"

"Especially Bestrei."

"Bestrei is getting old, they say."

"She can still deal with any two Mistresses of the Ship from any other Community."

"Perhaps. Who can tell? But that is moot. The Reugge will not challenge her. And how could the Serke challenge us? Would that not amount to a public admission that the Reugge have a right to leave the surface of this planet? I would so argue before the convention on behalf of all those sisterhoods denied access to space." Carefully, Marika admonished herself. This old silth speaks for a Community of dark-farers at least as powerful as the Serke.

"There is that. This thing you have about rogue males. This campaign you have undertaken in the rural territories. I wish to understand it better. In modern times the Redoriad have concentrated their attention offworld. We have leased our home territories to other sisterhoods and paid little attention to what is happening here."

"Are the Redoriad still calling for censure because the Reugge allow such flouting of the law within their provinces?" Marika lifted her upper lip enough to make it clear she was being facetious.

"Hardly. Today there is a fear that you may be going too far in the opposite direction. That you may be drawing the brethren in. Particularly since several Communities have begun emulating you."

"With less success."

"To be sure. But that is not the point. Marika, some of the Communities have become very uneasy with this."

"Because all paths lead one way?"

"Pardon?"

"Because each path through the rogue tangle eventually leads to a brethren enclave?"

"Exactly." Kiljar seemed reluctant to admit it.

"They are trying to destroy the sisterhoods, Mistress Kiljar. Nothing less than that. There is no doubt about it, much as so many would blind themselves to the fact. There is ample evidence. Even this winter that is devouring the world has become a weapon with which they weaken silthdom. They are manipulating the Communities, trying to bring on feuds like the one the Reugge have smoldering with the Serke. They are trying to gain control of natural resources properly belonging to the sisterhoods. They are doing everything within their power, if subtly, to crush us. We would be fools not to push back."

"The brethren are—"

"Essential to society as we know it? That is one of their weapons, too. That belief. They think that belief will stay our paws till it is too late for us. Come into the museum with me, Mistress Kiljar. Let me show you what you Redoriad have had here all the time. Nothing less than proof that silth can exist without the brethren."

"Marika…"

"I do not propose that they be destroyed. Not at all. But I believe they should be disarmed and controlled before they destroy us."

"Mistress?" Grauel said from behind Marika. "May I speak with you a moment? It is important."

Surprised, Marika dropped back. Barlog dropped even farther, to prevent the column from drawing close enough to overhear. "What? Have you seen something?"

"I have heard something. You are talking too much, Marika. That is not Barlog or myself, or even the most senior. That is the second of the Redoriad, a Community whose interests are not identical to those of the Reugge."

"You are right. Thank you for reminding me, Grauel. She's crafty. She knew just how to goad me. I'll watch my tongue." She overtook Kiljar. "My chief voctor reminds me that I did not come here to lay bare the Reugge breast. That we came entirely unofficially, to examine old darkships."

"I see." Kiljar seemed amused.

"May we proceed, and perhaps save the discussion for a time when I feel more comfortable with the Redoriad?"

"Certainly. I will remind you, though, that the Redoriad are no friends of the Serke."

"Mistress?"

"The Serke have been the next thing to rogue among silth for centuries. They have gotten away with it because they have always had a strong champion. They have become intolerable since they developed Bestrei. No sisterhood dares challenge them. There are many of us who follow the Reugge struggle with glee. You have embarrassed them many times."

"That is because we avoid confronting their strengths. We let them hurt themselves. The most senior is a crafty strategist."

"Perhaps she outsmarts herself."

"Mistress?"

"She is preparing a challenger for Bestrei. Buying time till you are ready. Do not argue. What is evident is evident. Certainly, it is possible that when you attain your full strength Bestrei will have aged so much she can no longer best you. It is said you are as strong as she was at your age. Perhaps stronger, because you have a brain and more than one talent. It is whispered that twice you have slain Serke who came from their ruling seven."

"Mistress, that is not—"

"Do not argue. These things are whispered but they are known. Let me tell you a thing I know. You are alive today only because you belong to a sisterhood without access to space. Because, as you mentioned, there would be extensive legal ramifications to a challenge."

Marika waited patiently through a long pause while Kiljar ordered her thoughts. They were on the doorstep of the museum. The door was open. She was eager to see what lay beyond, but waited while the old silth found what she wanted to say.

"You cannot hope to best Bestrei at her most senile without learning the ways of the dark, Marika. Handling a darkship out there is not the same as handling one on-planet. You are Reugge. You have no one to teach you those ways. You dare not teach yourself. The Serke will know if you go out on your own. And they will challenge immediately because you will in effect have challenged the sisterhoods who hold the starworlds. They will make it a challenge for the existence of the Reugge. And Bestrei will devour you."

Involuntarily, Marika glanced at the sky. And sensed the truth of what Kiljar said. She had not thought the situation through.

Had Gradwohl?

"I have a solution," Kiljar said. "But we will save that for another time. Today you came here only to look at old darkships." There was a light touch of mockery in her voice.

II

The Redoriad museum was as marvelous as Dorteka had claimed. Marika breezed through most of it, eager to reach the darkships, having saved them for last. She had done that with treats as a pup.

She did stop once to ask about a set of wooden balls. "What are these?"

"In primitive times one test for the presence of silth talents was juggling. All female pups were taught. Those who showed exceptional talent early often were managing the balls unconsciously. They were tested further. Today we have more subtle methods."

"May I touch them?"

"They are not breakable."

"I was a very good juggler. My littermate Kublin was, too. We would put on shows for the huntresses when they were in a mood to tolerate pups." She tossed a ball into the air, then a second and a third. Her muscles no longer recalled the rhythms. Her mind stepped in, made the balls float in slowed motion. She kept them moving for half a minute, then fumbled one and immediately lost them all. "I am a little out of practice." She returned the balls to the display.

Memories came back. Kublin. Her dam, Skiljan. The Degnan packstead. Juggling. Flute playing. She had been very good with the flute, too. She had not picked one up since fleeing Akard for Maksche. Maybe that deserved some attention. Playing the flute had been as relaxing as flying the darkship or fleeing into the realm of ghosts.

Enough. Thought could be too painful. In this instance it reminded her that her pack remained unMourned.

She went for her treat.

There were a dozen darkships, arranged to show stages of evolution. First a quarter scale model of a darkship similar to the newest flown by the Reugge.

Then another, similar yet different. The plaque said it was aluminum. There was only one more metal ship, also of aluminum, incredibly ornate.

"This one never got off the ground," Kiljar said. "The brethren created an exact copy of a famous golden-fleet darkship of the period, but it would not fly. It takes more effort to lift metal, even titanium, than it does golden fleet wood. Even though the wood is heavier. There is power in the wood itself. It pleases those-who-dwell. With the metal ships they come only under compulsion."

"Then why use brethren darkships? Why use a vessel less effective and made by someone we do not control?"

"Because building a wooden darkship, even in its most rudimentary, functional form, is a long and difficult process. Because the brethren can produce all we want almost as fast as we want them. Consider the Reugge experience with the nomads. My sources tell me you lost six darkships in the fighting. In the old days you could not have replaced those in two generations. Generations during which other sisterhoods might have devoured you. These days when you lose a darkship you just order another. The brethren take it out of stock."

"Sometimes. If you happen to be in favor."

"That is right. They would not replace yours. That is on the agenda for the next convention. They will be required to defend that decision."

"They could refuse all the Communities."

"The convention will sort it out."

"If there is one." It took a majority of sisterhoods agreeing one was needed before a convention could actually convene.

Marika moved along the line of darkships. The next was wooden, similar in style to the brethren ship that would not fly. It was a work of art, almost grotesque in its ornateness. She noted almost thronelike seats for the Mistress and bath.

The wooden darkships grew simpler and more primitive, ceased to be crossed. The last three were saddleships, also declining in complexity. The latest looked like an animal with an impossibly elongated neck. The oldest was little more than a pole with fletching at its rear.

Kiljar indicated the fanciest. "In this period silth imitated life. There was an animal called a redhage which was used as a riding beast. It has become extinct since. Saddleships of the period are stylized imitations with the neck elongated. The longer a saddleship was, the more stable it was in flight. As you can see, the oldest were stabilized the same as an arrow."

"But an arrow spins in flight."

"So it does. It may have been a clumsy way to travel. We do not know now for certain. The redhage type still gets taken up occasionally, though. Some of our Mistresses enjoy them. And they are much faster than anything in common use. The Mistress can lie on its neck and cut loose. The weakness of the darkship being the obvious: the Mistress is limited by her own endurance."

"Bath are that important?"

"That important. Well? Are you satisfied?"

"I think so. I have seen what I came to see. I should get back. There is no end to the work that awaits me at Maksche."

"Think on what I have said about the Serke, Bestrei, and learning the ways of the void. Mention it to Most Senior Gradwohl. Mention that I am interested in speaking with her."

"I will."

"There is, by the way, a voidship that belongs to the museum. An early one, now retired, but still far too big to bring inside. Would you like to see it?"

"Of course."

Marika followed Kiljar out a side door, into a large courtyard. Barlog and Grauel followed alertly, shading their eyes against the sudden change in lighting, searching for signs of an ambush. Marika reached through her loophole and checked. She made a gesture telling the huntresses all was well.

She stopped cold when she saw the void darkship. Her hopes for walking among the stars almost died. Yes. There was no way she was going to challenge a Bestrei anytime in the near future. "That is a small one, you say?" It was three times the size of the largest Reugge darkship.

"Yes. The voidships the Redoriad use today are twice this size. And the voidship we run in concert with the brethren is bigger still."

"If it is so difficult to move metal ships, how…?"

"Out there those-who-dwell are much bigger, too. And much more powerful. That is one thing you would have to learn before you dared face a Bestrei. How to manipulate the stronger ghosts."

"Thank you." Marika closed in upon herself, squeezing a knot of disappointment down into a tiny sphere. "I think I had best be off for Maksche. I have let my duties slide long enough."

"Very well. Do not forget to tell Gradwohl that Kiljar of the Redoriad wishes to speak with her."

Marika did not respond. With Grauel and Barlog and her train of bath and TelleRai silth keeping pace, she strode back to the steam coach. She climbed aboard, settled into her seat, and closed in upon herself again.

This required a lot of thinking. And rethinking.

III

It was very late when Marika returned to the Reugge cloister. She dismissed her bath with a grunt instead of the usual thank-yous, went straight to her quarters. Grauel and Barlog followed and stayed near, but she did not take advantage of their unspoken offer. She went to bed immediately, exhausted from the day's flights.

She had the dream again, of whipping through a vast darkness surrounded by uncountable numbers of stars. It wakened her. She was angry, knowing it to be false. She would not walk the stars.

Asleep again, she dreamed once more. And this time the dream was a true nightmare, a littermate of the one she had had soon after fleeing the overrun Degnan packstead. But in this dream a terrible shadow hunted her. It raced across the world like something out of myth, howling, slavering, tireless, faceless, murderous. It hunted her. It would devour her. It drew closer and closer, and she could not run fast enough to get away.

This time she wakened shaken, wondering if it were a true dream. Wondering what the shadow could represent. Not Bestrei. There had been a definite male odor to it. An almost familiar odor.

Warlock! something said in the back of her mind. Certainly it was a presentiment of sorts.

The rogue problem, which had seemed close to solution, took a dramatic turn for the worse. In places, outlying cloisters were surprised and suffered severe damage. It almost seemed her return from TelleRai signaled a new and more bitter phase in the struggle, one in which the rogue leadership was willing to sacrifice whatever strength it had left.

For a month it made no sense whatever. And nothing illuminating came off the signal networks of the Serke or brethren. Then the most senior returned to Maksche, making one of her ever more infrequent and brief visits.

"Think, Marika. Do not be so provincial, so narrow. You visited the Redoriad," Gradwohl said. "There are times you are so naive it surpasses belief. The Redoriad are in harsh competition with the Serke among the starworlds. The competition would become fiercer if there were a champion capable of challenging Bestrei. Your visit was no secret. Your strength is no secret. You have slain two of their best. It is no secret that the Reugge have no access to the void, and only slightly less well known that we covet an opportunity out there. If you were Serke, unable to see what transpired within the Redoriad cloister, had suffered several embarrassing setbacks at the paw of a Marika, what would you suspect?"

"You really believe the Redoriad want to train me?" It was a revelation, truly.

"Just as the Serke suspect."

Much of what Kiljar had said without saying it in so many words, and much of the attitude of the silth during her TelleRai excursion, became concrete with that reply. "They all thought—"

"And they were right. As you suggested, I got in touch with Kiljar. And that is exactly what she had in mind. An alliance between Reugge and Redoriad. Marika, you have to *think*. You have become an important factor in this world. Your every move is subject to endless interpretation."

"But an alliance...."

"It is not unprecedented. It makes sense on several levels. In fact, it is an obvious stratagem. So obvious that the Serke—yes, all right, and the brethren, too—must make some effort to counter or prevent it. Thus rogues who will devour your time while they hatch something more grim. Be very careful, Marika. I expect you will be spending a great deal of time in TelleRai soon. TelleRai will be far more dangerous than Maksche."

"And you?"

"I am fading away, am I not?" Gradwohl seemed amused.

"If you are trying to slip me the functions of most senior without having to rejoin the All, I want you to know that I do not want them. I have no intention of assuming that burden ever. I do not have the patience for the trivial."

"True. But patience is something you are going to have to learn anyway, pup." No one else called her "pup" these days. No one dared.

"Mistress?

"Consider a Reugge sisterhood without a Most Senior Gradwohl. It would not much benefit you without your being in charge. Would it?"

"Mistress...."

"I am not immortal. Neither am I all-powerful. And there are strong elements within the sisterhood who would not scruple to hasten my replacement, if only to prevent your becoming most senior. That danger is partly why I have made myself increasingly inaccessible."

"I thought you were spending all your time with the sisters trying to build us darkships of our own."

"I have been. In a place completely isolated. My bath are the only meth outside who know where it is. And there are times when I do not trust them to remain silent."

The bond between Gradwohl and her bath was legendary.

Marika said, "I did get the feeling that the TelleRai council are disturbed by your lack of visibility. One sister went so far as to hint that I might have done away with you."

"Ah?" Again Gradwohl was amused. "I should show myself, then. Lest someone get silly notions. I could adopt your approach. Go armed to the jaw."

Now Marika was amused. "They would accuse me of having acquired an unholy influence over you."

"They do that already." Gradwohl rose, went to a window, slipped a curtain aside. It was getting dark. Marika could see one of the smaller moons past the most senior's shoulder. "I believe it is time, " Gradwohl mused. "Yes. Definitely. It is time. Come with me, pup."

"Where are we going?"

"To my darkship manufactory."

Marika followed the most senior through the cloister, to the courtyard where the darkships landed. She felt uneasy. Grauel and Barlog were not with her.

Gradwohl's bath were waiting. Her darkship was ready for flight. Marika's uneasiness grew. Now it surrounded the most senior. Gradwohl had made this project her own. Her revealing it implied that she feared she might not be around much longer.

Had she had an intuition? Sometimes silth of high talent caught flashes of tomorrow.

Gradwohl said, "We are doing this on the sly, pup. No one is to know we are leaving the cloister. They may wonder why we do not appear for ceremonies, but I do not think our failure will make anyone suspicious. If we hurry. Come. Step aboard."

"I could use a coat."

"I will stay low. If the wind is too much for you, I will slow down."

"Yes, mistress."

In moments they were airborne, over the wall, heading across the snowbound plain.

Gradwohl became another person while flying, a Mistress of immense vigor and joy. She flew with the verve of a Marika at her wildest, shoving the darkship through the night at the greatest speed she dared. The countryside whipped away below, much of it speckled silvery with patches of snow-reflected moonlight.

The flight covered three hundred miles by Marika's estimate. She had the cold shakes when they arrived at their destination. She had not yielded to weakness and touched the most senior with a request that she slacken the pace.

Gradwohl's goal proved to be an abandoned packfast well north of the permanent snowline, far to the west, on the edge of Reugge territory. Even from quite close it appeared empty of life. Marika could detect no meth presence with her touch. She could smell no smoke.

But thirty sisters turned out for the most senior's arrival. Marika recognized none of them. None were from Maksche. Too, some wore the garb of other Communities, all minor orders like the Reugge. She was surprised.

She said nothing, but Gradwohl read her easily enough. "Yes. We do have allies." Amused, "You have been my chosen, but there is much that I have not told you. Come. Let me show you the progress we have made here."

They went down deep into the guts of the old fortress, to a level that had been dug out after its abandonment, to a vast open area lighted electrically. Scattered about were the frames of a score of partially assembled darkships.

"They are wooden!" Marika exclaimed. "I thought—"

"We discovered that while sisters could extract titanium as you suggested, the process was slow and difficult. With modern woodworking machinery, we could produce a wooden darkship faster. Not elegant ships like those of the high period before the brethren introduced their imitations, but functional and just as useful as anything they produce. Over here are the four craft we have completed so far. We are learning all the time. Using assembly-line techniques, we expect to produce a new ship each week once we are into production. That means that soon no sisterhood will be dependent upon the brethren for darkships. We expect to produce a large reserve before circumstances force us to reveal ourselves. Come over here."

Gradwohl led Marika to a large area separate from the remainder. It was empty except for a complex series of frameworks. "What is this?" Marika asked.

"This is where we will build our voidship. Our Reugge voidship."

"A wooden one?"

"Why not?"

"No reason, I guess."

"None whatsoever. And it would not be a first. Over here. Not exactly a darkship, but something I had put together for you. I thought it might prove useful."

"A saddleship."

"Yes."

"It is gorgeous, mistress."

"Thank you. I thought you would appreciate it. Want to try it?"

"Oh, yes."

"I thought you might take it back to Maksche."

"But mistress...."

"I will follow you in case you have trouble managing it. It is not difficult, though. I learned in minutes. You just have to get used to not having bath backing you."

"How do we get it out of here?"

"It disassembles. All these ships come apart into modules. We thought it would be useful to be able to take them inside, where they would be safer."

Marika thought of the brethren's airships and nodded. "Yes. All right. Let us do it."

Half an hour later she was riding the wooden steed through the night a thousand feet up, racing the north wind toward Maksche. She found the saddleship far more maneuverable and speedy than the conventional darkship, though more tiring.

The experience filled her with elation. Gradwohl had to press her to take the saddleship down before the cloister began rising for the day. The most senior wanted her to keep its existence secret. "Use it only when you are certain you will not be seen. It is for emergencies. For times when you have to go somewhere swiftly and secretly. Which I will be talking to you about more later."

CHAPTER TWENTY-FIVE

I

Most Senior Gradwohl's "later" came just two weeks after she gifted Marika with the saddleship.

Those two weeks saw rogue pressure rise markedly. Marika sent three hundred prisoners to the Reugge mines. The sisters responsible for managing them protested they could feed no more, had work for no more. And still the rogue movement found villains willing to risk silth wrath.

They came from everywhere, and though few recalled how they had come to Reugge territory, it was obvious they had been transported. They spoke openly, almost bragging, of the great wehrlen who was their champion. But Marika could learn nothing about him. Could not even gain concrete evidence of his existence as more than a legend being used to motivate the criminals.

The rogues succeeded in killing a number of silth. They overran one small, remote cloister and slaughtered everyone within. Marika was distressed. She could not understand how those attackers could have been so successful. Unless they had been led by this wehrlen himself.

The rogues were active elsewhere, too, for the first time, though to a lesser degree. But whomever they struck, wherever, friends of the Reugge Community were hurt.

Even the Redoriad suffered.

There was one assassination right in TelleRai.

The Serke hardly pretended noninvolvement anymore. Marika intercepted a message in which a rumor was quoted. It claimed a senior sister of the Serke had said in public that anyone who stood with the Reugge could expect to suffer as much as did they.

Marika remained baffled by the Serke determination. And angry. She had to ask Grauel to keep reminding her to control her temper. At one point she nearly flew off on a one-meth mission to destroy a Serke cloister in retaliation.

Two weeks after receiving her saddleship, she began to get less sleep.

Gradwohl visited her. She was direct. "I have spoken with Kiljar, Marika. An arrangement has been made. Each third night you will fly to TelleRai, directly

335

to the Redoriad cloister, where you will meet Kiljar. Your first few visits will be devoted to teaching you to pass as a Redoriad sister. When she is satisfied that you can do that, you will be introduced to the voidships."

Marika had seen it coming, Her furtive late-night flights aboard her saddle-ship, which she could assemble and slip out the largest window of her quarters, had shown her it was capable of velocities far beyond those of a standard darkship. If she used the saddle straps, and lay out upon the saddleship's neck, and bundled herself against the chill of passing air, she could reach TelleRai in two hours. Obviously, the most senior had had something in mind when she had the saddleship built.

"To the world's eye you will remain here, pursuing your normal routine. Only the most reliable silth on either end will be aware of what is happening. We hope the Serke and brethren will be lulled."

"I do not believe they will be, mistress. That is, they may not see what we are doing, but they already see the possibility. Otherwise they would not have resumed pressing so hard."

"That will come up at the convention. The Serke are trying to avoid one, but they will not be able to stall for long. They have made themselves im-mensely unpopular. Their behavior is no longer a matter of strictly parochial interest."

Marika went into TelleRai that night undetected, and joined Kiljar in her private quarters. She discovered that the Redoriad seniors lived very well, indeed. She did not learn much else that trip, except that she had limits. She barely had the strength to keep the saddleship aloft long enough to return to Maksche. She slept half the following day.

She returned to her work groggy of mind and aching in her joints. That she did not understand, for there had been nothing physical in her night.

The experience repeated itself each time Marika flew south, though each trip became easier. Developing endurance for flying was easier than developing it for running.

She had let her morning gym sessions lapse once Dorteka was no longer there to press her. She resumed those now.

Grauel caught on during Marika's third absence. Marika returned to her quarters to find her packmates awake and waiting. They eyed the saddleship without surprise. Marika disassembled it and concealed the sections. Still they said nothing.

"Does anyone else know? Or guess?" Marika asked.

"No," Grauel replied. "Even we do not know anything certain. It just seemed strange that you should be so tired each third day. Each time you looked like you had not had much sleep."

"I should learn to bar my door."

"That might be wise. Or you might have someone guard it from within. If there was anyone you could trust to do so."

Marika considered the huntresses. "I suppose I do owe you an explanation. Though the most senior would not approve."

Grauel and Barlog waited.

"I have been flying down to TelleRai. To train with the Redoriad silth. As soon as I can pass as a Redoriad sister I will begin learning the ways of their voidships."

"It is what you wanted," Barlog said.

"You sound disappointed."

"I am still a Ponath huntress at heart, Marika. Still Degnan. I was too old when I came to the silth. All this flying, this feuding, this witchcraft, this conspiring and maneuvering, they are foreign to me. I am as frightened now as I was when we arrived at Akard. I would as soon be back at the packstead, for all the wonders I have seen."

"I know. But we have been touched by the All. The three of us. We have no choice of our own."

"Touched how?" Grauel asked. "There are mornings when I rise wondering if it might not have been better had the nomads taken us all at the beginning."

"Why?"

"Things are happening, Marika. The world is changing. Too much of that change centers upon you, and you never seem fully aware of it. There are times when I believe those sisters who feared you as a Jiana sensed a truth."

"Grauel! Don't go superstitious on me."

"We will stand by you as long as we survive, Marika. We have no choice. But do not expect us to give unquestioning approval to everything you do."

"All right. Accepted. I never expected that. Did anything interesting happen while I was away?"

"It was a quiet night. I suspect you were right when you predicted the rogues would give up on Maksche. You'd better rest now. If you still plan to go flying with Bagnel this afternoon."

"I forgot all about that."

"You want to cancel?"

"No. I see him so seldom as it is."

Despite all else, she maintained her relationship with Bagnel. He maintained his end as well, despite hints that it was no longer fashionable with his superiors. He was, she felt, her one true friend. More so than Braydic, for he asked only that she be his friend in return. He stayed as close as Grauel and Barlog, in his way, without being compelled by their sense of obligation.

"Yes. Definitely. I'll be going. I wish I could show him the saddleship. Maybe someday. Waken me when it's time."

Thenceforth Grauel and Barlog watched her quarters while she was away.

II

Marika had just come to the end of her seventh visit. She asked, "How much longer do you think, mistress? I am getting impatient."

"I know. Gradwohl warned me you would be. Next time we will go aloft. The Mistress of the Ship and her bath will be preoccupied with the ascent. They should not notice your peculiarities. What they do note can be explained by telling them that you are from the wilderness. We will pass you off as a junior relative of mine. I come from a rural background myself, though I went into cloister younger than you did. We Redoriad keep a better watch on our dependents."

"Three days, then."

"No. Five this time. And find a reason for being out of sight longer. We will not be able to make an ascent and return in time to get you home in one night."

"That may be difficult. Maksche keeps a close eye on Marika."

"If you do not appear I will know that you were unable to make the arrangements."

"I will manage it. One way or another."

She did so by feigning ill health. She began three days early, pretending increasing discomfort. Grauel and Barlog aided in the deception. She received offers of help from the healer sisters, of course, but she put them off. Before departing, she told Grauel, "They will want to treat me when you tell them I am not feeling well enough to come out. If only so they can report my condition to my enemies. Stall them. I expect to be tired enough to look thoroughly ill when I get back. We can let them at me then. I'll make a swift recovery."

"Be careful, Marika." Grauel was both in awe and dread of what Marika was about to do. "Come back."

"It isn't that dangerous, Grauel." But, of course, she could not convince the huntress of that. Grauel was only a few years past not even being able to imagine walking among the stars.

Marika began assembling her saddleship, eager to be airborne, eager to be free of her mundane duties, eager to mount the voidship, and more than a little frightened. Her insides were tight with anticipation.

"This coming and going...." Grauel started, then tailed off.

"Yes?"

"I think some of the sisters are suspicious. You move at night, but the night is the time of the silth. Even at night there are eyes to see strange things moving above Maksche's towers. There has been talk about strange visions in the moonlight. Whenever strange things happen they somehow become attached to the name Marika, despite the evidence. Or lack of it. I may not be able to keep the sisters from entering if—"

"You may go to any extreme but violence. This has to be kept quiet as long as possible. A leak could bring both the Reugge and Redoriad into direct confrontation with the Serke. That would mean the end of us."

"I understand."

Marika finished assembling the saddleship. She bestrode it, strapped herself into a harness she had modified, lay down behind the windscreen she had installed. Windscreen and harness adaptations made it possible to fly at great speeds.

She reached for ghosts. The saddleship lifted and drifted through the window, brushing its stone frame. She glanced back once to wave to Grauel, and saw Barlog come rushing into her apartment. What did she want?

No matter. Nothing could be more important than tonight's flight.

She set her ghosts to work with a vengeance, raced away.

She thought she heard a far voice call her name, but decided it was just a trick of the air rushing around the windscreen.

Snow-splattered earth whipped past below.

III

Softly, Kiljar said, "Just stand there on the axis, the same as any passenger on any darkship."

"Will we get cold?" Marika asked question after question, all of which she had asked before and had had answered. She was too nervous to control her tongue. She recalled Grauel or Barlog telling her, long ago, that she betrayed her fear because she talked too much when she was frightened. She tried to clamp down.

The senior bath left the Mistress of the Ship and came to Marika and Kiljar carrying a pot like a miniature of the daram cauldron that stood inside the doorway to the grand ceremonial hall at Maksche. She held it out to Kiljar. The Redoriad took it and drank. The bath then offered it to Marika, who sipped till Kiljar said, "That is enough."

"It tastes like daram, but it is not as thick."

"There is essence of daram in it. Several other drugs as well. They make it possible for the Mistress to draw fully upon everyone aboard. You will see."

A feeling of peace crept over Marika, a feeling of oneness with the All. She turned into herself, went down through her loophole, watched as the Mistress gathered ghosts and drew upon her bath. The giant cross lifted slowly. Marika sensed the strain required to elevate so massive a darkship. She was tempted to help, overcame that temptation. Kiljar had admonished her repeatedly against doing anything but remaining an observer. There would be ample opportunity for participation later. First she had to experience being separated from her birth world, to explore a new realm of those-who-dwell.

The darkship rose straight toward Biter, which stood at zenith, glowing down from his pockmarked face. Higher and higher. For a time Marika did not realize how high, for there was no change in temperature nor of the rarity of the air she breathed.

Then she could see all TelleRai spread below her. She had flown very high aboard her saddleship, but never so high that she could see all the city and its satellites in their entirety. The satellites lay scattered over hundreds of square miles. To the west, clouds were moving in, rolling over the islands of light.

The Mistress of the Ship was surrounded by a golden glow. Turning, Marika saw that the same glow surrounded each of the bath. It was not intense, but it was there. She could detect nothing around Kiljar or herself.

She started to ask a question.

Touch, Kiljar sent. *Use nothing but the touch.*

Yes. The glow. What is it?

The screen that restrains the void. What some sisters call the Breath of the All.

We are surrounded, too?

We are. Watch now. Soon you will begin to see the horizon curve. Soon you will see the moonlight shining off the snow in the north. No. Not tonight. It is snowing there again. Off the backs of the clouds, then.

It is a rare night when it is not snowing north of Maksche, mistress. The darkship was gaining velocity rapidly. *What is that glow along the horizon?* The horizon had developed a definite bow.

Sunlight in the atmosphere and dust cloud.

Marika lost herself in growing awe. She could see almost all the moons. More than she had seen at one time before. She could discern a score of the satellites put up by the brethren and dark-faring sisterhoods. They were brilliant dots moving against the darkness.

What is that? She indicated a bright object rising from the glow along the edge of the world. It was too small to be a moon, yet larger than any satellite.

The Serke-brethren voidship Starstalker. *Just in from the dark this week. We will pass near it. By design. The Redoriad ship is out, but* Starstalker *is similar.*

Won't they...?

Be upset? Perhaps. But they have no basis for a protest. We can look. Inside Biter orbit is convention space.

Marika glanced back at the world—and was startled. The Mistress had reoriented the voidship. The planet was down no longer. The darkship was moving very fast now.

She was in the void. If the glow she could not see failed her, she would die quicker than the thought.

All sense of motion vanished, yet the world continued to grow more curved. The bright spark of the voidship *Starstalker* drew closer, though the ship upon which Marika stood seemed at rest.

She looked upon the naked universe, sparklingly bright, clearer than ever she had seen it from the surface, and surrendered to awe.

Kiljar touched her. *Over there. The darkness where there are almost no stars at all. That is the heart of the dust cloud. The direction our sun and world are traveling. It will become more dense before it clears. It will be five thousand years before we finish passing through.*

That is a long winter.

Yes. We are getting close to the voidship. Do nothing to attract attention to yourself. They will be displeased enough as it is.

The darkship turned till its long arm indicated a piece of sky ahead of the swelling voidship. It began to move, though Marika could tell only because the voidship skewed against the fixed stars. As they approached the shining object, she detected lesser brightnesses moving around it. Closer still. The voidship resolved into something more than a bright glow. Looking over her shoulder, Marika saw that the sun had risen above the edge of the world. The world itself, where it was daytime, was extremely bright—especially at the upper and lower ends of the arc of illumination. The snowfields, she supposed. The cloud cover looked heavier than in any photograph she had seen. A quick query to Kiljar, though, told her that it was a phenomenon of the moment.

It was impossible to discern the shapes of continents and islands. This world looked like no globe she had seen.

Turning to *Starstalker,* she found that the voidship had swollen into an egg shape. The surrounding sparks had become smaller ships. They looked like none she had seen before. Two were moving away, one of them well ahead of the other. Two were moving in. Another waited idly, matching orbit. Several were nosed up to the voidship like bloodsucking insects. Marika asked no questions for fear her touch would leak over and be detected.

But Kiljar looked as puzzled as was she. Marika felt a leak-over as she touched the Mistress of the Ship. Their approach slowed. Then the Redoriad darkship began to turn away. Marika looked at the Redoriad with her question plain upon her face.

Something is happening here that should not be, Kiljar sent. *Those little ships are like nothing I have ever seen, and I have been in space for three decades. They may be in violation of the conventions. Oh-oh. They have noticed us.*

Marika felt the questioning touch, felt it recoil in surprise, alarmed because the darkship was not Serke.

The touch returned. *Stop. Come here immediately.*

Kiljar waved at the Mistress of the Ship. *Starstalker* began to dwindle.

A spear of fire ripped through the great night, coming from one of the small ships. It touched nothing. Marika had no idea what it was, but felt the deadliness of it. So did the Mistress. She commenced a turn to her left and dove toward the planet.

What is happening? Marika asked.

I do not know. Do not distract me. I am trying to touch the cloister. They must know about this in case we do not survive.

Fright stole into Marika's throat. She stared back at the dwindling voidship. Another spear of light reached for the Redoriad darkship, came no closer than the last. The Mistress skewed around and took the darkship another direction, like a huntress dodging rifle fire.

Flames bloomed around one end of one of the small ships attendant upon *Starstalker*. It came after the darkship, its lance of light probing the darkness repeatedly. Behind it another such ship blossomed flame and joined the chase.

Marika nearly panicked. She hadn't the slightest notion of what was happening, except that it was obvious someone wanted to kill them. For no apparent reason.

Another spear of fire. And this one grazed the pommel end of the dagger that was the darkship. A silent scream filled Marika's head. The rear bath drifted away, tumbling. She disappeared in the great night, her glow gone.

Kiljar ran along the titanium beam to the spot where the bath had stood. And in her mind, Marika felt, *Use that vaunted talent for the dark side, Reugge. Use it!*

Marika had begun to get a grip on herself. Down through her loophole she went—and froze, awed.

They were huge out here! Not nearly so numerous as down below, but more vast even than the monsters she sometimes detected above while flying high in the chill upon her saddleship. Bigger than imagination.

Another beam snapped through the dark. The Mistress of the Ship was in the shadow of the planet now, trying to hide as she would from another darkship. But her maneuver proved more liability than asset. The pursuers had vanished into the darkness, too, but seemed able to locate the darkship, and had the muscle to keep after it.

A thousand questions plagued Marika. She shoved them aside. They had to wait. She had to survive before she dared ask them.

She grabbed the nearest ghost. She felt a definite, startled response to her seizure. Then she had it under control and began searching for a target.

A flare from one of the pursuing ships gave her that. She hurled the ghost, marveled at the swift cold way it dispatched the tradermales inside the ship.

Tradermales. That ship was crewed entirely by brethren. It was wholly a machine. Rage filled Marika. She clung to its fire and hurled her ghost toward another flare. Again brethren died.

All the ships around *Starstalker* were in the chase now, strung out in a long arc back around the planet's horizon. Only one more seemed to be close enough to reach the darkship with its deadly spear of light. Marika hurled her ghost again.

This time, after she finished its crew, she lingered over the ship's interior. Within minutes she understood its principles.

She explored its drive system. Brute force supplied by what Bagnel called rocket engines. She used her ghost, compressed to a point, to drill holes in a liquid-oxygen tank, then into another that carried a liquid she did not recognize, but which seemed to be a petroleum derivative.

The rear of the ship exploded.

She did the same to the other two vessels, though the last was difficult, for it was far away. She might die here in the realm of her dreams tonight, but she would make of it an expensive victory for the brethren.

She ducked back into reality to find the planet expanding below and the darkship headed back in a direction opposite that it had been flying when she went down. High above there were flares as brethren ships changed course. *Was that good enough, mistress?* she asked Kiljar.

More than adequate. A terrible awe informed the Redoriad's thought. *Now let us get down and start raising a stink.*

IV

It was not that easy. The tradermales came down after them. They plunged into atmosphere far faster than the Mistress of the Ship dared do. Spears of light ripped past the falling cross. But it fluttered and swayed in the wisps of air, making a difficult target.

Marika went back through her loophole and destroyed another two brethren ships. These proved more difficult. The tradermales were prepared for silth attack, and were very good flyers.

Nevertheless, she took them, blew them, and fragments of them raced past the darkship, beginning to glow.

Then she sensed something coming up from below. Several somethings, in fact, but one something far stronger than the others, rising on a fury like that of something elemental.

She slipped back into reality, saw that the darkship was over TelleRai now, at perhaps 250,000 feet. *Kiljar. Darkships are coming up. At least five of them.*

I know. I completed touch. The cloister is sending everyone able to come.

But it was not a Redoriad voidship that appeared moments later, shoved past, dropped like a stone, and matched fall. It bore Serke witch signs.

Marika tried to make herself small. She did not have to be told who was riding the tip of that dagger. The power of the silth reeked through the night.

Bestrei.

Bestrei, who was the destiny Gradwohl had determined for her. Bestrei, who could eat her alive right now. Bestrei, who made her feel tiny, vulnerable, without significance.

The darkship continued to fall.

Marika felt a leak of touch as something passed between Kiljar and the champion of the Serke. She was unable to read it. The ship fell, and she unslung her rifle, feeling foolish, doubting she could hit anything in her unsettled state, aware recoil might throw her off the darkship.

Another darkship materialized, coming out of the night below, not so much rising as not falling as fast till Bestrei and the Redoriad darkship caught up. It slid beneath the other darkships and took station on Bestrei's far side. Marika could not make out its witch signs, but felt it was friendly. Then another slid out of the deeps of night and fell in behind Bestrei.

344 — GLEN COOK

Marika sensed the tension slipping away. Below, the clouds began to have a touch of glow as the lights of TelleRai illuminated them from beneath. She guessed they were below one hundred thousand feet now, falling fast, but not as fast as before. The witch signs aboard her ship had begun to wobble as though in the passage of a high wind. At that altitude the air had be extremely rare, so the ship had to have a great deal of velocity left.

She leaned back to stare at the night above. *Starstalker* had passed beyond the horizon. The surviving brethren ships had gone with it. No more danger there.

Another Redoriad darkship had appeared, was on station below Bestrei. And now Marika could sense at least a score more darkships in the sky, all closing slowly, trying to match their rapid fall. They had to have come from half a dozen Communities, for none of the dark-faring sisterhoods had so many unoccupied.

Bestrei's voidship surged forward, out of the pocket formed by the Redoriad, tilted, went down like a comet, outpacing everyone.

We are safe, Kiljar sent.

She did not do anything, Marika responded. *Why?*

Bestrei may be stupid and vain, but she has a sense of honor, Kiljar returned. *She is very old-fashioned. There was nothing in what we did deserving of challenge. She was angry with those who wakened her and sent her up. I think she will cause a stir among her sisters today. They will talk her out of it, of course. They always do. But by then it will not matter. We will be long safe, and you will be on your way back to Maksche.*

Puzzled, Marika made a mental note to investigate Bestrei more closely. *Did she recognize me?*

I think not. I did my best to distract her. It was not wise of you to start waving a rifle. There is no known silth but Marika the Reugge who flies around armed like a voctor.

What now?

Now we return to the cloister. You rest till nightfall, then hasten home. Meanwhile, the Communities will get into a great fuss about what happened. You lie low till you hear from me. There can be no more lessons till less attention is turned toward the void. I think, after this, that the Serke will have great difficulty blocking the convening of a convention. And the brethren themselves will have some long explaining to do once that happens.

We must find out why they are so anxious.

Of course.

The darkship plunged into the clouds, slipped through. Another layer of clouds lay below, lighted more brightly by the city. The Mistress plunged down through it and into the night a few thousand feet above TelleRai.

The entire city was in a state of ferment. Touch scalded the air.

CHAPTER TWENTY-SIX

I

Marika wakened suddenly, completely, as though by alarm, two hours before sunset. The flight into the void returned. She shuddered. So close. And that Bestrei! The sheer malignant power of the witch!

Something called her from the north. An impulse to be gone, to head home? Now? Why so intense? That was not like her.

The urge grew stronger, almost compulsive.

She completed a rapid toilet and went to her saddleship. She was eager to get back to Braydic. There would have been a great many signals today. Braydic was bound to have intercepted something that would illuminate the behavior of the Serke and brethren. There had to be some outstanding reason for their having been so touchy about having their voidship observed.

She was supposed to wait for darkness, but she could not. The compulsion had grown overwhelming. She told herself that no one would notice one tiny saddleship ripping through the dusk.

As she flitted out the window, she sent a touch seeking Kiljar. Something came back, anxious, but by then Marika had attained full speed and was rushing away north too fast for Kiljar to catch the moving target.

The region of lakes appeared and fell behind. The Topol Cordillera passed below, speckled golden and orange in the fading light. She reached the Hainlin and turned upstream. Seventy miles south of Maksche she passed over a squadron of brethren dirigibles plowing along on a westward course. Seven? Eight? What in the world? The setting sun made great orange fingers of them. Some were as big as the first airship she had ever seen. What did that mean?

Minutes later she began to suspect.

The light of the setting sun painted the westward face of a pillar of smoke that rose in a great tower far ahead, leaning slightly with the breeze, vanishing into high cloud cover. The reverse face of the pillar was almost black, so dense was the smoke. As she drew nearer, she began to pick out the fires feeding it.

Maksche. All Maksche was aflame. That could not be. How?...

She forced her ghosts to stretch themselves, plowed down through thicker air so swiftly it howled around her.

She roared right through the smoke, so shocked she barely maintained sense enough to stay above the taller towers. The cloister was the heart of it. The Reugge bastion had been gutted. The main fires now burned among the factories and tinderbox homes of Reugge bonds.

Meth still scampered around down there, valiantly fighting the flames. They fought in a losing cause. Back over the cloister Marika passed, and saw scores upon scores of bodies scattered in the sooty courts, upon the blackened ramparts. She dropped lower, though the heat remained intense. The stone walls radiated like those of a kiln. She let her touch roam the remains, found nothing living.

She had not expected to find anything. Nothing could have lived through the inferno that raged down there.

Up she went, and across the city, touch-trolling, pain filling her. She hurt as she had not hurt since the day the nomads had crossed the packstead wall and left none but herself and Kublin living. And Grauel and Barlog.

Grauel! Barlog! No! She could not be alone now!

Touch could not find one silth mind.

She heard shooting as she rocketed over the tradermale enclave, certain it had had something to do with the disaster.

She went down, saw tradermales behind boxes and bales and corners of buildings firing at the gatehouse. Rifles barked back at them. Outside the gatehouse lay two dead meth in Reugge livery. Voctors. They had attacked the enclave.

She read the situation instantly. The huntresses were survivors of the holocaust. They had decided to die with honor, storming the source of their grief.

Tradermales in great numbers were closing a circle around the gatehouse. Machine guns yammered away, slowly gnawing at the structure. None of the brethren looked up.

They might not have seen her in the treacherous firelight anyway.

Marika lifted her saddleship a hundred feet, detached one large ghost, and sent it ravening while her conveyance settled toward the runway. By the time the carved legs of the wooden beast touched concrete, the male survivors were in full flight, headed for the one small dirigible cradled across the field.

Marika dismounted, sent the ghost after them. They died swiftly.

The firing from the gatehouse had ceased. Because the huntresses there were dead? Or because they had recognized her? She started that way.

A badly mauled Grauel slipped out a doorway, stood propped against the building. There was blood all over her.

Marika ran to her, threw her arms around her. "Grauel. By the All, what happened? This is insane."

Weakly, Grauel gasped into her ear, "Last night. During the night. The warlock came. With his rogues. Hundreds of them. He had a machine that neutralized the silth. He attacked the cloister. Some of us decided to break out and circle around. One of the sisters thought they had come in on tradermale dirigibles because a whole flight of airships dropped into the enclave after sunset."

"Where's Barlog?"

"Inside. She's hurt. You'll have to help her, Marika."

"Go on. Tell me the rest." She thought of that westbound squadron she had seen during her passage north. The same? Almost certainly. She had been within a few thousand feet of the warlock, that she had thought an imaginary beast.

"They destroyed the cloister. Surely you saw."

"I saw."

"Then they destroyed everything that belonged to the Reugge and Brown Paw Bond. The fires got out of control. I think they would have killed everyone in the city just so there would be no witnesses, but the fires drove them off. They left a couple of hours ago, just leaving the one airship load to finish up. I think they may have wanted to search the ruins after the fires died down, too."

"Come inside. You have to rest." Marika supported Grauel's weight. Inside she found most of a dozen huntresses. The majority were dead. Barlog was lying on her side, a froth of blood upon her muzzle. Only one very young voctor was uninjured. She was in a state bordering on hysteria.

Bagnel lay among the casualties. He had been bound and gagged. Marika leapt toward him.

He was not dead either, though he had several bullets in him. He regained consciousness briefly as she pulled the gag from his mouth. He croaked, " I am sorry, Marika. I did not know what was happening."

She recalled Grauel saying the raiders had destroyed Brown Paw Bond as well as Reugge properties. "For once I believe you. You are an honorable meth, for a male. We will talk later. I have things to do." She turned. "Grauel. You're in charge. Get this pup settled down and have her do what she can. And, Grauel? When I get back I want to find Bagnel healthy. Do you understand?"

"Yes. What are you doing, Marika?"

"I have a score to balance. This is going to become painfully costly for those responsible."

"You're going after them?"

"I am."

"Marika, there were hundreds of them. They had every sort of weapon you can imagine. And they had a machine that can keep silth from walking the dark side."

"That is of no import, Grauel. I will destroy them anyway. Or they will destroy me. This marks the end of my patience with them. And with anyone who defends them. You tell me the one called the warlock was with them. Did you see him?"

"He was. I saw him from very far away. He did not move far from the airships.

We tried very hard to shoot him, but the range was too great. He was very strong, Marika. Stronger than most silth."

"Not stronger than I am, I am sure. He will pay. The brethren will pay. Though I be declared an outlaw, though I stand alone, this is the first day of bloodfeud between myself and them. Stay here. I'll be back."

"And if you're not?"

"You do what you have to do. Sooner or later someone will come."

"And maybe not, Marika. Before we lost the signals section, we heard that they were attacking several other cloisters as well."

"That figures." Where did they gather their strength? She had been killing and imprisoning them for years.

"Braydic did have some advance warning, Marika. She tried to tell us. But you flew off to TelleRai too fast."

Marika recalled Barlog rushing into her quarters as she went out the window.

This was her fault, then. If she had waited a moment... Too late for regrets. It was time to give pain for pain received.

"Good-bye, Grauel." She stalked out of the gatehouse, and shut everything behind her out of mind, out of her life. Bloodfeud. There was nothing but the bloodfeud. From this moment till death. A short time, perhaps.

An entire squadron of dirigibles. How did one go about destroying them? Especially when they had some device capable of rendering a silth's talent impotent?

Worry about that in its time. First she had to find them again. She strapped herself on to her saddleship and rose into the night, raced to the southwest, cutting a course that would cross that last seen being made by the dirigibles.

II

Marika did not spare herself. In less than an hour she found the squadron, still doggedly flying westward, chasing the vanished sun. The ships were down low, hugging a barren landscape. They did not want to be seen.

She hung above them a few minutes, way up in the rare air. She was tempted to strike then, but desisted. She even refrained from probing, certain the wehrlen would detect her. Then she found her appropriate idea.

They had attacked silth using a device that stole the silth talent. She would requite them in similar coin.

Maps slipped through her mind. Yes. A major, remote brethren enclave lay nearly two hundred miles ahead. Their destination? Probably. There were no neighbors to witness what villainy was being launched from the enclave. She headed there as swiftly as she could, dropping to treetop level as she approached, flying slower because of the denser air and reduced visibility.

She hedgehopped because she was not sure her saddleship would be invisible to tradermale radar. What she had learned from Bagnel suggested she would not be seen, but now was no time to make such bets. Now she wanted to play the longer odds her own way.

She supposed she was an hour ahead of the dirigibles when she reached the edge of the enclave. There were hundreds of lights burning there, lots of activity. Yes. The base expected the raiders. Doubtless it had been the staging ground for all the attacks. The sheer number of males suggested something of vast proportion being managed from there. There were thousands of males. And the enclave bristled with weaponry. Whole squadrons of fighting aircraft sat upon the runway. Half a dozen dirigibles rested in the enclave's cradles, and there were cradles enough to take another score.

She gave herself ten minutes to rest, then she ducked through her loophole. Her anger was such that she wanted to go ravening among these brethren, killing all she could, but she did not yield to the red rage. She scouted instead, and was astounded by the magnitude of what she had found.

She did not let numbers intimidate her.

Once she was certain she knew where everything lay, she came back, checked the time, went out, and collected the most awesome monster of a ghost she could reach. She took it to the tradermale communications center.

It took her ten seconds to wreck the center and slay the technicians there. Then she drove the ghost to a workshop stocking instruments she suspected of being the devices the tradermales used to neutralize the silth. They resembled the box she had destroyed during the first confrontation on the airstrip at the Maksche enclave.

She wrecked them all, then scooted around the base, ruining anything that resembled them.

Only when that was done did she allow herself to go mad, to begin the killing.

There were so many of them that it took her half an hour. But when she finished there was not one live male inside the enclave. Hundreds had escaped, after panicking in typical male fashion. By now they were well on their ways to wherever they were trying to run. She did not expect them back.

She came back to her flesh, checked the time again. The dirigibles should arrive soon. Maybe fifteen minutes. By now they should be alert because they could make no radio contact.

She wanted to rest, to bring herself down from the nerve-wrecking high of the bloodletting, but she had no time. She trotted forward, catching a ghost once more and using it to slice a hole through the metal fence surrounding the enclave. She slipped through and raced toward the combat aircraft.

Every one was fully fueled and armed. The Stings even carried rockets. The males had been ready. Ready for anything but her. She examined several aircraft quickly, as Bagnel had taught her, and selected the one that looked soundest. Into it she climbed.

It was a well-maintained ship. Its starter turned over, and its engine caught immediately. She warmed it as Bagnel had taught her, a part of her blackly amused that one of the brethren had taught her to use the one weapon that would be effective for what she planned.

Eight minutes, roughly. They should be in sight soon. She jumped out of the aircraft, kicked the chocks away, piled back inside, harnessed herself, closed the canopy, and shoved forward on the throttle. Down the runway she rolled, and whipped upward into the night, without moonlight to help or hinder. Night was the time of the silth.

This would be a surprise for them. They seldom flew by night. Too dangerous. But they did not have the silth senses she did. Except for one.

Up. Up. Eight thousand feet. Where were they? They were showing no running lights. She caught a ghost, took it hunting.

There. The dirigibles were several minutes behind the schedule she had estimated. They were running more slowly than before. Perhaps they were concerned about the enclave's lack of response.

Down. Full throttle. Bagnel said you should fight at full throttle, though no one he knew ever had been in actual aerial combat. The brethren pilots skirmished with themselves, practicing.

She found the safeties for the guns and rockets. She was not quite sure what she was doing with those. Bagnel had not let her fire weapons.

A dark sausage shape appeared suddenly. She yanked back on the stick as she touched the firing button. Tracers reached, stitched the bag, rose above it. She barely avoided a collision.

Back on the throttle. Lesser speed and turn. At the speed she had been making there was no time to spot and maneuver.

Up and over in a loop. Grab a ghost during the maneuver. Use it to pick a target. Close in. Tracers reaching as she ran in from behind, along the airship's length, the belly of the Sting nearly touching it.

Still too fast. And doing no special damage.

She sideslipped between two dirigibles and came up from below, firing into a gondola, felt the pain of males hit, saw the flash of weapons as a few small arms fired back. Could they see her at all?

She felt the brush of one of the talent suppressors. For an instant it seemed half her mind had been turned off. But it did not bother her as much as she expected.

In the early days, at Akard, she had somehow learned to get around the worst effects of proximity to electromagnetic energies. This was something of the sort, and something inside her responded, pushing its worst effects away.

She turned away, found a ghost as soon as she could, reached in to study the airships more closely. This was not quite the same as seeing drawings in books.

She slammed the throttle forward and went after the airship out front.

Which ship carried the warlock? Would he respond to her attack?

She came in from the flank and fired a rocket. It drove well into the gasbag before blowing its warhead. Deeply enough to pass through the outer protective helium bag and reach the bigger hydrogen bag inside.

The brethren used hydrogen only when they wanted to move especially heavy cargoes. For this raid they had used hydrogen aboard all the airships, inside, where Reugge small arms could not penetrate.

She rolled under the dirigible as it exploded. The Sting was buffeted by the explosion. She fought for control, regained it, climbed, turned upon the rest of the squadron. She glanced over her shoulder, watched the airship burn and fall, meth with fur aflame leaping from its gondola.

"One gone," she said aloud, and found herself another ghost. She used it to spot another target.

This time the neutralizing weapon met her squarely. Its effect was like a blow from a fist. Yet she gasped, shook its worst effects, fired a rocket, climbed away. Small arms hammered the night. The very air was filled with panic. She came around and swept through the squadron, firing her guns, felt them firing back without regard for where their bullets might be going.

Back again. And again. And again. Till the Sting's munitions were exhausted. Five of the airships went toward the ground, four of them in flames, the fifth with gasbags so riddled it could no longer balance the leaks.

Now she was at risk. If she wished to continue attacking, she would have to go take another aircraft. If they came after her…

But they did not. Their vaunted warlock seemed as panicked as the rest. The survivors shifted course.

Marika put the Sting down fast and hard. She threw herself out of the cockpit even before it stopped rolling, hit the concrete running, and picked a second aircraft. In ten minutes she was aloft again, pursuing the remnants of the airship squadron.

One after another she sent them down and continued to attack till each had burned. She went back for the one that had descended for lack of lift, used her last two rockets to fire it.

Where was the warlock? Why did he not fight back? Was he staying low, sacrificing everything, because he knew the certain destruction he faced if he gave himself away? Or had he been killed early?

She returned to the enclave. And this time when she crawled into a cockpit, she went to sleep.

She did not have much left. They could have taken her then, easily.

She wakened before dawn, startled alert. Someone was nearby. She reached for a ghost rather than raise her head and betray herself.

Some of the males from the airships had found their way to the base. They were standing around stunned, unable to believe what had happened.

Marika's anger remained searing hot. Not enough blood had been spilled to quench the flames. She took them, adding them to the hundreds of corpses already littering the enclave. Then she started the Sting and went aloft, and in the light of dawn examined the wreckage of the dirigibles she had downed. She could not believe she had managed so much destruction.

She strafed survivors wherever she found them, like a pup torturing a crippled animal. She could have slaughtered them with her talent easily, but she was so filled with hatred that she took more pleasure in giving them a slow, taunting death, letting them run and run and run till she tracked them down.

But by midday that had lost its zest. She returned to the enclave and settled into a more systematic, businesslike revenge. After spending a few hours demolishing the base, she went to her saddleship and resumed hunting survivors again.

The brethren and rogues would not soon forget the cost of their treachery.

She wondered if she ought not to try taking a few prisoners. Questions really ought to be asked about the fate of the wehrlen. If he had existed at all, his survival might well keep the rogue movement alive despite her fury.

Toward sundown she suffered a horrible shock.

She was circling above woods where a dirigible had gone down, and… two things happened at once. She detected a small force of dirigibles approaching the enclave from the north, which fired her hatred anew, while below her she detected a moving meth spark that was all too familiar.

Kublin!

III

Kublin. More killer airships. Which way to throw herself?

Those airships would not be able to flee fast enough to escape her. She could catch them later. Kublin might vanish into the forest.

Down she went, among the trees, pushing through branches till her saddleship rode inches off the ground. She stalked him carefully, for he seemed quite aware that he was being hunted. He moved fast and quiet, with the skill of a huntress. Once, when she drew close, he sent a burst of automatic weapons fire so close one bullet nicked the neck of her saddleship.

Kublin. The treasured littermate for whom she had risked everything. Here. With the killers of her cloister.

Even now she did not want to harm him, though she remained possessed of a virulent hatred. She seized a small, feeble ghost and went hunting him, found him, struck quickly, and touched him lightly.

He brushed the ghost aside and threw a stronger back at her, almost knocking her off her saddle.

What?

Wehrlen!

Kublin?

Another blow as ferocious as the last. Yes. It could not be denied.

She dodged his blows and collected a stronger ghost, struck hard enough to knock him down. He struggled to fight off the effects.

He did have the talent, though he was no stronger than a weak sister.

In a way, it made sense. They were of the same litter, the same antecedents. He had shown a feel for the talent as a pup, a strong interest in her own early unfoldings of silth talents.

She grounded the saddleship, rushed him before he could recover, hit him physically several times, then slowly, forcibly, nullified his talent, reaching inside to depress that center of the brain where the talent lived.

Her attack left him too groggy to answer questions.

She sat down and waited, studying the uniform he wore.

She had seen its like several times before. The rogues wore uniforms occasionally. She had examined enough prisoners to have learned their uniform insignia.

Either Kublin had adopted insignia not properly his or he was very important among the rogues. Very important, indeed. If his insignia could be believed, he was a member of their ruling council.

She should have killed him in the Ponath. Before she asked the first question, she had the dark feeling the Maksche raid would not have occurred had she finished him there.

She ached inside. He was still Kublin, her littermate, with whom she had shared so much as a pup. He was the only meth for whom she had ever felt any love.

He recovered slowly, sat up weakly, shook the fuzziness from his mind, felt around for his weapon. Marika had thrown it into the brush. He seemed puzzled because it was not there beside him. Then his glance chanced upon Marika, sitting there with her own rifle trained upon him.

He froze. In mind and body.

"Yes. Me again. I did all that last night. And I have just begun. When I have finished, the brethren and rogues will be as desolate as Maksche. And you are going to help me destroy them."

Fear obliterated Kublins's defiance. He never did have much courage.

"How does a coward rise so high among fighters, Kublin? Ah. But of course. You rogues and brethren are all cowards. Stabbers in the back. Friends by day and murderers by night. But the night is the time of the silth.

"No! I do not want to hear your rationale, Kublin. I have heard it all before. I have been feeding on rogues for years. I am the Marika who has taken so many of your accomplices that we no longer have room for laborers in the Reugge mines. You know what I am doing with them now? Selling them to the Treiche. They have a hard time maintaining an adequate work force in their sulfur pits. The fumes. They use up workers quickly. I do not think it will be long before the Treiche have all the methpower they can handle."

"Stinking witch," he muttered, without force.

"Yes. I am. Also an enraged, bloodthirsty witch. So enraged I will destroy you brethren and your proxies, the rogues and this warlock, even if I die in the process. Now it is time for you to sleep. I have more airships to destroy. Later, I will return and ask you about this great warlock, this great cowardly murderer who animates you rogues so."

He gave her an odd look.

She continued, "This is the base from which the whole filthy thing was launched. It is fitting that the villains die here. I will wait here and slaughter your accomplices as they return." She snagged a ghost and touched him, left him in a coma.

She slew the crews of two airships. The others drove her off with the talent suppressors. She had made a mistake, destroying everything at the enclave. The Sting remained the best weapon against airships.

Later, she decided. She would find more fighting aircraft somewhere else.

The madness had begun to pass. She could not get her whole heart into the fight. It was time to move on. Time to take Kublin in and drain him of knowledge. Time to find the most senior and join her in assessing the damage to the Reugge Community.

Time to rest, to eat, to recover. She was little stronger than a young pup.

She returned to Kublin.

He had wakened and gnawed at his wrists in an effort to kill himself. Her touch had left him too groggy to succeed. She was astonished that he had had the will and nerve to try. This was her cowardly Kublin? Maybe his courage was selective.

She bandaged him with strips torn from his clothing, then threw him across the neck of her saddleship. She clambered aboard, called up ghosts, rose from the woods. Airships quartered the wind to the west, searching for those who had destroyed the enclave and attacked them. She bared her teeth in bitter amusement. Never would they believe that all that damage had been done by a single outraged silth.

"Have to be more careful next time," she mused. "The time after that for sure. They will be ready for any kind of trouble then."

As the saddleship limped eastward, slow and unstable with Kublin aboard, she fantasized about the Tovand, the main brethren enclave in TelleRai. A major strike there would make a dramatic statement. One that could not be misinterpreted. She imagined herself penetrating its halls by night, stalking them like death itself, leaving a trail of corpses for the survivors to find come sunup. Surely that would be something to make the villains think.

CHAPTER TWENTY-SEVEN

I

Marika's passage eastward was a slow one. The extra burden of her littermate added geometrically to her labor. And she had been expending her reserves for days.

Each fifty miles she descended for an hour of rest. One by one, the moons rose. She considered Biter and Chaser and a point that might be the Serke voidship *Starstalker*. The weather seemed better lately. Did clear skies signal a change for the better? Or just a brief respite?

It took her a while to recall that it was the tail end of summer. In a month the storm season would arrive. The snows would return. Below, scattered patches threw back silvery glimmers. Despite the season and latitude. It would get no better.

As Marika neared the Hainlin she sensed something ahead. It was little more than a premonition, but she took the saddleship down. Kublin whimpered as the bottom dropped out.

Too late. That something had sensed her presence, too. It moved toward her.

Silth.

She dropped to the surface, skipped off the saddleship, slithered into the brush, checked her rifle and pistol, ducked through her loophole to examine the ghost population. "Damn," she whispered without force. "Damn. Why now, when I'm too tired to face a novice?" The All laughed in the secret night.

She did her best to make herself invisible to silth senses.

The silth did miss her on her first passage, sliding over slightly to the north. Marika extended no probes, for she did not want to alert the hunting Mistress or her bath.

She felt the silth halt at the edge of perception, turn back. "Damn it again." She slipped the safety off her rifle, then collected a strong ghost.

She would not use the ghost offensively. She was too weak. She would fend attacks only, and use the rifle when she had the chance. Few silth expected rifle fire from other silth.

Not once did it occur to her that the prowler might be friendly.

The silth approached cautiously. Marika became more certain her intentions were unfriendly. And she was a strong one, for she masked herself well.

Almost overhead now. Low. Maybe she could get a killing burst off before… A shape moved in the moonlight, dark, low, slow….

That was no darkship! That was a saddleship like her own.

Marika?

There was no mistaking the odor of that touch. Gradwohl! A flood of relief. *Here, mistress. Right below you.* She left the brush and walked toward her own saddleship as the most senior descended.

"What are you doing here, mistress?"

"Looking for you. What have you been doing?"

"I went after the raiders. Have you been to Maksche, mistress?"

"I came from there."

"Then you know. I got them, mistress. All of them. And many more besides. Perhaps even their warlock. They have paid the first installment."

Gradwohl remained astride her saddleship, a twin of Marika's. Marika mounted her own. Gradwohl indicated Kublin. "What is that?"

"A high-ranking prisoner, mistress. Probably one of the leaders of the attack. I have not yet questioned him. I was considering a truthsaying after I have recovered my strength."

She felt rested after the few minutes down, despite the tension. She was eager to get back to Grauel and Barlog. She lifted her saddleship. Gradwohl followed, hastened to assume the position of honor. They rose into the moonlight and drifted eastward at a comfortable pace.

I want you to drink chaphe when we get back, Gradwohl sent. *I want you to rest long and well. We have much to discuss.*

Marika considered that thoroughly before she responded. Between them she and Gradwohl had seldom shifted from the formal mode, yet tonight there was an unusually odd, distant aroma to the most senior's sending. She was distressed about something.

What is wrong, mistress?

Later, Marika. After you have rested. I do not want to go into it when you are so exhausted you may not be in control of all your faculties.

Marika did not like the increased distance implied by the sending's tone. *I think we had best discuss what must be discussed now. In the privacy of the night. I sense a gulf opening between us. This I cannot comprehend. Why, mistress?*

If you insist, then. The Reugge have been crippled, Marika. This is what is wrong. This is what we must discuss. The Reugge have been hurt badly, and you want to make the situation worse.

Mistress? The Reugge have been hurt, that is true, but we have not been destroyed. I believe the cornerstones of our strength remain intact. We can turn it around on the brethren and—

We will turn it around, but not in blood. All the world knows what happened. No one believes rogues made the raids on their own, unsupported. Those, and Kiljar's experience with the Serke voidship, have been enough to cause a general clamor for a convention. Even by some elements within the brethren. The Brown Paw Bond nearly ceased to exist because of the raids. Their enemies within the brotherhood tried to exterminate them along with us. The Redoriad are going to demand dismemberment of the Serke and the banning of all brethren from space for at least a generation. Already some among the brethren are crawling sideways, whimpering as they try to bargain for special consideration for their particular Bonds. They have imprisoned a number of high masters, saying they acted on their own, without approval, in a conspiracy with the Serke. We have won the long struggle, Marika. At great expense, yes, but without resort to challenge or direct bloodletting—other than that in which you have indulged yourself. It is time now to back away and let the convention finish it for us.

You will accept that? After all these years? After all the Reugge have suffered? You will not extract payment in blood?

I will not.

Marika reflected a moment. *Mistress, will I be continuing my education with Kiljar?*

Gradwohl seemed reluctant to respond. Finally, she sent, *There will be no need, will there? Bestrei will have been disarmed by the dispersal of her Community.*

I see.

I am not sure you do. Your focus is sometimes too narrow. That is why I want you to rest under the influence of chaphe. To become totally recovered before we examine this in detail. I want you able to see the whole situation and all the options. We will be headed for a period of delicate negotiations.

What will become of Bestrei? She could not imagine a sisterhood being dismantled. But there were precedents. The Librach had been disbanded by force after a convention four centuries earlier, after considerable bloodshed.

She will be adopted into another Community. If she wishes.

And the Serke assets?

They will be dispersed according to outstanding claims.

The Reugge will possess the strongest of those. Yes? And because the brethren will pretend to have been used, and to be contrite, and will sacrifice a few factors, they will get off with a wrist slap. And in a generation, before you and I are even gone, they will be back stronger than ever, better prepared, more thoroughly insinuated into the fabric of society.

Marika. I told you you should rest before we discuss this. You are becoming unreasonably emotional.

I am sorry, mistress. I remain a Ponath bitch at heart. When I see bloodfeud directed my way, I have difficulty letting the declarer beg off if he sees that he is going to lose. Particularly when he will return as soon as he feels strong enough to try again.

The brethren were manipulated by the Serke.

You are a fool if you believe that, mistress. The brethren were the manipulators. You have seen the evidence. They used the Serke, and now I see them starting to use you even before they have shed their previous victims.

Marika! Do not anger me. You have been brought far in a very short time. You are a member of the ruling council of the Reugge, soon to be one of the major orders.

At the price of honor?

Do not harp on honor, pup. Yours remains indicted by the existence of the male lying before you.

Mistress? Coldness crept into Marika.

Would you subject him to a truthsaying? Really? Now?

It would provide the final proof of the villainy of the brethren.

Perhaps. And what would it prove about you?

Mistress?

You accuse me, Marika. By your tone you accuse me of crimes. Yet I have forgiven you yours. Dorteka was precious to me, pup, yet I forgave even that. For the sake of the Community.

You know?

I have known for more than a year. The Serke presented the evidence. You saved a littermate in the Ponath. The result was what has happened these past few days. But even that I can forgive. If you will shed the role of Jiana.

Jiana? And, You engineered this holocaust? This is where you were headed all along? You had no intention of challenging Bestrei? Of breaking into the void? I was just your distraction?

I pursued both goals equally, Marika. The success of either would have satisfied me. My mission is to preserve and strengthen the Reugge. I have done that. I will not permit you to diminish or destroy what I have won.

You called me Jiana. I do not like that.

There are times when you seem determined to fill the role.

Mistress?

Everywhere you go. Maksche is just the latest.

I had nothing to do with that. I was in TelleRai when—

You were. Yes. And that is the only reason you survived. The rhythm of your visits altered. The only reason the brethren attacked was to destroy you. You, Marika. The other attacks were diversions meant to keep aid from rushing to Maksche. But you were not there. You went off to TelleRai off schedule. You did not have the decency to perish. Accept, Marika. Do not continue to be a doomstalker.

I am no doomstalker, mistress.

Destruction walks in your shadow, pup.

This is foolishness, mistress.

First your packstead, Marika. Then your fortress, your packfast, Akard. Now Maksche. What has to happen before you see? The end of the world itself?

Marika was baffled. Gradwohl had been sound of mind always, spurning such superstitious nonsense. This made no sense. *All these things would have happened without me, mistress. The brethren and Serke began their game long before anyone ever heard of Marika.*

The All knew you. And the All moved them.

Marika gave up. No argument could change a closed, mad mind. She peered down at moonlight reflected off the Hainlin. That was as much of the void as she might see. *I want the stars, mistress.*

I know, Marika. Perhaps we can get something for you in the settlement.

I will not accept perhaps, Most Senior.

This is not the time to—

This is the time.

This is what I feared. This is why I did not want to discuss this with you now. I knew you would be unsettled.

When will this convention set the silth stamp of approval on the treacheries of the brethren?

The first session will meet as soon as I reach TelleRai. I will take my saddleship south as soon as I have won your promise to support me.

I cannot give you that, mistress. My conscience will not permit it. There is bloodfeud involved. You would betray all those sisters who have perished.

Damned stubborn savage. Put aside your primitive ways. We are not living in the upper Ponath. This is the real world. Allowances and adjustments have to be made.

Wrong.

I did not want it to come to this, pup.

Marika felt the otherworld stir. She was not surprised, nor even much frightened. The moment seemed destined.

She did not try her loophole. It was too late for that. She did what silth never seemed to expect. She squeezed the trigger of the rifle she had not returned to safety. The entire magazine hammered the air.

Gradwohl separated from her saddleship and tumbled toward the river.

Marika! Damn you, Jiana! Then the sensing of Gradwohl vanished into a fog of pain. And then that spark went out.

Marika circled twice, fixing the spot in her mind. Then she went on, composing herself for Maksche.

II

Marika had nothing left when she brought the saddleship down on the airstrip near Bagnel's quarters, Kublin still limp across its neck. Someone came out, recognized her, shouted back inside. In a moment Grauel limped forth. She reached out feebly, far too slowly, as Marika slipped off and fell to the concrete. "You're still here," Marika rasped.

"Yes." Grauel tried to lift her to her feet, could not. More meth gathered around. Marika recognized faces she had not seen last visit. Somehow, Grauel had assembled some survivors. "The most senior told us to remain."

"Gradwohl. Where is she?"

"She went looking for you."

"Oh. I got them, Grauel. Every one of them."

"Take her inside," Grauel told the others. "Where did you find him?" She indicated Kublin.

"With them. He may have been one of their commanders."

"Oh."

"Yes."

"Give her the chaphe," Grauel ordered as they entered the building.

"Grauel...."

"The most senior's orders, Marika. You get two days of enforced rest."

Marika surrendered. She did not have the strength to resist.

Several times she wakened, found Grauel nearby. She told the huntress about the brethren base in snatches. Grauel did not seem much interested. Marika allowed the enforced rest to continue, for she had stretched herself more than she had realized. But the third night she refused the drug. "Where is the most senior? Enough is enough. Things are happening and we are out of touch."

"She has not returned, Marika. I have become concerned. Sisters from TelleRai were here this morning, seeking her. I had thought she might have gone there."

"And?" Time to be cautious. Time to have a care with Grauel, who persisted in using the formal mode.

"They flew west, seeking some trace. I believe they called for more darkships to join in the search. They were very worried."

"Why?"

"The... You do not know, do you? A convention of the Communities has been called to bring the Serke and brethren to account. The most senior must be there. The Reugge are the principal grievants."

Marika struggled up from her cot. "That's happening? Gradwohl is missing? And you've kept me drugged? Grauel, what...?"

"Her orders, Marika."

"Orders or not, that's over. Bring me food. Bring me fresh clothing. Bring me my weapons and prepare my saddleship."

"Marika...."

"I have to go to TelleRai. Someone has to represent the most senior's view-point. Someone has to be there if the worst has happened. If the brethren have slain her and the wrong sisters hear of it first, her whole dream will die. Get me out of here, Grauel. I'll send for you as soon as I get there."

"As you command."

Marika did not like Grauel's tone. She let it slide. "How is Barlog doing?"

"Recovering. The most senior was able to save her."

There was an accusation behind those words. "I am sorry, Grauel. I was not myself that day."

"Are you ever, Marika? Are you now? Have you slaked your blood thirst yet?"

"I think so."

"I hope so. They say this convention is an opportunity to end what has been happening. I would not want to see it fail."

"How are Bagnel and Kublin doing?"

"Bagnel is recovering nicely. The most senior treated him, too, inasmuch as he seems to be the sole surviving Brown Paw Bonder from this enclave. Kublin is in chains. There were those who wanted to do him injury. I have protected him."

"Maybe you shouldn't have. I'm not sure why I brought him in. When the darkship comes, bring him to TelleRai. He may prove useful during the convention."

"Perhaps."

"What is the matter, Grauel? I feel…"

"I fear you, Marika. Since you returned from this vengeance, even I can see the look of doom upon you. And I fear you the more because Gradwohl is not here to temper your ferocity."

"Be about your business, Grauel." Marika stood. Her legs were weak. She ducked through her loophole to check her grasp of the otherworld, fearful she might not be strong enough to get to TelleRai in time.

She would manage. She was not weak in her grasp of the dark.

She visited Bagnel briefly. He apologized again. "It was despicable," she agreed. "But I think we're about to conclude that era. Keep well, Bagnel." Outside, as she prepared to mount her saddleship, Marika told Grauel, "Bring Bagnel, too."

"Yes, mistress."

Marika looked at Grauel grimly. She did not like it when the huntress took the formal mode. It meant Grauel did not approve.

Irked, she lifted the saddleship without another word.

She sped southward, paused briefly where Gradwohl had gone down. She found no trace of the most senior's body. She did find Gradwohl's saddleship, broken, in a tree. She dragged it out, dismantled it, threw the pieces into the river. Let them become driftwood, joining other flotsam come down from the dying north.

The sisters at TelleRai were not pleased with her advent. Many had hoped she had perished in the raid. More feared the most senior had perished sometime afterward. They dreaded the chance the savage northerner would lay claim to the most senior's mantle.

As strength goes. They were convinced none could challenge the outlander.

"I will not replace the most senior," Marika told anyone who would listen. "It has never been my wish to become most senior. But I will speak for Gradwohl till she returns. Her mind is my mind."

Word of what had happened at the enclave in the wilderness had reached TelleRai. Though Marika did not claim responsibility and no one made direct accusations, there were no doubts anywhere who had been responsible for the slaughter. Terror hung around her like a fog. No one would dispute anything she said.

Grauel and Barlog, Kublin and Bagnel arrived a day after Marika, near dawn, with the first group of survivors brought out of the ruins of Maksche. Marika had insisted that every survivor, including workers and Reugge bonds, be evacuated south. That earned her no friends, for it would strain the resources of the TelleRai cloister.

Barlog was somewhat recovered. She was not pleasant at all when Marika visited her.

There was a small fuss when Marika insisted Bagnel be assigned guest quarters. She had Kublin imprisoned. She did not visit him.

Grauel and Barlog retired to their new quarters to rest, or to hide. Marika was not certain which. They were attached to Marika's own, where she paced outside their door, wondering what she could do to recover their goodwill.

Someone knocked on the apartment door. Marika answered it, found a novice outside. "Yes?"

"Mistress, second Kiljar of the Redoriad wishes to speak with you."

"Is she here?"

"No, mistress. She sent a messenger. Will there be any reply?"

"Tell her yes. The second hour after noon, if that is convenient. In the usual place. She will understand what I mean."

"Yes, mistress."

Shortly after the novice departed, sisters Cyalgon and Tascil, the order's sixth and third chairs, in TelleRai for the convention, came calling. Marika knew Cyalgon. She had been with the party that had gone to the Redoriad museum. She presumed upon that now. After the appropriate greetings, Marika asked, "To what do I owe the honor of your visit?"

Cyalgon was direct. "First chair. You say you would refuse it. We wish to know if this is true or just a ploy."

"I have made no secret of the fact that I have no wish to bury myself in the petty details that plague a most senior. But for that I would not mind having a Community behind me."

"Perhaps something might be arranged."

"Oh?"

"Someone might assume the weight of detail."

"I will not become a figurehead in any task I assume. In any case, I would prefer being the power behind. I am young, mistress. I still have dreams. But this whole discussion is moot. The Reugge have a most senior."

"It begins to appear that Gradwohl is no longer with us."

"Mistress?"

"Even experts at the long touch cannot detect her."

"Perhaps she is hiding."

"From her own sisters? At a time like this? She would have responded if she could. She must be dead."

"Or possibly a prisoner? Suppose the brethren captured her. Or the Serke. They could have lifted her off-planet. She could be alive and there be no way to touch her."

"Amounts to the same thing."

"I fear it does not. I fear I do not want to be party to what could later be interpreted as an attempt to oust a most senior who has been very good to me. I think I would like stronger proof that she is not with us. But I will give the matter some thought. I will speak to you later."

They had not gotten what they wanted. They departed with shoulders angrily stiff.

"Starting to line up for a grab-off," Marika snarled after they departed. "I suppose I will hear from them all. I wish I knew them better."

She was speaking to herself. But a voice from behind said, "Perhaps if you had paid more attention to your duties here...."

"Enough, Grauel. I am going out. Take the names of any who ask to see me. Tell them I will contact them later."

"As you command, mistress."

Irked, Marika began assembling her saddleship.

III

Marika swept in over the Redoriad cloister as fast as she dared, hoping to remain unnoticed. Vain hope. There was an inconvenient break in the cloud cover. Her shadow ran across the courts below, catching the eyes of several Redoriad bonds. By the time she reached Kiljar's window, meth were running everywhere.

"You came," Kiljar said.

"Of course. Why not?"

"I received your message but doubted you would make it. My sources suggested there is a lot of maneuvering going on inside the Reugge."

"I have been approached," Marika admitted. "But only once. I will tell them all the same thing. First chair is not open. If it were, I would not take it. Though I do want someone philosophically compatible to be most senior. I am busy enough with the brethren and Serke."

"That is what I wanted to discuss with you."

"Mistress?"

"Do not become defensive, Marika. It is time you assessed your position. Time you shed this hard stance."

Marika's jaw tightened.

"Were you not satisfied with what you wrought at that brethren enclave?"

"No, mistress. That was not sufficient at all. That was an insect's sting. I am going to devour them. They destroyed a city. Without cause or justification. They will pay the price."

"I do not understand you, Marika. Victory is not enough. Why do you make this a personal vendetta?"

"Mistress?"

"You are not killing for the honor or salvation of your Community. You are more selfish than the run of silth. No! Do not deny it. For you your order is a ladder to climb toward personal goals. Gradwohl was crafty enough to use you to the benefit of the Reugge. But now Gradwohl is gone. We all fear...."

"Why does everyone insist that? For years Gradwohl has been in the habit of disappearing. Sometimes for months."

"This time it is for good, Marika."

"How can you know that?" A blade of ice slashed at her heart.

Kublin might know what had become of Gradwohl. That had not occurred to her before. Suppose he had not been unconscious throughout the whole flight? Indeed, all he needed to know was that she and Gradwohl had met.

"Come." Kiljar led her to another room. "Look." She indicated fragments of wood. Some retained bits of gaudy paint. "Parts from a saddleship not unlike yours. Some of our bonds found them drifting in the Hainlin yesterday. I have heard of only one saddleship other than yours. The one Gradwohl was flying when last seen."

Marika settled into a chair uninvited. "Does anyone else know?"

"My most senior. Do you accept this evidence?"

"Do I have any choice?"

"I think it is close enough to conclusive. It seems obvious Gradwohl went down in the Hainlin. How we may never know. What stance will you take now, Marika? Will you think of someone besides yourself?"

"Oh. I suppose. Yes. I have to." Was Kiljar suspicious?

"You had best reconsider your position on the Serke, the brethren, and the convention, then."

"But..."

"I will explain. I will show you why it can be in our interest to see the convention through to the conclusion you abhor. Let me begin with our passage near *Starstalker*."

"Mistress?"

"We were attacked. Without provocation. Unprecedented. Have you not wondered why? And the how was so startling."

"Those ships."

"Exactly. Nothing like them has been seen before. Yet they could not have been created overnight. And, sneaky as they are, the brethren could not have built them without the project having come to my attention."

"The brethren have done many things without attracting attention, mistress. Including putting satellites into orbit without the help or license of any Community."

"Yes. I know. They used rockets half as big as TelleRai, launched from the Cupple Islands. For all the organizing you have done, I have resources that you do not. The brethren are not monolithic. Some bonds can be penetrated with the wealth at my command. There are no secrets from me in TelleRai."

Kiljar paused. Marika did not care to comment.

"The brethren did not build those ships here. They came here aboard *Starstalker*. We were not supposed to see them because the brethren did not build them at all."

Startled, Marika asked, "What?"

"The brethren did not build them. It took great pressure upon my contacts and the spreading of much Redoriad largess, but I wormed out an amazing truth. A truth which has been before us all for years, unseen because it was so fantastic."

"You are toying with me, mistress."

"I suppose I am. Marika, the fact is, *Starstalker* crossed starpaths with another dark-faring species fifteen years ago. A species without silth. They are like the brethren, only more so. The Serke were unable to comprehend them, so they enlisted the help of those bonds with whom they had operated closely before. And the brethren took control. Much as you have claimed."

Marika could not keep her lips from peeling back in a snarl.

"At first only a few dark-faring bonds were in it with the Serke. Thus, overall brethren policy was inconsistent. The Serke began trying to seize Reugge territories because of advantages they hoped to gain from these aliens. Their ally bonds helped. At the same time the Brown Paw Bond, being uninformed, were battling the nomads the Serke and other brethren had armed. Do you follow?"

"I think I see the outline. Bagnel once said—"

"After Akard and Critza fell, but before you defeated the force near the ruins of Critza, the dark-faring bonds gained ascendancy over all the brethren. A smaller faction inimical to silth controlled *them*. Though you Reugge suffered, there was much quiet feuding among the bonds in private. Increasing bitterness, failure of communication, and outright disobedience on the part of a few highly placed individuals resulted in the ill-timed, ill-advised, much too massive attempt to kill you at Maksche."

"To kill me? They destroyed an entire city just to get me?"

"Absolutely. There was one among them who was quite mad."

"The warlock. We have been hearing about him for some time."

"The warlock. Yes. He engineered the whole thing. My contacts say he had an insane fear of you. Insanity bred insanity. And when it went sour it all went sour. His madness caused the overthrow of the dark-faring brethren. They have been replaced by conservatives who favor traditional relationships with the Communities. Now."

"Mistress?"

"Now is the time you must *listen* and *hear*. Timing is important now. If the convention moves fast the rogue faction can be disarmed forever. What the Serke found, and hoped to use to our detriment, can be exploited for the benefit of all meth. If we do not move fast the dark-faring brethren may regain their balance and attempt a counter-move. I have gotten hints that they received fearsome weapons and technologies from the aliens."

Marika left the chair, began to pace. She recalled once naively telling Dorteka or Gradwohl that the Reugge ought to try creating factions within the brethren.

"The pitchblende. These aliens wanted it?"

"The brethren believed so. Apparently they use it in power plants of the sort you once predicted in one of our discussions. It seems the Ponath deposit is a rich one indeed. It was because of it that the dark-faring brethren took control of all the brethren. They believed they could use the ore to buy technology. And thus the power to destroy all silth. But for you they might have succeeded."

"Me?"

"You have a friend among the brethren. You were open with him apparently, even when relationships were most strained. The brethren, like silth, are able to extract a great deal from very little evidence. Like the Serke and Gradwohl and everyone else who paid attention to you, they saw what you might become."

"Bestrei's replacement."

"Exactly. With a strong conservative bent and a tendency to do things your own way. The brethren foresaw a future in which they would lose privileges and powers. Also, you are more than Bestrei's potential successor. You have a reasonable amount of intelligence and a talent for intuiting whole pictures from the most miniscule specks of evidence. That you insisted on isolating yourself in a remote industrial setting only further disturbed those who feared you. You recall the stir at the time of your first visit here? You recall me remarking that everyone was following you closely? Had you spent more time in TelleRai you might have been more aware of what you are and how you are perceived."

"Such talk mystifies me, mistress. I have heard it for years. It always seems to be about someone else. I think I know myself fairly well. I am not this creature you are talking about. I am no different from anyone else."

"You compare yourself to older silth, perhaps. To sisters who have risen very high, but who are in the main within a few years of death. They have passed their prime. You have your whole life ahead of you. It is what you might become that scares everyone. Your potential plus your intellectual orientation. That can frighten meth who, to you, may seem unassailable."

Marika looked inside herself and did not find that she felt special. "Where do we stand now? Where are we headed? You wished specifically to know about my position on the convention."

"Yes. It is critical that none of us holds a hard line. We must not give the dark-faring brethren excuses to recapture control. We must be satisfied with recapturing yesterday. The ruling brethren are eager to please right now."

"They attacked—"

"I know what they did, pup! Damn you, *listen!* I know bloodfeud. I come from a rural background. But you cannot make enemies of all brethren. That will give the wicked among them ammunition. In that you risk defeat for all silth."

Marika moved toward her saddleship, suddenly aware that Kiljar was unusually tense. There was a threat implicit in her plea.

"Yes," Kiljar said, reading her well. "If you sustain your stance, you will find yourself very unpopular. It is my understanding that some elements within the Reugge have sent out feelers seeking aid in removing you."

"I see. And if I bend? If I go along? What is in this for me?"

"Probably anything you want, Marika. The Communities want to avoid further confrontation. You could name your price."

"You know what I want."

"I think so."

"That is the price. I will put it to the convention formally."

Kiljar seemed amused. "You will do nothing the easy way, will you?"

"Mistress?"

"The dark-faring Communities will shriek if you demand extraplanetary rights for the Reugge."

"Let them. That is the price. It is not negotiable."

"All right. I will warn those who should know beforetime. I suggest you present a list of throwaway demands if you wish to make them think they have gotten something in return."

"I will, mistress. I had better return to the cloister. I must shift my course there, too. Immediately."

Kiljar seemed puzzled.

Marika slipped astride her saddleship and took flight. She rose high above TelleRai and pushed the saddleship through violent, perilous maneuvers for an hour, venting her anger and frustration.

CHAPTER TWENTY-EIGHT

I

Marika told the gathered council of the Reugge Community, "I have changed my mind. I am laying claim to first chair. I have seen that there is no other way for the Community to properly benefit from the coming convention."

None of the sisters were willing to challenge her. Many looked angry or disappointed.

"I have been to the Redoriad cloister. They showed me evidence, collected upon their estates, that Most Senior Gradwohl is no longer with us. Despite my claim, however, my attitude toward the most senior's position has not altered. I intend to retain first chair only long enough to win us the best from the convention and to set our feet upon a new, star-walking path. Once I succeed, I will step aside, for I will have a task of my own to pursue."

Blank stares. Very blank stares. No one believed.

"Does anyone wish to contest my claim? On whatever grounds?"

No one did.

"Good. I will leave you, then. I have much to do before tomorrow morning. As long as you are all here, why not consider candidates for seventh chair?" She thought that a nice touch, allowing them an opportunity to strengthen themselves by enrolling another of her enemies in the council.

She truly did not care. Like Gradwohl before her, her strength was such that she could do what she liked without challenge.

She departed, joined Grauel, who had awaited her outside the council chamber. "Gradwohl's darkship crew is here in the cloister somewhere. Assemble them. We have a flight to make."

Grauel asked no questions. "As you command, mistress." She persisted in her formal role.

"Have Kublin and Bagnel brought to the darkship court. We will take them with us. And have someone you trust care for Barlog. Most of the Maksche survivors have arrived now, have they not?"

"Yes, mistress."

"Go."

Marika hurried to her quarters, quickly sketched out what she would demand from the convention. Space rights for the Reugge. Serke starworlds for the Reugge. The void-ship *Starstalker* for the Reugge. The other orders could squabble over Serke properties on-planet.

Bar the brethren from space forever, not just for a generation. Disarm the brethren except in areas where weapons were necessary to their survival. Allow them no weapons exceeding the technological covenants for any given area, so that brethren in a region like the Ponath, a Tech Two Zone, must carry bows and arrows and spears like the native packs. Demand mechanisms for observation and enforcement.

There would be screams. Loud and long. She expected to surrender on most all the issues except Reugge access to space and a Reugge share of Serke starholdings. As Kiljar had said, let them think they had won something.

"Ready, mistress," Grauel said from the doorway. "The bath were not pleased."

"They never are. They would prefer to spend their lives loafing. Kublin and Bagnel?"

"They are being transferred to the courtyard. I told the workers to break out a darkship. Everything should be ready when we arrive."

The flight was uneventful, though early on Marika had to lose a darkship following her at the edge of sensing. She crossed the snowline and continued north, and by moonlight descended into the courtyard of Gradwohl's hidden darkship factory. "Good evening, Edzeka," she said to the senior of the packfast. "Have you been following the news?" The fortress could send no messages out, except by touch, but could collect almost everything off almost every network. Gradwohl had established one of Braydic's interception teams there. She would miss Braydic more than anyone else who had died at Maksche.

"Yes, mistress. Congratulations. Though I was unhappy to hear that Most Senior Gradwohl has left us for the embrace of the All."

"There will be no changes here, Edzeka. We will continue to do what we can to make the Communities independent of the brethren. We will expand our operations when we can."

Edzeka seemed pleased. "Thank you, mistress. We were concerned when it seemed you would forego first chair."

"There is a great deal of pressure on me to abandon the ideals that drew Gradwohl and me together, and you to her. I may have to present the appearance of abandoning them. It will be appearance only. The fact that you continue your work will be my assurance that I have not changed in my heart."

"Thank you again, mistress. What can we do for you?"

"I need one of the new darkships. Tomorrow I must speak for the Reugge before a convention of the Communities. I thought I might make an unspoken statement by arriving aboard one of your darkships."

"You have males with you."

"Yes. Two very special males. The one who is not bound is a longtime friend, one of the few survivors of a bond friendly to the Reugge, who may be at risk in these times. I wish to keep him safe. He is to be accorded all consideration and honor."

"And the other?"

"A prisoner. One of the commanders of the attack upon Maksche. He is to be assigned to the communications-intercept section to translate messages out of the brethren cant. Do what you need to to enforce his cooperation. Otherwise do not harm him. I may have a use for him. Now. May I have one of the new ships?"

"Of course. I will give you the one prepared for the most senior."

"Good. I cannot spend time here, unfortunately, for I have to be back in TelleRai early. I will need to borrow bath as well. Mine need rest. I will need a Mistress of the Ship also, if I am to get any rest myself."

"As you wish."

"And something to eat."

"Never any problem there, mistress. Come down to the kitchen."

II

Grauel wakened Marika as the darkship approached TelleRai. She checked the time. Edzeka had not given her the strongest of Mistresses. It was later than she had hoped. There would be no time to pause at the cloister. She touched the Mistress, told her to proceed directly to convention ground. The convention would meet there despite the weather, which threatened snow.

The flight south had encountered patch after patch of snowfall, the Mistress being unwilling to climb above the clouds. She was young and unconfident.

It smelled like another hard winter, one that would push farther south than ever before.

A victory today, Marika reflected, and she would be in a position at last to do something about that.

The sky over TelleRai was crowded. Every darkship seemed to set a course identical to Marika's. She edged up to the tip of the wooden cross, touched the Mistress, took over.

The moment the silth reached the axis, Marika took the darkship up five thousand feet, well above traffic, and waited in the still chill till it seemed the crowd should have cleared. Then she dropped a few hundred feet at a time, feeling around in the clouds.

If something was to be tried, this was the time.

So many enemies.

She glanced over her shoulder. Grauel was alert, her weapon ready. She checked her own rifle, then allowed the darkship to sink till it had cleared the underbellies of the clouds.

Still a fair ceiling. The snow might hold off awhile.

The air was less crowded. In fact, the few darkships aloft seemed to be patrolling.

She let the bottom fall out.

Startled touches bounced off her, then she was swooping toward the heart of convention ground as faces turned to look. The glimpses she caught told her they were thinking of her as that show-off savage, making a late, flashy entrance.

Exactly.

She touched down fifty feet from the senior representatives of the Communities. Kiljar was the only silth she recognized. The Redoriad came toward her, skirting a small pond.

Tall, slim trees surrounded the area, winter-naked, probably dying. The heart of convention ground centered upon a group of fountains surrounded by statuary, exotic plantings, and benches where silth came to meditate in less exciting times. A dozen Serke waited near the trees in silence, eyes downcast, resigned. On the opposite side of the circle stood a larger group of males, most of whom were old. Marika spied the tradermales from Bagnel's quarters among them. She raised a paw in mocking greeting.

The males were sullen and hateful.

They were resigned, too, but theirs was not the resignation of the Serke. Marika sensed an undercurrent, something resembling the odor of triumph.

Was there something wrong here? A truthsaying might be in order.

"I had begun to be concerned," Kiljar said. "Where were you? Your cloister told me you were away." She eyed Marika's darkship. While not as fancy as those of times past, it was large and ornate. "Where did you get that?"

"Sisters made it. That was Gradwohl's legacy. A first step toward independence for the brethren."

"You might avoid that subject."

"Why did you wish to contact me?"

"Shortly after you announced you would become first chair of the Reugge, there was a rebellion among the brethren of the Cupple Islands. They have taken control there. What they do next depends upon what you say now."

"I see."

"I hope so."

"I thought it was foregone what would happen. Dismember the Serke and ban the brethren from space for a while."

"Essentially. But the details, Marika. The details. Your past attitude toward the brethren is well-known."

"These prisoners. They are the sacrificial victims?"

"You could call them that."

"The males are old. Those who will replace them are all younger?"

"I would not be surprised."

"Yes. Well. To be expected, I suspect. I have brought a list. As I said, I will negotiate on everything but a Reugge interest in the void."

"Understood. Come. I will introduce you. We will get into the details, then go to the convention for approval. Simply a matter of form, I assure you."

Marika scanned the encircling trees. Here, there, curious faces peeped forth. Silth by the hundred waited in the greater park outside. "Have those meth no work?"

"This is the event of the century, Marika. Of several centuries. I will gather everyone. Tell them what is on your mind."

Marika watched Kiljar closely, wondering about her part in the game. She was behaving as though there was some special alliance between herself and the new most senior of the Reugge.

Random snowflakes floated around. Marika glanced at the overcast. It would not be long.

"Speak, Marika," Kiljar told her. And in a whisper, "Demand what you like, but avoid being belligerent."

Marika spoke. The silth listened. She became uncomfortable as she sensed that they were trying to read into her tone, inflexion, and stance more than was there. She was too young to deal with these silth. They were too subtle for her.

Her speech caused a stir among the trees. Many silth hastened away to tell others farther back.

Kiljar announced, "The Redoriad endorse the Reugge proposal." More softly, she said, "Remember, Marika, this is an informal discussion, not the official convention. Do not take to heart everything that is said."

"Meaning your endorsement is a maneuver."

"That, and that some unpleasant attacks may be made by those opposed. Those who speak against will not be declaring bloodfeud."

The various representatives responded individually. Some felt compelled to do so at great length. Marika seated herself on a bench. She felt sleepy. Sitting did not help. She caught herself nodding.

The breeze became more chill. The snowflakes became more numerous, pellets of white that swirled around the heart of the park. They caught in the grass and whitened it till it looked like the fur of an old female. Kiljar settled beside Marika. "That fool Foxgar will never shut up."

"Who is she?"

"Second of the Furnvreit. A small Community from the far south with limited holdings in the outer system. In a convention the smallest order speaks with a voice equaling that of the largest. Unfortunately. She may be stalling in hopes her vote will be bought."

"Do the Furnvreit have any claim on the Serke?"

"None whatsoever. Few Communities do. But they all want a share of the plunder. And they will get it. Otherwise the convention will go nowhere."

"Wonderful."

A silth came from the trees, hastened to Kiljar, whispered. Kiljar looked grim.

"What is it?" Marika asked. A bad feeling twisted her insides.

"Somebody relayed your opening terms to the Cupple Islands. Those ships we saw around *Starstalker*. A great many of their type are lifting off, packed with brethren."

Marika's bad feeling worsened.

III

An old silth appeared, too excited to retain her cool dignity. "The darkships are leaving the cloister at Ruhaack! The Serke are... are..."

"You would deal with brethren!" Marika snapped at Kiljar. She raced to her darkship. "Grauel! Get aboard. Bath! Mistress! Get it airborne."

The remaining silth stood bewildered for a moment, then scattered.

Marika was well away before anyone else lifted off. She touched the Mistress of the Ship. *The Reugge cloister. Hurry.*

"What is it, Marika?" Grauel asked. She kept turning, weapon ready, seeking something she could not find.

"I don't know. But I don't like this. I have a bad feeling. A premonition. I don't want to be caught on the ground. We'll pick up Barlog, then head for Ruhaack." She was as confused as any of the silth aboard the darkships swarming up below.

Any course of action had to be positive.

The enemy was on the move.

She touched the Mistress of the Ship again, showed her where to go as Grauel protested, "Marika, Barlog is in no condition to—"

"I don't care. I want her with me till we see what's going to happen."

The Mistress of the Ship brought the darkship to rest beside the window to Marika's quarters. Marika gestured violently. The Mistress rotated the darkship, brought one arm into contact with the windowsill. "Hold it there!" Marika ordered. "We'll be back in a minute. Grauel, break that window."

Grauel tottered along the beam, eased past the bath at its tip, smashed glass with her rifle butt. She jumped through. Marika followed. "What now?" Grauel asked.

"Barlog." In her mind a clock was ticking, estimating the time it would take the brethren fugitives to rendezvous with *Starstalker*.

Intuition began shrieking at her. "Hurry!" she barked.

They found Barlog sleeping, still partially immobilized by the healer sisters. They pulled her out of bed and hustled her to the window. Marika leapt out onto the arm of the darkship. It sank beneath her weight. "Hold it steady!" she yelled. "All right, Grauel. Push her up. Come on, Barlog. You have to help a little."

Barlog was no help at all. Marika pulled, balanced the huntress upon her shoulder. For a moment she became conscious of the long plunge that awaited her slightest misstep, froze. Never before had she been particularly cognizant of the danger of falling. She turned carefully, gestured the bath to duck, eased past. "Come on, Grauel."

Grauel, too, was conscious of the emptiness beneath the darkship. She was slow about boarding and slower crossing to the axis. Marika had Barlog strapped down by the time she arrived. "Strap up fast," Marika said. "Mistress! Take us up! Go high and head toward Ruhaack."

Marika became aware that she was being observed from a darkship poised just beyond the boundary of the cloister. Kiljar. She waved, pointed. Kiljar's darkship rose.

The clock in Marika's mind told her the tradermale lifters would have reached *Starstalker*. She touched Kiljar. *I am going to the Ruhaack cloister. With any luck those left behind may be cooperative.*

Do not forget Bestrei.

How can I? Would you care to bet that she was not aboard the first voidship up?

Behind them, above the city, darkships swarmed like insects on a warm morning. Touches of panic fluttered the otherworld. There had been collisions and deaths by falling.

Marika reached, touched every sister she could, told them to get higher, to get away from the city.

She felt for the sky, for the Serke voidships, and to her surprise she found them. They were clustered, more than a dozen of them, and they were much higher than she could rise in pursuit. They were on the edge of the void and hurrying outward.

Marika felt *Starstalker* rise from behind the rim of the world. There was a deadly feel to the voidship, as though it had metamorphosed into something terrible. It radiated a threatening darkness. It climbed the sky rapidly.

It lost its deadly aura as it approached zenith, as Marika hurried to TelleRai's southwest, toward Ruhaack. That modest city, where the Serke made their headquarters, lay a hundred miles away. Its supporting satellites brushed those of greater TelleRai.

Why did *Starstalker* seem less black? Marika opened to the All. There! The deadliness remained, but it had separated from the voidship.

Kiljar. They have sent something down against us.

That something came down fast. Very fast. Streaks of fire burned the upper sky and backlighted the clouds. Thunder hammered the air.

They were forty miles from TelleRai when the first sword of fire smote the world.

The first flash blinded Marika momentarily. There were more flashes. A grisly globe of fire rolled upward above the city. Shuddering, fur bristling, Marika felt the thundering wind, the first shock wave raging toward her.

Another great flash illuminated the mushroom cloud.

The Mistress of the Ship lost control. The darkship twisted toward the ground.

CEREMONY

BOOK FIVE: METAL SUNS

CHAPTER TWENTY-NINE

I

Marika reached with the touch. *Mistress! Get hold of yourself!*

Her vision cleared. A quarter mile to her left Kiljar's darkship fluttered downward, too, but it stabilized soon after she spied it.

Marika felt Kiljar's touch. The Redoriad second sent, *What has happened?*

I do not know. The strange weapons you mentioned?

Marika looked back to the city so recently and hastily fled. A grisly glow backlighted the snowclouds. The world within, the ghost world of the touch and dark, was filled with terror and pain, unfocused, diffuse, yet centered upon dying TelleRai.

Marika sent, *What should we do, Kiljar?*

Go on. We must go on to Ruhaack. Already the touch tells me there is nothing we can do back there.

How bad is it?

Worse than you can imagine. How did you know?

I just felt something bad coming. Premonition. Silth set great store by intuition. *Not even that much when we started. I just knew we had to get away from the city. Then when Starstalker rose above the horizon I knew something terrible would happen. And it is not over yet. I feel a great hot wind coming.*

The Serke will pay for this.

The Serke did not do this, mistress.

They made it possible. It will be impossible to assemble a true convention now, for a while. Perhaps it is best that way. At the moment you could demand and receive anything.

What happened? Marika demanded again.

Kiljar sent a mental picture of what she imagined TelleRai must look like now, with the fires raging and the mushroom clouds rising. Marika pushed it away, unwilling to believe the disaster she had predicted.

Her Mistress of the Ship appealed for her attention. *Mistress? Coming up on Ruhaack.*

Go carefully. She shifted touch back to Kiljar. *What do you think? Do you sense any perils ahead? I do not.*

I sense emptiness within the Serke cloister. I sense death. I do not believe what I sense. No Community has committed kalerhag in centuries.

Kalerhag. Ritual suicide. The Ceremony. The ultimate silth ritual. The one that, at one time, had ended most silth lives.

In the packs of the wild, like that of Marika's puphood, the very old were put out of the packstead in hard times, after the less useful males and pups. In the sisterhoods of old the aged had retired themselves through kalerhag. And any sister had done so when she felt honor demanded it.

The two darkships moved in on the Serke cloister, losing altitude, slowing, watching it belch smoke that rolled up into the clouds, reminding Marika of Maksche aflame after the perfidious brethren attack there.

No sisterhood has committed kalerhag here, Kiljar sent, correcting herself, more distressed. *They took some with them and left the others poisoned.*

Marika instructed her Mistress of the Ship to drop lower still, to approach the Serke Ruhaack cloister below the worst of the heat. Inrushing air tugged at her clothing.

It is safe, Kiljar sent. *Set down.*

Marika had her darkship taken to ground. She stepped off. Her voctor, Grauel, stepped down beside her and stared at the cloister in awe. "What happened, Marika?"

"Kiljar says they poisoned everyone they could not take with them. I suppose the fires were meant to destroy evidence."

"Evidence? Of what?"

The earth beneath their feet was trembling, groaning, carrying news of the destruction of TelleRai.

"Who knows? Let's see what we can find."

As Marika unslung her rifle the hot wind from TelleRai overtook them. Most of its force had been spent, but still it was enough to stagger them. Marika regained her balance. She looked toward TelleRai. "That they could do such a thing," she snarled into the wind. Then, to her Mistress of the Ship, "Stay here. Remain prepared to lift off."

The Ruhaack Serke cloister stood at the heart of the city Ruhaack, surrounded by a broad belt of green. That belt was filling with meth. Marika considered the creatures, Serke bonds all. She felt no danger there. They were nothing more than bonds.

Kiljar left her own darkship and joined Marika. "You intend to go inside?"

"If I can." The cloister gate stood sealed. She ducked through her loophole, caught a small ghost attracted by the disaster, and used it to demolish the gate.

Grauel went in first, behind a short warning burst from her rifle.

There was no one to resist them, silth, voctor, or bond. They found most of the Serke still in their cells, apparently resting peacefully. The stench of death filled the place. Marika could not long stand the sight of dead novices bloating in the heat. She asked Kiljar, "Do you think they did this at all their cloisters? Or just here?"

"Probably just here. This was the beast's head."

"Why, Kiljar?" she asked as they retreated through the gate. "Why would they do such a thing?"

"I suspect to sever all ties that might allow us to trace them."

"But…"

"They are running. All the guilty of the Serke and the brethren. Together. I expect to the world where they found their aliens. I doubt that the Serke wanted to do it this way. They are not as wicked as we have painted them. Imagine the pain they will carry with them into exile. It would not surprise me to learn they had turned on the brethren. Bestrei is simple. She has her concepts of honor. She will demand that a price be paid. When we find them…"

"Find them?" Marika asked.

"You know we will. Someday. I have not seen TelleRai, but I have sensed it. What was done there cannot be forgiven. Ever. The voidpaths will be filled with silth on the hunt."

"And that explains this, I suppose. The brethren strike on TelleRai compelled the guilty Serke to burn their bridges in kalerhag."

"Exactly. There is nothing we can accomplish here. I suggest we return to TelleRai. We must join the bonds in Mourning. There will be time to worry about settling scores later."

Despite her own cold-blooded excesses against the base and rogue males the rebel brethren had used to attack and destroy her cloister in Maksche, Marika was sickened by what she saw in TelleRai. Broad patches of glassy, glowing desert had replaced miles of once proud and beautiful cloisters-including that of her own Community, the Reugge.

Six of the gruesome weapons, whatever they were, had come down upon the great city. One had fallen upon the convention ground where Marika and Kiljar had thought to disarm the villains forever. It had destroyed the highest sisters of scores of Communities. Others had fallen upon the Reugge cloister and the Redoriad. A fourth had fallen upon the Tovand, the headquarters of the brethren. The remaining two weapons seemed to have fallen where they would.

Touch brought the news that the brethren rebel facility in the Cupple Islands had been vaporized too. Another cutting off of backtrails.

Voidships from several dark-faring Communities had lifted in pursuit of the Serke already, but they would not reach orbital altitude in time. Already the great Serke-brethren voidship *Starstalker* and her convoy of darkships were departing into the great night between the suns.

Kiljar predicted, "We will hear from them again if we do not find and neutralize them first."

Marika did not believe that required any prophetic vision. "I insist on being trained to walk the void. I want to be there when they are found."

"It shall be as you wish."

A cold wind blew out of the north, bringing with it snow that melted as it approached the still-hot craters. The winter of the world was a slower enemy, but the fate it bore was as certain. The great glaciers were on the move. Nothing could withstand them.

Nothing? Marika reflected. That was not true. Now she was in a position to do something about the ice age. At last.

II

As years trickled into the well of time it seemed to Marika that her homeworld, and the meth who populated it, drifted backward into their own history, into an era of peace unlike any known since the system had entered the interstellar dust cloud responsible for the cooling cycle. The bonds of brethren who survived the terror after the destruction of TelleRai became extremely conservative and accommodating. They surrendered much of the power they had gained in recent generations and hunted out the heretics among themselves. The vestiges of the Serke Community were absorbed by sisterhoods with claims or were allowed kalerhag. Serke properties became reparations paid to Communities hurt at TelleRai.

The Reugge, with a prior and stronger claim, took the biggest bites. Marika successfully argued her right to claim Serke starworlds for the Reugge, though few of the established dark-faring orders were pleased. Only a tiny fraction of what the Serke had held off-planet, a mere token, those holdings nevertheless legitimized the Reugge as starfarers.

In the early going, while she was trying to take possession of the new holdings, Marika had to borrow voidships and crews from friendly sisterhoods. She had to borrow again in order to properly exploit the new far territories.

"Grauel, alert the darkship crew," Marika said.

The huntress asked, "Where to now, Marika? How much longer must we live paw to mouth, upon the charity of other sisterhoods?"

"Not long. Not long at all. Where is Barlog? Is she recovered enough to make a journey with us?"

"Try to leave her behind. Where are we going, anyway?"

"To visit Bagnel."

"*Oh.*"

"Don't take that tone. I am indifferent to Kublin."

"I do not want to call you a liar, Marika. I do understand. Somewhat. I would have difficulty dealing with a littermate myself. Yet he was at the very root of the crimes, one of the chief criminals."

"He will remain where he is. The rest of his natural life."

Grauel held her tongue, but it was obvious she did not find the risk of leaving him alive acceptable. Marika let the argument alone. As strength goes. She was most senior of the Reugge. Her word was law. That was enough.

The three bath reported immediately. The Mistress of the Ship delayed a few minutes. Marika was irked by the delay, but said nothing. Mistresses of the Ship were that way, even when they served a most senior. They felt compelled to assert themselves.

She was tempted, briefly, to take the command position herself. She did not get to fly as much as she liked now that she was trying to drag an entire Community out of the despair brought on by the destruction of TelleRai.

The darkship dropped into the landing court of a packfast hidden far to the north, in territories all other meth believed had been abandoned to the ice. Senior Edzeka came out to meet Marika. She did not have much to say. Just another example of the widespread emotional paralysis Marika encountered everywhere.

"How may we serve you?" Senior Edzeka asked, and when Marika told her she wanted to see her friend, the tradermale Bagnel, the senior assigned her a guide and disappeared.

Following Marika's instructions, Bagnel had been treated as an honored guest. "Really more an honored prisoner," he said. "But I should complain? If I hadn't been here I'd probably be among the dead."

"They have kept you posted on the news?" Marika asked.

"Those two arfts still shadow you, I see," Bagnel said, nodding toward Grauel and Barlog. "Yes. It was a form of taunting, I suspect. They were certain whatever favor I enjoyed would be withdrawn." The male looked haggard for a moment, betraying the fact that he feared *that* might be why Marika had come.

"I have come to bring you out of hiding, to send you back to the brethren. Those who destroyed your bond, and Maksche and TelleRai are dead, scattered, or on the run. The brethren need new leaders—rational and reasonable leaders."

"I would be no puppet."

"We have been friends long enough for me to know that, Bagnel. If you pretended to be I would become more suspicious of you than I normally am."

"Of me?"

"Of course. You are brethren. I am silth. There is no way our interests will ever approach identity. But we can live together amicably. We have done before."

Bagnel looked at Grauel and Barlog for a moment. Marika had the distinct feeling that, more than ever, he wished her two old packmates elsewhere.

"So," he said. "Tell me Marika's plans. I hear you are most senior of the Reugge now."

"A temporary inconvenience. I will shed the mantle as soon as I can. I have another destiny. Out there." She pointed skyward. "My dream." She had shared her dream of the stars with no one but Grauel, Barlog, Bagnel, and a few meth whose goodwill would be critical in achieving it. Only the named three knew how much an obsession the stars were.

"I see."

"I have made certain arrangements on your behalf. Wherever you go when you return to the brethren, a small number of aircraft will remain available. The arguments were bitter, and I had to lie to convince some members of the convention, but the fact is, they're there for you. Because I know what my life would be like if I could no longer fly."

Bagnel bowed his head and said nothing for a long time. Then, "I am sure they have said terrible things about you, Marika. After what you did at the base at… But they do not know you. Thank you."

"I remember my friends as well as my enemies. The sisters here have instructions to see you prepared for the journey. I have a few things to do here before we depart. I hope you do not mind traveling blindfold."

Bagnel snorted. "I expected nothing else. This place, with its secret manufactories, would be too precious to you for you to do otherwise."

Marika shrugged. "Darkships are too precious to we silth to allow control of production or distribution to rest in outside paws. Were it not for this place the Reugge would have none left but mine after the battles in the Ponath and the destruction of Maksche and TelleRai.

"I will see you later. We will fly together again, as we did when we were innocent."

Marika was barely out of Bagnel's hearing when Barlog remarked, "You told Grauel you were no longer interested in Kublin's fate."

"I said nothing of the sort. I am no longer interested in making special dispensations for him, but he is still my littermate, even though he turned rogue. He is still the meth who was closest and dearest to me during my puphood years. Those days cannot be regained, but they need not be discarded."

The two huntresses exchanged glances. Marika knew they were thinking they would never understand her. To them she must seem an incongruous and incompatible mixture of sentimentalism and deadly cold ambition, too often subject to masculine weaknesses.

They would never understand. For all they wore the dress of Reugge voctors of the leading rank and were accustomed to the technological and social marvels of the south, at heart they remained neolithic huntresses with a very primitive black-and-white view of the world's workings. Mostly they did not try to reconcile their beliefs with what they saw. They followed orders, often with sullenly silent or formal disapproval, and held themselves aloof from their effete and decadent surroundings and associates.

Their disapproval was graven on their faces, but neither said another word as Marika stalked into the packfast's signal intercept section.

Kublin was imprisoned there, compelled to translate brethren cant and coded messages Reugge technicians stole from the satellite network. "He is as isolated as if he had been sent to rejoin the All," Marika said. "And this way his blood is not on my conscience. Not to mention that we get some use out of him."

Grauel and Barlog did not speak to arguments they considered weak excuses. Blood meant little or nothing to a Ponath female dealing with males.

Kublin was at work when Marika arrived. She stood out of the way of the small team on duty, and signaled the supervisor to continue as though she were not there. She watched Kublin.

He did what he was supposed to do, no faster than he had to. He looked much older than he had when she had captured him. When she mentioned that to Grauel, the huntress remarked, "You look much older too. And you two look very much alike. Persons who did not know you nevertheless would suspect you were littermates."

The discussion, though whispered, caught Kublin's attention and he noticed Marika for the first time. Their gazes met. He betrayed no expression whatsoever.

Marika did not try to speak to him. There was nothing to say anymore. After a few minutes she left and collected Bagnel, and returned to warmer southern climes and the business of righting a Community decimated by the attack upon TelleRai.

III

The initial fury of the hunt for the fugitive Serke and brethren faded, but the search never ceased entirely. Nor did it enjoy any success. The villains had vanished as though they had never been, and surviving members of the Serke Community could provide no hints as to where they had gone.

Contrary to her announced intentions, Marika did not immediately step down as most senior of the Reugge Community. She claimed that was because there was no one qualified to replace her. All the Reugge ruling council excepting herself had been in TelleRai when death fell from the sky. So she remained on till she was confident that the order was no longer in disarray, by which she meant till it was made over to her own specifications. She sorted through the ruling councils of the surviving cloisters, identifying and elevating sisters whose philosophies mirrored her own.

In time she did yield first chair, to a silth named Bel-Keneke. Bel-Keneke hailed from a frontier province as remote as the Ponath. Her attitudes were very much like Marika's, though she was nowhere near as strong in the talents.

Marika collected Grauel and Barlog and retreated to the secret darkship factory in the snow wastes, there to continue interrupted studies and to pursue her slightly paranoid watch on signals traffic.

At first Marika came out of hiding regularly, to study with Kiljar, to fly with Bagnel, as had been their custom for years, except when broader events interrupted them. She learned to handle a voidship with the best of the starfaring

Mistresses of the Ship, though she never actually pursued her dream and traveled to any of the starworlds. She did not, in fact, go much beyond the orbits of the two larger moons, Biter and Chaser.

Once she had become proficient with the voidships her ventures out of isolation became even more infrequent, then not at all.

She fell out of the public eye for nearly three years.

The permanent snowline crept southward steadily till it reached the remains of TelleRai. The land of Marika's birth lay buried beneath a hundred feet of ice and snow. The ruins of Maksche were little more than lines beneath a cloak of white.

Hunger stalked the world for all the effort of the silth to care for their bonds, for all the abnormal cooperation that developed between disaster-besieged sisterhoods. Too many meth were being compressed into too little territory.

The population of the meth homeworld had never been large, but neither was much of its surface developed agriculturally. Development efforts started after the destruction of TelleRai were too little, too late. Land could not be brought into production quickly enough to support the shifting populace.

Marika watched from isolation. In time she lost patience with the efforts of others.

"Grauel, send word up to have my darkship prepared. Find Barlog. Arm yourselves."

Surprised, Grauel asked, "What are we doing, Marika?"

"We're going out. It is time I stopped waiting for others to do something. No one seems inclined to act."

"Really?" It had been three years since Grauel had been out of the fortress, which Marika had renamed Skiljansrode in honor of her dam, and which she had made over into an independent packfast populated by refugees, fugitives, and malcontents from a dozen sisterhoods. Viewed from a traditional silth perspective, Skiljansrode could be considered the germ of a new Community.

Marika never thought of breaking away from the Reugge.

Other silth contemptuously called those of Skiljansrode the brother-sisters because they worked with their paws. The principal product of the fortress remained darkships, but other, more technical items went out as well, increasingly in competition with the brethren. Most of the meth at Skiljansrode were curiosities like Marika herself, little interested in the fashions and forms of silthdom.

"Really, Grauel. Really. Have Kloreb message the cloister at Ruhaack that we'll be coming. I will want our quarters warmed. I will want a précis of the current political climate prepared. And I will want Kiljar of the Redoriad told that I will be in Ruhaack and that I would like an audience."

"Is something afoot, Marika?"

"In a sense. It's time we tried to do something about reversing the winter of the world."

Grauel looked at her long and hard. Finally she said, "Not even you have the witchcraft to make the sun burn hotter."

"No, but there are ways. What do you think I have been working on all this time? It can be done. I think the brethren knew that in the old days. Had they won, they might have taken steps. I suspect many of them know what to do even now, but they allow the long winter to go on because it weakens us."

"I believe you when you say... It's just..."

"Just?"

"I haven't been out of here for so long. I find I am very uncomfortable when you talk about going."

"I'm uncomfortable too, Grauel. And that is a sign that we have sat still too long. We have allowed ourselves to become sedentary. We have become like our dams. We have reverted to being the pack meth we once were. I think we're overdue to reenter the active world."

"Shall I have Bagnel messaged as well?"

"That can wait till after we reach Ruhaack."

In the past three years Bagnel had risen high among the brethren. Marika found she was excited about seeing him again. More excited than she was by any other prospect, including the possibility that she would mount a voidship again, and this time maybe actually fly off in pursuit of her dreams. After, of course, she had won the struggle to get a program started to reverse the long winter.

How many more years might that take?

She knew the exact cause of her excitement. She examined it with sardonic self-mockery.

Toghar ceremonies or not, she was female. And she was into a female's prime pupbearing years. Some hormones were produced despite Toghar.

"Not a distraction I need," she murmured to herself. There were silth who assuaged that natural need, who enjoyed a sort of false estrus, using male bonds. Marika refused. She considered that degraded, despicable, even perverted. She forced the need out of mind.

"Go on, Grauel."

She paced after the huntress departed, concerned that she had been gone from the world too long, that it might have passed her by during her three-year sabbatical.

CHAPTER THIRTY

I

Ruhaack had become the site of the new dam cloisters of several Communities bombed out of TelleRai. The city was a welter of construction. TelleRai itself had been abandoned. It was no longer healthy.

The Reugge had been awarded possession of the former Serke cloister. The reconstruction and refurbishing begun during Marika's administration were finished. The Reugge Community was back to business as usual—as much as it could be.

The Redoriad were building their new main cloister in one of Ruhaack's satellites. Construction was far advanced from what it had been at the time of Marika's last visit.

Though Marika had departed the immediate equation, the two orders remained closely allied. For a time, soon after the bombs, there had been talk of a merger. The main talkers had been Marika's enemies, who wished to keep her from taking control. Nothing had come of it. Marika's supporters and other conservatives within both Communities had scuttled the proposal.

The same conservatives supported the alliance, though. It had proved of great benefit to both orders. The Reugge, particularly, were now considered a force to be reckoned with in everything.

Marika nervously stalked around a hastily prepared apartment. Kiljar, now most senior of the Redoriad, was coming to see her. She felt like a pup again, as unsure of herself as she had been when first she had arrived at Akard.

"I shouldn't have locked myself up in Skiljansrode," she told Barlog. "Not so thoroughly. I've lost something."

Grauel entered. She looked sour. "Bagnel the tradermale is here, Marika." Which explained that. Grauel never had approved of Bagnel. "And the Redoriad say that mistress Kiljar has departed the Redoriad cloister."

"Good. Good. What of Bel-Keneke?"

"She will be here soon, I think more out of curiosity than because you implied that you were about to call in her debt to you."

"Fine."

Both huntresses considered her. She continued to pace.

"I spent too long in the safety and nonpressure of Skiljansrode," she explained again. "I have lost my edge. I am not comfortable being Marika. The weapons... I feel almost silly carrying them. But they were our sigil. Going around armed, making dramatic gestures. We are too old. I'm almost ready to become one of the Wise."

Grauel snorted. "Maybe in another twenty years. You're still hardly more than a pup." She spoke thus in defense of herself. She was much older than Marika, but she was not ready to lay down her huntress's role.

Barlog said, "I think I understand, Marika. When I am out in the cloister I too get the feeling that the world has left me behind."

Grauel agreed. "I encountered young voctors who didn't know who we are. Or were, perhaps I should say. Not that we were ever that famous. But there was a time when our being Marika's bodyguards meant a lot more than it does now."

"It slips away," Marika said.

"It hasn't been that long, Marika."

Bagnel arrived first. A group of baffled novices delivered him to Marika's door. A male in the cloister? Impossible. They were scandalized. They had heard stories about the bizarre doings of this silth called Marika, but had not believed them before this.

Marika was amused.

"Well," Bagnel said as the door closed behind him. "The living legend herself. Where have you been, Marika? We agreed to fly together at least once a month. One day there wasn't any more Marika. No message. No excuse. No apology. Nothing for years. Then out of nowhere a typically peremptory summons. And here I am, though I should have requited indifference with indifference."

It took Marika a moment to realize he was teasing, that he was glad to see her. "You're looking a little gray around the fringes, Bagnel."

"I have not had the privilege of taking an extended sabbatical. My brethren would gray the fur of a statue." He looked troubled.

"What is it?"

He glanced at Grauel and Barlog, as always disturbed by their presence. "Are they immortal?"

"They are as safe as ever, my friend. The Redoriad will join us presently, though I do not expect her immediately. Most Senior Bel-Keneke will wait till Kiljar has arrived before she makes her own entrance." She did not add that the room itself was safe, for she, Grauel, and Barlog had made independent sweeps in search of the sort of listening devices Marika herself had once used habitually.

"Nothing really remarkable. Just the persistent element that wishes the sisterhoods ill. It has been growing stronger recently. Nothing to be concerned about, mind you. Just aggravation enough to keep me on edge."

Marika considered him closely. "There's more than that, isn't there?"

"You read me better than ever. Yes. I have found evidence that those who fled have not broken entirely their ties to their homeworld. Evidence that they are in contact with those who are driving me gray."

"What?" A tendril of fright touched Marika. "How can that be?"

"It is easy enough. It is not difficult at all to slip a darkship through to the surface, to some remote rendezvous. Especially when I have no advance warning."

"Then it isn't over."

"It never was. You knew that. The Serke just fled to a safe place. I suspect their overall goals had to change somewhat once they were driven off the homeworld, simply by force of circumstance, but there was no reason for them to give up trying to seize control of everything."

Marika paced, mused, wondered that the Serke had gotten so entangled in a brethren scheme that they had allowed themselves to become the tools of their own destruction.

Bagnel added, "Unfortunately, nobody takes the threat seriously anymore. They have been quiet, so are forgotten. Nobody even hunts them now, except as a convenient side flight on a trip to the starworlds. But if they were hiding anywhere convenient they would have been found already."

"They aren't strong enough to try a comeback," Marika said. "Even with help from their supposed aliens."

"You think not?"

"If they were, they would have tried. Right? They have not. Therefore they are not."

"Irrefutable logic."

"Smart, Bagnel. I suspect they have no support from any alien—if one even exists. If one does, that relationship must be less intimate than we once thought. In my reflections I have begun to suspect that they may have no direct contact at all."

Bagnel looked startled.

"Yes?" Marika asked.

"You continue to amaze me."

"How have I managed that now?"

"You just struck close to the picture we have developed by questioning prisoners and others who may be in the know one way or another. What seems to have happened is that they did make a contact, but they could not deal with the alien because the alien *was* alien—though from other things we have learned they don't *seem* that alien. If you are following this."

"I'm trying."

"Apparently being unable to deal with the alien, they stole, possibly by killing the alien and appropriating everything that belonged to them. So it's possible they're hiding from the alien race too."

"If you are going to go rogue, why do it halfway?" Grauel asked. "Marika, mistress Kiljar is about to arrive. I hear the novices shuffling in the hallway."

"We'll talk more later, Bagnel. I'm happy to see you have become so important among the brethren. I cannot think of anyone more deserving."

Bagnel snorted derisively.

II

Kiljar, too, had aged, but she had been old when Marika had seen her last. Marika was shocked by what time had done to the Redoriad. Kiljar had lost large patches of fur, and what remained was mostly gray or white. She had lost a lot of weight, too, and begun to stoop, but her eyes remained brightly intelligent.

More than age, long-term ill health had diminished the Redoriad most senior. She had to walk with the aid of a cane. One side of her body was partially paralyzed. She responded to Marika's horrified glance with a lopsided expression of amusement. "A stroke," she explained, slurring her words. "Weakened the flesh but did nothing to the mind. I am recovering slowly."

"Could the healer sisters not...?"

"They assure me there is nothing more they can do without killing me. That seems too heroic a measure to effect a cure."

"At least you have been able to take it in good part."

"The hell I have. I resent it. It angers me so much I go into howling rages against the All. They think me quite mad at the Redoriad cloister. But none have yet found the courage to try ousting me from first chair. They think I am dying anyway. They spend their time trying to outmaneuver one another so as to stand at the head of the pack when I go. But I am going to disappoint them. I am going to outlive them all. You look good, Marika. I suspect that a few years beyond the edge of the world were just what you needed. You seem less driven, less saddled by doom."

Marika looked at her sharply, surprised that Kiljar read her so easily.

She suspected one unconscious reason she had isolated herself was because of self-doubt, an inclination, following the destruction of TelleRai, to credit those sisters who called her Jiana and doomstalker. Four sequential destructions of the place she called home, with those who dwelt there, was enough to make anyone ask questions.

"The most senior is approaching, Marika," Barlog said from the doorway.

"Leave it open. Sit somewhere." Barlog still had difficulty getting around, all these years after recovering from the wounds she had suffered at Maksche.

We have all been injured and left crippled, Marika thought. In the heart if not in the flesh.

Bel-Keneke arrived. Marika reached back in time to find greetings appropriate to a most senior of the Reugge. There had been no formalities, no ceremonials, no obsequies, observed at Skiljansrode. Marika held them in contempt because she considered most of them unearned.

Bel-Keneke, too, had changed, though now she seemed more secure in her role than when last Marika had seen her. "You can dispense with the ceremonials, Marika. I know they do not come from the heart. You are looking well." She ignored Bagnel and merely nodded to Kiljar. "You should be seen here more, Marika. There are times when we could use your slant on the world."

"I will be seen more," Marika said. "That is why I have come back."

"Direct as always. So. We are all here. Let us get to it. Tell us about the grand project you want to attempt."

Marika prowled while Bel-Keneke seated herself. Barlog, in the background, in her customary array of weapons, looked increasingly uncomfortable. Marika gestured for her to sit, as she had directed earlier.

She did not sit herself. She could not. She was about to broach the result of many years of thought and felt shy about doing so. It was not the usual sort of Marika idea, full of fire and blood and doom for enemies of the Reugge. She was afraid for its reception.

She moved to the center of the room and stood there with her guests watching from three directions. She ordered her thoughts, ran through calming mental exercises. Finally she attacked it. "I have an idea for stemming the snow and cold."

"What?" That was Bel-Keneke, who was least accustomed to Marika's ways. But the others looked at her askance.

"A major engineering project that might allow us to turn back the ice."

"Major?" Bagnel murmured. "You have a gift for understatement, Marika."

Kiljar said, "If you managed that you would be immortalized with…"

"It is not possible," Bel-Keneke said. "You are talking about halting a process of such a magnitude that…"

Bagnel added, "Perhaps we ought to hear her idea before we tell her it is impossible."

Marika gave him a nod of gratitude. "Excuse me, mistresses. I know it would be a large project and extremely difficult, but it is not impossible—except perhaps in that it presumes the cooperation of all the Communities and all the brethren bonds, working toward one end. Achieving that will be more difficult than the actual engineering and construction."

"Go on," Kiljar said before Bel-Keneke could interject negative comments.

"Review: The problem is that insufficient solar energy penetrates the dust and falls upon the planet. The solution—my solution—is to increase incident radiation."

"Do you plan to sweep the dust up?" Bel-Keneke asked. "Or to stoke the fires of the sun?"

"Not at all."

"Why so negative, sister?" Kiljar asked. "Do you feel threatened because your predecessor has come out of hiding?"

Marika ignored the sparks. Those two old arfts never had had much use for one another. She said, "We collect solar energies that are flinging off into the void and redirect them toward the planet. We do that by constructing large mirrors."

"Large mirrors," Bagnel said.

"*Very* large. Wait. I admit there will be difficulties. The orbital mechanics of our situation, because of the presence of so many moons, will make maintaining stable orbits for the mirrors difficult. But I have been studying this matter for some time. It is not impractical. If we can install the largest mirrors in the planet's leading and trailing solar trojan points and keep them stable..."

"Pardon me," Bagnel interrupted. "The idea is not original, Marika."

"I did not think it was. I assumed the brethren had thought of it long ago and had not brought it up because it was in their interest to have the weather help destabilize the social structure. It was no coincidence that the inclination to rebellion grew stronger as the cold crept down. I believe the factors behind the planning failed only because they got overeager."

"You are, perhaps, half right. In such an engineering program the brethren would have required the same level of cooperation you already mentioned. We would not have gotten it. There is, too, the sheer magnitude of the thing. I have heard that the necessary mirrors would have to be thousands of miles across. If you mean installing them in the trojan points where the sun's gravity and the world's balance, rather than in the lunar trojans, they would have to be almost unimaginably huge to reflect enough energy to make a difference."

"Those are the points I mean, as I said. The main mirrors would require less stabilization there. But, as you say, they would have to be more huge than anything any meth has imagined. I picture them on the order of five thousand miles in diameter."

"I fear you underestimate considerably."

"Utterly impossible," Bel-Keneke said.

"Let her talk, sister," Kiljar countered. "Marika is no fool. She would not have brought this up had she not worked most of it out already. If she says it can be done, then she has done enough calculation to convince herself."

"Thank you, Kiljar. Yes. The idea first occurred to me while I was still a novice, many years ago. There were too many other demands on my attention then, so I did not pursue it. Later, when I retreated to Skiljansrode, I did have the time. It is the major reason I have remained out of touch so long. I will admit that I have not done all the calculations necessary. The orbitals require calculations all but impossible with pencil and paper. But the brethren once developed a system for rapid calculation, else they could not have orbited their satellites. I am hoping that the system, or at least the knowledge to replace it, survived the bombing of the Cupple Islands. That system, skilled labor, the metals, technology, and such would be required of the brethren. The Communities will have to lift the materials into the void—and contribute the talent where necessary. Skiljansrode will provide the reflecting material."

"A grand stumbling block in the scheme as the brethren worked it out," Bagnel said.

"As I see it, we would need a web of titanium metal-work—or possibly one of golden fleet wood if that proves either impractical or the titanium cannot be produced in sufficient quantities—supporting an aluminized plastic surface no thicker than a hair."

"It's a possibility," Bagnel said. "I am amused by the notion of wooden satellites. But that is neither here nor there. Discounting for the moment all the other problems, where do we get this plastic? The same notion occurred to those who toyed with this among the brethren. They were unable to produce such a plastic and were reduced to thinking in terms of a heavy aluminum foil that proved too brittle in actual trials. The breakage ran better than fifty percent."

"We have developed the plastic already. You will be amused to learn that it is a petroleum derivative. I felt I had to have that before I broached the larger idea."

Bagnel began to look truly interested, not just speculative.

"Two main reflectors, as I said, to provide a steady, gross energy incidence. Then smaller ones, in geocentric orbit—and lunar trojan orbit—with which we can fine-tune the amount of energy delivered. With which we can deliver extra energy to specific localities. For instance, to keep threatened crop lands in production. We will want more energy in the beginning, anyway, to initiate the thaw cycle."

"It is crazy," Bel-Keneke said. "You have gone mad in isolation."

"It's not impossible at all," Bagnel countered, now so intrigued he forgot to use the formal mode. He got up and started pacing and muttering to himself.

"Do you really believe in this, Marika?" Kiljar asked. "Have you convinced yourself that, despite the obvious problems, it can actually be done?"

"My conviction is absolute, mistress. I have yet to find an insuperable barrier, though there were more problems than I at first expected. Yes, it can be done—if the Communities and the brethren are willing to invest the resources and the energies."

Bagnel's pacing took him to a window. He stared out at the frigid world. The most seniors watched him uneasily. "You have done it again, haven't you, Marika?"

"Done what, Bagnel?"

"You have overturned everything. And bigger than ever before. No wonder you had to take a few years off. You needed that long to wake the earthquake."

"What are you talking about?"

"Three meth are going to leave this room with your notion fixed in their minds. All three are going to find some reason to consult others about it. Those others will tell others. The news will spread. In time it will have reached those for whom it will represent an almost religious opportunity for salvation. It will become impossible for us, brethren and Communities alike, to do anything but attempt it, even if it proves impossible. For the alternative will be destruction at the paws of outraged bonds who will believe themselves betrayed."

"What are you talking about?"

"I am saying you have let a devil loose. That you proposed this with no thought for the social implications. I am saying that you have made undertaking the project mandatory simply by stating that you believe it is feasible. I am saying that such a project will reshape society as well as weather. I ask you to think about what you are asking."

Taken aback by his vehemence, Marika said, "Tell me."

"You are asking that the brethren be restored to grace. You are asking two dozen dark-faring Communities to join forces in one grand project instead of flying off in all directions, spending half their energies sabotaging and one-up-ping each other. You are proposing a project of such vast magnitude that bond meth will have to be given technical training because the brethren available to do the work are not numerous enough. You are letting devils out. Those are things I foresee just off the top of my head. More thought would produce more, surely. And the project is bound to have repercussions that cannot be foreseen at all—some just because of its scale. Did none of this occur to you?"

"No. I was not concerned with anything but the practical considerations." Marika took a turn at the window and thought of Jiana the doomstalker, reflecting on the fact that destruction need not be physical, as it had been with the Degnan packstead, Akard, Maksche, and TelleRai. She turned. "You really think so?"

"Yes."

"Given that, do you think it would be worth the effort?"

"Actually, I do. Because the alternative is a longer, slower, more certain doom. This cooling cycle is going to continue till the whole planet becomes too cold to support life. The permafrost line is within three thousand miles of the equator today. It shows no inclination to slow its advance, though I am sure it will in time—after it is too late for us. I suspect that we dare not waste many more years or for the meth it will be too late for anything but awaiting the end. Which will not come in our time, of course. But it will come."

Marika looked at Bel-Keneke and Kiljar. "Mistresses?"

Kiljar said, "I approve pushing ahead. Tentatively. Trusting your judgment, Marika, and that of your friend. I will want to see more solid data before I approach my Community with the proclamation that this project is the only way we can save our world."

"I understand. Bel-Keneke?"

"You are outside my expertise. You know that. All I know about the void is that it is cold and dark out there. I do very much share the male's social fears. I foresee great troubles and terrible changes. But I am in your debt, and I respect the opinion of mistress Kiljar. If you can convince her, I will follow her lead and back you."

Marika walked back to the window and stared out at the chill landscape. Once Ruhaack had been warm and lush. Now it was barren, except where meth had planted vegetation adapted to a near arctic climate. After a moment she turned.

"Bagnel may be right, about the social upheaval. I plead guilty to failing to consider that aspect. But we are in a corner from which there is no escape. There is no future without trying. If the race is to survive, we must pay the price."

She was amazed that the most seniors were so agreeable. Perhaps the world had grown more desperate than she knew.

"Bagnel, can the brethren provide the necessary calculators?"

"We call them computers. Yes, we have them. We may have to develop a breed designed specifically for the project, but that would not be an insurmountable problem. A matter of increasing capacity, I expect."

"What about the engineering? Do you have anyone capable of designing the mirrors?"

"That I cannot say, but I can find out. Given adequate time, I am sure, someone—more likely many someones—could be trained. I will find out and let you know."

"So that is that. We are agreed. We go ahead a step."

III

Marika gaped at Bagnel. "Eight years? Just to get the materials together?"

"It's a big project, Marika. I think that's too optimistic a figure, myself. It assumes total cooperation by all the Communities in providing the labor we'll need for getting the titanium out, building new plants to process the ore and metal, building new power plants to provide energy for those plants, and so on and so on and so on. I told you it would reshape society. And it *will*. My guess is that we'll be extremely fortunate to get even one mirror functional within ten years. There will be hitches, hang-ups, problems, delays, personality conflicts, bottlenecks, shortages…."

"I get the picture."

"The word is spreading already, just as I forecast. I keep running into brethren who know before I consult them, though I swear everyone to silence when I do consult them."

"We expected that. We chose to live with it."

"I have another scenario for you. In this one your old enemies get wind of the project. As inevitably they must."

"You think they would try to sabotage it?"

"I am certain they'll try. Wouldn't you? The cold is on their side."

"Then we must neutralize them."

"How, when no one has been able to find them?"

"No one has tried hard enough. A truly major effort…"

"There. You're talking about diverting energies from your project. Which means having to stretch it out a little."

Marika sighed. "Yes, I guess I am."

"You see? One thing affects another."

"We'll do what we have to. Are you ready to face Kiljar and Bel-Keneke? And beyond them, a convention of all the Communities?"

"I believe so."

"Good. Because Kiljar is failing and I believe that to have a chance the thing has to get rolling before she dies."

"Arrange for me to see her. I'll sell her."

"Just give her the truth. Let it argue for itself. You cannot mislead her. And she'll have to sell it to others on its provable merit."

"Of course. That's understood. Did you happen to notice that I flew down here in a Sting? We haven't flown together for a long time."

"I did notice that. And I was thinking of stealing you and it if you didn't come up with the suggestion yourself."

"This afternoon, then? After I have seen the most seniors?"

"Yes. Don't let them intimidate you. They may try, just to see what you're made of."

"Those old arfts? Not likely. Not when I have to deal with my factors and bond masters every day."

Bel-Keneke and Kiljar needed very little convincing. They had done their own investigating. "I am amazed," Kiljar admitted. "The response among the Communities has been almost messianic in intensity. They believe you are going to show them the pathway into a new age, Marika."

"It must be timing," Bagnel remarked. "Purely a matter of timing. Everyone is just frightened enough, just certain enough. Ten years ago no one would have taken the project seriously. Conservative elements would have killed it. But now the world is in desperate need of a hope, and this one fills the need. I find extremes of enthusiasm everywhere within the brethren. All the factors and masters, once they examined the data, showed uncharacteristic excitement. Even some who were very suspicious before. It has softened the appeal of the rogues tremendously. There have been almost no incidents at all this past month."

Bel-Keneke added, "I have consulted a number of senior sisters from a number of orders. My experience has been the same everywhere. Tremendous enthusiasm, discovering a hope where none was thought to exist, except in that the dark-faring sisterhoods might have established a few feeble colonies upon the starworlds. How long the enthusiasm will persist I cannot tell. Seldom has any meth devoted herself to a project for as long as this will require."

"There will be problems," Marika agreed. "The project will hurt some orders more than others. It will draw attention and energy away from the starworlds. None of those sisterhoods will be pleased by that. I do have a suggestion, though it may not prove popular."

"Yes?" Kiljar inquired.

"We could survey all the sisterhoods, including those without rights in the void. Then conscript every sister capable of serving aboard a darkship out there. We could even retrain some of the strongest bath as Mistresses for workships. We would then have to depend less heavily on those sisters normally preoccupied with the starworlds. Too, we will have to lift the ban on the brethren so they can participate as fully as possible. That is an absolute necessity. We will get nowhere without them because of the traditional silth resistance to becoming involved in physical labor. Also, ships of the sort that were associated with *Starstalker* before she vanished would be valuable if we could build them. That would ease our dependence upon a very small supply of void-capable Mistresses of the Ship."

Bagnel said, "We should be able to develop construction ships. I have suggested that it be given some thought. I doubt that anything we came up with would be as good as those rogue vessels, but because some saw them we know what has to be done. There are problems, though, Marika. Fuels. Energy. We're right down to it now, and you may not want to hear this. The fact is, one way or another, we have to tap the resources of the Ponath. It is going to take a tremendous amount of energy to produce the necessary titanium."

"You were going to look into the possibility of producing it in orbit, in solar-powered factories."

"I was and I did. There are no adequate titanium ores available anywhere in the system other than right here on the planet. I'm sorry. The girderwork will have to be produced down here and lifted into orbit."

Kiljar asked, "Who will manage all of this? Consider the politics. It will be an alliance of all the Communities and the brethren, and will represent and include most meth bonds. With that many interests, there is no hope of working in harmony for the time required. Many sisters will not tolerate taking orders from old enemies or from competitors in other orders. None will take directions from brethren, even where brethren are the competent experts. None will work with bonds as though they are equals."

"Setting this in motion will require a formal convention, as Senior Kiljar has said," Marika said. "Most of that will have to be fought out there. One possibility would be for the Communities to elect a most senior of most seniors for a fixed term and give her absolute powers and a group of judges to enforce them."

"The smaller sisterhoods would object strenuously," Kiljar said.

"Then, perhaps, a continuous convention in which grievances can be aired as they arise, given the understanding that work must go on uninterrupted."

Bagnel snorted derisively. "No, Marika. I see time stretching and stretching already. Nothing ever gets done while silth argue. The arguing has to be done before. During, there can be nothing but the project."

"Just how critical is the time frame?" Bel-Keneke asked. "Is there a time of no return? Of too late? We will be inside this dust cloud for millennia."

"I do not know exactly, mistress," Bagnel said. "One thing we will have to do is chart the density of the dust, just so we can estimate such things. I do know that we do not have millennia. Even now, tapping the petroleum in the Ponath will demand the creation of new engineering techniques. The longer we wait, the deeper the ice. And the greater the difficulties. Everywhere."

"No matter what we do there will be problems," Bel-Keneke mused. "No matter what else, then, we have to keep muddling ahead. An inch gained now may mean a foot saved later. Any progress will be better than none."

Kiljar said, "Our first trial will be assembling a convention capable of acting. That chore I will assume myself, being, you will admit, somewhat more tactful than any of my fellow conspirators."

Marika was startled. Humor? From Kiljar? You never learned everything about anyone.

Bel-Keneke remarked, "If the project takes twenty years instead of eight, so be it. The Reugge are committed."

Marika turned from one more look at the icy world. "Bagnel, I believe you promised to take me flying. Let's do it."

CHAPTER THIRTY-ONE

I

Marika's voidship drifted slowly through the clutter and confusion of the leading trojan point. She could make better speed down on the surface of the planet. Here she dared not fly herself, trusting only herself, for there were so many obstacles to navigation. Passage through the site required the combined efforts of a Mistress of the Ship and a Mistress-qualified pilot-passenger working from the axis. Marika could not imagine how the brethren kept track.

Three years had passed. Initial construction was just beginning. The support industry down on the planet's surface was not yet more than thirty percent of what it would have to be. Ninety percent of the off-planet effort, so far, had been devoted to the leading mirror.

It would be a demonstrator, in a sense. If it went active and did no apparent good, the rest of the project would collapse.

Marika reached with her touch and scanned the confusion. She remained awed by the magnitude of what she had set in motion. Designing it, planning it, talking about it was not the same as seeing it.

Flares of light speckled the night as crude brethren ships moved materials. Already Bagnel was complaining that they had chosen the most difficult way possible of building the mirror. He was agitating for a giant pack of balloons in the trailing trojan. His brethren had orbited a two-hundred-mile gas-filled reflector the week before. Its energy yield was directed at the developing oil field in the Ponath. Its value might have been more psychological than actual. The workers there claimed they sensed a change in the bitter cold already. Marika had visited and had been able to find no evidence of any local temperature increase. She suspected most of the energy was being absorbed before it reached the surface.

A remarkable vigor and an even more remarkable spirit of cooperation still animated the venture. There had been far fewer conflicts than anticipated. Yet even now Bagnel's best estimate had the leading mirror eight years from completion.

That protracted unity, in part, sprang from the project's single biggest problem, which existed down below—a sabotage campaign by those residual brethren still committed to the cause of the departed villains.

These criminals were more subtle than their predecessors. Marika's old tricks for digging them out did not work nearly as well. But still, enough were taken to keep the mines working at capacity.

Few of the taken had any direct connection with the brethren. More and more disturbing to Marika was the fact that the criminals were able to continue recruiting. And that they now were taking a few females into their ranks. The great hope of the mirror project had not adequately fired the hearts of the mass of bond meth. Marika was distressed, but did not know how to convince ordinary meth that they had as great a stake as the powerful who ruled their lives.

The mines were a problem not yet unraveled. In the past there had been no need for mechanization there. The structure of society had been such that no demand for ores had been so great that plain physical labor could not meet it. Meth did not mechanize simply for the sake of efficiency. They did so only where a task could not be performed by meth alone. But now...

Bagnel had been correct. The project was restructuring society. Traditionally labor-intensive areas like mining and agriculture had to be mechanized either to up volume or release labor for the project. Marika was, she feared, creating the possibility of compelling some of the changes the rogue brethren had aimed toward. Some could not be avoided. There were times when she agonized. She was in the incongruous position of being the principal defender of the silth ideal while not believing in it herself.

Marika's Mistress of the Ship reached the sunward position she desired, just miles from the heart of the expanding framework. The titanium beamwork sparkled, arms radiating from the anchor point. Marika recalled some old steel bridges, brethren-built, that spanned the river at TelleRai. Bridges constructed with incredibly complex girderwork intended to distribute load stresses. Bridges built in later times were much simpler in design. Was there a similar design problem here? Was the framework needlessly complex? Or, like those old bridges, was the design state of the art for the knowledge available, for the metallurgy of the moment?

Rotate your tip so the framework is overhead, Marika sent. *Your glow is obscuring my view.*

The framework rose, filling the sky.

A tinny voice spoke in Marika's ear, from the tiny radio earplug there. "Hello, the darkship. We will need you to pull back a few miles. We are coming through your space with girderwork."

There was a time when no male would have dared think of speaking so to silth. But in space the laws of physics often overruled tradition. Maybe these brethren would have to be destroyed in the end, lest their easygoing, not so subtly insubordinate ways infect the rest of the meth race.

Marika scanned the night for a brethren workship towing a string of bundles and spotted its flare. She touched her Mistress, relayed instructions. The darkship began to drift backward.

She was pleased with what she saw at that trojan.

She would be remembered. The meth race would recall that Marika the Reugge, wild silth of the Degnan pack of the upper Ponath, had lived. Even if the project failed, if it died in squabbling between the sisterhoods, it was something that would not be forgotten. She, its instigator, would be remembered with it.

Already the mass of materials reflected enough light to be visible from the planet's surface. In a few years it would be the brightest object in the heavens, bar the moons. When it was complete only the sun itself would outshine it.

There was nothing she could contribute here, other than encouragement. She touched several senior sisters who were working the site and sent her wholehearted approval, then touched her Mistress. *Proceed to the other site now, please.*

The darkship began easing out of the clutter.

It took an hour to reach space where the Mistress dared move swiftly. During the wait Marika ducked through her loophole into the realm of ghosts, through which she worked her silth magic, and continued a long-term effort to further familiarize herself with the odd those-who-dwell of the void.

She was accustomed to them now, and used them as she did the ghosts down below on her homeworld. Their immensity and power no longer disturbed and intimidated her, perhaps because by dealing with them she developed her own strength and power. There were none of them so mighty she could not take them into control and use them to pull her voidship or perform some task ordinary meth would perceive as witchery.

She knew them, and the void, but still she had not realized her dream. Still she had not traveled to an alien star, even as a passenger upon another Mistress's darkship. Still she had not dared breach the Up-and-Over, where light became a lagging pedestrian. For reasons deep within her, reasons she could not fathom herself, she was frightened of what she might encounter there.

Dark-farers told her hers was a problem all voidfaring Mistresses and bath faced before faring the Up-and-Over. They called the fear the Final Test. Those who conquered it joined the most elite sisterhood of all, the few score who flew the darkships to the starworlds. Those who did not conquer it seldom fared past the orbits of the meth homeworld's major moons.

Marika extended her touch, her sensing, farther and farther outward.... There it was, that dark something—remote, lying outside the system itself, vast, colder than the indifferent void. A sense of darkness radiated from it. And it terrified her.

She sensed it every time she passed outside Biter's orbit. Kiljar had told her it was the ultimate in those-who-dwell, more vast and powerful and deadly than anything she had yet experienced. It lurked in the gulf between the stars, and had to be appeased by any voidship that passed out of the system. It had appeared there soon after the first silth had penetrated the deep.

It was the thing that made Bestrei, the Serke champion, the most terrible of living silth. Three living silth could manipulate that great darkness. Bestrei could control it better than any other. She could call it and hurl it against any challenger. None had the strength to steal her control and drive it away.

Kiljar said Bestrei meshed with it so well because inside she was just as cold, deadly, and vacant.

Marika feared it because she sensed it in her future. The script was written. The very nature of meth, silth, and the silth ideal made certain eventualities inevitable.

Someday...

Unspoken by anyone, tacitly assumed and accepted by every silth, was the fact that one day Marika would have to meet Bestrei in darkwar. The confrontation was fated by the All. There was no escaping it.

When Marika reflected upon that chance she was afraid, for she was unsure of herself with the great black, with Bestrei. Most of her life she had been hearing about Bestrei and how terrible the Serke was. The one time their paths had crossed she had been awed by the raw power in the silth.

The Serke and their rogue brethren allies had mounted several incursions into the home system the past few months, attacking the mirror project. Bestrei had not participated. Bestrei would not participate in such trivialities, in the estimation of silth who knew her. She would be contemptuous of such nuisance tactics. She would not be seen till she was offered a traditional challenge with dramatically high stakes.

As seemed inevitable, fate stalked Marika's trail. As her Mistress of the Ship began to put on speed toward the trailing trojan point, Marika received a generalized touch from a far-toucher sister riding a picket darkship far out in the direction from which *Starstalker* and the raiders always appeared. It was brief, cut short.

Turn about, Marika sent to her Mistress. Starstalker *is coming.*

The plane of the touched reeked with the fear of the Mistress and bath. The Mistress returned, *This is not our proper task, mistress.*

Turn about. Set course upon the Manestar.

The darkship wheeled.

The speaker in Marika's ear began to babble as slower electromagnetic waves brought the warning.

II

They are very daring this time, Marika sent. Many minutes had passed. *Starstalker* and the raiders were closing with the leading trojan. Never before had *Starstalker* come in so close. The Serke had been afraid to risk her. Losing her would mean losing the brethren she had brought aboard her.

Marika's Mistress of the Ship returned, *They must be armed with more powerful weapons.*

The possibility had occurred to Marika. A few bombs of the kind that had destroyed TelleRai could kill the project. Having them delivered might seem worth risking *Starstalker.*

She opened to the universe, sensed the movement of everything nearby. A dozen brethren ships and five darkships accompanied *Starstalker.* For the moment Marika was alone, the only defender capable of intercepting the raiders. The sisters down below remained confused, as always. Those within the work site could not get out into free space in time to save themselves, let alone do any defending.

Did the Serke know she was here? Had they recognized her? There was no indication in their behavior. The rogue ships were headed toward the mirror. The silth were forming a screen meant to intercept help coming up from the planet. Marika was tempted to strike at *Starstalker* itself, to destroy any chance for the criminals to escape, but she feared that might allow the rogues a chance to kill her project.

The rogues had to be halted first.

She went out the long arm of the darkship, her specially built wooden darkship, her darkship that so amused the sisters of the great titanium crosses. The struts bore shields showing her own personal and Degnan witch signs instead of those of a particular cloister, as was the case with all other darkships. She reached the Mistress of the Ship and sent, *I will take it now. I am fresher. You guard while I attack. Do you understand?*

Yes, mistress. The silth responded with an absolute lack of enthusiasm, despite understanding the necessity presented by the situation.

Marika assumed control, urging the darkship onto a course that would cut that of the rogue vessels from behind.

She put on velocity till she felt her bath begin quivering with the strain of her demands, felt the displaced Mistress shuddering, wanting to tell her to ease back, that they were too near space cluttered with materials for the mirror.

Marika swooped into the wake of the rogues and tasted the bitter flavor of ions from their exhausts. She gained rapidly, reaching ahead to see what she faced.

Two ships carried no crew at all. She allowed the darkship to drift while she captured a stronger ghost and took it forward for a closer look.

The uncrewed two were loaded with what must be bombs, great cumbersome devices with a jury-rigged feel. She explored one rapidly, but could find no way to disarm it or to detonate it prematurely.

She took the ghost into the fuel stores of those two ships, compressed it to marble size, put spin on it, and used it to perforate the tanks. She returned to flesh in time to watch the second flower of fire blossom against the night.

She felt the rage explode among the thwarted rogues, felt them begin sweeping the surrounding night. She returned to the otherworld and began stalking them.

They could not see her! Their radars could not pick up her wooden darkship. She was running right up to them, and they could not see her!

She hit one ship after another, just as she had taken the bomb drones. They scattered so she could not massacre them all.

Mistress. Come out. The Serke have turned our way.

She had known that would come and had ignored it.

Five of them to her one plus a spare Mistress. The odds were too long, strong as she was. Yet there was no way to hide from them. To do that she would have to abandon the talent entirely. To do that in the void meant instant death.

She curved after a rogue ship belching flame in an effort to escape, closed up, killed it, began looking for another.

Mistress...

There is time. Do not distract me again. Six brethren ships had been negated. They would remember this raid as a disaster. *Just guard me.*

Let the Serke come. She was strong and treacherous. If nothing else, she could outrun them.

She was closing on another rogue when the Mistress touched her again. She suppressed her anger at being interrupted.

She did not need the warning.

Astounded, she forgot the rogue as she stared at a glowing darkship that had materialized only a few hundred yards away. She recovered barely in time to help the Mistress turn the attack.

This Serke Mistress was weaker than she. Grimly, Marika ducked through her loophole and seized a ghost, hurled it back.

The darkship vanished.

Another appeared an instant later, in another quarter, and vanished again before she could do it harm.

She finally understood. They were trying to attack her through the Up-and-Over.

How could she get out of this?

She could see no escape.

Decision came instantly. She swung the tip of the wooden dagger toward *Starstalker* and accelerated.

The Serke recognized her intent. They flung themselves into her path. She and the Mistress brushed their attacks aside and continued the drive toward the great voidship. Soon the sisters there would have to move or be rammed.

The Serke tried placing a preponderance of strength in Marika's path. But once they did that she knew where to expect their appearances. She recovered her advantage of her superior grasp of the dark side.

Short, sharp touch-shrieks filled the void as a Serke Mistress's heart exploded and her bath realized they had no hope.

Marika continued gaining velocity.

Starstalker vanished.

Marika searched the void, wondering where it would return from the Up-and-Over. If she chased it hard enough it might not be able to recover the rogues before darkships rose up from the planet's surface or came from other work sites. The rogues might have to be abandoned.

A lance of fire cut past her. She had not kept close enough track of the rogues. She had allowed one to sight her visually. Hurriedly, she threw a ghost its way, destroyed it, and returned to flesh to find her Mistress almost overwhelmed by the Serke. A pair of darkships drifted nearby, radiating elation, thinking they had her.

Marika hammered at one. Again the dark filled the despair.

The second darkship vanished.

Marika spotted *Starstalker* again, far away, and darted toward it.

It was going better than she had expected. She was as strong as ever she had been, as quick, as deadly, as finely tuned in her instincts. She had won the victory already, even if she were destroyed. The raiders could no longer damage the project.

The surviving Serke were gathering at extreme range. She suspected they would jump at her together. She could not see herself and one sadly weakened Mistress fending off all three.

She had to shatter the fear barriers and hazard the Up-and-Over herself. There was no other exit. They would make no more mistakes.

How long before help arrived? Surely there had been time for darkships to complete the long, slow climb from the planet's surface. Surely someone could have arrived from the moons or have wended her way out of the jungle of metal at the trojan point.

But a quick fling of the far-touch brought no response.

It was the Up-and-Over or death.

She knew what she was supposed to do. Technically. She had reached out and collected the appropriate ghosts occasionally, but had come up short on nerve. And never had she allowed herself to be taken through by someone else, though that was the customary way of learning.

There was no option. The Serke were poised.

She gathered ghosts.

The Serke darkships vanished.

Marika sealed her eyes and opened to the All, twisted her ghosts, and bid fear be gone. She reached for the Up-and-Over, twisted again.

The stars vanished. Everything vanished. For several seconds nothing surrounded her but a chaotic sense of ghosts and screaming. She had penetrated a vacancy that made the void seem warm and homey.

Stars reappeared, spinning. The darkship was tumbling. Marika looked for landmarks, and nearly panicked when she could spy nothing familiar. The world! Where was it? Where were the Serke darkships, the brethren ships, the mirror, *Starstalker,* the moons? She saw nothing at all. Only stars, distant stars. Had she hurled herself into the gulf between?

Something huge and dark stirred nearby, aware of her presence, so powerful she could feel it without reaching into the plane of ghosts. It was the great grim dark thing she had so often sensed waiting at the lip of the system. Her skip through the Up-and-Over had thrown her almost into its grasp!

Still battling panic, she steadied the darkship, polled her companions, found them frightened but safe. Her Mistress had no experience of the Up-and-Over either. *What do we do now?* she sent.

Find the direction home.

Marika scanned the void opposite the crawling darkness, and found a star that seemed brighter than any other. *That one?*

The Mistress knew where they were too. *Must be. Only the sun would be so bright from here. Hurry. It knows we are here and it is coming to see...*

The darkness had begun to move.

Marika turned the darkship toward the sun and began moving inward, accelerating. *Can we make it?* She did not have the courage to hazard the Up-and-Over again.

We must try. We cannot go through again. Another time, not knowing what we are doing, and we could be too far away to find our way. In the face of a problem less savage than the Serke the Mistress was perfectly calm. More rational than she, Marika thought.

The homeward passage took three days, despite the incredible velocities Marika attained. She reached lunar orbit at the edge of exhaustion, with her bath and Mistress all but burned out, and had to be rescued by brethren ships working the mirror, for she and her meth did not have enough left to take the darkship down.

III

Bagnel came to Marika where she lay in a bed aboard the workstation the brethren called the Hammer because of its shape, two pods upon the end of a long arm rotating to create an illusion of gravity. He said, "I heard you cut it pretty close this time."

She had not been awake long and he was her first visitor. "Very close. I wasn't sure I would make it this time."

He eyed her intently while shaking his head.

"I tried something I didn't know how to do and almost did myself in. Is that what you want me to say? I've said it. But I'll also say I didn't have any choice. It was the Up-and-Over or die. The Serke were closing in."

"I understand."

"How bad is it? How much damage did they do?"

"The raiders? None at all. Unless you count a little caused by one of the wrecks. It ploughed through an area where we had some materials tethered. We'll have to replace a few hundred sections of beam that got warped."

"That's all?"

"Evidently you took them completely by surprise. I hear there's a great deal of despair among the recidivists down on the planet. This was supposed to be a killer blow."

"Then the other darkships did get there in time to keep them from wrecking everything."

"Not exactly."

"What?"

"They ran away. The Serke. Before the darkships ever arrived. We heard the warning, but for a long time we did not know what had happened. Actually found out from a captured rogue."

"But…"

"Marika, nobody knew you were out there. I mean, some of the workers remembered a darkship nosing around, but they didn't know whose it was. You didn't tell anybody where you were going or what you were up to. Meth only started wondering about where you were after we captured the rogue and could not find any silth missing who were supposed to be out there at the time. Meth were talking about a ghost darkship for a while. Then when nobody could find you anywhere down below… Marika, you have to stop doing that kind of thing. You could have died trying to get back. If you had told somebody what you were up to, anybody, silth could have gone looking for you. It's hard to save somebody when you don't know they're in trouble."

"All right, Bagnel. Don't get excited. I get the message. It doesn't matter now, anyway. Everything turned out for the best. I'm safe."

He scowled. There was much more he wanted to say, but he held his tongue.

Marika said, "The problem has become how to protect the mirrors. They would have destroyed the project but for the accident of my having been out there. Two of those ships were carrying bombs like the ones they used on TelleRai."

"Accident? What accident?" There was an odd glint in Bagnel's eyes.

"What is it? I don't like the way you're looking at me."

"You always discount the notion that you are fated. I don't like superstition any more than you do, Marika, but this time I really have to wonder."

"Don't you start. I get enough of that nonsense from silth. Anyway, if you assume I am a fated thing then the mirror would have been destroyed. Isn't the pattern one of destruction? That's what they keep telling me."

"Maybe that was to prepare you for the turnaround."

"Enough of this, Bagnel. I won't have it from you. It's pure silliness."

"As you wish. I came to see how you are. I have my answer. You're as nasty as ever. And those who had hopes of your early demise will be disappointed again."

"Right. I intend to keep disappointing them, too, because I intend to outlive them all. I have too much to get done to waste time dying."

He looked at her hard, surprised by her intensity. "Things such as?"

"The project has reached takeoff. It is running itself. Not so?"

"Pretty much."

"This misadventure got me to thinking. There is very little I can contribute now, unless it's protection. Or if I just help lift materials from the surface. The rest of the engine is running on its own impetus."

"So?" He sounded suspicious.

"So I think it's time I went looking for trouble instead of waiting for it to come to me. No smart remarks! Remember when I was young? Remember how the novice Marika always jumped to the attack? She hasn't been doing that since she got older. That antique factor in your quarters that time was right."

"You're so old now? About to turn into one of your Ponath Wise meth? Eh? Eh? I know. You attacked even when you didn't know what you were attacking. Yes, I remember that Marika very well. She was a fool, sometimes. I think I like today's Marika a little better."

"Fool. *That* Marika made things happen. This Marika just sits around reacting. Mainly because she has been too cowardly to take what she knows to be necessary next steps. Before Kiljar finally gives up dying and actually yields up her spirit to the All—which may not happen for another century, the rate she's going, always going to die tomorrow and going on for another year—and maybe leaves the Redoriad Community in the paws of somebody less sympathetic, I'm going to learn the ways of the gulf and the Up-and-Over. I am determined. I will defeat fear, learn, then go hunt those who would destroy us."

"Marika, please understand when I say I don't approve. I don't think…"

"I know, Bagnel. And I appreciate your concern." Marika closed her eyes. For several minutes she did nothing but relax, comforted by his presence. Much of their friendship remained tacit, undefined by confining words.

"Bagnel?"

"Yes?"

"You have been a good friend. The thing we mean and wish when we use the word friend. The best… Oh, damn!"

Bagnel was startled. Marika so seldom used words like damn. "What is the matter?"

"There are things I want to say. That should be said, for the record. But I can't pry out the right words. Maybe they don't even exist in the common speech."

"Then don't try to say them. Don't look for them. I know. Just relax. You need rest more than talk."

"No. This is important. Even when we know things, sometimes it takes words to make them concrete. Like in some of our silth magics, where the name must be named before the witchery can be." She paused a time again. "If we had been anyone but the meth we are, Bagnel. Anyone but silth and brethren, southerner and packsteader…"

He touched her paw lightly, diffidently, actually squeezed it gently for a second, then hastened out of the cubicle.

Marika stared at the cold white door. Softly, she said, "They might have made legends." She could recall him having touched her only once before, for all they had been in close contact for so many years. "We will have to make them for them, for they will never be."

He had dared, at last. And fled.

One did not touch silth.

She had touched him once, before she had known him, atop a snowy ridge as they stared down upon the nomad-gutted remains of the place he had called home. It had been his responsibility to defend that place, and he had failed.

Silth did not show fear. Ponath huntresses did not show fear. Neither did either weep.

Marika wept.

CHAPTER THIRTY-TWO

I

For the first time in nearly six years Marika put the mirror project out of mind—though she debated with herself many days before admitting that it could get on without her there trying to run everything herself.

Kiljar allowed her to draft whomever she wanted from among the Redoriad dark-faring Mistresses of the Ship. She took the best as her instructresses.

She went up into the dark, out into the deep, and drove herself to exhaustion again and again, learning the Up-and-Over. She pushed herself as relentlessly as she had when she was younger, and she regained some of the enthusiasm that she had had then. She forced herself to learn the guile and craft that were needed to placate or elude the great darkness lurking at the edge of the system, waiting for no one knew what, filled with a hunger so alien it was impossible to comprehend.

"While we perceive them in countless ways they are all much the same, what you call ghosts," Kiljar said. Not once in all her years had Marika encountered another silth who called them that. Most called them those-who-dwell. A very few did not believe in them at all. "The farther from the world's surface you get, the larger they are, and fewer, till out in the gulf you find the rare black giants.

"Most of us do not worry about what they are or why. We just use them. But there are those sisters, seekers after knowledge, who have been debating about them for centuries. One popular hypothesis about their distribution says that they feed upon one another, like the creatures of the sea, larger upon smaller, and the largest are least able to withstand the distortion of space that occurs near large masses. The perceived size gradient does run right down to the surface here, each ghost seemingly pushing as close as it can. The feeding theory would say for safety from larger ghosts and because if they get closer they might catch something smaller.

"I do not accept an ecological-feeding hypothesis myself. I have been silth more years than you care to imagine and never have I witnessed one ghost preying upon another. And I know for a fact that the gradient, while generally true, will not hold up to close examination. Among the several thousand forms ghosts take there are those who refuse to follow theory. Even out near the big black there are several different small forms. I have seen them. Ones no bigger than my paw flashed about in swarms of millions.

"The hypothesis of our age, perhaps growing out of brethren disbelief in anything not subject to measurement and physical analysis, not yet widely accepted but becoming more so, is that they do not exist at all. This hypothesis says they exist only mentally, as reflections of silth minds trying to impose patterns upon the universe. The hypothesis makes of them nothing more than symbols by which powers entirely of the mind are able to manipulate the universe. This hypothesis would have it that silth trained that way could do everything the rest of us can without ever summoning those-who-dwell."

"No one actually has done that, though. Right?" Marika asked. She liked to believe she had an open mind, but she could not see this. She had seen ghosts before she had heard of silth or silth powers. Her very conception of them, as supernatural entities, came from that time, when nothing else in her experience could explain what she had sensed and experienced.

"Silth tend to be conservative, as well you know. They remain devoted to methods that work. From a purely pragmatic point of view it does not matter if those-who-dwell are real or symbolic. What counts is the result of the manipulation."

Marika reminded Kiljar, "I saw ghosts before I ever heard of silth. I still recall the first instance vividly. It was right after we found out that the nomads were watching our packstead. I had developed a feeble grasp on the touch and was trying to track my dam while she was out hunting them."

"That has been explained away as genetic imprinting, the argument being that the touch itself is proof enough that we rely on the powers of the mind. It has been pointed out that we never summon those-who-dwell to make a touch, only to physically affect our surroundings. And the summons itself is with the touch."

"Mistress, we are entering an age when meth, even silth, prefer explanations that are not mystical or magical. They will search for new reasons. I am content to accept what is, without explanation. If it works, I am satisfied. I do not need to know *how* it works. But, to change the subject, I believe I am ready for my solo star flight. What do the Mistresses who have been instructing me say?"

"They agree with you. Almost. But you have yet to make a supervised crossing to another star. It is a rule: The first time you go you must take someone with you who has experience. Just in case."

Marika was mildly irked, yet could not understand why she should be. Kiljar made perfect sense. She supposed it was the rebellious pup within her still, the pup with the overweening self-confidence. "Very well. I will go do that. If I can find a Mistress willing to go with me."

"Be careful, Marika."

"I shall. I have goals I have not yet achieved."

Kiljar's ragged face tightened momentarily. She was not pleased by the way Marika had fixed herself on stalking the Serke and rogue brethren. "Be very careful, pup."

"Pup, mistress?"

"Sometimes you are. Still. You came to your powers too early."

Grauel and Barlog looked grim as they took their places. They controlled the appearance of fear, but they were afraid. Grauel had been into the void only once, and that time she had not passed beyond the orbit of Biter. Once returned to the surface, she had stated a strong preference for remaining there the rest of her life. Barlog never had been up.

Now Marika wanted to drag them with her to one of the fabled starworlds. Worlds in which they still did not wholly believe.

"Relax," Marika told them. "It will seem strange, but it will be no more difficult or dangerous than a surface flight from Ruhaack to Skiljansrode."

"It isn't the same," Barlog insisted. "Not the same at all. Inside."

"We're still Ponath huntresses, Marika," Grauel said. "Very old ones, too. Very near the end of our value as huntresses. If we were in the Ponath still we would be on the edge of becoming Wise. A year or two more at the most. And you know the Wise. They are not inclined toward risk."

"I'll do my best to keep it from becoming too harrowing. After all, the purpose is to instruct me, not to take off on an adventure. That time lies a way down the river yet." She beckoned the senior bath, who brought a bowl of the golden drink. "Each of you drink about a cup of this elixir."

The Mistress who was to share and chaperone the journey tossed off a drink after Grauel and Barlog finished, then settled her tail upon the axis platform. She had been to the starworlds countless times. For her this journey would be routine.

The bath drank, then their senior brought the bowl to Marika. She finished it, feeling the drug taking effect immediately. "Have you finished your rites?"

The senior bath said she had.

"Good. Is everyone strapped?" She noted the tight grips Grauel and Barlog had upon their weapons. This was one time she had not needed to remind Barlog. The huntress had brought her arms as talismans against the unknown.

Marika touched her own weapons. Rifle across her back. Revolver inside the tattered otec coat that had been with her almost forever. She carried a knife in her boot, another on her belt, and a third concealed under her arm. She had ammunition enough for a small battle and dried meat enough for a week.

She felt foolish when she gave it a thought. She, too, was carrying amulets into the unknown.

"Take it up," the practiced Mistress said. "Time is wasting."

Marika closed her eyes, gathered the strongest of those-who-dwell, and began the long ascent into the void.

The dream of a lifetime was coming true. Her feet were upon the path to the stars.

She was terrified.

Though during the long climb she attained velocities not to be imagined on-planet, she became impatient. She wanted to get into it in a hurry, get through it, get it over, get the fright thoroughly tamed.

The void demanded new realms of thought of those who would navigate it. Mental habits from the surface could not be transferred. Often dared not be, lest they be fatal.

It was traditional not to enter the Up-and-Over before passing the orbit of Biter, the outer of the major moons. Seldom were the appropriate ghosts numerous enough closer to the planet. Impatient as she was, Marika began seeking those-who-dwell long before the proper time. Her guide refused to allow her to gather them. She pushed the darkship hard till she reached a point where her tutor found the ghost population acceptably dense.

Marika felt she could have called them to her much earlier, but she did not argue. She had not come to argue. She had come to get a final test over so she could walk the stars alone.

Sight on the star, the Mistress sent, and Marika fixed her gaze upon the Redoriad star she had chosen as her destination. *Gather those-who-dwell. Keep that star firmly fixed in your mind. Do you have them? Star and those-who-dwell?*

I do.

Make the star grow slowly larger in your mind's eye. Squeeze those-who-dwell with all the will you have. Let them know that you will not release them till that star has become a sun.

The horde of ghosts Marika gathered was larger than any she had seen any voidfaring Mistress gather before. She did as she was instructed, squeezing down with a mind strong on the dark side.

The stars around her went out like electric lights suddenly extinguished. For an instant she almost lost the spark that was her destination. She resurrected it in imagination, pounded it into those-who-dwell, who boiled around the darkship, frenzied by the effort she exerted, furious in their effort to escape.

The spark swelled swiftly in sudden jerks, as though she and the darkship were skipping vast tracts of intermediate void. That star became the size of a new coin.

Let go! the Mistress sent. *Let go now!* Marika had become so fixed upon driving toward her destination that she had not thought to release her bearers.

What did I do wrong?

You almost hurled us into that star. The Mistress was in a state approaching shock.

I apologize, Mistress. I was concentrating upon controlling those-who-dwell.

You did so. You definitely did. Never have I seen a passage made so swiftly, so suddenly. We will see how you manage the return journey. If you are more aware of your destination. If so, I will tell the most senior you are ready to fare on your own.

You seem distressed, Mistress.

I have experienced nothing like this. I have encountered no such overwhelming demonstration of power. You hardly needed the bath. She then let it drop, and refused to be drawn forth on the matter again. *Feel for the world. You are on the sunward side of its orbit.*

Marika found it, to the left of and slightly beyond the sun. *Up-and-Over?*

Carefully. You do not need to set records getting there.

Marika repeated her performance, though with a gentler touch. *How was that, Mistress?*

Less unsettling. But you need to develop a subtler touch. Take the darkship down. The Mistress presented a mind picture of their destination.

From orbit the planet looked little different from Marika's homeworld. Less icy, perhaps, but even here, according to her tutor, the interstellar cloud had begun to have its effect. In a few hundred years this world, too, would be gripped by an age of ice.

As stellar distances go, Marika, we are still very close to home. We see very few stars in our home sky. If we go out in the right direction, so that we pass beyond the cloud, we can see stars by the tens of thousands.

As Marika watched the world expand and become down, she realized, with a chilly feeling of déjà vu, that she had fulfilled her dream. She had walked among the stars. As a dream it had lost meaning and impact in the pressure of more immediate concerns.

"Stars beneath my feet," she whispered.

The darkship dropped through feeble clouds and turned out over a desert, an environment familiar to Marika only from photographs and tapes. There were no deserts in those parts of her own world that she knew. She realized that she had no broad, eyewitness familiarity with her native planet. She knew only a long, narrow band running from the Rift through the Ponath, Maksche, TelleRai, and on south to Ruhaack. She had seen perhaps a thousandth of her world. And now she was stalking the universe!

Toward the sun, Marika. Two points to your right. Can you feel it?

Yes.

This world felt nothing like her own. It felt incredibly empty, lonely. Her touch rang hollow here, except in one very well-defined direction, sharp as a knife stroke. She pushed the darkship forward, through a wind she found unnaturally warm even at that high altitude.

Barren mountains rose above the horizon. They were bizarre mountains, naked of vegetation, worn by the wind, each standing free in a forest of stone pillars. Some reached five hundred feet into the air, striated in shades of red and ocher, and each wore a skirt of detritus that climbed halfway up its thighs.

She found the cloister without further aid from her tutor. It lay atop one of the pillars. It was a rusty brown color, built of blocks of dried mud made on the banks of a trickle of a river running far below.

Sisters came into the central courtyard as the darkship slowed, hovered. They peered upward. Marika let the darkship settle.

"Welcome to Kim," her tutor said once the darkship had grounded. "We will rest for a day before we start back."

Marika stepped down onto alien rock, hot rock, under a sun too large and bright, and shuddered. She was here. There. Upon a starworld. The pup who had shivered in the chill wind licking the watchtower at the Degnan packstead and had stared at the nighttime sky, had achieved the impossible dream she had dreamed then.

She watched Grauel and Barlog dismount, their fur on end, their weapons gripped tightly, their eyes in unceasing flickering motion. They felt the strangeness too. They felt the absence of the background of unconscious touch that existed everywhere at home.

Marika met Redoriad silth whom she did not remember five minutes later. They asked questions about the homeworld, for their cloister was off the main starpaths and they had little news. She and the Mistress answered, but she paid little heed to them or what she said. She was unable to get over the fact that she had done what she had done.

Marika did not sleep much during the time set aside for resting. Her curiosity was too strong once the impact of achievement began to lessen. She spent hours learning everything she could about the world.

That was not much. The silth had little commerce with the natives, who were very primitive and had nothing to offer in trade. The Redoriad maintained the cloister on Kim only as a means of enforcing their claim upon the planet and as an intermediate base from which further starworlds could be explored and exploited.

II

The homeworld flashed into being. *Very good,* Marika's tutor sent. *Almost perfect this time. You will do, Marika. You will do. You need to study your stars now, so that you can recognize them from any distance and angle. Then you will be ready to roam on your own.*

Do darkships get lost?

Sometimes. Not so much anymore. The sisterhoods do not do much exploring these days.

Why not?

In the early days the voidfarers visited more than ten thousand stars and found little worth finding. There is little out there. Certainly little that can be profitably exploited. Nevertheless, in ten thousand stars there has been enough found that the few silth with the starfaring skill are kept quite busy. It has been a generation since anyone has had time for exploration.

Except for the Serke.

Perhaps. They found something, certainly.

Did they not, though.

Marika had her next step already planned. A thorough search of everything salvaged from the Serke before their disbandment. Somewhere in the records there might be a clue—though no one had yet found it.

The homeworld swelled, and with it a feeling of welcome, of returning to where she properly belonged, as the unconscious touch-world of all meth gradually enfolded her. She looked back at Grauel and Barlog, but could not see their faces. She sent a tendril of touch drifting over them, found them relaxed, pleased, almost comfortable. Out on the world called Kim they had been nervous and irritable all the time.

The darkship settled into the court of the new Redoriad cloister. There Marika's tutor immediately took her leave, heading for Mistress's quarters without a backward glance. As she rose to go on to her own cloister Marika wondered what new rumors would be spread about her now.

Hardly had she settled into the Reugge landing court, dismounted, formally thanked her bath, and begun soothing Grauel and Barlog, when Edzeka of Skiljansrode appeared. She hastened toward Marika with a portentous step.

"Something is wrong," Grauel said. "Bad wrong. Else she would not have come out of her den."

The joy had gone out of Barlog too. "I have an awful feeling, Marika. I do not think I want to hear this. Whatever it may be."

"Then go. It is time you took a ceremonial meal with the voctors anyway. Isn't it?"

Both huntresses gave her looks that suggested she was mad for saying they should leave her.

"Edzeka. What are you doing here? You look grim."

"A nasty problem, mistress. Very nasty."

Marika dismissed everyone else who had gathered around, who took it as a slight. She did not care. Never would she let herself fall into the manners and stylized forms of silth relationships. "Trouble at Skiljansrode?"

"Major, perhaps, mistress. The prisoner Kublin has escaped."

Marika did not permit her feelings to show. "How did this happen? And how long ago?"

"Shortly after you departed for the stars. Or maybe just before. It is not absolutely certain yet. There is some evidence he chose that moment to move specifically because you would be out of touch. There were copies of intercepts at his workstation mentioning you going out. We have not pinned down his time of escape because it came during his off-hours. When not at his workstation he remained in his cell, even if offered an opportunity to move around."

"I see. How did he manage it? Who was lax?"

"No one was lax, insofar as I could determine. He did it with the talent. There is no other explanation that will accommodate the facts, though not all of them are clear yet. Several voctors were injured or slain, and their injuries are all of the sort caused by one who wields the talent. It was the failure of those voctors to report that alerted us to the fact that something unusual was happening. We first thought someone had gotten in from outside, it making no sense for a prisoner to attempt escape. It was a while before someone noticed he was absent—by which time we did at least know that no one had come in from outside."

"A search is being made, of course?"

"Every darkship we could lift. I myself came here aboard a saddleship so no bath would be wasted on the carrying of a message. I thought you would want this reported directly, without it passing through the paws of anyone else."

"Thank you. That was thoughtful. How is the search progressing?"

"I do not know. I have been here awaiting you. Not well, though, I fear, else someone would have followed to tell me he has been recaptured."

"He will be difficult to take if he has been honing wehrlen's skills all this time." Already Marika had begun consulting a mental map. These days Skiljansrode lay far up in frozen country. It would be a long walk for anyone, getting from that packfast to country where one could live off the land. Almost impossible even for a skilled nomad huntress accustomed to the ways of the frozen wastes. Due south would be both the shortest and easiest route.

Edzeka would know that. No point telling her what she knew, or upbraiding her for what could not have been her fault. "How much food did he take out with him? What sort of clothing and equipment? Has that been determined yet?"

"It had not at the time I left, mistress."

"I know him. He would have prepared extensively. He would have made sure he knew all the risks and all the needs he would face. He would have prepared to the limit allowed by his situation. And he would not have moved unless he was convinced his chances were excellent, even with silth hunting him. He is a coward. But he doesn't make desperate moves. Knowing the fickleness of the All, we would be utter fools to hope the winter would take him for us. What is your method of search?"

"I positioned three of my darkships twenty miles farther south than I believed he could possibly have traveled, even with the best of luck. The middle darkship I stationed right on top of the base course he is going to have to make. The other two I placed to either paw, at the limits of sight, within strong touch. All three darkships are at one thousand feet. That places a barrier forty miles wide directly across his path. He cannot avoid being seen or sensed without going at least twenty miles out of his way. In that country, in that ice and snow, that would mean at least three days of extra work. That should give winter's paw a little extra edge."

"I like that. Go on."

"The other darkships are searching for him or physical evidence of his passage. The wind is blowing hard and there is fresh powder snow, but even so he cannot help leaving a trail."

"Very good. Very good indeed. Logically, that should do for him, one way or another. Keep pressing so that he has to keep going out of his way. He will not dare light a fire. His food supply will dwindle. When he becomes weakened and tired he will have more difficulty hiding from the touch."

Marika was not confident of that. She ought to claim a favor from Bagnel. His tradermales had tools more useful than silth talents. A few dirigibles prowling the wastes searching with heat detectors might locate Kublin more quickly than any hundred silth.

"Edzeka. The hard question. What chance that he had help? From inside or out?"

"From inside, none whatsoever. Any helper would have fled with him, knowing we would truthsay every prisoner left behind. Which we did, without result. And there never have been any friends of the brethren or Serke among the sisters. Help from outside? Maybe. If someone knew he was there and had a means of getting messages to and from him."

"A thought only." Another thought: the means of communication might have existed right inside Kublin's head. In all the years of isolation he would have had ample time to practice his far-touching. "Nothing came of the truthsaying?"

"Nothing had as of my departure. Final results will be available upon my return. Had they amounted to anything I am sure I would have heard."

"Yes, Well. You may break radio silence if anything critical develops. If you do not have the necessary equipment, requisition it before you leave."

"Thank you, mistress."

"Have you enjoyed Ruhaack? You ought to get out more."

"I have my work, mistress."

"Yes, as we all do. Thank you for the report. This bears thought." Marika extricated herself and hurried toward her apartment, lost in contemplation of what Kublin's escape might portend.

If he did make it out, he could become especially troublesome if he did know what had happened to Gradwohl. She could not be certain he had been unconscious throughout their confrontation.

She had to consult Bagnel. Bagnel knew a little about Kublin. He could judge what Kublin's escape could mean within the brethren.

Silth and huntresses who had survived the destruction of Maksche controlled that wing of the Ruhaack cloister where Marika dwelt. They were few, but intensely loyal to Marika, for they knew that she had tried to avenge their injury and knew she had not given up hope of further vengeance. They guarded her interests well. It was something of an amusing paradox. Marika had not been popular at all before the attack on Maksche.

A sister named Jancatch, who had been but a novice at the time of the Maksche disaster, awaited Marika at the entrance to her cloister within the cloister. Her face was taut. Her ears were down.

"Trouble?" Marika asked, thinking, what else?

"Perhaps, mistress. There was an urgent appeal for your presence from Most Senior Kiljar of the Redoriad some hours ago. An almost desperate call. We replied that you could not come because you had not returned from your travels. We were asked to inform you immediately when you did arrive, and to ask you to waste no time. No reason was stated, but there are rumors that she is dying."

"Kiljar has been dying for most of the time that I have known her. With one breath she predicts that she will not live to see the sun rise again, and with the next vows to outlive all the carrion eaters waiting to grab the Redoriad first chair."

"This time I believe that the crisis is genuine, mistress. The Redoriad have called in all their cloister councils and all their high ones who are inside the system. They have closed their gates to ordinary traffic."

"Call them back. Speak to Kiljar herself if that is possible. Tell her or them that I have returned. That I am available immediately if necessary. Grauel, Barlog, assemble my saddleship. I will go over right now if that is what she desires."

It was. Marika departed within minutes.

She was not welcomed at the Redoriad cloister. The halls were thick with important silth. One and all, they eyed her with hostility. She ignored them and the growls that came when she was granted immediate entry to Kiljar's apartment. Even the most powerful of them had not been permitted that.

III

Kiljar appeared very near the edge. Her voice was little more than a whisper. She could not lift her head, nor more than slightly stretch her lips in greeting. But she did manage to issue strong orders to her attendants to leave them alone.

Marika felt a sadness rise within her, a rare sadness, a rare sorrow. Few meth meant much to her, but Kiljar had become one of those few. She took the old silth's paw. "Mistress?"

Kiljar called upon her final reserves. "The All calls me, pup. This time there will be no deafening my ears to the summons."

"Yes." One did not hide such a truth from a Kiljar. "My heart is torn." One should not hide that truth either.

"It has been good to me, Marika. It gave me more years that I expected or had the right to hope. I hope I have used them as well as I believe I have."

"I think you have, mistress. I think you may have accomplished more than you suspect. I think you will be recalled as one of the great Redoriad."

"I am not sure I wish to be recalled that way, pup. I think I want to be one of the remembered names in your legend. I think I want to be remembered as your teacher, as the one who brought you to see your responsibilities, your importance, as she who taught you to harness your inclination to excess…" Kiljar succumbed to a racking cough. Unable to help, Marika clung to her paw and fought back the sorrow bringing the water to her eyes.

Kiljar's paw tightened upon hers. "I do not want to go into the darkness riding the fear that I have failed, Marika. You are not of my sisterhood. You are not of my blood. Yet I have made of you the favored pup of my pack. I have done much for you that you know, and much more that you do not. I have watched you grow, and have clung to life desperately in hopes that your growth would become complete and you would mature into a silth fit to stand beside Dra-Legit, Chahein, and Singer Harden. You are in the position, and these are the times. You have the power and the talent to shape the entire world. You are doing so, with your great metal suns. They are the one regret I know I will be carrying into the darkness. I would have lived to have seen them shedding their warmth."

Marika's throat had tightened till she could scarcely speak. She had to struggle to croak, "Mistress, you have been a true friend. I have found few of those. It is not a world for making friends."

"The great never have many friends, pup. Perhaps I have been less a friend than you think, for I have had the temerity to try to shape your destiny. One friend does not try to force a role upon another."

"You are a friend."

"As you will. You know what I want, do you not?"

"I think I do."

"You would, yes. You always know. But I will say it anyway. I do not want you to return to old hatreds once I can no longer be here to peer over your shoulder and be the whisper of your conscience. We have made a sound peace with the brethren. A peace that can last if it is given a chance. An accommodation with which the majority of silth and brethren both are content. To take up old grievances now would…"

"I will not, mistress. Though my stomach sours and my heart still fears their power, I will do nothing to alter the balance. I have reoriented my future toward the stars, as I had aimed during my novitiate. I have done what I can here. I will take my anger into the void in my search for the rogue Serke and their brethren masters. I will do nothing here unless others force me."

"Yes. That is well. Go stalk the stars. Find the criminals. That is where the true danger lies—though it must be growing weaker. They have not been back, except to sneak messengers in, since you drove *Starstalker* into the void. But do not allow that hunt to rule you entirely, Marika. The All has given you talents most silth would commit the thousand crimes to possess. You have learned to evade the consequences of the Jiana complex. I hope. Its aura does not hang so strongly upon you now. You have resurrected the Reugge from the ashes and have given them the potential to become one of the great sisterhoods of the future."

Kiljar coughed again, not so terribly. Marika waited in silence, knowing Kiljar was working hard to get said what she had to say.

"I suspect you now face an opportunity to do for the meth race what you have done for the Reugge. If you walk the stars in the proper frame of mind."

"Mistress?"

"I see three frames. Three great portraits sketched upon a canvas of time, perhaps overlapping one another, all forming a complete new life. The first is that of a pup. I foresee you dark-faring for the wonder, for the thrill of venturing where none have gone before. That is a thrill I knew well when I was young and first faring the void.

"A second frame surrounds your quest for revenge upon those who did you, the Reugge, and all silth so much evil. It is in your character to become fixed within that frame, and to lose the wonder and the grand potential of what could come of a successful stalk. You must carry with you always the knowledge that a successful hunt could define the entire future of our race. Have you thought at all about what might come of open intercourse between our world and that of these aliens the Serke discovered?"

"Only a little, mistress," Marika admitted. "My entire concentration has been devoted to the mirrors. But great evils or great benefits, surely."

"Indeed. One or the other, but nothing trivial. They will be very different, pup. Very different, indeed, from what I have been able to learn. You must realize that they will not all be magnificent and terrible weapons and technologies and whatnot that not even the brethren have begun to suspect. They will be modes of thought and slants of eye and ways of hearing that have not occurred even to our greatest thinkers. They will be the product of a distinct evolution, with all that implies in the way of millions of years of shaping minds as well as forms. They will infect us with ten thousand new ideas, new hopes, new fears—as, I am sure, we will infect them. Imagine the impact of the silth ideal upon a species that has no concept of that sort."

"I have seen the edges of such things, mistress, and I find them frightening."

"Indeed. And how much more frightening to silth who are narrower of mind? Who have known but one way since first rising to walk upon their legs alone? How threatening to them? There is great potential in this meeting of races, and its shaping for good or evil will lie strongly in the paws of the successor to Bestrei, for that successor will have the strength to determine anything she wishes in the void. You recall the frontier maxim you quoted to me so often. As strength goes."

"I understand, mistress."

"I hope you do, Marika. I pray you do. Truly. Like it or not, the future lies in your paws. You are the shaper. The eyes of all silth will be upon you after my passing. Your defeat of *Starstalker*'s raid and your mirrors have made of you the best known of silth, though you sought no notoriety. The world over, meth will look to you first. It is a heavy responsibility. Can you be a Dra-Legit? A Chahein? A Singer Harden for our times?"

Had Kiljar not been so close to dying, Marika might have become impatient. At the moment she could say only, "I will not disappoint you, mistress."

"Good. Good, pup. And do not disappoint yourself. Sit with me now. In silence. I believe I am ready. I have done all that I must do."

Kiljar closed her eyes. Marika felt her composing herself through the mental rituals. She continued to hold the old silth's paw.

The All was not long in claiming Kiljar, then. And for hours afterward Marika did not think of anything else, did not once calculate what Kiljar's passing might mean on the mundane level of what direction the Redoriad would now take. Even the importance of Kublin's escape did not penetrate her awareness till she had come to an accommodation of her loss.

In her grief she was reminded that even now, when she had acquired the power, she had not discharged a debt placed upon her when she was but ten years old. She had not seen to the Mourning of the Degnan pack. That was a thing that would have to be done. She would discuss it with Grauel and Barlog.

Kiljar gone. The world would not be the same.

CHAPTER THIRTY-THREE

I

Marika worked out her grief aboard her saddleship. She flew north, into the wilds below Skiljansrode, and spent three days in the hunt for Kublin. Three days during which few traces of the fugitive were found. He had planned well, her crafty little littermate. He traveled by night, in the dark of the moons, in snow storms, in high winds, seldom leaving a trail that could be seen from aloft the next day. Those who hunted him always knew where he had to be within a hundred square miles, but they could not pin him down more closely.

After three days Marika left the hunt, resigned. The All would will Kublin caught or not, according to its grand design. She had more pressing matters to attend.

She made daily pilgrimages into the void, studying the progress of the mirrors, learning the neighbor stars of her sun. Each of those, she discovered, had its unique flavor that she could identify instantly if she simply abandoned thought and opened to the All. Once she found the key the learning process accelerated till she could know a star in seconds.

All was well with the mirrors. Bagnel kept a firm paw on the project. She was not needed there looking over everyone's shoulder every moment.

She went out to Kim again and experimented there, and found she was able to learn the new, strange stars visible only from there in just a matter of hours.

Home again, after having intentionally stretched herself by not pausing to rest upon the planet. She returned to Ruhaack to catch up on the situation upon the homeworld.

Kublin had not been taken, though Bagnel had sent a squadron of dirigibles to help with the search. Their technological advantages had been of no value.

Marika began to suspect that her littermate had used the far-touch to call in help after all.

She learned that the new most senior of the Redoriad was a silth named Balbrach, who had been nominated by Kiljar before her passing. Balbrach had pledged to pursue her predecessor's policies, particularly in operating in concert with the Reugge. The alliance represented a concentration of power unseen for generations.

There had been a Serke courier incursion. The patrols hoping to jump the messenger had been insufficiently alert. The darkship had gotten past them and gotten down without betraying its landing site.

"We're still hunting for them," Bagnel told her. "We have traces picked up by satellite, but the optics just aren't what they should be. If our resources weren't so totally committed to the mirror project, we might develop an observation network...."

"It isn't really that critical. What we have will do the job. It's just a matter of forging better communications between your radar operators and our huntresses."

Bagnel was amused. "Of course. Just plant a qualified far-toucher in each of our installations. Or put one of our radio operators aboard each of your darkships. Nothing to it. Assuming you can get around however many millennia of tradition."

"Of course," Marika said, with sarcasm equaling his. "Nothing to it. There are times when I wonder how we meth have managed to survive."

Bagnel had come down from the Hammer soon after learning of her return. He had called her from the brethren legation at Ruhaack and they had flown together into the wastes to that remote base from which the Reugge cloister at Maksche had been attacked. The brethren still maintained a small establishment there, rebuilt after Marika destroyed the base, as a way station at the intersection of dirigible lines. Marika had gone out upon her saddleship, flying off the wing of Bagnel's increasingly venerable Sting fighter. Now they were aloft in the Sting, putting it through its paces.

"I hear you've been promoted again," Marika said.

"Yes. As always, the factors reward incompetence. The leading mirror is now all mine to demolish."

Marika was amused. He was so persistently negative about his own abilities. "I will be going away soon, Bagnel. As soon as modifications to my darkship are completed and I have trained a group of new bath." She had asked for the four strongest upcoming bath the Reugge and Redoriad could provide. The extra would be a reserve, would allow rest and rotation during extended interstellar passages. And she had a further experiment in mind that would require the presence of an extra silth. "I have the darkship at the dome on Biter being fitted to carry a detachable pod in which we can haul stores."

"Then you plan to be gone a long time."

"I'll be back in plenty of time to celebrate the triumphant completion of the first mirror."

"I see little enough of you now. If you disappear for years again..."

"I seriously doubt I will be gone that long. I was teasing."

"You're going after the Serke, aren't you?"

"That's the main reason. But also to see what's out there. Just to see it."

"Then the Serke are as much excuse as they are reason."

"Of course they are. I'm really going because that is what I've wanted to do from the moment we pups first heard stories of meth who went to the stars."

"I wish I could see…"

"You could. One more wouldn't make much difference. You might decrease our range, but not enough to concern me."

"I wish… I have too many responsibilities, Marika. We have reached a point where the mirrors definitely look practical. No, I couldn't. Yes, I would like to see the stars. Maybe later. After this is done and the warm is falling. After you have done what you have to do. And that frightens me."

"Why?"

"I am frightened by what you may find. What you have been doing cannot remain a secret. Those here who are still in contact with your enemies will hear about what you are doing. And they will relay the news. It will find the Serke before you do. And because you are Marika, and can do what other silth cannot, they will be afraid. They will prepare for you. They'll be waiting."

Marika had thought of that, and it was of concern to her. She did not know how to prevent it. "You'll just have to do better preventing contact. That's all I can say."

"You know I'll try. But do not forget that that is not my specific responsibility. I can only nudge and urge and appeal and beg and suggest. Others, perhaps with less concern for your welfare, will be in control."

"I have faith in you, Bagnel. Fear not. We will fly together again, in this same box of rusty bolts, over this same barren landscape. Let's hope it's on a day when fewer dooms shadow the world."

"That can't help but be, I think. Though the dooms breed."

Marika's eyes narrowed. "You are trying to tell me something."

"Perhaps… Being out at the mirror or the Hammer most of the time, I have little opportunity to keep track of what those who look for rogues are doing. But before I joined you a friend came to me with the latest rumor they had tapped."

"Yes?"

"The warlock is back."

Marika took a minute to get herself under control. Then she took another. "That is impossible. He perished when I destroyed those who had ravaged Maksche."

"I report only hearsay."

"The warlock?"

"The same one. The one who was the rogues' great hope a few years ago."

"I suppose it had to be," Marika murmured. "And I blinded myself."

"What?"

"I have done the unforgivable, Bagnel. I have made the same mistake twice. That is never forgiven."

But who could believe Kublin in the role of the warlock? A whimpering coward?

"What is it, Marika?"

"Nothing crucial. Let's fly a bit more, in silence, then take our leave."

There was something Marika had to do before departing, before pursuing her stalk among the stars, and she was afraid.

II

Marika brought the darkship out of the Up-and-Over virtually on top of the darkness that lurked at the edge of her home system. That blackness reeked to the touch, stinking of wickedness and death, of gnawed bones and ripped flesh and corrupt corpses and hatred unconstrained. If the void had a heart of evil, this ghost was its animate form.

This ghost was like no other she had encountered, and she had identified hundreds of different kinds. This ghost was, in a way, an absence. Most others seemed bright, flighty, sometimes curious, sometimes afraid, but always colorful and seldom inimical unless under silth direction.

This was an absence of color moved by its own grand malice. It was a thing that did not need direction to be inimical. It would strike out at the unwary. Only because it could not move as swiftly as lesser voidghosts, and because the silth had learned to appease and baffle and, rarely, to control it, did it not strike every darkship that tried to leave the system.

Control. That was Marika's goal. The highest or darkest of dark-sider sorceries, managed only by a dozen silth before her...

It moved toward her, almost as swiftly as thought. She squeezed the ghosts that carried her darkship, fleeing, pulling it along after her, staying out of its reach while she explored it with her touch.

She let it catch up.

Three times she recoiled from its cold, malignant vibration before she found sufficient courage to reach farther, to strive to control it.

Control came far more easily than she had expected. In some way she could not fathom, her dark side spoke to it, and meshed with it, and, in moments, the great monster became an extension of her will, a force she could hurl as simply as tossing a pebble with a flick of her wrist. She threw it at a piece of cometary debris. It struck savagely, compressed, caused gases to boil, to explode. A short-lived flare illuminated space.

Marika turned loose and backed away, awed. So much power! No wonder Bestrei was feared.

She reached again, lightly, and found the darkness possessed of a fearful respect for her, a vague, almost thoughtless admiration for her dark power. It acknowledged her its mistress after those few moments.

She backed away again. And now, at last, she began to see and understand what it was so many silth had seen in her, and had feared.

She reviewed the strongest silth she knew, and knew none of them could have done what she had. Few could have taken control of the ghost at all, let alone so swiftly, so easily, so thoroughly.

And she knew, then, what it was she had sensed about Bestrei that time when their trails had crossed. Bestrei could take a great dark ghost easily too—though hopefully without imagination, or cunning, or any especial ability to direct it with her intellect. Bestrei, too, was slanted far toward the dark side.

Marika turned and drove toward the homeworld, toward the dome upon Biter where her venture was being prepared, but she watched over her shoulder, considering a region about thirty degrees to one side of the Manestar. *Bestrei,* she sent, in a hopeless long touch. *I am coming, The long wait of the meth is nearly done. Soon we will meet.*

It was from that region that the Serke had come each time they had struck at the mirrors. Somewhere in that area she would cross their trail.

"Marika, you look terrible," Grauel said when she returned. "What did you do?"

And Barlog said, "She has that look of doom about her again."

"That is it. Isn't it? It's been absent for years. What did you do out there, Marika?"

Marika refused to explain. They would learn soon enough.

Grauel kept after her, but Barlog said little more. She looked terrified of what was to come, for she and Grauel, as always, would walk Marika's path with her.

Marika spent a busy few days contacting silth all across the world, silth with whom she had worked in her rogue-hunting days. She left suggestions and instructions, for there had been no further trace of Kublin. He had escaped for certain, though. The warlock rumor had begun to grow.

How could she have been so blind? The thought that he might be the one had never occurred to her.

Everyone who had investigated the destruction of Maksche, silth or brethren, agreed that that whole city had died because of the warlock's determination to kill her. And she had spared him twice.

Why did he hate her so? She had given him no cause, ever, that she knew.

He would not escape again. If he persisted, she would destroy him as surely as she would anyone else who rebelled against silth power.

The waiting was not a happy time.

III

Marika's first venture through the Up-and-Over was the most ambitious she had yet tried, three times the length of the journey to Kim. The magnitude of it overcame her.

She lost her nerve and turned loose before she should have, not maintaining the courage to follow what her talent told her was right. The star she sought still lay ahead, brighter now, but still far away. She searched the broad night, locating her home star and all the stars she already knew, then noted all those that she had not seen before. There in the heart of the dust cloud those were few, and she was able to inventory them in her mind with no trouble at all.

She dithered awhile, reveling in the glory of the void, till Grauel and Barlog began to disturb her with their increasing nervousness. Then she went down through her loophole again, gathered ghosts—which were scarce in the deep—and went on, pulling the darkship in close to the target sun.

It was not an inhabited or even habitable system. Marika had known before she jumped that it could be little more than a landmark on the trail the Serke walked, both because the system had been investigated often and because all logic said the Serke would have taken up residence in a system capable of sustaining life. Perhaps they shared it with the aliens or had taken control of the aliens' homeworld, as they wished to do with the homeworld of the meth.

In any case it did not seem plausible that two races of apparently similar needs would stumble into one another in the neighborhood of a giant or dwarf. Each would be seeking worlds of potential value, and those circled only certain types of stars. Only a small percentage of stars fit. Marika meant to concentrate upon those and use other types only as stellar landmarks.

Of course, all that had been reasoned and done before, in the hot, furious days after the bombing of TelleRai, when the might of all the dark-faring sisterhoods had been flung into the hunt. But Marika meant to carry the search far afield, avoiding stars already claimed or visited. The surviving Serke documents suggested that that sisterhood had been much more daring than any other, and that they had visited scores of starworlds to which they had laid no formal claim. That, unlike the other orders, they had kept exploring long after it had come to be deemed counterproductive.

It would be among those unnamed and unclaimed worlds that she would find her enemies.

She drifted near that first target star, a red giant, devouring its vast glory, extending her touch through its space in search of watchers, feeling for new or unusual ghosts or one of the great blacks, and found nothing of interest but the giant star itself. She scanned the night, learning the new stars she saw, then looked for and found her next target. This was another star on an almost straight line out from her homeworld. This one lay at the edge of explored space and would place her outside the dust cloud when she reached it. She would see the universe as she never had from home.

She faced that with trepidation, for the few silth who had been that far out had been unable to relate the marvel they had felt when they had been able to see the cloud and the galaxy from beyond the mask of dust.

Too, she was frightened because once she reached that star she would no longer be able to see her home sun. She would be cut off. The way home would rely upon memories impressed upon a few chemicals within her fragile brain.

She almost abandoned the quest then.

But she went on, defying fear, and those-who-dwell bore her well and quickly, and this time she did not allow her self-confidence to flag during the course of the jump.

She returned to the natural universe close to a white dwarf so brilliant she dared not look in its direction. It radiated so powerfully in the electromagnetic range that it threatened to disrupt her grip upon her talent. She did not stay long, though she did take in one awe-inspiring glimpse of a cloud of stars upon one paw and a vast darkness upon the other, only lightly speckled with points of light.

Grauel and Barlog practically whined with fear. The bath were unafraid, but stricken with awe.

Onward. And this time with care, for the next target was a wobbling star that, even from so far away, could be heard screaming as it died. A sister who had been there had told Marika that that star had an invisible companion that had to be treated with great respect, for it was a cannibal star, devouring the stuff of its visible sister the way some insects devoured the stuff of others.

The electromagnetic fog around that third target was more furious than anything Marika could have imagined. For minutes she remained disoriented, unable to select her next target, her last. It was hard to find. It was a normal little star much like her own sun, and it defined the outer known limits of exploration in this direction. It lay against the flank of the dust cloud.

Marika battled the numbness creeping over her. She recalled the most furious thunderstorms of her puphood in the Ponath. This was a hundred times more terrible.

She clung to her ghosts mostly by instinct and urged the darkship away, gaining velocity as the impact of the star lessened. In time she was able to think clearly enough to locate her target star. With head aching, she commanded her ghosts and pulled into the Up-and-Over.

The headache passed. Soon she found herself letting go almost automatically, almost without conscious calculation. The darkship fell into normal space, drifting toward her target.

This star boasted a world that could be used as a way station. It was a friendly world, the record said, but it was nothing like home. It was uninhabited. It would be a fair place to rest. A place where Grauel and Barlog could get solid ground beneath their boots once more.

She located the world and guided the darkship into orbit, released the massive stores pod after Grauel and Barlog and the extra bath had removed what might be needed below, then descended.

It was a hot, humid world with an atmospheric pressure much higher than that at home. Having descended to the level of discomfort, Marika cast about till she found a tall mountain. There she made her landing.

She had gone to the very bounds.

Soon the hunt would begin.

CHAPTER THIRTY-FOUR

I

"Marika!"

Grauel's tone startled Marika. She threw a hasty touch toward the huntress, fearing she had encountered something deadly. But it was not danger, just something she had found. Something that had her excited. Marika hastened to join her.

This was at least the hundredth habitable world and thousandth star they had visited since leaving home. The number of stars inside the radius Marika considered logically limiting, worth investigating, seemed infinite. She had lost track of time.

Time had little meaning when all worlds were different and each begged to be explored. She had thought the film Bagnel had given her, in rolls upon hundreds of rolls, was a ridiculous oversupply. But now most of it was gone, exposed, sealed, ready to be returned to those who would be avid to search it for the new, the weird, the terrible. The universe seemed capable of producing an infinitude of wonders.

More than three years had passed. None of Marika's original bath were with her anymore, having one by one proved out the value of her experiment or simply having grown homesick and opted to return on the Redoriad voidship *High Night Rider,* which resupplied Marika's base every few months.

Marika scrambled across a decomposed rock face where striations glistened unsettlingly alien blues, perched a hundred feet above a patch of tableland where Grauel crouched, studying something. "What have you got, Grauel?"

"A campfire site," the huntress called back. "Come down and see. Your talent might find something I cannot."

Marika's heartbeat picked up. Campfire site! There was no intelligent life on this world. And it had not been visited by any meth before, unless by the Serke. Maybe after all this time, chance had brought her to a warm trail.

She had discarded the world as a possible Serke hiding place only seconds after making orbit. The presence of silth would not have been hard to detect. These years among the stars, reaching out to find an enemy never there, had stretched her far-touching talent till it would have shamed the most talented of far-touchers back home. She did not believe anyone with the talent could hide from her long.

Aliens of the sort she sought should not have been hard to detect either, if only by the talent vacuum the brethren suspected should exist around them. She had grounded only because they all needed to rest, needed to feel a planet beneath their feet.

She was very strong now, able to make venture after venture without pause. She was not the least uncomfortable with the void or the Up-and-Over. It was as if she had been born to stalk the stars. But her bath reached their limits after six or seven passages and needed several days to recuperate. Grauel and Barlog never became comfortable with starfaring. She had taken them all to their limits this time. This site she had chosen only because it looked safe and comfortable.

Talus bounded around her boots as she slipped and slid down the slope, thanking Grauel's increased propensity for wandering while they were down, thanking the All for interesting the huntress in the oddities produced by the worlds they visited. It had paid a dividend.

Maybe.

Grauel remained crouched over a circle of stones blackened on one side. The circle lay away from the foot of the cliff, but was still sheltered from the prevailing winds. A glance told Marika it was an old site, barely recognizable for what it was.

Grauel glanced up. "It was not like this when I found it. I had to reconstruct it. I noticed some stones that looked smoked on one side scattered around. Then just a hint of a smell of smoke still in the ground here. Once I started looking around I found more stones. It all came together fairly easily."

Marika nodded. "What can you tell me about it?" Grauel was the huntress. This was her area of expertise.

"Very little, except that it's here. And it shouldn't be. But it did seem that this ledge would be a good place to ground a darkship."

"How far afield did you go?"

"Not far."

"Let's snoop around, see what we can find."

Careful visual search turned up nothing more.

"If they were here, they must have had a latrine and some place to dump their garbage," Grauel said.

"They may have had huntresses with them," Marika chided. Grauel and Barlog, treating the search as they would a hunt in their native Ponath, left every resting place pristine, naked of evidence that anyone had visited. Both huntresses believed the Serke were hunting for them in turn.

"One doubts it. No skilled huntress would have left a fire site so obvious to the eye. My thought was that you might use your talent to look where the eye cannot see."

"You are right, of course." Marika went down through her loophole and caught a suitable ghost, then searched the area again, using the altered perspective of the otherworld. She found what Grauel wanted in a crack to one side of the ledge. She returned to flesh. "You were right. Over here. Whoever they were, it looks like they used one natural hole for a garbage pit and a latrine both."

"Grab yourself a stick," Grauel said.

"A stick?"

"Do you want to stir through it with your paws?"

"Of course. All right." Marika collected pieces of dead wood. Grauel used one to dig at soil that had been used to cover the wastes.

"Been a while for sure," the huntress said. "It has all decayed away to nothing. It must not rain or snow much here, for the black on the rocks to have remained noticeable. But we're wasting our time. There's nothing.... Hello!" Grauel dropped onto her belly and reached into the hole. She wriggled forward, bent at the waist, got hold of something, wriggled back and sat up. She held a lump to the light. Marika saw nothing special till Grauel spat upon it and cleaned it on her sleeve.

"A button." It was a tarnished metal button with a few fibers of thread still attached. It was embossed. Grauel passed it to her. Marika studied it, then compared it to the five upon the left wrist of her jacket. "That is a Serke witch sign on it, Grauel. We're on the trail. They've been here. I have a premonition. We are within a few passages through the Up-and-Over of catching up with them."

"That's what you've been saying since we established our first base."

"This time I am right. I can feel it. I am convinced."

"I hope you are." Grauel sounded sour.

"Grauel?"

"I do not want to die out here, Marika. How would the All find me?"

"What?" This was a surprise.

"In fact, if I had my choice, I would spend my final days in the upper Ponath, at the packstead that gave me life."

Marika was baffled. What had brought this on?

"I am getting old, Marika. In the Ponath I might already be one of the Wise. Likewise Barlog. The witchery and medicine of the silth have kept us young beyond our time, but time never stops gnawing. Lately I find I cannot help remembering that we are the last of the Degnan pack, and that our pack lies beneath the northern ice still unMourned."

"Yes. I know all that. You are indeed old for the Ponath, but not old by standards of the silth. There will be time, Grauel. We will see to the Mourning. But we can't go now. We're finally making some headway out here. We've finally found something besides a place where they aren't and haven't ever been. Maybe this world is a regular stop. Maybe if we just sat here and waited.... I know what I'll do. I'll make this world our new base. We'll continue the hunt from here."

"Which means a whole new globe of space to search," Grauel countered, showing no excitement. "It will be like starting from the beginning."

"Think positively, Grauel. Think lucky. Let's go tell the others."

"What I think is I wish I had not called you down here."

That evening Marika climbed a peak while the others rested. She stood staring at the stars. There were few to be seen, for the dust cloud spanned the heavens of that world. She selected the next half-dozen stars that should be investigated. Into the cloud itself this time? Yes. What better place to hide?

For the most part she had avoided going into the cloud during her search. She was much less comfortable operating there because there were so few landmark stars. She had reasoned that the Serke explorers would have suffered the same reluctance. But perhaps one of their more-daring Mistresses of the Ship, possibly a Bestrei, might have dared the darkness and found the aliens.

What lay beyond the cloud? No one knew. No one had tried to reach its nether side. Maybe no one but the Serke had had any contact with the aliens because they were over there and they too were reluctant to enter the dust.

The dust cloud it would be, for a time.

II

Marika's bath had again been rotated. Grauel and Barlog had begun to show gray and even lose a little fur. Marika herself had begun to feel age in her bones when she rose some mornings. And there were moments when the homeworld called so strongly that her resolve almost broke. There were moments when she was tempted to go home just to discover what had happened in her absence. Sometimes, during the on-planet resting pauses, she lay awake when she was supposed to be sleeping, wondering about Bagnel, longing for his company, and wondering about the progress of the mirrors she had imagined into reality, and even about the warlock, her littermate, Kublin.

She knew very little about what had happened since her departure. But for the regular visit of *High Night Rider,* and the occasional appearance of a Mistress of the Ship with an adventurous spirit, a desire to visit the strange worlds Marika had reported, and a knack for assembling bath of like temperament, she had no ties with home.

Grauel and Barlog had recognized the process at work and had ceased their importunities for abandoning the quest, fearing their petitions would harden her resolve.

She was finding it increasingly difficult to convince herself that the hunt was worthwhile. There was no end to the universe, even within the dust cloud. There was always another star. And, inevitably, always another disappointment.

It was time for *High Night Rider* to come again. She felt she had reached a time of decision. If the news from home were bad, she would return.

The mirrors, insofar as she knew, were coming along well. A brief note half a year earlier, written by Bagnel, had told her the mirror in the leading trojan was well ahead of schedule. So much for his doubts about his management skills.

But he had mentioned trouble down on the homeworld's surface. The old rogue male trouble had begun to reassert itself. The Communities seemed unable to stem it. This time the outlaws seemed to be working independent of the brethren, under the dominance of their wehrlen, but there were those, according to Bagnel, who did not believe the warlock was the true source of their witchcraft. Silth did not want to believe a male could be so strong, so felt the rogues had to be getting aid and encouragement from silth smuggled in by the Serke.

On its last visit *High Night Rider* had brought word that the rogues were sabotaging the brethren as well as silth, that assassination had become their primary weapon. They were using their talent-suppressing device again, and the sisterhoods could not cope.

Marika suspected they could not cope because they did not feel motivated enough. Even now, after all the disaster they had wrought, it was difficult to get silth to take males seriously as a threat.

Marika did not want to take up that task again, but it seemed she might have to, if the vague reports she received indicated the way things were actually moving. If the Communities themselves would not spend the effort and energy to defend themselves adequately.

A wave of undirected touch passed over her. She looked at the sky as one of her bath called out, "Mistress, *High Night Rider* has come."

A blob of light moved across the sky, visible even in daylight. It slowed, maneuvered, fell into orbit. Marika rose and stalked through the camp, which today housed nearly a score of meth. Two other darkships were operating from her base, not participating in the hunt, but examining more closely the most interesting of the worlds that Marika had discovered. Their Mistresses were young ones, filled with a desire to expand the frontiers, and they had found themselves teams of bath willing to join their ventures.

Marika's reports home had had one effect: They had somewhat revivified the old spirit of exploration. Once she had blazed a trail others were eager to devote closer attention to what she had found.

She suspected Bagnel was irked. That meant darkships scattered about the void contributing nothing to the mirror project. She suspected the tedium of construction work was what had encouraged these younger Mistresses and bath to come out to the edge of beyond.

The explorers could do little to truly expand meth knowledge. There were more curiosities among the starworlds than could have been cataloged by ten thousand darkship crews in ten thousand lifetimes.

Of late even Marika had been spending more time looking at those curiosities than she had been being driven by her need to overhaul the Serke.

"Darkships coming down, mistress," someone called. "At least three of them. Maybe four."

That was to be expected. There were supplies to be delivered, and always there was another group of explorers who had saved themselves effort by scavenging a ride aboard the giant voidship.

Though the darkships would not ground for a long time yet, Marika went to the landing area with the others. They all stood around waiting, joining in speculation about what news would come from home.

The first darkship down carried a passenger.

"By the All! Bagnel!" Marika swore as the tradermale stepped down. He was shaking, numb with awe. "What are you doing here?" He did not hear her. Whether he was amazed to have arrived healthy, or overawed by having traveled so far, he was completely turned inside himself. She rushed over and repeated her question as meth yelled about clearing the area so the next darkship could ground.

Silth stared. A male! Out here!

Bagnel shuddered as though shaking water off, and said, "Marika." He looked her over. "You have changed."

"So have you. Is that gray I see there? Time gnaws, does it not? It must be fate. I was just thinking about you—and here you are. What are you doing here? Come with me. Before that Mistress gets impatient and plops down on our heads."

"Are you all right? You look tired."

"I am tired, Bagnel. I have looked at more stars than you can imagine even exist. Though you must have seen how many there are when you spanned the reach outside the cloud. Come. Let's get something to eat. You must be starved."

"My stomach is too unsettled. That passage... It was too much for me, I fear. The Up-and-Over... I find myself dreading the return trip already."

"You still haven't told me what you're doing here. Has something happened?"

"No. Except that I have been stripped of my job and prerogatives. Whoa! It's only temporary. A cabal of senior factors and high silth ganged up on me and ordered me to take a vacation. They said I was pushing myself too hard, that I was on the edge of a breakdown because I was trying too hard to keep the project ahead of schedule. They stripped me of my powers so I would have no choice. Since they wouldn't let me do anything at all, and the Redoriad were willing when I approached them, I decided to come walk the stars while I had a chance. You invited me, you'll recall. I think I am sorry I did it."

"I recall. I believe I invited you to come after I caught the Serke."

"But you haven't. You've been out here forever. It begins to seem unlikely, doesn't it?"

"I am narrowing it down, Bagnel. Narrowing it down. I have a very good idea where they're not."

"You are still able to be amused at yourself."

"Not often. But I don't think it will be too much longer."

"You sound like you're trying to convince yourself."

Marika noted Grauel and Barlog hovering. They were polite enough to remain out of earshot, but they were there, eager to discover the meaning of Bagnel's appearance. Marika asked, "You're sure this isn't business? That someone didn't send you out to get me to come home?"

He looked surprised. "No. Why do you ask that?"

"We get very little reliable news out here. What we have gotten are rumors about increasingly bad rogue trouble. Trouble nobody seems able—or maybe just willing—to solve. I thought maybe someone sent you to get me to come back and deal with it."

"Marika... I might as well put it bluntly. The vast majority of silth are very happy that you are out here instead of at home. That's why you get the support you do. The farther away you are, the happier they are."

"Oh."

"The rogues have become a problem again, though, that's for sure. They're much better organized this time. They learned a lot."

"I believe I predicted that. I believe no one would listen to me."

"Right. It's no longer possible to use the tactics you developed. One cannot be taken and forced to betray scores more by subjecting him to a truthsaying. They have structured their organization so that few members know any of the others. And they are careful to keep the risks low whenever they choose to strike."

"That was predictable too."

"And even where the hunters know who they are looking for it has been hard to track a culprit down. Your Kublin, for example."

"Kublin?" Marika had done her best not to think of her littermate over the years. It had been her thought to destroy his hope by shattering the support lent by the Serke and their rogue companions. But the Serke remained unshattered.

"He is rumored to be the mastermind, the one they call the warlock. Not one hunter has been able to find a trace of him since his escape from you. Whenever someone does get a line on him he is found to be gone by the time the hunt closes in. There is still strong support for him and those who fled with the Serke among the bond meth and even our worker brethren."

"I can find Kublin."

"No doubt. You have always done whatever you set your mind to. I will mention that to anyone who is interested. My own opinion is, you should continue the search for the Serke. Step it up, even. It could be important."

"Ah? Is that it?"

"What?"

"The true reason you put yourself through what it takes for a meth unfamiliar with the Up-and-Over to come out here?"

"I came for a vacation, Marika. I came where I could see a friend who has been missing from my life for far too long. I'm just trying to tell you what is happening at home. If you care to interpret that as an attempt at manipulation…"

"I'm sorry. Go ahead. Tell me the news."

"Last month we finally caught a courier from the rogues trying to sneak in. Two of them, actually. Both brethren who had gone into exile aboard *Starstalker*. I was brought in for their questioning because they had things to say about the project."

"And? Did you get any hints as to where they are hiding?"

"Just one. Inside the dust cloud. Which you suspect already. Naturally, they would not have been risked had they known more. I wish we could have taken the Mistress of the Ship who brought them in."

"Of course. What did they have to say otherwise?"

"We learned a lot about what they've been doing, which is mostly marking time and hoping the aliens find them before you do. They are no longer so confident of Bestrei."

"What?"

"It turns out that our estimates of the Serke situation were not quite right. They have no direct contact with the aliens. What they have is a very large alien ship orbiting a planet. They have been studying it and appropriating from it, while they wait for its builders to come looking for it."

"But…"

"Give me a chance, Marika. There is a story. I'd better tell it so you know what I'm talking about."

"I think you'd better. Starting from the beginning."

"All right. Here it is. Way back, a venturesome Serke Mistress of the Ship…"

"Kher-Thar Prevallin?"

"Exactly. That most famous of the farwanderers. A legend of our own times. But if you keep interrupting you will never hear the story."

"Sorry."

"Way back, Kher-Thar decided she wanted to see what lay on the far side of the dust cloud. While she was passing through she decided to rest her bath at a particular world. An almost optimally friendly one, by all accounts. After several days down she had just reached orbital distance departing when the alien ship appeared, I take it out of the Up-and-Over. The way I was told, it was not there one moment, and there the next. It detected the darkship and gave chase. Out of curiosity, apparently."

Marika grumbled beneath her breath. He was stretching it.

"No. There was no evidence the creatures aboard were hostile. But Kher-Thar, you will recall, was not known for her cool head. She panicked. Thinking she was being attacked, she attacked first. The aliens were unable to deal with her, though she was not known for the strength of her talent for the dark side. The aliens abandoned the chase. Kher-Thar scrambled into the Up-and-Over and scurried home, nearly killing her bath."

"I always thought she was overrated. She was a total misfit, which is why the Serke put up with her wandering in the first place. They wanted her out of their fur."

"You would understand that better than I."

"Vicious, Bagnel. Tell your story."

"Let me."

"Well?"

"The aliens who survived Kher-Thar's attack managed to get their ship into a stable orbit around the planet, but could not save themselves. When Kher-Thar returned, accompanied by a horde of Serke investigators, they were all dead. The investigators knew the importance of their find, but could make no sense of it. After long and often savage debate their ruling council voted to ask the dark-faring brethren bonds for help. Ever since, for more than twenty years, they have been studying the alien ship, appropriating equipment and technology, and waiting for another ship to come looking for the first."

"Why do they think one will come? We seldom send anyone to look for a lost darkship."

"I am not certain. But they are convinced one will. Perhaps because of the investment such a vessel would represent. The prisoners said it is huge. That for us to build, it would take an effort on the scale of the mirror project."

"Then everything they did to us in the Ponath was purely on speculation? They might have gotten nothing at all for their trouble?"

"Apparently. Even under truthsaying the prisoners insist that no meth has ever met one of the aliens alive."

"Idiots."

"Maybe. You don't know how you would have reacted in identical circumstances. One like your Gradwohl, obsessed with making the Reugge Community into a power, might have done the same. Or worse. You dare not fault the Serke without faulting all silth. They were being silth."

"I will not argue that. I will only say they behaved in the most stupid fashion possible in being silth. And they continue in their stupidity. All those years and no ship has come? And they have not given up?"

"How long have you been looking for them?"

"More years than some care to count. Grauel and Barlog are not happy with me."

"It is the only hope they have left, Marika. If the aliens do not come, sooner or later you will. And, as I said, they are afraid Bestrei is no longer what she was.

"Suppose that ship was an explorer, the same as Kher-Thar's? With no more fixed a routine than hers? Suppose she had been lost instead? How long have you looked, knowing the place existed?"

"Even so… I suppose I understand."

"So I think you should go on looking, though I am sure the search is wearing. You have to be getting closer, if only by the process of elimination. But so must the aliens. I wouldn't like to guess what might happen if the Serke were to make common cause with them."

"The weapons that destroyed TelleRai."

"Not to mention those mounted on the ships the rogues used. We have studied those endlessly, from fragments we captured, and we can make no sense of them. I fear we are just too far away in knowledge and technology. They might as well be your witchcraft. Nevertheless, brethren in the sciences believe larger weapons of the same sort could be used against planetary targets."

"I will admit I have been tempted to give up the hunt."

"I thought so when I saw you, Marika. You look tired. As if you're ready to accept defeat. But enough of that. I really did not come here on business. I'm dedicated to carrying out my orders, which are to spend a few months without worrying."

"How is the project coming?"

"Seventy percent completion on the leading mirror. Forty on the trailing. The orbitals for making fine and local adjustments are in place. We're getting almost forty percent of peak output. I understand that they have begun to have an effect. There was no measurable advance of the permafrost line this past winter."

"How far did it get?"

"Almost to the tropics. Well past Ruhaack. But it should begin to fall back soon. If the dust gets no thicker. And the probes we have run in the direction the sun is moving show no increase in density along the path to be followed for the next five hundred years. I think we will win the battle against the long winter. And, though you have spent very little time on it since you got it going, you will be remembered as the dam of the project."

"I am not much concerned about how the future recalls me, so long as there is a future. And I am still battling for it out here. In a hunt that, I am sure, will not be in vain, and that will not last much longer."

Bagnel bowed his head as if to mask his expression.

"Well, tradermale. Adventurer. Want to make it a working holiday? I can squeeze another body onto my darkship. You could be the first male ever to see new worlds."

III

Bagnel stepped down off the darkship and surveyed the encampment with the look of one returning home. "I'll confess this, Marika. I never once worried about the project."

Marika lifted a lip in amusement. "It could not have been that bad. It wasn't the same as traveling in *High Night Rider?*"

"No. It was not the same. As you know perfectly well. It was more like falling forever. It was more unnerving than riding a darkship at home. There is something under your feet there, even if it is several thousand feet down. Still…"

"What is that look in your eye?" Marika kept one eye on her bath and Grauel and Barlog, making sure *they* made sure the darkship was being readied for its next journey. She ruled the base strictly. She insisted all darkships be ready to lift at a moment's notice. The Serke could strike at any time. Would strike, she suspected, if they knew where to find her. She was stuck to their trail like the stubbornest hunting arft.

"Wonder, I suppose. I have to admit that, harrowing as it was, the experience touched something in me. I could develop a taste for exploration."

"Give up the mirrors, then. I am here. The darkship is here."

He looked at her narrowly, startled and tempted. "I think not, Marika. Your sisters would not understand."

"I suppose not. It was just a thought. Maybe someday. When the project is complete. When the Serke have been disposed of. When the aliens have been found and some sort of accommodation with them has been reached. Wouldn't it be in the grand tradition for us to fly away and never be seen again?"

He picked it up as a game. "Yes. We could just go on exploring, skipping from star to star, forever. We might be touched occasionally, in the far distance, and rumors would rise about a ghost darkship flitting out on the edge of the void. Young, fresh Mistresses would bring their darkships out to hunt the legend."

"But it couldn't be. We couldn't carry enough stores. And where would I find willing bath?"

"Oh, well."

"Tomorrow we will go out again. There is no end of stars in this sector—though those really worth investigating are running short."

But Marika returned to space much sooner.

The night was just hours old when a sudden, sharp, panicky touch smote Marika. *Darkship! Starting down. Not from home.*

Marika rushed from her hut. The base began coming to life around her. Darkship crews rushed to their ships. The touch came again. *Serke! Oh. They have detected us. They are starting back up. They are fleeing. They are very frightened. The otherworld reeks of their fear. Hurry!*

"Grauel! Barlog! Will you come on? We're going up!"

Sleepy-eyed, the untouched huntresses had come out to learn the cause of the commotion.

Marika's bath raced toward the wooden darkship, pre-flight rites forgotten.

Marika tossed her rifle across her shoulder and dashed after them, shouting, "Come, you two. The Serke."

Grauel and Barlog raced for the darkship after snatching their weapons.

One voidship was off the ground already, rising swiftly. Marika's eyes were fiery as she glared at her senior bath, who was not hustling the silver bowl around fast enough to suit her.

"Wait!"

Bagnel wobbled toward them, trying to keep his trousers from tripping him by holding them up with one paw.

"No," Marika said. "This is the real thing, Bagnel. There are Serke up there."

Bagnel played deaf. He lined up for his turn at the silver bowl. The bath muttered something unappreciative, let him sip. Grauel extracted another flask of liquid from the locker under the axis platform and dumped it into the bowl. Then she dug out a spare rifle and forced it upon him. "One I owe you, male."

"I see you still carry the one I gave you at Akard."

"It has been a faithful tool. Like me, though, it is getting old and cranky."

Marika swore. The other darkship was aloft now. The first had dwindled to a speck, its Mistress driving it hard. And she had not yet gathered her ghosts. "You meth strap down good," she said. "Everyone strap down. This is going to be the ride of your lives."

Bagnel was strapped already. He began disassembling the weapon Grauel had given him. The huntress nodded with approval. Seated, she and Barlog did likewise with their own weapons.

Marika snatched the bowl from the senior bath, gulped its contents, then bounced to her place at the tip of the wooden dagger. She went down through her loophole and snagged ghosts, lifted off, and continued gathering ghosts as she rose, dropping smaller specimens as she snatched ever bigger, stronger denizens of the otherworld. She pressed mercilessly.

She overhauled one darkship at fifty thousand feet and the other before it made orbital altitude. All the while she caressed the void with the touch, tracking the Serke darkship as it fled toward where it could clamber into the Up-and-Over. She soon had its line of retreat clearly defined in her mind.

It pointed toward a section of cloud she had not yet explored. She sketched an imaginary circle around that line, finding only four stars within it. She discarded the one farthest off center.

She reached with the touch and told the other two Mistresses of the Ship, *We will pursue. There are three stars close to their line of flight. I will take this one.* She sent a picture of the stars and indicated which she had chosen for herself, then assigned each of them one of the two remaining. *Push yourselves. Try to arrive before they do.*

That was unlikely, she thought. Even for her, with her advantages. Though time lapses in the Up-and-Over depended on the strength and talent of the individual Mistress of the Ship, the Serke Mistress had a long start and death raving behind her to motivate her.

Marika began pushing down her chosen course before she reached orbital altitude and began gathering ghosts for the Up-and-Over long before she reached the traditional jumping distance. She grabbed at the Up-and-Over only minutes behind the Serke—long before she should have. Echoes of silent terror came from her bath, whom she had pushed near hysteria already with her demands.

Blackness, twisting. A sensation of infinite nothing. A hint of a deep space ghost, a great black ghost, startled by the voidship's passage.

Then light again. The target star lay nearby. Marika struggled to gain her bearings, groggy from the violence of her plunge through the Up-and-Over.

The bath recovered more slowly than she. While she waited on them Marika reached into the surrounding void, searching for the Serke darkship.

Mentally righted, the senior bath left her station to prepare another silver bowl.

Marika's probe revealed that the star had no planets. It might have had at one time, but something had happened. Perhaps too close a brush with another star. The surrounding void teemed with rocky fragments, some of them bigger than the moon Biter back home. None were big enough to retain an atmosphere, and nowhere could Marika sense the betraying glow of life.

There were no Serke bases here.

And no Serke darkship.

She stalked up the blade of the wooden dagger to see how Grauel, Barlog, and Bagnel had fared. She had drawn upon them as well as upon the bath, though the strength they had to lend was feeble.

Bagnel looked sick, like he might vomit any second. He was down, clutching the framework with his eyes sealed. Grauel and Barlog looked strained and a little stunned by the savagery of the passage, but they had been with her long enough and had been through enough to be accustomed to the occasional violent passage. Though this had outdone everything that had gone before.

Marika touched Bagnel briefly, gently, encouragingly. The one silth ability for which she had very little talent was healing, but she tried to let well-being flow from her to him. He nodded. He was all right. He was just shaken.

She suspected, in her more dark moments, that she was a poor healer because she was not sufficiently whole and at peace within herself.

She started back toward her station.

Plop!

It had the feel of the sound of a pebble falling into water as heard from beneath the surface, only it fell upon the silth part of her mind.

The Serke darkship.

Where?

She searched, found a line, drove toward the enemy darkship. If she could strike before they recovered....

They sensed her coming, turned, gained velocity rapidly. Marika swept into their wake, skidding like an aircraft in a tight turn, began gaining, began snapping up stellar landmarks as she went. Those were few indeed. This deep in the cloud only a dozen stars were visible in any direction.

The Serke ship vanished. Marika fixed its line of flight and a target star and grabbed for the Up-and-Over herself.

She did not press as hard this time. She guessed she need not strain so to arrive first.

Correct.

From that second system, in the dense heartstream of the dust, only three stars were visible. One was that from which Marika had come.

There was no life in that system. Nor had there ever been any, for the star was a dwarf of a type never associated with planets. Marika scanned star and system only casually. Then she concentrated upon those two farther stars.

One was a red giant.

The other was a yellow, like the meth home sun.

Elation filled her.

She had sniffed out a hot trail at last.

She gathered everyone at the axis and had the senior bath pass the silver bowl again. Once everyone had sipped and taken a few moments to relax, she pulled the darkship into the Up-and-Over again and returned the way she had come. Back to the base world.

Let the Serke think they had eluded her.

CHAPTER THIRTY-FIVE

I

Bagnel left the wooden darkship at the Hammer. Marika scanned the surrounding void. The Hammer was just one of a dozen huge orbital stations now, and far from the largest. Near space seemed almost uncomfortably crowded. There had been many changes during the years she had been gone. Some she had heard about, of course, but the seeing was nothing like the hearing.

She wanted to make a pass by the leading trojan, to see her brainchild, but responded to the anxieties of Grauel and Barlog. They had not set foot on the homeworld in nearly seven years. It was time to be attentive to their needs. Time to take the darkship down. The mirror would be there forever.

Too, the huntresses wanted to move fast, lest some unpleasant welcome be arranged.

Marika did not arrive ahead of the news of her coming. Bagnel had not been able to keep her return quiet simply because there were meth who had known he was with her. Random touches, mostly unfamiliar, brushed her, curious. She descended toward Ruhaack, ignoring the touches, sending only one of her own ahead, to warn the Reugge cloister that she was coming in.

Most Senior Bel-Keneke herself came out to meet Marika. Marika fixed her gaze upon the Reugge first chair, ignoring the amused silth studying her wooden darkship and the firearms that she and her companions bore. She tried to read Bel-Keneke.

She had been gone so long. This would be a changed world, perhaps a different world....

Assuredly a different world. She could feel the difference. There were new smells in the air, smells of heavy industry, such as had plagued Maksche when the air was still. But Ruhaack was far from any industry. The smell must be everywhere.

Had it become a world remade in the image of a brethren dream? Had it become what she had battled to avoid, simply because that was what had to be to escape the grasp of the grauken winter?

She glanced up. The mirror in the leading trojan stood high in the sky, almost too bright for her eyes. Yet the air seemed colder than she remembered.

Snow lay everywhere. It looked very deep.

She could not recall what the season should be. She suspected the snow would be there no matter which. Bagnel had said the permafrost line had moved far south of Ruhaack before it halted.

The silth awaiting her looked thin and haggard. They had not been eating well. So, too, the bonds waiting to handle the darkship. So. How much worse for the run of meth?

Marika let the darkship drop the last few inches, formally reuniting her with her homeworld. When she stepped down she nearly collapsed. She had pushed herself too hard making the long journey homeward.

Bel-Keneke greeted her with elaborate honors. Marika returned the greeting formulas, pleased that her stature had not suffered in her absence.

"Welcome home, far-fared," Bel-Keneke said, now speaking for herself rather than as the voice of the Community. "We wondered if we would ever see you again. There have been repeated rumors that you had perished in the dark gulf, that you lived on only in legend, that the Redoriad were only pretending you were still alive to keep the warlock and his ilk afraid."

"I have gone farther afield than any silth before me, Bel-Keneke. I have seen ten thousand stars and marveled at ten thousand wonders. I can tell ten thousand stories that no one would believe. So. I have come back to the world of ice. I have come home."

"You have abandoned the hunt? You have given up? We surely can use your help here."

"No, I have not given up. Not exactly. Why would you need my help?"

"Rogues."

"Ah. And my friend Bagnel was convinced no one would want me around, poking my nose into that business. That everyone would be happier were I to stay a legend among the stars."

"No doubt there are a great many high silth who would feel that way. Your return is sure to be the topic of discussion in every cloister. It will be searched and researched endlessly for meaning. But I speak only for myself and the Reugge. We are glad to have you here, and we will welcome your help."

"Tell me."

"That can wait. We are standing in the weather. You have just set foot to earth. You need rest more than you need news."

"This is true. Are there quarters for me?"

"The same as always. They are being cleaned and the heat let in."

"Good. Will you attend me there at your earliest convenience? Would that be too much of an imposition?"

Bel-Keneke blinked, glanced at Grauel, Barlog, and Marika's bath, none of whom had departed for bath quarters. "I think not." She was feeling around, trying to recall how one dealt with the wild silth Marika.

Marika, too, was trying to remember. Seven years she had done without the artificial protocol and ceremonial of homeworld silthdom. Seven years since she had seen Bel-Keneke. Perhaps the most senior no longer felt indebted.

Marika nodded. "Please do not speculate. To anyone, or even within yourself. I am here. That is enough for now. Let other sisterhoods drive themselves silly trying to figure out what I am about."

"Yes." Bel-Keneke seemed amused. "Will you need anything? Other than your quarters, and food?"

"A roster of all the current most seniors and ruling councils of all the dark-faring sisterhoods. Eventually, I suppose, the interesting and relevant data on the rogue problem. Though I may not be inclined to help those who have not helped themselves."

"I will see to it." Bel-Keneke blinked some more. "Welcome home, Marika." She hurried away.

Marika watched her go, a little puzzled. She had not been able to read Bel-Keneke well. Had she lost the touch while away? Perhaps because she had been with so few meth for so long, and all of them well known?

Bel-Keneke vanished through a doorway. "Come." Marika gestured. Grauel, Barlog, and the bath followed her, trying to ignore the stares of the meth in the landing court. That the bath did not go to the bath dormitories would fuel wild speculation, Marika knew. But she doubted anyone would strike on the truth, and to allow them a chance to let that slip seemed a greater risk.

It was a strain, keeping her eyes open till Bel-Keneke arrived. The others she sent to rest as soon as they had eaten and the workers had been chased from the still frigid apartment. She tossed more wood on the fire, paced before it awhile. She had been on warmer worlds too long.

Pausing to gaze out the window, she watched a small brethren dirigible drift down and begin unloading firewood and what probably were food stores. Perhaps she had been unwise to take the old Serke cloister as the new Reugge main cloister. Maybe she should have chosen a site nearer the equator.

She had to give up. Her eyes refused to remain open. She put still more wood on the fire, then slouched in a chair before it.

Bel-Keneke's scratch at the door did not waken her. But the squeak of hinges as she let herself in did. Marika sprang up, rifle swinging to cover the most senior.

"Oh. I am sorry, mistress," she apologized. "I dozed, and out there we are accustomed to…"

"No matter," Bel-Keneke replied, regaining her composure. "I believe I understand. May I?" She indicated another chair.

"Of course. Come close. Singe your fur. It is very cold here. Is it winter, or has the weather turned this bad? Or have I just forgotten how bad it was?"

"It is the heart of winter. The coldest time. But these days the summers are little better. You could have forgotten. I do not recall the winters having been much more harsh when you left. And the mirror meth tell us that from orbit you can see that the project is beginning to have an effect."

"My friend Bagnel told me the permafrost line has been halted."

"So they say. The energy from the mirrors falls day and night. When both are finished there will be no more night. What will we silth do if we do not have the dark?" She twitched her ears to signify that that was a joke. "I have hopes of seeing another summer before I join my foredams in the embrace of the All."

"The project continues well? Asking Bagnel did me no good. He is as determined a pessimist as ever."

"Very well. It remains ahead of schedule, more or less. The sisterhoods and brethren remain unified and determined, much to my amazement. If you had asked me when we began I would have said there was no chance there would be any enthusiasm left at this time. But there is. I suppose because those with the training can see positive results. There is, however, that element I mentioned before."

"Yes. It is just possible I may have a cure for that. I have come home to…" Marika paused. Some great reluctance held her tongue. It was almost as if some part of her did not want an era to end.

Bel-Keneke waited expectantly.

Marika forced it. "I have found them."

"The rogues?"

"The rogues and Serke. Yes."

"Why are you here? You have dispatched them?"

"I have not. It is not something I wish to hazard alone. For many reasons. No. I have come home to ask for a convention. For this I want to gather all the voidfaring darkships of all the Communities."

"I was certain you would…"

"Go after them myself? Perhaps the Serke think the same. I hope so. It will keep them confident that they have not been found out. But I would not try it alone. I am not that wild novice from the Ponath anymore, Bel-Keneke. I have learned to regard consequences. And our enemies are not the Serke of yore. They are not true silth at all anymore."

Bel-Keneke did not care to comment. She just sat there toasting her boots, face composed in a mask of neutrality, waiting.

"Were I to go in alone, and challenge Bestrei alone, and were I to defeat her, still nothing would change. They would not accept the failure. They would destroy me and keep on. They put the old ways, the traditions, the laws, aside long ago, the day TelleRai died. Would the meth who cast down the fire upon TelleRai…"

"I understand. I do not like it, but I understand. They have backed themselves into a position where they must do what they must to survive."

"Then you understand why they must be approached with all the force that can be mustered."

"I see it, but I do not think you will win much support. Many of the old starfarers have retired now. They are content working the mirror project. They may be content letting the Serke lie. Those who do venture to the starworlds now are younger. They are not motivated by the hunt. For them, come from here, the grauken is a danger more to be feared than the legendary Serke. I believe times have changed. Though I could be wrong. Certainly there are those of us who do remember, and who still hurt."

"We shall see. What I would like, if possible, is a quiet gathering of the most seniors of the dark-faring silth. Those who do remember and who have the power to order done what needs doing. If we move quickly, we can strike before the news reaches the rogues."

"You are sure they do not know you have found them?"

"Only one meth outside my crew knows. And the crew only suspect. And them I intend to keep here in the apartment till decisions are made and action begun."

"Who is that one?"

"You, mistress."

Bel-Keneke gave her a strained glance.

"The story is a simple one. For the past several years I have made my base on a world where we stumbled across evidence that the Serke had once rested a darkship crew. Just recently a Serke darkship, possibly headed here, appeared. We pursued it and it pointed the way, though I allowed the Serke Mistress to believe she had lost me. She was not as strong as I."

"They will have defenses, Marika. They know you are hunting."

"Of course. That is another reason I do not care to undertake the final move alone. If I am lost, nothing is gained for anyone else."

"I will contact the most seniors immediately. I fear I cannot promise much, but I will do my best." Bel-Keneke passed Marika a large envelope. "These are my comments upon the various most seniors. As you asked. I think, though, that you should rest before you do anything else. You do not look ready to challenge the universe."

"I do not feel ready. You are right. I have driven myself hard for a long time. I will rest before I begin studying them. Thank you."

"Good. I will return tomorrow, then. I should have a response from the most seniors. I will tell them as little as I can, and what I do tell I will bind with oaths."

"Yes. That you must. Though the news will escape soon enough."

Bel-Keneke rose and moved toward the door. A few feet short of the exit she halted, turned, looked at Marika oddly.

"Yes?" Marika asked.

"A random thought. About how you have become a huntress despite having become silth."

"I have had similar thoughts often enough. But what game I stalk. Eh?"

"Yes. Tomorrow, then."

"Tomorrow."

II

Marika wakened in the night, cold but somehow more comfortable than she had been in years. She had missed being enfolded in the homeworld's unconscious background of touch. Even the base, with its population of transients, had not become comfortable.

She entered the room where Grauel and Barlog were sleeping and found them resting peacefully. She studied them in the light cast by the coals in their fireplace, wondering that they had remained with her so long, through so much. She knew they would continue till the All reclaimed them, though it was past time they moved on into the role of the Wise. Both had gone gray. Barlog had lost more spots of fur.

She considered ordering them to remain behind when she returned to the void. But she knew she would not. She could not, for they would be hurt beyond measure. They were her pack. They were her only true sisterhood. Her loyalties beyond those two attenuated very quickly. And they had none but to her and to a dream of yesterday.

She went back to the fireplace in the main room, added firewood, settled in her chair. She opened Bel-Keneke's envelope.

Few of the names had changed. Death had not been busy during her absence. She wondered what time had done to change those old silth. Attitudes were most important. Had they lost their desire to finish the question of the Serke?

Attitudes could not be gotten from pieces of paper. Those she would not know till she had faced the meth themselves.... She became restless.

She missed Bagnel.

Already? She mocked herself. It had been but hours since their parting.

For how long this time? Years again? Somehow, that seemed insupportable.

She went to the window and stared at endless vistas of white, skeletal in the moonlight. Biter grinned down like a skull, Chaser like something hungry in close pursuit. That was a change, if noticeable only to one who had been gone a long time. There was no permanent overcast.

She looked past the moons, and all the roving dots of light that had not been there before, in the direction whence she had come. She would be going out there again, soon. And this time she might not come back. Win *or* lose.

"How old are you, Bestrei?" she whispered. "Too old? Or still young enough?" Her restlessness increased. Finally she could stand it no more.

She went to the cabinet where she had stored her saddleship in times long gone, times that seemed to belong to another's past. Who had that been, that pup-silth who had drawn a bloody paw across the face of the world?

The saddleship was there still, ready for assembly. It had not been touched. She brushed dust from her personal witch signs.

She considered only a moment more.

The outside air was more bitter than she remembered. She ignored the chill, drifting above the rooftops of Ruhaack, between pillars of smoke, looking longingly on winter-bound streets where nothing moved.

An occasional curious touch brushed her and departed satisfied. Her presence was accepted. She was home.

She was pleased. They were alert, for all that they could not be seen.

Where was Kublin now? What was he thinking? He must have had word of her return by this time. Could he guess its significance? Would his rogues react?

She should let it be whispered that she had come home to break their backs again. They would believe it. Kublin the warlock would believe it. He was mad. He feared her. Feared her as he feared nothing else, for he knew that he had strained her mercy beyond endurance.

They all feared her. For them she was the grauken, the stalker of the night without mercy, without pity. She was the hunger that would devour them all.

The rogue problem had been of great concern to Bagnel. She ought to examine it while she was here. Ought to get back into touch with it. Perhaps she could again find a fresh approach that would give these earthbound silth a novel way to defend themselves while she hunted down the ultimate authors of the dissatisfaction that produced the rogues.

She looked to the stars.

After Bestrei, perhaps. After a probe to the far face of the dust cloud, to look for the aliens. Then a short time home, to eliminate Kublin and secure her bridgeheads behind her.

This time she must. This time the world would be watching. This time there could be no mercy even were she so inclined.

She had slain Gradwohl, her mentor, rather than be thwarted. Why not Kublin? In terms of her own wild frontier culture, let alone that of the silth, a male meant less. Even a littermate. Even a male who was the last surviving male of the Degnan pack.

Soon sunlight set the eastern sky aglow. It was time to return, to catch a nap before Bel-Keneke brought the results of her contacts with the most seniors. Below, meth had begun moving through the snowy streets. An occasional startled eye or paw of greeting rose when her shadow passed.

She considered the soft silver brightness of the mirror in the trailing trojan, which had risen before the sun. Unlike the mirror in the leading trojan, it did not yet appear impressive.

The smaller mirrors in geocentric orbit formed a necklace across the morning. Where they doing any real good? Was the project all wishful thinking, despite Bagnel's positive reports?

She drifted in through her window and, after dismantling her saddleship, stoked up the fire and sat before it, warming her paws. A glance around at ancient stone, piled into a structure by Serke bonds and engineers thousands of years before her birth. It was a fortress haunted by time. A long way from a Ponath loghouse, she thought. A long, long way.

She knew she was aging. She had not been very reflective when she was younger.

Much to Marika's surprise, Bel-Keneke arrived before anyone else stirred. Marika responded to her scratch, let her in, then returned to her place before the fire. "You are up and about early, mistress."

After hesitating Bel-Keneke took the other chair. "I have been up awhile. I heard you were out on your saddleship. I thought if you were up and around already we might as well get started. I have spoken to all the appropriate most seniors. It took rather less time than I anticipated. None of them were surprised. They had their decisions made."

"Yes?" Marika was surprised, if the several dark-faring most seniors were not.

"They had heard of your return and suspected its import. From those who were more talkative I gathered that it has long been an article of faith that Marika the Huntress would not return till she had sniffed out her quarry's den. You will be pleased to hear that, without exception, they have issued orders to their starfaring Mistresses of the Ship to assemble at your base world."

Marika faced Bel-Keneke. "I honestly did not expect such a quick, affirmative response. Certainly not a unanimous one. From what Bagnel had to say I gathered that my return would not be greeted with unreserved joy. I expected to have to argue and threaten for weeks."

"Some decisions have been debated on the quiet for years, Marika. I think every most senior knew in her heart what she would say when the time came. Too, as some mentioned, a formal convention would cost valuable time and would draw unwanted attention. So the thing was done entirely informally, quietly, and the darkships will join you as quickly as they can be redirected."

"I have missed something, I suspect. All this without debate. Without consulting me to see if I might have been touched by the All and gone raving mad? I have a feeling I must do some reflecting."

"It is a thing that needs doing, Marika. That is long overdue to be done. We cannot survive if this shadow persists. The rogue problem is about to go out of control. Defeat of the Serke and those brethren rebels who fled with them would deal the warlock's followers a crippling emotional blow. Suddenly they would stand alone, with no hope of gaining the technology they believe will give them victory. Their only weapon would be the sorcery of the warlock—the very thing they are fighting to destroy."

Marika nodded and waited. The rogue problem did deserve more examination before she departed.

Bel-Keneke continued, "All are agreed. Destroy the Serke and break the back of rogue hope. As for debate, what have we been doing? Everything has been debated a thousand times in your absence. Every nuance has been brought forward and laid open and the entrails read. Every most senior has had ample opportunity to examine her heart and determine where she must stand. And stand for this we must."

"It seems—almost disappointing. From the moment I turned homeward I have been steeling myself for a grand battle. All that worry wasted."

"The fact is, they think they know you, Marika. As I said, you coming home meant you had found the Serke. And they were confident that you would, one day. So some policy had to be established. Perhaps you could have had your big battle four, or even three, years ago. There are ancient enmities to be gotten around. Some cannot, even now, consult directly with others. Tacit agreement formed, and eventually solidified into fixed policy. If there was any way to manage it, every sisterhood would be there when the final confrontation came."

Marika had begun to catch a glimmer. "To make certain that the Reugge do not take up what the Serke began?"

"Probably. In part. You see some of it now, I think. There is always more to everything than meets the eye. You must set aside the simplicities of your life over the past seven years and recall the complexities of life on this world. All unity is born of fear. Have a care that you do not move before you are politically ready, able to do the thing backed by a mix of sisters that is above reproach."

"I understand."

"I am told that some voidships are headed out already. How soon will you leave to guide them?"

"Ah-ha," Marika murmured. "Glad to see you, so sad you have to leave."

"What?"

"I get the feeling that, whatever else it may signify, there is not great joy at Marika's return."

"To be honest, there is very little. As I have said, you have become a legend in your absence. And that legend is not entirely a positive one. Your great violences are the things that are remembered. As the legend grows, so grows the fear of what you may do next."

"I see." Marika reflected for a moment. "I will be staying a few days for sure. My huntresses and bath need to get into touch with the homeworld once more. I need to do that myself. When you return from so long out there you are almost stricken by the realization that something has been missing." She thought a moment more. "When I leave, it will be by night, secretly. Do not tell anyone that I have gone. Meantime, have bonds begin whispering that I have come home to silence the rogue menace."

"Are you sure?"

"They will hear of it quickly. The warlock will respond one of two ways. He will attack wildly, in which case you will decimate his followers, or he will go into hiding, taking his vermin with him, in which case you will have a breathing space in which to regain your balance. Further, if the world believes that I am here to hunt, it will not concern itself with other possibilities. It will not watch for me to slip off to the stars. Perhaps, even with the delay for assembly at my base, I can strike before the Serke learn that they have been found."

"Perhaps you should have remained most senior. You have the twisted bend of mind, like Gradwohl before you. You go at things no more directly than did she."

"I am happier being Marika. I never wanted first chair."

"For which I remain in your debt. Will I see you again?"

"Again?"

"Will you come back after you have subdued the Serke?"

"I expect to. There are the rogues. There is the warlock, with whom I have an especial grievance. He has been allowed to make free with his villainies for far too long."

Bel-Keneke did not seem pleased. Marika was surprised. After all this time she still did not feel secure in first chair?

She might be wise to watch her back once the Serke threat ceased to be. "Come to morning ceremonies with me," Marika suggested. "It has been half a generation since I celebrated them properly. It seems an appropriate time to petition the indulgence of the All."

"Very well," Bel-Keneke replied. Reluctantly. "I am behind in my own obligations."

They slipped out of the apartment quietly. But not so quietly that their departure went unremarked. Grauel took up a revolver and trailed them through the cloister halls.

III

Marika stood before the window, contemplating falling snow. Huge, slowly drifting flakes. Chill drifted in around the window frame and lapped across her toes. There were no real thoughts in her mind except that, out there somewhere, there was a pup whom she had loved more than any other creature. Her littermate. Her only ally when she was small. And now her most deadly, most intractable enemy.

And she did not understand.

What had happened in his life to make him change so? To shape him to such iron hatred?

For all she had sworn to herself, so many times, to forget, she still recalled the pup that was. That was the Kublin she knew, not this incredible monster called the warlock. This male *thing* with the skills of a silth and a mind so far askew that...

Some would say she was his mirror image. That she was mad too. So who knew?...

A feather of touch brushed her. It was time.

She retreated to the chair before the fire. The fire had died to coals barely putting out heat. She slipped her boots on, donned her coats, collected her personal arsenal, extended her touch to see if anyone was in the hallway.

All clear.

When first they had come among silth, Grauel and Barlog had been terrified of sisters who, they believed, could move about invisibly. This was not possible in reality. But a talented and cunning silth could use the touch below a conscious level to direct the gaze of others away, so that she might walk unnoticed except by those she did not notice herself. Marika extended that low level of touch as she passed through the cloister to the landing court.

It was the heart of night. Her precaution was unnecessary. No one was stirring.

Grauel and Barlog had the darkship prepared. The bath were ready. She strode to her place at the tip of the dagger. The senior bath touched her, asked about the bowl.

It will not be necessary this time. She had not told anyone anything about the flight. *We will not be going off planet.* The cloister would rise in the morning to find her gone, with nothing save a brief note saying she would return soon.

She surveyed the others. The snow was falling faster. The bath at the hilt of the dagger was the vaguest of dark shapes. They were ready. She secured herself with her straps. Seldom would she do without anymore, unlike the rash Marika who had dared fate every flight when first she had learned the darkships.

Up. Away. Low, over the steep slate rooftops. Here and there a brush of startled touch as some silth sensed a darkship passing. She brushed them aside, gained speed.

Her initial flight took her southwest, till she was beyond touch from the cloister, then she turned north and drove as hard as she dared into the fangs of the wind. It was as vicious as ever it had been.

The wooden darkship settled into the courtyard of Skiljansrode. Nothing seemed changed there, except that the surrounding snows were deeper and the old fortress harder to pinpoint. To the west there was a wall of ice, a massive glacial finger, forerunning the even more massive accumulations to the north. How much longer would the silth of Skiljansrode hang on? Till the ice groaned against the roots of the wall? Was secrecy worth so much?

The darkship touched down. As Marika stepped from the dagger there was one sharp touch from one of the bath: *Watch out!*

What had appeared to be banked snow exploded. Heavily armed voctors stepped forward, weapons ready. *Careful,* Marika sent, especially to Grauel and Barlog. She allowed herself to be disarmed, feeling little trepidation. It was impossible to disarm her truly without killing her. The others accepted disarmament with less grace.

A sleepy-eyed Edzeka appeared from the doorway leading to the inner fortress, way below the ice and earth. "Some greeting for your patron," Marika chided.

"You should have sent warning," Edzeka said without a hint of apology. "The visitors we get are seldom friendly. You are lucky the voctors gave you time to be recognized. Come. Cferemojt, return their weapons."

After the chill of the flight from Ruhaack Skiljansrode's interior seemed stiflingly hot. "That bears a little elucidation," Marika said. "That you seldom get friendly visitors. Do you get unfriendly ones?"

"Only the enemy knows where to find us. Three times he has sent forces against us. Three times we have devoured them, leaving none to take him their woe. But he will try again, because this place means much to him. It is more than just a place where he was held in bondage. This is a place that defies his technology. I believe he has been shocked. His talent suppressors have meant nothing here. We do not need the talent to obliterate his brigands. Intelligence is adequate. That must frighten him. That must make him suspect his doom may spring from this place."

"His doom will spring from *here*," Marika said, tapping her skull. "He is the reason I have come. Skiljansrode, though isolated, is the best place to begin taking those steps necessary to eliminate the rogue threat—assuming you have continued in the fashion set when I dwelt here myself."

"We go on. We seldom change."

Marika noted and ignored the continued disdain of ceremony and formality. Her own fault, of course. Gradwohl had created Skiljansrode, but she had shaped it, and she had had little use for ceremony or formality in those days. Or even now, most times, though sometimes a part of her insisted that it was her due. Was she not—though she never felt it herself—the preeminent silth of her generation?

"The intercept section is still in place?"

"It is. Though reduced. There is very little on which to eavesdrop these days. The brethren have changed their codes and signals since they now know we eavesdrop, but we have kept up with their honest side. Only the rogues themselves give us much trouble. But their traffic is seldom significant. *He* knows we are listening. He must have his important messages paw-delivered."

"Very well. I will be spending most of my time in communications and intercept, arranging some unpleasantries for him."

"How long may we expect to share your company?"

"You will not have to endure me long. Perhaps two days. Three at the most. How long depends on how quickly I make my contacts and how cooperative I find those who have not seen or heard from me in ages."

Edzeka understood that well enough. "And it is true, what they are saying?"

"Is what true? What are they saying?"

"That you have found the Serke."

"Where did you get that idea?"

"Off intercept. It is the topic of the day. Did Marika return to the homeworld because she has found the Serke at last? Has she destroyed them? Has she not? In either case, if they have indeed been found, what will that mean to silth, to rogues, to the honest brethren, to meth in general? Will the Reugge arrogate to themselves the technology of the aliens, as they arrogated the Serke starworlds?"

"What? We received three poor planets and a begrudged right to venture beyond the homeworld's atmosphere. Hardly an arrogation, considering what we suffered at the paws of the Serke and their allies. We should have gotten it all. We would have taken it all had I been then what I am now. There would have been no negotiation, no convention, no nothing but the obliteration of the Serke and their allies."

"Calm yourself, mistress. I merely repeat what I have overheard. Those Communities that have been in the void for generations naturally resent the intrusion of the Reugge. They make accusations, take positions. Would they be silth if they did otherwise?"

"True. Of course. Posturing. Always posturing." But there was food for thought in what Edzeka had said. The solution of the Serke problem would raise new troubles possibly as dangerous. She had refused to face that before. It was time she invested in some reflection.

Marika had set herself a task. And for the first time she feared she had found one she could not handle. A simple job: Contact those silth who had worked with her in her days as the Reugge charged with bringing the rogue under control. Enlist them in a new and similar effort, gathering intelligence against her return from the meeting with the Serke.

But it was not simple. Many years had passed. All those silth had moved around, been promoted, passed into the embrace of the All, changed their names. Many were impossible to trace. Silth were not strong on keeping records.

Of those she did find, few were interested in helping. New duties, new responsibilities, new perquisites. Older and more sedentary, in some cases. Plain laziness in others. And complacency. The curse of most silth, complacency. How could anyone remain complacent after the events of recent decades?

The internal workings of the Reugge were more orderly than those of most Communities. Marika had less trouble finding old allies and agents. But even there she had trouble recruiting. Many did not wish to be identified with her anymore. She was not in power and not upon the pathway to power. She had abdicated.

Yet she did locate a few score old accomplices willing to strive for the communal defense, who recalled the old hard ways and who were willing to seek and implement new hard ways of excising the cancer surrounding the warlock.

Probably most of those thought they saw a chance to improve their places.

"The world changes," Marika told Grauel. "But silth do not. Not in any way that matters. I think we may be living in the last years, at the end of time, as silth history goes. And those fools do not begin to suspect." She leaned back in a chair. Grauel and Barlog watched with faces of stone. "They cannot see anything in the mirror of the world. They cannot foresee with the simple intellect the All has given them. In one way it does not matter if the warlock is eliminated. I can obliterate him and everyone who serves him, to the last rogue meth, and still what he symbolizes will live on, just as strong. It is a poison in the heart of the race. Why do I even bother?"

Barlog said, "Because you must. Because you are what you are."

"Profound, I think, Barlog. You are saying more than you think you say. Because I must. Yes. And perhaps all those dead silth who declared me a Jiana were also saying something they did not know they said. Maybe I will, in a way they could not imagine, preside over the downfall of silthdom. I think I may be the doomstalker, but not so much the cause as the product of the event."

Grauel and Barlog had no further remarks. Marika didn't need to read their minds to know they did not doubt that the fall of the silth would be a universal benefice. Most of the world felt that way. In battling to preserve what she herself did not love she was battling the very tides of time.

This world had seen that there were other ways.

And that *could* be her fault. *She* had put those artificial suns up there where even the most remote savage could see that mystery and magic were not all the answers. Could see that they were not even the best answers. Could sense that they were not answers in which any but the very privileged few could share....

It could be that she had written the doom of silthdom in an effort to save the race on whose backs silthdom rested.

"I am grateful for your aid and cooperation," Marika told Edzeka. "I believe these few days may have made it possible for us to concoct a few unpleasant surprises for the warlock once I return."

"Now you go to meet Bestrei, eh?"

Marika did not answer that. She asked, "All the world is convinced that it has come to that?"

"That is the message of the intercepts. The Serke have been found, and Marika is going out to meet their champion."

"Then the warlock may believe it too. He will be considering moves. Beware, Edzeka. You are right about his attitude toward this place. Skiljansrode does much valuable work, and most of it hurts him. Do not let me hear that you have been called into the embrace of the All before your time."

"If I am lost, many rogues will light my path into the darkness, Marika. You have a care where you are going. The race can ill afford to lose you, little as many value you. You are probably the only silth who could deal with these aliens reasonably."

"I will be most careful. I am nearing the end of the list of those things I must do for others. I am on the brink of freedom. I have no intention of wasting that. Grauel, is the darkship prepared?"

"We are waiting on your pleasure."

"Very well. Edzeka, fare you well."

"Where to, Marika?" Barlog asked as she and Marika approached the darkship. Night held the world in shroud.

"Ruhaack, where we will reappear as we disappeared. Without announcement or ceremony."

"And then?"

Marika pointed upward. "And then we go out there again. The dark-faring Communities have begun assembling their strength. I will lead it in the final run of the long hunt."

"And then?"

"Kublin, I suppose."

"And then?"

Irked, Marika snapped, "That is enough! Until the time comes. Let be, Barlog. Let be."

"As you command, mistress. As you command."

That night Marika took the darkship into the high cold and rode with the wind, without strapping down, letting the freedom and risk of flight leech away the uncertainty and anger.

CHAPTER THIRTY-SIX

I

There were nineteen voidships waiting at Marika's baseworld when she arrived. A challenge greeted her the instant she came out of the Up-and-Over. Several of those ships were in the deep, patrolling. The others, on the ground, were so packed together that they could not have lifted off in any hurry. There was little room to bring more down. Few voidships could be dismantled or folded the way on-planet darkships could.

High Night Rider was in orbit. Kiljar's successor, Balbrach, was aboard. In fact, Marika soon discovered that Bel-Keneke was among the pawful of most seniors of dark-faring Communities who had chosen not to appear.

She was surprised. So much interest by so many who stood so high.

Nineteen darkships. And a twentieth arrived before Marika had completed her descent to the surface. Nearly all the dark-faring sisterhoods were represented, including several with which Marika had had no prior contact. She was impressed. In both scale and scope the gathering was more than she had hoped it would be.

With the exception of the Redoriad, the most seniors were down on the surface, awaiting her. She was surprised and pleased to find that they treated her as the most senior of the baseworld. She had anticipated having to face down several too arrogant to accept that.

Once Marika had eaten and rested and refreshed herself she led her high visitors down to the place where Grauel had discovered the old fire site. There was nothing to see, but it was a good, isolated place where leaders could talk, free of the watchful eyes of those they ruled. And it had symbolic significance as the first step upon a long trail.

Another two darkships arrived. The newcomers had to ground where they could. There was no more room at the main site.

Marika carried her weapons and wore her most barbarous garb. She and Grauel and Barlog wore bloodfeud dyes. With the most seniors assembled, Marika said, "What we are about to attempt will not be easy. Our enemies have had a decade to prepare for our coming. Much as we might wish tradition to hold, they will not be satisfied to have the matter settled by the outcome of a meeting between Bestrei and myself—if their champion fails them. We may expect to face alien weapons. We may have to face the talent suppressor we have seen used by rogues at home. We may expect almost anything—including the fact that some of us are going to die."

She marched back and forth, trying to look fierce, and something in Grauel's eye gave her pause. Then she realized what it was. Grauel was seeing yesterday. Just this way had her dam, Skiljan, paced in the hours of decision before the nomad had come down upon the Degnan packstead. This was the tone, the tenor, Skiljan had used on speaking to her huntresses before leading them out of the packstead to attack a nomad gathering below Machen Cave.

She gave Grauel a slight bow to indicate that she knew what the old huntress was thinking. She growled, "If you are not prepared to die, are not prepared to face the worst you can imagine, you may go now. But hear my spoken word. My blood pledge. She who does not partake of the risk will not partake of the profit. There will be no caviling of carrion eaters over the corpse as there was when the Serke properties were divided. We go to hunt, sisters! Those who will not hunt will not feast afterward. This is spoken by Marika of the Reugge. Is there one here who would argue?"

She was in a fine, ferocious mood. No one would have argued with her had she told the most outrageous lie. "Good. There was a saying in my home province, 'As strength goes.' I have never been one to brag. I will remind you this once. I am the strength. I am in my prime. When this has ended there will be no more Bestrei. I will have replaced her. My will shall rule that new starworld, as it does this one. And I will decide how we share in what we take from the rogues."

Now they did respond, and the response was bitter and protracted. Once Grauel took her weapon off her shoulder. That quieted the silth somewhat. Marika said, "I told you, I am the strength. But if you wish to dispute me, you may. Now or later. Ah? What? No takers? That is what I thought."

She continued, "Listen. I have grown weary of the way the sisterhoods feud with one another. I am not going to permit that out there. Bury your secret ambitions in the soil of this sad world. No one sisterhood is going to oust the Serke and leave the rest facing an unchanged situation. I say I will decide who shares what. What I mean is, I am going to hold that starworld in trust for all meth. With the exception of those who side with or do not help suppress the rogues."

She paced awhile, letting them bicker among themselves, then interrupted. "You may save your arguing and scheming for later. For now I only want to hammer upon one theme: that this is not going to be the simple bloodduel some expect. It is going to be darkwar, sisters, and darkwar as has never been seen in all the history of silthdom. The prize will be the future of the race. There will be many deaths. I hope most of those will be among our enemies. That is all I have to tell you now. Go. Prepare your hearts and minds. We will begin when we have twenty-five voidships rested and ready and willing."

She turned her back upon them and stood staring out across the hills of the world everyone but she accepted as hers.

Marika delayed till there were thirty darkships ready. And there was the promise of more to come. During the wait she visited *High Night Rider* and the Redoriad most senior, and arranged for a special role for the great voidship.

The day came when she felt she was stalling. She took her fears by the throat. Next morning, before dawn, the darkships began lifting, unhurriedly, and in some cases reluctantly. Perhaps she had waited too long. Too many of the silth had had time to reflect on what they might face. The fever of the hunt had begun to fade. Many were going on now only because they did not wish their orders to be cut out of the plunder.

Marika went up last—counting daggers.

The attack force numbered twenty-five ships, including her own and the Redoriad *High Night Rider*. The others would form a second wave, a reserve. *High Night Rider* would return for them and any who joined them too late for the first wave.

The darkships assembled around *High Night Rider,* forming the greatest concentration of voidships ever seen. That fact alone awed the silth. Only the mirror project had ever drawn more, and those were never gathered in a single drop of space. Marika peered at them, so many titanium daggers glistening in the light of a foreign sun, and she was awed herself. Once again she faced the fact that she was remarkable. Who else, with a word, could have drawn so many here? And so many of the mighty, at that?

Who was working the mirror project?

That could be set back years if the Serke had the perfect trap set at the far end of the Up-and-Over.

Marika closed her eyes, shunned all doubts, opened to the All, reached with a general touch, felt other minds grow aware. She opened her eyes again and fixed her gaze upon the first milestar of their journey. *See with me. This is our first target star. I will lead off. Come you behind me one by one. We will assemble again before continuing.*

She felt a murmur of assent, like the soft rush of water over sand. They, too, had put all doubts and reservations aside.

I am going.

She gathered her ghosts and went.

Blackness. Then the reality of stars again. She was drifting down toward the heart of the system. She felt for a foreign presence and found none. Good.

A darkship came through. So long, she thought. Were they really that slow? She touched the Mistress of the Ship to let her know where she was, and that the system was clear and safe. She repeated that over and over while the others gathered, till *High Night Rider* had come through.

The ships finally completed reassembly. Nearly four hours had passed since her own arrival. That was not good. It meant an erratic appearance at the business end of the quest too.

There was a way for darkships to travel in concert, though it was used seldom, and never had been tried with so many voidships. Still, she was tempted to try. If they exited the Up-and-Over in no more orderly a manner next passage, she would, third time.

She repeated the general touch, picturing the next target star and went, and came out well ahead, and again had satisfied herself that the system was untenanted before the next ship appeared.

Again it took four hours to gather them preparatory to the final jump, and this time yet another hour for each of the senior baths to pass fresh draughts of the golden fluid. She wanted no crew to arrive in need.

We face the final leg, Marika sent. *This time, to avoid the disorder we have suffered thus far, I will mesh all Mistresses in a general touch before we go into the Up-and-Over. We will go it together, as a lot, traveling with the slowest. Open to me, and to the All. It is time to go.*

There were protests. Marika ignored them, *Open to me,* she sent. And *Prepare your souls. It is time for the final jump.* She reached out and collected ghosts, waiting for others to do the same. She was amazed that they should be so slow, should have to labor so hard. For her it was a task done almost without thought.

At last they were ready. At last even the most reluctant surrendered to control. She gathered them in a tight formation, nearly touching, surrounding her, and sent, *Here we go.*

She fired one last arrow of touch at the Mistress of *High Night Rider,* and went.

Behind her, *High Night Rider* also disappeared, but bound back to the base world, to assemble and guide the second wave.

II

It was a dragging passage, making the pace of the weakest Mistress. Marika became restless. It gave her too long to become concerned about what might await her.

She began to question her conviction that she stalked the sun of the world where the Serke were hiding. She had no concrete proof that her target was the Serke star. Suppose she had been set upon a false trail? How discredited would she be if the star proved to be just another blank milestar on the secret pathway?

And there was Bestrei. Always in her thoughts there was Bestrei. She was not eager to meet the Serke champion, old as she must be now. Bestrei was three times victorious in darkwar over the strongest challengers of her time.

And there were all those surprises desperate meth might prepare.... But the Serke could not expect a raid in such strength. Could they? Would they not expect her to come alone, thinking she, as most silth would, would want to claim the prize for herself?

She found a part of her counting the time, flashing away too swiftly for all it ran so slowly. She crouched, as though to offer a smaller target.

Time ran down. Ran out. Her will wavered as the last second approached.... She let go.

A star flared into being. The disorientation was strong because she caught echoes of that suffered by other Mistresses of the Ships. She wrenched herself out of touch, got a grip on herself, gasped in awe the moment she had herself fixed in space and time.

They had come out of the Up-and-Over within spitting distance of a world, a greenish-blue planet shrouded in cloud.... There! Rising.

I have it! she sent. *Coming over the horizon. I sense silth. Let us move.* She pushed her darkship forward. Others followed as they regained their composure. The formation stretched and became ragged.

She felt the alarm rise ahead, the terror spread as lashes of touch whipped from her target to the world below, and into the depths of the system. She followed those touches and learned that she had come out of the Up-and-Over well inside a picket maintained by two darkships. Down on the world itself she detected a huge base beside a river. Already meth had begun evacuating farms and factories in panic.

The Serke had done well, Marika thought. Their courier flights must have been collecting meth on the homeworld. How else to explain the numbers she sensed? They could not have bred their workers here.

She faced the approaching object, which had to be the alien ship.

And she recoiled in awe.

Nothing made ought to be that huge.

It was a great ripped and rent thing half a mile long. A hundred *High Night Riders* would fit inside it.

Touch brushed Marika. She responded, *I have come, rogues. It is time for you to pay your debts.*

Who?

Marika. Of the Reugge.

Panic redoubled.

Something flashed on the great ship. Marika sensed rather than saw the beam, She began flying an erratic course, projecting that undercurrent of touch that might make her invisible to some silth minds.

She touched her companions as well, detailed five Mistresses to meet the two darkships rushing in from picket duty, ordered five more to go down to the planet, and another five to stand off and intercept any darkships that came up. The remaining darkships she led toward the alien vessel.

More beams crisped the darkness, never quite touching their target.

Something was wrong. She could detect no darkships save the two out on patrol. At least a dozen had escaped, of which only three were known to have been lost. With the brethren to help, they could have built more had they the sisters to crew them. And *Starstalker* was nowhere in evidence.

Give it up, she sent. *Let us not waste any more lives. Your situation is hopeless. Surrender to the inevitable.*

Beams flared around her.

Pinpoints of light winked around the alien ship. Marika grabbed ghosts and flung them forward to investigate, found the void aswarm with tiny ships. They had machine minds and carried explosives.

She detonated two score in rapid succession and drove her darkship through a cloud of expanding gases. But she stopped only those missiles directed toward her. Others slipped past. A scream tortured the otherworld as a darkship died.

Marika hurled ghosts toward the alien vessel, found tradermales working the weapons there, and began neutralizing them. She sensed others following her example.

Something ripped near her, jiggling her grip on her ghosts. Talent suppressor. Behind her another silth crew screamed and died. She regained her self-control and ghosts and hunted for the operators of the suppressor. She found several weapons and crews.

She received a broken touch from the atmosphere, where another silth crew had lost their darkship. The rogues had suppressors down there too. She withdrew, left that problem to those who had to face it, and pushed her own ship up to the hull of the alien.

She set the wooden darkship down upon a flat area, out of danger from the ship's armaments, and sent ghosts ravening through its innards, dispatching tradermale after tradermale, and a few Serke as well. There were not many silth.

Still, there was something wrong. There were males in there who were immune to her ghosts. They wore space suits similar to those used by workers on the mirror project. Each radiated a suppressor field.

She sensed many more suits of that kind. The dead males had not had time to don them. She sabotaged all she could find while they remained inactive.

She felt another darkship die and grew afraid that the rogues were too thoroughly prepared.

But no. Surprise had been hers. The alien ship could no longer fire upon its attackers. Its weapons had been disarmed. Inside, those who did not wear the suppressor suits were dying. The task was not complete, but the anchor of rogue strength had been neutralized.

Marika reached for the planet, where the darkships had scattered and were descending amid a welter of beams. No darkships rose to meet them. The darkships Marika had detailed to support them had elected to join the descent, to help stifle the defense. She touched her surviving companions and ordered all but one darkship to join her. The remaining darkship she detailed to stand off the alien to thwart any escape attempt.

The screams of perishing silth filled the otherworld. It took Marika a moment to realize that she had sensed several crews perishing at once. She reached…. And was astonished by the nothingness she found.

All five ships she had sent to intercept the patrol! All gone in an instant!

Something cold and dark and hungry lurked behind the inward-bound Serke, death on a tether.

She found an aura she recalled from long ago. From her first flight aboard a dark-faring darkship.

Bestrei.

Bestrei was aboard one of the picket ships. She was coming in.

Fear filled Marika.

Bestrei. The undefeated champion. Arrowing toward the world. Dragging the heart of the deep behind her.

Marika murmured mantras, calming herself. The inevitable had come upon her, as she had known it must. It was time to face it.

She unslung her rifle and gripped it tightly, swung the wooden dagger toward the Serke champion. She touched Grauel, Barlog, and her bath. *We go to meet Bestrei. I must have your best.*

*
*

III

Marika turned her conscious mind off, opened to the All, maneuvered without calculation.

She gathered ghosts, climbed into the Up-and-Over, let go an instant later, raced toward the Serke. She sent a strong ghost whirling ahead.

She had to release the ghost and bounce into the Up-and-Over to evade the pounce of Bestrei's great black. She came out again. The great black surged toward her, trailing her by just a few seconds. She barely had time to recover her equilibrium.

It was to be hammers, then, and no finesse. Strength against strength.

Of course. Raw power was Bestrei's strength.

Marika touched the black ghost, grabbed at it, tried to wrest it away from Bestrei. The great black was the most real of ghosts, the most responsive to stimuli. This one screamed in touch, radiating cold rage and frustration. Bestrei had it on an unbreakable chain, and now it was being torn another way.

Marika darted closer, sweeping around the vacancy where the great black lurked. Vaguely, her eyes caught the glimmer of sunlight skipping off titanium darkships. Bestrei moved, too, remaining opposite her beyond the great black, leaking a bit of touch that betrayed her amazement. She could not believe she had encountered one so strong.

Where had she been this past generation? Did she not know that the Reugge had raised up a champion against her?

Marika could not take control of the ghost. She felt she was stronger than Bestrei, but the great black was attuned to the Serke champion and remained inclined to serve her interest. Perhaps Bestrei better suited its bleak, dark taste.

The ghost drew in upon itself as it recoiled from the demands placed upon it. The Serke were not three hundred yards from Marika, beyond the ghost. Her wooden darkship rocked and jerked. Grauel and Barlog were firing, using vacuum ammunition Bagnel had given them. Their fire did little but distract Marika. They seemed unable to calculate the ballistics between moving darkships.

Marika recalled the Serke she had bested in the Ponath, during the fighting at the ruins of Critza. She squeezed the great black viciously, then broke away to fling a burst of her own Bestrei's way. Her tracers flew so wide one ricocheted off the second Serke voidship.

Marika's senior bath touched her with an appeal. The second Serke ship was trying to harm her while she was preoccupied with Bestrei.

Suns, stars, planet wheeled as darkships danced around the sullen great black, locked in a stalemate. Marika found the duel somehow anticlimactic. All those years anticipating this encounter. It did not seem as dramatic as it should. But such was life. Anticipation, then disappointment or anticlimax.

What was the story? Bestrei was a sport, overpoweringly strong. She, the upstart, was strong, too, but she supposedly had a brain as well. Why was she not using it? Why had she locked herself into a reactionary role? Was it her fear? Or a misplaced respect for the great?

She *was* afraid. Terribly afraid. And that *had* crippled her ability to reason and plan.

She turned the tip of the wooden dagger toward Bestrei and pushed forward, trying to drive through the great black, trying to part it as if it were some dark, noisome fog.

She failed. Bestrei forced her back, though she had to strain to her limits. Marika sensed Bestrei's growing concern. Never before had the Serke champion encountered an opponent she could not overpower immediately.

Marika allowed Bestrei to force her back. She withdrew from the contest of strength gradually and devoted her freed strength to gathering ghosts for a jump into the Up-and-Over.

That took more effort than she had anticipated. Lesser ghosts were scarce where the great black prowled.

Marika gathered enough. She sighted on the nearest neighboring star and climbed into the Up-and-Over, drove with all her strength. A tendril of victory touch from the Serke trailed her.

Only seconds passed. She reached her destination, regained her equilibrium, felt the void.

There. It was very far out, but it was there. Another great black. She scrambled into the Up-and-Over again, and came out near it, grasping desperately for balance before it pounced. For a moment she feared she would lose the gamble. Cold hunger, dark hatred engulfed her. Then she found the place to touch, to grab, to command, and took control.

Marika rotated her darkship and sighted upon the Serke star. She fixed Bestrei's darkship in her mind, then climbed into the Up-and-Over.

Her bath projected a whining complaint about the load she imposed upon them. She was drawing upon them heavily, conserving her own strength.

She dragged the black along with her. It went with great reluctance.

Out of the Up-and-Over again. Closer to the planet now. The otherworld was astenchful with fear. Those who had come with Marika were in flight from the Serke champion.

Marika rushed the Serke, flinging her great black ahead.

Bestrei wavered, then turned back.

Marika's darkship and Bestrei's hurtled toward one another. A silth scream filled the otherworld as Marika dispatched Bestrei's companion, then fended the Serke's great black.

If anything, the ambience was colder, more dark and hate-filled with the second black added. The two great ghosts slid around one another like slippery water creatures never touching, though those who wielded them tried to use them like swords.

For a time Marika and Bestrei traded blows like fighting huntresses standing toe to toe, hammering one another with doubled paws. Neither could harm the other.

Brains, Marika reminded herself. The reason silth feared her more than Bestrei. Supposedly because she had brains. She should use her head as well as her hatred.

She used the reluctance of the blacks to touch to force Bestrei's monster to one side. Those demons of the void twisted around one another, well out of the way. Bestrei concentrated upon that struggle, for that was what she had been taught and that was her great strength. Marika nudged her darkship nearer Bestrei's, letting it drift, keeping most of her strength with the great black. She let the Serke think she was winning the test of strength slowly.

Fifty yards separated the darkships. Then twenty-five. Marika lifted her ship slightly relative to the other. In seconds she would be over Bestrei, just yards from the Serke. Ten yards away.

Bestrei finally sensed her danger. She tried to pull out.

Marika leaned and fired short, rapid bursts that raked the titanium cross, sent sparks scattering into the void. She emptied her magazine. Grauel and Barlog laced the night with tracers.

Bestrei pulled away. Marika slapped another magazine into her weapon and pushed after the Serke, firing down the length of her darkship.

Bestrei almost got her with a surprise strike from her black. Marika turned the blow, but barely, and had to abandon the chase. Bestrei withdrew several miles.

Then she turned and started back, accelerating—straight toward Marika. Marika watched with her eyes and silth senses, dumbfounded. What was Bestrei doing? It seemed she meant to collide with her, taking them both out in one magnificent crash.

Then she understood.

A bullet had found one of Bestrei's bath, and another Bestrei herself. Neither wound was mortal or incapacitating, but they had weakened and distracted the Serke, and she was no longer confident of victory.

She *did* mean to go out in a glorious suicide, taking her Reugge opponent with her.

It was an act worthy of a legend. Worthy of the noble silth Bestrei was supposed to be.

Kalerhag.

The only hope for the Serke who had fled the homeworld.

Marika wrenched her darkship away. The Serke dagger passed within inches, Bestrei trying to roll it so an arm would tangle with one on Marika's ship. Marika rolled too. Bestrei missed.

Tracers streaked around her.

Bestrei's black struck. Marika pushed it away. By the time she freed her attention the Serke was coming at her again, a silvery streak driving toward her heart.

She dodged.

But this time Bestrei made it even closer.

Marika emptied her rifle as the titanium cross ripped past. Grauel and Barlog did likewise. This time it was the recoil that saved the wooden darkship, for it skewed away, twisting, barely sliding beneath the sweep of Bestrei's voidship.

Somebody got lucky. The storm of bullets tore one of Bestrei's bath apart. The performance of the Serke darkship declined immediately.

Marika stabilized her ship, faced Bestrei, waited. Bestrei waited too.

This is hardly traditional darkwar, Marika thought. We cheat on our silthdom. Especially I. Bestrei must be scandalized.

She felt for the great blacks. Hers had fled into the void. Bestrei's was going. The Serke champion seemed too weak to recall it.

Bestrei seemed to have strength enough only to guide her darkship toward the planet.

Marika reached for Bestrei's great black.

It did not want to be ruled again. And she was not at her strongest. She needed another draught of the golden drink. But she did take the great ghost, and brought it back, and drove it toward the Serke.

Bestrei tried to force it back. But wounded herself, with one bath wounded and another dead, she could not withstand Marika's greater strength.

Silth screams filled the otherworld.

Before long the Serke voidship was a fiery meteor plunging toward the surface of the planet.

The song of Bestrei was sung.

BOOK SIX: STARSHIPS

CHAPTER THIRTY-SEVEN

I

Marika neither mourned the Serke champion nor waited for her dying to end. She gripped Bestrei's great black ghost tightly and drove it at the alien starship.

The suppressor suits worn by the brethren were powerful, but they could not withstand the great black. Images of insects in campfire coals crossed Marika's mind as she listened to dying cries haunting the otherworld.

She reached out to her allies—those who had not yet vanished into the Up-and-Over—and summoned them back to the struggle. *Bestrei is no more, cowards! Come! Let us put an end to this tale.*

Marika directed her darkship to orbit, following Bestrei, watching as the Serke's titanium voidship heated white hot and began to burn. She felt those on the planet below pause, watch the glow streak across their sky, and realize what it meant. She reached, pulled the great black toward her.

Could she force it down there, to the surface itself, to complete the conquest of the brethren? She tried, but the black's resistance was too much for her. She did not have the strength to overcome its will to avoid large masses. But she believed she could force it down if she were fresh.

She released it with a stroke of gratitude. It flashed away across the void to resume its place on the edge of the system.

Marika sent her allies down to complete the subjugation of the planet. She drifted across to the alien starship and forced her way inside. The last minutes before she succeeded were desperate ones, for she had no strength left and was beyond help from the senior bath and her golden fluid—even had the bath had strength enough to leave her station. Had she tried to descend to the planet's surface she would have followed Bestrei as a shooting star.

She led her huntresses and bath into halls filled with breathable air. The moment they were safe she sat down, her back against metal, and sighed. "That was close. As close as ever I want to get."

It was very strange in there. Very spartan and spare, all metal and cold and electronic lighting and the hollow sound of feet shuffling on deckplates. Her curiosity was intense but she hadn't the strength to pursue it. "Grauel. Barlog," she whispered. "I *must* rest. Stand watch. Please."

The bath, except their senior, had collapsed into sleep already.

Grauel and Barlog shared their remaining ammunition and stood guard, though they themselves were near collapse from exhaustion. Marika had drawn upon them as well as her bath.

Marika wakened ten hours later, feeling little better than when she had closed her eyes. Barlog was snoring. Grauel had the watch. The bath were all still asleep. "Any trouble?" Marika asked.

"None yet," Grauel replied. "Not a sign of life. But this place makes me nervous. It vibrates all the time, and makes sounds you cannot hear unless you listen. It makes me think of putting my ear against someone's stomach and listening to what is going on inside. It makes me feel as if I am inside the belly of some mythological monster."

When Marika listened she could hear and feel what Grauel meant. It was disconcerting. She opened to the All, seeking those who had come to the system with her.

Dead ships were adrift everywhere. A disaster? She counted carefully. There were only ten derelict or missing. Not as bad as she had feared. But *only* ten? Was that not disaster enough? That was almost half the force she had brought. A massive loss of dark-faring silth. Virtually every voidfaring Community would be plunged into Mourning.

And the expense of victory did not stop totally with a count of darkships lost. The survivors down below, upon the planet's surface, resting and inventorying what had been taken, numbered only enough to cobble together crews for seven or eight darkships. The fall of the Serke might mark the end of an era in more ways than one.

"Is there anything to eat?" Marika asked. "Did anyone think to bring anything in? I'm ravenous." The struggle had consumed her body's energy reserves.

"There is cold meat," Grauel replied. "The bath remembered to bring it in, but I have found no way to cook it."

Marika was amused by a vision of nomads cooking over a dung fire in the middle of the floor of an electric kitchen. Neither she nor any of those with her had any idea what anything aboard the alien might do.

"Did we take any captives who know anything about the ship?"

Grauel shrugged. "I'm not silth, Marika. I can't communicate with those below."

"Of course. It was foolish of me to ask. Get some rest now. I'm going exploring."

"Marika…"

"Give me your ammunition. I'll be fine."

Grauel did not argue, which indicated just how far she and Grauel had extended themselves. Marika moved the ammunition from Grauel's weapon to her own, then settled down to gnaw on cold, half-cooked preserved meat. Her stomach rumbled a greeting as sustenance finally arrived.

Having eaten, she reached out to the planet and tracked down a Mistress who was alert enough to be touched. She sent a series of queries and learned that only a pawful of Serke had been taken captive. Few of the rogue brethren had survived either. There had been a lot of anger in the struggle down there, and each death scream of another allied darkship had heightened the fury of the attackers. The majority of the prisoners were bonds. They would know little or nothing.

Some who had been interviewed were unaware that they were not still upon the meth homeworld.

But we did capture the records of the investigation of the alien ship, apparently intact.

That is wonderful, Marika responded. *I will come down to examine them as soon as my bath are rested enough to make the descent. We will want hot food, and lots of it, when we arrive.* She broke touch and began to wander through the dead ship.

She found dead brethren everywhere. Those who had not gotten themselves into their suppressor suits had begun to bloat, to stink. The first order of business would be to get rid of them before they polluted the environment permanently. She stepped over and around them, ignoring them, as she examined alien hardware.

The ship was a Jiana, she reflected. Or, if not a doomstalker, certainly accursed. Twice those it sustained had been slaughtered by enemies from without. She sped an admonitory prayer to the All, suggesting that that not be made a tradition.

The starship was a tradermale's dream. It recalled the wonder she had felt the first time she had entered the control cabin of a dirigible, now so long ago the moment seemed excised from another life. The line of descent from that crude array to this was obvious at the control stations.

Much of what she saw was recognizable in terms of function, if not of actual operation. She saw several places where tradermales had made repairs and brought parts of the starship back to life.

The subliminal throb of the vessel continued, almost unnoticed, like her own heartbeat. The ship was crippled but far from dead. She wondered how much the rogue brethren had hoped to restore it. There had to be limits to what they could comprehend.

How broad those limits, though? They had had more than two decades to study it.

She wandered for more than two hours, growing ever more awed by the ship's size. In that time she was unable to see everything that had been restored, and that part of the vessel represented but a fraction of the whole. She could duck through her loophole, capture a ghost, and sail through vast sections still unreclaimed, seeing ten thousand wonders that were absolute mysteries.

Wouldn't Bagnel love it?

A worthy next project for him and his loyal brethren? There must be studies enough here to occupy generations.

Something touched her. She had a vague, general sense of something having gone wrong. She opened to the All.

A darkship had arrived.

She probed more closely. It was *High Night Rider*, at last come from the baseworld with the second wave.... No. When she scanned the surrounding void she found the Redoriad voidship alone, and limping discernibly.

II

Feeble touch brushed the starship. Marika thought she recognized its flavor. *Balbrach. Are you there? Is that you? What is wrong? Where are the other darkships?*

The weak touch focused. *I am here, Marika.* Balbrach's touch did not become much stronger. *We jumped into an ambush. The Serke were attacking your base when we arrived. They had destroyed everyone caught on the ground and were dueling two darkships. We tried to help and nearly were destroyed ourselves. We lost bath. We managed to shake them returning here. But they could appear at any time. Our very direction of flight would unnerve them.*

Do they know we have found them?

I do not know. It is likely they will learn, if they do not guess from the way we fled. We did learn that they were trying to destroy you with their attack. They were disappointed because you were not on your baseworld. My impression was that they planned to remain there till you returned. But if they guess that you have come here they will bring all their strength back. Come help us, Marika. We may not have the strength to make orbit.

I will be there as soon as I can. How many darkships did they have?

Five still functional when we fled.

Hold on. I am going to collect my bath now.

Marika withdrew into herself and hurried to rejoin her crew. But soon she learned that she was lost in the corridors. She had to go down through her loophole and catch a ghost and ride it through the starship, scouting a pathway.

She touched her senior bath. *We have to go out.* High Night Rider *has arrived after skirmishing with the missing Serke darkships. They lost bath and are in trouble. We are the only ones able to get there. Get your sisters up and ready.*

The senior bath grumbled to herself, but prepared.

Marika debated having her let Grauel and Barlog lie where they were, but decided against it. They needed the rest, but they might waken, find themselves alone, and think that they had been abandoned.

Marika joined them as the senior bath passed the silver bowl and led the way through the airlock to the darkship. While she waited for the bath to untie and push away, Marika reached down and touched a Mistress on the planet to relay Balbrach's news.

We could have unfriendly visitors at any time. All darkships must lift off immediately, lest they be caught on the surface. Assemble near the starship.

The response below was not one of great joy, but the silth down there sorted themselves out and got seven darkships off the ground. Marika was not pleased. Only seven surviving. She touched the silth who remained, telling them to keep a firm paw on their captives.

Her senior bath touched her. *We are clear, Mistress. You may drive when you will.*

Marika marked the location of *High Night Rider* and surged away from the alien. She gathered more ghosts and did the unthinkable: skipped through the Up-and-Over. She matched courses with the voidship, took her darkship inside, and loaned one of her bath to the senior Redoriad bath. Then she put her head together with Balbrach's.

The Serke darkships materialized only hours after *High Night Rider* made orbit in the starship's shadow. Marika and the others were waiting. They rushed in. The struggle was fierce, bitter, and without mercy asked or given. Though they were tired, the Serke showed well. They destroyed another three darkships. Marika had to summon the great black to end it.

The survivors limped back to the alien starship. Marika found Balbrach wandering the cold metal passageways of the ship. Balbrach greeted her by gesturing, saying, "This reminds me of the ice in a brethren factor's heart. There is nothing here but function. Is this species a race without a soul?"

"I do not know, mistress. I have not had time to learn. Come with me. I can show you what they look like."

"You have one of them?"

"No. An image."

As they walked, Balbrach asked, "And what will you do now?"

"We have broken the Serke threat at last," Marika replied, scarcely able to believe that the long hunt had come to an end. "Now we go on to…"

"You have fulfilled the role for which you were shaped by Gradwohl. Where will you go from there?"

Marika temporized. "I think nowhere. I will return to the homeworld, briefly, to gather meth to study the starship. Maybe I will come back here and stay here, awaiting the advent of the creatures who built this ship—if ever they come seeking their brethren."

"Brethren?"

"Most seem to have been males, though their crew was mixed. Actually more like bonds at work than silth or brethren. Or I may hunt some rogues. There is one in particular with whom I have a grievance."

"For a long time there have been close ties between Marika and the Redoriad first chair," Balbrach observed. Her body language suggested that she was imparting an important secret. In a softer voice, she continued, "I suggest that you not spend much time at home, Marika. That you be very careful and abnormally alert if you do visit."

"Why?"

"There are many sisters who feel that we should not have to endure the continuous threat represented by one silth who is able to impose her will upon anyone. Bestrei was tolerated because she did not interfere. She enforced the Serke will in the void, but according to a rigid and ancient noble code. They will see the silth who defeated Bestrei as more flexible, less predictable, and more likely to interfere in areas considered none of her business."

"I see. You fear someone might try to eliminate that unpredictable silth."

"Certainly the rogues would make that effort. The warlock will have been planning your fate from the moment he heard a rumor that his stellar allies had been found. And if he failed, then those sisters would take up the blade."

"And?"

"And another thought strikes me now. This ship has proven to be a treasure that inspires madness. And you have made statements already sure to arouse the enmity of the greedy."

"I see what you mean. I also sense that you speak not on the impulse of the moment, and that you do so without guessing. That you know whereof you speak."

"Perhaps. I am sure there were Mistresses who came out here with orders to close the legend of Marika the savage if that was possible. The Serke ended their tales instead in this great slaughter. That in itself is going to cause considerable dismay. A useful villain has vanished. A third of all voidships in existence have been lost, and with them the most seniors of many dark-faring sisterhoods. There will be chaos when the news reaches home."

Marika reflected. "Yes. Not only within the Communities bereft, too. If he has prepared as you suggest, and recognizes it, that would be a great moment for the warlock to strike."

"So I have thought."

"Then I shall race the news homeward. I shall arrive before he hears and complete my business there before the Communities can recover sufficiently to turn upon me."

Looking within herself, Marika found her ties to her homeworld attenuated. But for wanting to see Bagnel again, and hoping to encounter Kublin, she had little desire to return. She hardly missed the enfolding subconscious touch of the planet. In fact, if she could convince Bagnel to come out to help unlock the secrets of the alien ship, she would be content to spend the rest of her life there, perhaps using it as a base from which to continue her explorations and to fare beyond the dust cloud in search of the creatures who had built the starship.

If she could fulfill her responsibilities toward Grauel and Barlog... She was stricken by an old guilt. "Whatever else I may do, Balbrach, there is one task I am compelled to undertake upon the homeworld. In one sense, now that the Serke have been overcome, I no longer have any excuse for delaying."

The Redoriad most senior awarded her a baffled look, confused by her body language. Marika had ceased to be silth. She had lapsed into the upper Ponath savage she had been as a pup. Balbrach said, "I sense that some old haunt has recalled itself to you."

"You know my background. You know I never completely rejected it. Nor have my two voctors, my packmates, who have been with me since we escaped the nomads the Serke sent down upon our homeland. It has taken us all our lives to avenge our packmates. But with that done, we still owe them one obligation. And we cannot complete that without returning to the place where they died." She tried to explain a Mourning to Balbrach. The Redoriad could not encompass the savage practice. It was unlike anything in the silth experience. But she managed better than most because of her own rural background. Most silth would have mocked the notion of rites for a band of savages.

"I wish you could engineer it so you did not have to do this thing, Marika. I wish you could stay here and never again venture homeward. But I cannot presume to tell you what to do. I can only warn you of the dangers to your person."

Marika nodded. "Here we are. This is the place from which the vessel was controlled. Where their equivalent of the Mistress of the Ship was posted."

The chamber was large. It had three separate levels, with seating for forty beings. Most of the chairs faced screens similar to those meth used for communications. Balbrach said, "It looks like an oversize comm center."

"Look here." Marika touched a switch. One of the screens assumed life. A creature peered out at them. Balbrach made a startled sound when it began talking. The sounds it made were more liquid and round than any that could be formed by the meth mouth and tongue.

"That is one ugly beast," Balbrach said in an attempt at humor. "Such a flat face. Like someone smashed it in with a frying pan. And no fur, except on top. It looks like a badly deformed pup. Look at those ears. They are ears, are they not?"

"I suspect so. They are taller than we are, in the main, judging from the size of their chairs and doorways. That one seems to be male. The one in the background behind him, though, may be female."

"Do you have any idea what he is saying?"

"No. At a guess, this is a recorded report to whoever finds the ship. This is the reason the Serke were certain someone would come. As it progresses you will see what appears to be a report about what crippled the ship, followed by regular reports on the fates of individual crew members as they perished."

"You could tell all that?"

"Some things do not need words. A picture says more."

"True." Balbrach turned from the screen. "So. What are your plans?"

"As I said. I will go home briefly. I will assemble a team to study the ship. I will close out my life there. I think it will be my last visit, unless I go home to die. I will leave soon, to arrive before anyone who slips off with the news. Can *High Night Rider* carry darkships and Mistresses who have had to loan their bath?"

"If necessary. That leaves me with only one question, Marika. Perhaps the most important question of all."

"Yes?"

"What about *Starstalker*?"

It was a question Marika had been avoiding, even within her mind. *Starstalker* had not been among the Serke voidships destroyed. "What about *Starstalker*? I do not know. I think that will have to answer itself. Possibly at a time and place of their choosing."

III

The first rest stop on the path home came at the former baseworld. Marika drifted in through space scattered with broken voidships and dead silth. One third of all voidfaring silth lost. One third of the best and brightest of all silth. And the warlock had not had to lift a paw.

What would the disaster mean to the mirror project?

She took the wooden darkship down to her old camp. And there she found more of the same, twisted darkships and decomposing corpses. The Serke had been thorough. She walked with her memories of her years there, rested as best she could with haunted dreams, then climbed to the stars again, running out hours ahead of *High Night Rider* and the survivors of the struggle.

Her thoughts kept turning to *Starstalker*. What had become of *High Night Rider*'s littermate and the one or two ordinary Serke darkships that remained unaccounted for? Nothing could be found of them at the baseworld, and they had not participated in the counterattack upon the system of their exile.

Were they on the run again, that last dozen or so? Had they another hiding place still? Would *Starstalker*'s survival leave a hope where she wanted all hope slain?

Marika felt very old when her home sun materialized and she saw her birthworld again. Very old and very useless. Yet she was convinced that she was far from playing out the role that had been decreed for her by the All. Beyond the few remaining tasks imposed upon her by circumstance lay her own life. She might yet have something for herself, if she was not still a tool of fate.

She directed her darkship toward the Hammer.

Bagnel met her in the airlock. He directed brethren to care for her companions. The moment they were alone, he said, "The news is spreading already. You have destroyed the rogues."

Baffled, she asked, "How can that be? I *must* be the first ship back."

"You came back. That was evidence enough. It was on every radio network within minutes of your coming out of the Up-and-Over. At least that speculation. So. Did you do it?"

"We destroyed most of them. But it was very expensive. There will be little joy of it. I am exhausted, trying to beat the news home. And I'm depressed, old friend. Yet I am elated too. For once and all I have refuted the Jiana accusation. I have led the race out of its darkest hour."

"Have you?"

"What?"

"I don't like the look of you, Marika. There is a new darkness behind your eyes. It is the darkness I saw there when you were young."

Marika was not pleased. "It must be the darkness that comes of battle, Bagnel. It will be a long time before I can shake my memories of my meeting with Bestrei. There was darkness incarnate, for all her nobility."

"There is an old saying among the meth with whom I spent my puphood. It goes, 'We become that which we would destroy.' "

"I've heard it before. It's not always true. I will not become a new Bestrei."

"You're much more. You're a thing that cannot be understood. There has been much discussion of you in your absence. Undertaken in complete confidence that you would succeed in doing what you have done. That discussion has been underlaid by fear of Marika, the wild silth, the dark-walking sister with no allegiance and no limit to her power. I know you will do what you will do and nothing I can say will shift your course an inch. So I will only beg of you, be careful. The frightened do desperate things."

"So I have been warned already. Yet I have been given no specifics."

"There are no specifics to be had. At least by those of us who might be tempted to relate them to their target. Only rumors."

"What of Kublin and the rogues?"

"They have been quiet. Surprisingly so. Again, though, there have been rumors. That they have been preparing for your return, come you in triumph or defeat. It is said that they are convinced that by killing you they can start a scramble for control of the alien ship that will so embroil the attentions of the dark-faring silth that they will be left with a free paw here at home. I have a feeling their estimate is close to the truth. The rumor mill also has much to say about undercover planning in various Communities for an effort to seize and exploit the alien."

Marika folded a lip in sardonic amusement. "So I have no friends at all. Not that I ever had. And my death would serve everyone's purpose. I think we belong to a sad race, Bagnel."

"I could have told you that truth the day we first faced one another on Akard's wall."

"Does the project continue well?"

"As well as might be expected, considering that we have had to do without the voidships that accompanied you and the fact that so many meth have become distracted by other matters. We brethren persevere."

"Has it reached a stage where it could survive without you?"

"Everything can survive without me. I am wholly disposable."

"A matter I would debate strongly, with you or anyone else. Would you like a new challenge? A challenge greater than putting new suns in the sky?"

"You intrigue me, Marika. If anyone but you made a statement like that… What is it?"

"How would you like to unravel the secrets of the alien starship?"

He examined her intently. "What are you saying?"

"One of the reasons I've come home is to recruit replacements for the rogue scientists who were studying the starship. I want you to be in charge."

"You found it? You have it? It wasn't just speculation?"

"It's very real. And very strange, in the way things are strange when they are similar." She began describing the ship.

"Ah."

She saw the marvel he tried to conceal. The eagerness. The excitement.

"If you want it, the job is yours. But it could be dangerous. I have declared that the vessel is going to be mine, held in trust for all meth. As you suggested yourself, some Communities do not feel it should be that way. They feel they should have it for themselves, and I have been warned that more than one might try to seize it."

"Of course. No might about it. There will be efforts to grab it. Even with the lesson of the project before them, silth are unable to comprehend the notion of working together for the good of the species. They have trouble enough working together for the good of their orders."

"It may be a difficult thing, Bagnel. I am strong, but I stand alone out there. I will have to have support. Any team I put into the starship will be dependent upon my remaining on friendly terms with the Reugge and Redoriad. They will have to supply us. I cannot carry that load alone."

"Even them I would not count on completely were I you, Marika. But consider: How did the Serke and rogues support themselves without supplies from the homeworld? Theirs may be the path you'll want to follow yourself. Sever the ties entirely. Go ahead and be what they have called you, a Community unto yourself."

"It may come to that, though I still refuse to believe that the silth can remain so narrow."

"Refuse if you like. I will refuse to believe that you have become so naive during your absence. Are you acting? To me? You know that the unity forged for the mirror project is a harbinger of nothing. That was and remains desperation, the only answer in a struggle for survival. It has come so far even the rogues would not dream of destroying them. But their very nature makes them vulnerable in other ways, to those who seek power and profit. Among all the other accusations thrown your way over the years the secret dreams of some have been betrayed by their canards about your intentions in regard to the mirrors."

"I have no intentions. My intentions were satisfied when I convinced everyone to build them."

"True. But still some whisper that you intend to seize them when they are complete and use them to hold the race hostage."

"That's stupid. If I wanted to hold the race hostage I could do so right now, without mirrors. I am the greatest walker of the dark side this race has ever produced. If it was in me to extort something, I could scourge the population till everyone surrendered and there would not be a thing anyone could do."

Marika bit her lip, forcing herself to shut up. This was not something that needed to be said even to Bagnel.

"I know. You don't have to convince me. And I suspect that there is no point trying to convince others. They will believe what they want to believe, or, even knowing the truth, will say what they want to say to serve their own ends. Do what you have to do here, Marika, guarding yourself every second, then get out. Resign yourself to a life far from the homeworld. You may indeed be the strongest darksider ever to have lived, but you are not strong enough to survive here. I am not Degnan, nor even of the upper Ponath, but I would feel compelled to give you rituals of Mourning if you fell. And I don't know how."

"Enough. I appreciate your concern, as always. Will you go back with me once I finish my business here? Will you break all precedents and traditions and be second chair of my new star-roving Community?"

"I will."

"Then examine your brethren and pick out those you think will be most useful. Prepare to travel. I won't be long here."

CHAPTER THIRTY-EIGHT

I

Marika surveyed Grauel, Barlog, and her bath as the wooden darkship tumbled over the edge of the world and plunged into atmosphere. They were as ragged a bunch of meth as ever she had seen. Worse-looking than any randomly assembled band of bonds. Worse-looking even than those desperate nomads who had driven her from the Ponath, all hide, bones, and tatters. This time she had to spend long enough down for them to flesh out, to acquire decent apparel, and to prove up their health. They were next to useless in their present state.

Touches reached for her. Some she recognized as those of skilled far-touchers with whom she had communicated before, from her own Reugge and the Redoriad Communities. She ignored them all. Let them wonder.

How was it that they could find her so easily, yet when a Serke courier came in they could see nothing? Did she cast so great a shadow? Or was it that they were just looking for her more seriously?

They stopped trying to communicate as she dropped below one hundred thousand feet. She supposed they would be scurrying around at Ruhaack, getting ready for her. She could imagine Bel-Keneke's consternation when she did not appear as expected.

The world was an expanse of white that changed not at all as she descended. For all Bagnel's assurances, she found it difficult emotionally to believe the mirrors were doing any good. He said it was like trying to reheat a loghouse with one cooking fire. It was easier to maintain a temperature than it was to raise it once the loghouse had cooled off. You had to do more than warm just the air. The snows of the world and all that lay beneath were great reservoirs of cold that would take years to thaw. The cooling had not happened overnight. Neither could the warming. Unless she was unnaturally lucky she would not live long enough to see the ghost of normalcy restored.

Below fifty thousand feet Marika began pushing the darkship northward, toward Skiljansrode. She flung a touch ahead, to Edzeka, for she did not feel up to one of the fortress's welcomes.

Edzeka was in the landing court waiting, though Skiljansrode was besieged by a blizzard. voctors ran to hold the darkship down and secure it, for the wind was fierce. Marika dismounted, strode toward Edzeka, and shouted against the wind, "Let us go somewhere where it is warm. I am not up to this weather."

"Is it not cold in the void?"

Grauel, Barlog, and the bath practically shoved them into the underground installation. They were starved for a decent meal. Bagnel had tried on the Hammer, but what the brethren served was no better than meals aboard the voidship.

"Yes. But it does not touch you. There is no wind out there. Not much of anything at all. I would appreciate it beyond measure if you would see that my meth are given the best food possible. We have gone and come a long way, and have barely set foot upon a world since our visit here before. They are starved for something hot and real. Their bellies are shrunken smaller than fists. They need to be reminded that they are live meth, not some ghostly denizens of the void."

Edzeka seemed mildly amused. "Indeed? Then you have come to the wrong side of the world. We survive on plain, spare rations here. As you and they know."

"As we know. But those rations are feast stuff compared to what we eat out there."

Edzeka led them directly to the cafeteria. She joined Marika at table. When the grauken in Marika's belly had been soothed, she asked, "Why did you come here first? The impression I got was that you wanted to arrive before the news of your victory. Which you have done, more or less, though speculation will disarm the value of your effort since you have chosen not to appear among the courts of the mighty."

"When I go among those courts I want to do so armed with the knowledge you have gleaned in my absence. About the rogue problem. I have a fixed public policy I wave like a banner, but I have no real strategy. That will be the great issue before us after I announce my success. I must have something to offer."

"If you were counting on me to arm you I fear I am going to send you off on the hunt naked. The sisters you recruited were quite imaginative in their search for information, but the warlock is obsessive in his quest for security. I wonder that his organization grows, he is so fearful of spies."

"I will examine what has been gathered."

Edzeka was right. There was nothing useful in the filed reports. Marika contacted those she had recruited in hopes they had learned things they had been reluctant to impart to anyone but herself. They had very little to say that was useful. Unanimously, they did warn her that the rogue apparently had wicked designs on her life. She told them to intensify their efforts, to keep a closer watch on anything or anyone even remotely suspect. Her return should instigate movement by the warlock. Something would happen, and that something might betray him.

In discussion with Edzeka later, Marika said, "I almost fear I have wasted my time. I could have gone directly to Ruhaack and been no more ignorant. Still, there was a chance. I had to know. I suppose the absence of information is information in itself. I know him. Something is moving beneath the dark waters. I would suggest you concentrate on producing darkships. There will be a demand for replacements if things go as I suspect they will."

Edzeka nodded curtly. "There are those that have not returned.... I wonder, Marika, how popular you will be when the extent of the disaster out there is known. An entire generation of dark-faring silth gone, to all practical purposes. Whatever the gain, there will be those who will not forgive you the price you paid." She strained to phrase herself politely. It was clear she preferred having Marika elsewhere.

"I will pluck myself out of your fur after one more good sleep, Edzeka. My rogue hunters will move their center of operations to Ruhaack. Your Community will be yours once more."

Edzeka neither thanked her nor acknowledged the implicit rebuke.

It was impossible to slip into the Reugge cloister unnoticed aboard a voidfaring darkship. Marika cursed that state of affairs. She would have preferred having the cloister rise one morning to find her reestablished in her quarters, come like a haunt or breath of conscience out of the darkness. But she had to arrive amid all the ceremony Bel-Keneke could lay on, with representatives of all the Ruhaack cloisters watching.

Practically before her feet left the tip of the dagger there were demands for her time and news. She made one general statement announcing the defeat of the Serke fugitives, the extermination of their rogue allies, and the taking of the alien starship on behalf of all meth. Then she retreated to her apartment, allowing only Bel-Keneke to accompany her. And her bath, at their request. She had given them permission to go to bath's quarters this time, but after considering the pressures and attentions they might face, they elected to remain with her, hiding within her fortress within the cloister.

Marika closed the door. "I have said it in public. Now it is known and sure. Now the excitement of the aftermath begins. I suggest you be more alert than ever before."

"How bad was it out there, Marika?"

"There are no words. Edzeka, perhaps, said it best. A generation of dark-faring silth spent to end the Serke terror. And possibly with very little actually gained. The starship, though, is impressive. I wish every meth alive could be taken to see it. It is going to change our lives as much as the age of ice has."

"And you intend keeping your pledge to hold it in trust for all meth?"

"I do. We may part somewhat on this. I do not know your exact attitude. But yes, I mean it. You will recall that I come of a region where my pack was held in primitive straits for the advantage of other meth. I resented that greatly when

I learned it, and I do still, though now I am one of the other meth. I cannot allow one small group to seize this starship. It is too important to us all. How it is exploited may shape the entire race for ages to come. I do not want it to become the grauken of the age, dam of a tyranny to beggar that of the most vicious sisterhood. In the past we have allowed the land and oceans and even the stars to be seized for the advantage of the strongest few, but with this we cannot keep on in the same old way."

Bel-Keneke seated herself before the fireplace. She said, "I read in you a deep undercurrent of fear. Never before have I known you to be frightened of the future. Not in the way I sense it now."

"You are probably right. I would not call it that, but even the wisest of us sometimes lie to ourselves. Do we not?"

"Yes."

"These days I am often confused about who and what I am in the grand picture painted by the All. Sometimes it seems I am the only silth alive willing to battle to preserve our traditions. And at other times I feel I am exactly what they accused me of being when I was younger, the new Jiana who will preside over the collapse of silthdom.

"And still I do not feel stronger or different. I just feel as if I am on the outside.... I talk too much. We face ever more interesting and exciting times. But maybe we are over the summit now, with the mirrors in place and the Serke defeated. Perhaps a semblance of normalcy will reassert itself after we dispose of the warlock."

"You might reflect on the fact that for most meth now living, silth included, this *is* normalcy. They are not old enough to recall anything else."

"I suppose you are right. Let me rest awhile. Let me become attuned to where and when I am. Then I can get on with trying to reshape my world in the image of its past. Amusing, no? Me, trying to back into the future."

Bel-Keneke did not understand her words or mood. Marika suspected that she did not understand them herself, though she pretended otherwise. Maybe it was all just age sneaking up on her.

II

Marika brought the darkship southward over the tops of dead trees, barely high enough to clear the reaching branches. She cleared the edge of the woods, then dropped till the wooden cross hurtled along inches above the snow. The landing struts sometimes dragged. The wind of her passage whipped up and scattered loose powder snow behind her.

She brought the darkship to a violent halt and dropped it into the snow. She and Grauel and Barlog piled off, ran low to the edge of a ravine, flopped.

Below, a dozen rogues were reloading a rocket launcher. The females opened fire with their rifles. Bodies jerked and spun. Two of the males got off shots of their own before they were hit, but did no damage. Some tried to flee. Marika seized a ghost and overtook them. Then she led the huntresses in a wild scramble down into the ravine, snow flying, to finish the wounded.

"This one is faking, Marika," Barlog said, yanking a youngster upright.

"Hold him. We'll take him with us." She examined the others. All dead or soon to die. She kicked the nearest rocket launcher. "A fine piece of machinery."

The first rocket had hit the Reugge cloister only moments before, wrecking the tower Marika customarily occupied. There had been no warning. Marika and her huntresses had been out almost by chance, down with the bath mapping a search sweep of rogue territory northeast of Ruhaack.

She had been airborne before the second rocket arrived.

"They look like the machines made by those aliens," Grauel said.

"Don't they, though? I wonder how much knowledge they spirited out over the years?"

"What shall I do with this pup?" She had the captive cringing at her feet.

"We'll truthsay him. For what that's worth." Marika did not expect to learn much.

She had been back to Ruhaack five days. This was the third attempt upon her life. One she had been unable to trace. She believed silth might have been behind it. The other had been brethren in inspiration, but her search for those behind it had dead-ended. Her enemies were careful to cover their trails these days.

"Here? Now?"

"Here is fine. We can leave him with his friends."

Truthsaying the youngster was easy. He had no resistance. And was almost an empty vessel where knowledge was concerned, though Marika nursed his entire rogue history from him.

"They are pulling them in young, now," she said. "He was barely more than a pup when they enlisted him. That damned Kublin is insane."

Grauel looked at her expectantly.

"We'll backtrack him. At least he knew where he'd been. Somewhere there'll be a rogue who hasn't moved on. We'll grab him and hope he gives us another lead."

"The slow, hard way," Barlog said. "One villain at a time."

"That may be the only way."

"Kill him?" Grauel asked.

"Yes."

Grauel broke his neck. "I'm old," she said. "But the strength remains."

Marika replied, "Yes, you're still strong. But you *are* old. It's decision time."

"Marika?"

"I will be going back to the alien ship soon. Chances are that it will be many years before I return to the homeworld again. You have often expressed a desire to spend your last days as near the Ponath as can be."

Neither Grauel nor Barlog responded. Marika waited till the gawking bath had returned to the darkship to ask, "Have you nothing to say?"

"Is that what you wish? That we remain behind?"

"You know it isn't. We have been together for a lifetime. I don't know what I would do without you. You're my pack. But I don't want to stand in your way if you are ready to assume the mantle of the Wise. If I had any conscience I would, in fact, urge you to do so. The young voctors at the cloister are in desperate need of firm and intelligent guidance. By staying with me you'll only see more of the same, and probably come to no good end. Half the race wishes me dead, and half that half might try doing something about it."

"We will do as you command, Marika," Barlog said.

"No. No. No. You will do what you *want* to do. It's your future. Don't you understand?"

"Yes, mistress," Grauel said.

Marika favored her with a scowl. "You are baiting me. You are not as dense as you pretend. Come. We will discuss this later." She stalked toward the darkship.

She took the darkship up and turned out across the snowy wastes, toward the ruins of TelleRai. The rogues had come from there in a ground-effect vehicle still hidden among the dead trees of the woods.

The rogues who had sent them had moved out of their hiding place, but had not moved fast or far enough. Marika overtook them. She captured two, truthsaid them, and continued her hunt.

Before day's end the trail had taken her most of the way to the eastern seaboard. A dozen scatters of defeated rogues lay behind her. She found herself wondering why her sister silth had so much trouble suppressing them. They needed only to invest vigor and determination.

She took the darkship up and let her far-touch roam the wilderness. Somewhere in those icy badlands there was a major rogue hiding place, one they had believed could not be traced back through the levels of their organization.

She sensed a place where many meth were gathered, deep beneath the surface. She captured a strong ghost, rode it through a long, twisting tunnel, and found herself inside a weapons manufactory. More than two hundred meth were at work there, including bond females...

Females!

Marika considered them closely. They were not prisoners. Some even seemed to be supervisors.

Anger seized her. She set the ghost ravening.

The massacre lasted fifteen seconds. A screaming electromagnetic surge severed her connection with the ghost. She suffered a moment of disorientation. The darkship plunged fifty feet before she regained her equilibrium and control.

So. They had adapted a suppressor field so it would shield an entire installation. It was to be anticipated. They had adapted it so it would protect individuals upon the alien starship.

No matter. These meth were dead. Voctors would come to cleanse the place once she reported it.

She took her darkship up high and sent a general far-touch roaming that face of the continent. *Kublin. The game is about to end. I am coming for you this time.*

She expected no response and received none, but was certain Kublin would receive the message if there were as many wehrlen among the rogues as some silth suspected.

She drifted away westward, to continue the hunt elsewhere.

III

"How long do you plan to stay this time?" Bel-Keneke asked from what had become her customary seat before the fireplace in Marika's quarters, though now those quarters had been shifted.

"Until I find the rogue I seek," Marika said. "A day or a decade." It had been a month since her return to Ruhaack. A dozen attempts on her life had failed. The cloister had suffered damage on several occasions. "Do not be distressed. Do not be frightened. I wish there were some way I could stem your fear that I intend to wrest the Reugge away from you."

Bel-Keneke was startled. "I do not..."

"Of course you do. Because your one weakness is insufficient imagination. If I have such wicked intentions, why have I not displaced you already? Do you doubt that I could in a test of strength? Entertain, for the sake of argument, the remote chance that I would not want to endure the responsibilities of being a most senior. Assume that I have a task to complete here and then I shall depart for the Serke starworld. I really would rather spend my time nursing secrets from the alien starship."

Bel-Keneke seemed mildly embarrassed.

"Shall we drop the matter and turn our attention to the rogue problem?"

That problem had become one silth dared not ignore. In the past month the rogues had become violently active, betraying a level of strength and organization unsuspected even by those few silth who had taken them seriously. Their weaponry was a shock, and they had made excellent tactical use of their talent suppressors. A lot of damage had been done and many silth had died.

It was, of course, all Marika's fault. So the word ran among those who refused to see their own failures.

"All right," Bel-Keneke said. "The rogues."

"They can be beaten. They can be wiped out. If the Communities would cease blinding themselves, pretending they are only a nuisance. The problem must be recognized for what it is and approached in the same cooperative spirit as the mirror project."

"That is a matter of survival, Marika."

"Stubborn folly. Stubborn folly. Things are not so because we wish them so. They have to be made so. *This* is a matter of survival, Bel-Keneke. Those rogues are determined to obliterate all silthdom. And they are going to manage it if someone does not wake up."

"They are but males."

"True. Absolutely true. Are you any less dead when a male puts a bullet through your brain?"

"Marika, you credit them too much...."

"Ask yourself who unleashed the fire that consumed TelleRai. Mere males. They will not go away because we wish them away. They will not go away because we turn our backs and refuse to see them. Those are the very reasons they come back again and again. I smash them, then the rest of you pretend they do not exist after I have gone on to something else, and the disease reestablishes itself. It was not imagination that destroyed my tower."

Bel-Keneke looked like one patiently suffering the ravings of one touched by the All.

Irked, Marika continued, "They now have an unknown number of hidden bases and manufactories. I have revealed several of those already. You have seen the things they were stockpiling. And you will still insist that they are just a nuisance? Must they kill you in order to gain your attention?"

Bel-Keneke shook her head.

"Try to imagine what they may be preparing in more remote places, safer from searchers."

Bel-Keneke showed no enthusiasm, even so. Marika was disturbed. Was all silthdom paralyzed by some mad suicidal urge? She feared she would have to call on the terror of her name to mobilize a real effort to overcome the rogues.

She was convinced that Kublin had built a movement so strong it no longer needed the support of the defeated Serke. It would attain its goals without it if silth continued to blind themselves to the threat.

Kublin, she was convinced, was not just the warlock; he was the driving force behind the rogue movement. She knew Kublin because she knew herself. Kublin might be cowardly at times, but he was very much like her. He was every bit as determined, if for reasons she could not fathom. In a way battling him, she battled her mirror image. She had acted, thus far, as though she *was* dueling herself, guessing what she would have done in Kublin's place before she made a move. And that had allowed her to deal this new crop of rogues numerous and frequent disasters.

The difference between Kublin and herself was that he was less willing to risk his person. In his place she would have come out to kill herself instead of sending assassins.

As a test she had tried an offer of rich rewards for information. She had had few takers. As she had expected. That revealed the real strength of the rogues. They were so strong and so feared that few ordinary meth would dare betray them.

"It is time to put the fear of silth back into the populace," Marika said.

Bel-Keneke looked startled.

"I do not want to press anyone, but I will if I must. I do not tolerate willful blindness in myself and I will not tolerate it in anyone else. We will destroy the rogue if I have to *compel* the Communities to join in the hunt."

Bel-Keneke sighed. "There is a great deal of confusion yet, Marika. You know very well that many of the strongest Communities lost their most seniors during your adventure against the Serke. They have not yet stabilized into any fixed hierarchy. You cannot expect them to have formed policies."

"The lack of a certain meth in control should not rob a Community of direction at mundane levels. You... Never mind. Argument accomplishes nothing. As strength goes. I would appreciate it if you would contact those Communities that do have most seniors and tell them that I plan a major rogue hunt directed to the northeast. Tell them I want all the darkships that can be mustered. My intention is to mount a sweep that will cripple the rogue's offensive capacity. If in the course of the sweep I find the one rogue I am hunting myself, his loss will set his movement back so far the rogues will present no threat for years. You all will be rid of me, for I will disappear into the void once more. And you can all go back to your somnolent pretense."

Bel-Keneke refused to be angered. "Very well. As you wish. I will see that your fleet is assembled." Bel-Keneke's tone recalled that of Marika's dam Skiljan when she was discussing tribute that had to be paid to the silth at Akard. A little something yielded grudgingly so a greater power would leave one alone.

Damned blind fool. They were all damned blind fools. Maybe they deserved... "Thank you, mistress. I appreciate your efforts. I must go now. I have to visit the comm center." She left Bel-Keneke there, served and observed by Grauel and Barlog.

She stalked the hallways of the cloister, irked with herself. She was growing too intolerant and impatient, she feared. In younger days she would have tried to maneuver, to manipulate, to get what she wanted more slyly. These days the impulse was to turn to power at the first impediment.

From the comm center she contacted the Hammer, ostensibly to see how Bagnel's preparations were coming, actually to turn off her thoughts for a while while talking with someone who wanted nothing from her and from whom she wanted nothing. She left the conversation pleased. Bagnel had assembled a scientific team that, he assured her, was more than respectable in knowledge, ability, and reliability.

She began to feel anxious to move into deep space once again.

The homeworld was not home anymore.

If anywhere ever had been.

CHAPTER THIRTY-NINE

I

Grauel returned from the window. "The sky is filled with darkships, Marika. They are grounded in the streets and on the open ground around the cloister. I never imagined there were so many."

"I am amazed," Marika admitted. She looked at Bel-Keneke. "What did you tell them?" In one week more than three hundred darkships, of the planet-bound sort, carrying as many as a half-dozen voctors each, had gathered at Ruhaack.

"I told them what you told me to tell them." Bel-Keneke was not surprised at the response. "You are much feared, in more ways than you can imagine."

"Whatever moves them, I had better take them out before the spirit falters. Is there a place where they can be gathered so that I can speak to them all? Tomorrow I will lead them out against the rogue."

"I thought you would want to address them. I have made arrangements with the Redoriad. The west wall of their cloister overlooks open ground. Nearly half of them are grounded there anyway."

"Thank you."

Marika examined the weather auspices. It would be a clear night, and the major moons would be in near conjunction. She set her speechmaking for that hour.

She said nothing new or particularly inspiring, nor did she try to whip the assembly into a froth of hatred. She simply told the silth that they had a job of work to do, and if they carried it out properly they would end this rogue threat that had begun to seem like a reign of terror. An hour before dawn she raised her wooden darkship and led the airborne horde northeast, to that region she believed to be the heartland of Kublin's shadow empire.

She expected heavy action and she was not disappointed. In that region the rogues had invested heavily in time and labor and resources, and so felt compelled to resist instead of to run.

The Mistresses accompanying Marika learned quickly after several darkships had been downed by suppressor beams. Fear inspired cooperation. The moment a Mistress detected anything inimical she summoned aid. When superior strength had gathered the Mistresses grounded and sent in their voctors to do the killing, supporting them with their talents.

In the six hours following the first contact fourteen installations were captured and more than a thousand rogues slain.

Marika did not participate directly. She remained high above the hunt, probing the far distances with her touch, occasionally sending, *Kublin, I am coming for you.* She was certain he was out there, cowering in some secret command center, watching his fastnesses fall.

Grauel and Barlog watched her and became increasingly unsettled. They began to prowl the arms of the darkship, restless, watching her closely. They sensed a darkness growing in her.

The more stubborn the rogue resistance, the more angry and hate-filled she became. Something had twisted inside her. She was no longer able to think of Kublin as the fragile, sweet littermate she had known as a pup. She could not remember him as the youngster she had saved in the Ponath at the risk of her entire future, nor as the adult she had spared by imprisonment and murder after his raid upon Maksche.

He would not learn. He would not recant. He would not cease his misdeeds. She had risked everything for him, and he had given nothing but pain in return. She had no more love for him. Not a spark. She wanted only to hurt him in return.

Splash the plains of snow with blood. If he did not join the dead, maybe he would read a message he would finally understand.

A squadron of latecomers arrived from Ruhaack. Marika touched them. They seemed eager to join the hunt, like pups racing after the panicky denizens exploding out of an opened leiter nest. She was pleased. Slow as silth were to start, she had no trouble inspiring them once they decided to move.

An eagerness for plunder animated many of the hunting crews. The rogues had betrayed several advanced technologies in their attempts to defend themselves—technologies that, locally, almost offset the overpowering silth sorcery.

Maybe that was the answer. Survival never had been much of a motivator when she had tried to get them to do something. But appeal to their greed and they swarmed.

She would never understand. But, then, she had been involved in a struggle for survival all her life.

She directed the newcomers to places in the sweep line, then turned her attention to a lone darkship at the limit of vision, rising and racing toward her. In a moment she recognized Balbrach's aura.

She flung a questioning touch. Balbrach was supposed to be aboard *High Night Rider*, in orbit, refitting after surviving the Serke.

Wait, Balbrach sent back, and continued her swift approach.

Marika waited, her nerves beginning to fray. Balbrach's tone intimated bad news.

The Redoriad darkship drifted close to her own till arms touched. Balbrach stepped aboard Marika's darkship and joined her at the tip of the dagger. "What news can be so bad that you have to meet me face to face up here?" Marika asked.

"Yes. You guess well. It is bad news, though not surprising."

"What is it?"

"A Chorada darkship has just arrived from the Serke starworld. They brought word that three voidships of the Groshega—their entire fleet, none of which joined us in the struggle out there—have seized the alien starship and claimed it for their Community."

"The fools. How stupid can meth be?"

"The universe is filled with fools, Marika."

"How do they expect to hold it? They must have support. I am here, and can cut them off…"

"I do not know. But something must be done."

"Must be done by me, you mean?"

"For two reasons, one being that no one will even begin to believe the noble motives of anyone but you. For all they may say otherwise, many silth at least grudgingly suspect you may actually mean it when you say you intend this find to benefit all meth."

"And the other reason?"

"The Groshega have a champion, Brodyphe, who was thought to be second to Bestrei before you proved that Bestrei was not first. No Community would dare challenge her. We Redoriad are strongest in the dark now in numbers, but I would not send all my Mistresses against her."

Silently, Marika appealed to the All. Why now? Was this a sign? Was she never to be allowed to extinguish the rogue plague?

"The dark-faring sisterhoods appeal to you to end this usurpation, Marika. Before a precedent is set. You said you would hold the alien starship and its secrets in trust. Grudgingly, most of us have accepted that. But you are compelled to enforce that if you wish to maintain that acquiescence."

"I know. But I have a task here. It will not get done if I leave it."

"Have you not crippled the rogue enough?"

"No. Not enough. Far from enough to satisfy me. There is one I especially want to remove from the social equation. Without him the movement will become blind and halt."

"Can one male be so important?"

"This one can. He is very much like me. He is wehrlen, Balbrach. He is strong and smart and very dangerous. What is your hurry? Those Groshega will be there whenever I get to them."

"We dare not wait long. Any significant delay will give some meth the idea you have accepted the fiat. That would dissolve whatever unanimity of thought exists...."

"Is *High Night Rider* ready?"

"Yes. I contacted your male Bagnel and directed him to begin sending his scientific team aboard. I intend to leave, with all the voidships I can gather, as soon as I return to the cloister and make arrangements for another extended absence."

"All right. Let it be known that your movements have my full approval and are my first move against the Groshega. Do not rush, but move with deliberation. I will continue here for a few days more, then will overtake you along the starpaths." Marika looked to the sky and silently asked the All what it wanted of her.

Balbrach nodded curtly. "That should appease the majority."

"This land should never have been abandoned," Marika said. "We Reugge never pulled out of our territories. We still have our outposts. Leaving the land unwatched only encouraged the rogues..." She was talking to empty air. Balbrach had returned to her darkship. It separated, turned, hurried toward Ruhaack.

Marika checked the progress of the sweep. Another rogue installation had been located. The darkships were settling in the snows and the killers were gathering. It was a large base and would be stoutly defended. But it was not the base she sought, the one where Kublin the warlock sat at the heart of his villainous web.

She did not waste time on anger or frustration when she did not find that one. It seemed fated that the worst would happen.

In the end, after taking three more days, during which her hunting teams exterminated another four thousand rogues, she gave up and hurried back to Ruhaack and her wooden voidship. She left the hunt in care of a sister she had known in the days when she had battled the rogue out of Maksche, a silth almost as stubborn and determined as she. But she did not expect the campaign to retain its momentum long after her departure. The Communities would convince themselves that they had struck a mortal blow and no longer need be concerned. They would begin withdrawing their darkships.

II

Marika came out of the Up-and-Over well away from the alien starship. She waited and probed the dark till *High Night Rider* and its escort of five Redoriad voidships materialized. She gave the Groshega sisters time to think about the advent of the force. Then she sent, *Brodyphe. I am here. If you do not leave peaceably, I will have to send you down the dark path after Bestrei. Go. There has been too much death here already.*

There was no response from the silth aboard the starship.

Marika had not expected one, really, though she had hoped that an attack of sense would smite the Groshega once they knew she was there to evict them. She drifted closer. The Redoriad darkships spread out. She glanced back at Grauel and Barlog, who had refused to be left behind, no matter their dreams of ending their days at home.

Go! she sent.

Three Redoriad darkships darted toward the alien starship.

Beams and rockets leaped to meet them. They pranced away, unharmed.

Marika scanned the surrounding space. The great black still lurked at the system's fringe, but it was not under control, not moving. It seemed disinterested in what was happening down near the sun.

Did the Groshega intend to maintain their claim with technical weapons?

Marika vacillated. There was something wrong with the whole situation. How could the Groshega hope to best her with alien armaments? They could not have the use of the suppressor suits and weapons developed by the rogue scientists. She had had those removed to the surface of the planet before departing. They were in the care of one of Balbrach's most trusted Mistresses...

She hardly thought about what she did. She grabbed ghosts and clambered into the Up-and-Over, bringing herself out beside the great black.

Was she mad? Had she begun seeing plots where none could exist?

Or had she been guided gently into a trap?

The Groshega had a strong champion. The Redoriad had numbers. They were silth, as subject to pestilential silth blindnesses and shortcomings as sisters of any other order. The Redoriad had been allies for years, but that did not guarantee an alliance forever.

And nobody loved Marika, who had the strength to thwart greed and crush schemes.

She took the great black under control almost without direct thought and leaped back to the heart of the system.

She dropped into an atmosphere of confusion. They did not know where she had gone, or why. Marika sent, *Balbrach, I want you to take* High Night Rider *and your darkships back to the last milestar. Wait there three hours, then return.*

Why, Marika? Balbrach could not disguise the disappointment in her touch.

This is an uncomfortable situation. It has some very unpredictable aspects. To avoid potential problems arising from the uncertainties I have decided to handle it alone. I believe I can accomplish our ends more quickly that way, and with fewer silth killed.

Balbrach understood the message behind the message. She sensed the great black roiling around Marika, angry at being disturbed, eager to rip and slay. She sent, *As you wish, Marika.*

Marika did not move until the Redoriad had vanished.

Now she must move quickly, lest they not do as she had ordered, and try to surprise her.

Brodyphe. Are you coming out? Must I come after you? You have no chance against me.

She nudged her darkship toward the alien. No beams or rockets greeted her. After ten minutes two darkships left the derelict.

There should be another. Hurry. I am impatient. Come to me here.

Another darkship left the alien. Marika eased closer. She sent a lesser ghost into the starship and detected no Groshega silth.

The Groshega voidships floated toward her, into visual range. She sent, *Who were your allies in this venture?*

They did not respond.

She touched the great black.

Aboard Brodyphe's darkship silth screamed into the otherworld. Their bodies twisted, tore apart. The golden glow faded around them. Blood crystals and flesh fragments scattered.

Marika touched the Mistresses of the remaining ships. *Who were your allies in this venture?*

They confirmed her worst suspicion.

She touched the great black again, then turned away before it was over. Down to the alien starship she went, sending before her small ghosts to locate and disarm booby traps. Then she went aboard.

The moment they could talk, Grauel demanded, "Did you have to kill them?"

"Are you getting soft, Grauel? They intended to kill us." Huntresses were not wont to mourn enemies, nor to give them a second chance.

"No. It just did not seem necessary."

"It was, Grauel. I struck a blow at an idea when I eliminated them."

"What idea?"

"The idea that one sisterhood or a cabal of Communities can seize this ship for the purpose of limiting its benefits."

Grauel nodded, but was not entirely mollified. Marika reminded herself that in some ways the Wise were more tolerant than were younger females, who had to face danger more directly.

Barlog asked, "Are you sure you were not more interested in crushing any doubts about your own invincibility?"

Marika scowled at her and turned away. She stalked through the alien ship to the control area. She did not relax her hold upon the great black, which she moved far enough away that its presence would not be immediately obvious. She replayed the final message from the alien crew, again studying their smooth-faced strangeness, their methlike yet alien forms. How well had the brethren unraveled their language with the times and clues they had had available?

She settled into an alien chair and wondered what the rogues really had hoped to accomplish, wondered what had become of the few Serke who remained unaccounted for. *Starstalker* and one or two darkships. Where had they gone?

She sensed the return of *High Night Rider* and its escort and sighed. She did not look forward to the next few hours.

Balbrach. Come to the alien. I must speak with you.

III

High Night Rider departed the system unaccompanied, without Balbrach aboard. It carried Marika's message to the most seniors of all the dark-faring silth. It had left behind the brethren scientists and the darkship crews who had accompanied it out. Marika touched the great black, told it to let the voidship pass.

She had made that monster her creature entirely, a deadly sentinel guarding her system.

She told the Redoriad crews that they could not leave the system, that the great black would devour them if they tried to go. They would be released in time if they behaved. In the interim they must do ferry duty between the starship and the planet, where former Serke bonds continued farming and manufacturing, their lives little touched by changes in ruling Communities.

Marika made her home in the starship's control section. The brethren she assigned to the quarters that had been occupied by their rogue predecessors.

The very typical bit of silth treachery that had brought her back to the alien ship sent her into a depression that lasted for weeks. Her homeworld, and her deadly littermate with his bloodthirsty movement filled with hatred, slipped from her thoughts entirely. When she recovered she found she had very little interest in her roots.

She did not leave the starship for a year, not until she was convinced that her control would not be disputed by any element of the meth race.

During that year she mourned Balbrach often, for theirs had been a good partnership while it had lasted. At times it had approached the friendship she had had with Kiljar. But Balbrach had not had Kiljar's mental scope or character and had not been able, in the end, to resist typical silth greed. She had made her move. She had lost. Though it hurt still, Marika had had to demand that she pay the price of failure.

Darkships came and went, their movements carefully monitored by Marika's tame great black. The dark-faring sisterhoods were keeping a sharp watch upon her. After that year, though, even the most suspicious and paranoid of Communities had become convinced that she did indeed mean the starship to benefit all meth. The watchers came less frequently, but their visits lasted longer, and they joined in the unraveling of alien secrets. Each departing darkship carried a full report of everything that had been learned about the starship and the aliens who had built it. Which was not that much, considering the time and effort that had gone into opening it up.

One day Marika went looking for Bagnel, whom she seemed to see no more than when they had not been living on the same ship. "Hello, stranger."

"Me? I am not the one whose thoughts cannot remain where I am, who is always wandering somewhere else."

"Somewhere else? I have not been out of this ship..."

"Your heart has been."

"Have you reached any major conclusions yet?"

"Not really. Unless you do not know that this vessel was built by creatures who do not think like meth."

"You've had more than a year."

"Most of which we have spent relearning what the rogues learned."

"And?"

"They did find out more than anyone suspected, Marika. If the Communities did not follow through on the hunt you initiated at home last year they are going to be in for some very nasty surprises."

"I am sure they did not. Oh, Dhervhil will have tried. Is still trying, no doubt. They accused her of being as rogue-obsessed as Marika. But the Communities refuse to learn. Without some overpowering personality there to drive them, they will just go on being the same petty backstabbers trying to steal a moment's advantage. How soon can you start some really original research work? And how has the repair work been going?" Most of the planetary industrial base developed by the Serke had been created for the purpose of refurbishing the starship.

"Sometime within the next few months I expect to okay a couple of projects my meth have proposed. Mostly attempts at getting to information stored in the ship's systems. The repairs go forward, but they are all gross things like sealing broken hull plates. The more subtle things are waiting for us to get into the information banks. The drive system, for example, is something I am not going to let anyone near until we have drawn out, examined, and come to understand every morsel of information available. By tinkering with it we might smash it beyond hope."

Marika thought a moment. "Bagnel, you were right. My heart is not here. Its feet have been wandering for a long time. I've decided to surrender to it. I'm going to sneak away and do something I have been promising myself to do for a long time. I don't think you'll have any trouble while I'm away."

"Yes?"

"Yes, what?"

"Where are you going? Or is that a secret?"

"To look at the far side of the cloud."

"That is a long passage. Are you sure... You're convinced we won't be troubled?" He was afraid. He had become important among meth, but he would remain important only so long as he enjoyed her protection.

"It'll be all right. Don't let on that I've gone. If somebody wants me, tell them

I'm being moody again and won't see anyone. They're used to me. And I don't intend to be away long."

"You never do. But... All right. Be careful."

"I will. Indeed I will. There is much I want to see before I rejoin the All."

Marika's first exploration was a four-star voyage rapidly taken. It did not lead her out of the dust. She did not find a world suitable for resting her bath. She returned to the starship with her crew strained to their limits.

She found that her absence had gone unnoticed.

She tried another route a month later, with no more success. The dust was deep and the stars in that direction unfriendly.

Not until her sixth venture outward, late in the second year after she had reclaimed the alien ship from the Groshega, did she establish an advance base and begin preparations for venturing beyond it. By then it was common knowledge that she slipped away occasionally, but she kept her comings and goings unpredictable. She did so mainly out of habit, for she no longer feared trouble from the dark-faring silth. Her hold on the system had been accepted because she had fulfilled her promises.

Midway into her third year of ruling the alien ship she finally broke out of the far side of the cloud and caught her first glimpse of skies ablaze with stars numerous beyond any imagining, great reefs of starlight that beggared anything she had seen on the nether side. Her awe remained undiminished when she returned to the alien ship.

Bagnel was impressed by the film she brought back. "Incredible," he breathed. "Absolutely incredible. Who would have guessed?"

"Bagnel, you have to *see* it. I don't care what you have going here. I don't care what you have to do. Come see it. This will make your life. Remember how we talked about flying off into eternity when we retired? Come. See this. It will make you lust to do that now."

Bagnel looked at the film again, and he quivered all over. But he was the most responsible of meth, bound by his notions of duty. It took her a week to pry him away from his work.

He had become enamored of the alien mysteries. But pry him away she did, and get him aboard her fey darkship she did, and carry him through the cloud she did. And his response to those shoals of stars was all she expected. He could find no words to describe his feelings when he saw them, even months after he had returned to his mundane work.

For months after that venture Marika stifled herself and did not go out again, though those stars called to her incessantly. She concentrated on making her presence felt among visitors from the homeworld, who were becoming more numerous now that the starship had begun to yield some of its secrets.

She anticipated being away a long time on her next voyage.

CHAPTER FORTY

I

"I do not think this journey is wise, Marika," Bagnel said. "Still, if you *must* go, take me with you."

"Not this time. This is going to be a far journey. Every pound of weight will have to be useful."

Grauel and Barlog were startled. Barlog asked, "Does that mean you are leaving us behind too?"

"I'm sorry. This time, yes. I must go without you. I will be taking extra bath and supplies instead. Do not look at me that way. I will behave and be careful."

She had no trouble finding herself a double set of bath. Bath from all the dark-faring sisterhoods journeyed to the starship in hopes of spending some time on her darkship. Bath who had served with Marika were much in demand. Somehow she opened hidden channels in their minds, and strengthened them immensely, so that many became immune to the weaknesses plaguing most bath, and a few even found that with her guidance they could grow enough to become Mistresses of the Ship themselves.

There were times when Marika had to resist pressures to become a teacher and trainer of dark-faring silth. "Can you imagine me an instructress?" she complained to Bagnel. "Spending the rest of my life developing crews for the Communities?"

The notion had amused him.

Pursued by his displeasure and the unhappiness of Grauel and Barlog, Marika left the starship on her first far flight of exploration.

Double-crewed, she could make vastly extended flights, hopping as many as twelve stars before having to take a rest landing. She needed that capability if she was to venture beyond the dust cloud into that vastness on the other side, to satisfy the exploration bug that had been tormenting her since she had discovered those endless shoals of stars.

It was to be a voyage of terrible moment.

She was in the seventh hop of her second twelve-star run out from the edge of the dust. For this venture distance was her principal concern. She wanted to see how far she could travel before conscience and dwindling stores compelled her to turn back. A fever of excitement rolled along with the darkship. The bath were animated by the emotions surrounding the doing of a thing never before tried. Instead of becoming increasingly uneasy as they ventured even farther from home, the opposite was true. Every hop outward raised the level of excitement.

The darkship dropped out of the Up-and-Over, and even before Marika regained her equilibrium she knew that they. had made an enormous discovery. *Listen!*

Awe gripped the bath.

The void reeked with electromagnetic radiation. It was not natural. In moments Marika detected a world in the star's life zone. A satellite network surrounded it. The space of that system sported moving objects that could be nothing but ships. Closed ships of the sort built by tradermales and others who did not have the talent. She nudged the darkship inward, caught ghosts and sent them ahead.

The creatures of the system were the creatures of the alien starship.

Marika turned toward the nearest ship, reaching with the touch. She could get no response. The creatures were deaf to the touch!

She considered climbing back into the Up-and-Over, to make a hop to planetary orbit.

The bath inundated her with a babble of touch, urging her to be more cautious in her thinking.

They were right. She knew little about these creatures. The one contact they had had with meth had proven disastrous. She continued to drift, probing with ghosts.

The world ahead was not the alien homeworld, that was evident immediately. It had all the roughness and wildness of a colony, like the world the crippled starship orbited. The aliens were numerous, but they occupied only limited areas—those apparently most hospitable to their species.

The colonies had the rough new look of settlements perhaps only a few decades old. Marika saw much that looked familiar, and as much more that she did not understand. She allowed the bath to ride the back of her thoughts to get their reactions to what she saw, but they were more baffled than she. They had not studied the information gained from the derelict and they had not lived on the frontier at home.

Everything supported Bagnel's conviction that the alien was not just deaf to the touch but ignorant of its existence, and equally ignorant of those-who-dwell, the otherworld, and what, for want of a better term, meth called the silth ideal.

They are a bunch of tradermales, Marika thought.

Males and females appeared to be equal in number and status, though that was difficult to determine while riding a ghost. They lived in simple structures easily understandable by meth, but the guts of the planet contained far more complex installations that recalled those of the rogue brethren she had seen during the last sweep. Those places were not places to live.

She had to communicate with the creatures. But how?

Fear grew down deep inside her, a knot that tightened yet swelled like a cancer, feeding on the fear already gnawing at the bath and tainting the aura of touch around them. The primitive in all of them wanted to flee from the monsters. It insisted that she forget she had found them. *Grauken, grauken, grauken,* it chanted.

This is silly, she sent. *Are we pups, to be terrified of the unknown? Are we going to whine at sounds in the dark? The dark is the time of the silth.*

Silth had contacted alien creatures many times before, on the starworlds claimed by the dark-faring orders. Nothing evil had come of those meetings.

The trouble was that these creatures were not savages, as all those others had been. These creatures represented a potentially real threat. They boasted weapons like none any meth had imagined before the Serke had encountered their starship.

She selected a ghost with great care. She tamed it well. Then she slipped it into the control section of the nearest alien ship, into the electronics there, commanded it to switch a comm screen on, then used the ghost to imagine herself appearing upon that screen. It was something Bagnel had postulated as possible in one of their rambling conversations, but something she had not tested for practicality.

She did not have the skill to do more, except to show her paws raised and empty of weapons. She clung to the picture for ten seconds, then had to let it go. The effort to hold it took too much attention from the darkship and her awareness of the surrounding void.

After resting, she sent another ghost, just to observe. She found the aliens extremely excited.

She was near their ship now, but they had not spotted her. Her wooden darkship was as invisible to their radar as it was to that of the brethren.

Her bath begged her to withdraw now. They had seen enough. They did not want to suffer the same fate the aliens of the starship had.

Marika ignored them. She swung in close to the alien ship and with half her mind kept a strong ghost in their control center, there to strike if they panicked and attacked her. They remained oblivious to its presence.

She took the darkship in so close they could not help but see her. When her ghost revealed that they had done so she waved politely and again showed them her empty paws. She wondered what they would make of the rifles she and the bath carried slung across their backs.

The aliens did not know what to make of her and the darkship. They babbled at one another. They pointed at screens where she appeared. They argued. Their vessel trailed spurts of electromagnetic energies.

Marika reached with the touch, searched mind after mind, found every one closed and deaf till she located a pup she guessed to be three or four years old. To that one she sent her message. *I am Marika. I come in peace. We have searched for you long and long, since we discovered one of your voidships years and years ago.* She tagged on a strong picture of the crippled starship, emphasizing the characters painted upon its exterior.

She did not expect the pup to understand her message, except that she was friendly, but she hoped those characters might attract attention. She tried to impress the pup with the importance of relating the fact of the touch to its elders.

She withdrew and watched. Aboard the ship, they went to their battle positions, but made no threatening move. She maintained her position beside them, being careful to do nothing to panic them. Once again she reached out to the confused pup.

In time it related its experience to its elders, who immediately discounted it. Marika gently prodded the pup to draw a picture.

It did not have the motor skills of a meth pup its own age. It was a long, hard job getting it to draw the alien starship with its hull characters plain enough to recognize. But, finally, it did create something recognizable. Marika prodded it to approach its elders again.

One who seemed to be Mistress of the Ship, despite being male, examined the picture. Marika judged that some part of her message had gotten through. She raised a paw again, gathered ghosts, and went into the Up-and-Over. She hurried homeward, pausing only when she had to rest her bath.

II

"You really found them?" Bagnel asked.

"Yes. It was a colony world like this one. Only more so, because they were moving in, actually making the world their home."

"It must have been far away. You were gone a long time. I worried. You tempted the All. There were those who visited who were tempted by your absence."

"They know better than to yield to that temptation. Bagnel, I am more excited than I have ever been."

"So I see." That very fact seemed to frighten him.

"They weren't hostile—just astonished. I don't know if they have encountered dark-faring races before, but they've surely never encountered anyone like us. They seemed unable to believe what they saw."

"You think they'll come here now?"

"I don't know. I left bait, but I don't know. Have you made any progress deciphering their language?"

"Some. On the simplest level. That tape you're so fond of, for example. We can translate most of what the creature says, but that doesn't tell us much. The tape is exactly what it appears to be, a report to anyone who finds the ship. It implies that there is a lot more information stored in the ship's data banks, but we can't get to them without the unlocking codes, and we don't have any idea how to decipher those. The books we've found, once we realized what they were, all proved to be technical manuals. They are valuable, but so far they have proven much more resistant to translation. It has been suggested that they are written in a language other than the one the creature spoke."

"Maybe they have castes with secret languages. Like the brethren."

"There is no evidence of that, Marika. Our principal difficulty is that we have no one trained for the kind of work we're having to do. The skills needed have to be found by trial and error. It is a slow business. And the language we are dealing with is not precise. We have found a number of words that, while identical in print, can possess multiple meanings. There are also words that, when spoken, sound the same, but appear differently in print. It isn't always possible to guess what they were trying to say."

"All right."

"Excitement running down?"

"No. Never, now. The gateway to the future is open. Before long we are going to be inundated with dark-faring sisters, all eager to pass through it."

"I know. And I don't look forward to that."

"Oh?"

"Silth will be silth, Marika."

"What do you mean?"

"It will be the same old story. Flocks of darkships will race out there and try to make first contact in order to lock up the benefits for their particular sisterhoods."

"Not this time. The All has decreed the impossibility. In order to reach these aliens one has to cross a desert of stars. There is no silth but I who has the strength to manage that crossing. The bath who accompanied me will attest to that. And even if one such did exist, no one but me knows the way. My bath didn't have the training to recall the sequence."

Bagnel appeared doubtful.

"Believe me. Call it chance or the will of the All. The alien's whereabouts is my secret. If the sisterhoods wish to participate in whatever comes of the contact, they had better try hard to keep me alive. You might let that drop occasionally, especially in your reports, just so the fact isn't overlooked or forgotten."

"Of course." He seemed amused. "You will play your games with the whole race, won't you?"

"With the most seniors, yes. There are times when I enjoy manipulating them. But don't you ever tell anyone I said that."

"I don't need to. They know already. Are you going there again? To that alien world?"

"Of course. But not right away. I'll let you know when. One thing I'll need from you is some simple messages prepared in their language."

"Why don't I go with you?"

"Who's getting bitten by the adventure bug at this stage in his life?"

Bagnel pretended to look around. "Who are you talking to?"

"Nobody here but me and thee, old-timer. Of course you can go. I hoped you would ask because I did not want to conscript you. It will be our grandest flight ever. Something they can write epics about."

"Epics are for silth. I don't care about epics. I want to see these aliens. I want to smell and touch them."

"You'd better find us some way to communicate."

"On the most basic level that may prove easier than you imagine. Assuming you can transport the equipment. Dare you trade bath for equipment?"

"Not really. The desert of stars is too wide."

"Suppose you spied out an alternate and easier route?"

"No. I won't do that. If only one is believed to exist, and that only within the confines of my mind, then my hold remains firm. Should it ever become necessary to transport large masses of equipment we'll have the Redoriad loan us *High Night Rider.*"

"That would not make them happy."

"They haven't been happy with me for years. That doesn't concern me. They have earned their unhappiness. You will have to excuse me. I must go see Grauel and Barlog and smooth their ruffled fur. They are extremely displeased because I left them behind and they missed out on a memorable mission. Though they would have been just as displeased had I insisted they fly off with me on one of my mad exploratory jaunts. With those two I can't win."

"You should…"

"Don't even suggest it. They are my pack. Damn it, Bagnel, they are as good as my dams. I have known no other since before I first met you."

"Go. I will not pretend I understand the relationship between you three."

"We don't either. But it keeps us alive."

III

A year passed before Marika dared take the time to visit the alien world again.

Her discovery had excited the sisterhoods into a scramble. Till it waned she stood fast, guarding the treasure already in paw. She shook her head often that year, unable to believe grown silth could behave so, that they would so stubbornly cling to old values and ways in the face of a screaming need to adapt to altered realities.

Bagnel did not believe her when she informed him that she was ready for the trip. "I will pack my things when I see you step into the airlock."

"This is the real thing this time." There had been false alarms before, times when she had changed her mind at the last minute. "There are no schemes afoot, here or on the homeworld." Though it was difficult to manage from so far away, she had kept her small group of dedicated antirogue silth operating and had used them to acquire intelligence about other plots as well. "I am going this time."

He awarded her a doubtful look.

"Really," she said. "It's under control. Grauel and Barlog can hold it down here. Everyone is preoccupied elsewhere. Do I have to make the trip without you?"

"You jest. Try it. You will find your darkship on a tether with me reeling it in."

Adding Bagnel and the equipment he needed made the journey much more difficult. Marika stretched herself farther than ever before—and was surprised to find that she could stretch that far.

She continued to develop endurance and strength. And those bath who remained with her did so too.

Even so, she entered the alien system uncertain she could manage the return.

They were alert this time, though so much time had passed. Perhaps they were watching for something else. Whatever, although she rode the wooden darkship, they soon detected her. Ships hurried to meet her. She sent a covey of ghosts ahead to probe their temper.

She was disturbed by what she saw. She sensed only nervousness and fear. As a precaution she gathered and held ghosts enough for a fast climb into the Up-and-Over.

She let the darkship drift directly toward the alien world. Starships took station around her, having some difficulty keeping position because they were not as maneuverable as a darkship. She pushed in and assumed a high orbit, then had the senior bath pass the bowl of golden fluid. She wanted to be ready to flee.

A return, though, would be far easier if she had a chance to rest her bath before departing.

Her discomfort increased as she examined the starships and cataloged the array of weapons trained upon her as she sensed the fear and disbelief filling the ships. She probed mind after mind and could not find one receptive to the touch. These creatures were all adult, and all voctor.

Throughout the system ships less heavily armed were scurrying toward cover.

Why? What could they fear from one darkship? Had they had contact with silth before, to their dismay? Did they know what had become of the lost starship after all?

She reached back to the bounds of the system and, yes, there was a great black ghost patrolling the brink of the deep. It seemed there was a black wherever intelligence paused, one monster to a star system. She stroked that thing and sensitized it to herself so it would answer more quickly if she had to summon it.

She signaled Bagnel. It was time to try talking.

Bagnel fiddled with his communicator until she lost patience, ordered the strongest of her reserve bath to the tip of the dagger, had her take over as Mistress of the Ship. The bath had experience, but she did not want control while they faced a potential enemy. Marika had to insist.

She joined Bagnel. "What's the problem? Won't they respond?"

"I don't know if they are ignoring me or if I just can't find the right frequency. It should not be so difficult. I began with the range of frequencies used on the derelict."

Marika sent a ghost into the nearest ship. The creatures there were clustered around their communications screens. She returned. "You have their attention. Maybe they just don't want to answer. Keep with it."

Bagnel made a face. He was as frightened as any of the aliens. "Right now I think I made a mistake coming out here. This isn't the same as talking about it. Well, here's something." His tiny vision screen had come to life. A female alien looked out at him. The communication speaker squeaked.

Marika said, "Run your tape."

Bagnel snapped, "Marika, mistress of the ship, will you? Let me alone. I know my task."

"I'm sorry." But apology did nothing to soothe her frayed nerves.

This could be the greatest moment of meth history. Its success or failure rested squarely upon her—and yet it might be entirely outside her control. The aliens might panic.

Bagnel had prepared a tape that began with a simple print message protesting the peaceful intent of those aboard the darkship. That looped ten times, then followed with a copy of the last message left by the folk of the derelict alien.

When that ran Marika was inside the nearest starship with a ghost, watching. The message stirred considerable response, but not of the sort she expected. Well, they were aliens. She had no cause to expect them to respond as meth might.

A message came back once Bagnel finished sending. It arrived too rapidly for him to follow. He used a tiny light stylus to letter a response on the screen of his communicator, asking them to go much slower. Then he requested permission to set the darkship down on the world below.

Again the response was too swift to yield any sense. Again Bagnel relayed his request for a slower information feed and permission to set down.

Permission came in the form of a map with a landing site indicated by a pulsing point of red light. Marika soon matched the map with the face of the world below. The site indicated was near the largest of the alien underground installations, in a barren area.

There was a grim, deadly feel to that region. The area hummed with modulated electromagnetic radiation. A rapid scout with a ghost revealed scores of weapons similar to those that had destroyed TelleRai, all mounted upon huge rockets.

Marika began to have doubts about making contact with these creatures.

But they had no grasp of the otherworld, no suspicion that it existed. If the worst happened she could call down the great black. She extended her touch to it again, shocked it, attuned it to herself more closely, until she was certain she could summon it if that became necessary. "Continue trying to get sense from them as we go down, Bagnel." She returned to the tip of the dagger, resumed control, dropped away from the alien ships.

They paced her to the edge of atmosphere, then turned away.

For a time Marika dropped alone, but when she reached 150,000 feet aircraft began arcing past her, and lower down they began circling. Bagnel observed them with awe. They were like no aircraft he knew. Their airframes were long and slim. Their long, narrow wings were rooted far back on the fuselage and angled forward, so that the craft looked almost like the head of a trident. They seemed to be rocket-powered.

Marika was impressed too. Nothing like them existed in the meth technical arsenal.

At fifty thousand feet she resumed exploring the assigned landing area. Already it was thick with aliens, all of them come up out of the ground and all of them armed. Again she wondered if she had stepped into something nasty.

At last the darkship touched down after she had floated a moment, seeing if the mob would rush her. The aliens surrounded the darkship, but kept their distance and held their weapons casually. She hoped that was a good sign. She touched the bath. *Keep your rifles slung. Do not unsettle them. I will guard us through the otherworld. But see you to assembling your own protective ghosts. Bagnel. Be circumspect in your communications. Do not give them something for nothing.*

Meth and alien eyed one another till an alien senior stepped forward. Marika was mildly surprised. This one was male. He presented a bare palm as he approached.

Marika replied by raising both paws, then indicated Bagnel. Bagnel put his communicator aside, produced pen and paper.

"How well have you learned their language?" Marika asked. Not well at all, she knew, but she had to say something to vent some of her nervousness.

"Not well. I don't know if it's the right one. What I'm hearing spoken here doesn't sound like what we've been hearing aboard the starship."

Marika fought to keep her ears from twitching, though she was sure the aliens could not read her body language.

The alien senior examined what Bagnel printed out so laboriously, frowned, summoned another alien. They chattered briskly. Then the second alien wrote something upon paper he carried. Bagnel studied it for a long time.

"Problems, Marika."

"What?"

"I am almost convinced that these creatures do not use this language. Or if they do, I am using it entirely wrong. But if I understand what this note says, then our starship belongs to their enemies."

"Trouble?"

He shrugged.

"Make it clear that we are enemies of no one. In fact, try to get across the notion that we do not quite understand what an enemy is. Also tell them that we never saw those starship folk alive."

"That is a lot to get across at a reading-primer level."

"You're a genius."

"I wish I had your faith in me."

"You can do it."

"I'll try. That's all I can promise."

"And tell them that all that deadly hardware makes me nervous. Tell them who I am."

"You expect them to understand or care?"

"No. But if you do it right they might be impressed."

"You expect too much of me." He resumed writing in curiously blocklike letters, passing small sheets of paper after each few sentences. "I'm telling them who I am too."

"Of course."

It was slow work. The strange-colored sun of that world moved. It, too, was slow, as the world moved more slowly than that which had given Marika birth. Not, she reflected, that she was much familiar with sunrises and sunsets anymore. How many of the homeworld's sunrises had she seen in the last twenty years?

The bath began to relax. Several stepped down from the darkship and began prowling. Marika reached with the touch. *Remain alert. Do not allow any of these creatures to place themselves between you and the darkship.*

Their response did not go unnoticed. Bagnel said, "They're full of questions about us. Especially about how we can take a ship through the void while exposed to the breath of the All."

"We have questions about them too," Marika said. "Evade. Ask them about them. There's something not right here."

"I am. I'm not stupid, Marika. But neither are they. I am certain they intend to be evasive too."

Marika grunted. She was growing more unsettled by the minute. *Rest!* she sent to the bath. *We may need to get out of here at any moment.* There was a wrongness here that had little to do with these creatures' alienness.

She shrugged. Maybe she was imagining it. She climbed aboard the darkship while Bagnel struggled on, rummaged through a locker, and found the photographic equipment he had brought. She loaded a camera and began photographing the alien beings.

They became very agitated.

"Bagnel, what's the matter with them?" Some had begun shouting and shaking weapons.

"I'm trying to find out. Stop bothering me." After a minute he said, "They don't want you taking photographs."

"Why not? They've been photographing us."

Bagnel exchanged notes rapidly. It did seem to be getting easier for him. "They say this is a secret installation. They want no photographs to leave the system."

"Oh." Marika settled on the arm of the darkship and considered the implications for a moment. "Bagnel, what do you think of them?"

"I'm not sure. I have the feeling they're hiding more than we are. I have a growing feeling that they may be more trouble than they're worth. I am trying to be neutral but I find myself beginning to dislike them."

"Yes. There's something in the air here. An aura that reminds me of those places where rogues hide. Did you ever get down into one of those underground... No. Of course not. We may have made a mistake, coming here without looking at them more closely first. But keep talking. See what comes of it."

"Stall?"

"Some. But learn whatever you can. I want time to rest the bath." She touched the silth again, ordered them to rest. They boarded the darkship, stretched out near their stations, performed rituals of relaxation, went to sleep. Marika pushed herself into a half sleep, leaving everything in Bagnel's paws.

The sun of that world eventually set. The aliens kept the landing site brightly illuminated. Some of the curious drifted away and were replaced by others. Always there were weapons in evidence. Marika went past half sleep into little naps several times. Bagnel continued valiantly, facing the same aliens who had come to the fore at the beginning. The speed of communication continued to improve.

Soon after the morning sun rose Marika asked, "Have we learned anything significant?"

"They're rogues of a sort. They have tried again and again to explain, but the situation is beyond my comprehension. It's something like what we would call bloodfeud, only every member of their society is a participant. Without choice. There are cognates with the Serke situation, in that one group is trying to take territory from another, but the motives make no sense."

"I did not expect to understand them that way. What else?"

"I have established that their society includes nothing like sisterhoods or brethren, or even our bond working castes. Their thinking vaguely resembles that of the brethren who joined the Serke in exile. It may have affected the thinking of those rogues back when they first entered the derelict."

"We suspected that."

"They have no consciousness of the All, the touch, nor any silth skills, except as the contrivance of fantasy. Their words. I have betrayed nothing by mentioning such skills because they refuse to believe they can exist. They call such skills superstition and directly accuse me of lying. They believe, and fear, that we are greatly advanced beyond them technically."

"What is their interest in the ship we found?"

"It belonged to their enemies. They suspect it was searching for their hiding places. They aren't interested, really. It vanished long ago by their standards. They're very interested in us, though. They have never met another dark-faring race. I suspect they would like to find a way to manipulate us into helping them in their struggle."

"No doubt. Just as the Serke would have enlisted them. But I have no interest in that. Especially if they're rogues. We're going to leave, Bagnel. I made a mistake. These are not creatures with whom I care to be associated. Our search will have to lead elsewhere. Did they tell you much about their enemies?"

"They're very reticent on the subject."

"That is understandable." She extended her touch, wakening those bath who remained asleep. She sent the strongest to their stations. The senior passed the bowl. Wearily, Bagnel continued his exchange. Marika said, "You will make certain you are soundly strapped down. You are exhausted and I may be forced into violent maneuvering."

"They want to know what we are doing, Marika."

"Express our regrets. Tell them we have decided that we made a mistake in pursuing this contact. Tell them we do not wish to become embroiled in the affairs of an embattled race. Tell them we are going home. Then get aboard and strap down." She passed the bowl to him, let him sip, then consumed what remained and took her station at the tip of the dagger. *Strap securely,* she sent to the bath.

Bagnel concluded his final note, passed it over, and climbed to his place at the axis. The aliens did not understand until Marika lifted the darkship.

They began shouting and running around and making threatening gestures.

Marika ignored them.

There were a few wild shots from handheld beamer weapons. They came nowhere near.

Marika took the darkship up fast.

She could not climb nearly as swiftly as the alien aircraft. A flight overtook her before she reached fifty thousand feet. She was in no mood to play. She sent ghosts to still their engines. They fell toward the surface. Their pilots eventually left the craft to float toward the ground on parachutes.

Rockets leaped up. Marika was prepared for them. She stopped them long before they neared her. After a dozen tries the aliens stopped sending them.

Above, voidships moved to intercept her. She did not want to make enemies needlessly, but they seemed determined to stop her, and that she would not permit.

She reached out to the fringe of the system and summoned the great black. It came to her struggling, wriggling, protesting, never having encountered silth before. She held it in abeyance, not loosing it till the starships fired upon her.

She silenced three ships in fifteen seconds, then shifted her course. Dimly, she sensed Bagnel laboring over his communicator, sending crude messages, trying to assure the aliens that the meth meant them no harm, that they wanted nothing but to return home and forget the whole thing.

The strike of the great black paralyzed the aliens' decision makers long enough for Marika to reach orbital altitude and gather ghosts for the Up-and-Over. Bagnel was apologizing for their having defended themselves when she climbed into it.

CHAPTER FORTY-ONE

I

Trouble did not end with escape from the alien world.

The homeward journey became an epic of endurance and determination, and there were moments when even Marika doubted she would have strength enough to bring the darkship safely to the starship.

She succeeded—only to learn that her absence had been noted and someone had tried to take advantage.

She was barely able to stand when she came through the airlock, to be greeted by Grauel and Barlog, who had remained in a frenzy days after the event. They stumbled over each other explaining. "Someone tried to sneak in on us. We did not know what was happening till the killing started. We fired back, but if we had not gotten help from silth who were here, visiting… We managed to destroy them. Barely. At least fifty died here. We have not accounted for everyone yet."

"You did well," Marika said, leaning against a passageway wall. "But did you have to keep shooting till there wasn't a fragment of darkship left with identifiable witch signs?" She had spied the debris during her approach and had wondered about it.

The huntresses were not overcome with remorse. Grauel said, "We know who it was. We saw their witch signs. They were Serke."

"Serke? You must be mistaken. Or it was someone who had assumed the guise of Serke? There aren't any Serke…"

"Tell that to the dead brethren, silth, and voctors. They were Serke, Marika."

"Or masquerading as Serke," Marika insisted. But who would?

"It is a ruse that might make sense," Grauel admitted, sounding as if she believed nothing of the sort. "But even pretending to be Serke, what other sisterhood would unleash such indiscriminate slaughter? Any other order would want the starship for what it contained, and that has to include the minds of those who have been unearthing its secrets. Not so?"

"I suppose. I guess I just don't want that old haunt lifting its head again."

519

How many Serke remained unaccounted for? *Starstalker* and one, possibly two darkships. But it had been years. Even she had forgotten them. They all had to be old, possibly on the edge of becoming harmless. But if the attackers had come from the dozen or so surviving Serke silth, then they must have some contacts inside the meth civilization. Else how had they known she was away?

"I should return to the homeworld," Marika mused. "What I learned among and about the aliens is important enough to be reported directly. And I really should see what is happening with the rogues. I did not catch Kublin. He must be up to something. But I dare not go, do I? This could happen again."

Bagnel had been muttering with one of his associates. Scarcely able to contain his grief, he said, "I fear we have flown our last probe among alien stars, Marika. I have lost thirty of my best meth. It might not have happened had I remained here. I will not go out again. Not while meth remain meth and silth remain silth. It is… What do you silth call ritual suicide? Kalerhag? It is an invitation to kalerhag. Exposing your back to the knife. I am too old to run through the snow with the grauken baying at my heels."

Marika nodded curtly. She drew herself together, willing her weariness away, and stalked off. She went into her quarters and isolated herself there, and opened to the All, and stayed opened longer than ever she had before. Despite her exhaustion, when she returned into herself she went looking for Grauel and Barlog.

"I have a mission for you two," she announced. "A tough one. Feel free to refuse it if you like."

They eyed her expectantly, without eagerness.

"I want you to accompany Bagnel to the homeworld. I want you to watch over him as you would me while he reports on our visit to the aliens and recruits brethren to replace those lost in this attack. I also want you to assess the situation there. Especially as regards the warlock."

Barlog remained as still as stone, not a ghost of expression touching her face. Grauel exposed her teeth slightly.

They were not happy.

"I know no one else I can trust. And I dare not send him unprotected."

"I see," Grauel said.

And Barlog said, "As you command, Marika."

"I command nothing. I ask. You can refuse if you wish."

"Can we? How? We are your voctors. We must go if that is what you want."

"I could wish for more enthusiasm and understanding, but I'll take what I can get. I'll assemble a crew and talk to Bagnel. I am certain he will be as thrilled as you are. But you must go soon. Quickness may be essential."

She spent a long time with Bagnel, wobbly with weariness, first convincing him—he was more stubborn than Grauel and Barlog—then detailing what she wanted said and what she wanted investigated.

"You will do fine," she said to his latest protest of ineptitude.

"Fine or not, I do not want to go. I have work to do here. Have you seen what they did to my meth?"

"I know, Bagnel. I know. And I think you will be better for recruiting replacements personally and bringing them out to undo what has been done. You've already agreed to go. Stop trying to change my mind."

"All right. All right. Will you get some rest now? Before they find you collapsed in a passageway somewhere?"

"Soon. Soon. I have one more thing to do."

She assembled the bath with whom she had ventured to the alien world. They were little more rested than she, though they had been sleeping. She told them what she needed, and told the strongest of the bath she now had her own darkship and a mission to fly it on as soon as she was ready.

All of the bath volunteered to accompany her, though a passage with a Mistress of the Ship who was not completely tested was risky. They all wanted to see the homeworld again. For several it had been years.

They bickered about who had the most right.

"All of you go," Marika said. "What's the difference? There are six of you and four will have to go to make a crew. What could I do with the two who are left?"

That settled, and everything she could do anything about done, she was able to rest at last.

It was a long time before she came out of her quarters again.

II

Marika became intolerable to those who remained aboard the starship and to those who came to visit, though visitors were not common. Few silth believed the attack had been delivered by the Serke who had survived Marika's capture of the derelict. The dark-faring Communities all eyed each other suspiciously and poked around in the shadows seeking those with guilty knowledge.

Bagnel did not return, and still did not return. She became more difficult after he became overdue, and the longer overdue he was, the more intolerable was she. More than once she caught herself on the brink of taking a darkship out alone, in a mad effort at limping through the homeward passage by herself. But that was impossible even for one of her strength.

She was strong enough to make a short passage, one star to another, on her own. But she would need long periods of rest between passages, and there were no resting places at many of the homeward milestars. Moreover, rests would consume too much time. Bagnel, Grauel, and Barlog, even with a weak Mistress, could make the journey several times over while she limped along.

A daring silth came to her quarters while she slept and wakened her. Marika did not so much as growl. Something dire had to be afoot if the female dared this. "What is it?"

"Darkship just came out of the Up-and-Over, mistress. Your darkship. It is in trouble."

Marika leaped up. "Send out…"

"Every darkship available is headed that way, mistress. We expect to save them, but it will be close. They came through with only two bath."

Marika settled her nerves carefully, turning to old rituals seldom used since her novitiate. She reached with the touch, lightly, for it would not do to rattle a novice Mistress in trouble.

She found the darkship drifting inward, unstable in flight, damaged. Bagnel was not aboard. Neither was Grauel. Three bath were indeed missing. Barlog was there, at the axis, lying down, apparently injured. The darkships rushing to help had skipped through the Up-and-Over and were closing in. Marika remained close till all four meth had been transferred to safety aboard other darkships.

Her ship. Her precious oddball wooden dark-faring ship. It had been crippled. The signs were unmistakable. Someone had attacked it.

She began stalking the passageways of the alien starship, boots hammering angrily. This was it. This was the end of all patience. She would not tolerate any more. Those responsible for this would pay. "I am the successor to Bestrei. Would they have dared this with her? No." She would make them remember. That fact would become painfully apparent to those responsible. The silth would change if she had to send half the sisterhoods into the dark…. Rage sapped by vigorous exercise began to fade into worry. Where was Bagnel? What had become of Grauel?

She was at the lock when they brought the survivors inside. She said nothing. She just stood there letting the healer sisters get on with their work, spurred by her dark, angry glare.

More and more meth gathered as the word spread. The atmosphere aboard the starship grew depressing. Marika sensed little anger. That fed her own rage. They were depressed because they knew she would avenge this. Because they knew this outrage meant the beginning of a new era of friction.

They were *not* outraged, and that angered her almost as much as the fact of the attack itself. All this time with her and they had given no loyalty to herself or to the project. Or maybe only to the project. They might not care who was in control so long as they could proceed with their studies undisturbed.

"Move them into the games room," she instructed the healer sisters. "Prepare sleeping arrangements for five. One of you will be there, on duty with them, at all times."

As she started away one of the healer sisters expressed her mystification with a simple, "Mistress?"

"I want them kept together, in one place. And I want to be there with them. I am going for a few things. Have them in the games room when I get there."

And she did move in with them, watching them every instant, scarcely napping. If there was an enemy aboard the starship, he or she would not reach them.

There were moments when she marveled at her own paranoia, but they were far between. And even then she understood that paranoia was justified.

The bath she had made Mistress recovered first. She wakened and saw Marika hovering. Relief overcame her. Then embarrassment. Then silth training took hold and she began a formal report.

"Back up," Marika said. "Give it to me the way it happened—from the time you arrived on the homeworld."

"It is simple, mistress. Your male friend pursued his assignment with great vigor. He irritated many silth by his manner, and was tolerated only because he was your agent. But they are trying to forget you on the homeworld. They are angered by constant reminders of your power, though they have benefited much from what you have done. Already it can be seen where brethren have adapted knowledge we have gained here and have employed it to the benefit of all meth.

"But no one believed in our mission. Everyone believed we were spies sent to prepare the way for your return. No one would cooperate. Bagnel garnered what information he could by trading what we learned about the aliens for gossip. He worked long hours comparing what one order said to what others told him."

"Am I to assume that lack of cooperation was the reason you took so long?"

"Yes, mistress. That and the male's insistence on frequent visits to the mirrors. He learned more there than he did among those who have a logical interest in treating us honestly."

"Us. You keep saying us and we. Explain."

"We are not of the same Community, Marika, and that has stood between us. There have been moments of friction within our crew. But when we returned home we all found ourselves considered suspect by our seniors. None of our Communities welcomed us. We were all treated coolly and with suspicion, as though we were of an enemy order. Even your own most senior, Bel-Keneke, would have little to do with us."

"So what happened? Where are the others?"

"We were on a flight to Ruhaack from Khartyth, where we had spoken with the Frodharsch seniors, when we were attacked by rogue aircraft. They were much like the alien craft we saw when we visited that world. I amazed myself. I was able to gather those-who-dwell and strike at them. I had not been able to manipulate on the dark side before."

"Fear can inspire wonderful things. Rogue aircraft, eh? The Communities have let things go that far? Why do I bother trying to educate the fools?"

"Terrible things have happened, mistress. A fourth of the world is in rogue paws, mostly wilderness country, snow country, but held as firmly as any

Community territory. More firmly, because it was from silth they took the land. The sisterhoods have ignored that, except for the few you organized to fight back. Many have become so frightened that they will not *try* to control the rogues. But you will find all that in Bagnel's reports. Let me continue.

"There were four rogue aircraft. I opened to the All and let it carry the struggle through me. I took the darkship down into rugged valleys where they could not follow, gathered and sent those-who-dwell. The rogue pilots were shielded by suppressor suits. But their aircraft were not protected. I downed three by damaging their control systems. The fourth fled. We sustained only minor damage.

"But as we neared Ruhaack we were hit by a suppressor beam. We were just two miles from the Redoriad cloister. I reached with the touch and appealed for help. None came. Rogues attacked on foot. There were at least a hundred of them, there in the shadow of that great cloister. It was a long, fierce fight. I slew many who were not protected by suppressor suits. But in the end we ran out of ammunition and they overwhelmed us.

"During the fighting I appealed repeatedly to both the Redoriad and Reugge cloisters. Finally the Reugge responded to my touch. Several darkships came out. They scattered the rogues and drove them off, but when they fled they took with them the voctor Grauel, the bath Silba, and the male Bagnel. The baths Rextab and Nigel were left dead. The rest of us were uninjured but in poor condition mentally."

The Mistress turned inward upon herself, remembering, radiating pain. Marika had to prod her. "Go on, please." She had a feeling there was more, and maybe worse, though her imagination had difficulty enough encompassing the disaster already set forth.

"Everyone refused to help us, then. We had been reduced to harmlessness, they thought, and that was enough for them. If they ignored us long enough, we would die eventually, I guess." A trace of sarcasm. "The threat of Marika's wrath would have no substance. She would be isolated in a far place. In time, I expect, messages would have gone out for all darkships to stay away from here, and recalling those few Mistresses who were with you. You would have been left to live out your life in exile."

Marika controlled the emotions boiling inside her. "I see. But?"

"I freely admit that some of us would have permitted that to happen had our own orders not treated us like bearers of pestilence. We suffered that for a few days only. Your voctor Barlog was enraged. She was also very determined to rectify the situation and to do something to recover our companions from the rogues—or at the very least to have vengeance. But as matters stood we were powerless. When even your own Community would do nothing... We argued long hours and decided we had to come for you. Still, we were short of crew. And still we could recruit no aid of any sort. Finally our anger and disgust grew so boundless we decided to attempt the passage, feeble though we thought our chances were. The voctor Barlog, with no talent at all, volunteered to risk herself completely by standing bath.

"But before we departed, she insisted we had to recover Bagnel's reports from the Reugge cloister. At that point, I think, she was in full command, though she was not silth. We bowed to her age, wisdom, and, most of all, her determination, which is not unlike your own when your mind is set."

Marika was mildly amused. It had been a long time since any junior had dared speak so frankly. She found she approved.

The Mistress continued, "We slipped in by darkship, hovered outside the window of our quarters there, and Barlog broke in. It took her several trips to bring all the reports aboard. During the last of those several Reugge sisters tried to compel us to return them. Barlog was out of patience with silth political nonsense. Her words. She gunned them down. Their voctors fired back before she finished them, too, and she was wounded. I then took the darkship up and headed here. There was no pursuit, probably because they expected us to perish. It was a difficult passage, but we made it."

"It was a heroic passage," Marika said. "If it does not spawn a legend it will be because of the fool nature of silth." Secretly, she was amazed that the Mistress had made it through—with almost no practical experience, only two bath, and a talent that was marginal at best. Her chances should have been nil. "There is a lesson in it that should not be lost. Determination counts for as much as any other factor. Where are Bagnel's reports?"

"Still aboard the darkship. In the carrier baskets."

"Thank you. This will not be forgotten. There will be great rewards and terrible reprisals because of what you have suffered. It has destroyed the last of my patience and mercy. You rest. You treat yourself well. I appoint you my deputy in my absence, with full powers to speak as I would speak."

"You are going back?"

"There are debts to be collected. There are friends in durance. This I will not tolerate." Within the hour Marika had conscripted a darkship crew and had had them ferry her out to her wooden voidship.

III

The homeworld of the meth swam before her. She drifted past the mirror in the leading trojan, noting that it was complete and in full operation. Afar, the second was so near completion it would be finished within a month.

Bagnel's report declared the long winter beaten. It was in retreat, though it would be a long time yet before it could be declared fully conquered.

The project was winding down. Briefly Marika wondered what impact that would have upon meth society. Perhaps the unity could be kept alive in projects designed to recover lands and resources the winter had given up.

She wondered for a moment about her place in history. It did mean something to her, despite her protests to the contrary. It concerned her a little because she had no friends among those who would do the remembering. She feared the silth would recall her for things that seemed to her of little real consequence, and others not for her accomplishments but her tyrannies.

She did not worry about it long. She was silth enough to have little attention to devote to far futures.

She drifted past Biter, past Chaser and the lesser moons, past the Hammer and all the stations and satellites that had been orbited during the erection of the mirrors. She moved into position above the New Continent, well inside geocentric orbit, but remaining stationary with respect to the planetary surface, a fraction of her mind devoted to controlling those-who-dwell, who maintained her position.

They did not know she had come, down there. They did not know out there on the edge of the void. She had come with the stealth of a huntress intent on counting coup upon a rival packstead. They were not watching, anyway. They did not expect her. How could they believe that one novice Mistress with only two bath and a wounded voctor in support could run the long reach out to the alien starship?

She sent ghosts to explore the world below, carefully, carefully, lest their passage be detected. She found very little besides disappointment.

Skiljansrode—that Gradwohl had created, and she had shaped into an engine of silth-managed technology, and that Edzeka had developed into her personal technical Community—was no more. A gutted ruin, the surrounding snows littered with the corpses and machines and airships of those who had brought it low. Edzeka had been overconfident of her fortress, it seemed. But as she had promised, the warlock had paid a high price for his vengeance.

He had survived the quirky engine she had created in hopes of controlling him. Had outlived it and had prospered. As Bagnel had reported.

Bagnel's pessimistic reports were not pessimistic enough. Exploring the rogue areas, she found them stronger and more numerous than he had suspected. They had installations everywhere. But, she was pleased to note, not all were protected by suppressor systems.

She found no trace of Grauel, Bagnel, or the missing bath. That did not surprise or dismay her. She had not expected to find them easily.

She pinpointed the rogue installations upon a mental map, then went on to explore everything the meth had in orbit. She was quite surprised to discover that no weapons had been orbited since the defeat of the Serke. Perhaps silth disunity was of some value after all. Maybe they had not been able to agree on the best ways to shut her out.

She sent stealthy ghosts out to cripple what few systems did exist in tiny sabotages that would not become apparent till the weapons were actually used. She sent more down to the world to do the same to the rogues' suppressor systems. She pursued her quiet, undetected guerrilla campaign till she neared collapse from exhaustion. Then she rested. And when she could do so, she went on.

She was not discovered during her preparations. It was what she wanted, and yet she was not entirely pleased. What she could do so could the pawful of Serke exiles hidden with *Starstalker*.

It was time to begin the scourging, the scouring, the cleansing. Time to let the fire fall, though it was no wind she sent down upon the world of her birth and hatred.

She did what no other silth had ever imagined or tried. She summoned the system's great black and sent it down against her enemies.

The death screams of rogue minds reached her there in the void, so numerous were they and so terrible were their deaths. So great was the horror that it reached that deeply hidden place where her compassion lay. She called out her hatred, hardened the shell around it, and continued the killing till she had cleansed every installation she had been able to locate.

At the desert base of the brethren, after their destruction of Maksche, her rage had led her to a slaughter of thousands. A slaughter so great it had shaken the world almost as much as the bombing of TelleRai. Against this kill that was but a fleck in the eye of a murdered beast.

The rogue world went mad. The airwaves went insane with confused messages, frequently cut short. And because Skiljansrode was dead and there was no one else to intercept their messages, the silth remained ignorant of the terror that had been loosed.

Black and terrible as the killing was, rogues survived. Marika released the great black, rested, allowed the remaining rogues to absorb her message. Recovered, she searched again, and found many more installations, every one defended by active suppressors.

Panic fogged the New Continent. It was so powerful she could not see how the silth could not sense it.

She summoned the great black, sent it down again, and delivered a new message. Only the most powerful batteries of suppressors could withstand its grand, dark fury.

Again she released it. And still there were rogues. She nurtured her hatred, lest it bleed away before the task she had set herself was done. No half measures this time. No getting distracted and going away before the job was finished. No matter the cost to herself or the homeworld.

She reached with the far-touch, probed those installations that had withstood the great black. *Kublin. Littermate. I have come home. You have roused me this time. This time there is only one way you can survive. Return me my meth.* She gave nothing away by admitting her presence. By now they would know their enemy down there. Who else had the dark-sider strength to do such slaughter?

The rogues responded just as she had expected. They tried to destroy her. But it took them hours to locate her, hours she used to recover her spent strength.

Then they discovered that most of their weapons had been incapacitated. Their beamers did nothing. Their missiles exploded in their silos. And when they had failed in their counterattack the far-touch came down again.

I am here, Kublin. Littermate. Warlock. And you are dead unless I receive my meth. Think of sleeping with the worms, coward. Think of this whole world sleeping with the worms. It will, if that is what it takes.

By now the Communities were aware that something terrible was happening. Their best far-touchers found her there in orbit and recognized her. Panic spread with the speed of lightning. It exceeded that of the rogues, who remained armed with the illusion that they could fight back.

Voidships rose from the surface. Marika sent one harsh, intransigent warning.

Most of the voidships turned back. The few that did not perished in the grasp of the great black.

Marika searched for and found Bel-Keneke and prodded her with the far-touch. *Gather the most seniors of the Communities. There will be a convention.* She closed herself to any response.

She reached elsewhere. *Kublin. Littermate. Deliver Grauel, Bagnel, and the bath named Silba to the Reugge cloister at Ruhaack. You have one day. Then you die. And all who stand by you die with you.*

She continued launching periodic attacks upon rogue centers where she had been unable to detect the presence of her comrades. With practice she found that the great black could be pushed through the shielding of even the most powerful battery of suppressors.

She rested yet again while her senior bath managed the wooden voidship, then sent, *Bel-Keneke. I will be coming down soon. The most seniors had better be gathered. I will have no mercy upon those who do not appear before me.*

Then back to another message for Kublin. *Kublin. Littermate. I am coming down. If my meth are not at the Reugge cloister I will have no mercy at all. There will be no place you can hide. I will hunt you down to the very last of you.*

She began a leisurely descent, allowing those below ample time to respond, either with attacks or surrender to her will.

There were no attacks.

CHAPTER FORTY-TWO

I

There were darkships everywhere around the Reugge cloister, and scattered about the fields outside the town. Fields, she noted, that showed signs of beginning to thaw. Maybe the mirrors *were* working. The air did not have its customary toothy bite.

She saw witch signs of orders of which she had never heard, of Communities great and small, gathered from the ends of the world. She sensed more darkships in the air, hastening to the gathering, coming from afar. Her command had been unrealistic. It was physically impossible for some to reach Ruhaack in so short a time.

She drifted into the landing court, noting that the cloister itself was free of snow. The court had been cleared for her arrival. Silth were arrayed in accordance with the demands of ceremony for the arrival of a great most senior. She was grimly amused because they accorded her that honor.

She sent ghosts scurrying through the cloister, detected no signs of treachery or foolishness. For all the talent amassed, not a whiff of a trap. "As strength goes," she murmured. When the wooden voidship grounded she told her bath, "All of you stay close to me. For your own protection." She glanced skyward. Both mirrors were visible. Each seemed as brilliant as the sun itself. A world with three suns. Nowhere in her far travels had she encountered anything as strange as that.

Purely for the drama of the moment she pulled down ghosts from the upper air and made them shimmer about her. She stepped down from the darkship.

Bel-Keneke came to meet her, a silth grown old in a very short time, fur ragged, gray, body quaking as she approached alone. Marika glared, unable to restrain her feelings completely. She stood with ghosts glimmering around her, crawling through her fur, motionless, speechless, waiting.

Bel-Keneke croaked, "The convention has begun assembling in the great hall, Marika. Not all have arrived yet, some being impossibly far to begin. But all have promised to come, and I am told that all who have not yet arrived are in fact hurrying here as fast…"

"I am aware of that. Hear this. Henceforth you will address me as mistress of mistresses. That which you feared has befallen you, and that which you fled has overtaken you. Lonely, lonely, the stars come down, and the fire washes away the sins upon the earth…." What in the name of the All was she saying? Marika controlled herself. "You stirred the darkness and wakened its wrath. You have brought it upon yourselves. You would not let be. You have forced me. From this moment I am most senior of most seniors. And I intend to proclaim a new order. Those who find they have no desire to embrace it will soon be reunited with the All. I am out of patience, out of tolerance, out of understanding. Lead on to the great hall, Bel-Keneke. My old friend, upon whom I bestowed all blessings."

Bel-Keneke turned. She walked, bowed as though by the weight of time, her shoulders drawn as though she expected to be struck. Fear trailed her like an evil perfume.

The most seniors were gathered in the great hall, indeed. As Marika stepped in she recalled it as it had been after the kalerhag of the Serke and the fire set by those who had taken themselves into exile. Half ruined, choked with burned corpses. Alive with the stench of death.

Death lurked there now, slithering around behind the smell of meth fear.

She examined the silent silth in their shivering scores. So many. And so many of them so very old. And all of them so very frightened.

She stalked to the high seat that Bel-Keneke occupied in ordinary meetings of the Reugge council and seated herself. Her bath and Barlog moved in behind her, their weapons held ready. Barlog, she sensed, moved back behind everyone, not really trusting the bath to stick. She waited silently, her touch roaming the cloister. She could find no Grauel. No Bagnel. No Silba.

So.

Some shaking, deputized silth moved toward her. She raised a paw, freezing them where they stood. They dropped their gazes and waited.

She grasped a powerful ghost from high above, drew it down, tamed it, and sent it wandering rogue territory, into the installations she had not yet destroyed, amid the enduring terror and confusion. And she found an old gray male who could be none other than Kublin.

So old… But she, too, was aging, for all silth had their ways of staying the teeth of time. How many years did she have to tame this mad civilization and prepare it for what would come upon it from the stars? Maybe not enough.

That was the task left her, after she had fulfilled her duty to her own. To sculpt this world a single face. For the alien was coming. Sooner or later. The meth were known, now, through her own doing. Seekers would find, as she had found the Serke, given determination and time.

Kublin. Littermate. I see you there. You are running out of time. Where are my meth?

He started, amazed that she had found him. He shouted panicky orders. Rogues ran hither and yon.

There is no mercy in me this time, Kublin. Littermate. This time, if I must, I will make you die a death that will balance my past foolish mercies. Unless you surrender Grauel, Bagnel, and Silba, you are doomed and damned. Do not persist in your stupidity. You are strong, but I am stronger. I cannot be stopped. I am the successor to Bestrei, and I am ten times stronger than ever she was. I am not constrained by her ancient codes of honor. I have a hunger in me, littermate. It is a hunger for your soul, like the hunger of the grauken, and I am barely able to restrain it. Bring them to me, Kublin. Bring me my meth. Or I surrender to the grauken within me.

Immensely powerful suppressor fields rose around the installation, forcing her out. But she was strong, and went more slowly than they hoped. Before she lost touch she saw females, silth, moving near Kublin. They were all very old, very ragged. Their apparel was Serke.

So. As she had suspected, that struggle was not at an end either. Only a pawful remained, but they went on, trapped in the destiny they had woven for themselves.

What better place to hide than upon the world that had spawned them, far from the deadly hunter of stars? Was *Starstalker* concealed right here in the system? In the shadow of a distant asteroid, somewhere where no voidfaring silth bothered to go?

That answer would come soon enough.

Marika stationed her tame ghost near the installation and held it there with a thread of touch while she returned herself to flesh and the grand convention she had summoned.

They were conversing, some in soft tones or whispers, most with the touch. Snatches quickly patched together in one grand consensus. *Doomfarer. Jiana. That look is upon her, stronger than ever before. Something dire is about to happen.*

The reek of fear in that great hall was ten times what it had been upon her entry.

From her place Bel-Keneke made a sign, sped a feeble, frightened touch that told her that the last of the most seniors had arrived. Marika rose. She chose to speak instead of touch, and to speak in the tongue of common meth instead of any silth language. "Pups in gray mange, with your fur falling out, why are you so afraid? What is one savage from the wilds of the upper Ponath? Look. See how amusing, in her country clothing, her savage bloodfeud paints, carrying her weapons like some common fur trapper. Is this an object of fright?"

Her voice hardened. "I am reality, who has been baying along your backtrail so long. I am that which you fear, and I have overtaken you. I am not pleased with you. You have been in command. You are responsible. Your Communities have done foolish, stupid things, over and over and over, and then you have insisted on compounding them with more follies and stupidities. The story is always the same. Always the story of silth greed. Always the story of silth manipulation and maneuvering and treachery, never the story of meth thinking of tomorrow, never of meth facing reality and the future and *seeing* what lies there. I have preserved you and preserved you, and for what? Why? You will not learn. Perhaps you cannot learn.

"This is a new age, sisters. Can you not understand that? We are alone in this universe no more. We must sculpt a single outward face.

"I sent you a messenger, to apprise you of that, and you saw in him only one more opportunity to vent the greed and treachery that lies coiled about your hearts. You saw nothing else, and you heard nothing at all."

She glared down at the packed, silent, frightened silth. She sensed that some were considering attacking her. If they dared, as a group, they might end their terror forever. But not one among them had the courage to be the first to move.

"I read your hearts. As you are afraid of me now, so you stand convicted of the crime of cowardice in the face of the rogues who would have wrested your world from you. *Had* wrested it from you, save for small regions where they allowed you to abide till they chose to eliminate you. Again and again I gave you the chance to destroy those who would devour you, and always you squandered it. Again and again you allowed them to regain their strength, and each time become stronger, while you snapped at one another's backs and tried to steal starships or lands or whatever it was that for the moment seemed more important than the survival of your Communities. You will not save yourselves."

She stared, dared. No one responded.

"You do not protest the indictment. Not one of you, though some are less guilty than the rest." She reached into the void, pulled. "You would not learn, would not live together, would not defend yourselves. If you have no other value, then you might at least serve as examples of the cost of stupidity to those who will come after you." She yanked viciously. The great black struggled, but it came. "We cannot rebuild the world with you, that is obvious. We will see if it can be done without you."

They did not understand for a while. Then they understood only too well. The otherworld filled with outraged, terrified touch. And they remained true to what they were. They panicked rather than do what they needed to save themselves. They would not join even then.

Marika hammered another layer of armor around her heart. She told herself they were poor silth, that they truly deserved what was to come. But she hurt. She could no longer love herself.

She drew Barlog and her bath close to her, to envelop them in her own protection, then unleashed the fury of the great black.

You experience true darkwar, she flung into the horror of screaming mouths and twisting bodies and flying blood. *I bring it down upon you, for the race.*

It lasted far longer than she expected. When it was over she felt hollow, wasted, as though the massacre had been a futile and pointless gesture, little more than a pup's destructive tantrum.

Her companions did not speak to her. The bath eased away, overcome with horror. Barlog seemed more disgusted than horrified. Marika did not think much of herself at that moment, but she refused to turn inward, to scrutinize her feelings and motives.

"They wanted a doomstalker. A Jiana. They insisted. I have given them one. Come, you. We have business with the rogue."

As she walked to the courtyard and darkship, stepping over and around still forms, Barlog finally said, "Marika, they will not suffer this. You have sealed your doom. You have cried bloodfeud upon all silthdom."

"I know, Barlog. I know. But they'll have to work together if they're going to finish it, won't they? They'll have to eliminate the rogue at their backs before they dare turn upon me, won't they? In order to destroy me they will have to become what I want them to be, won't they?"

A wild awe filled Barlog's eyes as she realized that Marika had walked into this knowing exactly what she did.

"I have them by their cropped tails, Barlog. And I am not going to let go till they have remade themselves in the image I want. I have more surprises waiting for them…. But you need not be any part of this. You can retire to the packsteads on our world out there. It's not the Ponath, but it's…"

"No. We have lived together—so many trouble-filled years. So much blood. We will die together. I insist. I have nothing else."

"If that is what you wish. Come. Let's go find our friends. And lay my family to rest."

Barlog shuddered.

II

Kublin had not exhausted his arsenal, nor would he surrender. He was as stubborn, was as much Jiana, as Marika was. He had his own dream of the shape of the future and was as determined to give it form.

But he did yield. A little.

Marika hammered at him a week, reducing his final strongholds one by one, slaughtering his followers. Then she laid siege to his final redoubt, a place far beneath the earth shielded by suppressors so powerful even the great black could not penetrate them. Marika brought in laborers and voctors by the thousand, began digging.

A deputation of terrified rogues came out. They brought Grauel, Bagnel, and the bath Silba.

Only Silba was alive.

She then understood why the coward had been so stubbornly determined.

He had had little with which to trade.

Grauel and Bagnel had died before her return to the homeworld. Kublin had had no counters with which to play a trading game.

He had feared her fury would be inflamed all the more.

It was. But it became a directionless fury, a rage against circumstance, which burned bright swiftly and soon guttered into despair.

Marika took up Silba and the bodies of her loved ones and withdrew into the void. Bagnel she set sailing among the stars.

"Go, old friend," she whispered, and fought a sorrow greater than she dared admit. They might have been wonders. One death, among all the thousands she had engineered and witnessed, had stolen away all purpose, all caring. "Sail among your dreams. Among our dreams. And may the All reward you with more than all you lost for my sake."

A small part of her urged her to go back and ravage the world as she had ravaged the rogues and most seniors and her own Community, to take a vengeance that would not be forgotten while eternity lasted. But Bagnel's ghost visited her and whispered to her in sorrow, in the gentle way he had learned in his later years. He was never tilted to the dark side, for all he had shared her life. He would not have himself avenged. He could forgive even stupidity.

She battled her hatred for her world, her past, and all that had been denied her because she was what she was. She thought often of pups never born, and wondered what they might have become.

She watched Bagnel's body drift till she could no longer find it with the touch, then climbed into the Up-and-Over and fled toward her far stronghold, her alien starship fortress that orbited a foreign world and star.

"Let *them* deal with Kublin," she said. "I have no home and no race. I will go back there only one more time."

She would keep Grauel there, preserved in the void. And when the time came for Barlog to become one with the All she would go back, and the two old huntresses would go down to the Ponath, to the Degnan packstead. They would receive a proper Mourning, with all the Degnan unMourned, and their ashes would be scattered as was fitting for the most respected of the Wise. That she would do, though it cost her everything. They had kept their faith. She would keep hers.

On the resting worlds Marika questioned the bath Silba, and learned that the rogue had subjected her, and Grauel, and Bagnel, to every torment and indignity in an effort to learn about the aliens and about her. Bagnel and Grauel had died by Kublin's paw, as he had used his wehrlen's talent to force a crude truthsaying. Silba had been immune, being silth-trained. She believed that Kublin had learned everything known by the other two, and much from her as well, for he had been a crafty interrogator.

Marika worried, for she did not know how much Grauel and Bagnel had known, nor could she predict what Kublin might make of it. She should have gone ahead and destroyed him.

Already her most ferocious oaths were sliding from her mind. She was thinking that, one day, she would venture back with some of those weapons the rogues had dropped upon TelleRai. A few of those would dig Kublin out of his last fastness. If the silth themselves did not complete what she had started, to free themselves of one half the family so they could devote their attention to the other.

III

A nasty surprise awaited Marika.

She might have made a heat-of-the-moment vow to retreat from the universe. The universe had made no such promise to her.

The starship was not alone in orbit.

It took her a minute to comprehend what she was seeing.

Starstalker. The long-missing Serke voidship. Here! But that could not be. It had to be hidden in-system back… Maybe. And maybe it had been waiting for her to show, and had pulled out while she was preoccupied.

She sent ghosts skipping across the void, felt them rebound. *Starstalker* was bound by suppressor fields as powerful as those shielding Kublin's headquarters. The voidship bristled with technological armaments.

She did not waste a second. She summoned the system's great black and hurled it. *Starstalker*'s suppressor fields bowed, but held. A trickle of silth distress leaked into the otherworld.

Marika overcame the great black's reluctance and slammed it in again, harder. *Starstalker*'s fields creaked. Panic radiated from the voidship, from the orbiting alien derelict. Marika pressed harder still, and kept the entire Serke compliment preoccupied with resisting the great black while she pushed her darkship to one of the alien's locks. She touched Barlog. *Go inside and kill Serke. They will be too preoccupied to defend themselves.*

Barlog went. She stalked passages, firing short bursts at Serke sisters, and exchanged shots with a pawful of unskilled rogues not directly involved in resisting Marika's assault.

Each silth slain weakened Serke resistance to the great black. It was now clear that the suppressors would hold only while the Serke supported them by pushing at the black themselves.

The Mistress aboard *Starstalker* panicked. She broke away, abandoning her sisters aboard the alien. Marika touched Barlog. *Take care.* Starstalker *is running. I must pursue.* But once *Starstalker* pulled away it no longer lent suppressor protection to those aboard the alien. Marika flung a pawful of lesser ghosts into the starship's passageways.

But then *Starstalker,* under lessened pressure from the great black, opened fire with its brethren-type weapons and forced Marika to dodge while it ducked into the Up-and-Over on a line she could not calculate. In parting, the voidship dispatched a covey of rockets toward the alien.

Marika could not stop them all.

She threw her darkship toward the alien, flinging a touch ahead. *Barlog! Are you there?*

Barlog could not respond. She was not silth.

Marika snatched a ghost and sent it inside. She found Barlog trapped in a damaged sector, still alive, but unlikely to remain so for long if not helped. She sped an enraged promise of damnation after *Starstalker*, a promise to end its tale.

She took the voidship in hard, quickly, and sought a lock through which she could enter. The first few she examined were damaged beyond use.

Inside. She raced along metal corridors, climbed ladders that rang beneath her boots, skipped past dead meth, flung ghosts this way and that, searching out safe pathways....

She arrived too late.

Barlog lay sandwiched between buckled plates of steel. She screamed when Marika tried to shift the weight. Marika screamed with her, cursing the All. There was nothing she could do. She did not have a healer sister's skills. She had not taken time to learn them. None of her bath had the talent.

She settled down and gripped Barlog's paw. Over and over she apologized. "I'm sorry, Barlog, that I brought you to this end."

Barlog replied, "Do not blame yourself, Marika. I chose. Grauel and I both chose. You gave us a chance to return home. We chose not to go. It has been a long life filled with wonders no Degnan ever dreamed of. By rights none of us should have survived the invasion of the Ponath. So we cannot complain. We had many borrowed years. Our deaths have been honorable, and we will be recalled as long as Marika is recalled, for were we not her right and left paws, her shadows in the lights of Biter and Chaser?"

Barlog gathered her strength. Marika gripped her paw more tightly. She said, "I do not want you to die, Barlog. I do not want you to leave me here alone."

Finally Barlog replied, "You were always alone, Marika. We but followed you down the pathway of your destiny. We leave one request. Take us back to the Ponath. Not now, but someday."

"That will be. You know it will be. If it is the only thing I accomplish in what life is left me."

"Thank you, Marika."

Neither said anything more. Marika did not want to speak for fear grief would betray her, and she lose the concentration she lent to watching for a return of *Starstalker*.

In time Barlog shuddered, whimpered, clutched her paw tightly, and went to join the All.

Marika could maintain control no longer.

CHAPTER FORTY-THREE

I

Marika presided over an abbreviated Mourning down upon the colony world. She had the ashes of Grauel and Barlog stored in flasks that she placed aboard her darkship. Then she took the darkship up and out, to the stars, and till her bath rebelled she hunted Serke. She became more cold, more deadly than ever before, and saw little purpose to life other than the final destruction of the last six or seven of the old enemy.

When the bath refused to be driven farther she returned to the battered starship and lurked there sullenly, solitarily, becoming social only when preparing to launch another search foray. She often talked to herself when alone, debating taking her huntresses home. The part of her that insisted on waiting till they were avenged always won.

If she would not go of her own choosing, the homeworld would summon her.

There was a flight into the dust cloud, sniffing cold spoor, and another team of bath who tired of fruitless, driven pursuit. She turned back to the starship, and as she approached it she received a touch.

A darkship with a crew symbolically selected from four dark-faring orders awaited her. It bore a desperate petition from the new most seniors of the various Communities, the silth she had expected to come hunting, but who never had.

What was this? Some cunningly laid trap?

She approached the meeting with extreme caution.

The Mistress of the courier ship was a Redoriad survivor of the battles with the Serke, one Marika knew and had little cause to suspect—though she had participated in Balbrach's attempt to steal the derelict. Her skills in the void were second only to Marika's own. She said, "You see before you the only Mistress of five sent who survived the effort to escape the homeworld. We all carried the same plea. Your talent is needed at home, Marika."

"For what? What has happened now?"

"The brethren. Of course. You were right about them. Somewhere, somehow, while silthdom diverted itself with other matters, they built a starship modeled on the alien. It appeared a month ago. It carried many brethren whom we could not harm and weapons of the alien sort. Many silth have perished. They seized the mirrors and orbital stations. Now they are down on the planet, attacking us everywhere. They have powerful suppressors that take our talents away and force us to battle them in their own fashion. Though you hurt them badly before, they have gained strength because they have won the sympathy of the bonded population."

Marika recalled the attitudes of her elders when she was a pup. The Communities had not ever had the hearts of common meth. "You would not listen, you silth. You would not learn. I do not want to come. The homeworld has done nothing but cause me grief. Yet I have made promises to my dead. I will come. And I will die, I think, for if none of you can destroy them, what hope for me alone? For if this is a lure into a web to avenge those I punished for their stupidity and cupidity, what chance that I will prevail? The bait would not be set out till the trappers felt certain of their ground."

The Redoriad ignored her suggestion of potential treachery. "You have the wooden darkship. The rogue cannot see you in the void."

"Little good may that do."

"You will come? For certain?"

"I said I would. Let me rest. Let me grieve for myself and all my stupid sisters who would not hear my warnings, so beg me now to kalerhag for their salvation. I should allow them to be eradicated. I should hope a smarter generation would arise after them. But I will come. I have nothing for which to live. Nothing but the destruction of my enemies."

"This is not true, mistress. It has taken a disaster of grand magnitude to convince the sisterhoods that the solitary voice crying warning held more wisdom than all their ruling generation. They believe, Marika. They beg you to take the mantle and show the way, to forge the new unity...."

"I do not want to lead. I never wanted that. Had I wished, I could have taken command long ago. All I ever wanted was to walk the starpaths with my friends, finding new things. I have been allowed little opportunity to chase that dream. The wickednesses of silth have compelled me always to turn elsewhere. And now they have robbed me of all who were dearest to me. Then when they must pay the price of their folly they beg me to save them."

"You are bitter."

"Of course I am. But enough of that. Tell me what you know of the orbits occupied by the rogues." She did not believe treacherous silth would have craft enough to weave a luring tale with sufficient verisimilitude to include properly shaped imaginary rogue orbits. She would go, but the Redoriad's report would tell her what she faced.

II

Marika paused on a world a short jump from home. She rested her bath well. She carried a doubled and heavily armed crew. The Redoriad she sent ahead to scout. Shortly before she expected the Redoriad to return she took her darkship up and gathered ghosts for the Up-and-Over.

The Redoriad appeared. *They are in polar orbit*, she reported. *Inside the orbits of the smallest moons. They are arming the mirrors and stations, though there are not really enough of them to operate all the systems. Touch I had with the surface was grim. Several small sisterhoods have been entirely destroyed. All the larger are in trouble. The only damage done the rogue ship was by a homecoming Mistress who committed kalerhag when she saw she could not reach the surface. After her rites she plunged her darkship into the rogue's drives. It cannot maneuver. Unfortunately, it remained in a stable orbit.*

Marika thanked the Mistress, then questioned her closely about the rogue ship's orbit. She wanted to arrive near it, to allow it no time to respond to her appearance.

She skipped to the edge of the system, took control of a great black, then made the long jump, mind tight upon the innermost of the home world's minor moons, which orbited inside geocentric altitude and well askew from the equator.

She came out within a mile of the moon and hid behind it. It was fewer than a thousand miles from the rogue, and would move closer. She hurled the great black the moment she regained her equilibrium. She drove it with all the strength her hatred could inspire. She ignored the rest of the system. If she did not beat that ship nothing else would matter.

The Redoriad Mistress was right. The ship was brethren from its conception and mimicked the alien in line and armament, though it was smaller. It began firing soon after she started her approach. It had not had much trouble detecting her.

She moved in fast, though, directly toward the ship's stern, where there was a cone of space in which it was difficult for the ship's weapons to track her. She evaded or destroyed what little did threaten her, then entered a smaller cone where no weapon could reach her at all.

She probed the ship's suppressor fields and found a crack where the sister had smashed her darkship. She flung the great black at it, set it to ripping metal and the flesh beyond.

She brought her darkship into physical contact with the rogue's stern. Rogue weaponry on the moons and stations dared not fire upon her there.

Marika touched her reserve bath, who would have to play the roles so long filled by Grauel and Barlog. *Plant a charge.* They hurried out the arm touching the starship. Once they returned Marika drifted a short distance away.

This would surprise the brethren. They still expected silth to think like silth. That made them vulnerable to more mundane techniques.

The explosion left a satisfactory hole in the starship's skin. Marika drifted to that gap, tethered her darkship, and threw herself in amid the twisted metal. Her bath followed her.

The great black made the ship's interior a place of madness. So condensed was it there that the place seemed thick with a noisome, hate-filled fog. The bath teetered on the edge of insanity. Marika had difficulty maintaining her sense of direction.

She found a pressure door through which she could enter that part of the starship that retained hull integrity and opened it.

Rogues waited on the other side. Their determination collapsed, though, in the fog of the great black. They did not wear suppressor suits. Perhaps they had grown lax within their orbiting fortress.

Marika allowed the great black to spread through the vessel, overcoming without killing. Many of the crew went mad. They fired at one another or shot themselves. They screamed and screamed and screamed. The bath captured and restrained those they could.

The control center was a greater problem. It was shielded by independent fields. Marika could find no weak points. She did not want to damage the ship any more, but had no choice if she wanted her way. She sent two bath to fetch more explosives.

Rogues in suppressor suits counterattacked from the command center while they were away. Marika and the remaining bath exchanged fire with them till they lost their nerve. One bath and three rogues were killed.

The explosives arrived. The moment the charges blew Marika shoved the great black into the control center. She followed. She had to slay only one more of the brethren to force their surrender. Five minutes later she had them out of their suits and the great black off seeking other rogues' nests.

She found those everywhere. Most she did not attack because they held too many hostages. She would not force grand sacrifices unless she could break the rogues no other way.

She set the shadow loose upon the world, in places where the rogues were strong, till all was confusion down below. Then she sent the great black off to its home system.

She examined the ship's control center. It duplicated that in which she had lived so long, reduced in size. "Wake them up," she told the bath, indicating prisoners who were unconscious. Those who retained consciousness she told, "Take your stations."

They moved reluctantly. A few refused. She drew a small ghost inside, chose a male at random, and made him die slowly.

She demanded, "Anyone else want to be a martyr to an idiot cause?" She extended a paw toward one who seemed senior.

He moved to a position.

"Good. Now activate all secured systems. This ship is going to do what it was designed to do."

Males eyed her blankly.

"You'll buy your lives by destroying those who summoned you." She wrinkled a lip in amusement.

No one argued, though many sets of shoulders tightened in anger and resentment.

"Good. You know me well enough not to waste time arguing. You may begin by recalling those who have taken control of the stations and mirrors."

The senior male replied, "They will not come. They have orders."

"They will not come, *mistress.* Recall your upbringing. Annoy me again and you will enjoy a long life as my personal bond. I am not pleased with you meth. I am tempted to see that your lives are very long and extremely unpleasant."

"They will not come, mistress. They have orders to remain where they are, no matter what they hear."

"Very inventive. We shall have to convince them, then. Prepare a rocket. We will destroy the Hammer. Send the order. Give them one minute to respond. Then launch."

The senior rogue started shaking.

Typical male fear fit. They had no choice but to entrust tasks to cowards. They were all cowards.

"I am watching you. While you work recall that I have spent years studying the ship on which this one was patterned. I will know what you are doing." She stopped, flipped a ghost at a male doing something surreptitious. He screamed. "You see?" She ordered the bath to hang him from the overhead. "Your friend will sing songs of agony while you work. His screams will serve to remind you who rules and who obeys."

She patted the senior's shoulder. He shuddered. "This time you pushed too hard. You made the Communities beg me to deal with you. You sealed the doom of all brethren. Even those we silth think good, I suppose. You were given countless chances to learn and refused all of them. In the Ponath, where I was whelped, we destroyed an animal that threatened us. Immediately. Sentiment did not stand in the way. Life was too fragile, too difficult." She patted his shoulder again. "Be of good cheer. You will participate in great events. You will see the end of an era. You may become the only brethren left alive. I might set you loose later, to wander the world and bear witness to the fury of silth aroused, to the fury of the All, when meth dare defy the natural order."

Some of the males looked at her as though she were mad. Most tried to evade her attention. The senior started to rise, lips back in anger. Marika gestured. The hanging male shrieked. "Such is the fate of those who will not obey. Those who will will survive. Destroy the Hammer. The dome on Little Fang will be next." She whispered to her senior bath, "I am leaving for a moment. Watch them."

She stepped out of the control section, closed her eyes, opened to the weak touch she had felt a moment before.

The Redoriad Mistress had entered the home system.

III

What is it? Marika sent.

You may have sprung a trap.

I knew that when I came. But the males were here. How otherwise?

I came back too soon, too tired, hoping to be of aid. I dropped out of the Up-and-Over too soon, and askew from the ecliptic. Chance showed me three starships very like that which attacked the world. They are lying quietly out there.

Marika grunted, reflected a moment. *So. Did they detect you?*

I think not. I remained only a moment. Barely long enough to note them, probe them, and get out. They are not alert.

Interesting. Were they shielded?

No.

Stay where you are. It is dangerous here still.

Marika paced. A trap. With the deadly part awaiting a signal from in here. A signal already going out at the velocity of light. How far? She queried the Redoriad Mistress. Many, many hours. Too far for them. They had been too careful in hiding themselves.

The fools. She closed her eyes and summoned the system's great black. It did not take long.

She returned to the control center afterward. "Have they been stalling?" The rocket had not launched.

"I think so, mistress."

"So." She waved a paw. "Like that. That easily. Your ships in hiding have been destroyed. They were not alert. They did not have their shields up. You gain nothing by trying to stall till they get here." She faced the bath. "I want all the brethren aboard gathered here. I will give them the chance to die for their beliefs, or to make their peace."

The senior male looked grim. Marika said, "I told you to destroy the Hammer. You have not done so." She waved. The dangling male howled till the senior closed a circuit that launched a rocket.

"Now the dome on Little Fang. Orders to return here, then one minute, then launch. I want the orders sent on a frequency open to everyone."

The senior growled, "You are enjoying this."

"Very much." And she was. She was free of restraint. There was no one whose opinion concerned her. This would be done her way entirely. She would shatter their power, and humiliate them in the process. And she would enjoy doing it.

There would be no mercy this time. This time she would redesign the world.

It took only four rockets to convince the brethren that their position was hopeless. Marika made it seem obvious that she was willing to sacrifice everyone in the stations.

A few hundred meth died. And the void around the homeworld was hers.

Once the brethren from the mirrors were safely away, inward bound, she loosed the great black and finished everyone who had held the stations.

The senior male protested.

"I promised them nothing. Only you who are here." She stared down at the homeworld, at the place where Kublin cowered. He would not respond to the touch. But he never did.

She had a rocket carry a greeting down.

The explosion, half an hour later, was most gratifying. But it did not neutralize Kublin's installation. She sent another.

A tendril of touch reached her. A far-toucher sister down below sent her the gratitude of the Communities. The message sounded terribly contrived. Marika responded, *You are not yet saved. That from which you fled has overtaken you. That which you feared has befallen you. I have the rogue ship now. And there will be real changes before I abandon it. You had a choice. The brethren way or Marika's. You chose mine as the lesser evil. Now you must live or die with it.*

The second missile detonated over Kublin's headquarters, highlighting her position of strength.

That weapon did not break through either. She ordered a third launched.

She reached with the touch. *Kublin, this is only the beginning. The bombs will fall forever unless you surrender. There is no other way to save the brethren. Your trap has been broken. Your ships are destroyed. You are powerless. It is you, or all tradermales.*

His response would reveal the extent of his commitment to his dream. If cowardice ruled him completely, he would stay down there till the bombs reached him. If he screwed up his courage and came forth, and surrendered, she might allow his followers life.

He would receive her message, of that she was certain.

She watched the senior tradermale closely as he released each of the missiles. The ship boasted a great many. The rogues must have found themselves a world rich in uranium, and must have developed the skills to manufacture them. She recalled those they had used to try destroying the mirror project. How primitive they had been!

After the twelfth bomb struck down into the molten fury left by its predecessors Marika received a touch. *Enough, Marika. Stop. I am coming up. Full surrender. Just stop destroying the world.*

A darkship will pick you up. She touched the Redoriad Mistress, instructed her to descend and collect Kublin.

It would be hours. She took the opportunity to rest.

IV

A touch from the Redoriad. *I have him, Marika. In chains. He is cooperating.*

He seems shocked.

Bring him up. Touch me when you clear atmosphere.

When that touch came she resumed bombing the more stubborn brethren facilities. She expended all the remaining rockets, without much concern for whom they might harm. Installations across the world perished. The surviving tradermales would find themselves hammered back into the past century.

That ought to convince all meth that she ruled the future, that she would accept no arguments.

The rogue senior reached his limit. He could not believe she had done what she had done. She asked, "You would not have employed the weapons against different targets? Is your thinking so parochial? If meth are to be changed, they must be convinced that they have suffered from the fury of the All itself." She ordered him to prepare beam weapons for use against surface targets. "I wield that fury. Let the world placate me."

He refused. Even in the face of unending shrieks from the hanging male, she refused. "String him up," Marika ordered. Once he was up she made him scream too. She told his crew, "I need meth able to operate the beam weapons."

They would not aid her. Killing some did not move them. They believed they would be slain anyway. Why help her?

A touch reached her. She told her bath, "Our guest is about to arrive. Meet him. Be careful. He is wehrlen."

Kublin entered ten minutes later. Marika did not recognize the creature he had become. For an instant she feared she had been tricked. But on closer examination she found the feel of the pup well-hidden behind the surface of this ragged, graying male.

"Marika, you broke your word. I surrendered. You sent bombs down anyway."

"What would you have done differently? I gave you countless chances. You abused them all. Each time you made the reestablishment of order more costly."

"You are destroying everything, Marika."

"Perhaps."

"Do not obliterate the memory of the good you have done, Marika."

"The good has been forgotten. No one cares. I turned back the ice, and they fight for the power to control it. Meth care about me only because I represent power. They either want to take it from me or want to profit from my possessing it."

"Then why do you fight those who would free the world from the old silth wickedness?"

"Some things are worse, Kublin. Some things go against nature."

"It is too late for you, Marika. You are one meth trying to slow a flooding stream by bailing with a bucket. You cannot halt what has been set in motion. Silthdom is dying. And you are more to blame than I."

Marika leveled her rifle.

"You initiated the mirror project, which required so many changes in society. You made it possible for those who share my beliefs to move freely, telling males and bonds that there is hope for a world not always crushed beneath silth paws."

"It was you tradermales who made an unholy alliance with Serke and..."

"Perhaps. But we would not have won the hearts of millions without your contributions, Marika. Without you we would have been nothing but what those old ones planned to become: replacements for silth. New oppressors. You made us over into liberators."

Marika slipped her weapon off safety. Her paws shook. Old memories from her early days at Akard howled in the back of her mind. Madness peeped out of its deeps. Ghosts of silth long gone muttered *Jiana!*

"Killing me will solve nothing, littermate."

"I will not be betrayed by my softness toward you again, Kublin. If you counted on that when you surrendered..."

"I did not. I never have. You can kill every tradermale there is, Marika, but you will not stop it. Because you yourself have been the principal agent of the change. I have done nothing but channel it. You are the Jiana and you have reshaped the world already."

"Do not call me Jiana!"

"Why not? Can't you face the truth?"

"Do not!"

"You know the truth in your heart, Marika. Who but a doomstalker leaves all who cross her path dead upon her backtrail?"

Marika's bullets ripped into him. Her aim climbed. Bullets hammered the control center, racketed around, cut brethren and silth down. Even she was grazed by a ricochet.

The pain restored her sanity. She flung her weapon away, leaped to a silth she had injured, tried to help her. Her fury was spent. She became businesslike, shouting orders. The other bath eyed her warily. "Do not stand around! Help these meth."

She was disgusted with herself. In a moment anger returned, but it was a cold, reasoning anger that had little to do with hatred, that was turned inward.

Jiana, yes. At least on this small scale. Many meth had been injured need-lessly.

To escape her shame she ducked through her loophole, into the peace of the otherworld. After a time she grabbed a ghost and raced through the dark, flitting from station to station, mirror to mirror. The crews there had begun to recover. Electronic chatter filled the ether.

Electronic communications. How things had changed during her lifetime. In her young years, at Akard, telecommunications had been a rarity, a carefully kept secret. There had been little of anything technical or mechanical in silth life.

The whole world had been, in a way, a restricted technological zone. Roaming the world now, she found new technology everywhere, affecting every life, brought on by the demands of the long winter and the mirror project.

Electrical, petroleum, or gas heating had replaced coal and wood in the homes of many meth. Agriculture and mining had become mechanized. Once even the vast cloister farms had been worked by methods little different than those the Degnan had used in the Ponath. Only wealthy orders had possessed draft animals. Industry did not at all resemble what she recalled. She had to look long and hard to find a true dirigible airship. The great sausages had been retired from all but the most remote enterprises.

She should have paid more heed during her rare visits home. A drop to Ruhaack, on the borders of civilization, and a monomaniacal hunt for rogues beyond those borders had not been enough to show her the broader picture.

All that. All her fault, in a way.

The past was gone. And the past was silth.

Kublin might be right. Unless in her madness she had destabilized the new civilization so far that it would collapse.

She returned to her self, surveyed the control center briefly, stared at Kublin's still, mutilated form. That, at least, she had accomplished. The future would not be his. Down on the homeworld the rogues were on the run. This time the silth would show little mercy. They had learned. They would finish the job before returning to their feuds and their fear of her.

She no longer cared. Let them go on. Let them hunt her. It did not matter now, and once she was gone it would not matter ever.

She reached down to the world with the touch and announced that she was returning to the starship.

She sabotaged the brethren ship so it could not use its weapons and left the males alive as promised. She took to her darkship and the stars. But her heart kept swinging back to Kublin and she knew that dead he would haunt her more virulently than ever he had alive.

CHAPTER FORTY-FOUR

I

Years came and went and were lonely. Marika grew older, and was all too conscious of aging. Contrary to her expectations, darkships continued visiting the alien. Few had permission from home.

In the quiet following the horror on the homeworld all voidfaring silth turned outward, away from yesterday. A new era of exploration began. Silth soon probed far beyond limits reached in older times. Marika herself occasionally ventured out, guiding favored Mistresses through the cloud to see the shoals of stars beyond.

She undertook no new explorations. She did not stray far. *Starstalker* remained unconquered. But she listened to others avidly, and insisted explorers maintain meticulous records.

Many who visited came to learn. She taught, if less than eagerly. These were young silth, of a new generation, less shaped by ancient thinking, more flexible and less afraid. They wanted to pick her brain for what she had discovered about those-who-dwell, about the dark side, about undertaking extended journeys through the void. Many wanted to serve her as bath, for she continued growing stronger as she aged. Those who served with her could expect to grow stronger themselves. Somehow she opened new paths in their minds.

She was alone seldom, yet always lonely, like some legendary hermit of old tales, seated on her mountain, tutoring all who came seeking knowledge. She had no joy of it, but taught all comers, hoping to shape the new generation. They paid for their education by helping to recover, rebuild, and unravel the mysteries of the alien starship.

"We must cease to be narrow," she preached. "Narrowness nearly brought us to destruction. We must know the tradermale mentality as we know our own. We must eschew contempt, for others have skills of their own that are as wonderful and mysterious as our own." Her use of old-fashioned backcountry words like tradermale amused the new silth. Such language was an anachronism. The ice had devoured those who had used it.

Marika had become a bridge to a vanished culture, last of her kind. The far frontiers of civilization, the low-tech zones, were gone forever.

She had peace, but there was no Bagnel, no Grauel, no Barlog with whom to share it. There was no friend to help cushion the future.

She retreated increasingly into ritualistic patterns set by her foresisters. The young silth were baffled by the paradox: Marika proselytized new ways while devoting herself privately to rituals and mysteries already old at the beginning of history. There were whole days she spent open to the All, alone in celebrating traditional mysteries.

Old ways banished the troubles of the spirit haunting her. She now understood the old sisters who had tried to force her into certain shapes when she was young.

There were times, too, when she took the wooden darkship out alone and drifted through the system contemplating the void. She could not believe that, had it not been for the endless winter and the fury of the nomad, she would now be among the oldest of the Degnan Wise. The Marika within did not *feel* old. Only the flesh did.

She was waiting too. Marking time. She knew the All had not finished with her yet.

II

A Mistress named Henahpla, a footloose explorer such as Marika once had hoped to become, brought the word. Aliens in the cloud. Far down the heartstream of the dust and gas, where it was densest, giving birth to new stars.

The cloud was Henahpla's stalking ground. She knew it better than did Marika. Marika closeted herself with the Mistress. "Where?"

Henahpla sorted charts for which she was primarily responsible, indicated a particular star. "Here. One ship, like this one."

Marika knew the star. Hers had been the first voidship to visit it. It had one planet in its life zone. "A resting place. I will post it off limits till we see what they are doing."

"They are looking for something, mistress. They are searching, not exploring."

"How do you know?"

"I am an explorer, mistress. There are ways things are done. If you do not fall into one pattern you fall into another. I know searching. I search before I explore, lest I stumble upon *Starstalker*."

"Uhm." Marika had a theory about *Starstalker*'s disappearance. Would this encounter confirm it? "I want you to do a reconstruction of that ship. Some of the sisters who were with me when I visited the rogue aliens are still here. We will see.... But I should go see for myself, should I not?"

"Mistress?"

"There are aliens we do not wish to meet again. And there are those who built this ship. The enemies of the others. Did you get any feel for their plans?"

"None. I stayed only long enough to see what was happening. I think I departed undetected."

"I had better eliminate any information pointing toward the homeworld. Just in case. Then we will go see these aliens."

Marika passed the word. Silth began examining mountains of records. No questions were asked—in Marika's realm orders were carried out without them.

When she rejoined Henahpla she found half a dozen darkship crews assembled, eager to share the adventure. Marika could not in good conscience deny them.

They would venture out anyway, under pretext of going somewhere else.

She followed Henahpla into the Up-and-Over, nervous, yet feeling refreshingly alive. Was this the mission for which the All had saved her?

The voidships plunged into a system naked of an alien. There was no evidence that any had visited.

Searchers for sure. How long before they located her derelict? *Home,* she sent. *Let them come to us.*

The alien was there waiting when she returned. His ship was almost identical to her derelict. It was approaching the wreck, but had to do so constrained by physical laws that did not inhibit silth. Marika skipped through the Up-and-Over, hastened home.

The alien matched orbit, but did nothing else immediately. The creatures were cautious.

Marika hastened to the communications section of the derelict's control center. That had been in use for years. "Have they tried to communicate?"

"Frequently," an old male replied. "We acknowledged receipt, but put them off pending your return."

"Open channel and proceed. Test your knowledge of their speech."

The ensuing dialogue went more easily than had Bagnel's on the alien world. These creatures used the language of the derelict's crew. They were more polite. Marika suggested several direct questions. The aliens responded directly. "They have my permission to come aboard if they like."

The aliens accepted immediately.

Marika met them as they entered the ship. She felt young again, fired by the old excitement. *This* was what had lured her to stalk the stars.

The aliens wore suits recalling those the rogue brethren had worn in battle. They removed their helmets and stood looking at the meth looking at them. Marika lifted both paws. An alien female responded by raising her right, stretching thin pink lips over very white teeth. Marika nodded, indicated that they should follow her. She led them to the control center.

Sometimes the aliens seemed amused, sometimes they seemed baffled, by the repairs and modifications the males had made. Marika watched closely, but did not trust her judgment of their reactions. They were too similar to meth in appearance. It was too easy to assume they should think like meth.

In the control center she told the old male, "Ask them if they are of the Community that built this ship."

The senior alien seemed to understand the question. She responded affirmatively. Marika said, "Tell them they may examine the machinery. Watch them closely." She herself activated the alien's final report.

The six outsiders divided, began doing this and that. Marika suggested, "Tell them about the encounter with the Serke so they may see our perspective."

The outsiders paid little attention. They chattered excitedly as they brought up data no meth had been able to access. They seemed pleased by what they found, and not at all distressed by the vessel's fatal encounter with a startled Serke Mistress.

"They call it a piece of living history," the translator told Marika. "A ship lost for several of their generations. I suspect they are not inclined to long-term feuds. After all, the event antedates your own birth."

Marika grunted, not entirely satisfied. The roots of her feud with the Serke antedated her birth. Today six or seven of them survived. And she was the last of the Reugge, more or less.

She had made several efforts to learn what was known of the alien language. She had had little success. Now she determined to try again.

Silth intuition told her good things were about to happen, that she had come at last to the time for which the All had saved her.

A species from another star! A species created by an entirely different evolution, yet starfaring like the meth!

Puplike wonder overcame her.

III

They called themselves humans. Their forebears sprang from a far sun they called Sol, more distant than Marika could imagine. None of these humans had seen their dam sun. Their race occupied a hundred colony worlds, in numbers that left Marika agog. She could not imagine creatures by the trillion. At their peak, before the coming of the ice, the meth had numbered only a few hundred million.

Marika was much more comfortable with these aliens than those she had met before. She learned their language well enough to converse with their senior, who called herself Commander Gayola Jackson.

The outsiders could not believe silth did what they did. "It smacks of witchcraft," Jackson insisted. Though the word translated, the two races invested it with widely different emotional value. What was fearful fact to one was almost contemptible fantasy to the other.

Marika envied the aliens their independence. Their starship could stay in space indefinitely. Commander Jackson had no intention of departing before exhausting the potential of the contact. She sent a messenger drone to her seniors.

Marika felt comfortable enough with the "woman" to permit the drone's departure.

Four years fled. The living legend began to shun mirrors.

Marika rolled her voidship, sideslipped, surged forward. Her students slid behind and beneath, nearly collided. She was amused. They were learning, but the hard way.

She glanced at the axis platform. Commander Jackson was shaking. The only human ever to dare it, she could not acclimate herself to silth dark-faring. Marika began rolling as she aimed the tip of her flying dagger at the heart of the system. *Go home,* she sent.

The touch was another thing the humans had difficulty accepting.

So much for enjoying herself. She could stall no longer. It was time to hear the latest bad news.

Marika gathered ghosts and hit the Up-and-Over. Stars twisted. The derelict materialized. Jackson's dread formed a miasma around the darkship. But she would not yield to it. She ventured out as often as Marika would permit. There was a bit of silth in her, Marika thought. The stubbornness of silth.

Marika left the alien female in the paws of her bath, entered the derelict. Now, more than ever, the old starship was the heart of dark-faring silthdom. An incredible sixty voidships called the relic home....

It was a completely unforeseen result of Marika's struggles with the landbound silth of the homeworld. The terrors she had loosed back when had birthed an isolationism with which starfaring silth could not and would not deal. One by one, one darkship after another had broken with its dam Community rather than give up faring the void. Only a very few Mistresses fared homeward anymore.

A dying breed, Marika feared. No more were in training.

Marika entered the situation room, which had been refurbished by Jackson's people. A half-dozen of her folk's starships orbited with the derelict now. Each of the room's ends boasted a vast three-dimensional star chart. Each time Marika viewed one she felt a pang of loss. That Bagnel should have missed this!

The meth end of the room was crowded with agitated silth.

"Ruthgar gone," Marika observed. "And Arlghor?"

An elder sister replied, "It is as you suspected, mistress. Someone is sealing the voidpaths." Golden trails emanated from Marika's star and zigzagged toward the meth homeworld. Though Marika's folk had little intercourse with the dam planet, anomalies in that direction had caught their attention and had led them to investigate. Eight of the marked routes boasted stars hidden inside magenta haze. Those stars were the primaries of the worlds where dark-faring silth rested. Darkships sent to investigate those worlds had not returned.

The elder sister asked, "Will you do something now?"

"No." She did not know what to do. Sending more investigators would be like throwing stones down a well.

Everyone assumed *Starstalker* was responsible. Marika had grimmer suspicions. The old enemy, with no more than seven very ancient silth to operate it, could not have the power to make deathtraps of so many worlds.

"And Arlghor?" she repeated.

"Nothing yet."

She grunted. It was not yet Arlghor's time. Soon, though. Soon. She strode to the far end of the room. Commander Jackson was considering her own portrait of peril.

Hers was a more vast star chart, filled with clouds of light. Individual pinpricks were hard to discern. The magenta there floated in puffs and streamers. "No change?"

"No. No incoming information."

"That disturbs you?"

"We are a minor mission, far from home space, but there should be courier drones. All we hear is what your people bring us. They don't understand us so their reports make little sense."

For three years Marika's protégés had been visiting and trading with the human starworlds. Marika did not understand the news they brought either, but it was evident that the human rogues had come out of hiding and there was a great struggle on.

"Ruthgar is gone," Marika said. "Arlghor is next. If it goes I may leave this ship to you."

"Would that be wise? If what you suspect is true..." Jackson paused. "To hell with regulations. Marika, you've never seen a warship. These ships here are scientific and exploratory craft. Small ships, armed only lightly. I'm not supposed to admit that anything nastier exists, but I don't want you jumping into something blind."

Marika eyed Jackson. Small ships? Lightly armed? That world she had visited had not shown her anything more sinister.

"They'll be ready for you if they're working with your enemies."

True, Marika reflected. The sealing of the homeward starlanes might be meant to draw her into a trap. But just *Starstalker?* Would the alien rogues think her worth the bother?

Where did she stand? Damn! She had sworn to ignore the homeworld, to let it go to the All. If the Communities allowed yet another rogue resurgence, so be it. She owed the fools nothing more. But if *Starstalker* had acquired outside allies... Had she an obligation to defend the race?

This would become more than a power struggle. Humans were enough like meth that they could not ignore a power vacuum. Jackson's people, nominally friendly, were trouble enough.

She and the woman had become friends, but there was little love lost elsewhere. Silth would be silth, especially in the far reaches of the dark, too often upon the human worlds they visited. Admonitions had little effect. They inundated the humans with arrogance and contempt, for the creatures had no silth class. They were little more than brethren technicians, working with their hands.

Marika sometimes wanted to shriek in frustration.

Perhaps it was in their genes. Perhaps she was more a sport than she suspected.

CHAPTER FORTY-FIVE

I

Marika sensed a darkship approaching. She ignored it. She continued guiding three young Mistresses through maneuvers. They were doing well in their ghost-fencing.

She was old and feeling it, and thinking of recording all she had learned, all that had made her first among silth. All that had made her the most terrible silth of all time. She was considering revealing all her secrets. She thought such a document might illuminate a pathway, might betray the pitfalls and long ways around that she had encountered.

What might she have become had she lived in another time, free of constant strife? What might she not have done?

Mistress?

Yes, Henahpla?

The last route has been closed.

I suspected as much. Excellent move, Flagis! The youngest Mistress had used the Up-and-Over to seize a position of advantage. *You have the makings of a strategist.* She fended Flagis's ghosts deftly. From the summit of age each probe seemed entirely predictable. *Practice among yourselves now. Exercise restraint. I will tolerate no accidents.* The young occasionally let pride carry them away and began trading blows seriously.

Marika brought her darkship beside Henahpla's. Rude wood beside finely machined titanium. But the witch signs attached to Henahpla's darkship were as old as time, crafted and blessed in the ancient ways.

My voidship has more character, Marika thought. More style.

The human senior is concerned.

Then we must ease her mind. Marika slipped into the Up-and-Over. She was inside the derelict before Henahpla reached orbit.

Jackson did seem rattled. "What is it?" Marika asked.

"A darkship returned from the human side of the cloud."

"Bad news?"

"There was a big battle. My people were not victorious."

"But still no message direct?"

"No. They've forgotten us."

"What might this defeat mean?"

"That depends on the magnitude of the disaster. The rebels are outnumbered. They were never likely to succeed. The aftershocks will be more political than military."

Marika nodded an understanding she did not quite possess. She guided Commander Jackson to the situation room and pointed out the fact that the last route to the meth homeworld had been closed. "The last route they know," she added softly. "I can get there if I have to."

Jackson sucked spittle between her teeth. The habit irritated Marika. The creatures possessed no self-discipline. "Will you flank them, then?"

"No. I'll wait."

"I wonder."

"What?"

"I can see that you want them to come to you. But that might not be wise. You are not familiar with our warships."

"We shall see who distresses whom." She foresaw no difficulty dealing with human ships if it came to that. She was silth, darkwalker, strongest Mistress of the ages. The void was hers to command.

Those who had put the stopper into the bottle lost patience when she did not try to break out. Ten days after they closed the last route they invaded Marika's star system.

Alarms howled in ship-night. Mistresses and bath scrambled from their quarters, raced to their darkships. Calmly, Marika strode to the situation room. Commander Jackson arrived before her. Already the human end, bustling, had adjusted to local scale.

It was real! Not the false alarm Marika had expected. But...

"One ship," Jackson told her. "Destroyer size. Already deploying riders. We'll have singleships in our hair in an hour. I hope it's just a recon pass." She indicated dots radiating from a common origin. "I have to get my ships out of orbit."

Marika was irked. Why hadn't her patrols warned her? They should have done so long before the humans detected the arrivals. She hurled anger outsystem, though her pickets were too distant to receive a general touch. "They're going to run?" she asked.

"I have to protect my people." The human scientists were evacuating the derelict hurriedly. "We can't do much more than get killed if they attack."

Baffled, Marika shook her head. She examined the situation, wheeled, stamped away to her wooden darkship. She cut the bath's ceremonies short, drove into the void toward the incoming raiders.

A picket's touch found her then, reporting the arrival with overtones of bewilderment. The Mistress had detected nothing until a small human ship almost overran her.

Marika shivered with a chill that penetrated her golden shield. The aliens did not touch. The touch's absence rendered them invisible to Mistresses less talented than she. She should have realized.

She deployed her companion Mistresses.

Ghosts flung outward discovered an inward-bound formation of six small ships. Behind them, more sedately, came a second formation of one large ship, two a third its size, and four more small ships. Marika did not understand. Commander Jackson had spoken of one ship, a "destroyer," arriving.

Go!

Darkships vanished into the Up-and-Over.

Marika emerged into fiery confusion. Webs of light clawed the void. Missiles were everywhere. The smaller human ships were almost as nimble as darkships. She drove toward the biggest ship. A moment later she felt the touch-screams of dying silth.

The size of the main enemy ship awed her. It was long and lean and cruel, like some monster ocean predator. Its mass had to be several times that of Jackson's biggest ship.

A small ship exploded.

Another darkship died.

She had underestimated them. Terribly.

She flung a wild touch across the void, grabbed the system's great black, yanked. This was no time for finesse.

A medium ship turned her way, accelerated incredibly. How had it detected her so easily? She grabbed the Up-and-Over, skipped, regained control of the great black. The ship found her again and closed swiftly, but the great black came too. Marika skipped again, flung the great black.

A strange screaming filled the void.

These humans touched when they died!

Their screams went on and on and on as their ship began breaking up.

Why so long?

Their dying tore at her nerves, distracted her from the broader struggle....
Crewed by the dying, the disintegrating human ship ripped past, drives accelerating still, carrying the remains outsystem.

A bolt of light stabbed so close Marika imagined crisping heat. She tore her attention from her victim.

A small ship was almost atop her. She ducked reflexively, fired her rifle as it screamed past, and only then thought to fling the great black.

Tortured screams flooded the touch.

That was the last small ship of the main force. Marika probed for the leading group. It too had been hard hit. Three survivors were streaking back toward their dam ship.

Victory. But at a terrible price. She could not find half a dozen Mistresses.

The main force turned. Marika ordered pursuit abandoned. She wanted no more losses.

She trailed the enemy's withdrawal, watched him recover his surviving rider, then his singleships. The smaller vessels all nestled into recesses in the larger's flanks.

She tried for the main ship's drives, but it kept her too busy evading fire to concentrate.

Riders recovered, the destroyer pulled away. Marika found its acceleration astounding. Such power!

The starship vanished. Like a darkship leaping into the Up-and-Over, yet with a twist that seemed to rend the fabric of the void itself. Marika shuddered to a shock that recalled nearby thunder. But there was no sound out there in the dark.

II

"They got whipped, but they'll be back," Commander Jackson prophesied. "They learned what they wanted to know."

"Uhm." Marika conversed in monosyllables, gruffly concealing her uncertainty. Seldom had she been so uncertain of her capacity to cope. The incredible, powerful technology behind that killing machine!

"They'll come ready to fight, Marika. I wish I had orders."

"Why did the smaller ships cling to the large one?"

"Economy. Military grade hyperdrives are costly and bulky. So each hypership carries riders equipped only with cheaper, less massive system drives. *Military* grade system drives. A Main Battle carries riders on its riders."

Marika sighed. Despair began worming its way deep into her soul.

The destroyer had been gone four days. A ragtag fleet of voidships dropped from the Up-and-Over, badly mauled. Marika hustled her Mistresses out to meet them.

"They're from my homeworld," she told Jackson. "All who were able to fight their way through." They were, in fact, the last starfaring silth save a few crews exploring and not yet aware that the beast was afoot.

"The voidship *Starstalker* has returned to home space. Accompanied by your enemies." The news the touch carried was almost too grim to bear. "Silth talents have been of little value against alien technology in fighting on the surface." The Communities were struggling bravely and desperately, but with scant hope. The general populace was giving no help. Even the long-loyal brethren faction was making only token efforts at resisting.

Marika cursed the All within the shadows of her heart. She, the rebel within silthdom, had been by time and circumstance hammered into a symbol of everything silth. She had become the adhesive bonding harried silthdom together. How had she come to this?

She knew the message borne by the homeworld Mistresses. The Communities were struggling on in hopes she could, once again, stay the jaws of doom.

What was the point? The All seemed determined to see an end to the silth ideal.

She took the wooden darkship into the void alone, beyond the touch of those waiting aboard the derelict. The ashes of Grauel and Barlog rested at the axis. She faced the urns.

Grauel. Barlog. We are returned to where we began. Savages surround us. And this time there is no Akard to send help.

There is a difference, Marika. They war upon silth alone.

True. But without us what would meth be? And how long will it be silth alone?

Silence.

She cruised the dark till exhaustion turned her homeward, not once finding an answer she wanted. There were options, possibilities, and some things that had to be attempted whatever befell, but all outcomes depended upon Jackson's people.

She strode down the arm of the voidship, poised over the last of her pack.

There was no choice. She had promised. She had to take them home.

Jackson told her, "It's insane," after Marika dismissed the assembled Mistresses. "Your silth sorcery won't mean a thing against a rebel fleet. Please wait."

"Your people have shown no interest in what is happening here. There is no point in waiting."

"They must be hard-pressed. It's hard to defend everything when marauders..."

"Take the struggle to the marauder. That is what I have done all my life. To the sorrow of thousands. No. No, my human friend. This I must do, though it means my end. I have my obligations. To my huntresses who have fallen, to my Community that is no more, to all meth and silth still living. I was created by the All to act. If I achieve no greater victory, I must break through and scatter these ashes before I rejoin the All." None of the Mistresses had questioned that. They understood.

"What you call kalerhag is an obligation?"

Marika eyed Jackson warily. Even the humans? "What makes you mention kalerhag? It is a forgotten rite."

"I doubt that. I cannot speak your language, but I can follow conversations. Kalerhag is a growing theme. The bath especially are talking mass suicide if your mission fails."

Was it engraved on the genes? Kalerhag had been out of vogue for ages, and most recently discredited by Serke behavior in the face of absolute defeat. Yet it became attractive in the face of the terrors borne by these aliens. "It could be," she murmured in her own language. "Should honor and the need of the race demand."

Forget that. That was not a good way to think when there was a strike to mount. She dared think of nothing but conflict. The voidships were poised. The best of the best Mistresses, Henahpla, Cherish, and Satter, were ready to launch the first phase, down interdicted voidpaths, behind a trio of great blacks. Soon horror would stalk the stars.

Marika's own approach would pursue a starway only she knew, only she had the strength to fly.

"Where there is life there is hope. An old saying among my people."

"We meth are fatalists and mystics. Symbol is always more important than substance."

"But suicide…"

"Not suicide. Kalerhag. Sometimes to defy, deny, even defeat fate, one must rob it of its prey."

Jackson shrugged. "Perhaps. Some of our ancestors venerated such gestures."

Marika grunted, withdrew. She assembled her crew, including redundant bath and a back-up Mistress, in the sanctity of a small compartment set aside for ritual. Soon most of the silth aboard had crowded in or were watching from beyond the hatchway. The humans respected that time and stayed away.

Henahpla, Cherish, and Satter were long gone. The principal follow-up forces had departed. The passageways aboard the derelict were naked of silth. Only a few old brethren researchers maintained a meth presence. Marika was about to leave.

She did not expect to return.

Jackson's messenger caught her at the lock, about to share golden liquid. "Mistress, the Commander must see you before you leave."

"Must I?" She did not need her despair reinforced by Jackson's negativity.

"It's critical."

Marika found the Commander in Communications. She sensed bad news immediately.

"My superiors have spoken at last, Marika."

"Sending bad news, of course." She had ignored the arrival of the courier drone.

"It's not good. There has been a change of government." Government was a concept Marika still did not understand. "General orders to the Fleet Arm are to undertake no hostile action till the State stabilizes and determines policy. I am able to defend myself. Nothing more."

"It could have been worse."

Jackson lifted an eyebrow.

"You could have been ordered to turn on us." She strode out, using old drills to calm herself as she hastened to rejoin her bath.

Alone.

In the void there would be little time to worry about betrayal.

III

Marika drove the darkship as hard as ever she had, hastily scouting the strike points assigned Henahpla, Cherish, and Satter. Each had employed her great black properly. A dead ridership drifted off each rest world, still tainted by last touch-screams. She snarled, an ice-hearted Ponath huntress with the blood of foes upon her fangs. The last weapon.

She grabbed the Up-and-Over, racing along the secret pathway to the homeworld, satisfied that her strategy was sound.

She should arrive first, armed with a great black dragged in from another system. Henahpla and Cherish should appear shortly afterward, armed with great blacks of their own. Satter would grab control of the home system's own black. Four of those monsters ought to be able to overwhelm everything in their way.

She drove hard. Her bath protested. She rested when she must, and resented every minute. Later, she rested one jump from home, after neutralizing a ridership.

All was timing now. The others had to be in position. If they were delayed, her next move would prove disastrous.

The time came.

Nervousness fled during the passage. She maintained an iron grip on her great black. Elation grew. The wait was at an end.

She paused on the brink of the home system briefly, wishing she dared make certain of the others. But the Serke aboard *Starstalker* were certain to sense the new great black.

Into the Up-and-Over, her mind fixed on Biter. She would use the moon for cover. Out of the Up-and-Over.

She almost lost the black in her astonishment.

The void was aswarm with aliens. Several of their ships were as dreadful as Commander Jackson had promised.

An electromagnetic storm exploded. Her appearance had been detected.

She hurled the great black.

She eased nearer Biter till she hovered in shadow just yards above its barren surface. Spears of light stabbed the night, coming nowhere near her. Beyond the moon, *Starstalker* flung panicky signals at its allies. The voidship began to move.

Terror and agony flooded the otherworld as a huge alien ship died. Thousands aboard, Marika reflected. The agony of their dying seemed to touch other humans elsewhere on a subconscious level. Their reactions were slow, tentative.

She yanked the great black and hurled it at *Starstalker*.

Panic filled the otherworld.

The Serke voidship vanished. Marika was astonished. She had not thought those old witches possessed the nerve to take the Up-and-Over so close in.

She threw the great black at the largest alien she sensed.

Fire erupted upon Biter's face. Light lances dragged drunken scarlet feet across the monochromatic moonscape. Glowing balls welled by the dozen, yielded by missiles unable to target the wooden darkship.

Marika shifted her attack to a third warship.

A beam struck close by, followed by another. They might be guessing, but they were guessing well.

Out on the margin of touch she sensed another great black. One of her point Mistresses had arrived.

Where was *Starstalker*?

A beam seared the void only yards away. A missile boiled Biter's face close enough for the fringe gases to buffet her. All through nearby space small attack vessels were closing in.

She flung the great black once more, then gathered smaller ghosts and darted into the Up-and-Over. A missile erupted close by as she went, disturbing her concentration. She lost the great black. It fled before she stabilized her darkship and reached for it again. She cursed, moving nearer the surface of Chaser.

She sensed two great blacks under control out on the lip of the system. Soon, now.

Still no evidence of *Starstalker*.

She captured a large ghost and flung it into the drive of a medium-size alien hustling toward Biter. It went drifting toward the homeworld, unable to alter course.

She turned to another, again ruined a drive.

The crowd around Biter began turning her way. She ruined a third drive, aboard a ship headed toward her, then grabbed for the Up-and-Over, darting well inside the orbits of the smallest moons. That far in she would be unable to take the Up-and-Over again.

She started down. Best deliver the ashes while the alien remained distracted and confused.

Her latest victim bored into Chaser, igniting a geyser of fire.

Alien ships darted around, trying to locate her. Angry radio blasts filled the ether. Marika continued to marvel at their numbers and sizes. The damage she had done amounted to nothing. Everything they had must be here.

She felt *Starstalker* return, felt Serke minds questing. And in the same second two great blacks arrived among the foe. A third appeared only two minutes later. One set upon *Starstalker*. Terrified, the Serke fled again.

The rest of the starfarers should arrive soon.

Marika had no time to follow the struggle. She was going down as fast as she dared, yet not fast enough. The touch of a weary surface silth reached her, warned her that ground-based aircraft were being prepared to intercept her.

She raced toward the sea east of the New Continent, holding that touch with the surface.

The news from below was not good. Only a pawful of silth survived. Most were in hiding, scattered among the populace, pretending to be displaced workers. The alien was in complete control and looked likely to break faith with his Serke allies.

Perfidious males.

Marika felt the approach of the enemy aircraft while she was yet two hundred thousand feet up. She hurled ghosts. Aircraft dropped. How arrogant of them! Not one of their starships or aircraft was equipped with suppressors.

Maybe they did not know. Maybe the Serke were exercising duplicity of their own, counting upon her to batter the alien, and the alien to destroy her, leaving them to pick up the pieces.

She reached the surface unscathed and raced over gray waves edged with fire. One of the ships she had injured was coming down, trailing thunder.

The action beyond the sky was brisk. Three great blacks had ruined the alien's confidence. And now the main forces of darkships were arriving.

But their ships, all their ships, were titanium.

IV

The shore cliffline reared ahead, giants wearing boots of foam. Beyond, the land betrayed patches of green. Marika was pleased. Here the ice had lain fifty feet thick the last time she had come by. For all that had happened, the mirrors remained active.

She was a long way from the Ponath. Fast as she rushed along, the night was faster. It overtook her before she reached her ancestral territory. There in moonlight the land yet lay skeletal, not all the ice gone, but enough so the heads of hills and bones of dead forests had begun to show through. She slowed, searched for the packstead.

Again and again aircraft came to challenge. None of those that detected her ever came within eyeshot.

The ice had changed the land. Little seemed familiar, though the hills above the Ponath reared naked above the remaining ice. Bald heads where once had stood impenetrable forests. She slowed, uncertain she had reached the right country.

She had flown too far west, for she came upon the promontory where Akard had stood. The ice had left no trace of the fortress. She turned eastward, thinking how puny were the works of meth in the face of the slow fury of nature.

She found the packstead easily, then, for something turned within her, connecting with the land of her birth. Her life there rushed through her mind, a torrent. How did that pup become the hard, cruel bitch riding the night above?

She summoned her backup and ordered her to take over as Mistress, to drift slowly above the site, fifty feet up. Marika went to the axis and collected the urns containing Grauel and Barlog.

Holding those urns, she gazed at the sky. The continuing struggle scarred the outer darkness. She opened, allowed the touch to overwhelm her.

Half her Mistresses had been destroyed. Satter was among those lost. No other Mistress had been able to take control of the system's great black. But the survivors battled on.

The alien had suffered as heavily. A score of crewless starships drifted aimlessly, complicating the battle situation. The struggle remained close despite the technology and numbers ranged against the silth. Henahpla and Cherish, recalling what Commander Jackson had told them about warships, were trying to intimidate the enemy by concentrating on vessels capable of carrying riders away.

Perhaps that was not the wisest tactic, Marika reflected. But she let them continue, with just a light touch to let them know she would be back among them soon.

She opened the urns and sang an ill-remembered memorial chant. The breeze around the darkship wafted bits of meth dust. She continued on into rites of Mourning for the entire Degnan pack, which she had owed for so long.

"I kept my promise, as you kept yours," Marika whispered to the spirits of the huntresses. "We kept faith. Fare you well wherever, and I pray we meet in another life, to hunt the same trails."

Fighter aircraft were coming up from the south and in from the west. Another flight circled over the distant sea, hoping she would flee that way. Up in orbit others were thinking of her too. *Starstalker* was keeping close track.

She scattered the last ashes, sped one final farewell, then resumed her place at the tip of the dagger, well satisfied that she had fulfilled her principal obligation. Now she could join the rest of silthdom in death.

She had the golden bowl passed, for she felt a need of renewed strength. She had begun to feel her years. And she could not convince herself that self-sacrifice was the only remaining answer.

Ready?

Her crew responded affirmatively. Some even seemed eager to fling themselves into the jaws of the All. There were no doubts in their minds. They would die here, heroically, or later, if vanquished but unslain, in some grand and foolish ceremony.

Marika hurled ghosts wherever aircraft were approaching, scattering wreckage over land and sea. Then she climbed rapidly, calling on her backup to assume the Mistress's duties again.

She stretched herself to the system's bounds, searching for her old dark ally. The great black fought her angrily. She refused to acknowledge its desire to be left alone. She dragged it toward her.

Then she opened to the battle.

It was even no longer. Henahpla had been slain. Cherish had but two bath remaining and could not manage her black while struggling to control her voidship. Several fainthearts had fled for the derelict.

The outcome was no longer in doubt if one were silth enough to read it.

Starstalker began guiding alien warships to intercept Marika.

She whipped the great black in on the Serke voidship. They shrieked and jumped away, but not without having smelled the rotten breath of death. Not distracted by having to manage the darkship, Marika kept watch. She hurled the black the instant she sensed *Starstalker* returning from the Up-and-Over. Again she got her blow in. Then again, and again, and the fifth time *Starstalker* did not gather ghosts fast enough to escape.

Marika brushed the Serke voidship once more to make sure it would not recover, then let be. Let them think, and worry, and wonder if their allies would save them or let them die, adrift a few thousand miles from the homeworld they had come so close to recapturing.

The warships above were sniping at the wooden darkship, though Cherish valiantly strove to distract them. Rather than assume control of the darkship, Marika began flinging the great black among those who awaited her. Her hammer blows caught them off guard. In minutes they began to scatter.

Despite the evidence that the struggle would end in their favor, alien ships began leaving the inner orbits. A quick scan told Marika they were removing their jump ships from danger. The ouderships would have to carry the brunt.

She might die here. She might be defeated. But already she had won a great victory for Commander Jackson's people. If they took advantage.

She reached orbital altitude despite all that could be thrown her way, though she lost two bath and had to resume control of the voidship before she wanted. She clawed her way into the shadow of one of the smaller moons, dodged from it to another farther out, part of her mind wielding the great black, part seeking ghosts with which to take the Up-and-Over. She wanted to get into open space now, to steal maneuvering room.

Ghosts were scarce. Most of the surviving Mistresses had fled, stripping the surrounding void. She would have to wait till more drifted in.

She pranced around the little moons, among the wrecks of alien ships, at times pretending to be debris. She sent a dozen ridership crews to whatever those creatures recognized as their maker. Always she inched away from the homeworld. Always the All stalked with her, though she was so weary she thought she would collapse any moment.

Cherish died, her soul parting from her flesh with a last scream of touch encouraging Marika to fly away, to regain the derelict and thence mount another offensive. There were a few Mistresses among the stars, wandering. She could bring them in, train them to the great blacks, and finish the massacre begun here.

Marika returned a gentle, thankful touch as Cherish melded into the All. There was one silth who, like herself, never yielded.

She gathered ghosts.

She was alone in the home system, the only darkship still in action. The aliens were closing in. Even those vessels that had withdrawn were returning to taste the kill.

She threw the great black one last time, then jumped, dragging the monster with her a hundred million miles outward.

She waited.

They did not come. They had lost touch.

She had the senior bath pass the golden liquid again. And then she jumped inward again, dropping not four miles from *Starstalker* and a bevy of small alien attendants.

Good-bye, old witches. Old enemies. You lose again. She loosed the great black and took pleasure in the screams of the dying till enemy fire came so near one of her bath complained of scorched fur.

She skipped into the Up-and-Over, reversing the route she had used to approach the homeworld.

CHAPTER FORTY-SIX

I

For all good news there must be bad, for all good fortune balancing evil. That which Marika garnered a week after fighting her way free of the homeworld was the worst.

Alien warships had beaten her to the derelict. A Main Battle was there, with riderships deployed, and it was evident that several Mistresses had stumbled in to their deaths already.

Tired of fighting, of killing, of struggling on when there seemed no end to the struggle, Marika nevertheless jumped in, leaving the Up-and-Over so near the derelict the aliens remained ignorant of her advent.

The starship had been pounded into scrap, as had the starships belonging to Jackson's expedition. Nothing lived except on the planet below. Marika reached with the touch and found a few silth, but no starfarers. All those had been driven away.

She drew the system's great black, disposed of the crew of the Main Battle, then took the Up-and-Over while the riderships bustled about in panic. She jumped to another world and found another alien waiting there, fully alert. She departed rather than fight. She needed rest.

A second and third world proved equally perilous. The supply of golden liquid was getting low. And her bath had been exposed to space too long. She had to get down.

There was but one place left to flee, a world Henahpla had discovered, hidden on the far side of the cloud. She had designated it as a last hiding place if ever she were ousted from the derelict.

Could she survive so long a passage?

She made it, barely, but had to be aided down to the surface by the few silth who had reached the world already. She collapsed once she was down, was only vaguely aware of the chatter of silth afraid she would be lost to them.

She wakened occasionally, took a bit of broth. She suffered spates of delirium in which she believed she was arguing with Grauel, Barlog, Bagnel, Gradwohl, Kiljar, or even Kublin. She believed she was delirious when she

566

overheard the ongoing argument polarizing the makeshift encampment.

Once she staggered from her shelter and tongue-lashed the Mistresses and bath, damning them for yielding to despair, but they did not understand her tangled Ponath dialect. She collapsed before she could make them understand. They restored her to her pallet and resumed their defeatist chatter.

Later, a Mistress came to inform her that another two darkships had come in. She observed, "I think you are suffering from more than exhaustion, mistress. A pity we have no healer sister."

Marika tried to rise. "I cannot be sick. I do not have time."

The Mistress pushed her back down. "A tired body is fertile for disease, mistress. Rest."

"I have never been sick. Not a day."

"Good. You have a strong soul. You will recover more quickly."

Perhaps. And perhaps her malaise was all of the soul, she thought. Lying there, she had too much time to reflect. Jiana. How she had bristled at that label in younger years. But how right they had been. They had smelled the stench of death in her fur. She could deny it no longer. Doom had come irrespective of her conviction.

Even now she fought confession. But how could she deny truth? She had been the heart of it all along, and her backtrail was strewn with bones and ruined cities. Yea, with ruined planets.

She should have perished in the Ponath with the rest of the Degnan pack. Grauel and Barlog should have abandoned her when first she had offended them with her wickedness. She should not have been born. She or Kublin.

The debate among the sisters continued without respite, swinging sometimes this way, sometimes that, toward resumption of the struggle against the alien invaders, or away. Marika charged into the lists in a rare lucid moment, after days of introspection.

"It is too late for our kind. We are obsolete. The doom of silthdom was sealed when first the Serke encountered the alien. We can struggle on but gain nothing, like the Serke themselves after they were found out. We are what? Eight darkships? Nine? Can so few turn the tide? Of course not. Why even try? We are not wanted at home. Time has passed us by. The race have turned their backs upon us. We are orphaned and exiled."

They heard her without interrupting, as befitted a most senior. Their deference irked her. She was not deserving. "Do you understand? We are silth. Silth have no tomorrows. If we live, we leave no legacy. The homeworld and colonies are lost to us. We cannot breed. We cannot recruit. We are the last of our kind. Understand that. The last. Representatives of the end of an age. If we continue the struggle we will serve no one well, silth or the race. In the broader view of the race, we can do nothing but harm. We must let the race go. Let them learn the new ways of rogue and alien. We must not torture them further, for they will need every hope to survive."

Marika settled to the barren, rocky earth of the campsite, her energy expended.

Not one sister spoke in opposition, though in a strictly silth context her remarks amounted to heresy. She took a series of deep, relaxing breaths.

"Good, then. Let us examine our position. I doubt we will find we have supplies enough to last long. Decisions will have to be made around that fact. I have a task for a volunteer. A darkship will have to sneak back to the homeworld, to the edge of touch, to carry the news that Jiana will lead till the end."

Still no sister spoke.

"We have all been doomstalkers," Marika suggested. "Making tomorrow by fighting it. Come, sisters. Let us see what supplies we have and can recover."

They began to murmur as they worked, questioning her sanity. Those who had argued against going on had, perhaps, counted on her to overrule them. Now they wondered what had become of Marika the tireless, the unyielding, the savage, feral silth who had grown up to become the very symbol of conservative silthdom.

II

The date Marika chose was an anniversary of that on which the nomads had stormed the palisade of the Degnan packstead for the final time. So many years ago. Her silth life had been hard, but life would have been much harder even in a peaceful Ponath. She would not have lived this long had she not been driven forth.

The place Marika chose lay on the far side of the dust cloud, facing the banks of stars she had hoped one day to explore. She viewed those silvery reefs and shivered with lonely sorrow. So much missed because she was Marika. Talent was more curse than gift. Only lesser Mistresses had won free and had gone thither in stalk of wonder.

That vast starscape recalled Bagnel and shared dreams, and things that never were, and thoughts of Bagnel stirred other sorrows. She did not want to face those now. Not at a time like this. She would face Bagnel soon enough.

Come together.

One by one, nineteen voidships drifted together, till each dagger tip floated just feet from Marika. A thistle head of darkships. Their refurbished and polished witch signs glittered in the light of massed stars. And not a one present but by choice.

Nineteen voidships. Certainly all that still existed. Marika had gathered them for months. Not one voidship remained unaccounted for. But for a scatter of ground-bound silth in hiding among the turbulent underclasses, these constituted all surviving silthdom.

Jiana. Jiana indeed.

A short distance away a silvery speck glistened as it shifted slightly. It was a captured messenger drone, reprogrammed. It was observing. Recording, for the posterity of a race about to enter upon an entirely new age. Marika wanted this hour remembered.

The drone would carry its tale to the homeworld. Marika supposed the few surviving rogues would cheer when they deciphered its message.

Thistledown adrift among the stars. She was afraid. All the sisters were. But it was too late to turn back. It had been designed that way. There could be no changes of heart. The golden fluid was gone.

Let she who knows the song begin to sing. Let the All harken. The final ritual is begun.

For all the talk, for so long, not one of the sisters had known the Ceremony entire. It had been that long since its formal usage. But snippets gathered from the memories of nineteen crews had been enough to restore it.

Marika made her responses abstractedly, contributing to a growing envelope of touch that softened the fear. In a way it reminded her of her Toghar, the ceremony by which she had achieved her official entry into adult silthhood.

Kalerhag. *The* Ceremony. The most ancient rite, dating back to prehistory. It could be and could mean so many things. This time, stepping aside to make way for the new and the young, the oldest of its functions.

Not the end she had foreseen. But now, surely, the best thing for the race, sending the old ways out in honor rather than hanging on and hanging on the way the Serke had done, working only evil. Let the new way have the full use of its energies. It would need them to deal with these rogue aliens, and with Commander Jackson's people, who were sure to come hunting their enemies.

As peace enveloped her, Marika found she could wish her successors the best of luck. Anger and hatred went with the fear, and she found she could forgive them most of their wickedness.

Momentarily, she wondered if Kublin had settled into the same frame of mind in his final minutes.

The golden glow surrounding the sisters began to fray. Their fur stirred in the breath of the All. The darkness closed in. Marika, whelped of Skiljan, a savage huntress of the upper Ponath, possibly the strongest and greatest silth ever to have lived, faded quietly into the All, her battles finally done. Her last thought was a curiosity as to whether or not she would find Bagnel waiting on the other side.

III

Courier departs.

Nineteen darkships drift on the edge of the cloud, very, very slowly separating. They are lost, but they will not be forgotten. They will become legend.

And the legend says that Marika did not die at all, that she is only sleeping, and that when the race of meth have fallen into their darkest hour she will come out of the great void with her witch signs shining, her bloodfeud dyes fresh, and her old rifle newly oiled. And the enemies of the meth will be swept away before her.

So ends an ancient age.